DESCENDANT

DESCENDANT

The Complete Nikki Glass Series

JENNA BLACK

Gallery Books

New York   London   Toronto   Sydney   New Delhi

G

Gallery Books
An Imprint of Simon & Schuster, Inc.
1230 Avenue of the Americas
New York, NY 10020

This Gallery Books trade paperback edition June 2016

GALLERY BOOKS and colophon are registered trademarks
of Simon & Schuster, Inc.

For information about special discounts for bulk purchases,
please contact Simon & Schuster Special Sales at 1-866-506-1949
or business@simonandschuster.com.

The Simon & Schuster Speakers Bureau can bring authors to your live event.
For more information or to book an event, contact the Simon & Schuster
Speakers Bureau at 1-866-248-3049 or visit our website at
www.simonspeakers.com.

Manufactured in the United States of America

1   3   5   7   9   10   8   6   4   2

Library of Congress Cataloging-in-Publication Data is available.

ISBN 978-1-4767-0012-0

Contents

DARK
DESCENDANT

In loving memory of Albert Barlow

ONE

My entire world shattered on a cold, rainy, miserable night in early December.

The evening started off depressingly normal with a blind date arranged by my sister, Steph. Now, I love Steph to death, and I know she means well, but her ability to pick just the kind of man I'm least likely to hit it off with is legendary.

My date *du jour,* Jim, was good-looking, unattached, and conspicuously charming, at least on the surface. In Steph's book, that made him perfect for me. Little details like his self-absorption and thinly veiled disrespect for women had apparently escaped her notice. They did not, however, escape mine.

When my cell phone rang, I practically dove into my purse to find it, praying the call would grant me a reprieve from the date from hell. I did a mental happy dance when I glanced at the caller ID and saw the name Emmitt Cartwright.

I gave Jim my best imitation of a chagrined expression. "I'm so sorry," I said, hoping I didn't sound relieved. "It's a client. I have to take it."

He indicated it was okay with a magnanimous sweep of his arm. His face conveyed another message—something along the lines of how much he loathed people who interrupted romantic dinners for something so crass as business. Considering some of the views he'd expressed over appetizers, I wouldn't have been surprised if he were a charter member of the "women belong in the kitchen, barefoot, and pregnant" club.

I dismissed Jim's disapproval and answered the call as I pushed away from the table, heading for a quiet corner near the back of the restaurant where I could talk in something resembling privacy.

"Nikki Glass," I said.

"Miss Glass," Emmitt said, sounding relieved to have reached me. I'd tried to convince him to call me Nikki, but he had the quaintly old-fashioned habit of reverting to "Miss Glass" whenever I failed to remind him. It made him sound almost grandfatherly, although he was younger than me. "I hope I'm not interrupting anything."

I smiled, glancing over at the table where Jim sat with his legs crossed and his fingers tapping impatiently. "Nothing that didn't badly need interrupting," I assured him. "Is everything all right?"

He hesitated a moment. "I . . . don't know."

I raised an eyebrow at that hesitation. I'd only met him in person once, but that was enough to leave a strong impression. He wasn't the hesitant type. The man practically had "alpha male" tattooed on his forehead.

"Maggie called me," he said quietly.

I leaned against the wall and bit my lip, trying to figure out what to make of this new development. Maggie was his ex-girlfriend, and he obviously hadn't gotten over her yet. He'd originally hired me to track her down after she'd left him for a guy he suspected of belonging to a weird cult of some kind. He'd said he was worried the cult was going to indoctrinate her.

"What did she have to say?" I asked, genuinely curious. I'd had very little luck in my investigations so far. Maggie and the other members of this so-called cult lived together in a massive mansion in Arlington, Virginia, and discreet inquiries in the neighborhood had revealed only that they "kept to themselves." Real helpful. All I had to show for my investigation so far were names and a handful of surveillance photos, and I'd been lucky to get those.

"She said she wanted out. She wants me to come get her."

I frowned. This seemed like exactly the kind of break Emmitt had been hoping for, and I wondered why he hadn't already whisked her away.

"She's going to wedge the front gate open, and I'm supposed to drive up to the back and pick her up," Emmitt continued.

Ah. Now I had a hint why he hadn't already run to the rescue.

"In other words, she thinks someone might try to stop her, so she's trying to make a fast, quiet getaway."

"Yeah. Something like that. I'd like you to come with me. I want another witness there in case things get . . . weird."

All right, *that* I hadn't been expecting. "I'm not really sure I'd be much help," I said. Emmitt was about as imposing a human being as I could imagine. I'm five foot two, fine-boned, and female. Anyone not intimidated by Emmitt wouldn't even give me a second glance. "Maybe you should call the police."

"And tell them what? I have no proof of anything, and Maggie didn't even say she was being threatened. I'm probably just being paranoid, but I don't like the idea of going up there alone. Just in case. This cult believes some very strange stuff, and I don't think it's smart to expect them to act rationally."

Everything substantive I'd learned about the cult's beliefs had come from Emmitt himself, though he'd always been a little vague about how he'd learned the details. Apparently, they believed themselves to be descended of gods and therefore immortal. I didn't doubt that these nut jobs were dangerous, but my gut was telling me to turn Emmitt down. This wasn't a job for a private investigator. At least, not for *this* private investigator.

"I'll pay double your fee," Emmitt said, sounding almost desperate. "But I don't want to keep her waiting too long. I don't want to give her time to change her mind."

"Money isn't the issue," I assured him. "I just don't think . . ."

"Please humor me, okay? I don't have anyone else I can ask on short notice."

I glanced over at the table, where Jim's body language was screaming even more loudly that he resented me taking this call. The server had brought our entrees while I was talking. My stomach gave an unhappy grumble at the thought of going hungry, but I wasn't anxious to spend the next hour or so gnashing my teeth to keep from telling Jim exactly what I thought of him. Emmitt was giving me a perfect excuse to cut the evening short, and he was going to pay me, to boot.

I decided to ignore my gut instinct and agreed to meet Emmitt at the gate in front of the house.

I'm twenty-five years old and have been listening to my gut all my life. I should have known better than to ignore it.

A little more than half an hour later, my gut was insisting even more loudly that this was a piss-poor idea.

The skies opened up as soon as I left the restaurant, and by the time I pulled up to the gate in Arlington, the rain was mixed with sleet and the streets were growing slick. All the worst moments of my life have been associated with rain, so this should have been another clue it was time for me to turn around. My windshield wipers squeaked and squealed as they tried their best to dash the rain away. I'd meant to replace the wiper blades months ago.

The neighborhood was dark and quiet. Most of the houses were set far enough back from the road that they were hidden from view, and the streetlights were few and far between. Close to D.C. as it was, the neighborhood still felt distant from all the hustle and bustle, and I seemed to be the only person out and about in this weather.

I'd expected Emmitt to be waiting for me at the gate, but when I pulled up, I saw no sign of his car, nor of him. The gate stood open, however, making me wonder if Emmitt had gotten impatient and decided not to wait for me.

I pulled off to the side of the road, keeping the car running and the headlights pointing at the gate, then dug out my phone and called Emmitt's cell. There was no answer. A chill that had nothing to do with the frigid weather or the sleet crept down my spine. I knew he had his cell phone with him, since that was the number he'd called me from. So why wasn't he answering?

"Damn it," I muttered under my breath. This was *so* not my type of gig.

I sat there for a good ten minutes, debating what to do between repeated attempts to get Emmitt on the phone. The rain had turned to sleet, and icicles were forming on the gate. The branches of the trees beside the road hung low, weighted down by a thin coating of ice. There was no sound except the steady ping of the sleet bouncing off the windshield and the roof of my car.

Finally, I blew out a deep breath and put the car in drive. I couldn't sit idling forever. My choices were to turn around and go home, or drive through the gate and make sure everything was okay. Doing so was technically trespassing, but the gate *was* hanging open like an invitation. Emmitt had almost certainly gone in without me, and if he had, his failure to answer the phone was a bad sign.

"Screw it," I decided, and maneuvered the car carefully down the driveway, my tires struggling to find a grip on the ice-slicked asphalt.

I gave the ice the respect it deserved, driving slowly and trying not to make any sudden moves. Even so, my car slipped and slid, and I gripped the steering wheel tightly as I struggled to keep control. The damn driveway meandered through trees too evenly spaced to be natural growth. I wished whoever had done the landscaping had kept the trees farther back from the road. There wasn't a hell of a lot of room for error if I lost control of the car. Streetlights would have been a nice touch, too.

My nerves were taut, and I had to remind myself to breathe every once in a while. Driving in snow I can handle, but the sleet was a nightmare. I worked my way around yet another curve in the driveway, one that seemed specifically designed to send cars careening into the trees. I let out a sigh when the driveway finally straightened out, the lights of the house itself just visible in the distance. Anxious to find Emmitt and get out of there, I gave the car a little more gas than was strictly wise.

My only warning was a glimpse of movement in the trees off to my right. Then, as if he'd appeared literally out of nowhere, a figure stood in the middle of the road, barely two yards from my car.

With a shriek of alarm, I instinctively slammed on the brakes. If I'd had half a second to think about it, I'd have remembered that slamming brakes on an icy road was a bad idea. The wheels locked up, and the car skidded forward, the back slewing to one side.

The figure in the road made no attempt to get out of the way. At the last moment, he raised his head, and I recognized Emmitt's face in the glare of the headlights. His eyes met mine, and I'll never forget the small smile that curved his lips. Then the car slammed into him with a sickening wet thunk.

I screamed again, my car now spinning like a top as the airbag exploded out toward my face. The impact slammed my head back against the headrest. Though I tried to turn the wheel into the skid, I was so disoriented, I didn't know which way that was.

Out of the side window, I saw a tree trunk heading my way. The side of the car crunched with the impact, safety glass shattering and peppering my face as I held up my hand to protect my eyes. The car door crumpled under the pressure, and something sharp and hard stabbed into my side, the pain blinding. Even as my head snapped to one side, the car caromed into another tree. Something struck the other side of my head, and everything went black.

Two

When I came to, the engine was off and the air bag had deflated. My whole body hurt, and with the windows all broken, frigid air and sleet had frozen me to the marrow. With a groan, I looked down at myself to assess my injuries. My vision swam and my stomach lurched when I saw the huge gash in my side. Blood soaked my sweater and the top of my pants and coated the crumpled door.

My brain was working in slow motion, my head throbbing. I suspected I had a concussion in addition to my other injuries. Shivering, sick, and scared, I forced my nearly frozen fingers to release my seat belt. I didn't need a medical degree to know I needed help, but when I reached for my cell phone, I found it hadn't survived the crash.

The door was far too badly damaged to open, so I had to drag myself out the broken window. It hurt so much that I wondered if I wouldn't be better off just keeping still. Surely the people in the house had heard the accident. Someone would come to check it out, and then they could call an ambulance for me.

By the time this brilliant thought occurred to me, I was more than halfway out the window, and gravity took the decision out of my hands. I came close to blacking out when I hit the ground, but I fought for consciousness. I couldn't be *sure* anyone in the house heard the accident, and if I didn't find shelter soon, the sleet and cold would finish me off even if I didn't bleed to death.

I staggered to my feet, swallowing a cry of pain. Clutching my side, hoping I wasn't killing myself by making the wound bleed faster, I limped and stumbled back to the road.

Without the headlights, the dark was thick and oppressive, but the ambient light was just enough to illuminate Emmitt's body. He lay by the far side of the road, where he must have been tossed by the impact. He wasn't moving, and the angle of his neck was all wrong, but I had to check on him, just in case I was wrong and he was still alive.

My feet slid out from under me the moment they hit the icy road, and I slipped and slid the rest of the way on my hands and knees, leaving a trail of blood. In the distance, I could see three small yellow lights bobbing up and down from the direction of the house. Flashlights, I decided with relief. Good.

Someone in the house *had* heard the accident, and help was on the way. I'd be a dead woman otherwise, because I didn't think I'd be able to make it to the house on my own before I collapsed and the elements had their way with me.

I came to a stop beside Emmitt's body and let out a sob at what I saw. His neck was obviously broken, his eyes wide and staring. The sob hurt like hell, but once I'd let go of one, I couldn't restrain the rest.

I was on my knees, clutching my side, which oozed more blood, and crying uncontrollably when the beam of a flashlight hit me square in the face. The light sent a stabbing pain through my head that almost made me vomit. My vision still blurred with tears, I held up one bloody hand to shield my eyes from the flashlight's glare. There were three flashlights, though only one was focused on me. The other two illuminated Emmitt's ruined body.

"Aw, shit," said a man's voice softly.

One of the men behind the flashlights knelt beside Emmitt. I recognized Blake Porter, one of the supposed cultists I'd been doing such a fabulous job of investigating. He was the quintessential pretty boy, though he didn't look so pretty now with his blond hair plastered to his scalp and the look of raw sorrow on his beautiful face. He brushed his hand gently over Emmitt's face.

"Keep your fucking hands off him!" one of the other two growled, the one who insisted on shining his light right in my eyes. He took a menacing step in Blake's direction.

Blake looked up at the speaker blandly. "I was just closing his eyes." He sat back on his heels and held his hands innocently to his sides.

My head was still spinning from a combination of concussion, shock, and blood loss, but everything around me had taken on a surreal quality that had nothing to do with my injuries. These men weren't acting at all like first responders to an accident. There was no sense of urgency or shock. No one had spoken to me, asked if I was all right. And the man who'd ordered Blake to keep his hands to himself had sounded distinctly protective. But why would the cultists—*any* of the cultists—feel protective of the man who'd been trying to lure one of their members away? Did they even know who he was?

My teeth were chattering, my feet and hands almost completely numb. The wound in my side was anything but. I didn't know how long hypothermia would take to kill me, but if I had to guess, I'd say I was halfway to the grave already.

"C-call an ambulance," I stammered, since it obviously hadn't occurred to these wingnuts that I was in need of medical assistance.

"Shut up, you fucking bitch!" roared Mr. Hostility, the flashlight in my eyes still keeping me from seeing his face.

"Jamaal, no!" Blake suddenly yelled, reaching out, but he was too late.

I didn't see the kick coming until the heavy boot connected with my face, and the world went dark again.

When I came to, I wished I hadn't. My side still screamed in pain. I was still freezing, and soaked, and light-headed. And now my jaw felt not so much broken as crushed. I tasted blood in my mouth as I forced my eyes open.

I was lying on the road, being pelted by sleet. All three of the cultists' flashlights were on the ground. With none of the beams directly in my eyes, I could actually see what was going on around me.

The man who had kicked me—Jamaal—was being held back by a third man, who I recognized as Logan Fields, the man Maggie had run off with. It was hard to believe that Logan was physically capable of restraining Jamaal, who was even bigger and more imposing than Emmitt.

I had no idea what Jamaal had against me, but whatever it was, he was beyond livid. His face was twisted into a feral snarl, and he was struggling against Logan's hold with every ounce of strength, his head lashing back and forth, whipping the beads at the ends of his braids across Logan's face. Somehow, Logan held on, though his face was dotted with welts, and the uncertain footing should have seen them both sprawling on the ground.

"Take it easy, Jamaal," Blake said. He was standing between me and the two struggling men, but he looked even less able to hold off Jamaal than Logan did. "You're not helping Emmitt by acting like a mad dog."

That enraged Jamaal even more. His howl sounded scarcely human, sending a superstitious shiver down my spine.

Incongruously, Logan laughed, even as he struggled to hold Jamaal back. "You sure have a way with words, bud."

Blake looked sheepish. "Sorry."

Again, my sluggish brain struggled to make sense of things. Why were these guys talking about Emmitt like he was a friend of theirs? He was supposed to be the enemy. At least, that's what he'd told me. But I was beginning to wonder if anything Emmitt had told me was the truth.

"Jamaal," Logan said sharply, trying to get the other man's attention. "I don't want to hurt you, man, but I'm getting pretty damn tired of playing referee."

"Then let me go!" Jamaal snarled in reply, his eyes fixed on me with such hatred it was amazing I didn't go up in a puff of smoke.

"Enough!" Logan said, but Jamaal continued to struggle. Logan heaved a sigh, and then . . . I'm not really sure what happened. Maybe it was the multiple blows to my head, or the shock, or a cold-induced hallucination, but it looked to me like Logan shoved the bigger man forward so hard that he flew all the way across the road and slammed into the trunk of a tree on the other side. And when I say flew, I don't mean stumbled—I mean he flew through the air with the greatest of ease.

Impossible, of course. Even if the men had been more evenly matched, it wasn't possible for one human being to throw another human being that far and with such force. Icicles rained from the branches of the tree as it shuddered with the impact. When Jamaal collapsed to the ground over the knotty roots, he didn't get up.

Logan gave me a quick glance, his face registering mild distaste—which I much preferred to Jamaal's rabid hostility—then turned his attention back to Blake. "Take her to the house. I'll hang out here until Jamaal comes to. And I'll try to talk him down a bit when he does."

Blake looked at Jamaal's crumpled form doubtfully. "I think she may have just killed the only person capable of talking him down."

Logan looked grim. "Maybe. But I might have a chance if you just get her out of sight."

Blake didn't look convinced. "Good luck with that."

I tried to form some kind of protest. I didn't need to go to the house—I needed to go to the *hospital*. I didn't know just how badly I was wounded, but I was sure it was pretty damn bad. Even before Jamaal kicked me in the face.

I doubt Blake would have listened to my protest, even if I'd managed to muster one. My jaw sent spears of agony through my head the moment I tried to move it, and I was now shivering so violently I wasn't sure I'd be able to get words out anyway.

Blake squatted beside me, slipping one arm behind my shoulders and one behind my knees. Then he rose easily to his feet, making no particular effort not to jostle me. I couldn't help crying out at the pain, but Blake ignored me.

Behind us, Jamaal let out a little groan.

"Shit," Blake and Logan said in unison. And then Blake began jogging back toward the house, slipping and sliding like mad, and I was in too much pain to think of anything other than how much I wished I would pass out for a third time.

Blake carried me all the way around the house to a back entrance. He knocked on the door with his foot, and moments later I heard footsteps approaching. The lights went on, and the door swung open.

I was barely conscious, my clothes soaked through with melted ice and blood. I felt I'd never be warm again, sure I was going to die if I didn't get medical attention stat. Through eyes narrowed in pain, I saw a few more cultists—including Maggie—standing in the hall with anxious looks on their faces.

"What happened?" one of them asked as Blake stepped inside.

He shook his head. "Emmitt's dead."

Someone gasped, and Maggie covered her mouth to stifle a cry. Even in my shocked, semi-lucid state, I was once again aware of how off everything seemed. Not only did everyone seem to know and care about Emmitt, but Blake was carrying the obviously battered body of a woman soaked in blood, and no one seemed to even consider calling an ambulance. What was wrong with these people?

My eyes finally adjusted to the brightly lit hallway, and I did a mental double take. Despite my distinct lack of success in investigating the cult, I had at least managed to identify and get photos of each member. In those photos, the only member of the cult who'd had a tattoo was Blake, who had a corny cartoon Cupid on his biceps. But as I blinked water out of my eyes, I saw that each person in the hall had a tattoo visible somewhere, mostly on their faces or necks.

The tattoos were like nothing I'd ever seen before. They looked like hieroglyphics or cuneiform or some other incomprehensible script, and though I stared, I couldn't for the life of me come up with a word to describe their color. In fact, the colors seemed to change with every minute shift of the light.

"What should I do with this one?" Blake asked, indicating me with a curl of his lip.

His question was directed at Anderson Kane, a man my observations had led me to believe was their leader, despite his laid-back demeanor; a suspicion that was even now being confirmed.

Anderson barely spared me a glance. "We'll deal with her later," he said dismissively. "Put her downstairs for now."

I voiced a protest at that, but no one listened to me. Oh, God. These guys were just going to dump me in a room somewhere and let me bleed to death!

I tried to find something I could say to persuade Blake he needed to call an ambulance, but if he heard a word I said, he made no sign of it. He carried me down a narrow flight of stairs into a huge basement, then into a drafty corridor punctuated with several doors, each of which came equipped with multiple deadbolt locks on the outside. None of those doors was locked, but the sight instantly called to mind a prison cellblock.

Blake stopped in front of the first door, pushing it open with his foot to reveal a small, barren room with a stone floor and a single thin cot in one corner. There was a sink and a toilet in another corner, but other than that, the room was empty.

Blake dropped me unceremoniously onto the cot, and I couldn't stifle a cry of pain as my side and my head both screamed in agony. Without another word, he turned his back on me and left the room, closing the door behind him.

With a moan of utter despair, I heard the dead bolts being thrown and realized that even if my wounds didn't kill me, I was still in big, big trouble.

THREE

I don't know how long I lay on that cot, shivering, bleeding, sure I was going to die. As far as I could tell, I didn't lose consciousness again, but my mind wasn't exactly all there. I suspected more time was passing than I could account for.

Feeling returned to my hands and feet, which was a relief. I'd been halfway convinced that even if I survived, I'd lose a few fingers and toes to frostbite. The pain in my side and my head faded to manageable levels, as long as I held absolutely still. The shivering didn't stop, but since my clothes were soaked through, that wasn't a surprise.

What the hell had happened out there?

I remembered my headlights illuminating Emmitt's face as he stood in the path of my car, remembered the little smile on his lips, and how he hadn't made the slightest attempt to get out of the way. The evidence suggested he had *wanted* me to hit him. But hell, if he was bent on committing suicide, surely he could have found an easier way!

After lying on that cot for who knows how long, I finally decided I couldn't stand the feel of wet fabric against my skin for another moment. Bracing myself for the pain, I made a tentative effort to push myself into a sitting position.

It was easier than I'd expected. Yeah, it hurt. My side screamed, and my head throbbed, and the whole room spun for a moment, but it was bearable. I glanced down at my sopping, bloodstained sweater and swallowed hard to keep from throwing up. Maybe moving around wasn't such a great idea after all. The blended scents of wet wool and coppery blood gave my stomach added incentive to rebel. I closed my eyes and breathed through my mouth until the nausea receded.

Wincing in anticipation, I grabbed the hem of the sweater and started slowly, carefully peeling it away from my skin. It stuck to my wound, but it was wet enough to come loose with little effort. I stifled a whimper, my stomach rolling again. I've never been that crazy about the sight of blood, especially my own.

Getting the sweater off over my head was pure torture; every movement of my left arm pulled on the muscles around the wound. Even so, I was determined to get the wet wool away from my skin.

Finally, I managed to drag the sweater off, dropping it to the floor with a plop. I sat still, breathing hard from the exertion. Each breath made my side hurt. I forced myself to open my eyes and examine the wound to see how bad it was and whether I'd started it bleeding again.

I expected to see a jagged, deep gash, based both on how much it hurt and how much I'd bled. The wound that met my eyes stretched from the bottom of my rib cage all the way down to my hip. Blood smeared my skin all the way around it, but the wound itself . . .

I blinked in confusion. The wound was an angry red seam, but the edges were kind of puckered together, as if there were a whole lot of invisible stitches holding it closed.

What the hell?

Gently, I touched the edge of the wound with one trembling finger, sure I must have passed out after all and been stitched up while I was unconscious. But I neither saw nor felt any stitches. Besides, if someone had stitched me up, they wouldn't have put the sodden sweater back on me.

I shuddered and decided to think about it later. I still had more wet clothing to get out of.

The pants came off more easily than the sweater. It was a relief to be out of the wet clothes, but I was still shivering in a residual chill, and there was nothing to wrap up in. The thin sheets of the cot were soaked and bloodstained and of no use. I wanted to take off the wet bra and panties, too, but there was no way I was sitting around this room naked. Bad enough that I was down to my underwear. At least I'd chosen a black satin matching set on the off chance Steph had set me up with a man I would hit it off with. Wishful thinking at its finest.

The date with Jim seemed so long ago, it had taken on an almost dreamlike quality. I checked my watch to get some feel for how long I'd been here, but the crystal was completely shattered, the hands bent so badly they couldn't move.

I looked across the room at the sink, thinking about running some hot water over my hands to warm up a little. Assuming there *was* any hot water in this dungeon.

I was trying to decide if it was worth the effort to drag myself to my feet to find out, when I heard footsteps approaching from down the hall. I quickly glanced around me, but no suitable cover-up had magically appeared. I settled for grabbing the soggy pillow, turning it so the dry side was against my skin and clasping it against my chest and belly. It wasn't much of a shield, but it was all I had.

My heart was in my throat as I heard the locks on my door clicking open. I sat up as straight as I could manage and raised my chin, hoping I looked braver than I felt.

The door swung open, and Anderson Kane stepped into the room, followed closely by Blake, who had changed into clean, dry clothes. The light revealed an iridescent tattoo beside Blake's left eye. The shape was vaguely phallic, and like the tattoos I'd seen on the other cultists, it hadn't been there when I'd taken the surveillance photos. Blake was carrying a chair, which he set on the floor before moving to stand in front of the door as if to block my escape.

Making a dash for it might have been tempting if I'd thought I had the least chance in hell of getting to safety. But even if I could miraculously get by both Blake and Anderson, it was unlikely that I'd get past the other cultists and out of the house. And even if I did, running out into the sleet on foot wearing nothing but a bra and panties was somewhere between insane and outright suicidal.

Anderson adjusted the angle of the chair until it was squarely facing me, then sat down. He didn't speak, instead giving me a slow and thorough once-over. Not knowing what to say—I wasn't going to repeat the "call an ambulance" line yet again only to have it ignored—I followed suit.

At first glance, Anderson was unprepossessing. Medium height, medium build, medium brown hair. Not bad looking, in a bland vanilla sort of way. He wore a pair of tan cords with a slightly wrinkled blue Oxford shirt, and his hair was shaggy and past due for a cut. His five o'clock shadow looked scruffy, rather than sexy. He was the kind of guy you'd pass in the street without giving a second glance.

Except for the weird tattoo, that is.

It was on his neck, just above the collar of his shirt, and I still couldn't tell what color it was. Part of it looked kind of silver, another part flashed red, but then he tilted his head to the side and the silver turned green and the red turned gold. I blinked a couple of times, trying to clear my vision. The tattoo looked more like a hologram than ink, but I'd never heard of a wearable hologram.

"You're staring," Anderson said, his voice startling me so much I jumped and almost dropped the pillow.

I jerked my eyes away from the tattoo, which I had, indeed, been staring at. I swallowed and clutched the pillow a little more tightly against me.

I didn't know how to respond to his statement, so I didn't. "Is there some reason you're so dead set against calling me an ambulance?" I asked instead.

He raised his eyebrows. "I would think that's obvious."

I didn't like the sound of that. His reasoning was far from obvious, but nothing I came up with on my own—like he was going to kill me anyway—was in the least bit comforting.

"I was in a car accident and then kicked in the head," I said. "Even if it's obvious, I'm not getting it. Please humor me and explain."

He sat back in his chair, looking thoughtful.

Blake snorted, drawing my attention. He was leaning against the closed door, arms crossed over his chest. His blue eyes pierced me, his anger as cold as Jamaal's had been hot.

"Playing dumb isn't going to win you any brownie points," he said with a sneer. I'd never known a pretty boy could look that menacing. The sneer changed to a leer that was just as unpleasant. "Dropping the pillow might, though."

Blood heated my cheeks. It pissed me off that I was letting him get to me that easily, but I couldn't seem to help it. I dropped my gaze and held the pillow even more tightly.

Anderson sighed. "Please forgive Blake's bedside manner. Sometimes he just can't help himself when a pretty woman's around."

Anderson had his back to Blake and therefore couldn't see the look on the other man's face, but I didn't for a moment believe he hadn't heard the malice in Blake's tone of voice. Flirtation had been the furthest thing from Blake's mind, and Anderson knew that. Besides, I wasn't exactly a ravishing beauty, even when I wasn't wet, dirty, bruised, and bedraggled. I was kind of like Anderson, come to think of it—not bad to look at, but completely unremarkable.

"So you have no idea why we didn't call an ambulance?" Anderson asked, bringing us back on topic.

I shook my head. "It's generally what people do when there's been a car accident and someone's hurt."

"Oh, please!" Blake said. "Cut the bullshit."

"Ease down, Blake," Anderson said in a low, calming voice. "It's always possible she's telling the truth."

"Oh yeah, like this is all some big fucking coincidence."

"Blake!" Anderson said with a little more heat, and Blake shut up. Anderson smiled at me, but the expression didn't reach his eyes. "Do you still think you need an ambulance?"

The question stopped me cold. My sense of time was completely out of whack, but it couldn't have been more than an hour or so ago that I'd stumbled out onto the road, bleeding so badly I left a trail across the ice. Now I was still in pain and feeling badly beat up, but the wound seemed to have almost closed itself, and I seemed to be suffering no aftereffects from having lost so much blood. All of which was, of course, impossible.

Anderson didn't wait for me to answer. "What were you doing on our property?"

There was no heat or anger in his voice, and yet there was a studied intensity to his question. He looked at me like a lawyer might look at a witness he was sure was about to lie.

I wasn't sure what to say. The reason I was here was a long story, and one Anderson wasn't going to like. Plus, the more I thought about it, the more full of holes it sounded, especially if I accepted that Emmitt must have been lying to me about at least some of the stuff he'd told me.

"I was here to meet Emmitt," I finally said, deciding to keep my answer simple but true.

"Like hell you were!" Blake snapped. "Hey, Anderson, maybe you should get her a towel or something to wrap up in. I'll stay here and keep watch." He gave me another creepy leer. His pants were so tight I couldn't help seeing the evidence of why he was really suggesting Anderson leave the room.

Anderson apparently didn't need to see Blake to know what he was thinking. He smiled that mild smile of his. "I'm sure the pillow will suffice." His eyes met mine, and there was no missing the threat in his next softly spoken words. "For now."

My gut cramped with fear as I recognized the good cop/bad cop tactics. If you'd told me before tonight that Blake Porter would make an effective bad cop, I'd probably have laughed at you. He was just too goddamn pretty to be scary, with his smooth, flawless skin that probably never grew more than peach fuzz, and his Cupid's bow mouth. But right now, the absolute last thing I wanted was to be left alone with him. Unfortunately, my story sounded unbelievable even to my own ears, so why should these guys believe it?

"Why were you here to meet Emmitt?" Anderson prompted.

I decided that no matter how weird my story was going to sound under the circumstances, I had no alternative but to start talking and hope for the best.

Slowly, trying not to stammer, I told them a carefully edited version of how and why Emmitt had hired me, leaving out any mention of crazy cultists. Anderson's face gave away nothing, but Blake made repeated little snorts of disbelief and rolled his eyes a couple of times.

When I explained that Emmitt had asked me to meet him

in front of the gates, and that I'd found the gates open and driven through, both men fell silent, the silence an oppressive weight that made me want to sink under the bed and disappear. I forced myself to keep talking, though I didn't want to relive the nightmare of seeing Emmitt standing there in the road with that little smile.

"So what you're saying is that it was an accident?" Anderson asked when I finished talking.

I blinked at him. "Of course it was an accident! At least on my part. Did you think I ran him down on purpose?"

"What do you mean, at least on your part?"

I was momentarily taken aback by the question. I thought I'd made it perfectly clear when I'd explained. But despite everything Emmitt had told me, I was now convinced these people were actually friends of his, and it must have been shocking for them to hear that he'd basically killed himself. Maybe they didn't want to hear it and had subconsciously filtered that part out.

"I mean he just stood there in the middle of the road, looking at me and smiling, waiting for me to hit him. I don't know if he could have gotten out of the way if he'd tried, but he didn't even try."

There was a howl of rage from just outside the room. The door slammed open with such force that Blake, who was standing in front of it, went flying. He hit the floor hard and came up cursing.

Jamaal stormed into the cell in the same towering rage I'd seen by the side of the road. If he was suffering any ill effects from his tussle with Logan, I saw no sign of them.

His eyes locked on me, and he came at me like a guided missile. Leader or not, Anderson scrambled out from between us, leaving me to fend for myself.

If Anderson was the good cop, and Blake was the bad cop, Jamaal was the complete psycho cop. I'm physically fit and fairly athletic. I also know enough basic self-defense not to be completely useless in a fight. But I would have been no match for Jamaal even without my injuries. I couldn't even manage to get to my feet before he was on me, grabbing me by the throat.

I dropped the pillow and tried to loosen Jamaal's grip, digging my fingernails into his hand as hard as I could. I'd have gone for his face, only his arms were longer than mine and I couldn't reach. When clawing at him didn't work, I tried to separate one of his fingers from the herd and throw all my strength into peeling it away, willing to break it if necessary. My efforts didn't bother him in the least, and he hauled me off of the cot until my feet dangled.

I stopped trying to loosen his fingers and merely held on to his arm, trying to pull myself up a bit so I didn't strangle. It was a useless effort, and his hand squeezed hard enough to cut off my air completely.

Still easily holding me off the floor, he stepped around the cot so he could slam me against the wall so hard I saw stars. Or maybe the stars were just because I couldn't breathe. My struggles weakened as my brain starved for oxygen.

Anderson came to stand beside Jamaal, his expression one of gentle concern. Concern for Jamaal, that is, not for me.

"She can't talk while you're choking her."

Jamaal bared his teeth in a feral smile. "That's a shame." He pulled me forward then slammed me into the wall again to show how heartbroken he was. I could hardly believe I hadn't passed out from lack of oxygen yet.

"We need to get answers out of her," Anderson said, still in that mild voice.

"You can get answers out of her when I'm finished!" Jamaal snarled, and the look on Anderson's face hardened.

"I'm giving you an order, Jamaal. Let go. Now!"

"Fuck you!"

Across the room, Blake cursed again. The whole mild-mannered leader act Anderson had been putting on suddenly dissolved. His back straightened, his eyes flashed with anger, and his face took on an expression that said someone was about to die—or *wish* for death.

"Wrong answer," Anderson said, his voice dropping about an octave and filled with a power that made my teeth ache.

My vision was beginning to fade around the edges, but I saw Anderson reach out and clap his hand on Jamaal's shoulder, right at the base of his neck. The hatred faded from Jamaal's face as his eyes widened in what looked like alarm, though I couldn't see why. Then suddenly, he let go of me and screamed.

My feet hit the floor. I crumpled to my knees, gagging and coughing as I tried to draw air into my lungs.

Jamaal collapsed, too, trying to pull away from Anderson's grip as he did. Anderson must have been stronger than he looked, maintaining his grip as he lowered himself into a crouch so he could keep his hand on Jamaal's shoulder. Anderson's face had turned to stone, all expression bleeding away as Jamaal continued to scream in obvious pain. In that moment, Anderson looked almost inhuman, an ice-cold predator who could kill without hesitation or remorse.

Blake appeared in the periphery of my vision. He moved with caution, but he didn't look scared or surprised by whatever Anderson was doing. "Go easy on him, boss," he said with a wince of sympathy. "He just lost his best friend."

The expression on Anderson's face thawed, a hint of humanity returning to his eyes, but he didn't let go. Jamaal's screams were weakening. What the hell was Anderson doing that caused such intense pain? His grip didn't even look all that tight.

"He'll pass out soon enough," Anderson said, and moments later Jamaal's whole body went limp. Anderson let go of his shoulder, and even on Jamaal's coffee-colored skin, I could see the bright red hand mark where Anderson had been touching him.

"Sorry, my friend," Anderson said so softly I barely heard him. The stone-cold killer was gone, and the mild-mannered human being was back. He stood up and looked at Blake. "Put him next door," he said. "Then gather the troops in my study."

Blake didn't look happy with the order, but he complied, gently picking up Jamaal's limp body and carrying him out of the room. Anderson looked down his nose at me. I was still coughing, but the gagging seemed to have stopped, and my vision had cleared.

"I'll be back in a couple of hours," he told me. "Think carefully about your story and whether you'd like to amend it. Unless you're a very skilled actress, I'm pretty sure you were not familiar with the power I just used against Jamaal. If I come back later and don't like your answers, I'll let you experience it firsthand."

I swallowed hard. So much for the "good cop" act.

Without a backward glance, he marched out the door, slamming it behind him. Once again, the locks clicked shut.

No doubt about it. I was in deep shit.

FOUR

My throat hurt every time I swallowed, but other than that, I didn't feel as bad as I expected after nearly being choked to death. Especially considering that beforehand I'd been seriously injured in a car accident, then been kicked in the face, then nearly perished from exposure.

Do you still think you need an ambulance? Anderson's voice echoed in my head.

Rubbing my bruised throat, I sat down on the edge of the cot and tried to absorb everything I'd seen and heard tonight.

Emmitt, appearing in front of my car from out of nowhere.

Logan, lifting Jamaal off his feet and flinging him all the way across the road and into the trees beyond.

My wound sealing itself with invisible stitches.

Anderson's fire-red handprint on Jamaal's shoulder.

I've never been much into all that woo-woo stuff, but either I was having the longest, weirdest dream in the history of mankind, or something decidedly woo-woo was going on.

I hoped for the former, but suspected the latter.

I looked down at the gash in my side and was only dully surprised to see the entire line scabbed over. I imagined the *Twilight Zone* music playing in the background, then shook off the thought before I made myself hysterical.

I decided to make a cursory examination of my cell. I tried the door, of course, but the sound of those locks clicking shut had been no illusion. I tried the sink and discovered that yes, blessedly, I could get hot water. I picked up my bloody, ruined sweater, rinsed out as much of the blood as possible, then used the sleeve like a washcloth to clean myself up.

I was painfully aware that Anderson was planning to come back and question me later. The kid gloves were going to come off, but I couldn't figure out what he wanted to hear. If I thought about how our next interview was going to go, all I would do was send myself into a panic. Instead I stripped the sheets off the cot and rinsed them in the sink. Then I flipped the mattress over and was relieved to find I hadn't soaked it through. With nothing left to do, I reluctantly lay down, terrified of being alone with my thoughts.

I hadn't been lying down for more than five minutes when I heard footsteps out in the hall again, and I was struck with a far more virulent terror. I shot to my feet, heart pounding and adrenaline flooding my system as I waited in dread for Anderson to finally carry out his threat.

But when the door opened, it wasn't Anderson after all.

The word that had first come to my mind when Emmitt had shown me a picture of Maggie Burnham was *statuesque*. I guessed her height at about five-eleven, and she was built like an athlete. She had absolutely gorgeous curly auburn hair, and a pretty, heart-shaped face.

She wasn't looking her best tonight, though. Not with those

red-rimmed eyes and the sorrowful droop of her shoulders. I had no clue what her real relationship with Emmitt had been, but it was clear she was grieving.

"Hi," she said, smiling weakly. "I'm Maggie."

"Nice to meet you," I said automatically, though I mentally grimaced at the empty pleasantry. "I'm Nikki Glass."

She nodded. "I thought maybe you could use this." She held out a plush terrycloth robe, and I was so happy I could have hugged her. Considering that she was mourning Emmitt and that I'd been the instrument of his death, I wouldn't have been surprised if her first move had been to slap me.

"Thanks," I said, taking the robe from her outstretched hand. My voice came out a little scratchy. I told myself that it was an aftereffect of Jamaal's attempt to choke me to death, not a sign that I was about to burst into tears at the first hint of kindness. Cynically, I couldn't help wondering if she'd taken up the mantle of "good cop" now that Anderson had dispensed with it.

Maggie considerately turned her back as I removed my undies and slipped into the robe. I wouldn't have died of embarrassment if she hadn't, but under the circumstances, I was feeling vulnerable enough to appreciate the gesture. I had to take a deep breath to keep control of my emotions before I told her it was okay to turn around.

She took in the stripped bed and the wet, still-stained sheets that I'd draped over the sink to dry, and frowned.

"I see the boys are in major hard-ass mode," she commented in obvious disapproval. As far as I'd been able to determine, she was the only woman living here.

I crossed my arms over my chest, pulling the warm, soft robe close around me. "Yeah, well, they seem to think I killed Emmitt on purpose." The last word came out in something almost like a sob as the full weight of what had happened hit me.

I'd killed someone.

No, of course I hadn't meant to. And from where I was

standing, it sure looked like he'd deliberately put himself in harm's way. But still . . . He was dead, and it was my fault.

To my surprise, Maggie stepped forward and gave my shoulder a warm squeeze. "It's all right," she said, though her own eyes shone with unshed tears. "Anderson told us your story. The boys are all huffing and puffing with conspiracy theories, but I believe you."

I had to swallow hard a couple of times before I found my voice. "You do? Why?"

She smiled sadly and gestured at the cot. "Why don't we sit down? This might take a few minutes."

We both sat, backs to the wall. I gathered the robe around my legs and wrapped my arms around my knees.

"You told Anderson that Emmitt hired you to investigate me," Maggie said.

I shook my head. "Not exactly. He originally hired me to find you, then he asked me to try to learn more about . . . um . . ." I'd kind of glossed over the whole cult thing when I'd explained to Anderson, and I didn't want to blurt out anything tactless now, either.

Maggie grinned at me, a surprisingly genuine expression, considering her obvious sorrow. "I can only guess what he might have told you. He claimed that I'd fallen in with a bunch of loonies. Is that the gist of it?"

I couldn't help returning her grin. "Yeah, basically."

"And then tonight . . . ?"

"Tonight he said you'd called him and were ready to leave. I was supposed to meet him here as an extra witness." I frowned as I realized how flimsy Emmitt's story had been. There was a reason my gut had been telling me to say no, but my desire to escape from my bad date had overridden my common sense. It would have been so much better if I'd told Jim I had to meet a client and then driven straight home. Why hadn't I thought of that?

"Then he surprised you on a dark, icy road when you had no time to stop or swerve."

I nodded, but couldn't find the voice to speak.

"The goddamn selfish bastard," Maggie said thickly, shaking her head as a single tear snaked down her cheek. She reached up and dashed it away angrily.

"Do you . . . Do you know why he did it?" I asked softly, wondering if it was any of my business.

She let out a heavy sigh. "He was getting old. Old and tired. I knew that, but he was too much of a tough guy to admit how bad it was."

"Old?" I cried, totally confused. "The guy couldn't have been more than twenty-five, tops." Truthfully, I thought he was closer to twenty-two.

Her lips twisted into a wry smile. "He was more than twenty-five. Trust me."

I gaped. "Even if I'm off by a bit, there's no way in hell he qualified as 'old.'"

"What if you're off by an order of magnitude?"

"I don't believe in woo-woo," I said, without great conviction.

Another wry smile. "You might want to start. I'm afraid right now you're neck-deep in woo-woo and still sinking."

I grimaced. Yeah, that was kind of what I was afraid of. "Where's a life vest when you need it?" I joked feebly.

Maggie reached into the back pocket of her jeans and pulled out a slim compact. "There's something I think you should see," she said, thumbing the compact open and then handing it to me.

Hesitantly, I took the compact from her hand. The makeup inside looked ordinary enough, so I guessed that the something I needed to see would be in the mirror. Holding my breath, I opened the compact all the way and looked at my reflection.

I looked awful. There was a big lump on my temple, and my right eye was thoroughly blackened. The entire left side of my face was one big bruise from where Jamaal had kicked me—though the bruise looked like it was about three days old. But clearly, that wasn't what Maggie had wanted me to see.

No, what Maggie wanted me to see was the iridescent mark on my forehead. It vaguely resembled a half-moon with an arrow through its middle. My mouth dropped open and my eyes widened as I reached up to touch the mark that quite obviously was not a tattoo.

"What the fuck is that?" I whispered.

"It's a glyph," Maggie explained, holding out her hand so I could see the mark on the back of it. Hers looked like a stylized circular lightning bolt. "It represents whose line you're descended from."

"Line?" My voice sounded hollow, and I stared intently at the mirror. The glyph wouldn't go away, no matter how many times I blinked or how I rubbed it.

Out of the corner of my eye, I saw Maggie run a finger over the glyph on her hand. "Mine represents Zeus," she said. "I've never seen one like yours before, but Anderson says it's Artemis. I didn't think she had any descendants—she was supposed to be a virgin goddess—but I'll take his word for it."

"Artemis." I sounded like a mentally challenged myna bird, but none of this was quite sinking in. My rational mind threw in the towel, deciding to go hide somewhere safe until the world returned to order.

"Emmitt was from Hades' line. Jamaal's a descendant of Kali, and he and Emmitt bonded like brothers because both of them possessed death magic. Emmitt was mentoring him, teaching him control, but Jamaal still had a long way to go. Without Emmitt to balance him, it's hard to know if he'll be able to hold it together.

"You also met Logan, right?" She didn't wait for my answer. "He's Tyr." She cocked her head at me. "Are you familiar with Tyr?"

Totally numb—and not comprehending a word of what I was hearing—I shook my head.

"He was an old Germanic war god. Descendants of war gods tend to be kind of cranky, but Logan is one of the most easygoing people I know. Oh, and I almost forgot Blake." She made a face, making it clear Blake was not her favorite person. "He's a descendant of Eros. Despite that cutesy Cupid tattoo he's got, there's nothing even remotely cherubic about him. He's easily as deadly as Jamaal. He's just not as in-your-face about it."

I remembered the way Blake had looked at me while he was playing bad cop. That was plenty in-your-face for me.

Maggie gave my shoulder another sympathetic squeeze. "I know this has got to be overwhelming, and you probably don't believe half of what I've said. I'll give you the quick highlights and then give you some time to try to absorb it all.

"Anderson and the rest of us are what is known as *Liberi Deorum,* which means 'children of the gods' in Latin. A long time ago, when the ancient gods were still around, they had children with mortals. Before the gods left Earth, they gave each of their children a seed from the Tree of Life. This seed made them immortal, and the *Liberi* thought they were gods themselves as a result. The only limitation they had—as far as they knew—was that they couldn't make their own children immortal, because the gods took the Tree of Life with them when they left. What the first *Liberi* didn't know until too late was that anyone with even a drop of divine blood—in other words, all their children and descendants—could steal their immortality by killing them."

Wow. That was one hell of a detailed delusion. I had to admit, there was something decidedly weird going on. But come on, children of the gods? Really?

"The glyph on your forehead marks you as a descendant of Artemis," Maggie continued. "When you killed Emmitt, you also stole his immortality. Not on purpose, I know," she hastened to add.

"So I'm immortal now?" I asked, trying to hide my skepticism the best I could—which wasn't well at all.

"I know it sounds crazy. But yes, you are."

"Uh-huh."

"The guys—especially Jamaal—think you already knew all this and staged the accident to steal Emmitt's immortality deliberately."

Perfectly logical—if you bought into the craziness in the first place, which I wasn't about to do. "But *you* think Emmitt committed suicide, because he knew I was a descendant of Artemis and was actually capable of killing him?" I was well aware of my tone of voice, that I was talking to her like I was humoring a dangerous psycho, but I couldn't help it.

Maggie nodded. "I don't know how he found you, but he must have seen the glyph on your face and decided to use you."

"But the glyph only showed up a little while ago!" Had I caught an inconsistency in her story?

"It's been there all along. It's just that only *Liberi* can see it."

Some of this was beginning to make a weird kind of sense, and I began to worry about my own sanity. Maybe the blows to my head had rattled my brain around more than I knew. But Maggie was the closest thing I had to an ally in this loony bin, and I needed to take advantage of that while I could.

"It's all a little much to take in," I said, because I didn't have it in me to actually say I believed her.

"I know," she said with a gentle smile. "And it's all right. You don't have to pretend to believe me. I'm not offended."

Maggie was definitely the nicest of the cultists. It was time to test just *how* nice.

"Thanks for being so understanding," I said.

"Hey, we girls have to stick together here in Testosteroneville."

"Yeah, about that . . ."

"I'm sorry, but I can't let you out," Maggie said.

"Please, Maggie. I think Anderson's going to . . . interrogate me. And I don't think that's going to go so well for me." I didn't have to force the shudder.

She gave me a sympathetic smile. "It'll be all right. I'd let you out if I could, but Anderson gave me an order, and disobeying his orders isn't such a great idea."

I remembered Jamaal's scream, and felt just a little guilty for asking Maggie to defy Anderson. Not enough to stop asking, though.

"Maggie, I—"

But she'd had enough, rising to her feet and cutting me off. "I can't, Nikki. I just can't. I'll get you some clean bedding, some towels, and some toiletries, but that's the best I can do."

She started toward the door, and I slid off the bed, wondering if I could barrel past her and escape. I didn't like my odds, but I might have tried it anyway if my wounded side hadn't screamed in pain. Apparently, I'd stood too fast. By the time I was able to breathe through the pain, Maggie was gone and the door was closed.

FIVE

Maggie brought the supplies she had promised. If I had been inclined to stick my head in the sand and pretend nothing out of the ordinary was happening, I might have been able to curl up on the cot in something resembling comfort and gotten some sleep. Of course, sleeping was the last thing on my mind; I kept thinking Anderson was going to come back to "question" me.

He never showed. Maybe Maggie convinced him that I was telling the truth. Or maybe he just thought the anticipation of pain would crack me faster than the pain itself.

Whatever the reason, no one came for me through the long hours of the night. For a while, I was treated to the comforting sound of Jamaal pounding on a door and yelling at the top of his lungs. Apparently, Anderson had locked *him* in one of these basement rooms, too, and he wasn't shy about letting everyone know he was unhappy about it.

Every time I heard his voice, I found myself self-consciously rubbing my throat, where I should have had bruises galore from his attempt to strangle me to death. I didn't have a mirror, but as far as I could tell by touch, there wasn't any bruising at all.

Of course, everything Maggie had told me had to be bullshit. Right? There was a perfectly rational explanation for everything that had happened tonight. Damned if I could figure out what it was, though.

Locked as I was in a room without windows, and wearing a broken watch, my internal clock was my only way to keep track of time. No matter how scared and freaked out I was, as the hours crept by, exhaustion sat more and more heavily on my shoulders. When the pillow started to look inviting, I forced myself to the sink and splashed some cold water on my face. It helped me feel more alert for all of about five seconds.

I never consciously made the decision to lie down and sleep, but when the door to my cell next cracked open, the sound of squealing hinges woke me up with a start. My heart instantly went on red alert, pounding adrenaline through my system. I leapt to my feet, wide awake. My side didn't scream at me for the sudden movement, but I was too alarmed to be relieved.

Standing in the doorway, grinning as if my terror was the funniest thing he'd ever seen, was yet another one of Emmitt's "cult members." This one was Jack Gillespie, and he looked a bit like a transplanted surfer-dude. His curly, dark blond hair was streaked with lighter blond—an effect that was probably supposed to look like sun-bleaching, but was a little too even to be anything but man-made. His skin was a deep, skin-cancer tan, and in the handful of times I'd seen him, he'd always been wearing torn jeans and a short-sleeved T-shirt, despite the cold.

I shook off my fear and narrowed my eyes at him. "Has Anderson ordered you guys to take turns coming to see me, or what?" I asked. Unless there was another cultist I wasn't aware of, I had now met all but one of the men Emmitt had had me "investigating."

Jack's grin didn't falter. "If Anderson had ordered me to come down here and talk to you, I probably wouldn't be here. I'm not too good with orders."

I rubbed my eyes. Now that the first surge of adrenaline had faded, I remembered how utterly exhausted I was. I had no idea what time it was, or how long I'd been asleep, but I felt like I could sleep another six or eight hours, easy. I wasn't in the mood for witty banter.

"Are you just here to stare at me like I'm an animal in a zoo, or is there something you want?"

He leaned casually against the doorjamb and crossed his arms over what his tight T-shirt advertised was a very nice chest. "I'll go away if I'm interrupting your beauty sleep. But I thought you might sleep better in your own bed."

My heart leapt at the thought, though my rational mind immediately proclaimed the suggestion too good to be true.

"So you're letting me go?" I asked, making no attempt to mask my skepticism.

"I'm going to do better than that. I'm going to drive you home, seeing as what's left of your car has been towed. And there's not much in the way of public transportation out here even in the daytime."

I examined his words for hidden nuances, but couldn't find any. Still, there was something decidedly fishy going on. If Anderson had decided to release me, I was pretty sure I'd have been gone hours ago. Jack showing up here in what my body clock told me was the middle of the night or very early morning screamed of ulterior motives. Unfortunately, I had no idea what those motives could be.

"Why would you do that?" I asked suspiciously.

The grin came back full force. "Because it'll make Jamaal shit bricks." He rubbed the glyph on his forearm. "I'm of Loki's line, so making trouble is in my blood. And Jamaal is the easiest target ever."

I wasn't much of an expert on mythology, but if memory

served, Loki was a Norse trickster-god. But since I didn't buy this whole descended-from-the-gods bullshit, I didn't buy Jack's explanation, either. Still, letting him drive me home sounded like an excellent idea.

"Real nice of you to pick on someone whose best friend just died," I said, deciding that even if he was letting me go, I didn't much like him.

"Isn't it, though?" he responded, unperturbed.

"And you're not worried about what Anderson will do when he finds out?" Maggie had seemed awfully sympathetic to me, but she had categorically refused to defy Anderson's orders.

"Descendant of Loki, remember? We tend not to trouble ourselves about consequences. If I didn't piss Anderson off at least once a week, I'd feel like a disgrace to my divine ancestor."

I looked at him like he was crazy. Even crazier than the rest of the crazies here, that is.

He straightened up and gave an exaggerated shrug. "Hey, no skin off my teeth if you'd rather stay locked up down here. Make yourself comfortable. Anderson's going to come talk to you in the morning, and I'm sure that'll be just *loads* of fun."

I felt myself pale on cue, a hard knot of fear twisting in my gut.

"I won't look a gift horse in the mouth," I told Jack hurriedly, hoping I didn't look as scared as I felt. I'd never thought of myself as a shrinking violet, but I'd been scared so many times over the last few hours I might have to reassess my own toughness.

Jack nodded briskly. "I thought you'd come to see it my way." He reached behind him to pick something up from the floor. He held it out to me, and I saw that it was my pocketbook.

At least, it had been a pocketbook once upon a time. The tan leather was soaked through, turning it almost chocolate brown, there was a slash all the way across the front, and one of the straps was gone. I took a moment to mourn the loss—I love my bags, and this one had been my favorite—then took the ruined pocketbook from Jack.

"I couldn't get your car key out of the ignition," he told me, "but I got the rest of the keys off the ring and put them in the inside zipper compartment."

Numbly, I checked the pocket in question and was glad to see that my apartment keys had survived the crash. I was tempted to check the rest of the contents of the purse, but decided that might be rude, implying that Jack might have taken something. I didn't know why he was helping me—if that was really what he was doing—but if he was going to take me home, I didn't want to do anything to risk pissing him off.

"Ready to go?" he asked, stepping away from the door.

Way more than ready, I hurried out of the cell and into the hallway beyond.

Jack drove me home in a surprisingly bland black BMW. I'd have figured him for the red sports car kind of guy, but maybe he didn't like to be predictable. Or maybe he was "borrowing" someone else's car. I wouldn't have put it past him.

The clock on the dashboard informed me it was four a.m. I fought a yawn. God, I was tired! My body felt ridiculously good, considering the abuse it had taken, but if I really was now possessed of supernatural healing ability—a fact that I was going to have trouble continuing to deny—I must have burned extra energy to do it. I could hardly hold my head up.

The streets of Arlington were deserted at that time of night, and Jack made good time into Bethesda. He seemed to consider the speed limit merely a suggestion. Same with red lights and stop signs. If I weren't exhausted down to my bones, I might have been alarmed.

The good news was that we didn't get stopped by cops, and that Jack was blessedly quiet for the whole ride. I wasn't up to either an encounter with the police or another conversation that would make my head hurt. The bad news was that Jack never bothered to ask me where I lived. He drove straight to my apartment building, barely even looking at street signs.

The obvious conclusion was that even if he hadn't taken anything from my pocketbook, he'd obviously looked in it. My driver's license would conveniently provide my address, which made the fact that he was willing to let me go a little less surprising. As long as he knew where I lived, he—and his crazy friends—could get to me. The smirk he gave me as I dragged myself out of the car made me wish I had the energy—and the guts—to smack him.

"Be seeing you around," he said with a wave just before I slammed my door closed. The smile and the twinkle in his eye failed to hide the warning behind the words.

Moments later, I was safe inside my own home and could have wept in relief. My body still cried out for sleep, but I didn't have time for it. I had no illusions that the folks at Nutso Central were going to leave me alone, and that meant I had some preparations to make.

First, I had to get out of the apartment, much though it pained me to admit it. The feeling of safety that enveloped me when I stepped in the door was nothing but an illusion when Jack knew where I lived. He might or might not have been releasing me behind Anderson's back, but either way, I knew he wasn't doing it out of the goodness of his heart. I also knew he wasn't going to keep my address a secret.

I went into the kitchen to brew a pot of coffee—I was never going to stay awake otherwise—while I tried to figure out where to go. The light on my answering machine was blinking, and I hit it by reflex.

"Hey there, Nikki," said Steph's perky voice. "You know I hate it when you keep me in suspense. How'd it go tonight?"

I groaned and pinched the bridge of my nose. The Date from Hell seemed like it had happened in another lifetime. And any date Steph arranged for me came with a mandatory debriefing afterward, one that I could have done without in the best of times. In my current state of mind, I couldn't bear to face it. The answering machine beeped, then moved on to the next message. Steph again. What a surprise.

"It's midnight, and you haven't called me back yet," she scolded. "I promise to forgive you, but only if you're not calling because you're in the middle of some hot and heavy sex."

I snorted, both at the ridiculousness of the idea of me having hot and heavy sex with Jim, and at the ridiculousness of my real reason for not having called.

"I wish," I muttered.

I briefly considered going to stay with Steph for a while, just until I got things sorted out. Unlike me, she was willing to dip into her trust fund, and her house was more than big enough for the two of us. Not that my condo was a humble shack. My adoptive parents, the Glasses, had set up a trust fund for me at the same time they'd set up Steph's. When I'd refused to touch it, they'd bought this condo and offered to rent it to me for a ridiculously small sum. I should have turned it down, but I'd fallen in love with the place. I assuaged my guilty conscience by paying them three times what they asked, although they didn't need the money.

Mr. Glass had built a start-up company into a multinational corporation when he was young, and he had money to burn. I know it bothers him that I won't use the trust fund—he'd grown up poor and always dreamed of giving his children a better life. But as much as I loved my adoptive family, I can't help feeling like an interloper who doesn't deserve a share of their wealth.

Frowning fiercely as I packed a small roll-aboard bag, I decided that although Steph had plenty of room, I didn't dare stay at her place. It wouldn't be hard for Anderson and crew to find her connection to me and to track me there. I didn't want to put her in danger. Which meant I couldn't stay at the Glasses' house, either, even though they were away on a round the world cruise and I'd have had the place to myself. That left a hotel.

I took a long, hot shower before I left. Afterward, I stood naked in front of the foggy, full-length mirror. The wound was nothing but a faint red line. I couldn't even find a bruise anywhere. I didn't know whether to be thankful, or just freaked out.

Worse, the glyph was still there, despite my attempt to wash and exfoliate it away. Gone was my hope that it had all been a frighteningly realistic nightmare.

The sun was just beginning to rise when I cautiously set foot outside my apartment building, dragging the roll-aboard and carrying my laptop in a backpack. Along with the laptop, the backpack held my .38 Special and several boxes of ammo. I had never once needed to use it in my line of work, but I did sometimes have to venture into neighborhoods where I didn't feel safe. Having a gun gave me a sense of security. I wasn't a very good shot, and I wasn't sure I'd actually be able to pull the trigger if I were pointing it at a human being, but it was comforting to know I had the option. Of course, since I was headed for D.C.—the better to lose myself in the crowds—carrying a handgun was risky. I had concealed carry permits for Maryland and Virginia, but there was no such thing available for a civilian in D.C. Still, given the mess I was in, I wasn't leaving home without it.

I looked carefully up and down the street, but didn't see anyone suspicious lurking around. I then headed for the closest Metro stop and took the train to Dupont Circle, where I took a room at the Holiday Inn. The fact that no one on the train or in the hotel gave me a second glance suggested that Maggie had been telling the truth and ordinary people couldn't see the glyph. I refused to allow myself to speculate about which of the other outlandish things she'd said might be true.

As soon as it was late enough for businesses to open, I located the nearest shooting range—which, of course, was outside the D.C. city limits, making me thankful for our efficient public transportation. I had a feeling that with Anderson and his crazies potentially after me, I might need to use the gun whether I wanted to or not, and it wouldn't hurt to try to up-grade my shooting ability from "poor" to "okay."

I picked up a new cell phone to replace the one that was destroyed in the accident. Then I showed up at the shooting range by ten o'clock, my nerves taut with one hell of a caffeine buzz even while I found myself yawning every two point five seconds. There were three other people shooting—all men—and even through the earplugs, the sound of all those gunshots made me jumpy. Probably just the caffeine. Or the fact that the guy standing nearest to me was firing an assault rifle, which sounded rather like a cannon.

I figured with the exhaustion, the caffeine, and the way I jumped every time the assault rifle fired, I was going to have one of my worst shooting performances ever. I took aim at the target, taking a few slow, deep breaths in hopes that it would soothe my frazzled nerves. The guy with the cannon fired off a shot right as I was squeezing the trigger. My attempt to go Zen notwithstanding, my arms jerked as I jumped at the noise.

I almost laughed when I saw that my shot had hit the bull's-eye. Maybe I should take target practice while exhausted and jumpy more often. I took another couple of deep breaths to dispel the remainder of the adrenaline, then fired again. This time, my hands were steady.

And I hit the bull's-eye again.

Luck, I told myself. Even a bad shot had to hit the bull's-eye occasionally. That I'd just done it two times in a row was nothing more than a freaky coincidence. I lowered the gun so I could roll my shoulders a little bit to work out the tension. Then I took my shooter's stance again and squeezed the trigger.

I swallowed a yelp when I saw that for the third time, I'd hit the bull's-eye. If two times in a row was a freaky coincidence, what was three times in a row?

I lowered the gun again, this time looking it over as though I might find some magical can't-go-wrong gizmo had been attached while I wasn't looking. Of course, there was nothing different about the gun. I couldn't help remembering Maggie telling me that my glyph meant I was a descendant of Artemis, the Greek goddess of the hunt. Crazy talk, right? But if it *was* crazy talk, then it seemed like an awfully strange coincidence that suddenly I seemed to have become a sharpshooter.

Telling myself three bull's-eyes in a row was statistically within the realm of possibility even for a lousy shot like me, I raised my shaking hands and took aim again.

I was considerably less surprised this time when I hit dead center.

I took about twenty shots after that, experimenting. I tried aiming at things other than the bull's-eye. Being nowhere close to ambidextrous, I tried firing with my left hand. I even tried shooting with my eyes closed.

Whatever I aimed at, whatever crappy technique I used, I hit my target one hundred percent of the time, once and for all dismissing the statistical realm of possibility.

There was no more denying that I'd become a supernaturally good shot.

I headed back to the hotel in a daze, spaced out enough that I missed my stop on the Metro. I decided to walk the rest of the way, figuring the fresh air might do me good. I'm generally pretty good at denial, but the evidence was piling up too high. I might have been able to talk myself out of believing the things I'd seen the cultists do last night. They could have been tricks, after all, though who would go through such elaborate lengths to pull a trick like that on me? But it was much harder to explain away the glyph on my face, or the way my body had healed overnight, or the way I had suddenly become an expert marksman.

What am I talking about, "much harder"? It was *impossible* to explain away.

Much as I tried to convince myself that there had to be a rational explanation that didn't involve woo-woo, I failed. I didn't know where that left me—except with an aching head and an urge to give in to hysteria—but I'd had to learn to accept some very unpalatable truths in my life, so I would eventually find a way to accept this one.

I was in too much of a stupor to pay attention to what was going on around me, so at first I didn't notice the black Mercedes with the tinted windows that was pacing me. Even when the car behind it started honking indignantly, it barely registered on my conscious mind. Then, the Mercedes sped up a little, getting ahead of me and pulling into what would have been a parking space if it weren't for the fire hydrant.

The Mercedes's door opened and a man in an expensive charcoal gray suit got out. I froze in my tracks when I saw the stylized lightning-bolt glyph on the back of his hand.

SIX

He was not one of Anderson's people. He was a complete stranger to me, and the warm smile that curved his lips as he looked me up and down did nothing to ease my instant, instinctive dislike.

Many women would find him handsome. I supposed that objectively he was—tall, nicely muscled, manly square jaw softened by dimples when he smiled, and lovely gray-blue eyes. But the way he carried himself reminded me of every arrogant, entitled, self-centered country club asshole Steph had ever introduced me to, all rolled up into one pretty package.

I considered trying to walk past him, but the look in his eye told me he had no intention of letting me ignore him. There was nothing overtly threatening about him, but my gut was screaming "danger, danger" even so. I'd ignored my gut instincts last night, and look where it had gotten me.

"What do you want?" I growled at the stranger.

He blinked in what I suspected was surprise. I bet that smile of his had charmed every woman he'd ever used it on, but I was made of sterner stuff.

The smile flickered for a moment, then came back at full force as he took a step toward me. "My name is Alexis Colonomos," he said, holding out his hand for me to shake.

Instead of shaking his hand, I stepped backward, trying to keep a safe distance between us. I had no idea what a safe distance might be, however. Despite my recent skepticism, I had no doubt Alexis Colonomos would turn out to have supernatural powers of some sort.

"Nice to meet you," I said, making no attempt to sound like I meant it. "Now what do you want?"

The smile flickered again, and his eyes narrowed in what might have been anger as he let his hand fall back to his side. When he put the smiley face back on, it had lost some of its wattage, and there was a hard glint in his eye that suggested he was a man used to getting what he wanted.

"I just wanted to introduce myself," he said, and there was an edge in his voice that hadn't been there before. "And have a little talk." He gestured toward the open door of the Mercedes.

"If you think I'm going to get into a car with a total stranger, you're nuts." I took another step back, prepared to turn and bolt if he made a hostile move.

He didn't, but his smile lost even more wattage, until it started to look more like a snarl. "You're *Liberi*," he said from between gritted teeth. What were the chances he and Maggie would use the same unusual term to describe what I apparently was if it were all some freaky cult delusion? Yet another nail in the coffin of denial. "I couldn't hurt you if I wanted to." And everything about his body language said he wanted to very much.

Personally, I didn't think I'd been rude enough to warrant the level of hostility that radiated from this guy, but based on the behavior I'd witnessed last night, either it didn't take much to set a *Liberi* off, or I just had a natural knack for it.

"You can't kill me," I clarified, though I felt ridiculous making the claim. It was one thing to almost kind of believe it, and quite another to truly *accept* it. "That doesn't mean you can't *hurt* me." I'd seen evidence enough of that last night.

The smile turned into a sneer. "Cowardice isn't becoming to a descendant of Artemis."

I guess I was supposed to be so insulted by the suggestion I was a coward that I would meekly climb into the car. "There's a difference between cowardice and caution," I told him. "If you want to talk to me, then do it. If you don't want to do it standing here in the street, then offer to buy me a cup of coffee. I might take you up on it."

Maybe the smartest thing for me to have done was to turn around and run away. The vibe I was getting off this guy was anything but friendly. But I didn't know what he wanted from me, and I wasn't sure that ignorance was bliss. Plus, I had no idea how he'd found me. Even if he was some friend of Anderson's—a friend I'd never seen hanging around the mansion—he shouldn't have been able to locate me when I was nowhere near any of my usual stomping grounds.

Obviously, he *could* find me, and if I ran off now, he'd probably be even less friendly the next time he did. Which was why I was prepared to at least listen to what he had to say.

"Then may I buy you a cup of coffee?" he asked, and it looked like it physically hurt him to concede.

"I'd love one. How 'bout we head over to that diner?" I pointed at a greasy spoon on the opposite side of the street. It was doing a brisk business, so I figured it had good bad food and served bottomless cups of coffee.

Alexis looked at the place and curled his lip in disdain. I pegged him for the kind of guy who thought he was slumming it if he ate in a restaurant that charged less than five bucks for a cup of coffee. "Fine," he said, then slammed the door of the Mercedes with more force than necessary.

I hate sore losers.

I kept just enough space between us to be out of arm's reach as we crossed the street and headed to the diner. He probably wasn't going to try anything in broad daylight, in front of tons of witnesses, but you can never be too careful.

When he reached the diner, he pushed the door open and held it for me. It meant I had to brush by him to get inside, and I didn't like it. I reminded myself once again that he wouldn't dare try anything on a crowded street. His expression darkened as he noticed my hesitation, but I went inside before he could make an issue of it.

A waitress was clearing a table for two just as we walked in the door. The hostess directed us to that table with a wave of her hand, and we slid into the booth in silence while the waitress gathered up the remains of the previous patrons' meal.

"Be right back," she said with a distracted smile, then carried her loaded tray to the kitchen. As far as I could see, there was only one other waitress in the whole place, which explained why they were both moving so fast and looked so wild-eyed.

There were crumbs all over the place, and a smear of ketchup looking rather like a bloodstain threatened to drip over the edge and onto my lap. I grabbed a napkin from the dispenser to wipe it away, watching Alexis surreptitiously as I did. His lip remained curled in that singularly disdainful sneer, and his arms were crossed over his chest as if he were trying to minimize contact between himself and the diner. To say he looked out of place was an understatement. No one else was even wearing a dress shirt, much less a suit and tie.

The waitress came back and wiped off our table with a damp rag, but she had a harried look and wasn't very careful about it. A couple of crumbs tumbled off the table and onto Alexis's lap. His face reddened and his eyes sparked and I thought sure he was about to make a big scene. He restrained himself, however, and settled for staring daggers at her. It was all I could do not to smile.

Have I mentioned that this guy rubbed me the wrong way?

"What can I get you?" the waitress asked, pulling out her pen and order pad without making eye contact.

"Two cups of coffee, please," I said, because I was afraid that if Alexis opened his mouth he was going to be a total asshole.

"Anything else?"

"That'll do it," I said, and Alexis didn't contradict me. I suspected he'd rather starve to death than eat anything served at this place.

She was walking away before the last word left my mouth. If I couldn't see with my own two eyes how overworked she was, I'd have thought she was being rude.

I leaned back in my seat and eyed the dangerous-looking *Liberi* who sat across from me. I got the distinct impression that he'd been planning to charm me when he'd stepped out of that car, but I figured my attitude had killed that plan by now. Maybe I shouldn't have come on so strong right from the start, but I had a right to be grumpy after everything that had happened.

"So, what was it you wanted to talk about?" I asked as the waitress put two ceramic cups on the table and filled them with dark-as-pitch coffee. She reached into her apron and pulled out a handful of creamers, leaving them in a pile in the center of the table. She opened her mouth—I think she was going to ask if we needed anything else—but shut it again when she saw the forbidding expression on Alexis's face. He waited until she'd walked away to answer me.

"You're new in town," he said, and it wasn't a question.

I raised my eyebrows as I took a sip of coffee. "I am?"

He frowned at me, dark eyebrows forming a severe V. "You have to be. You're not one of ours, and you're not one of Anderson's." He said Anderson's name with another one of those little sneers of his.

I sipped my coffee, wishing I'd been able to believe Maggie last night so I could have asked her a lot more questions.

There was a hell of a lot I didn't know about being a *Liberi*. For instance, I had no idea what Alexis was talking about when he referred to "one of ours." Nor did I have any idea what—if anything—I should tell him about myself.

"Let's say for the sake of argument that I *am* new in town. What's it to you?"

He leaned forward, resting his elbows on the table and pushing his untouched coffee out of the way. "You'd best have a care how you talk to me," he said in a menacing whisper that carried just fine even in the noisy diner. "Descendants of Artemis are rare, and therefore valuable to us, but that will protect you only so far."

Ah, we'd reached the threat-making stage of the conversation. I'd had a feeling this was coming. Maybe if I hadn't just had the scariest night of my life, I'd have been more intimidated. Maybe it would have been *smart* to be more intimidated.

I let my hand slide under the table and smiled broadly—not the reaction Alexis was hoping for, if his scowl was anything to go by. "You know what I was doing before you ambushed me?" I asked, keeping my body language completely relaxed as I unzipped the front compartment of my backpack. I rested my hand lightly on the .38 Special. "I was at a gun range, polishing my skills. Turns out I'm a very good shot. Feel like giving me some more target practice?"

I had no intention of actually shooting the guy, or even taking the gun out. I wasn't even sure I'd be able to shoot a person in the heat of battle, much less in cold blood, and I sure as hell wasn't waving a gun around in a crowded D.C. diner. Felony charges and a prison stay would *not* improve my situation. But part of being a good P.I. is being a good actress.

I was a good P.I.

"You wouldn't dare," he growled at me.

I blinked at him innocently. "I wouldn't? How the hell would you know that? You don't even know my name, do you?" I'd seen no reason to introduce myself, and if he'd already known my name, I suspected he'd have flaunted the knowledge by now. "I could be sweet as sunshine or a total psycho bitch for all you know."

I leaned forward till I was almost nose-to-nose with him, meeting his glare with a good bit of steel. "Back the hell off, or you're going to find out the hard way," I said as I cocked the gun, making as much noise about it as possible. The diner was kind of noisy, but not so much that Alexis couldn't hear and recognize the sound.

I got the feeling Alexis desperately wanted to come across the table at me, but he just sat there glaring instead. Then his gaze flicked to something over my shoulder, and his eyes widened.

It was a classic distraction technique, but I couldn't help taking a peek over my shoulder anyway.

Alexis hadn't been trying to trick me. Standing in the doorway, giving me a decidedly neutral look, was Blake.

The hostess—who had to be pushing fifty—was giving him goo-goo eyes, and practically every adult female in the place, not to mention a few men, were surreptitiously looking him over. There's nothing like a well-built pretty-boy to get the hormones working overtime.

Blake ignored all of them—even the hostess, who was trying to direct him to an open seat at the counter—and started toward our table. I uncocked the gun, then scooted over in my seat so I could have the wall at my back while keeping an eye on both men.

Blake had been only slightly less hostile than Jamaal last night, but he was barely paying attention to me today. He and Alexis engaged in a hot and heavy alpha-male staring contest. I could practically smell the testosterone in the air, even over the bacon grease and coffee. I'd have liked to get out from between them, but there wasn't anywhere to go.

When Blake reached the table, he casually leaned against my side of the booth, never taking his eyes off Alexis.

"She's one of ours," Blake said, his voice as challenging as his stare. "Tell Konstantin to mind his own business."

Konstantin? Who the hell was Konstantin? And what was this "one of ours" crap?

Alexis raised his eyebrows. "If she's one of yours, then why are you letting her wander around the city unaccompanied before notifying Konstantin about her?"

"Get out. And leave her alone."

I'd have snapped at Blake for trying to protect the "little woman," only I wasn't sure that was what he was trying to do. It felt more like he was claiming his territory.

"I don't answer to you," Alexis countered. "And if she really belonged to Anderson, I'm sure she would have mentioned the fact by now."

"For the record," I said, though I wondered if drawing attention to myself was a bad idea, "I don't belong to anybody, especially you assholes."

Both men ignored me.

Blake shrugged. "Anderson has already decided she belongs to him. He sent me to fetch her, so that's what I'm doing. You have a problem with that, take it up with him."

Still barely sparing me a glance, Blake reached out and grabbed my arm in a bruising grip. I, of course, tried to pull away. But he was damn strong.

Alexis leaned forward, putting both his hands on the tabletop, his eyes practically glowing with menace. "Let go of her and get the fuck out of here, or you'll be sorry," he growled. "Konstantin wants to talk to her, and only a fool would get in his way."

Blake let go of my arm and smiled. He, too, leaned forward and put his hands on the table. He was crowding my personal space, but he was doing the same to Alexis. If this went much further, people around us were going to notice and try to break it up or call the cops.

I was considering how I might bring the tension down a notch when I felt a change in the air. The diner suddenly felt about ten degrees hotter, and the crowd and traffic noise became muted and dull.

Blake ran his tongue over those full, sensual lips of his, and even though I'd never been particularly attracted to him, I felt a tug of desire in my nether regions. My pulse kicked up and my breath hitched. The air filled with the musky scent of sex, and I pressed my thighs together in hopes of erasing the ache that had built without warning.

Across from me, Alexis's eyes darkened, and his mouth fell open. His breaths came in excited little puffs, and sweat dewed his face. The look he was giving Blake screamed of something very different from anger, and I'd bet anything he was sporting quite a tent pole under the table.

"Don't ever forget who I am," Blake said in a chilling croon as he leaned in even closer to Alexis. "Zeus's line may be powerful, but even Zeus was helpless against Eros. Unless you'd like me to take you into the men's room and fuck you till you scream for mercy, you'd better go tell Konstantin that this one is ours. Understand?"

Whatever Blake had been doing, he stopped abruptly. The temperature dropped, the musky scent evaporated, and the crowd noise returned to normal.

Across the table from me, Alexis recoiled, his back slamming against the backrest as he tried to put distance between himself and Blake. There was a wild look in his eyes, the lust that had been there only moments ago completely gone.

"Konstantin would have your balls for a trophy if you tried it," Alexis whispered, but though that was supposed to sound like a threat, it wasn't very effective when his face was so white, and his eyes so wide.

Blake smiled easily. "Wouldn't do *you* any good, now would it? Besides, you'd have to tell him what happened, and I don't see you admitting it. Now get out. If you're still here when I've counted to five, we'll be partying in the men's room, and that's a promise."

Alexis made a hasty exit before Blake got to two.

I'd have liked nothing better than to follow Alexis's example, but I was under no illusion that Blake would let me go that easily. He slid into the booth across from me. He beckoned to the harried waitress, and she stopped everything to bring him a fresh cup of coffee.

"Would you really have done it?" I found myself asking, not sure why I cared one way or another.

"Hell yes," he answered with a sharklike grin as he poured an indecent amount of sugar into his cup. "I've always hated that holier-than-thou bastard. He'd have loved every minute of it, too, until his head cleared."

I sure as hell didn't like Alexis, but I couldn't help thinking that what Blake had planned to do to him was downright evil. I guess that thought must have shown on my face.

"Oh, please. Don't feel sorry for him," Blake said. "The Olympians have embraced rape and torture as a goddamn art form, and he's totally on board with that. As long as he's not the victim, of course."

"The Olympians?"

"A bunch of descendants of Greek gods. They envision themselves as some kind of master race. They also consider themselves to be the ruling body for all the *Liberi*." He flashed me a sarcastic smile. "Not all of us see it that way."

"And who's Konstantin?"

"Their leader. He styles himself as their king, but I refused to call him that even when I *was* an Olympian. I'm sure as hell not going to call him that now."

My mind boiled with an endless stream of questions. I settled for the one I decided was of most immediate importance. "How did you find me? And how did *he* find me?"

Blake leaned back in his seat. "I'm guessing he found you because their Oracle had a vision. And before you ask, the Oracle is a descendant of Apollo, and she sometimes sees the future. Most of her visions are so vague and confusing you can't understand what they mean until whatever it is has already happened. But every once in a while, she sees something clearly."

I nodded, swallowing my skepticism for the millionth time. "That doesn't explain how *you* found me."

He smiled and didn't answer. He was definitely being less hostile now than he had been last night, but there was a hint of malice in his eyes; he wanted the mystery of how he had found me to creep me out. Unfortunately, I was giving him exactly what he wanted.

"All right," I said, trying not to show my discomfort, "*why* did you find me?"

"Anderson promised you a follow-up conversation, remember?"

I had a feeling my effort to hide the chill that ran through me was in vain.

"Jack merely delayed the inevitable when he pulled his juvenile little trick and snuck you out," Blake continued. "I'll give you a ride back to the house. You'll be safer there anyway. It's off-limits to the Olympians."

Another conversation with Anderson was not on my to-do list, and no matter how much I'd disliked Alexis, I couldn't imagine feeling "safer" at Anderson's mansion. "What if I decide to decline your generous offer?"

"I know you caught the edge of my aura when I used it against Alexis," he said, his nostrils flaring as if he scented my weakness. "The effect would be a hell of a lot more intense if I directed it at you. You'd follow me anywhere, begging me to fuck you. I wouldn't do it, but I'd magnanimously offer to let you suck my cock during the ride to the house. You'd have a grand ol' time." He smiled pleasantly.

I was sick and tired of being scared. The threat made my stomach do flip-flops, but I did my best not to let my face show it. "Is threatening people with rape your answer to every problem?"

"I do find it's remarkably effective," he responded with a dry edge in his voice. "And it's far less ostentatious than grabbing you and dragging you kicking and screaming out the door."

I hated being bullied, but I didn't have much choice but to give in—for the moment. "Fine," I said. "Let's go see Anderson."

Blake fixed me with a long, penetrating stare. I had a feeling he knew I wasn't the type to give up so easily. I gave him my best innocent look. I had no intention of setting foot within ten miles of Anderson and his Hand of Doom, but I didn't want to give Blake an excuse to practice his unique method of coercion on me. I'd never realized sex could be so effectively weaponized.

I don't know if my feigned innocence convinced Blake, or if he merely decided he was in too strong a position for me to give him trouble. Whatever the reason, he slipped out of the booth, and I was mildly surprised to see him throw a ten-dollar bill on the table. He hadn't struck me as the generous type, but not only was he paying for my coffee—and Alexis's—he was leaving the waitress a sizeable tip. He reached for my arm as I stood up, but I quickly danced out of reach.

"Keep your hands to yourself," I warned. "I'm coming with you peacefully, but you touch me and all bets are off."

He gave me one of his malicious grins. My threat was an empty one when he could use his creepy power to force me to come along, but I didn't want him touching me if I could help it. Getting away from him was going to be hard enough without having to break free of his grasp.

My threat might have had no teeth, but Blake didn't try to grab me again. He led me out of the diner and onto K Street, keeping a careful eye on me. I hoped he wasn't parked too close, because I needed some time to come up with an escape plan. The gun was in my backpack, so even if I were willing to wave it around on a crowded street, I couldn't. He was walking close enough that I doubted I'd have the foot-speed to just bolt and hope to outrun him. Which meant I needed a distraction of some kind. Something to keep him busy long enough to give me a sizeable head start.

I scanned the streets and sidewalks for something that could help. Finally, I caught sight of two tough-looking guys leaning against a wall as they eyed Blake's approach. Both were big and imposing, and at just the right age to be eager to prove their manhood. There was a predatory light in their eyes as they looked Blake up and down.

Like I said, Blake was a pretty boy, his hair moussed to look casually tousled, his clothes obviously expensive. The classic metrosexual. To a bigoted young punk looking for trouble, "metrosexual" meant "gay." Despite the fact that he'd used his aura against Alexis, I was pretty sure Blake didn't swing that way.

Blake didn't seem to notice the punks, not even when one of them whistled at him and the other made kissy noises. From their body language, I doubted they were planning to do anything more than harass Blake, unless he was hot-headed enough to engage with them. But I suspected they would be just the kind of distraction I needed.

I looked straight ahead, pretending not to pay any attention to them. There was a dangerous glitter in Blake's eyes, one that said he was seriously considering stopping to teach the punks some manners. I didn't know if he had any powers beyond lust, but I suspected he was more than a match for these two, despite appearances. I also suspected he was going to control his aggressive urges, knowing full well that I'd make a run for it if he tried anything. So I decided to take the choice out of his hands.

Timing my move carefully, I waited until we were just a couple feet short of the punks. Then I slung my backpack off my shoulder and swung it as hard as I could at Blake's back.

Since I hadn't wanted to leave my expensive laptop sitting around the hotel, there was plenty of oomph behind the blow. Blake grunted in surprise as he flew forward—right into the two punks.

I didn't wait to see what happened. I whirled around, shoving my arms back into the straps of my backpack, then ran for all I was worth. There was a lot of yelling behind me, but I ignored it, my arms and legs pumping for maximum speed. I probably should have dropped the backpack so it wouldn't slow me down, but it had my wallet, my gun, and my laptop in it, and I wasn't willing to part with it.

I whipped around the nearest corner, sneaking a glance behind me as I turned. One of the punks punched Blake right on that luscious mouth of his, but it didn't seem to bother him much. He shoved the guy away hard enough to send him to the pavement.

I kept running at top speed. There was a parking garage a few yards ahead of me and another street a few yards past that. If Blake managed to get away from the punks—which I suspected he would soon, if he hadn't already—he was going to catch up with me quickly. I'm a relatively fast runner given my size, but at five-two, my stride is pretty short.

I ducked into the garage, hoping Blake would assume I'd run all the way to the corner before turning.

My breath was coming in frantic gasps, the muscles in my legs burning like hell. There was a fair amount of activity on the ground level of the garage, people cruising for spaces or trying to remember where they'd parked. A few of them glanced at me curiously as I blew past, but no one seemed particularly alarmed.

The muscles in my legs complained even more as I forced them to carry me up the ramp to the next level of the garage. I was still hoping Blake would run right past the place, but with my luck these days, I wasn't counting on it. If he found me, he could use his special power to force me to go with him, right under the noses of any number of witnesses, and they would never know anything was wrong. I, however, would need my gun to defend myself, and that meant getting away from potential witnesses.

There were fewer cars on the second level, but there was still enough activity that I didn't dare draw the gun.

My pace wasn't much faster than a brisk walk as I forced

myself onward, climbing the ramp to the third level. There were only a handful of cars up there, and no people.

Finally allowing myself to slow down, I examined my options as I sucked in air. If Blake managed to follow me up here, I'd pretty much run myself into a corner, but that wasn't entirely by accident. Best to be in a place where I could keep an eye on all the entrances.

There was a bank of elevators to my right, and a stairwell to my left, but other than the ramp, those appeared to be the only two ways up to this level. If Blake was following me, he'd have to use the ramp, otherwise it would be too easy for him to go right past me in the enclosed stairwell or the elevator.

I crossed the garage at a halfhearted trot, my legs feeling like they weighed about ten tons each. I can jog for miles if I have to, but the all-out sprint with the extra weight of the backpack had exhausted me.

When I reached the cluster of cars near the stairwell, I ducked down between them and crept forward until I was crouched between one car's bumper and the wall. I then quietly unzipped my pack and pulled out the gun. If Blake cornered me up here, I'd have to find the guts to shoot him. I didn't *want* to shoot him, but I doubted I'd have a lot of options if he found me. I couldn't risk letting him use his nasty special power on me.

I crouched in the shadow of the car for what felt like forever, my body practically vibrating with tension. The day wasn't particularly cold, but the air still felt icy against my sweaty skin. I was finally beginning to catch my breath after the long run, but my heart was still tripping on adrenaline.

It was all I could do not to groan when I saw Blake's silhouette as he stalked through a patch of sunlight. Goddammit! Why couldn't he have just kept on running? Or better yet, given up the chase? I should theoretically have had enough of a head start that I could be anywhere by now, so why was he *here*?

I carefully slid over so that I was in the deepest pool of shadow available. I kept my entire body hidden behind one front wheel—the driver hadn't bothered to straighten out once he'd pulled in, so the wheel gave me a gratifying amount of cover—and peeked from under the bumper to monitor Blake's progress as he approached.

He was moving slowly, staring at something in his hand. At first, I had no idea what he was doing, but when he got closer, I could see he was looking at the screen of a phone. I didn't think he was checking his email or surfing the Internet.

I mentally let out a stream of curses as I remembered Jack handing me my pocketbook. The purse itself had been ruined, but when I'd gotten home, I'd transferred its contents into my backpack. Evidence suggested there'd been something in that purse that wasn't mine. Like, say, some kind of tracking device.

I was sure the jig was up, but even so, I remained stubbornly hidden. Blake was so close now I could see the thin, angry line of his lips, and the dangerous intensity of his eyes. He stood at the top of the ramp and turned a full circle, looking back and forth between the phone screen and his surroundings.

Maybe the smart thing to do would have been to leap to my feet the moment his back was turned and fire. I would have to take Maggie's word for it that he was immortal and I couldn't kill him by shooting him. I urged myself to do it, picturing myself as an action movie heroine blasting away, but the mental picture was so absurd it almost made me laugh.

It would have taken at least an hour for me to talk myself into shooting, and I had about two seconds. Blake had finished his circle before I'd gotten through preliminary arguments. I thought for sure the tracker was going to lead him straight to me, but he just stood there, scowling and shaking his head in frustration.

Blake hit a button on his phone, then held it to his ear. I took a wild guess that he was calling Anderson, and that guess was confirmed by the conversation I overheard.

"She's in here somewhere," he said into the phone. "Or at least her bag is. The tracker can't tell me which floor she's on. Jack gave you a cell phone number for her, didn't he?"

Oh, shit! My heart shot into my throat, and I reached for my backpack. I tried to hurry, but I was hampered by having to hold on to the gun and by having to be quiet. If I just yanked open the zipper, that sound would give me away just as effectively as the stupid cell phone.

I didn't make it.

Before I'd even gotten the zipper halfway open, my cell phone played the opening riff of George Thorogood's "Bad to the Bone." It had been Steph's idea of a joke, but I kinda liked it. At least under normal circumstances.

There was no point in hiding anymore, so I stood up and pointed the gun at Blake, praying that no one else would come along and become an inconvenient witness. I'd be in deep trouble if I got caught carrying a gun. Blake's expression was somewhere between a sneer and a grin. I guess the lighting was kind of dim and he didn't see the gun at first. When he did, the grin disappeared.

Half a second later, heat suffused my body. My nipples hardened to aching peaks, moisture flooded my core, and my eyes started to glaze over.

The effect was almost instantaneous. One moment, I was staring down the barrel of my gun trying to work up the nerve to pull the trigger, the next, I wanted to fling the gun to the ground and tear off my clothes. I had only an instant to realize what was happening before I was under his spell, but that was enough.

Desperation gave me the will I needed, and my finger squeezed the trigger.

The tide of lust stopped as fast as it had started, and my vision cleared as Blake clutched the bleeding wound in his chest, gave me a wide-eyed look, and fell to the floor of the garage.

SEVEN

To say I was shocked by what I'd done was an understatement. For a long, breathless moment, I just stood there and stared, hardly believing I'd actually shot someone. Blake's face was squinched in pain, and his hands were stained crimson as he tried to stanch the flow of blood.

My hands were shaking as I lowered the gun, and I blinked furiously to hold back tears. I couldn't afford to wallow. A .38 Special isn't exactly a quiet gun, and people on the lower levels of the garage had to have heard the shot. Maybe they'd assume it was just a car backfiring, but I couldn't count on it.

I grabbed my backpack and shoved the gun back inside. There was a tracker in my pack somewhere, but I didn't have time to look for it now, and all the reasons I'd had previously for not dropping the backpack still applied.

Heart in my throat, I stepped around the protection of the car, keeping a wary eye on Blake. His face was still tight with pain, and his skin was a bloodless shade of white, but he was conscious. I hoped that meant he wasn't going to die.

"I'm sorry," I said lamely, then rolled my eyes. What kind of action movie heroine apologized to the enemy for hurting him? If I was going to play the part of a badass, I was going to need some serious practice.

I slung the backpack over my shoulder and opened the door to the stairwell. Blake's eyes glittered as he glared at me, but when he tried to stand up, his face went even whiter and I thought he might pass out. I bit my tongue to stave off another apology, then slipped into the stairwell and let the door slam behind me. The echoing sound made me jump, and it took a healthy dose of self-control to keep myself from running down the stairs, which would only draw attention. I had enough people chasing me without adding the police to the list.

I hurried to the nearest Metro station, and got on the first train that arrived, not caring where it was going as long as it was away from the scene of the crime. Once the train was moving, I sat down and started examining the contents of my backpack—making sure the gun stayed safely concealed, naturally.

Eventually I found the tracker. Jack had done an impressive job of hiding it. I'd gone through everything twice and was beginning to think I'd have to dump the whole backpack after all, when I finally noticed that my purse-sized package of tissues weighed more than it should. I pulled out the first few tissues, then found a white, rectangular device, about two inches long, tucked into the center of the pack.

I left the tracker on the train—that ought to keep Anderson and crew occupied for a while—then got off at the next stop and took a cab back to my hotel.

Just in case the tracker had allowed Blake to figure out which hotel I was staying in, I decided to get out of there. My cell phone rang while I was packing. I checked caller ID: Steph. I groaned. There was no way I could talk to her now without her figuring out something was wrong, and I couldn't explain my situation without sounding like a lunatic.

I was going to have to talk to her eventually, but I couldn't handle Steph now.

Deciding I'd call her in a couple of hours, I checked out of the Holiday Inn and found myself a new hotel halfway across town. I took a hot bath, hoping that would calm my nerves, but nothing short of a horse tranquilizer could have done the trick.

I had no idea what my next step should be. Apparently, I had two factions of *Liberi* after me, and they had the financial and magical resources to make my life really difficult. I couldn't evade them forever, not unless I decided to run away and make myself disappear.

I'd had enough experience tracking people who didn't want

to be found to cover my own tracks if I needed to. I could disappear from D.C. and create a new identity for myself somewhere else. But I'd spent most of my childhood being shuffled from foster home to foster home, and here in the D.C. area with the Glasses, I'd experienced the only true stability I'd ever known. I couldn't face the prospect of digging up my roots and leaving everything and everyone I'd come to love behind. Not unless it was absolutely the last resort.

Which meant that somehow, I was going to have to find a way to convince both factions of *Liberi* to leave me alone.

To be perfectly honest, I already had a sinking feeling that life as I had known it was over. I didn't have a clue how to get the *Liberi* to back off, and even if I did . . . Let's face it, I wasn't the same person I'd been just twenty-four hours ago. I believed in the supernatural. I'd become immortal with supernatural powers myself. And I'd shot a man. In cold blood.

I have to admit, I was wallowing. But then, who could possibly argue that I didn't have the right?

My phone rang again, and I snapped out of my funk enough to check caller ID. A nervous shiver ran through me when I saw the name Anderson Kane.

Naturally, my first instinct was to ignore the call, just as I'd ignored Steph's. I had, after all, gone to rather extreme lengths to avoid being forced to talk to him. But I was desperately in need of more information, and my available sources were pretty limited. Anderson couldn't hurt me over the phone—at least I hoped not—so I answered.

I'm not much of a badass. Hard to be, when you're only five-two. In spite of that, I've never been one to let people push me around and I'd had enough pushing already from the various *Liberi* I'd met, so instead of answering with a pleasant or neutral greeting, I said, "How's Blake?"

My stomach flip-flopped at the memory of Blake clutching his bleeding chest, at the memory that I'd actually pointed a gun at another human being and pulled the trigger. Good thing Anderson couldn't see my face, or he'd have known how much I was bluffing with my tough girl act. Hell, maybe he knew anyway.

He was silent for a long moment, and I wondered if he was more surprised or angry at my bravado.

"He'll recover," Anderson finally said, his voice perfectly neutral. "I suppose sending him after you was a miscalculation on my part. He has a unique ability to get under people's skin, and he still believes you killed Emmitt on purpose."

I raised an eyebrow, though of course he couldn't see. "You say that as if you *don't* believe it anymore."

He sighed, and it may have been my imagination, but I heard a world of sorrow in that sigh. "I don't know," he admitted. "Maggie is convinced Emmitt had grown weary and set you up, and I was beginning to agree with her. Then you up and shot Blake. I have to say that seems more like the act of a cold-blooded schemer than an innocent victim."

Internally, I cringed at the accusation in his voice. I didn't want to feel guilty about shooting Blake, but I couldn't help it. I'd already killed a man last night, and the fact that it had been an accident on my part didn't do much to ease my conscience. I couldn't help wondering . . . If I hadn't sped up when the driveway had straightened out, would I have been able to swerve in time to avoid hitting him? I hadn't thought I'd been going that fast, but the airbag *did* deploy, which suggested I'd been going faster than I'd realized.

I tried to summon a surge of anger to counter the guilt. "What was I supposed to do? Let him use that creepy power of his to violate me and then drag me to you so you could torture me? Are you suggesting only a cold-blooded schemer would do everything in her power to avoid that?"

There was such a long silence on the other end of the line I thought I might have lost the signal on my phone.

"I'm sorry," he finally said, and he actually sounded like he meant it. Whether he *did* or not was anyone's guess. "I don't suppose any of us are thinking as clearly as we should at the moment, especially me. Emmitt was my friend for a long, long time. I should have—" His voice cracked, and he cleared his throat.

My own eyes stung at the pain in Anderson's voice. I'm such a bleeding heart. But I couldn't help mentally putting myself in his shoes. I'd stolen his friend's life and immortality. Worse, I claimed that friend had used me to commit suicide. If I were in Anderson's shoes, I'd probably lash out at me, too.

"If he was really weary enough to end his life," Anderson continued, his voice steadier, "I should have seen it. I should have been able to help him. I'd much rather you were lying about it than to accept that I was so blind."

I took a deep, quiet breath, trying to distance myself from Anderson's pain. Yes, I could understand he was grieving for his friend, and I could even understand why he didn't want Emmitt's death to have been suicide. But none of that could forgive the threats and the strong-arm tactics.

"But the reasons for my behavior don't matter much to you, do they?" Anderson asked as if he'd read my mind. "I treated you like your guilt was a foregone conclusion last night, and for that I'm sorry. From now on, how about I presume you're innocent until proven guilty. And if you really are innocent, then we need to talk. There's a lot you don't know."

I resisted the urge to snort at the understatement. "I'm happy to talk on the phone for as long as my battery holds out."

"In person would be better."

I laughed. "Maybe for you."

"For you, too. Nikki, you have no idea the kind of danger you're in. I know I haven't exactly come off to you as one of the good guys, but I am. At least in comparison to Konstantin and the rest of the Olympians. They will stop at nothing to get their hands on you. You can't go up against them alone; and I promise you, you wouldn't like what would happen if they captured you."

"Why would they want to capture me?"

"Because descendants of Artemis are exceedingly rare. Contrary to popular belief, she wasn't literally a virgin goddess, but she bore only one child, and her line has nearly died out. She was a goddess of the hunt, and a lot of the skills her descendants possess would be of great use to the Olympians."

"Go on," I prompted. "Prove to me that you're a good source of information."

"I believe in the proverb that with great power comes great responsibility. The Olympians believe that with great power comes great privilege and no responsibility whatsoever. From their perspective, they are better than everyone else, and that's the natural order of the universe. They are selfishness incarnate, but as reprehensible as I find that, it's not why I oppose them as I do.

"I understand that Maggie explained the origins of the *Liberi Deorum* last night."

"Yeah," I said, swallowing hard. Even after all I'd seen, there was a part of me that desperately wanted to deny I believed what Maggie had told me.

"So she explained that anyone descended from the ancient gods can steal the immortality of a *Liberi*?"

"Yes."

"Because Descendants can potentially steal their immortality, the Olympians see them as a threat that needs to be eliminated. For centuries, they have hunted Descendants. Generally, when they find a family of Descendants, they kill all the adults and all the children over the age of five. They then raise those youngest children themselves, indoctrinating them into their beliefs. If the children show any signs that they question the 'natural order,' they are disposed of."

I sank down onto the edge of my bed, knees suddenly weak at the images Anderson's words brought to mind. "By disposed of, you mean killed."

"Yes. Remember, as far as the Olympians are concerned,

they are the pinnacle of perfection, and everyone else is expendable. Even children they have raised themselves."

"Why do they raise the children at all? Why not . . ." I let the question trail off because I couldn't put the horror into words.

"Because only a mortal Descendant can kill a *Liberi*. The Olympians can't kill rival *Liberi* themselves, so they need pet Descendants to do the dirty work for them. That's how they raise these children—with the philosophy that if they are good enough, the Olympians will one day give them a sacrificial *Liberi* so they can become immortal themselves.

"And if you don't find all of this distasteful enough, know also that only those descended from the *Greek* gods are considered worthy to become *Liberi*. If the Olympians find a family descended from one of the other pantheons, they leave no survivors.

"They want you to join them because they believe they can use your skills to help them hunt down and slaughter more Descendants. Without a descendant of Artemis in their employ, the Olympians have to hunt Descendants using only conventional methods. They're always on the lookout for unfamiliar people with visible glyphs. If they find a Descendant, they'll extract a family history and go looking for all the relatives. If you join them, they'll use your powers to track down the ones they can't find."

"That's never going to happen," I said immediately. "I wouldn't help them kill *anyone,* much less helpless children!"

"That's what you think now," Anderson countered, "but the Olympians are very good at . . . persuasion. Come back to the house. You'll be much safer with us than you would be out on your own."

I laughed briefly, then swallowed it before it could turn into hysteria. "You've got to be kidding me! You let Jamaal practically choke me to death last night, you yourself threatened to torture me, and then you sent Blake with his slimy lust power after me, and you expect me to just hand myself over because you claim the other guys are worse?"

"I realize that—"

"You don't realize a goddamn thing!" I squeezed the phone so hard I accidentally hung up on Anderson. Then I decided my subconscious had the right idea, and I turned the phone off.

Maybe he was telling me the truth. But I had no way of knowing. And even if he *was,* I saw no reason why I would be better off hanging out at Psycho Central. Jamaal had made it crystal clear that he wanted to make me suffer, and Blake no doubt hated my guts after what I'd done to him this morning.

Geez, I was just making friends all over the place.

I lay down on the bed and closed my eyes, pinching the bridge of my nose where an exhaustion headache was starting up. I might not be willing to hand myself over to Anderson, but I was no closer to figuring out what I *should* do.

As a child, I'd been a real pro at getting into trouble. There was a good reason I'd been bounced from foster home to foster home so often before I'd landed with the Glasses. I couldn't blame the other foster families for getting rid of me. I'd been well on my way to becoming a juvenile delinquent, getting angrier and angrier each time a family gave up on me, my behavior worsening each time. But as much trouble as I'd gotten into, as close as I'd come to spending some quality time in juvie, none of it came close to preparing me for the trouble I was in now.

Between the physical exhaustion and the sense of hopelessness that enveloped me, I couldn't help curling up on my side, clutching a pillow to my chest. In no time, I was fast asleep.

The dream was familiar, one that I'd had countless times over the years. More a memory than a dream, really, though I wasn't sure how much of the memory was real, and how much was pieced together by my subconscious. I'd been awfully young at the time, but in my dreams, at least, the memory was crystal clear.

It was a nasty, rainy day, the air so thick with moisture you could drown in it. The rain should have made it cooler, but instead it merely made it feel like we were walking through a steam room.

I don't know where we were, exactly, except that it was in the South somewhere and that it was a long way from home. My mom was carrying my baby brother, Billy, his chubby little arms lost under her thick hair as he wailed and tried to hide from the rain. Momma murmured assurances, shielding his face with her other hand. Until Billy had started to cry, she'd been holding my hand. I kept plucking at her sleeve, wanting her to take my hand again, but she was too busy with Billy.

We'd been walking for what felt like miles, after having spent a day and a night riding on a stinky, crowded bus. I was hungry. I was soaked through. My feet hurt. And I wanted to curl up to sleep in my cozy, comfortable bed at home.

"Momma! Pick me up!" I whined, at the end of what little patience I had at the age of four. "My feet hurt."

"Hush, sweetheart," she said, absently reaching down to brush a dripping lock of hair out of my eyes. The stupid baby cried even louder once Momma wasn't holding him with both hands. I hated him for it even though I knew I was supposed to love him. "We're almost there."

I didn't know where "there" was, but I didn't see anything familiar on this run-down city street, so I knew "there" wasn't home, and home was the only "there" I wanted.

"Wanna go home!" I yelled, stamping my foot. Then I decided to see if I could out-wail my brother. If I was loud enough, maybe Momma would give me what I wanted. It always seemed to work for stupid Billy.

Momma closed her eyes in pain and weariness when I started to cry, but she didn't take me home. Instead, we continued to trudge through the rain. I tried going on a sit-down strike, but Momma grabbed my hand and dragged me along. I was too old to be carried, she informed me, so I was just going to have to walk.

Finally, when I was sure I couldn't walk another step even

with Momma pulling on me, we climbed a set of weathered stone steps. Momma pushed open a door, and I followed her into a cool, dark entryway. It seemed we were finally "there."

I wiped my dripping hair away from my face as my eyes adjusted to the low light, which seemed to come almost entirely from candles. Ahead of us, a pair of doors were propped open to reveal a long aisle with rows of pews on either side. The rain had darkened the afternoon skies so that only the faintest glow of light shone through the stained glass windows, but a discreet spotlight illuminated a gruesome statue of Christ on the cross.

I shivered in the air-conditioned breeze. Seconds ago, I'd have done anything to get inside out of the rain, and to sit down, but I didn't like this church. Maybe it was a premonition. Or maybe it was just that I was reliving the memory/dream from my adult perspective, knowing what was going to happen.

Momma led me down the aisle, to a pew in the middle of the church. There were a couple of old ladies sitting at the very front, but other than them we were the only people in the place. Our footsteps echoed, despite the strip of carpet down the center of the aisle. It was then that I realized the baby had finally stopped crying.

Momma nudged me into the pew, and I sat down gratefully, no matter how uneasy the church made me. I thought she'd sit next to me, but she didn't. She knelt in the aisle, still cradling Billy in her arms. He made a little sound of protest, like he was about to start screaming again, but then stuck his thumb firmly in his mouth instead. The quiet made the patter of the rain on the windows seem loud.

Momma let go of Billy with one hand, and he was too busy sucking his thumb to complain. She brushed my cheek with the back of her hand, and the light glinted off the moisture in her eyes.

"I want you to sit here and be a good girl, Nikki," she said in a low whisper, the sound barely loud enough to hear over the patter of the rain. "I have to go change Billy's diaper," she continued, and her eyes shone even brighter. "I'll be right back, okay?"

A tear escaped her eye and trickled down her cheek. I didn't know why she was crying now that both Billy and I had stopped. I knew it was a bad sign, but I didn't know what to do about it. Momma was supposed to comfort *me* when *I* cried, not the other way around. The confusion was more than I could deal with, so I just nodded and didn't ask why she was so sad.

"I love you so much, baby," she said, leaning forward so she could plant a soft kiss on my forehead. "Never doubt that. Never."

When she pulled away from me, tears were streaming down her cheeks. And there was an iridescent glyph on her forehead.

She stroked my wet, tangled hair one last time and stood up. Then she wrapped both arms around Billy, and hurried down the aisle.

I never saw her again.

I awoke with a start and a gasp. I'd dreamed of my abandonment about a zillion times. The details varied here and there, which was what made me wonder how much was really memory, but never before had the dream included a glyph on my mother's forehead.

I sat up slowly, my head foggy and confused. The bright sunlight of the afternoon had faded to blue twilight while I'd slept, leaving the room in shadows. Still groggy, I reached over and switched on the bedside lamp, squinting in the sudden brightness.

Of course, it made sense for me to dream about my mom having a glyph on her forehead after all I'd gone through in the last twenty-four hours or so. Surely it was nothing more than the power of suggestion.

But what if it wasn't? Anderson said the Olympians hunted down Descendant families and killed them. What if I'd gotten my divine heritage through my mother's side of the family?

And what if she'd found out the Olympians were after her? Could that explain why she'd abandoned me?

We'd been on that bus a day and a night—if my memory was accurate—which meant she'd traveled hundreds of miles away from our home, before she left me sitting on that church pew. When I'd finally realized she wasn't coming back and the old ladies at the front of the church had called the police, I was so hysterical I couldn't even tell them my own name, much less my mother's. Nor could I tell them where I lived. My mom had made me memorize our address and phone number once, but I didn't remember it.

Eventually, I calmed down enough to remember the address, but it was just the street address—no city or state. The street name was common enough—Main, or Broad, or something like that—that the police were able to take me to the address, but since it was the wrong city, it didn't help.

My mother had not only abandoned me, she'd severed all ties to me. I was found so far from where I'd grown up that no one could possibly recognize me, and I was young enough to think my mother's name was "Momma." There was no way anyone could identify me, or associate me with my mother in any way. And if anyone was hunting her, if anyone *found* her, they'd still never have found *me*.

Most likely, it was just wishful thinking that built this scenario in my mind. After all, my mother hadn't left *Billy* at the church. Maybe she didn't think the old women at the front would have let her leave a crying baby and a four-year-old alone in the pews. Or maybe she'd left Billy somewhere else, hiding her tracks even more.

"Or maybe she just abandoned you because you were too much damn trouble," I muttered, disgusted with myself for the stupid fantasy. Odds were, my mom had known nothing whatsoever about the Olympians. I couldn't fathom why she was so desperate to get rid of me—I didn't become a hellion until I started living in foster care—but there is, sadly, no shortage of women who abandon their children, one way or another. There was no reason to believe my own mother wasn't just one more.

Eight

I felt even more tired now than I had before I'd taken my unintentional nap. I brewed a pot of the terrible in-room coffee, made even more terrible by non-dairy creamer. Then I took another shower, hoping it would clear my head.

It didn't.

Afterward, I reluctantly turned my phone back on and checked messages. As I'd expected, Anderson had tried calling back a couple of times, though he hadn't left any voice mails. Also as expected, I had a couple of messages from Steph, wondering where the hell I was and why I wasn't calling her back. Her third message revealed that her slight concern was well on its way to becoming full-out worry.

"Nikki. I talked to Jim, and he said you ducked out early last night. No one has seen or heard from you since. Please call me back as soon as you get this. If I don't hear from you soon, I'm going to call the police. Please call."

I winced in guilt as I heard the quaver in my sister's voice. It wasn't like me not to return phone calls, and after what must have seemed like a somewhat mysterious exit from the restaurant last night, I couldn't blame Steph for being worried. I might not run into the kind of daily danger that cops did, but my profession was not without its risks. She'd probably come up with a boatload of worst-case scenarios already. I prayed to God she hadn't gotten worried enough to try to call the Glasses yet. Surely she wouldn't interrupt their cruise unless she were *certain* there was something wrong. At least, I hoped not.

Knowing I could put it off no longer, I put on my big-girl panties and called Steph's house. She answered on the first ring, like she'd been hovering over the phone willing me to call. Maybe she had.

"Oh, thank God!" she said in lieu of a greeting, then immediately burst into tears.

Another wave of guilt rolled over me, even as I was momentarily annoyed at the melodrama. Steph bursts into tears at the drop of a hat. Which is probably healthier than my stoic reserve, but it gets on my nerves anyway.

In a lot of ways, it's a minor miracle that Steph and I are so close, seeing as we're polar opposites. Steph is a true blond bombshell, the kind that makes anyone with a Y chromosome start drooling. She's perky as hell, and everyone seems to like her. She'd always run with the popular clique at school—naturally, she'd been a cheerleader—but she'd been friendly with just about everyone, even the kids at whom cheerleaders traditionally looked down their noses. Steph may have been a card-carrying member of the popular crowd, but behind the frothy façade, she had a backbone of steel. No amount of peer pressure was going to make her be cruel to people who were outside her usual social circle. And heaven help anyone who dared to be cruel to her adopted little sister, even when said little sister made being an outsider a point of pride.

"I'm sorry I worried you," I told Steph as she fought to control her tears. I hadn't yet figured out what I was going to tell her—if I'd waited until I dreamed up the perfect explanation, I'd never have gotten around to calling—but I knew I had to come up with something fast.

"I'm fine," I continued. "I promise. Not a scratch on me. But I was in a car accident last night."

"What?" she shrieked, and I had to hold the phone away from my ear.

"I'm fine!" I repeated. "My car has gone on to its heavenly reward, but I'm not hurt, so please don't be upset."

"Don't be upset? You're joking, right?"

Please, please, please let her not have called the Glasses yet. Mrs. Glass was the quintessential overprotective mother hen, and she mothered me every bit as thoroughly as she did Steph. Dealing with Steph's distress was enough already—I couldn't bear the thought of having to call and reassure Mrs. Glass afterward.

"If you were in an accident last night," Steph continued, and there was a hint of anger seeping into her voice, "then why am I just hearing about it now? Why haven't you answered any of my calls? You *knew* I was going to call to ask you how things went, and you had to know I'd get worried when you didn't call back."

I sighed and wished I'd forced myself to call earlier. I couldn't blame her for being upset with me. If the situation had been reversed, I'd have been furious.

"I'm sorry," I said again. "I wasn't hurt, but I was pretty badly shaken up. I haven't been quite myself, and I just didn't think. My phone was turned off all day, and I didn't even notice until just now."

"Have you eaten yet?"

I blinked and shook my head at the non sequitur. "Huh?"

"Meet me at Angelo's at seven. A phone call doesn't cut it for this conversation, kiddo."

I groaned, thinking I should have drunk more coffee before picking up the phone. If my brain had been fully awake, I'd have known Steph wouldn't settle for a phone call. Angelo's was her favorite Italian restaurant, a real dive that served great food and mediocre wine. My body was too confused to know whether it was hungry or not, but I knew I wasn't up to the level of scrutiny I would undergo over dinner.

"I'm really not up to—" I started.

"Be there at seven, or I'm going to call Mom and tell her you totaled the car."

"You bitch!" I cried. "Don't you dare!"

I knew Mrs. Glass would have to find out about it eventually, but the more time that passed before she heard about it, the less chance that she would become hysterical.

"Show up for dinner, and I won't have to," Steph said, sounding smug. "You owe me for scaring the life out of me."

I considered trying to argue some more. There was no way I could behave as if nothing was wrong if I talked to Steph in person, and I still had no clue what I could use as a convincing cover story. But as I mentioned, Steph has quite a backbone beneath her deceptively sweet exterior. If she was determined to talk to me in person, nothing would change her mind. And if I didn't show up, she really would call her mom and rat me out.

"Fine," I said with poor grace. "I'll see you at seven."

I almost decided to skip the dinner, despite Steph's threat. I didn't like the idea that I might lead that creep Alexis right to her, and I didn't want him anywhere near my sister. However, Blake had told me that the Oracle's visions were rarely clear, so I figured the odds that Alexis would find me twice in one day were low. The odds that Steph would rat me out if I didn't show up were a hundred percent. Besides, I couldn't avoid her forever.

I pushed open the door to Angelo's at 7:15, and the scent of garlic and tomatoes set my mouth to watering instantly. A quick glance around the chipped Formica tables showed me what I'd already expected to find: Steph wasn't here yet. She is biologically incapable of showing up anywhere on time, despite all Mrs. Glass's best efforts to train her to punctuality. She also has a sixth sense about what time I'll arrive. Even when I specifically try to be late enough for her to get there before me, she's always just a little bit later.

The hostess led me to a table for two near the back. There was no longer any smoking allowed inside, but the walls themselves must have absorbed the stink of cigarette smoke over the years, because I could still catch a whiff of it in the air. Or maybe it was just because I'd been coming here so long I knew the table was in the old smoking section.

Steph made her grand entrance about five minutes later, rushing through the door and scanning the restaurant anxiously, like she was afraid I'd have bolted by now. I waved, and saw her sigh of relief.

The Glasses had already made their fortune by the time Steph was in her formative years, so she'd grown up with the best fashion sense money could buy. She was wearing perfectly tailored slate gray slacks and a luxurious red cashmere sweater that clung to her near-flawless figure. She'd finished the outfit with a black swing coat and a pair of stiletto-heeled boots that I'd have broken my neck trying to walk in.

As usual, every male over the age of twelve gave her at least one or two appreciative glances as she snaked her way through the tables toward me. I told myself I was *not* jealous, but it was a lie. She was just so damn . . . perfect. If only she were a bitch, so I could hate her like she deserved to be hated . . .

Steph's mischievous smile said she had an inkling what was running through my mind. She draped her coat over the back of her chair, then sat across from me and gave me a penetrating stare. It took every ounce of my willpower not to look away.

Steph leaned back in her chair and crossed her arms. "Something happened," she said with great authority. "Something other than a car accident. What is it?"

Great. I hadn't even opened my mouth yet, and already Steph saw through me.

I considered trying to bluff my way through it. When I was on the job, people always seemed to believe whatever pretext I made up, but Steph and her parents knew me too well, and I was rarely able to slip a lie past any of them.

"Yeah," I admitted. "I've got some stuff going on. But it's not anything I can talk about." Not without getting carted off to the loony bin, that is.

Steph uncrossed her arms and began tapping the table with her perfectly manicured nails.

"I mean it, Steph. I can't talk about it. I'm not willfully holding out on you." Well, not too much, anyway.

She continued tapping her fingers and staring at me, not saying a word. I recognized the ploy for what it was: she was hoping that the pressure of her silent scrutiny would make me blurt something out. It was a tactic she'd learned from her mom, and under normal circumstances, it might even have worked.

The waitress interrupted our silent standoff to take our orders. Neither one of us had even consulted the menu, but then we'd memorized it years ago.

"Are you in some kind of trouble?" Steph finally asked when the waitress was out of earshot.

"I can't—"

"Talk about it. Yeah, I heard you. I'm not asking for details. I just want to know if you're in trouble, and if there's anything I can do to help."

My throat tightened briefly. There were times when Steph bugged the hell out of me, but she was one of the nicest people I'd ever met. She could have resented me for inserting myself into her family when she'd had thirteen years of being an only child, but she'd been nothing but supportive even from the very beginning, when I'd been a sullen, sulky troublemaker.

"Thanks, Steph," I said, my voice a bit gruff. "But there's nothing you can do." I forced a grin. "Except stop setting me up on blind dates with assholes."

For a moment, I thought she was going to resist my attempt to deflect the conversation. Then her shoulders slumped in defeat.

"What's wrong with Jim?" she asked, though her heart wasn't in the question. "He's nice, he's handsome, he's successful, and he's single."

I rolled my eyes. One of the reasons everyone likes Steph is that she's so good at turning a blind eye to people's flaws. Which is why I should know better than to let her set me up with anyone.

"You honestly think he's a nice guy?" I asked. "Have you ever *talked* with him?"

She looked annoyed. "Of course I talked with him. I wouldn't set you up with someone if I didn't know him well enough to think you'd get on."

I bit back a caustic response, realizing that Jim might not have shown Steph the side of him I'd seen at dinner. After all, Steph was a sexist jerk's idea of feminine perfection, so she wouldn't have elicited the kind of reactions I'd gotten. She was beautiful, and put a lot of time and effort into keeping herself that way. She was sweet-natured enough that people who didn't know her might think her weak or submissive, though they'd be wrong. And because she didn't have my hang-ups about living off her trust fund, she'd never had a career to inconvenience a man who wanted her full attention.

"The problem with you," I told Steph, "is that you like everyone. I'm a little more particular."

She laughed. "To put it mildly."

"No more blind dates, okay? It never turns out well."

"You never give it a chance to."

"Please, Steph," I said, suddenly feeling exhausted again. "I don't want to fight."

Steph leaned across the table and squeezed my hand, smiling gently. "We're not fighting. I'm trying to give you sage, older-sister advice."

The advice might have been more convincing if Steph's love life had been any more successful than my own. Beauty and wealth attracted a lot of men, not all of them for the right reasons. Not to mention the men who made the mistake of thinking that because she was nice, pretty, and blond, she'd be a pushover and put up with crappy behavior. The door hit those guys on the ass pretty hard on their way out.

"Since when has giving me advice been a productive use of your time?" I asked, returning Steph's smile with a wry grin.

"Good point."

The rest of the meal was much more relaxed. Steph and I stayed away from sensitive subjects and just enjoyed our food. Steph talked about her upcoming charity project, a dinner and auction to support the American Cancer Society, and extracted a promise from me that I'd be there. Steph might not work a paying job, but with the stable of charities she actively supported, she worked a hell of a lot more than most of the nine-to-fivers I'd ever met.

Things didn't go to hell until we were sipping our after-dinner coffee and picking at the remains of the slice of cheesecake we'd shared. Steph's phone rang, and she frowned in annoyance.

"I should've turned the damn thing off," she mumbled, but I knew she couldn't quite bear to do that. The big auction was less than two weeks away, and she had to be available for crisis management at the drop of a hat.

I smiled as I took another sip of my rich, dark coffee. "Don't mind me," I assured her. "It could be important."

She acknowledged my point with a nod, then dug her phone out from her tiny designer handbag. She looked at the caller ID and frowned.

"I have no idea who this is," she said, but she answered anyway.

Her frown deepened at whatever the caller said. I don't know what it was about her expression that made me sit up and take notice, but the hair on the back of my neck prickled.

"Who is this?" Steph asked, her voice tight with what sounded like alarm. Our eyes met over the table, and the prickle at the back of my neck turned into a chill of fear.

Steph lowered the phone and covered the microphone with her thumb. "He says his name is Alexis, and he wants to talk to *you*."

My hands clenched so hard it was a wonder I didn't break the coffee cup I was holding. How dare that bastard drag my sister into this? Even without talking to him, I knew his decision to call on Steph's phone had been a deliberate threat. I used my cell phone for business all the time, so if he'd learned my identity—which he obviously had—he'd have had no trouble finding my number.

I put my cup down so hard that coffee sloshed out and spilled on the table, but I didn't care. I reached for the phone, ignoring the combination of alarm and curiosity on Steph's face. There wasn't anywhere I could talk truly privately, but I got up from the table and moved a few paces away anyway. I was painfully aware of Steph's eyes boring through the back of my head as I tried to calm myself down enough to talk. The last thing I wanted was to let Alexis know he'd gotten to me.

"What do you want?" I asked, and despite my best efforts, no one could have missed the fury in my voice.

"We didn't get to finish our conversation this afternoon," he said, and I could hear how much he was enjoying my reaction.

"I was finished with it even before Blake showed up."

"But I wasn't, and that's all that matters. You are not living in Anderson's mansion, therefore you're not covered under our agreement with him. I tried playing nice with you this afternoon, but you made it clear that playing nice wouldn't work.

"Meet me tomorrow at twelve noon in the lobby of the Sofitel. Konstantin requires your services. If you cooperate, you'll be rewarded more than generously. I doubt you've ever had a client who can pay you the sums we can.

"But make no mistake, Nikki Glass: you *will* do what we ask, whether it's to gain the financial rewards of cooperation, or to avoid the consequences of refusal. Are we clear?"

I wanted to crawl down the phone line and kill him right then and there. This afternoon when I'd shot Blake, I'd felt bad about it even though Blake was a jerk. Right now, I wouldn't have hesitated a moment to shoot Alexis. And no, I would not have felt bad.

I couldn't help sneaking a quick glance over my shoulder at Steph. She was chewing her lip with worry as she watched me. If Alexis or one of his cronies laid so much as a finger on her . . .

I must have been taking too long to answer, because Alexis spoke again.

"Your sister is truly a lovely woman," he said, his voice oozing slime. "I'm sure Konstantin would be delighted to make her acquaintance. He can be a little rough with his women, but I'm sure she'll still be at least marginally attractive when he tires of her and passes her on to me."

My blood boiled in my veins, and I bit down, hard, on my tongue to keep from giving him any more satisfaction than I already had.

"I'll see you tomorrow at noon?" he asked, back to using the pleasant, friendly tone he'd first tried on me, as if he hadn't just made such an ugly, revolting threat.

"Yes," I said through gritted teeth, because what else could I do? I had no clear picture of what Alexis and the Olympians were capable of, but I knew they had more power and resources to draw on than I did. I was under no illusion that I could single-handedly protect Steph.

"I knew you would make the right decision. I'll look forward to chatting with you again, without the interruptions."

Luckily for me, he hung up before I said any of the stupid, vitriolic things that came to mind.

NINE

I stood with the phone against my ear, my back turned to Steph, long after Alexis hung up. I needed time to regain control of myself, to tamp down the toxic combination of rage and fear that bubbled in my gut. I wished the earth would open up and swallow every one of the *Liberi*. With the exception of myself, of course.

Eventually, I could stall no longer, and I turned around to face Steph.

What the hell was I going to tell her? I couldn't possibly pretend nothing was wrong, but I couldn't tell her the truth. And I knew there was no way in hell Steph was going to let me go without an explanation of some sort.

I returned to the table and sat down, handing Steph back her phone. She took it from me in silence, tucking it back in her bag without looking. It must have taken a lot of willpower, but she managed not to question me, instead giving me a little more time to pull myself together. She could obviously see I wasn't ready to talk yet.

The problem was I would *never* be ready. I usually think pretty fast on my feet—again, an important trait for a P.I.—but I couldn't think fast enough to keep up with this mess.

"I'm . . . sorry about that," I said, figuring that was a safe place to start.

Steph raised her delicately curved brows. "Care to tell me who that was? And why he was calling *me* when he wanted to talk to *you?*"

Steph sometimes likes to play the spoiled, rich socialite, but there is a sharp mind under her fluffy exterior. I could see in her eyes that she'd made a number of assumptions—including the one that she'd just been subtly threatened. I didn't want to scare her, but I supposed it was better that I tell her something so she'd be extra careful. Alexis obviously knew Steph and I were together right now. I was damn sure no one had followed me here, so either someone had followed Steph, or the Oracle was more reliable than Blake had led me to believe.

"It was a wannabe client," I told her, which I supposed was something close to the truth. "I turned down his case, but he's not taking no for an answer."

"Have you called the police?"

I swallowed the urge to laugh. Somehow, I didn't think the police were going to be much use against the *Liberi*.

"He hasn't done anything the police would be interested

in." Which was also true, even if it wasn't really the reason I didn't call the cops.

Steph frowned and chewed her lip. "You could report him as a stalker, couldn't you?"

I dismissed that with a wave. "He's being a pain in the ass, but he's not technically stalking me."

She leaned forward, resting her arms on the table and dropping her voice. "I know you're not telling me everything, Nikki. Come on. Spit it out."

"I told you before, I can't."

Anger sparked in her eyes. "That man just threatened me, didn't he? That's why he called my phone instead of yours, right?"

I winced, which pretty much precluded the possibility of bluffing my way out of this.

"If people are threatening me, I have a right to know what's going on, don't I?"

I rubbed my eyes as a headache threatened to form behind them. "It's complicated, Steph. Please trust me that I have good reasons for not telling you more." I forced my hand back down to my side and met my sister's angry stare. "I won't let anything happen to you. No matter what."

She shook her head and looked disgusted. "That's not good enough."

"I'm sorry, but it's the best I can do."

Steph glared at me, but I was unmoved. I wasn't in a position to tell her the truth, and in all honesty, I didn't know if the truth would have done her any good. I didn't know a whole lot about the *Liberi* and what they could do yet, but if even half of what I'd been told was true, Steph was no match for them. Hell, *I* was no match for them, and I was supposedly one of them.

I walked Steph to her car on the pretense of being sociable when in reality I was looking for lurking *Liberi*. I didn't spot anyone, nor did I see any mysterious cars following when Steph pulled out of her parking space. I returned to my hotel, still trying to figure out how I was going to keep Steph safe. Too bad I didn't have the faintest idea how to go about it.

A good night's sleep failed to miraculously solve my problems, although I did feel fresher and more optimistic when I woke up the next day. For all that the *Liberi* were dangerous, and for all that I had no idea what their range of power was, they operated in secret, doing their best to blend in with the mortal population. That had to put some limits on their actions, and it suggested I'd be relatively safe meeting with Alexis in a public place later. Not that I was looking forward to it by any stretch of the imagination, but maybe when I talked to him again and got the details about what he wanted me to do, I'd be able to form a plan.

I'd turned off my phone for the night, but when I switched it back on in the morning, I found that I'd received another couple of calls from Anderson. I briefly considered calling him back and giving him an update on my upcoming meeting with Alexis, but thought better of it almost at once. I had no more reason to trust Anderson and his people than I did to trust Alexis. Though I might at some point find it to my advantage to play one against the other, right now I wanted to face one problem at a time.

I arrived at the Sofitel an hour before the appointment with Alexis. Not because I was anxious to meet him, of course, but because I wanted to give myself every possible advantage. I'd never been inside before, but I knew it was one of the more luxurious hotels in D.C. Of course, Alexis struck me as the kind of man who insisted on the best of everything.

I'm sure Alexis picked the place specifically for its lavish décor, but if he'd been looking for a place ideally suited for surveillance, I'm not sure he could have done better if he'd tried. The lobby was large, but there were a number of secluded nooks that were almost cozy. There were also a fair number of rectangular pillars, greatly cutting down on visibility, especially for someone coming in the front doors.

I took a seat on a not particularly comfortable sofa in one of the sitting areas. My seat was in a corner, where a pillar conveniently blocked me from view. Alexis would have to walk down a long hallway past the elevators before he'd be able to see me. I then pretended to drop something—not that anyone was paying particular attention to me—and positioned a small spy camera under the legs of the chair across from me. The camera gave me a perfect view of the hall leading up to the front desk.

Sitting once again in my secluded position, I opened my laptop and pretended to work as I scrutinized the feed from the camera. I watched every person who came in the front doors, without ever having to lift my head from my computer screen. If I saw anyone who tweaked my radar, there was room for me to retreat down another hallway, and I could leave another spy camera right next to my current position so I could keep up my surveillance. But carefully though I watched, I saw no sign that anyone was getting into position for an ambush.

At noon exactly, Alexis strode through the front doors of the hotel. He was not alone, although I didn't recognize his companion, a tall, imposing guy with olive skin and a neat black beard. I couldn't tell much from the somewhat grainy surveillance video, but it looked like his suit was as expensive as Alexis's, and he carried himself with the confidence of a man used to being in charge. Konstantin, I wondered?

The two of them stopped halfway down the hall, both standing there with expressions of impatience. A few more steps and they would see me, but I guess they figured it was my responsibility to come to them; they weren't about to expend the effort to look for me.

I watched them for another five minutes. Their body language got progressively more impatient as they waited. I didn't see anyone else come in after them—not anyone who acted like they were slipping in on the sly, that is—so I closed my laptop and shoved it back in my backpack. Then I took a deep breath and stepped into the main part of the lobby, where they could see me.

"Oh!" I said in feigned surprise when Alexis caught sight of me. "Have you been standing here the whole time? I was right over there waiting." I jerked a thumb toward the seating area.

Alexis narrowed his eyes at me. I had to resist the urge to glance at the spy camera, which I would have to come back later to collect. It was inconspicuous enough that I doubted Alexis would notice it unless I drew attention to it.

"You must be Ms. Glass," Alexis's companion said, and I took a closer look at him. He wasn't particularly good-looking in a traditional sense, but he fairly reeked of power, and I suspected women fell at his feet in droves. I saw no sign of a glyph on him, but perhaps it was hidden by his clothing, or even by his beard. His Mediterranean dark hair was just starting to gray at the temples, and there were the beginnings of crow's-feet at the corners of his eyes. On another man, they might have looked like laugh lines, but not on him. His smile was warm as he reached out his hand for me to shake, but I couldn't miss the hint of danger in his eyes. This was not a man to mess with, those eyes said, and I was inclined to believe them.

"I am Konstantin," he said as I reluctantly placed my hand in his. Not surprisingly, his handshake was crushing, though I gave back as much as I could before I remembered I'd decided not to mess with him. "It is truly a pleasure to meet you."

He released my hand, and I had to resist the urge to rub my now-sore knuckles. The predatory amusement in his eyes told me he was quite aware of his own strength; the crushing grip had been no accident. I hate bullies with a passion, and it took some serious willpower to keep myself from going on the offensive. I wasn't in a position to fight back, not yet, so for now I was determined to keep my cool and not be any more antagonistic than necessary.

"Alexis was quite insistent I make this meeting," I said, which was far more diplomatic than what I *wanted* to say.

Konstantin's face showed regret, but I had the strong suspicion it was only skin deep. "I apologize for the draconian tactics, but I understand Anderson has attempted to poison you against us already. I think it only fair that we be able to argue our case, which is difficult to manage if you refuse to meet with us."

Oh, yeah, right. He'd forced me into meeting with him because it was the *fair* thing to do. I'd convinced myself I had to stay as civil as possible, but that didn't mean I had to roll over and show him my belly. "You've done a better job of poisoning me against you than Anderson could ever have done. Hasn't anyone ever told you that threatening someone's family is a sure way to get a relationship off to a bad start?"

Konstantin shot a quick look in Alexis's direction. There was no missing the reproach in that glance. Alexis looked away. "Again, I apologize. Alexis can be rather impetuous at times. He should have cleared it with me before making threats. We have had a long talk, and he's assured me nothing like that will happen again."

Alexis's shoulders tightened at the rebuke, and his gaze remained pinned to the floor. All very convincing, but I had a hard time believing Konstantin really had a problem with what Alexis had done. Maybe he'd have preferred it if Alexis tried a little harder to make contact peacefully before resorting to threats, but the threats would have come eventually, one way or another. And if Konstantin were really sorry about it, he'd have said so right from the start.

"So are you retracting the threat?"

He smiled at me, the expression condescending, though his tone remained completely pleasant. "My friend threatened harm to your sister if you didn't show up today. You're here, so the threat is no longer valid."

I wondered if he thought he was being subtle. Some people are such good liars that they can respond to questions with a complete non sequitur and make you believe they actually answered you. Konstantin wasn't one of them.

"So if I walked out of here right now, we wouldn't have a problem anymore?" I asked, pressing the issue even though I knew the answer.

"Let's not make this meeting a waste of both my time and yours," he said. "We can have a civilized conversation over lunch."

He gestured in the direction I presumed was toward the restaurant, but I didn't budge. I didn't want to spend a moment more than necessary in the company of these men, and I sure as hell couldn't see sitting down to lunch with them.

"I've got a very busy afternoon," I told Konstantin, still trying to be at least relatively diplomatic. "I don't have time for a fancy lunch. Why don't we have a seat over there," I continued, gesturing toward the nook where I'd been sitting, "and we can get right down to business."

Konstantin was clearly taken aback by my refusal. Guess he was surprised I didn't automatically do what he wanted. He paused for a long moment before he spoke again.

"I can see how you and Alexis would rub each other the wrong way," he said with a wry smile that didn't reach his eyes. He may have been genuinely trying to create some kind of rapport based on shared humor, but the attempt was too forced to be effective. Beneath his urbane veneer, an aura of cruelty clung to him.

"Yeah, I don't think he and I will ever be on each other's Christmas lists," I said.

Alexis said nothing, merely stood to the side and glared at me, his arms crossed over his chest.

"Then perhaps it would be best if you and I spoke alone," Konstantin said. Without waiting for my response, he headed toward the sofa in the corner of the seating area. I guessed I was supposed to follow.

I felt Alexis's glare on the back of my head the moment I turned away from him. He hadn't uttered a sound of protest, but I knew he was majorly pissed off that he was being left out of the conversation. And he hadn't appreciated Konstantin's public rebukes, either, no matter how insincere they might have been. Like he needed another reason to hate me.

I sat gingerly on the edge of the sofa, feeling anything but relaxed around this self-proclaimed king of the *Liberi Deorum,* but he sprawled in the seat at the other end as if he owned the place. For all I knew, he did. I knew nothing about this man, not even his last name. Not that I *wanted* to know anything about him.

"So what was it you were so desperate to talk to me about?" I asked, trying to release some of the tension in my spine. We were in a very public place. I could hardly expect Konstantin to try to attack me here. Still, I couldn't dismiss the possibility out of hand, which was why I'd done my surveillance before the meeting. There was just too damn much I didn't know, and the only people who could give me information were people I didn't want to talk to. "Alexis suggested you wanted to hire me for something?"

Konstantin nodded. "Yes. As a descendant of Artemis, your skills would be a great asset to us."

I wondered if his "us" was a royal "we," or if he actually meant the Olympians as a whole. "Go on," I said. I already knew there was no way in hell I was working for him, but I figured it behooved me to hear him out for diplomacy's sake.

"We Olympians function as something of a police force for the *Liberi Deorum.* As such, we often find ourselves needing to track down people who do not wish to be found. Ordinarily, we use private investigators to help us locate these fugitives, but even a skilled private investigator has limitations, especially considering the level of secrecy we require. You, however, would be perfect for the position. Not only a descendant of Artemis, but already an experienced private investigator. You would make it infinitely easier for us to track down our fugitives."

He made it all sound terribly . . . benign. Of course, even

if everything Anderson had told me about the Olympians was true, they were no doubt the heroes of their own stories. What I might see as a ruthless slaughter of innocents, they might consider a necessary purge to protect their own people. Even so, I didn't think that was what *Konstantin* believed. He might have started his crusade against Descendants under the pretext of protecting the *Liberi,* but these days it was all about enjoying the power. Maybe I was reading things into his tone and body language, but his words carried no sense of self-righteousness or conviction like they should if he really believed them.

"What would happen to these 'fugitives' once I found them for you?" I asked.

"They would be dealt with in an appropriate manner."

"Would dealing with them in the 'appropriate manner' involve killing them, by any chance?"

"It would depend on the circumstances. However, it would be your job to find them, not to carry out their sentences, whatever those sentences might be."

Maybe that was supposed to allow me to soothe my conscience if I accepted the job. As if the fact that I wasn't personally killing anyone would make me feel better about tracking people down so the Olympians could kill them.

"The rewards you would reap if you chose to work with us are considerable," Konstantin said. "We are richer than many countries, and we are generous with those riches. Your pay would be in seven figures, with bonuses for success. You could live like a queen." He sounded much more passionate about this argument than he had about the "it's for a good cause" thing.

I shrugged. "Money doesn't tempt me."

He laughed, like I'd just made the funniest joke in the world. "Oh, Nikki, money tempts everyone."

And just like that, I'd heard enough. I'd listened to what he had to say, and there was no hint of doubt in my mind that I wanted nothing to do with Konstantin or his Olympians. The time for diplomacy was over. "Let me rephrase that: I don't want your money."

Konstantin's urbane veneer thinned a little more, until it was practically nonexistent. "Perhaps you don't understand. I am the king of the *Liberi Deorum*. I realize you have only been recently introduced to the *Liberi,* but that doesn't exempt you from our laws. You are *Liberi,* and therefore you answer to me."

I snorted softly. "Most of the *Liberi* I've met *don't* answer to you."

He went completely still, shedding the last vestiges of his pseudo-friendly persona. The darkness in his eyes spoke of power and of deadly danger. "I have a treaty with Anderson and his people. That treaty does not extend to *you*."

He leaned toward me on the sofa, and it was all I could do not to recoil. His anger wasn't as ostentatious as Alexis's, but it was all the more chilling for its calculated control.

"Make no mistake, Nikki," he said, his calm, unruffled voice at odds with the fury that radiated from his every pore. "I have presented you with a choice, but the consequences of making the wrong one are beyond the limits of your imagination."

I swallowed hard, hating that I couldn't hide my fear. "I thought you weren't into making threats."

He shrugged and sat back, banishing all signs of anger in a fraction of a second. The veneer was back, but I'd already gotten a clear view of what lay beneath it. "I prefer to catch my flies with honey, when possible." He gave me a charming smile that scared me almost as much as his glare. "But a good king must sometimes make compromises to ensure the well-being of his people. It is important to our people that we find these fugitives, and therefore I'm not in the position to take no for an answer."

He reached into the inner pocket of his jacket and pulled out a folded piece of paper. "On this paper are three names, those of our most wanted." He tried to hand me the paper, but I refused to take it from him. Then he grabbed my wrist in a crushing grip and forced the paper into my fingers, smiling pleasantly all the while.

"I know they will be difficult to locate," he continued, still holding my wrist so hard I felt like my bones were scraping together. "I'll be generous and give you one week to find your first fugitive. It can be any of the ones on that list, although eventually you must find all three. When you have the location of the first fugitive, you will call Alexis with your information, and he will send a squad to confirm you're telling the truth. When you find that first fugitive, I will pay you one million dollars." He smiled again and let go of my wrist. "In case that isn't incentive enough, I'll have you know that Alexis has taken quite a liking to your sister.

"If you refuse, or if you fail, I will give Alexis permission to do whatever he wants with her. Let your imagination run wild. He won't kill her, though. He'll let her live so that you can see the wretched ruin he has made of her. If that doesn't motivate you . . . then we will have to get more creative. I have walked this earth for many centuries, my dear. Let me assure you, when it comes to cruelty, I've seen every form imaginable in my day, and there is nothing I would not scruple to do."

His eyes bored into me as I sat there in horrified silence, unable to force a single word from my mouth.

Konstantin reached over and patted my shoulder. I was too frozen to react. Then the lines of his face softened and he gave me what looked like a sad smile. Another veneer, no more convincing than the other.

"It doesn't have to be like this," he said softly. "You can join with us and work in a spirit of cooperation. No one need get hurt. You are *Liberi Deorum,* Nikki Glass, and you will live forever. The choice is yours whether that life will be one of pleasure and privilege, or pain and strife."

I still couldn't speak, didn't know what I could say in the

face of such blatant evil. Words of defiance might get Steph hurt, but it was beyond me to in any way suggest I was in agreement with him. About *anything* he had said.

I remained silent as Konstantin rose to his feet, headed toward the front door, and beckoned Alexis to follow.

T<small>EN</small>

I sat in the hotel lobby for a good half hour after Konstantin and Alexis left, trying to pull myself together and think clearly. I didn't have much luck.

What was I going to do now? I couldn't let Alexis hurt Steph. And yet I couldn't live with myself if I tracked down the people on Konstantin's list and thereby got them killed.

Of course, it was still possible Anderson had been lying. Maybe the people on Konstantin's list were all bad guys, fugitives from justice, just as he had described them. I didn't actually believe it—the threats he'd made against Steph told me all I needed to know about the strength of his moral fiber—but I clung to the unlikely possibility.

I finally managed to get myself moving again. I collected my spy camera from under the chair, then left the Sofitel, keeping a careful eye out for any sign that I was being followed. I was pretty sure Konstantin was convinced he had me over a barrel and therefore wouldn't waste his time having me tailed, but you never can be too sure.

I took a very long and roundabout route back to my hotel, then retreated to my room to do a little research. I couldn't see complying with Konstantin's demands—surely I would find some other way out of this mess without endangering Steph— but I figured it couldn't hurt to see what I could dig up on the people he was asking me to find.

He'd given me very little to go on. Just names, and dates and places of birth. Under normal circumstances, I would have refused to try to locate someone with so little information. I'm good, but I'm not *that* good. But these were not normal circumstances. And besides, everyone seemed to think I had some kind of supernatural hunting ability. I'd seen the evidence that I'd become a ridiculously good shot, but so far I had no idea how that could translate into finding someone. Maybe once I tried, I'd unlock a special ability I didn't know I had.

I started with the first name on the list: Joseph Swift. Born March 15, 1955, in Madison, WI. At least that gave me a starting place for my search, although it was obvious Joseph Swift wasn't in Madison anymore, or the Olympians could have found him easily without my help.

I didn't need any fancy new supernatural abilities to find out some basic information about Swift, not when the local papers had a gruesome story to revel in.

Swift had lived a fairly ordinary life as a child. His parents were working class, but steadily employed. He was a straight-A student, and a star of his high school football team. Colleges were recruiting him aggressively, and his future looked almost unbearably bright. Until the spring of his senior year in high school, that is.

Just a few days shy of his eighteenth birthday, there was what was described as a failed burglary attempt at Joseph Swift's home. Several masked men broke into the house around midnight. According to Joseph, everyone in the household had gone to bed, and all the lights in the house were out. He, however, had been having trouble sleeping and had gone downstairs for a glass of water. He was in the kitchen drinking his water when he heard his father's startled cry, and then his mother's scream.

Joseph sprinted to his parents' aid, having no idea what was happening. When he was halfway up the stairs, his eight-year-old sister came running out of her bedroom, pursued by one of the masked intruders. The girl was stabbed to death before Joseph's eyes. When he saw two more masked men with bloody knives emerging from his parents' room, Joseph ran for his life. He managed to escape, but his entire family had been slaughtered.

I read several newspaper accounts of the murders. Everyone seemed to think that the masked men were burglars, and that Joseph's father had surprised them at their work. But the theory made little sense. The "burglars" sounded like a sophisticated crew, but the Swifts hardly seemed wealthy enough to attract them. Plus, what self-respecting professional burglars would break into a house when they knew there were four people inside? Far less risky to wait until the house was empty.

It was hard to see the murders as anything other than a premeditated slaughter of a family of Descendants perpetrated by the Olympians.

Joseph seemed to drop off the face of the Earth after the murders, which I supposed was why the Olympians wanted my help to find him. I tried locating other members of his extended family, thinking maybe he'd gone to live with them, but not only did I not find any sign of him, I found even more evidence that pointed to a purge. I couldn't find evidence of a single surviving family member on his father's side. There was one maternal aunt who survived until 1963, when she died of natural causes, and a couple of distant cousins—also on his mother's side—who seemed to have lived—or still be living—long and ordinary lives. But the more I delved into his father's family, the more unexplained deaths I discovered. Car accidents. House fires. Mysterious disappearances. Everything led me to the conclusion that Joseph's divine blood had come through his father's side, and that the Olympians had managed to eliminate them all one by one.

I never got around to doing any serious research on Swift's current location, because I'd already learned everything I wanted to know. There was not a single doubt left in my mind:

if I located Joseph Swift, he was a dead man. And if he had any children, they, too, would either die or be kidnapped and indoctrinated by the Olympians.

I couldn't do it. Not even to save Steph. And as horrible as Konstantin's threat had been, I knew my sister well enough to be certain she'd agree with my decision. I was just going to have to find some other way to protect her. Reluctant as I was to admit it, that meant I was going to need help. And there was only one person I could go to for said help.

Perhaps I was digging the hole deeper, both for myself and for Steph. Perhaps Anderson was just as cruel and ruthless as Konstantin. But there was only one way to find out.

It was almost five before I found the nerve to pick up the phone and call Anderson. I couldn't help remembering all the hostility he and Blake and Jamaal had shown me the other night, and the idea of placing myself at their mercy made me want to hide under the bed. But honestly, I could see no other option, aside from giving up my entire life and making myself disappear, which still wouldn't guarantee Steph's safety. It was possible that by calling Anderson, I was handing myself over to the enemy. It was also possible that I'd already soured any potential we'd ever had of working together. But I had to try.

My heart raced and my palms sweated as I waited for Anderson to answer. Was this my gut trying to warn me away? Or was it just a very natural fear reaction, after all I'd gone through in the past forty-eight hours? I couldn't tell.

Anderson finally picked up the phone just when I thought sure my call was about to go to voice mail.

"Nikki," he said by way of greeting. Guess he had caller ID. "What a pleasant surprise." There was a dry humor to his voice, but no hint of irritation. I chose to take that as a good sign. "To what do I owe the pleasure?"

I'd debated how much to tell him about my current situation, but decided that full disclosure might be my best shot at getting the help I needed. "I met Konstantin today."

He grunted softly. "My condolences."

I surprised myself by smiling. "Yeah. I'm not a big fan."

"Neither am I."

"So I gathered."

"Let me guess what he wanted: he's asked you to use your unique abilities to find some people for him."

Not that impressive a guess, considering he'd pretty much predicted it earlier. "There wasn't really any asking involved."

Anderson sighed. "No, of course not. Konstantin considers his desires to be everyone else's commands. Is he still trying to court you, or has he begun making threats yet?"

"I wouldn't even have met with him today if there hadn't been a threat involved." My heart constricted with fear for Steph. "He's threatened to let Alexis . . . hurt my sister if I don't do what he wants."

Anderson hesitated a moment before answering. "I didn't know you had a sister," he said. "If she's still alive, it's only because Konstantin thinks he can use her to control you for the time being. He won't allow another Descendant—even a descendant of Artemis—to survive when he can harvest her immortality for one of his pets. He won't destroy you as long as you're useful, but your sister . . ."

"Steph and I aren't related by blood," I clarified. "I'm adopted."

"Ah. Good. Otherwise, all your family members would be in danger."

Yeah, I'd already figured that out. But if Konstantin was going to use Steph against me, I had no doubt that he'd be just as happy to threaten my adoptive parents if he thought that might make me more pliable. I could only thank my lucky stars that they were out of the country and out of his reach, at least for now.

"If I do what Konstantin wants, he's going to kill anyone I track down for him. Right?"

"Yes. He always makes his purges of Descendant families

as thorough as possible, but sometimes people slip through his fingers. I suspect he's worked up detailed genealogies of all the families he's ever identified and has extensive lists of people he'd like to locate."

"He gave me a list of three."

"Trust me, that's not even the tip of the iceberg. He'd rather present you with a short list and try to lull you into a sense of complacency than let you know that once he's got the leverage he needs, he'll set you to tracking down hundreds of people for him to kill."

I winced. "Hundreds?"

"At least. The Olympians have been around a long time. Konstantin has been their leader since the early fifteenth century."

I felt momentarily dizzy at the concept. I was finally getting around to accepting that the *Liberi* were immortal, but it was still hard to absorb the idea that I'd talked to a man who'd been alive since before Columbus discovered America.

"He was bent on destroying Descendants even then, though of course it was a lot harder before the days of modern transportation and computerized records. But just think—if he missed a family member in one of those Descendant purges back in the fifteenth century, how many descendants might that person have running around today?"

I saw his point. And I once again saw that I couldn't do what Konstantin ordered, no matter what the risk. I blew out a frustrated breath. "Listen, I need your help."

"Oh, do you now?" he responded, and there was no missing the calculation in his voice.

"You keep trying to convince me you're one of the good guys," I forged on. "If that's the truth, then you won't let Konstantin and Alexis hurt an innocent woman, right?"

He thought about that a long while before he answered. "I hate to sound like a mercenary. But I can't forget you're the woman who killed Emmitt and shot Blake. I'm not a hundred percent sure that *you're* one of the good guys. I'm sure your sister is a lovely woman, and she doesn't deserve whatever Konstantin has threatened. But why should I stick my neck out for her when you've been so terribly . . . disobliging?"

"Because it's the right thing to do." I swallowed the lump of anger that rose in my throat. He had a point, and I knew it. He wasn't even fully convinced I hadn't killed Emmitt on purpose, so there wasn't any particular reason for him to feel kindly toward me. That didn't mean I had to admit it.

"I'm sure that's very clear-cut from where you're standing, but from where I'm standing . . . not so much."

"So that's it? I didn't fall at your feet and adore you after you threatened to torture me, and therefore to hell with me? And to hell with Steph? If that's the way you feel, then why the hell have you called me about a billion times?"

"I didn't say to hell with you," Anderson responded quietly, his calm making me feel like a child throwing a tantrum. "I was explaining why I'm not going to help your sister unless you give me something in return."

I guess it had been foolish of me to hope that Anderson would help me out of the goodness of his heart. It sucked that I wasn't in a position to tell him where to shove it.

"What do you want?" I asked through gritted teeth.

"I want you to find someone for me as well, but I promise it's not for nefarious purposes."

Too bad I didn't have a clue what Anderson's promises were worth. But I also didn't have a whole lot of options.

"Who?" I asked, trying not to sound as wary as I felt. "And why? And please don't give me the runaround the way Konstantin did."

"I won't. But it's rather a long story. Perhaps you should come to the house so we can talk in person. I'll make dinner, and we can have a civilized conversation."

"We can have a civilized conversation anywhere," I countered, not at all anxious to set foot in the mansion again. The place didn't exactly fill me with warm, fuzzy memories. "If you want to make it a dinner meeting, choose a restaurant."

He hesitated a moment before answering. "If we come to an agreement and I am to protect your sister, then you will have to come live here. My . . . arrangement with Konstantin is that he will not harm those who live under my roof or the families of those who live under my roof. It's not a perfect arrangement, and he wouldn't hesitate to break it if he thought he could get away with it, but it would provide your sister a great deal of protection."

As usual anytime I had a conversation with one of the *Liberi,* I had about a million questions. However, they were all drowned out by my outrage.

"You want me to come *live* with you?" I cried. "Are you crazy?"

"Perhaps so," he said drily. "Offering you my protection won't be my most popular decision ever, but this is my house, and my rules.

"At least come have dinner with me. I promise you'll have safe passage, even if you and I can't agree on a single thing."

I shook my head, though of course he couldn't see. "Why should I believe you won't just shove me back in that basement jail of yours the minute I show my face?"

"You're asking for my help. What good is that if you trust me so little?"

Reality check time. I couldn't protect Steph on my own. Sure, I could warn her that my problem-client had threatened her, and she could hire some security. But I couldn't warn her without having to give her an explanation of the threat. If I told her the truth, she'd never believe me. If I made up an explanation that left out all the supernatural stuff, she'd insist we call the police. And even if I thought of a way to overcome those obstacles, who was to say human security would be able to protect her? I had no idea what Konstantin and the rest of the Olympians were capable of.

But Anderson did.

"All right," I said reluctantly. "I'll come to the house. But you'd better guarantee you won't let Blake or Jamaal near me. I catch sight of either one of them, and all bets are off. Got it?"

It was an empty threat, of course. We'd already established that I needed Anderson's help, which left me very little bargaining power. But Anderson didn't press the issue.

"I'll make sure you don't run into them," he promised.

That didn't make me feel a whole lot better. Anderson might be the leader of his people, but they hadn't so far shown themselves to be the most obedient lot.

"Would seven o'clock work for you?" Anderson asked. "Or do you need more time?"

The sooner we got this over with, the better. "I'll be there at seven."

"I look forward to it."

Too bad I didn't share the sentiment.

Eleven

Having been suddenly turned into an immortal caught between two warring factions of the *Liberi Deorum,* I hadn't exactly had time to deal with the mundane challenges presented by having my car totaled. I had a suspicion that wasn't going to be changing anytime soon. My car had been towed, but I had no idea where or by whom, nor did I know how Anderson had explained the accident. He'd have had to offer *some* explanation, right? I mean, there was blood all over the place—both mine and Emmitt's—and I didn't imagine a wrecker service would haul the car away without any questions being asked.

If I thought there were any chance of going through legal channels peacefully, I'd have called my insurance company about the accident. They might even have reimbursed me for car rental. As it was, I decided that at least for now, I would ignore the whole problem. I rented a shiny new silver Taurus, then drove out to Anderson's mansion in Arlington.

Renting the car had taken less time than I'd thought, so I was a little early. The warmer weather of the last couple of days had melted all the ice, but I couldn't help the chill that ran down my spine when I caught sight of the iron gates at the head of the driveway. A big part of me longed to turn the car around and just go home. Pretend none of this had happened. Pretend Steph wasn't in danger, and I was just an ordinary woman.

Shoving down my disquiet, I lowered my window and hit the button on the intercom outside the gates. I wasn't sure what to say, but apparently silence was good enough. Moments after I hit the button, there was a faint buzzing noise, and the gates parted. I dried my sweaty palms on my pants legs as I waited for the opening to be large enough to drive through.

The visibility was a lot better today than it had been the last time I'd navigated the twisting driveway that led to the house. Even so, I drove like a nearsighted granny, my hands clutching the steering wheel way too tightly. My heart rate jacked up as I fought against the memory of driving through the sleet. When I rounded the final curve and hit the straightaway, I slowed to a crawl.

Everything had happened so fast the other night that I couldn't really say where the exact spot was that Emmitt had suddenly appeared in the middle of the road, nor where his body had lain when I'd crawled out of my car. My headlights illuminated gouges in a couple of trees beside the road—the trees that I'd plowed into. My stomach lurched, and for a moment, it as was if I were living at both times simultaneously. I could have sworn I smelled blood and scorched rubber.

I brought the car to a complete stop, then lowered my head to the steering wheel and closed my eyes, forcing myself to take slow, deep breaths. My head was spinning and my skin was clammy with sweat. I wondered if I was having a real live panic attack. Obviously, I had yet to deal with the horror of that night, and I wished I could have told Steph about it. She wouldn't have been able to say magic words to make it all better, but just the act of talking might have eased some of the pressure inside me.

After a while, my heart rate slowed to something just a little faster than normal, and I no longer felt like I might pass out behind the wheel. Cautiously, I raised my head, half expecting to find sleet clattering against the windshield. But no, the sky was clear. The past was back in the past where it belonged, at least for now.

Blowing out a deep breath, I put the car in drive again and proceeded to the house. I parked in a circular drive that surrounded a decorative fountain, then got out of the car, my legs still a little shaky from my brush with panic.

As I've mentioned, the house was easily big enough to be termed a mansion, and I wouldn't have been surprised if it turned out to be a renovated pre–Civil War plantation. The front door was framed by a series of columns and featured a porch that was bigger than some houses I'd lived in. A cluster of elegant outdoor furniture formed an almost cozy seating area on one half of the porch. The other half featured a white-washed swing and several dozen potted plants, all of hearty varieties that could survive a Virginia winter outdoors.

Anderson was waiting for me on that swing, one leg curled under him, while his other foot pushed on the porch floor just enough to create a little motion. He was dressed in a pair of faded denim jeans and a navy blue sweatshirt, his feet tucked into sneakers that had seen better days. The casual, comfortable outfit seemed almost out of place with the majestic mansion in the background.

Moving slowly, as if trying not to alarm me, Anderson rose to his feet. I had to admit, I felt extremely wary. If he'd made anything I could have interpreted as a hostile move, I'd have been running for my car in a heartbeat. But he kept his distance, and even stuffed his hands in his pockets for good measure.

"What happened out there?" he asked, jerking his chin toward the driveway.

I felt the blood rush to my face as I realized he'd been sitting here watching while I had my little panic attack. If I wanted Anderson to think of me as a tough chick he didn't want to mess with, I wasn't exactly going about it the best way.

I licked my lips, then regretted the nervous gesture. "I couldn't help . . . remembering," I said, because I had to say something.

Maybe I was just seeing what I wanted to see, but I thought there was a softening in Anderson's expression. "Why don't you come inside," he beckoned, heading toward the door. "It's a little chilly out here."

At that point, I was eager to comply. If I was inside the house, I wouldn't be able to see the spot where I had killed Emmitt, and maybe I'd be able to keep the memory at a more comfortable distance. I forgot to be wary as I hurried to cross the threshold while Anderson held the door open. Luckily, there was no mob of angry *Liberi* waiting to jump me, or I'd have blundered into them blindly without even a hint of a fight.

The foyer was everything you would expect in an enormous mansion. The floor was of intricately patterned green marble, and the walls were decorated by oil paintings that might well have been the work of grand masters—I'm not enough of an art aficionado to tell an imitation from the real thing. There was even a crystal chandelier that looked like something right out of *Phantom of the Opera*.

If Anderson took any particular pride in the grandeur of his home, he didn't show it. He barely seemed to glance at the house, or notice my reaction to it, as he led me through room after elegant room until we came to a huge state-of-the-art kitchen.

The rooms we had passed through on the way to the kitchen had all been pristine and formal, almost like they were more for show than for actual living. The kitchen was a different story. It was as large and well-appointed as any other room I'd seen, but there was no missing the signs of habitation. A couple of dirty cups in the sink. Some crumbs on the counter near the toaster. A walk-in pantry crammed with a disorganized array of boxes and cans and bags.

The air was rich with the smell of spices, and I saw a huge vat of something simmering on the stove. I couldn't be certain, but it smelled a lot like chili. My stomach grumbled its approval, and my mouth started watering. Who'd have thought the leader of a group of such powerful immortals would cook chili for dinner, just like an ordinary single guy? I bet neither Konstantin nor Alexis had ever let such peasant food cross their lips.

At one end of the kitchen, there was a breakfast nook, surrounded on three sides by windows looking out onto the back lawn. A butcher block table occupied the nook; Anderson had laid out a couple of place settings there. An open bottle of wine breathed in the center of the table.

"Please, have a seat," Anderson said.

I was strangely glad he didn't try to pull out my chair for me. Both Konstantin and Alexis were such stuffed shirts I couldn't help appreciating Anderson's more casual manners. I sat down while Anderson gave the pot on the stove a stir.

"I hope you like chili," he said. "It's about the only thing I can cook that anyone other than me would willingly put in their mouths." He shot me a self-deprecating smile over his shoulder.

"Chili's great," I assured him. "Can I help with something?" I asked, belatedly remembering my manners. Then I was surprised at myself for asking. Ever since I'd first met him, I'd been considering Anderson an enemy, or at the very least an antagonist, but over the course of just a few minutes, I seemed to have dropped my guard entirely.

"No, no," he answered. "One of the advantages of chili is that all I have to do is scoop it into a bowl. Strictly a one-person job."

He got a couple of bowls out of one of the cabinets and generously ladled in the chili. Then he reached into the oven and pulled out a foil-wrapped bundle, which turned out to be cornbread. He put the bowls and cornbread on a couple of plates, then carried them into the nook and set them down. The chili smelled heavenly.

"Don't worry," Anderson said, one side of his mouth curling up in another of his wry smiles. "I didn't cook the cornbread, so it's safe to eat."

The meal was surprisingly pleasant. We didn't talk about the Olympians or Emmitt's death or what either faction wanted from me. Instead, we talked about the kind of trivialities that almost reminded me of the getting-to-know-you part of a first date. We learned we were both Redskins fans, and I was appropriately jealous to discover he had season tickets. He had typically male tastes in movies—action flicks good, anything remotely mushy bad—but showed no hint of the veiled sexism I'd seen in Alexis and Konstantin. He didn't even make a face when I admitted I liked romance novels. And, unlike Jim, the Date from Hell, Anderson showed interest in what I was saying and didn't try the steer to conversation toward himself.

If it really *had* been a first date, and nothing had come before, I'd have said I had a good time. Too bad it wasn't a first date.

Observing Anderson's "cult" in the days before I'd joined the ranks of the *Liberi*, I'd noted that although he served as their leader, Anderson had a remarkably laid-back manner. That manner was very much in evidence tonight. I kept reminding myself that Anderson was dangerous and not to be trusted. I even forcibly reminded myself of the way he'd hurt Jamaal, and the way he'd threatened to hurt me. But it was hard to reconcile that memory with the man who sat across the table from me, chatting amiably and smiling easily.

I stuffed myself on chili and cornbread, both of which were blazing hot. I was half expecting it from the chili, but the cornbread took me by surprise, since I didn't see the jalapeños until

I'd shoved a big hunk in my mouth. Good thing I like spicy food, though I'd have preferred to wash it down with a cold beer rather than room temperature red wine. I'm pretty sure the wine was good stuff, but my taste buds were burning too much to notice.

When I could eat no more, Anderson made a pot of after-dinner coffee, which he served with a generous splash of Bailey's. When he returned to the table, I could tell by the serious look on his face that social hour was over, and we were about to get down to business. The strength of my regret surprised me.

Being in no hurry to put an end to the festivities, I sipped my coffee in silence, waiting for Anderson to begin. I didn't have to wait long.

"Your sister and anyone else you care about is going to be in some amount of danger, no matter what you do," he started, and the baldness of his statement made me wince. There was sympathy in his voice, but he made no particular attempt to soften the blow. "I figure it does neither of us any good if I make promises I can't keep."

At least he was honest about it. "So if you can't protect Steph, what's the point of me coming here?"

"I'm not saying I can't protect her. I'm just saying that even if I do, there will always be some danger. Konstantin and I have agreed to tolerate each other for the sake of expediency, but if at any time he should decide our truce is more trouble than it's worth, he could break it. That's a reality all of us in this house have to live with. We don't have any Descendants at our beck and call, which means we can't kill Konstantin or any of his people. If he decides to break his truce with us, he'll do it by having his pet Descendants attack us, and even if we win the battle, it's likely some of us will die—and increase the Olympians' strength by doing so."

I frowned as I thought this over. "Then why did he agree to a truce with you in the first place?"

Anderson smiled, and in his eyes I saw a flash of the ruthlessness that was usually well hidden beneath his friendly demeanor. "Consider that a trade secret."

I decided not to press. "Okay. So you have a shaky truce with the Olympians, but you're not confident enough in it to promise you can keep Steph safe."

"That's it in a nutshell. But I *can* promise to keep her a whole lot safer than she is right now. Even if you agree to hunt the people on the list Konstantin gave you, that won't guarantee her safety. If you ever balk at anything he commands you to do, he'll trot the threat out again. I can't imagine you could have spoken to him for more than five minutes and not know I'm telling the truth about this."

Unfortunately, he was right. Konstantin had tried to make it sound like we could be best buds if only I'd do this one little thing for him. But I knew a bully when I saw one, and I knew Konstantin was the kind of guy who'd enjoy flexing his muscles on a regular basis.

I had to suppress a shudder at the thought of Steph being subjected to Konstantin's malice. There were times I couldn't help being jealous of my sister's relatively easy life. She'd been born beautiful and personable, to a wealthy family who doted on her. Sure, she'd had her share of heartbreaks, just like any normal person, but nothing really *bad* had ever happened to her. She'd never been abandoned by her mother, or been passed from foster home to foster home, or been threatened with juvie.

The downside to this gilded life was that she'd never had to develop the kind of armor I had. There's a difference between knowing that there's ugliness in this world and being subjected to that ugliness yourself. My early life had inoculated me against some of the worst the world had to offer. I was reeling under the stress of what had happened to me the other night, but I was at least *coping* with it. Steph wouldn't have those kinds of coping skills. Even a small dose of violence would be a terrible shock to her system. I feared that if Alexis got his hands on her, he wouldn't have to work very hard to break her.

"The best thing you can do for your sister," Anderson said softly, "is to ally with me. I'm not a tyrant like Konstantin, and my people do what we can to make the world a better place."

I pushed my fears for Steph to the side and met Anderson's eyes. Maybe it was just my imagination, but I thought I saw something warm and wise in those medium brown eyes of his. Eyes I'd once dismissed as ordinary.

But as friendly and non-threatening as he was being now, I'd seen another side of him that first night. I wanted to trust him, if only because it would make my own life so much easier, but I couldn't allow myself to forget how little I knew about him.

"So that Hand of Doom thing you did to Jamaal isn't something you consider tyrannical?" I challenged, watching his face carefully in hopes his expression would reveal more of his hidden depths. No such luck.

"Hand of Doom?" he asked with a little smile. "I've never heard it called that before."

"You think it's funny?"

His smile faded, replaced by an almost sad expression. "No. No, it's not funny at all." He sighed and reached for his cup of coffee, which was almost empty. I think he was just stalling for time as he tipped the last few drops into his mouth.

"I suppose I have my own tyrannical moments," he admitted, staring into his empty cup. He seemed to catch himself doing it, then carefully placed the cup on the table and looked at me once more. "Gentle rebukes don't have much of an effect on most *Liberi,* especially not on someone like Jamaal. I know you've seen no evidence to support this, but he's a good man at heart. He *wants* to control his dark side, but he isn't always able to, especially without Emmitt to help him. When he loses control, there have to be consequences."

"So that was special treatment you reserve just for Jamaal?" Instinct told me the answer was no.

"I don't run around hurting my people on a regular basis, if that's what you're asking. But I am their leader, and I do expect them to obey me when I make a direct order." He leaned forward, his expression intense. "Understand this, Nikki: you're very new to being *Liberi,* but the rest of my people are not. Being immortal and having supernatural powers will change you over time, will corrupt you, if you let it. If I let my people get away with defying me, then I risk losing them. Not right away, but over time, as they find they can do anything they want without suffering any consequences, year after year after year. I've seen it happen too many times, and so have my people. They're with me because they don't want to go down that road, and they believe I can keep it from happening."

"And what's to keep *you* from going down that road? Or do you punish yourself when you've been a bad boy?"

I thought my sarcastic question might piss him off, but Anderson just smiled. "There are some checks and balances in place."

Not the most specific answer in the world, but it was apparently all I was going to get.

"All right. Let's say I accept that you're not a tyrant and that becoming your ally is the best way to protect my family. What would I have to do to join up?"

"First, you would have to move into the house, because those are the terms of my agreement with Konstantin. Any *Liberi* who lives in this house is considered to be one of mine."

I had no intention of moving into the mansion permanently. I loved my condo, and there was no way I was giving it up. I also loved my freedom, and sharing communal quarters with Anderson and his flock of *Liberi* would be like living in a barracks. A luxurious, beautiful barracks, but a barracks all the same.

However, I'd already established that I needed Anderson's help, and if temporarily moving into the mansion was what I had to do to get it, then I was going to have to suck it up, at least for a while. I'd just have to consider it as an indefinite hotel stay.

Unfortunately, Anderson had already let me know there was another condition I had to meet to earn his help.

"And second," I continued for him, "there's someone you want me to find for you. Who? And why?"

The corners of his eyes tightened with what looked like pain. "Her name is Emma Poindexter," he said. He swallowed hard, then took a deep breath and let it out slowly. "She's been missing for almost ten years. And I want you to find her because she's my wife."

TWELVE

I sat in stunned silence at Anderson's kitchen table. I don't know why I was so surprised. He might not be drop-dead gorgeous, but Anderson was certainly attractive enough, and he obviously had money and power. Why would I assume a man like him was single? Especially when he was most likely centuries old?

"Your wife," I repeated when I could find my voice. I glanced at his left hand, but there was no ring on his finger. At least I hadn't missed so obvious a clue as that.

He nodded. "She's a *Liberi,* descended of Nyx—the Greek goddess of night." He shifted in his seat, no longer meeting my eyes. "Konstantin and I may not be at open war with each other now, but that wasn't always the case. Konstantin hates me more than words can express for challenging his 'rule.' So to punish me for luring some of his Olympians out of the fold, he kidnapped Emma."

Anderson closed his eyes. His fists were clenched in his lap, his shoulders tight with strain. I felt a very feminine urge to comfort him, but I managed to stifle it. I didn't know him well enough to offer comfort.

When he opened his eyes, there was a hint of red around the edges, like he'd been crying, although I saw no evidence of tears. "He claims he interred her. Buried her alive."

I couldn't help the little gasp that escaped me. "But she's *Liberi* . . ." I whispered.

"Yes. She's *Liberi*. If he's telling the truth, if he didn't just have one of his pet Descendants kill her, then she's been in the ground, unable to escape even through death, for almost ten years."

He blinked rapidly, as if trying to stave off tears. His voice was steadier when he resumed, but there was a faint, husky tone to it. "You see, Nikki, I know what it's like to have someone you love used as a weapon against you. I'll do everything in my power to help you protect your family if you will do everything in *your* power to help me find Emma."

In all honesty, it's a case I might well have taken on without any need for threat or ultimatum. How could I not take pity on someone who'd suffered so horribly? Even if Emma was a raving bitch, I'd have felt sorry for her, but since I didn't know her it was even easier to picture her as the innocent victim of an evil, vindictive bastard.

As a P.I., I'd always specialized in locates and skip traces—basically, finding people who didn't want to be found. But this wasn't going to be a typical locate. None of the tools I used to find missing persons—things like online searches and interviews with people who might have heard from her—was going to help me find someone who was buried, and had been in the ground for almost ten years. Everyone seemed to assume I had some kind of supernatural hunting powers, but other than my sudden improvement in marksmanship, I'd seen no sign of them.

"Will you help me, Nikki?" Anderson asked, and the plea in his voice made something in my chest hurt. I wasn't trusting enough to believe everything he'd said, and I had the distinct impression there were plenty of things he'd left out of the story, but I *did* believe he was hurting. A lot.

"Yes," I said, because what else could I possibly answer? Even if I didn't need his help myself, I doubt I could have resisted that plea. Never mind that I hadn't the faintest idea how

I could actually go about helping him. "If you'll help me protect my family, I'll do everything I can to help find Emma."

"Thank you," he said, then heaved a big sigh. "I've been without hope for so long I'd forgotten what it feels like."

The knot in my chest tightened. I hated to get his hopes up when the chances that I could find Emma seemed so slim.

Anderson smiled wanly. "Don't worry. Unlike Konstantin, I am not prone to unrealistic expectations. I know there's a chance he's lying to me and she's been dead all along. I also know there's a chance even *your* skills won't prove equal to finding her, and that even if we find her, she may be irreparably damaged by what she's been through."

Anderson shook off some of his sadness. He sat up straighter in his chair, and his hands finally relaxed in his lap. I wondered if he'd been clenching them hard enough to leave nail marks on his palms.

"You'll need to move in as soon as possible," he said. "If Konstantin finds out you and I have reached an agreement before you're actually under my roof, he'll declare open season on you."

I was in no hurry to install myself in the mansion, and I didn't like the sense that Anderson was trying to rush me. However, the idea of spending another night in the hotel didn't have much appeal, either, and I still wouldn't feel safe going home. I had to stay *somewhere* tonight. Besides, I reminded myself, I was planning to consider this mansion an ultra-luxurious hotel. A stopgap measure until I could figure out a better way to protect Steph.

"I'm ready whenever you are."

He nodded briskly. "Good. I'll open up one of the spare bedrooms for you."

"Thanks. What about Jamaal? And Blake?"

He raised an eyebrow. "What about them?" I would have thought he was playing stupid, except he looked genuinely puzzled by my question.

"You might have noticed they don't like me much. How are they going to feel if I move in under your roof?"

Anderson shrugged. "Their feelings about it don't enter into the equation. This is *my* house, and I can invite whomever I please." He seemed to notice the severity in his voice and flashed me a rueful smile. "There I go being tyrannical again, huh?"

I smiled back. "I wasn't going to say it."

He acknowledged that with a nod. "Blake might not like it, but he'll understand. Jamaal will need some careful handling, but I'll have a long talk with him while you're gone. I'll make it very clear that he's to play nice with you."

"Even though he still thinks I killed Emmitt on purpose?"

Anderson's brow furrowed. "I have to wonder if he really believes that. It would be awfully hard for a Descendant not affiliated with the Olympians to find out we existed at all, much less understand her own heritage and our vulnerability, then arrange to kill one of us."

"Who said she's not affiliated with the Olympians?" a voice asked from the hall just outside the kitchen, and we both jumped a little.

The adrenaline kept pumping as I turned to watch Jamaal walk casually into the kitchen. He was looking much more sane today. There was still an unmistakable spark of anger in his eyes, but he no longer looked crazed by it. That didn't make him any less lethal.

On the scale of male beauty as judged by Nikki Glass, Jamaal was the most gorgeous of all the *Liberi* I'd met. Tall and broad-shouldered, he had the build and the grace of an athlete. He wore his hair in shoulder-length beaded braids, the braids following the contours of his elegantly shaped skull up to about his ears. High cheekbones, luxuriously long eyelashes, and full, sensual lips made his face into a work of art. I'd never seen him smile, but I suspected the effect would be devastating.

Of course, I'd have found him a lot more attractive if he weren't looking at me with such loathing. At least he wasn't charging at me with murder in his eyes.

Anderson pushed his chair back from the table, watching Jamaal carefully although he didn't get up.

"I thought I made it clear that I wasn't to be disturbed," he said, and though his voice was mild, there was a threat implied in his words.

Jamaal didn't come any closer, but he didn't go away, either. "Sounded to me like you were wrapping up."

"Eavesdropping?" Anderson asked with a quirk of his eyebrow. "You've been hanging around Jack too long."

Jamaal grimaced in distaste. "Low blow, boss."

I gathered that Jamaal and Jack weren't great friends, which I supposed made sense. Jack was a trickster, and I'd seen no evidence to date that Jamaal even knew what a sense of humor was.

"I call 'em like I see 'em," was Anderson's unrepentant reply. "How long have you been listening?"

Jamaal hunched his shoulders like a little kid getting scolded by his dad. "Long enough to think it was time to let you know I was here. Sorry." He flicked a glance at me, his expression no warmer than it had ever been when he looked at me. "My question stands: who says she's not working for the Olympians? Wouldn't Konstantin just laugh his ass off if we accepted his murdering little spy into our house with open arms!"

"If I had my choice," I said before Anderson could answer, "I'd have nothing to do with any of you. I want my life back."

"So you say," Jamaal countered. "But talk is cheap."

"Children . . ." Anderson chided, making a long-suffering face. I chose not to respond to Jamaal's jibe, and he subsided. Anderson nodded his approval.

"If it turns out she's a spy working for Konstantin," Anderson said, "we'll deal with it when we have proof." The look he shot me then spoke volumes about just how he would "deal with it." He might be giving me the benefit of the doubt, but he wasn't wholly convinced of my innocence.

I was too stubborn to drop my gaze, though it was hard to look into his eyes when his expression was so forbidding. Apparently satisfied with what he saw, he turned to Jamaal.

"I need you to prove to me that you can keep it together without Emmitt around to balance your temper. Nikki is now under my protection, and I won't have her being threatened or harassed by one of my own people."

Jamaal's chin jutted out stubbornly, and the look in his eyes was downright mutinous, though he didn't argue. At least not out loud. Anderson apparently read his expression the same way I did.

"I don't want to lose you," he said, "but you have no place under this roof if you can't accept my authority."

I squirmed and wished I could be anywhere else but here. The sudden pain on Jamaal's face was too much to bear. He was still grieving for his friend, still furious at me, and Anderson had just delivered a threat that caused a soul-deep hurt.

I didn't like Jamaal, of course. But I *could* empathize with him. I wasn't sure what the relationship had been between him and Emmitt—had they been more than friends?—but the pain of that loss was obviously agonizing. I knew what it was like to act out when in pain. I'd spent years doing it after my mother abandoned me. I suspected Jamaal was feeling abandoned himself right now, and to have Anderson threaten to kick him out for my sake must have been like a dagger to his heart.

"So," Anderson prompted when Jamaal just stood there looking devastated, "are you going to accept Nikki's right to stay in my house? Or are we going to have a problem?"

Jamaal shot me a look of pure loathing. "There's no problem," he replied. "As long as you don't expect me to *like* it, I can accept her presence."

Internally, I groaned. I was supposed to stay in the same

house with this guy? That meant I'd probably have to come face-to-face with him on a regular basis, which seemed like a recipe for disaster.

But I was only going to move in for a little while, I told myself. Just until I could figure out some other way to protect Steph. If putting up with Jamaal and his hostility was the price I had to pay for her safety, then I was ready to pay it.

But I had a sneaking suspicion matters were not settled between Jamaal and me, no matter what Anderson had ordered, or what Jamaal had grudgingly promised.

THIRTEEN

After dinner, I went back to my hotel and packed up my meager belongings. I hadn't brought a whole lot of stuff, but I was reluctant to go home and pack a bigger suitcase. It wouldn't surprise me if Konstantin was having my place watched, and I wasn't foolish enough to ignore Anderson's warnings. I needed to establish myself as being under Anderson's protection before I ran into Konstantin or Alexis again. Anderson had promised to call Konstantin and "register" me as being under his protection as soon as I arrived back at the mansion.

I called Steph before I left and let her know I wasn't going to be at my home number for at least a few days. Naturally, she tried to wring details out of me, but there were none I could give her. I just told her the same thing I'd told her at dinner last night, that a disgruntled wannabe client was giving me trouble. She was far from satisfied, but she let the subject drop, for which I was profoundly grateful.

It was almost eleven o'clock by the time I pulled up in front of the gates of the mansion again. Fate decided to screw with my head and dumped a bunch of unexpected rain on Arlington the moment the gates opened to admit me. My hands squeezed tight on the steering wheel, and I swallowed a lump of dread that formed in my throat. I did *not* want a repeat of the evening's near panic attack. I sucked in a deep breath and hit the gas, concentrating hard to keep any potential flashbacks at bay.

When I parked once again on the circular drive, I was pleasantly surprised to find Maggie waiting for me under the shelter of the porch roof. She was by far the nicest of the *Liberi* I'd met so far, and I couldn't help liking her. The rain pounded down relentlessly as I got out of the car and popped the trunk. It wasn't terribly cold out, but the rain came with a generous dose of wind, and I wished I'd worn a heavier coat.

Maggie could have stayed safely under the porch roof and kept dry, but instead she beat me to the trunk and was lifting my suitcase out before I could get to it. The suitcase wasn't particularly heavy, being a small roll-aboard and only lightly packed, but I was still surprised by how easily Maggie plucked it out of the trunk and scampered up the front steps with it.

I slammed the trunk shut and hurried to follow, eager to be out of the rain. When I caught up with Maggie on the porch, I reached for my bag.

"Let me take that," I said. "You don't have to carry my bag for me."

She grinned at me. "Anderson's got you on the third floor. Trust me, you don't want to haul your suitcase all the way up there."

I put my hand on the handle of the suitcase and gave a gentle tug, but she didn't let go. I rolled my eyes. "Come on, I'm supposed to be living here now, right? So it's not like I'm a guest and you have to carry my bag."

"You don't understand," Maggie said, still grinning at me, a cheerful twinkle in her eye. She twisted the suitcase's handle out of my grip, then lifted it one-handed over her head like it weighed no more than an empty grocery sack. "I'm descended from Zeus, through Heracles. I don't have any storm magic, but I am seriously strong." Yes, I could see that. "I even carry things for the guys sometimes, though it offends their masculine sensibilities so much it's an argument every time."

She said it lightly, and there was no change in her expression I could put my finger on, but I got the feeling that it bugged her. I guess it had to be kind of tough to be a strong woman in a household full of supernatural alpha males, most, if not all, of whom had been born in times when society accepted it as fact that women were lesser beings.

I followed Maggie up the grand front staircase, which featured a remarkably genuine-looking reproduction of Winged Victory on the landing, making me feel like I had been magically transported to a museum. When we reached the second floor, Maggie gestured with her free hand toward the long hall leading to the right.

"That's the east wing, which is Anderson's. The first door on the left is his study, and you can go in there whenever you want as long as the door is open. If the door is closed, knock first or he'll get cranky. The rest of the wing is off-limits unless you're invited or unless there's an emergency."

This information naturally set my suspicious mind to wondering what Anderson might be hiding in the east wing, but maybe I'd just seen *Beauty and the Beast* too many times. It was, as he had pointed out, his house, and it was only fair that he have his own private space within it, even if he was living with a bunch of other *Liberi*.

"The west wing is where Jamaal, Blake, and Logan's apartments are," Maggie continued, gesturing to the left and then starting up the next set of stairs. "Jack, Leo, and I all have rooms on the third floor."

"I haven't met Leo yet," I said. I was beginning to think he was a bit of a recluse, because even when I'd been in the process of investigating Emmitt's so-called "cult," I'd rarely caught sight of him.

"He's not very sociable," Maggie responded. "He's a descendant of Hermes, who was a god of commerce. If we didn't remind him to eat and sleep every once in a while, he'd spend every second of every day sitting at his computer scrutinizing the market. We tease him about it, but the kind of money he brings in makes it possible for us to do a lot of good. And live well ourselves, while we're at it."

"Who's Anderson descended from?" I asked. "You've told me everyone else's ancestor, but not his."

"That's because I don't know. He's very mysterious about it. No one recognizes his glyph, and he's not saying."

"Any idea why not?"

"Nope," Maggie replied cheerfully. "But if you want to see if you can pry the secret out of him, have at it."

My only response was a soft snort. If Anderson wasn't going to tell his closest friends, I was damn sure he wouldn't tell me, so there was no point in even asking.

We'd finally reached the third floor, and Maggie led me down another long hallway. Even with eight or nine people living in the mansion, there were plenty of rooms to spare. Dust covers draped the furniture in many of the upstairs rooms.

The "guest room" Anderson had assigned me was actually a generous suite, with a huge bedroom, a luxurious bathroom, and a cozy sitting room, complete with a rectangular table against one wall that could serve as either a desk or a dining table. It was a hell of a lot nicer and more comfortable than my hotel had been.

"Do you want to take some time to unpack and freshen up?" Maggie asked. "Or would you rather have the grand tour first?"

I stifled a yawn. I hadn't had a good night's sleep in what felt like forever, and the king-sized four-poster in the bedroom was calling to me. However, I doubted I could sleep comfortably without thoroughly examining my surroundings first.

"Let's do the grand tour," I said. "I'm going to crash if I hold still for too long."

"All right then. Follow me!"

The tour of the house lasted the better part of an hour, and it left me wishing I'd drawn a map as we went along. I'd been right about the house's origins—it had once been a plantation. Which meant that it was huge, with a zillion rooms, and also meant that there were servants' corridors and staircases all over the place. Combine those classic plantation features with a century's worth of additions and renovations, and you had a dizzying maze. Or maybe it was just my own fatigue that made everything so confusing.

By the time I got back to my room, I doubted I could find my way to the front door without help, and I was so tired my eyes ached. I locked both the door to my suite and the door to my bedroom before finally allowing myself to collapse into bed and fall into a deep, untroubled sleep.

It was still pitch dark out when I awoke. A nightlight glowed faintly from the open bathroom door, and there was a little light cast by the digital clock by the bedside, but otherwise the room was oppressively dark. I was used to the lights of the city creeping around the edges of my curtains, and to the sound of cars passing by at all hours of the day and night. Here in Anderson's mansion, I felt cut off from humanity, alone and out of my element.

I didn't know what had awakened me, but the shiver of unease trailing down my spine told me *something was wrong*. I lay still and peered into the darkness, checking to see if anything was amiss. When nothing immediately tweaked my threat radar, I almost let my eyes slide closed again. I was still dead tired.

But there's something inherently disturbing about sleeping in an unfamiliar room, especially when that room is part of a huge, pre–Civil War mansion inhabited by supernatural beings, and I couldn't just dismiss my nerves. I stifled a yawn and sat up, wishing the room weren't so damn dark.

I started to reach for the bedside lamp, and then froze as my eyes picked out a man-shaped patch of shadow in the darkness. A man-shaped shadow that wasn't looming over me, as I'd half expected, but that was lying on his side on the bed beside me, his head propped on his hand.

I couldn't make out his features in the dark, and so I had no idea who it was. Until he moved and I heard the telltale clicking of the beads in his hair.

With a yelp of alarm, I tried to throw myself off the bed, reaching for the lamp as I did so. I figured Jamaal knew the layout of this room better than I did, and I'd have a better chance of making it out the door if I could see where I was going. But Jamaal was faster than me, and before I could pull the chain on the lamp, he'd grabbed my arm and yanked me back onto the bed.

I tried to get in an elbow jab, but my movements were hampered by the sheets tangled around my legs. My jab missed, and moments later I found myself pinned facedown with my arm wrenched up behind my back. Jamaal was big and powerful, and my struggles were useless. I considered screaming for help, but then decided against it. I doubted anyone else in the house was close enough to hear, just as I doubted there were a whole lot of them who would be eager to help me against Jamaal, who was one of their own.

"How did you get in here?" I gasped. "I locked the doors."

Okay, it was probably a pretty dumb question under the circumstances. It really didn't matter how he got in my room. But I guess I wasn't eager to face the important question—what was he going to do to me?—so I ignored it in favor of the trivial one.

Jamaal laughed humorlessly, but at least he wasn't actively hurting me. Yet.

"There is no lock strong enough nor wall thick enough to keep Death out," he murmured, his lips close to my ear so that I could feel the puff of his breath against my skin. The ends of a couple of his braids had found their way under the collar of my flannel nightshirt and tickled the base of my neck.

"Are you speaking literally or metaphorically?"

I felt his slight jerk of surprise. I guess he'd expected me to cower in fear at his menacing words, and there was certainly a part of me that was afraid. But there was another part of me that was getting just plain fed up with all the bullying and threatening, and that part was keeping my fear at bay.

Jamaal's hand tightened around my wrist, although his grip had not yet gone from uncomfortable to painful. "You think because I can't kill you that I can't make you suffer?"

I snorted. "I'm not an idiot. But you're going to do whatever you're going to do no matter what I say, so I figure I might as well speak my mind."

I no longer made any attempt to struggle against his hold. What was the point? "Fair enough," he said, still talking into my ear. I noticed his breath smelled faintly of clove cigarettes. I guessed as an immortal, he didn't have to worry about lung cancer. "I'll speak my mind, too. I think you're a lying, murdering spy who works for the Olympians." His grip on my wrist tightened at the words, and I clenched my teeth to suppress a whimper of pain.

"I think you murdered my friend and that you're going to string Anderson along with hopes of finding Emma while you gather information for your boss. And I think Anderson is too desperate to believe in you to think straight."

"Ever considered that *you* might be the one not thinking straight?" I asked, my voice tight enough that he couldn't miss the fact that I was in pain. He surprised me by loosening his grip.

"I'll be watching you," he continued, ignoring my question. "If I see even the slightest hint that you're playing us false, there will be hell to pay."

He rolled off of me and sprang to his feet in one fluid motion. My lizard brain urged me not to move from where he'd left me, fearing any movement might incite him, but I couldn't just lie there on my stomach being Little Miss Submissive.

Swallowing the lump of fear in my throat, I carefully turned over onto my side and pushed up onto my elbow. Jamaal didn't pounce, but he didn't go away, either.

"I was speaking literally," Jamaal said, and for a moment I had no idea what he was talking about. "Locks can't keep me out. If you fuck with us, there's nowhere you can hide that I can't get to you. If you're out of here by the time the sun rises, I'll give you a free pass no matter what you deserve for killing Emmitt. But if you stay in this house and I find out you're working for Konstantin . . ."

Before I could even think what to say, he stalked away from me. I could barely pick out his shadow in the darkness of the room, but I was pretty sure he passed through my bedroom door without even bothering to open it.

FOURTEEN

After Jamaal left, I got up and turned on the light. I'd never be able to get to sleep if I didn't explore every nook and cranny of my room to make sure I was alone. I was not at all comforted to find that the bedroom door and the entrance to my suite were both locked. I wished I could believe I'd dreamed Jamaal's visit, but I knew I hadn't. If he could pass through locked doors, then I supposed he could have escaped from his basement cell on the night of Emmitt's death, despite all the pounding and shouting I'd heard. Of course, if passing through the locked door would have earned him another date with the Hand of Doom, I didn't blame him for choosing a different form of protest.

I made a halfhearted attempt to go back to sleep, but I failed miserably. The dark was too oppressive, and my fears were too overwhelming.

Jamaal had threatened to hurt me only if I double-crossed

Anderson, but it was obvious he'd be looking for the slightest excuse to condemn me. What if I couldn't find Emma? After all, I had as yet found no evidence of any supernatural hunting ability, and with Emma I didn't even know how to start. Would Jamaal take my lack of progress as evidence of betrayal?

I shoved the covers away and got out of bed, turning on the light. Sleep was an impossibility, no matter how much I might prefer to escape my situation by slipping into dreamland.

It was almost five in the morning, so at least I'd gotten a few solid hours of sleep before Jamaal had awakened me. I tended to be an early riser anyway, so I tried to tell myself I wasn't really getting up in the middle of the night, even though my body cried out for more rest.

A part of me was beginning to suspect I should cut my losses and run. Earlier, I'd talked myself out of disappearing because of all the things I didn't want to give up. Unfortunately, I seemed to be giving up a lot of those things anyway. I hadn't spent the night in my own home since the accident, and I'd put so little thought into my job that I hadn't even checked phone messages. I put referring my current clients to other investigators on my day's to-do list. It was easier to face than figuring out what to do with the rest of my life.

I decided I needed a serious coffee infusion before I made any life-altering decisions. If I'd really felt like I *lived* in the mansion, I wouldn't have hesitated to go downstairs in my nightshirt. But no matter what my supposed status, I felt more like a reluctant guest at an oversized B&B, which meant I wasn't going anywhere until I was showered and dressed.

I only made two wrong turns before I found my way to the kitchen.

The coffee didn't magically make all my problems go away, but it was warm, delicious, and caffeinated. That was all that mattered.

I spent the remainder of the wee hours of the morning

doing some basic Internet research on Emma Poindexter of Arlington, Virginia. I assumed most of what I learned was pure fiction. Depending on how old she was, she could have dozens of different assumed identities. None of which would have much to do with who she really was. Still, it was a start.

At around eight there was a knock on my door. I answered cautiously, hoping it would be Maggie, because so far she was the only one of the *Liberi* I could actually say I liked. Instead, it turned out to be Blake, probably my least favorite of Anderson's *Liberi*. Jamaal was hostility personified, but at least I understood where he was coming from. Blake just seemed slimy.

I probably made a face, but if so, Blake ignored it, holding up a manila envelope.

"Anderson sent me to give you this," he said. "I believe the subtext was 'kiss and make up.'"

This time I was *sure* I made a face. "I'd rather kiss a copperhead." I grabbed the envelope from his hand.

He laughed and held up his hands in surrender. "Don't worry. It was only a figure of speech."

He didn't seem particularly perturbed that I'd shot him yesterday, but I didn't believe he'd gotten over it that easily.

"How's your boo-boo?" I asked. I don't know if I was trying to rile him, or trying to remind him I wasn't someone he wanted to mess with.

He touched his chest, presumably where the bullet had hit him. "Still a little sore, but not too bad. I'm touched by your concern."

He said it with a self-deprecating smile, as if there were no hard feelings, but I still didn't believe it. I'd seen too much malice in him to think he'd let me off the hook that easily. Even so, I couldn't help feeling guilty about what I'd done, and I couldn't force myself to be as indifferent as I wanted to be.

"I really am sorry about that," I found myself saying, though it made me feel like a wuss.

Blake waved off my apology. "As Anderson pointed out, I

had it coming. If I'd left my attitude in the car, I probably could have persuaded you to come with me without the strong-arm tactics."

I was momentarily at a loss for words. This was not the reaction I'd expected from him.

"Alexis brings out the worst in me," Blake continued. "When I saw him sitting there with you, I started to wonder if Jamaal was right and you were a plant."

It wasn't quite an apology, but it was close. "And now you've changed your mind about me?"

"I don't know what to make of you," he said with refreshing honesty. "But if there's a chance you're telling the truth and can find Emma, then I'm willing to give you the benefit of the doubt."

"Sounds like you're as anxious to get her back as Anderson is." I belatedly realized that sounded accusatory, like I thought he and Emma were lovers, when all I'd really meant to do was fish for information.

He hesitated a beat, but didn't respond to my unintentional implication. "Anderson hasn't come close to getting over her yet. And the longer she's been gone, the more saintly she's become in his memory."

"Meaning she wasn't that saintly in real life?"

"Let's just say she was a bit high-maintenance. And it had been a long, long time since she and Anderson were happy together. By the end, they weren't even sharing a bed anymore. But you know what they say—absence makes the heart grow fonder."

He pointed at the manila envelope, which I hadn't bothered to open yet. "There's a full dossier on Emma's current identity in there. There's also an outline of Anderson's security plan for your sister. He's hired a private security firm we've worked with in the past, and the rest of us are going to help out as time permits. She'll be as safe as we can possibly make her, and she'll never even know her guardian angels are there."

"Angels, huh?" I asked with a lift of my brow. That wasn't a term I'd associate with any of the *Liberi* I'd met.

Blake just laughed.

Over the next couple of days, I spent countless hours chained to my computer, looking for something that might help. I figured that since my non-supernatural abilities to find people had stemmed largely from my computer skills, maybe my supernatural ones would as well.

I had Anderson compile a list of all the known Olympians and all the Descendants who worked for them. The list was long and intimidating, but I started doing methodical searches on each person. It was true that Konstantin could have buried Emma anywhere, including out in some national park miles from civilization, but instinct told me he'd want to have easier access to her. Which meant wherever she was, it was most likely on property owned by Konstantin or one of his many toadies.

When you watch TV shows featuring private investigators, the job always looks like it's exciting and full of action. The reality is somewhat different. Scouring databases looking for properties that belong to one of about thirty people—many of whom had multiple names as they changed identities over the years—was the antithesis of exciting.

The list of properties grew depressingly long, and though in theory I was making progress, it felt more like I was running in place. Even if I identified the right property, how would I find Emma once I got there? If I was a supernatural tracker, the power was taking its own sweet time to manifest.

On Saturday afternoon, I decided to take a break and get out of the mansion for a while.

Actually, it wasn't so much my decision, as Steph's. Her charity auction was on Wednesday night, and she called to remind me. Then she asked me what I would wear, and when I didn't answer fast enough, she declared we were going shopping.

I could have fought her on it. Although Steph has a steel backbone, I have a pretty good streak of stubbornness in me, too. But one thing I'd learned over years of working as a P.I. was that it really was possible to work too hard. The brain needs to take a break every once in a while, or you start missing things that are right in front of your face. So I let myself be persuaded.

Steph's favorite store is the Saks out in Chevy Chase, but I didn't make enough money from my P.I. business to buy so much as a single shoe there. Trust me, if I was ever going to be persuaded to tap into my trust fund, it wouldn't be for the sake of designer clothes. In deference to my budget concerns, we hit the shops and boutiques of Georgetown instead.

I enjoy shopping as much as the next girl, and I'd been on countless excursions with Steph over the years, but there was nothing like watching my beautiful sister trying on clothes to make me feel like an ugly duckling.

I know I'm not ugly. But I'm no Steph, either. Usually, I do a pretty good job of shoving my jealousy into a back corner of my mind, where I can ignore it. But the stress of recent events, and my relentless worries about the future, made it impossible to keep the green monster completely under control. Especially when Steph came out of her dressing room wearing a stunning, fire-engine red cocktail dress that clung perfectly to her curves without looking even remotely slutty. I swear, if you'd teleported her to the red carpet before the Oscars, she wouldn't have looked out of place.

I had on a simple black number at the time, and I couldn't help comparing our reflections in the mirror. Steph, tall and blond and sophisticated, wearing a dress that would draw every eye in the room. Me, short and average-looking, in a dress meant to blend in with the inevitable sea of little black dresses. And then, of course, there was the glyph that only I could see. The glyph that meant I had to give up even the semblance of a normal life that I had built.

We went out for coffee afterward. I kept trying to spot Anderson's private security team, but I hadn't caught sight of anyone following us. Maybe they felt Steph was safe enough with me. Or maybe they really were just really good at being inconspicuous. I knew the typical tricks of covert surveillance, but even knowing what to look for, I couldn't spot anyone.

"So," Steph said when we sat down in a cozy corner with our coffees, "what's going on with your stalker-client? I'm guessing since you're still not at home and you're in a crappy mood that he's still giving you trouble."

I grimaced and took a sip of my coffee, burning my tongue. I thought I'd been hiding my state of mind better than that. Probably if it had been anyone but Steph, they would have been fooled.

"Yeah," I admitted, because there was no reason not to. "The situation's still complicated." I gave her a half smile. "And I still can't talk about it."

"You ever consider that talking about it might help?"

My half smile turned to a full one, though I doubted Steph would miss the strain behind it. "No, I never considered that possibility."

She rolled her eyes. "Whoever said 'no man is an island' obviously never met *you*."

I bit back the urge to go defensive, but it was hard. If she'd been through what I'd been through as a kid, she'd understand why I didn't make a habit of blabbing out my problems. You learn to talk about your problems when you have a sympathetic ear available. I hadn't had any truly awful foster parents. No one molested me or beat me, at least not beyond the occasional spanking. But until I'd moved in with the Glasses at age eleven, there'd been no real warmth, either. My fault, entirely. I was one hell of an angry little girl. But by the time I had something like a warm, supportive family environment, I had already settled into the habit of keeping to myself.

Steph reached over and put a hand on my arm, the touch

light and brief. "Sorry. I didn't mean that to hurt. I was just teasing."

I did my best to shake off the gloom. "I know. I'm just grumpy and not very good company today."

"Think it might cheer you up if I told you about this new guy I'm seeing?"

I'm sure my eyes lit up at the idea. For all my unworthy jealousy of Steph, I really, truly loved her. I wanted to see her happy, and though so far she hadn't shown the greatest taste in men, I was always hoping she'd meet Mr. Right.

"Ooh yes, do tell!" I urged.

There was a twinkle in her eye as she smiled at me. She was proud of herself for chasing away the little black thundercloud that had been hovering over my head.

"It's all very preliminary," she warned. "Maybe saying I'm 'seeing' him is a bit of an exaggeration. I only met him a couple of days ago, and we've been on exactly one date."

"I have a feeling I've just been conned," I muttered, but I couldn't go back to being as surly as I'd been. I'd much rather talk about Steph's love life than keep evading her questions about my "stalker."

"Where and how did you meet? Details, please."

"You know that little bakery around the corner from my house?"

I nodded. It was the kind of place I didn't dare set foot in for fear of surrendering to I-want-one-of-everything syndrome.

"Well, I've gotten into the habit of going over there every morning. I take my laptop and do a lot of my correspondence. It's got a nice atmosphere, and it smells heavenly."

And unlike me, Steph could smell the various pies, cakes, breads, and assorted goodies and resist gorging herself. Just one more reason to hate her.

"Well, Blake came in to pick up a cake he'd ordered, and we got to talking, and . . ." Steph frowned as she watched my face go white. "What's wrong?"

"Please tell me his name isn't Blake Porter."

"You know him?" she asked, looking both confused and worried. "Oh, God, is he someone *you're* interested in?"

"Blake?" I cried with a comical squeak. "Hell no!" The blood that had drained from my face when Steph said Blake's name came back in a rush, my cheeks heating with rage I did my best to tamp down. "I am going to kill him," I muttered under my breath, though of course I wasn't physically capable of killing him. But shooting him a couple more times might turn out to be therapeutic. No wonder he'd taken to playing friendly with me lately—he must have found it really amusing to hold out an olive branch while secretly stabbing me in the back.

"What's going on?" Steph asked, shaking her head. "This isn't the stalker guy, is it? Please tell me my taste in men isn't *that* bad."

For a split second, I was tempted to lie, tempted to tell Steph that yes, indeed, Blake was the wannabe client who was making my life miserable and who had indirectly threatened her. I resisted the temptation, but it wasn't due to any goodwill toward Blake. I just didn't want Steph to let her guard down because she thought she knew who the bad guy was.

"No, he's not the guy," I said through gritted teeth. "But he's bad news anyway. He's messed up in this whole business."

"You've got to give me more to go on than that."

"I can't," I told her for the millionth time. She was getting sick of hearing it, and I was getting sick of saying it.

"Fine," Steph retorted, thumping her coffee cup back down on the table. "If you're not going to tell me why you think he's bad news, then there's no reason for me not to see him again."

"Please just trust me on this."

She folded her arms. "I've had enough, Nikki. I like Blake a lot, and it's going to take more than your cryptic warnings to make me give up on him before we even have a chance."

I wanted to kick the table in frustration. I almost wished Steph really *were* my biological sister. Then I'd have a good reason to tell her everything I'd learned about Descendants and the *Liberi*. But that was selfish of me. If I could go back to the days when I'd been blissfully ignorant, I'd have done so in an instant, immortality be damned. I wasn't going to shatter Steph's perfect world, even if I thought there was any chance she'd believe me.

"He's not what he seems, Steph," I said, knowing I was still being too vague to convince her of anything. "Just like Alexis called me on your phone to get to me, Blake is trying to seduce you to get even with me for . . . something I did." I was slipping a bit—I'd almost said "for shooting him," which would have left me majorly screwed.

Steph pushed back her chair with a loud scrape. "You know, Nikki, the world doesn't actually revolve around you, no matter what you might think."

I gaped at her, shocked into silence by her accusation. I didn't think the world revolved around me. What the hell was she talking about?

"You don't get to order me around and expect me to do whatever you say just because. I'm an adult, and capable of making my own decisions. You won't tell me what you think is wrong with Blake? Then I'll just have to find out for myself."

"Steph, it's not—"

"Stop it, okay? I don't know what kind of power trip you're on with all these mysterious secrets and threats, but I'm not playing that game anymore. I'm sick to death of being treated like some ditzy blonde who can't handle the truth. You have two choices: tell me the truth, or butt out."

There was nothing I could say that was going to fix this. I couldn't explain what Blake was, what he could do, or why he might want to do it. And if I couldn't explain, Steph was going to ignore any warning I tried to give her.

"I'm just trying to look out for you, Steph," I told her, though her closed-off expression said she didn't want to hear anything I had to say just then.

Steph shook her head and picked up her shopping bags. "I know you think I've led this easy, charmed life and I need someone stronger and more worldly, like you, to take care of me. I'm sorry you had such a sucky childhood before you became part of our family, but just because I haven't been through that kind of hell doesn't make me the weakling you've always thought. I don't need your protection, and I don't want it, either."

With one last angry look, Steph headed for the door, leaving me sitting at the table feeling utterly wretched.

FIFTEEN

I drove back to the mansion in something of a daze. I had never seen Steph so angry before. And the things she'd said . . .

I knew I was carrying around a load of baggage everywhere I went. How could I not have baggage after everything I'd been through as a kid? But I'd never realized how it had affected Steph. I could freely admit to myself that I was jealous of her at times, but I thought I kept those unworthy emotions well hidden. It had never occurred to me that *she* might have any ill feelings toward *me*.

Steph had been the ideal older sister from the moment I'd moved into the Glasses' house. I was a sullen handful of bad behavior during that first year, when I was sure the Glasses would be as temporary as any of my other foster families. Not that we hadn't ever fought—she was ideal, but she wasn't perfect, and a saint couldn't have put up with all the crap I pulled when I first moved in. But she'd never seemed to harbor any real resentment.

Had her words today meant I'd been seeing her through rose-colored glasses this whole time? Deep inside, did she hate me for having usurped a portion of her parents' love? Surely she didn't really think I was self-centered. Did she? I mean, I was self-*sufficient,* but that wasn't the same thing. I was almost sure of it.

I brooded and wallowed right up until I reached the gates of the mansion. Then, as I waited for the gates to open, I swallowed my hurt feelings and summoned up my righteous indignation. I might not have been able to convince Steph that Blake was bad news, but I could sure as hell make him rue the day he decided to mess with my sister.

I entered the house like a guided missile.

I climbed the stairs two at a time, practically sprinting to my room to get my gun. I hadn't liked leaving it behind, but I'd worried what Steph would say if she saw it. A physical sensation of relief flowed though me when my hand closed around the butt of the gun, and I cocked it with vicious glee.

I pounded down the stairs to the second floor, angrier than I'd ever been in my life. Angrier even than I'd been when Alexis threatened Steph. It was one thing to have the bad guy make threats; it was another when the supposed good guys did it.

When Maggie had taken me on the tour of the house, we'd only gone through the public rooms, so I didn't know which of the rooms in the west wing belonged to Blake. Come to think of it, I had no way of knowing if he was even home. That didn't stop me from marching up to the second door on the left and pounding on it. Don't ask me why I chose that particular door—it just kinda happened that way.

"Blake, you son of a bitch!" I yelled. "Open this door!" I was going to feel like an idiot if this wasn't his room, but I was running on adrenaline and instinct and ignored all logical concerns.

The door cracked open and I lunged forward, holding it open with my body so Blake couldn't slam it on me. He took a startled step back, and by the time he recovered, my gun was aimed squarely at his forehead. His eyes widened, and he held his hands up as if to show he wasn't armed. I was fully prepared to shoot if I felt the slightest hint he was about to use his aura against me, but he wasn't an idiot. We'd already established that I could pull the trigger faster than he could put me under.

"You stay the hell away from my sister," I ordered, and though my hands were shaking with fury, I didn't for a moment doubt my aim.

"Take it easy, Nikki," he said. "I was just—"

"You were just *what*?" I interrupted. "Taking a page out of Alexis's book and threatening Steph to keep me under control?"

"I didn't threaten her!" he snapped, putting his hands down. "I was helping keep an eye on her, and she happened to notice me. Women do, you know, and it's not something I can control."

"You took her out on a date." I kept the gun pointed steadily at his forehead.

"I didn't sleep with her, if that's what you're freaking out about. I asked her out because I'd already blown my cover, and I figured that way I could help protect her without having to try to hide."

He sounded perfectly sincere, but how could I believe him? I'd seen how ruthlessly he'd used that aura before, and the idea of him turning it on Steph made me sick to my stomach.

"I don't believe you," I said, moving my aim from his forehead to his crotch. His eyes went a little wider, and he swallowed hard. I was glad to know he was less scared of me blowing his brains out than shooting him somewhere *really* important.

"I'm telling the truth," he said, a little desperately. "If I were the kind of guy who preyed on innocent bystanders like that, I'd be with the Olympians, not with Anderson."

For some reason, his words had a ring of truth to them, and I took a baby step back from the edge. I still kept the gun pointed at his family jewels, but I didn't feel like I was moments away from pulling the trigger.

"I don't want you anywhere near her."

"I'm one of the few people Alexis is actually afraid of. You saw how he reacted to me in the diner. He's not getting within a hundred yards of her as long as I'm around."

I shook my head. "And I'm supposed to think that letting you seduce her is okay as long as you keep Alexis away?"

Blake rolled his eyes. "I'm not going to seduce her. I won't let things go further than a little flirtation."

"Why not? Don't you like women?" I couldn't imagine there were a whole lot of straight men who wouldn't leap at the chance of getting Steph into bed.

To my surprise, Blake blushed. "Yeah, I like women. Look, any chance we can continue this conversation without you threatening to shoot me? Because you're almost as berserk as Jamaal, and it's getting old."

Crap. I *was* acting a bit like Jamaal, come to think of it. Assuming the worst and threatening violence. That wasn't the kind of person I wanted to be, but I'd already really stuck my foot in it. "What's to stop you from doing something nasty with your aura if I put the gun away?"

"The fact that Anderson would 'lay hands' on me if I did. He takes a pretty dim view of infighting."

Again, there was that ring of truth. Plus, there was the fact that I couldn't keep him at gunpoint forever. Reluctantly, I uncocked the gun and lowered my arm.

Blake let out a sigh of relief. "Just to clarify something: I made some threats to you at the diner, but I wouldn't have followed through on them. I'd have used my aura to lower your inhibitions and get you to go with me, but I wouldn't have taken advantage of it. I could do it to Alexis without my conscience uttering a peep, but that's because I know exactly what he's capable of. Rampant abuse of power is an Olympian thing."

I wasn't sure whether I believed him or not, but at least he wasn't on the attack at the moment.

"So, if you like women, then why aren't you interested in Steph?"

Once again, he blushed. It was almost cute. Emphasis on "almost."

"I never said I wasn't interested. It's just . . ." He cleared his throat and looked at the floor. "As a descendant of Eros, I have certain . . . skills. If a woman has too much exposure to those skills, she'll have a hard time being satisfied with normal men."

I gaped at him. "I've heard men brag about their sexual prowess before, but you take the cake."

"It's not a boast, and I'd turn it off if I could. If I were an Olympian, it wouldn't bother me to make a woman unable to achieve satisfaction with another man for the rest of her life, as long as I enjoyed myself. But I'm not an Olympian, and it *would* bother me. As far as sex is concerned, I will always have to be a one-night-stand kind of guy. That's nothing to boast about."

I'd never thought learning the guy who was dating Steph was into one night stands would be a relief. "If you decide to make Steph one of those one night stands, we'll be having this conversation again. And I might find myself pulling the trigger by accident. Got it?"

Blake gave me a wide-eyed innocent look. "I got it. Now how about you and your gun do an about-face and get out of my apartment?"

By that point, I was happy to oblige.

Sixteen

I spent the next couple of days splitting my time between Internet research, locating every piece of Olympian property within driving distance, and doing some preliminary reconnaissance. Good old Google Maps let me get satellite views, and I weeded out the properties that didn't look like they had convenient burial spots. Of course, for all I knew, Emma was buried under someone's basement, but I figured I'd try the places with significant amounts of land first.

I did a series of drive-bys, hoping for some kind of super-natural X-Marks-the-Spot, but no such luck. I tried not to worry about what would happen to me—and to Steph—if I didn't make any demonstrable progress soon. Jamaal wasn't the most sociable of Anderson's *Liberi,* so I didn't run into him often. But each time I did, his expression seemed darker, more full of accusation. And a little less sane.

One day, when I returned to the mansion after another round of fruitless drive-bys, I noticed that the potted plants on the porch were looking ragged and overgrown. Hoping that manual labor would shut down the gerbil wheel in my brain and help me Zen out enough to think straight, I decided to do a little impromptu gardening. Anything to escape the feeling of futility that kept trying to creep up on me.

I started off by plucking dead leaves, of which there were many. Shortly afterward, Maggie came out to join me. Without a word, she set to plucking leaves by my side. When I looked over at her, I saw a sheen of tears in her eyes.

"Maggie? Are you all right?"

She sniffed and nodded, a faint smile on her face. "Yeah. It's just that these plants were Emmitt's babies. Big, macho death-god Descendant that he was, he'd talk to them like he thought they'd talk back."

I guessed that explained why they were starting to look ragged now that Emmitt was dead. "Should I keep my hands off them?" I asked, worried that someone would be offended at the idea of Emmitt's killer touching his beloved plants.

"Emmitt would want them taken care of," was her re-sponse, so we continued plucking.

There were several plants that needed pruning, and a cou-ple that needed repotting. Possibly, I should have been using my time more productively, but I was enjoying the peace of playing in the dirt too much to quit. When Maggie dabbed at her eyes, I pretended to ignore it.

In the back corner, there was one plant that looked completely dead. I pulled the pot out of the corner, then looked up at Maggie's gasp of dismay.

"Oh!" she said. "We should have brought that inside before the sleet storm the other night. I guess Emmitt was too busy killing himself to take care of it." Her eyes looked all wet and shiny again.

I poked at the dead foliage, not recognizing the plant. "Maybe it's just dormant and will come back in the spring." I grabbed a pair of shears and started snipping, hoping to find something green and alive at the core. We'd only had one really cold night so far, so there was always a chance . . .

Maggie shook her head. "It's a night blooming jasmine. They aren't cut out for Virginia winters. It was Emma's. And Anderson is going to be very unhappy if he sees it's dead."

I wasn't finding any signs of life, but I kept snipping compulsively anyway, until I'd removed enough dead leaves to see the soil. There was something shiny in the dirt, and for reasons unknown, I found myself poking at it.

Probably a piece of mica in the dirt, I told myself, but my fingernail caught on something, and it wasn't mica. I dug my finger into the soil and pulled out a silver band, dotted with moonstones and what looked like diamonds.

"Look what I found," I said, scraping some of the dirt away as I laid the ring on my palm to show it to Maggie.

"Where did you get that?" Maggie asked, and there was something off about her voice.

"It was in the pot. Why? Do you recognize it?"

She nodded. I didn't like the way she was looking at me, like she suddenly thought I was scum. "It's Emma's wedding ring."

I shivered, though I wasn't cold. Finding Emma's ring while I was searching for Emma had to be some weird sort of coincidence, right? I just happened to be in the mood to prune plants, and I just happened to pick up the dead jasmine, and I just happened to keep snipping at it even when I knew it was dead. It could happen.

But what if it wasn't coincidence? What if it was a sign that my supposed supernatural powers were coming out?

Maggie was still looking at me strangely. Her usually friendly face was closed off, and there was suspicion in her eyes.

"Anderson and Emma had marital problems," she said, and there was a caution in her voice that hadn't been there before. "But Emma *never* took off that ring. She was wearing it on the day she disappeared."

I swallowed hard, realizing that my finding the ring like this could look bad, especially to people who didn't entirely trust me in the first place.

"You can't possibly have that ring," Maggie continued. "Not unless you have access to Emma."

"Come on, Maggie," I said. "You've been with me the whole time. You *saw* me find it."

"I saw you poking around at the pot. That's not the same thing."

"If I'm working for the Olympians, then why would I pretend to find the ring when I knew Emma was wearing it when she was taken?"

"You were going to use it as a sign of progress. 'Hey, I haven't found Emma, but I've found her ring.'"

"Do you really think I'm that stupid?"

She bit her lip and shook her head, though I could tell she wasn't entirely convinced. If someone like Maggie, who'd given me the benefit of the doubt since day one, thought finding the ring made me look guilty, I didn't want to imagine how someone like Jamaal would take it.

"Maggie, I swear to you, I just found it in the pot. You said this was Emma's plant. Maybe she repotted it and lost her ring in the dirt on the day she disappeared." According to Anderson, no one was sure exactly when Emma was captured. She'd apparently been prone to storming out in a huff when she and Anderson argued, and it had been hours before anyone had realized she wasn't anywhere in the house or on the grounds.

"Maybe she was pissed at Anderson and hid the ring there so she could pretend she tossed it or pawned it—without having to actually toss it or pawn it."

"That does sound like something Emma would do," Maggie agreed. "Maybe it happened exactly that way. But maybe it didn't."

"I'm not one of the Olympians."

Her look of polite skepticism hurt. She'd been the closest thing I had to a friend in this house, and it sucked to lose her over something like this.

"Are you going to tell Anderson about this?" I asked. "I haven't done anything wrong, but my job's going to be a lot harder if he starts being all suspicious again."

She crossed her arms over her chest. "I really *should* tell him. He has a right to know. And I'm sure he'd want the ring back."

"I'm not asking you to keep him in the dark forever," I assured her. "I just need a little more time to locate Emma, and I won't be able to do that if Anderson decides I'm a spy after all."

"How much time?"

That was the million-dollar question, wasn't it? Should I take the finding of the ring as some kind of good sign? I had no way of knowing.

What I *did* know was that Maggie wasn't going to keep her mouth shut forever.

"Give me one week," I said, wondering if the ticking clock was going to make the job even harder. "If I haven't found her in a week, I'll talk to Anderson myself."

Maggie thought about it a minute, then nodded. "All right. You have one week. Make it count."

Tick tock, tick tock, tick tock.

Despite the looming deadline, Wednesday night rolled around, and I reluctantly got ready for Steph's charity auction. I'd held out a faint hope that our fight would get me out of it, but no. Steph called and informed me in no uncertain terms that I was going. She seemed content to pretend our fight had never happened, and I was happy to go along with it.

I wore the admittedly nondescript little black dress I'd bought on our shopping trip and a pair of stiletto-heeled pumps that would have my feet hurting in fifteen minutes flat. Remembering Steph's gorgeous red dress, I knew I was going to spend most of the night feeling like one of the ugly stepsisters from a fairy tale. I'd have to try to keep to myself as much as possible, because I wasn't exactly feeling like Little Miss Sunshine.

I left the house around six thirty to get to the pre-dinner cocktail party. That would be the most painful part of the evening—I wasn't a big fan of mingling with the rich and snooty. But I knew Steph would want me there the whole time, and I'd have done just about anything to smooth the waters. Even stand around in high heels drinking cocktails and talking to people with whom I had nothing in common.

The country club that was hosting Steph's auction reminded me a bit of Anderson's mansion, if only in its attempt to hide from the sight of passersby. There was even a set of gates—though these were usually kept open and were more ornamental—and an artificial forest lining the driveway. The "forest" was as well-manicured as the one at the mansion, devoid of the weeds and underbrush that would accompany natural growth. The driveway, however, was a lot straighter, and there were actually streetlamps to guide the way.

The patch of woods didn't last long, giving way to the inevitable golf course. This being the height of winter, it was already too dark for even the most fanatical of golfers, so at least I didn't have to dodge golf carts on my way in. There was convenient valet parking if I drove right up to the clubhouse, but I chose to park myself in one of the outer lots. It meant an uncomfortable walk in my high heels, but by the time the night was over, the last thing I would want to do was wait for someone to retrieve my car for me.

The glittering crowd was just starting to trickle in as I headed into the bar and lounge area. My eyes were immediately drawn to Steph in her fire-engine-red dress. She looked even more fabulous than usual, with her blond hair swept into an elegant up-do and her long neck adorned by a pearl and diamond necklace.

Standing right beside Steph, with a proprietary hand resting on her lower back, was Blake. I had to admit, he looked good enough to eat in his conservative black tux, the perfect Ken to Steph's Barbie. I didn't like the way he was touching her, though, not one bit. Despite Blake's promise that he would behave like a gentleman, I was all too aware of the malice that lurked beneath his cultured exterior. He was a dangerous man who used sex as a weapon. Was it any shock I didn't want him around my sister?

Steph caught sight of me while I was giving Blake the evil eye. I tried to blank my expression as she made her way across the room toward me, Blake following in her wake. She stopped right in front of me and smiled brilliantly, and I wondered if she'd thought I was going to stand her up. Sad to say if I had, it wouldn't have been the first time. Have I mentioned how much I hate these affairs?

"You look gorgeous!" Steph said, giving me a warm hug. She was busy enough hugging me not to see the way Blake rolled his eyes at her words.

Steph released me from the hug, then looked back and forth between me and Blake. His expression was one of polite disinterest. I have no idea what my own face looked like. I hoped my flush of embarrassment had faded. Bad enough to be pathetically insecure about my looks, but to have others know it was almost unbearable.

"I take it you two know each other," Steph said with a raise of her eyebrows. I could tell by the sparkle of curiosity in her eyes that Blake hadn't made up a story about how we'd met. Which was a good thing, since I'd have had no idea what the cover story was and would probably have blown it the moment I opened my mouth.

"We've met," Blake said drily, but he held out his hand for me to shake.

It felt like a challenge, so I didn't hesitate. Of course, he then lifted my hand to his mouth and kissed my knuckles. It was all I could do not to jerk my hand out of his grip and make a scene.

"Charming," I muttered under my breath, and he laughed softly at this evidence that he'd gotten to me.

Steph kept looking back and forth between us, no doubt hoping one of us would cave and tell her how we knew each other. She knew, of course, that I didn't like Blake, but Blake wasn't giving any overt signs of how he felt about me. Not signs that *Steph* could read, that is.

Blake held on to my hand a little longer than necessary, and Steph looped her arm through his, forcing him to let go. Her action might have been subtle, but I knew beyond doubt she'd done it because I looked uncomfortable.

"We still have some serious mingling to do," she said, and I was just as happy to let her and Blake go.

I hoped the look in my eyes gave Blake the message that I would feed him his balls if he hurt my sister. There was no way of telling from the little smirk on his face as he and Steph stepped away into the burgeoning crowd.

I worked my way to the bar and ordered a glass of white wine, then found myself a convenient corner shadowed by a large potted plant where I could mingle by myself without drawing too much attention. Yes, I was playing the part of wallflower and wasn't particularly bothered by the fact.

For the record, standing in a corner by yourself in a snooty country club watching the filthy rich strut around in their one-of-a-kind designer gowns and ostentatious jewelry is not my idea of a good time. The wine helped a bit, taking the edge off, but after I'd finished my first glass, I didn't dare get another.

I'm a bit of a lightweight when it comes to drinking, and I did have to drive home when the evening's fun and games were done.

Steph and Blake, young and good-looking, were quite a striking pair in the midst of the decidedly older crowd. Steph flitted around like an anxious hummingbird, making sure she talked to everyone, smiling and vivacious. Blake stuck close to her and I was pleased to see that, while he made social when necessary, he spent most of his time scanning the crowd, alert for any threats. I'd checked the guest list against the list of known Olympians Anderson had given me, but just because I hadn't identified any Olympians on the list didn't necessarily mean none would show up. After all, Konstantin had made it abundantly clear that the Olympians had money to burn. Someone with that kind of money could probably find a way to get themselves on the guest list at the last minute. So, much as I didn't like Blake, I had to reluctantly admit I was glad he was there.

The cocktail party was only an hour long, but it felt like an eternity. My feet were killing me, and I was bored out of my skull. I wasn't exactly looking forward to the dinner and auction parts of the evening, but at least then I would be able to sit down.

When eight o'clock finally rolled around, I followed the herd into the sumptuously appointed dining room. Annoyingly, there were assigned seats, so I had to either wander around the tables looking for the place card with my name on it, or stand in line to ask the nice man by the doorway to check his alphabetized list. I chose to wander.

Steph knew how much I enjoyed these affairs. She also knew I didn't like mingling with the sort of people who attended them. I made an educated guess that she would have been her usual considerate self and seated me at her table. I scanned the room, figuring that red dress of hers would stand out like a beacon, but I didn't see her.

At first, I wasn't even remotely concerned. She was, after all, in charge of this event, not a guest. I figured she was taking care of administrative details, or just talking to the stragglers who hadn't come into the dining room yet. But as the seats at the tables filled up and I still saw no sign of her, a niggle of alarm ran through me.

I located the table that Steph and Blake were going to be sitting at—right at the front, of course—and I found my own place card directly opposite hers. But still no Steph. No Blake, either. Maybe that meant they'd slipped away for a quick make-out session, but I didn't think so. Steph wasn't what I would call a control freak, but she did put a lot of time and energy into these events, and she wouldn't just wander away for a little me-time. Unless Blake used his nasty power on her, but that was a thought I could hardly bear to contemplate.

Telling myself I was being paranoid and overprotective, I slipped out of the dining room toward the bar and lounge. There were still a few people out there, ignoring the signals that dinner was nigh. But no Steph. I was going to start questioning the staff to see if they could tell me her last known location, but my cell rang, sending a shiver down my spine. True, the call could be completely innocuous, from anyone. But in my heart, I knew it was bad news.

My instinct was confirmed when I pulled out my cell phone and saw the caller ID: Alexis. What were the chances I would mysteriously lose sight of Steph, Alexis would call me moments later, and the two were not related? I prayed for a miracle as I reluctantly answered.

"What do you want?" I asked, my voice harsh with a fear I couldn't hide.

Alexis laughed. "What's the matter, Nikki? You sound tense."

"I'm not in the mood to banter with you. What do you want?"

"Do exactly as I tell you, and I promise no harm will come to dear Stephanie."

I swallowed a cry of anguish as he confirmed my worst

fears. "You can't hurt Steph!" I said. "My family and I are under Anderson's protection."

Alexis laughed again. "Is that how he told you it would work? Or just wishful thinking on your part?"

"He and Konstantin have a deal!" Oh, please, God, let that be true, let me not have been a complete dupe.

"A deal that doesn't include Stephanie. She isn't *really* your family, after all."

"She's my sister!"

"But adopted. Not related by blood. A technicality, per-haps, but one we mean to exploit. Because you chose to seek asylum with Anderson, we cannot touch you. But Stephanie is fair game."

"Let her go, you bastard! She has nothing to do with this."

"I'll be happy to let her go. No one has to get hurt in this scenario. Come to me, renounce Anderson's protection, and she'll go her own merry way, none the worse for wear."

What were the chances I could trust Alexis's word? Slim and none. The problem was, I didn't see that I had any alter-native. Alexis had Steph, and that left me with precious few options.

"How do I know you really have Steph?" I asked. I knew deep down in my gut that he was telling the truth, at least about that. But stalling for time seemed like a better alternative than rolling over.

There was a little scuffling noise on the other end of the line. Then I heard Alexis's voice in the background, saying "Let your sister know you're all right."

My entire body went tense as I braced myself for the im-pact of my sister's terrified voice. But Steph is made of sterner stuff than that, and she was every bit as protective of me as I was of her.

I knew she was there, knew Alexis wasn't lying, but she didn't make a sound. My throat tightened as I understood what she was doing: keeping her mouth shut in hopes that by not giving Alexis proof that he had her, she would keep me from coming after her. My eyes teared up.

"I'm not going to let him hurt you," I said, the words feeling hollow. Even *I* didn't believe I could protect her from Alexis. Why should I expect *her* to be convinced?

Alexis didn't like her show of defiance. I heard a harsh slap, and Steph's involuntary gasp of shock and pain.

"You'd best learn to do as you're told," Alexis growled in the background.

Steph still didn't say anything, though her gasp had already given her away. I cursed myself for asking Alexis for proof when I had believed him all along.

"I believe you!" I shouted into the phone, hoping my voice was loud enough for Alexis to hear.

There was a little more shuffling around, and his voice came back on the line. "You have thirty minutes to get to 28 Hillsboro Road in D.C. The door will be unlocked, so you just come right in. You come in, your sister goes out. If you don't get here in thirty minutes, the party will start without you."

I recognized the address from my list of Olympian properties. It was in Woodley Park and, if memory served, it was up for sale. I mentally calculated the distance and fought another jolt of terror. "That's not enough time," I told him. Maybe if I drove like a maniac and hit every light green, but . . .

"You'll have to *make* it enough."

"Please," I said, hating to beg, but willing to do it for Steph's sake. "It'll take me ten minutes just to get my car. Give me forty minutes to get there." I was already hurrying toward the exit. "I'm on my way now. Please don't hurt her."

"All right," he answered in an almost sensual purr, "I'm feeling generous tonight. You have your forty minutes. I look forward to seeing you again."

I turned my phone off before I was tempted to answer him with too much honesty.

Seventeen

Forty minutes gave me a fighting chance of making it to the rendezvous on time, but I was still going to be cutting it damn close. Despite the wintry temperature, I slipped my heels off as I burst through the front door and ran toward the parking lot. I'd run faster carrying them than wearing them, even if I ended up with a collection of pebbles buried in the balls of my feet. I stayed on the grass instead of the sidewalks whenever possible.

It was a long sprint to the parking lot, made longer, no doubt, by my fear. The cold air burned my lungs and stung the skin of my bare arms. I hadn't even considered stopping to pick up my coat on the way out, and little black dresses with spaghetti straps aren't great cold-weather gear.

Where the hell was Blake? I wondered belatedly. He'd been sticking to Steph like glue the whole evening. How had he let Alexis snatch her out from under his nose?

My gut cramped with fear again. Had Blake sold her out? Had he come with her tonight so he could more easily separate her from the crowd and hand her over to Alexis?

I shoved that thought out of the way. For the moment, it didn't matter. What mattered was getting to that damn house before Alexis went to work on Steph, and it was going to be a close call. Gravel tore the bottoms of my feet, and my breath formed frosty clouds in the night air as I continued to sprint. I was so focused on my ultimate goal that I didn't immediately notice that all four streetlights in the lot were out, not until the waxing moon slid behind a bank of clouds and made me suddenly aware of the darkness.

I stumbled to a halt just as my feet hit the asphalt. This was a country club, not some neglected inner city parking lot. If even *one* streetlight had burned out, they'd have fixed it within the hour. For all four to be burned out at the same time seemed so unlikely as to be impossible.

The little hairs at the back of my neck prickled, but I decided I didn't have time to be cautious. My silver rental was parked in the rear corner of the lot, and I started forward again at a brisk jog, too winded to manage another sprint.

I made it about halfway across the lot before I ran into something like an invisible wall. I hit it full force, rebounding wildly. My arms flailed for balance, and the shoes I'd been carrying in my left hand went flying. The impact had knocked what little wind I had left in my lungs out of me, and my legs were too quivery from the long run to hold me.

I sprawled inelegantly on the asphalt, my dress making an alarming ripping sound as the skirt hiked up my thighs. I broke the fall with my hands, scraping the skin off the heels and grinding dirt and pebbles into the wounds.

When I looked up to see what I'd hit, Jamaal's body seemed to coalesce out of thin air. I belatedly recognized the uniquely yielding properties of flesh and bone that had characterized my invisible wall.

Jamaal grinned down at me, the expression fierce as any snarl. "Going somewhere?"

I tried to draw some air into my lungs, but I hadn't recovered from the impact yet and could only stare up at him, imploring him with my eyes to get out of my way.

"You shouldn't have fucked with us, Nikki," he said, the grin/snarl growing wider.

I had no idea what he was talking about, of course. I also didn't give a damn, not now, not when Steph was in danger.

I finally filled my lungs enough to get some words out. "We can do this later," I gasped. "My sister's in trouble."

He snorted, the cold air making his breath a soft white cloud like the puff of smoke from the fire-breathing dragon's nostrils. "You don't get to decide when we do this."

He reached for me, and I rolled violently to my left, scraping more skin off my bare arms as I avoided his grasp. I'd torn my dress enough when I'd fallen to give me some freedom of movement, and I managed to lurch to my feet.

"Alexis has my sister!" I tried again, though I didn't have high hopes of getting through to Jamaal. Maybe he and Blake were in this thing together, Blake to hand Steph over to Alexis, Jamaal to delay my rescue attempt and give Alexis time to . . .

I didn't want to think about what he might do to Steph if I didn't make it there in time. "Please, Jamaal!" It came out a sob, but he didn't strike me as the kind to be moved by feminine tears. "Let me go!"

"You think I believe a single word that comes out of that lying mouth of yours?" he asked. "You'd say anything to get out of taking your medicine."

Because of my profession, I'd taken pains to learn a fair amount of self-defense. However, I knew I couldn't defend against Jamaal, at least not for very long. If he were an ordinary person in an ordinary situation, maybe I'd be able to fight him off long enough to make a run for it, but I couldn't *afford* to run for it. I *had* to get to my car, and he was in my way.

"I don't have time for this," I muttered under my breath as my heart kicked frantically behind my ribs. I had no hope that I could fight Jamaal off in hand-to-hand combat. That meant I had to try to reason with him. But how could I reason with a half-crazed death-god descendant who was convinced I was the enemy?

I held up my hands in a gesture that was supposed to indicate surrender, hoping Jamaal would take a step back from the edge. "Look, I don't know what you think I've done this time, but—"

"I heard you talking to Maggie," he replied, stalking toward me, muscles bunched to pounce, eyes practically glowing with his hatred.

It took me a minute to figure out what he was referring to. When I did, my eyes widened. He was talking about the day

I'd found Emma's ring. I suppose he'd been eavesdropping. I'd speculated at the time that Jamaal would jump to the worst possible conclusion if he found out, and it looked like I was right. I backed away from his approach but forced myself not to run, despite the dangerous intensity of his expression.

His lips pulled back from his teeth in a snarl. "I'm *glad* Maggie didn't tell Anderson. Glad she left you to me."

"I know you don't want to believe it, but I found that ring in the pot, just like I said."

He shook his head hard enough to rattle his beads. "The truth is your boss Konstantin sent you to kill Emmitt, then ordered you to spy on us. You've been leading Anderson on, telling him you would find his Emma, but you never had any intention of finding anyone, did you?"

Sweat dewed my skin, despite the cold. Every moment I stood here talking to Jamaal was a moment I lost in my race against time. If only I'd thought to bring my gun.

"If it's within my power, I swear I will find Emma," I said. "But right now, I have to help my sister. She's an innocent by-stander, Jamaal, whatever you might think about me. Please let me go to her, before Alexis hurts her."

Jamaal turned his head to the side and spat like there was a bad taste in his mouth. "Don't try to sell me that crock of shit! Blake is with her, so Alexis wouldn't get within a hundred yards of her. You think you can lie to us, kill one of our own, and I'm just going to let you run away? True, I'd catch up with you eventually. But I'm tired of waiting for my pound of flesh."

I wanted to scream with my overwhelming frustration. In the distance, a car engine gunned, and headlights headed down the main driveway toward the gates. This lot was too far away from the clubhouse for anyone there to hear me if I screamed, but maybe when the car got close enough, I'd be able to get the driver's attention.

I sucked air into my lungs, preparing to let loose the lon-gest, loudest, most blood-curdling scream in the history of the universe. Tires squealed as the car I'd spotted gunned the engine again, hurtling forward at a speed that would do a NASCAR driver proud.

Before I managed to get any sound past my lips, Jamaal's fist connected with my jaw.

He'd been well out of arm's reach when I'd allowed my attention to stray to the approaching car for that brief fraction of a second, but that moment of distraction was all he'd needed. His punch lifted me off my feet and threw me backward. Pain exploded through my head, my vision dancing with fireworks as my legs turned into jelly.

My back slammed into one of the parked cars, foiling my second attempt to force out a scream as the impact knocked the air from my lungs. The scream probably wouldn't have done me much good anyway, I decided as I sat on my butt and tried to blink the fireworks away. The car I'd been hoping to flag down was going so fast I expected a sonic boom to follow in its wake. It was well past us by the time I staggered to my feet to avoid Jamaal's next attack.

My head was swimming from that first punch, but my desperation helped me hold on to consciousness. If I blacked out, Jamaal would be on me in a heartbeat, and I'd never make it to Steph in time.

Something trickled over my upper lip. I brushed at it with the back of my hand. Blood. For the moment, I was glad it was dark, or I might have gone even more lightheaded with the sight.

Jamaal was grinning like a madman—which is pretty much what he was at that moment. As he closed the distance between us, both his hands clenched into heavy, dangerous fists. He swung at me again, his right fist aiming for my nose. This time, I managed to duck. Unfortunately, I wasn't prepared for the follow-up from his left, which caught me right in the gut.

Gagging, desperate for air, I collapsed to the ground once again. I retained just enough brain power to roll, this time avoiding a vicious kick from Jamaal's booted foot.

I pushed myself up to my hands and knees, scanning the parking lot to regain my bearings. My car was only a few yards away. I lurched to my feet and flung myself toward the car, but Jamaal caught me in a flying tackle before I took more than two steps.

Despite my breathlessness, I did manage a rough imitation of a scream of frustration as I went down once again. I kicked out blindly and got lucky, hitting Jamaal in the nose by the crunchy sound of it. He absorbed the pain with no more than a stoic grunt, but at least it distracted him enough to let me get to my feet again.

I had closed the remaining distance between myself and my car before I realized the fatal flaw in my plan. My evening bag, which had been draped bandolier-style across my chest while I ran, had come off sometime during the struggle. My car keys were in that bag.

Blood continued to trickle from my nose as I turned to face Jamaal once more. His nosebleed looked even worse than mine, but I saw no sign that it bothered him. He had drawn a knife from somewhere—his boot, maybe?—and was brandishing it in the occasional glimmers of moonlight that escaped the clouds.

I swallowed hard, tasting blood in the back of my throat. I hurt everywhere, from the punches, from the barefoot run, and from scraping off skin as I rolled around on the rough asphalt. My dress was in tatters, most likely indecent. Jamaal stood between me and the evening bag, and I was so hurt and exhausted already I didn't know how I could hold him off a moment longer. But I had to. Somehow.

Jamaal wasn't going to let me go. He'd long ago closed his mind to me, decided I was a traitor and that I was lying about Steph. Which meant that if I wanted to get into my car and drive away, I had to take him out.

It occurred to me that I'd been handling my fight with Ja-maal as if I were no more than human. Perhaps I was shrugging off my injuries better than I might have before, not worrying that they would cause permanent damage, but I had abilities now that I hadn't had when I was mortal. And maybe those abilities would help me now.

If Jamaal closed with me, I was a goner, and probably would have been even if he didn't have the knife. So I didn't dare let him close.

I started darting glances left and right, quick glances that were meant to suggest to Jamaal that I was picking out an escape route. Only I knew better than to think I could escape. I edged around the car at my back, giving myself room to move. Then, I feinted to the left.

Jamaal had been thinking of me as little more than a puny human female himself. A not-too-bright one at that. When I feinted, he fell for it, lunging forward on what would have been an intercept course if I'd really been making a run for it.

Instead, I took advantage of his distraction and threw myself forward, heedless of the pain that seared my already tender skin as I slid face-first across the asphalt. My hand closed around the discarded shoe I'd caught sight of when I'd been pretending to look for an escape route. I rolled over onto my back.

The feint hadn't bought me much time. I hadn't expected it to. Jamaal had checked his charge and now whirled to face me.

I hesitated for a fraction of a second, a part of me horrified by what I was about to do. But it was for Steph, and it was necessary. Wincing in anticipation, I took aim and hurled the shoe at Jamaal's face with as much force as I could muster.

I had gambled that my throwing would be as accurate as my shooting had been. The gamble paid off.

Not surprisingly, Jamaal didn't immediately think of a thrown shoe as a dangerous weapon, and he made only a half-hearted attempt to avoid it. But my supernatural aim could make a dangerous weapon out of a lot of ordinary objects, and those heels were fashionably pointy.

The spiky, three-inch heel slammed into Jamaal's eye and lodged there. He screamed, a sound full of pain and rage. Even a tough guy like him wasn't able to retain his calm after having his eye put out. He fell, wrenching the shoe out of the bloody socket and hurling it away. His hands clasped the wound and he bent over until his forehead almost touched the asphalt, unable to suppress his agonized moans.

Sobbing in pain, in terror, and in horror, I limped to my evening bag to get the car keys. Jamaal was still down when I collapsed into the driver's seat and started the engine. My stomach wanted to take a minute to empty itself out, but I'd run out of spare minutes about ten minutes ago, and I swallowed to keep my gorge down.

Trying not to look at Jamaal and what I had done to him, I slammed the pedal to the floor and pulled out of the parking lot at top speed.

EIGHTEEN

My hands shook and my teeth chattered as I drove, fear chewing a hole in my gut. How much time had Jamaal cost me? It seemed like forever, but my sense of time was completely out of whack.

My entire body throbbed from the beating I'd taken, and my stomach was still attempting to stage a rebellion. I'd fully intended to take out Jamaal's eye when I threw that shoe at him, but even in my fear for Steph, I couldn't help shuddering at the memory.

"He's *Liberi,* Nikki," I told myself, clenching my teeth, hoping that would make them stop chattering. "He'll heal."

At least, I hoped he would. For all I knew, the wound would heal and leave an empty socket. My gorge rose, and I swallowed fiercely. I'd done what I had to do. Besides, who knew what Jamaal would have done to me if I'd given him the chance? I suspected he had more than a beating in mind, a suspicion made stronger by the knife he'd brandished at me. He couldn't have killed me, but I knew I'd have been in for a world of hurt.

I've said before I'm a bleeding heart. No matter how much I told myself Jamaal had deserved what I'd done to him, I couldn't help feeling awful about it. Which is why I called Anderson while I was barreling down the street, trying to keep my speed to something that wouldn't inspire the cops to pull me over. If the way my own wound had healed after the car accident was any indication, Jamaal would be in pain and without an eye for at least a couple of hours, and I didn't want to leave him alone in that parking lot. Aside from any pity I might feel for his pain, I also didn't want any innocent bystanders to stumble on him. I didn't imagine having his eye taken out had improved his mental health.

Anderson answered on the first ring. "Nikki! Where are you?"

I blinked in surprise at the alarm in his voice. "On the road," I said. "Alexis—"

"Has your sister. I know. I just got off the phone with Blake."

Anger overwhelmed my fear, turning everything red. "Where the fuck was he?" I yelled. "He was supposed to be *protecting* her." I couldn't restrain a sob, and I had to blink away the tears that obscured my vision. I couldn't afford tears, not now.

"Explanations later," Anderson said curtly. "Do you know where he's taken her?"

I blurted out the address. If one of Anderson's people was closer than I was, then maybe they could get there in time to help Steph.

"And where are *you*?" he asked.

"Still in Chevy Chase, but going as fast as I can."

There was a hesitation on the other end of the line, as though Anderson was surprised by my answer. But then, if he'd already talked to Blake, he knew when Steph was taken, and he had to wonder why I wasn't already halfway to the rendezvous.

"Jamaal delayed me," I said, no longer caring if that made me a tattletale. "You might want to send someone to the country club to pick him up. He's not in very good shape at the moment."

"I'll call you back," Anderson said, then hung up abruptly.

I frowned at the phone. Why had he hung up on me like that? Even in those few words, I'd been able to hear the rage in his voice, but it was *Jamaal* he was angry at, not me. Right?

I closed the phone and tossed it onto the passenger seat. It didn't matter who Anderson was angry at or why he'd hung up. He was at the mansion, too far away to help. I'd deal with the fallout from my fight with Jamaal later.

The phone rang a couple of times as I sped through the streets of the city, cursing every red light I couldn't afford to run for fear of police intervention. I ignored it, because at the speed I was driving, it was safer to keep all my attention on the road. I wouldn't do Steph much more good if I wrecked the car than if I got stopped by the cops.

The minutes ticked away, and though I tried not to, I couldn't help checking the clock on the dashboard every time I could spare the attention. I let out a sob when Alexis's deadline came and went, although I'd known from the moment I'd run into Jamaal that I wouldn't make it in time. I prayed Alexis would hold off for just a little while, give me a little grace period, since he knew just how unreasonable his deadline had been.

I turned the final corner a good ten minutes past the deadline. The street was quiet and secluded—which, of course, suited Alexis's purpose. There weren't any legal parking spaces available, but I wasn't about to sweat legalities at this point.

As I pulled into a "space" blocking a narrow alley, the door to the house across the street—the one where Alexis had instructed me to meet him—flew open. I blinked in surprise when Alexis charged out at a dead run, vaulting the ornamental railing that lined the stoop and taking off down the street like the hounds of hell were after him.

Maybe I'd watched too many movies, but my immediate thought was that he'd planted a bomb in the house and was running to avoid the explosion. I slammed the car into park and decided I didn't care why Alexis was running. I only cared about Steph.

The wounds on the bottoms of my feet had been superficial enough that they had already healed, but it wouldn't have mattered if they'd been raw and bleeding. I still would have leapt out of the car and dashed up the steps. Alexis had left the door open when he fled, so I burst right in, not pausing for even a moment to consider the possibility of ambush.

"Steph!" I screamed, desperate to hear her voice, to know that she was alive and okay.

"In here!" answered a voice that most definitely was not Steph's.

Dread making me shiver, I followed the sound of Blake's voice.

I found them on the floor in a room toward the back. The house was up for sale and completely empty, but I suspected the room was meant to be an office, based on the desk-and-shelf combo built in to the wall.

Blake was kneeling on the floor, leaning protectively over Steph, her head on his lap. Her elegantly coiffed hair was a bedraggled mess and draped her face like a veil. She was naked, though Blake was doing his best to tuck her torn dress around her body to restore her modesty. Her shoulders were shaking with silent sobs.

I stopped in the doorway, clapping my hand over my mouth to stifle my cry. *She's alive,* I told myself over and over, though the nudity and the tears reminded me of the difference between *alive* and *well.*

"Oh, Steph," I whispered, my heart breaking.

Blake pulled her gently into his arms, rocking her as he cradled her head against his chest. His own eyes when he looked at me were rimmed with red, the evidence of his sincere distress giving me another shock. He did a double take when he caught sight of me. I'm sure I looked like I'd been dragged behind a pickup truck on a gravel road, and I felt drafts in places I shouldn't feel drafts while fully clothed, but I didn't give a damn about my appearance.

"I'm going to kill him," I growled, not sure if I meant Alexis or Jamaal at the moment. Maybe both.

I remembered seeing Alexis fleeing the scene, and my anger rose another notch. "You let Alexis get away. And where the hell were you, anyway? You were supposed to keep her safe!"

He flinched at the virulence of my tone, but rebounded quickly. "Somebody spilled a whole glass of red wine on me," he said. "I went to the men's room to clean up. She was right outside . . ." His voice trailed off and he gathered Steph even closer. "He locked me in, and he took her," he said. "I wasn't delayed for long, but I had to hurry after him. I couldn't stop to look for you, didn't have time."

The expression in his eyes hardened. "As for why I let the bastard get away, would you really rather I left Steph alone and chased after him?"

I let out a harsh breath, wishing I could hit rewind on my life. "No. Of course not."

I forced myself farther into the room, though seeing Steph's pain was almost unbearable. Blake stroked her hair away from her face, and the hollow ache inside me went from bad to worse. I staggered and almost fell.

He'd beaten her. Badly. Both of her eyes were blackened, and her lip was split and swollen. A ring of bruises circled her neck, where Alexis must have choked her.

All at once, it was too much. The beating I had taken. The horror of putting out Jamaal's eye. The constant pump of adrenaline through my system as I ran my losing race against time. And the awful, sickening revelation of what that sadistic bastard had done to my sister.

The room spun and bucked around me, and my brain shut down. My legs crumpled and I fell to my knees on the carpeted floor. I didn't quite pass out, but it was a near thing.

"Nikki," Steph rasped.

I fought to push back the gray fog that surrounded my mind. Falling to pieces would be the easy way out, and I was never one to do things the easy way. I swallowed the huge, aching lump in my throat and blinked to hold back tears.

Steph was holding her hand out to me, and I shuffled toward her on my knees until I was close enough to take it. Her fingers curled around mine in a surprisingly firm grip.

"Are you okay?" she asked. Her voice was rough and hoarse, either from screaming, from crying, or from being choked nearly to death.

My jaw dropped as I looked at her battered face, at the tears that stained her cheeks. "Am *I* okay?" I fought a hysterical laugh. After everything Steph had been through, she was worried about *me*?

She sniffled and blinked away some tears. "You look like someone shoved you through a paper shredder."

For a moment, I'd actually forgotten what a wreck I must look. But I would be healed in a few hours, and Steph . . .

"I'm fine," I assured her, the sound breaking in my throat as I struggled not to cry.

"You are not. And you have a lot of explaining to do."

Even in her obvious distress and with her ravaged voice, Steph managed to imbue those words with a tone of command. I wondered if Alexis had revealed his supernatural nature to Steph while he . . .

I stopped myself from going there, although the question remained in my mind. If his threats were anything to go by, he'd never intended to kill her, figuring that leaving her alive and suffering would hurt me more. But he was an arrogant bastard, and he might have figured she'd be too terrified and traumatized to say anything about any supernatural powers he might reveal.

"Let's get you taken care of first," Blake said gently when I took too long to answer. "We can do explanations later."

"Have you called an ambulance?" I asked Blake.

"No!" he and Steph answered at the same time.

I understood why Blake would object—he was worried about the potential of police getting involved in *Liberi* business—but if he thought I was going to let him stand in the way of Steph getting the medical care she needed, he was sorely mistaken. I squeezed her hand a little harder.

"You need help, hon," I said, but Steph shook her head.

"No doctors," she said firmly. She forced her swollen eyes open enough to meet my gaze squarely. "He didn't do anything to me that won't heal on its own in time. And I suspect siccing the police on him would probably get them killed. I don't know what he was, except that it's not human."

Crap. That meant Alexis had spilled at least some of the beans. I wanted to pretend I had no idea what she was talking about, to keep her sheltered from the knowledge of how formidable a foe Alexis was. I wanted to urge her to go to the hospital, to talk to the police, to do all the normal things that a rape victim should do. But I was too run-down to manage it. I might be able to say the words, but I wouldn't be able to make them convincing.

"We'll bring her back to the house," Blake told me. "She'll be safe there."

I was too depressed and guilt-stricken to argue. We helped Steph get back into what was left of her dress, and then Blake gave her his tuxedo jacket to cover up in. I retrieved my car from its illegal parking space and pulled up right in front of the door as Blake carried Steph out and bundled her into the backseat.

"I could have walked," I heard her grumble as Blake climbed in after her. I supposed he'd come back to get his own car some other time.

"But carrying you made me feel less useless," he said.

I glanced at his face in the rearview mirror, then had to look away from his raw expression. He couldn't know Steph very well, but despite my earlier suspicions, it seemed obvious he genuinely cared about her. And that he felt almost as guilty as I did about failing her.

NINETEEN

I drove back to the mansion in a daze. Steph lay curled in the back-seat, her head once again on Blake's lap as he soothed and petted her. Her tears had dried up long ago, but I knew there would be more to come. The wounds Alexis had inflicted on her psyche were far worse than the physical pain, and I wished like hell I were still a mortal so I could have the pleasure of killing him.

Blake called Anderson while we were en route, giving him an update. I couldn't hear anything Anderson said over the phone, of course, but I swear I could *sense* his anger. I wasn't sure who he was angry with, and I wasn't sure I cared. I did my best to retreat into a numb sense of unreality, not ready to deal with the emotions that roiled within me.

When we got to the house, Blake once again insisted on car-rying Steph, despite her protests that she could walk. Maybe it made him feel better to be gallant, though I couldn't help notic-ing how she curled into him, her arm slung around his neck, her head resting just below his chin. Protests aside, it seemed she needed the comfort, too. Maybe he was doing it for her sake after all. I raced ahead to hold the front door for him, then fol-lowed him into the entryway and came to a dead stop.

Anderson was waiting there for us, and he wasn't alone. Jamaal stood beside him, his eye thoroughly bandaged. I expected him to be in a towering rage after what I'd done to him. Instead, he took one look at Steph's battered form as she cuddled against Blake's chest, and lowered his head in what looked a hell of a lot like shame.

The rage I'd been fighting since the moment I'd seen what Alexis had done to my sister came boiling up through my chest. It was all I could do not to hurl myself at Jamaal and try to scratch his other eye out.

"Take her upstairs," Anderson ordered Blake, who nodded and headed toward the grand staircase. "Not you," Anderson continued when I made to follow Blake.

"But—" The look in Anderson's eyes made me swallow my protest. I didn't want to let Steph out of my sight, but a part of me knew my own emotional turmoil might do her more harm than good. The last thing she needed was to worry herself over my well-being after what she'd been through, and she was enough of a mother hen to do it. Curling my hands into fists, I stayed where I was and watched as Blake carried her upstairs.

Slowly, I turned back to Anderson and Jamaal. Jamaal still stood with his head bowed, his shoulders hunched like he was trying to make himself smaller. Maybe he sensed me looking at him, because he raised his head and met my gaze for a moment. The expression in his unbandaged eye was bleak. He opened his mouth to say something, then shook his head and returned his gaze to the floor.

"There are no words," I thought I heard him say under his breath.

One thing I can say for Jamaal, he's no actor. I doubted he could fake remorse if his life depended on it, and I knew what I was seeing was genuine. He had convinced himself every word out of my mouth was a lie, and therefore he had never believed holding me up would actually hurt anyone but me. Now that he was faced with the truth, his malice had drained away.

He might be genuinely sorry for what he'd done, but that didn't do Steph any good, and therefore I didn't give a damn.

"Tomorrow morning at nine," Anderson said to Jamaal, his voice cold steel, "we will hold a tribunal in my study to determine your punishment." Jamaal nodded his acceptance without looking up. "You'll spend the night downstairs." In one of the cells, I presumed. "Go. Now."

Jamaal bowed from the waist and, still keeping his gaze fixed on the floor, backed out of the room and away. It was as submissive a gesture as I'd ever seen, and it made me wonder just what kind of punishment this tribunal might sentence him to. For all that I was nominally a part of Anderson's merry band, I didn't know all that much about them.

Anderson turned to me when Jamaal was gone, his expression somber. Had Jamaal told him about the ring? Was I going to be having a tribunal of my own? At the moment, I wasn't sure I cared.

Anderson looked me up and down, inspecting the damage. The cuts and scrapes I'd suffered from rolling around on the asphalt were all well on their way to healing, but from the feel of it, several of the deeper bruises still had a ways to go. My head ached fiercely, but I suspected much of that was the aftermath of the stress rather than real physical injury.

Anderson shook his head. "I never would have guessed he'd do that," he said. "I knew he still suspected you, and I knew he was unstable, but . . ." He let his voice trail off, and for the first time since I'd met him, a look of true uncertainty crossed his face.

I heaved out a sigh. "It's not your fault," I told him, and despite my anger at the *Liberi* in general, I realized I meant it. Maybe if I had told him about Jamaal's nocturnal visit, he'd have been able to head off tonight's disaster. Keeping quiet had seemed like the honorable thing to do, but I'd had even more evidence than Anderson that Jamaal was out of control. I should have done something about it, and Steph had suffered because I hadn't.

"What are you going to do to him?" I asked, crossing

my arms and shivering in a phantom chill. Despite his mild-mannered affect, I'd seen hints that Anderson had a ruthless side. No matter how angry I was at Jamaal, I wasn't sure I wanted to see that ruthless side unleashed.

"We'll decide that tomorrow." There was no give in his tone, and I knew the subject was closed.

"And his eye . . ." I swallowed hard, sickened once again at the memory of what I had done. "Will it heal?"

Anderson looked at me in surprise. "Don't tell me you're feeling sorry for him!"

Logic said I shouldn't. I never wanted to be so bloodthirsty that I reveled in another's pain, no matter what that other had done, but that didn't mean I should feel sorry for him. And yet still I couldn't help being aware of the deep river of pain that ran beneath Jamaal's hostility. He needed someone to blame for Emmitt's death, and I was the obvious candidate. I knew too well what it was like to try to offload pain onto someone else. Just ask some of the unfortunate foster families who got stuck with me before the Glasses tamed me.

I glanced at the doorway through which Jamaal had disappeared. "What was he like before Emmitt died?" I asked instead of answering Anderson's question.

Anderson sighed and ran a hand through his already disheveled hair. "Not like this," he muttered, confirming what I'd already guessed. "He was always strung pretty tight, but Emmitt helped balance him. Emmitt had centuries of experience dealing with the effects of his death magic, and Jamaal's only had a couple of decades. It isn't an easy adjustment."

Despite the situation, I couldn't help being curious. I'd seen firsthand what Maggie and Blake could do, and I was pretty sure I'd seen Jamaal walk through a closed door, but other than that, I had very little grasp of the powers of my fellow *Liberi*. "Death magic?"

Anderson nodded. "It's a very . . . dark power, particularly in Jamaal. He can kill people without even touching them, and the power practically has a mind of its own. It *wants* to be used, and it's always a struggle to keep it contained. Emmitt had some of the same power, and he'd learned to master it. He was teaching Jamaal his techniques, and Jamaal was stabilizing." His jaw clenched. "Then the bastard decided to shuffle off this mortal coil with the job unfinished."

I hadn't known Emmitt very well, and most of what I'd known had been a fiction anyway. He'd seemed like a pretty nice guy, at least on the surface. But truly nice guys didn't walk out on people who needed them.

"Too bad we can't bring him back from the dead and give *him* a tribunal," I said, and Anderson cracked a small smile.

"Indeed." The smile faded before it had a chance to take hold. "You should get cleaned up and tend your wounds. We'll have an early day tomorrow."

"Look, I don't know if Jamaal told you—"

"That you found Emma's ring?"

Well, that answered that. "Um, yeah."

Anderson met my eyes. "If you tell me you found that ring in the pot, then I'll take you at your word. For now."

I wasn't sure if saying he believed me was legitimate when it was paired with "for now," but at least he wasn't threatening me with the Hand of Doom. "I found the ring in the pot," I said, looking him straight in the eye. "I swear it."

He stared at me a long while, but I didn't look away. Finally, he nodded. "All right then. We'll say no more."

I knew a dismissal when I heard one. I didn't much want to be alone with my thoughts, but I headed upstairs anyway. I took a shower and changed, avoiding taking too close a look at myself in the mirror, then went looking for Steph.

Not surprisingly, she was in Blake's suite. He was in his sitting room, sipping from a tumbler of amber liquid and pacing. The door to his bedroom was ajar, but the lights inside were out.

He stopped pacing when he saw me, putting his finger to his lips in a shushing motion. "She's sleeping," he whispered.

I wanted to go to her, to look her over and assure myself that she was all right. But of course, she *wasn't* all right, and if she'd temporarily escaped her misery in sleep, I wasn't about to wake her.

"You should get some sleep, too," Blake continued, still in that soft whisper. "You look like you're about to keel over."

I felt like it. Healing definitely seemed to take a lot out of my body, and I felt like I hadn't slept in three days. "Take good care of her," I urged, surprised to find I felt perfectly comfortable leaving Steph in his care. Just a few short hours earlier, I'd have said I didn't trust Blake as far as I could throw him. He'd failed to protect Steph, but he'd done more for her than *I* had. Who knew how much worse it would have been if Blake hadn't shown up at the scene when he did?

Hoping that I could find oblivion in sleep, at least for a little while, I headed back to my own room and collapsed on the bed fully clothed.

I've had more than my fair share of bad nights throughout my life, but that night was among the worst. As exhausted as I was, I couldn't sleep. I could barely even keep my eyes closed. Instead, I lay there on my back in the dark, cataloging the sins of my past and wondering how Steph had had the bad luck to get stuck with such a crappy adoptive sister. As I lay there wallowing in guilt, I realized that this wasn't the first time someone had gotten hurt because of my misguided desire not to be a tattletale. Considering how horribly wrong things had gone the last time I'd made the fateful decision to keep my mouth shut, you'd think I'd have known better by now.

I was eight years old, and was already on my eighth foster family, the Garcias. They had a twelve-year-old son, Dave, who had been every bit as much of a problem child as I was, so they were sure they could "fix" me. The thing was, they hadn't "fixed" Dave as much as they'd thought.

Mr. Garcia was a gun enthusiast, but a very responsible one.

He kept his guns safely locked away, with the ammo in a different safe and both keys hidden. Dave was fascinated with those damn guns, and one summer day when Mr. Garcia was off at work, Dave figured out where the keys were hidden. He was very proud of himself and excited about being able to handle the guns with impunity. He showed off for me and even let me hold one myself.

Playing with guns had appealed to my wild nature, and of course I thought of Dave as older and wiser. To tell the truth, I never even considered telling on him.

About a month later, Dave had some of his friends from school over. I was out shopping with Mrs. Garcia. Mr. Garcia was supposed to be keeping an eye on the boys, but they were old enough not to need constant supervision. He was comfortable sitting down in the living room and watching a baseball game while the boys played video games in Dave's room.

Dave was now making a habit of sneaking into the gun safe. Wanting to impress his friends, he'd stuck a gun into his dresser drawer. I'm pretty sure he thought it wasn't loaded, or that he'd fired all the bullets the last time he'd snuck it out for some target practice in the woods. One of his friends found out the hard way that there was one bullet left. The gun went off in Dave's hand, and he'd have his friend's death on his conscience for the rest of his life.

Dave told all in the aftermath, and when the Garcias found out I'd known about the gun, they couldn't wait to get rid of me. They couldn't find it in their hearts to be mad at Dave, their flesh and blood. So instead, they heaped all the blame on me. It was blame I'd never accepted, and my bitterness and anger when they packed me off was monumental.

I should have learned my lesson. No, the death hadn't been my fault, and yes, it had been wrong of the Garcias to blame me. Even so, there'd been a life lesson I could have learned if only I'd opened my eyes to it. I wasn't to blame for the death, but I could have prevented it.

Now that it was too late, I'd finally figured it out: I should have told Anderson the truth about Jamaal's threats. But even the best hindsight couldn't change the past.

TWENTY

I managed to doze fitfully through the darkest hours of the night, but was up and out of bed as soon as the sun peeked up over the horizon. I was tired, dejected, and on the verge of a headache, but I knew I wasn't getting any more sleep. I ventured down to the kitchen and made a pot of coffee, then fixed myself two hearty mugs full and took them back upstairs to my suite. With the tribunal at nine, I knew the rest of Anderson's clan would be getting up earlier than usual, and I didn't want to run in to anyone.

If I'd thought I could avoid the tribunal, I'd have done it in a heartbeat. Pissed off as I was at Jamaal, I thought that having his eye put out and then having to live with the guilt of leaving Steph to Alexis's tender mercies was punishment enough. He might still think I was a spy—Steph getting hurt proved that Konstantin was a bastard, but not that I wasn't in league with him—but I seriously doubted Jamaal would make another unsanctioned attack against me.

I wasn't really one of Anderson's people, no matter what he claimed to Konstantin. And moving into the house hadn't even saved Steph. There was no good reason for me to follow Anderson's orders and attend the tribunal. Maybe I should have just packed my bags and gone home. But Jamaal was being punished on my behalf, so when nine o'clock rolled around, I headed for Anderson's study.

Anderson had pulled in additional chairs from somewhere and pushed his usual furniture to the walls. Jamaal sat with his back to the wall on a metal folding chair, and the rest of the chairs were set up in a semicircle around him. In the center, directly facing Jamaal, was Anderson, his chair larger and more comfortable-looking than all the rest, looking almost like a throne. The others were all ranged around him, and there was only one empty seat, between Maggie and Blake. Apparently, I was the last to arrive.

Dragging my feet a bit, I made my way over to the empty seat. No one was talking, the tension in the room so thick I could almost feel it sliding against my skin.

Jamaal sat with his head bowed and his hands clasped in his lap, the picture of penitence. His eye was no longer bandaged, but it wasn't finished healing yet, either. The flesh all around the socket was swollen and bruised, but the eye itself seemed to have regenerated. I breathed a little sigh of relief at that. Like I said, a bleeding heart.

"Where's Steph?" I whispered to Blake as I took my seat. I didn't like the idea of leaving her alone, although I supposed having her sit in on the tribunal wouldn't be such a hot idea.

"Still sleeping," he answered, his voice equally soft. "She took a Valium, so she'll be out for a while."

I wanted to ask where Steph had gotten a Valium—it didn't seem like something the *Liberi* would have around—but just then Anderson called the tribunal to order. He asked me to tell everyone exactly what had happened last night, and I squirmed. Silly, perhaps, seeing as it was after the fact and everyone already knew, but I didn't want to sit there and publicly rat Jamaal out. Guess I *still* wasn't over my fear of being seen as a tattletale.

"Is that really necessary?" I asked. "We all know what happened."

"It's necessary," Anderson said in a clipped voice that told me he didn't appreciate his orders being questioned. Gone entirely was his usual, easygoing manner. This morning, he was all alpha-male leader, grim and intimidating.

I struggled to come up with a tactful way to explain the situation, but to my surprise, Jamaal put me out of my misery.

"I fucked up," he said quietly. He raised his head and looked us squarely in the eye, one by one. It wasn't a gesture of defiance, but one of accountability.

"I convinced myself Nikki was working for Konstantin, and I decided to teach her a lesson," he continued. There was misery in his eyes, but his voice was flat as he recounted the facts. "I thought if I ambushed her at the auction, I'd have the time to do what I wanted without fear of being interrupted. I waited by her car, and when she came running into the parking lot, I jumped her. She tried to tell me Alexis had her sister, but I wouldn't listen. I told myself she was lying again, and I wouldn't let her leave. She managed to fight me off." Was there a hint of approval in his voice when he said that? Hard to believe he'd approve of me taking out his eye.

"But my attack delayed her, and she was unable to get to her sister in time. Because of me, Alexis brutalized an innocent woman." His voice wasn't so flat anymore, and the words rasped out of his throat. "I have no excuse for anything I've done, and I'll willingly take whatever punishment you think I deserve."

A long, tense silence followed Jamaal's speech. I glanced at the other *Liberi,* trying to be subtle as I read their faces. There were a couple of people—specifically, Maggie and Jack—who regarded Jamaal with expressions of sympathy. Logan and Leo looked neutral, like they didn't care what happened to Jamaal one way or another. Blake was giving him a death glare, and Anderson looked cold and deadly.

"You've broken our trust," Anderson said, and he sounded about as warm as an iceberg. "You disobeyed my direct orders, and you hurt someone who was under my protection. Pack your bags. I want you out by noon."

Jamaal's jaw dropped, and his face turned ashen gray. "No," he whispered, not in refusal but in dismay. "Please." He gripped the seat of his chair until his knuckles turned white, as if he were holding on to it for dear life. "Anything but that."

My throat tightened in sympathy. Damn it, it was too easy

for me to empathize with him! I'd been kicked out of too many homes in my life not to know the sickening lurch of it. And most of the homes I'd been kicked out of hadn't really felt so much like homes to me as way stations. Jamaal might not have an easy rapport with the rest of Anderson's people, and he definitely held himself a bit aloof, but this was truly his home.

What would he do if he were no longer part of Anderson's crew? His divine ancestor wasn't Greek, so he couldn't become an Olympian even if he wanted to. And if being separated from Emmitt had worsened the effects the death magic had on him, I couldn't imagine what being separated from all his friends and his home would do to him.

"Maybe he deserves another chance," Jack said into the silence.

That surprised me—and everyone else, too, by the look of it. Jack seemed to have embraced his trickster heritage with gusto, and I'd never seen him be serious about anything. Of course Jamaal, with his nonexistent sense of humor, was Jack's favorite target. The jokes sometimes had some pretty sharp teeth, but he wouldn't have teased Jamaal so much if he didn't like him.

"He's had enough chances," Blake countered with a snarl. "He's proven he can't control himself—or *won't*—and there's no place for him here."

"Surely he's learned his lesson," Maggie put in softly, and I was glad I wasn't the only bleeding heart in the room.

"Too late!" Blake snapped.

The tribunal was about to devolve into a free-for-all, but Anderson nipped that in the bud.

"Show of hands. How many of you think we should give Jamaal another chance?"

Maggie, Jack, and I all raised our hands. I got a couple of startled looks—and a sneer from Blake—but I was sure giving Jamaal another chance was the right thing to do. I didn't think he would fall over himself in gratitude because I supported him, nor did I think he would suddenly be convinced I didn't work for Konstantin. Maybe I'd end up regretting the decision later, but I couldn't vote to throw him to the wolves. Steph might have been hurt because of him, but that certainly wasn't what he'd *meant* to happen. And there was no guarantee Steph wouldn't have been hurt if I'd made the rendezvous in time.

Blake, Logan, and Leo didn't raise their hands, despite the sad look in Leo's eyes. That left us deadlocked, though in truth I wasn't sure how much our opinions really counted. Anderson had made it very clear: his house, his rules.

Anderson thought about it for a long moment, then nodded. "Since Nikki, as the injured party, is willing to give you another chance, I'll let you choose your punishment. You can either pack your bags and leave. Or you can submit to an execution once a day for the next three days."

There were gasps and winces all around the semicircle of *Liberi,* and I saw the flicker of fear in Jamaal's eyes. Nevertheless, he didn't hesitate in his answer.

"I'll submit to whatever I have to if you'll let me stay."

I wasn't sure exactly what it all meant. Obviously, the *Liberi* couldn't die, so this wasn't a real execution we were talking about. (Not to mention that a real execution is a one-time deal.) But something about it sure gave the rest of the *Liberi* the shivers.

Anderson nodded regally. "Logan will perform the executions," he continued. "I'll leave it to him to decide the methods." He looked at his watch. "We'll convene at sunset at the clearing. Attendance is mandatory." He shot a look at me, as if knowing how little I'd want to watch whatever was going to happen. "Jamaal, you will remain downstairs until the sentence has been fully carried out. No passing through the door, or you're out. Clear?"

Jamaal held his chin high. "Clear."

Anderson stood from his chair, still running arctic cold. "Everyone out," he said as he turned his back on all of us and headed toward his desk to pull it out of the corner it had been shoved into. I think more than one of us considered offering to help him put the room back to rights, but we all thought better of it.

I gave Maggie a significant look as we left the room, and she got the message, following me up to my own suite.

"I don't want to go into this thing tonight uninformed," I told her as soon as I'd closed the sitting room door. "Jamaal can't die, so what's with the execution thing? And why did everyone look so sick about it?"

Maggie shuddered as she dropped onto the sofa, wrapping her arms about herself like she was cold. "It's not true that we can't die," she said. "We just don't stay dead."

I joined her on the sofa, feeling a similar chill. "Huh?"

"If we're dealt a serious enough wound, we die. Our bodies will heal the damage eventually, and we'll revive, so it's not permanent. But it is dead.

"I've never had a fatal wound myself, but from what I've heard, it's horrible. It has nothing to do with the pain of the wound or of the healing—though that can be considerable in itself, depending on the cause of death—but dying itself is a massively unpleasant experience. Even as an immortal, you want to avoid dying at all costs."

I salted this information away for later. I probably wasn't cruel enough to kill Alexis over and over again if I ever got my hands on him. But at least for now, it made a comforting, if gruesome, fantasy.

TWENTY-ONE

I checked on Steph every couple of hours until the Valium had worn off and she was awake and alert. I had to admit, Blake seemed to be taking good care of her. Her face and throat were still darkly bruised, but judicious applications of ice had reduced the swelling. There was also a bottle of Advil on the bed-side table, beside a cheerful flower arrangement exactly like the kind you might send someone in the hospital.

He'd given her an oversized T-shirt to wear, along with a pair of drawstring running shorts that would probably fall off if she tried to walk around in them. She was propped up in his bed, surrounded by mounds of pillows as she sipped from a mug of hot chocolate, when I came in.

Blake, still in guardian angel mode, was sitting on the side of the bed, his hand stroking idly up and down the covers over her legs as he kept her silent company. They both looked up when I knocked on the bedroom door, but Blake spared me only a brief glance before he turned his attention back to his patient.

Steph cupped her hands around her mug as if they were cold, then looked me up and down, her head cocked to the side. There was no way she could miss how my injuries had disappeared overnight. She didn't look completely shocked, so I suspected Blake had told her all the secrets I'd been unwilling to share. Just one more thing to feel guilty about, though truthfully, if I could have gone back in time I'd probably have made the same decision.

"How are you feeling?" I asked, though it felt like a dumb question.

She raised one shoulder in a halfhearted shrug. "To tell you the truth, right now I'm kind of numb. I don't suppose it'll last, but I'll take what I can get."

The flatness of her voice made her sound as numb as she said she felt, and I wished to God I'd been able to save her. It took about a thousand wrong decisions on my part to put her in this situation, and I couldn't stop myself from mentally recalling and regretting each one.

"How about you?" Steph asked. "You looked pretty rough last night."

"I'm fine now," I answered, which was true as long as we

were talking only about my physical injuries. The emotional wounds left me in a state that was very far from fine.

Steph set her mug down on the bedside table, then lightly touched the back of Blake's hand. "Could you give us a few minutes alone?"

I could tell by the look on his face that Blake was reluctant to leave her side, but he sighed and nodded. "I'll be right outside if you need anything," he said. "Just give me a holler."

She managed a small smile. "I will."

He leaned over and kissed her forehead, like a father comforting a little girl, before he left the room, but I didn't think his affection for her was exactly paternal. Was it just his guilt over having failed her last night that made him act so devoted, or had he really formed such a quick, strong attachment?

"Come and sit down, Nikki," Steph beckoned.

I hadn't realized until that moment that I was hovering near the door as if ready to make a quick escape. It was almost impossibly hard to face my sister and be forced to see what had been done to her because of me. But she needed every ounce of support she could get, so I manned up and took Blake's place at the side of the bed. She reached out and took my hand, giving it a firm, comforting squeeze.

"I'll survive," she told me softly even as she squeezed my hand harder. "You know that, right?"

My throat ached so much I couldn't answer, and if I wasn't careful I was going to start bawling. Steph shouldn't need to comfort me after what she'd been through. I should be strong enough to hide my own pain and guilt, deal with it on my own rather than burdening her with it.

"I'm not as fragile as you think I am, Nikki," she said when I still couldn't force myself to speak. "It's going to be rough for a while, but I swear to you, I'm going to get over it."

I sucked in a breath, and it loosened my throat enough to let me speak. "I'm so sorry . . ."

Steph shook her head. "There was nothing you could have

done. This Alexis creep was never going to just let me go. You know that, don't you?"

Actually, I hadn't thought about it, about what he would have done if I'd gotten there on time. I had a suspicion Steph was right. Alexis wasn't what you'd call the honorable type, so expecting him to keep his word was wishful thinking. But having not made the rendezvous, I couldn't be sure. I guess I didn't look convinced, because Steph continued.

"Blake says Alexis wants you to track down a bunch of innocent people so he can slaughter them. Do you think for a moment that's what I'd have wanted you to do?"

I scrubbed at my eyes, wiping away the hint of tears that had gathered in them, wishing I could wipe away the aching exhaustion as easily. Obviously, Blake had done a lot of talking. And been very convincing. "No, of course not."

"I'd like to take you and Blake and knock both your heads together. The self-flagellation the two of you are doing is getting on my last nerve. Bad things happen to people, and unless you've got an infallible crystal ball, you aren't always going to be able to stop them. Just deal with it and move on, because let me tell you, knowing you're miserable about it doesn't help me one iota."

I flinched from the anger in her voice. The numbness appeared to be gone for now. "What do you want me to do? Smile and act like nothing's wrong? I'm not a good enough actress to pull that off."

"No," she replied with exaggerated patience, "I want you to stop wasting your time and energy feeling guilty about it and start figuring out how you're going to get the *son of a bitch who did this to me!*"

There was nothing I wanted to do more. The problem was, how do you "get" someone who's immortal? Unlike the Olympians, Anderson didn't have a bunch of indoctrinated Descendants sitting around waiting for the opportunity to kill a *Liberi.*

An idea struck me before I even managed to finish the thought. "The list," I murmured, not meaning to say it aloud.

"Huh?"

"Konstantin gave me a list of Descendants he wanted me to find. Maybe if I could find one of them, we can use him to kill Alexis." What a sweet irony it would be if the very list the Olympians gave me turned out to be the key to destroying Alexis! I'd enjoy rubbing his smug face in it, right before—

"Wait a minute," Steph interrupted before my thoughts could gallop too far ahead. "Your plan is to hunt down some random civilian who probably has no idea that the *Liberi* even exist, then . . . what, exactly? Hope he's a homicidal maniac who'll be happy to kill Alexis at your command? Or were you thinking of kidnapping him and forcing him to kill Alexis? Or maybe doing to him what this Emmitt character did to you, somehow *tricking* him into killing Alexis?"

Damn. Steph had a few too many good questions for my taste. I frowned. "I only came up with this idea like five seconds ago. Give me some time to work out the kinks. Besides, how else are we supposed to make Alexis pay for what he did? There's no other way to kill him."

"Who says you have to kill him? Blake told me you've been searching for a woman the Olympians have had interred for ten years. Why not give them a taste of their own medicine?"

There was a sense of poetic justice to the idea, except—

"If we bury him, somebody could dig him up someday just like we plan to dig up Emma." Assuming I could ever find her, which wasn't looking too likely. "I never thought of myself as bloodthirsty before, but I want that man dead."

"And the world would probably be a better place without him." Her voice softened. "But Nikki, you aren't a killer. I want Alexis to pay for what he did, but not at the price of putting a black mark on your soul."

I'd always suspected Steph was so damn nice because she'd had such an easy life. It's easy to be magnanimous toward others when everything is going your way, or at least that's what I'd thought. But here she was, being nice, worrying about the state of my soul after having been through a trauma worse than any I'd experienced. Maybe her niceness had nothing to do with her charmed life after all. Maybe it was just *her*.

"You can't possibly believe you're the only woman he's hurt," I said instead of voicing any of my true thoughts. "There's not a question in my mind that he deserves to die." *And killing him would make me feel so much better*, thought the woman who felt guilty about taking Jamaal's eye out. Maybe Steph had a point, but damned if I was going to admit it.

"So you're going to turn vigilante? Use your superpowers to hunt down the baddies one by one?"

She meant for me to respond to the vigilante comment—I guess it was supposed to shame me into seeing things her way—but I didn't want to argue with her, not now of all times. So I deflected the question.

"You're presuming I even have superpowers. I do seem to have acquired really good aim, but the hunting/tracking thing has been a total bust." Unless I counted finding the ring as part of my "superpowers," but that hadn't exactly turned out so well.

Despite her misery, there was a spark of interest in Steph's eyes. I suppose learning about the secret world that existed just beneath the surface of the ordinary one was a good way to distract herself from her present situation.

"How is the power supposed to work?" she asked.

"Beats me," I answered with a shrug. "I didn't get an instruction manual."

She gave me an exasperated look. "No kidding? What have you tried?"

I resisted the urge to give her another flippant answer. I couldn't do near as much as I wanted to help her, but I could at least talk to her and keep her mind occupied. "To tell you the truth, I'm not really sure *what* to try," I admitted. "I've approached the search just like I would if I were using my ordinary everyday skills and hoped I'd figure something out. So far, it hasn't worked. It's not like I've suddenly developed a hound's sense of smell or can tell which way someone went by a blade of broken grass."

Her brow furrowed in thought. "But you've always been good at finding things, even when you weren't *Liberi*. How did you do it?"

I waved her point off. "Yeah, I was good at it, but there was nothing supernatural about it. Like you said, I wasn't *Liberi*."

"But it seems unlikely it's a coincidence that you're descended from a goddess of the hunt and you've always been good at . . . well, hunting."

"I suppose," I said doubtfully.

"Remember that time back in high school when I lost my wallet?"

I frowned at the unexpected question. "Um, yeah. I guess." When we were kids, Steph had always been pretty bad about losing things, though it was a habit she'd outgrown. In fact, she'd lost enough stuff that I wasn't immediately sure which incident she was talking about.

"I was walking back from school and stopped at a coffee shop because a couple of my friends were in there."

I nodded, the memory sparking in my mind. "You got home and realized you didn't have your wallet. We retraced your steps back to the shop, assuming you must have left it there when you paid for your coffee."

"Right. Only it wasn't there."

We'd searched the place thoroughly, even asking the manager if we could look in the trash cans in case someone had found the wallet, taken all the good stuff, and thrown it away. We'd had no luck, and Steph had been in tears because she'd just gotten her first credit card. She was afraid her mom wouldn't let her replace it if she lost it so fast.

Steph was sure someone had stolen the wallet and it would

never be seen again. That seemed like a pretty logical conclusion, but I suggested that maybe she'd dropped it somewhere between the coffee shop and home.

We started walking back home, scanning the pavement and the gutters, although Steph wasn't exactly holding out much hope. When we still didn't find it, Steph gave up and went to her room, miserably waiting for her mom to get home and scold her for being so careless with her belongings.

On a hunch, I headed back out. I remember it was in the early spring, the kind of day where you need a coat in the morning but it's too hot to wear by afternoon. Steph had a habit of absently stuffing things in pockets—it seemed like half the things she lost turned up eventually in a pocket somewhere—and I thought it was possible she'd stuffed the wallet in her coat pocket after paying for her coffee. Because it was too hot to wear the coat, she'd have been carrying it over her arm, and it was possible the wallet had dropped out.

We'd checked the sidewalk carefully when we'd retraced her steps, but what if a Good Samaritan had found the wallet? This was D.C., not the kind of place you could leave a wallet lying around on the sidewalk for very long before someone helped themselves to it. That Good Samaritan would have either taken it with them in hopes of finding the owner—which might be hard, since the only identification in there was the credit card, and that gave nothing but a name—or handed it in to the closest shop.

It seemed like a long shot, but I didn't think it would hurt to check. Figuring the wallet would have fallen out pretty close to the coffee shop, I went into the tiny little shoe store a couple of doors down and asked if anyone had turned in a wallet—and wouldn't you know it, they had.

"How did you find that wallet?" Steph asked me.

"You know the story as well as I do."

"Not really. I wasn't inside your head, you know. Why did you decide to go into a shoe store that you knew I hadn't been in myself to look for the wallet I'd supposedly lost at the coffee shop?"

"Well, uh, it just seemed logical is all." But I had to admit, as sound as my logic had been, the shoe store hadn't exactly been a *likely* place to look.

"It was more logical to assume someone had walked off with it than to assume I'd put it in my coat pocket, that it had fallen out close to the coffee shop, that a Good Samaritan had found it, and that that Good Samaritan would turn it in at the shoe store. I'd given up, so why didn't you?"

I shrugged. "It was just a hunch is all," I said, unable to explain it better than that. I cracked a smile that felt fragile and tenuous. "Besides, I was trying to impress my big sister, and I wasn't going to do that by assuming the wallet was gone for good."

She returned the smile. "And do you have those same kind of hunches when you're searching for people that other investigators have been unable to find?"

"Well, yeah. But it's really just thinking a little outside the box. I figure everyone's tried the most likely places already, so I try to come up with someplace less immediately obvious."

"So have you had any hunches about where Emma is buried?"

I sighed. "Not really."

"Do you think she's buried at one of the properties you checked out?"

"Yeah, probably, but I have no idea which one."

She nodded sagely. "There are a million other places she could be. What makes you think she's at one of those properties?"

I saw what she was getting at, but I was far from convinced. "It's either a hunch, or it's wishful thinking because if she's somewhere else, I've got nothing. And even if it is a hunch, and even if my hunches are supernaturally fueled somehow, I don't have it narrowed down enough to matter."

"Yet."

I appreciated her faith in me, but honestly, I didn't exactly feel hopeful. Would Anderson still have his people protect

Steph if I turned out not to be able to find Emma? The warm, easygoing Anderson might, but I had my doubts about the cold, implacable leader who'd presided over this morning's tribunal. I told myself not to worry about that, but I didn't listen.

"I hope you're right," I told Steph. I had no idea if Blake had told her that she was under Anderson's protection only because I'd agreed to search for Emma. Even if *I* couldn't stop worrying about what would happen if I failed, there was no reason why *Steph* should worry, so I didn't elaborate.

"Big sisters are always right," she said with a grin.

I snorted. "You've been trying to convince me of that for years."

"Can't blame a girl for trying. Now I think it's time for you to stop coddling me and get back to work."

If she weren't so beat up already, I'd have given her a good smack on the arm for that. "I'm not coddling you!"

"You're hovering. I'm going to be fine. If I feel like I'm going to break down and need a shoulder to cry on other than Blake's, I'll come find you, okay?"

I knew I wasn't doing Steph any particular good by being at her bedside. Though I hid it fairly well—at least I thought I did—every time I caught sight of the bruises on her face, I suffered a hammer-strike of guilt. So I let her talk me into leaving her bedside no matter how convinced I was that I should have stayed.

I spent the rest of my afternoon at the desk in my suite, eyes glued to the computer screen as I tried not to think too much. I looked over all the information I had on the Olympian properties, searching for something I'd missed, something that might point me toward one choice over all the others. I also looked for some subconscious hint that one was more likely to be Emma's gravesite, but discovered it was really hard to *look* for a subconscious hint. My conscious mind kept yammering away at me, arguing logic and casting doubt, until I had to give up or go mad.

Hoping to clear my mind, I decided to take a different tack and did some research on Artemis. Maybe if I learned more about the goddess who was my ancestor—a concept I still had trouble wrapping my brain around—I'd be able to figure out how to use the powers I supposedly had.

I read through a lot of Greek and Roman mythology that afternoon, scouring the stories for something that might hint at a secret power I was missing. The only thing that rang anything like a bell with me was the fact that Artemis, aside from being a huntress, was also a goddess of the moon. It made me wonder if any of her descendants' powers were moon-based. If that were the case, then perhaps I'd been making a mistake by doing all of my investigating during the daylight hours.

I felt like I was grasping at straws. It seemed more likely that my newly enhanced aim was my only supernatural power. Then again, it had seemed more likely Steph's wallet had been stolen, but I'd gone with my gut all those years ago and my gut had been right.

I can't say I exactly got my hopes up. But I at least tried to keep something resembling a positive attitude as I gathered the paperwork for some of the most likely properties and mapped out a route I would travel tonight, after the moon had risen. A faint hope was better than no hope. Whether Anderson would kick me out if I failed or not, my position here would still be stronger if I somehow managed to find Emma. I would do anything in my power to strengthen my position and protect myself—and Steph—from the Olympians.

TWENTY-TWO

Sunset officially came around five that night, but it took half an hour more before most of us were gathered in the kitchen, which was near the back door that would lead us to the clearing where Jamaal's first execution would take place. Everyone was in a grim, nervous mood. Maybe I was being paranoid, but I felt like everyone except Maggie was giving me a mild version of the cold shoulder. They might not have been all one happy family before I came along, but they'd been a lot happier than they were now. I couldn't blame them for holding me at least partially responsible.

Someone had left a bunch of lanterns on the kitchen table—actual oil-fueled lanterns, not the Coleman variety. I picked one up because everyone else did, lighting it with the long-barreled lighter that was being passed around.

We were milling about, no one talking, when Logan stepped into the room.

"Head on out to the clearing," he told us. "We'll meet you there."

"We" apparently referred to Logan, Jamaal, and Anderson, because the rest of us were all present and accounted for. If anyone objected to being ordered around by Logan, they kept their mouths shut. Still tense and unnaturally quiet, we filed out the back door.

When I'd first arrived at the mansion, Maggie had given me a thorough tour of the house, but I'd never been out on the grounds. I had no idea where we were going. I glanced up at the sky as we walked, but though it was a clear night, the moon hadn't yet risen.

We walked past the nicely manicured garden that dominated the view from the kitchen windows, plunging into the woods behind it. The woods were as meticulously pruned as those that surrounded the driveway. Although we weren't following a path, it was a simple matter to slip between the trees without tripping on undergrowth.

It was an eerie sight, this silent procession of grim-faced *Liberi*. The lanterns barely penetrated the dark, and it was easy for the mind to imagine terrors that lay just beyond the reach of the lanterns' glow. Or maybe that was just me and my nerves. Except for that terrible night when I'd killed Emmitt, I'd never seen anyone die before, and though I knew Jamaal would not stay dead, I desperately wanted to run back to the house and hide in my room. But Anderson had been very clear this morning, and I knew I had to bear witness, just as the rest of the *Liberi* did. I might not feel like I was truly one of them, but just as I'd had to in my many foster homes, I had to go through the motions and pretend I belonged.

We walked what I estimated was about one hundred yards before the trees gave way to a perfectly circular clearing. Someone—probably Logan—had already set the stage. A double row of torches flickered just far enough from the edge of the trees to avoid being a fire hazard.

My heart leapt into my throat when I saw what was in the center of the clearing: a low wooden block with a semicircular notch carved into the top. I might have been able to convince myself it was a stool or something else innocuous, if it weren't for the huge sword, held upright in a black iron stand just to the left of it.

I swallowed hard and sweat trickled down my back despite the brisk temperature. Maggie had walked beside me the entire way, offering her silent moral support. I didn't think she'd completely gotten over the suspicions that awakened when I'd found Emma's ring, but she was still friendly, even if not as warm. I reached out to clutch her arm.

"Tell me that's not what I think it is," I hissed, too freaked out to speak above a whisper.

She spared me a sympathetic glance. "Sorry, no can do."

"They're going to cut his head off?" This time, my voice came out in something more like a squeal. Nausea roiled in my stomach at the thought of it.

Maggie patted my back in a gesture that might have been comforting if I'd been capable of being comforted. "It's a mercy," she said. "It'll be over too quickly for Jamaal to suffer any pain."

I swallowed again, hoping to keep my gorge down. Maybe it was a mercy for Jamaal, but it sure as hell wasn't one for me. I looked around at the other *Liberi*. Although everyone still looked grim, I seemed to be the only one close to passing out or hurling. Even Leo, with his mild-mannered accountant look, didn't seem particularly disturbed by what was about to happen.

"We are none of us young, nor have we led sheltered lives," Maggie said, correctly reading the expression on my face as usual. "We've seen horrors you wouldn't believe, especially those of us who were Olympians for a time."

I took a deep breath, wishing it would settle my nerves. "How the hell can he survive being beheaded?"

"He can't. That's the point."

"You know what I mean!" I snapped, nerves making my temper brittle.

Luckily, Maggie wasn't put off by my snappishness. "It's magic, Nikki. I don't know exactly *how* he'll come back. All I know is that he will."

I was saved from further embarrassing myself when Anderson entered the clearing, closely followed by Blake and Jamaal. Jamaal held his head up proudly, no flicker of emotion on his face when he caught sight of the block and the sword. If he was afraid, he was hiding it well.

I expected speeches and ceremony, but Anderson merely joined our silent ranks while Logan gestured Jamaal to the block. Jamaal scanned the assembled *Liberi* and caught my eyes. I wanted to look away, too squeamish to deal with what I was about to witness—and too afraid of his continued anger. I managed to hold on to my courage and meet his gaze.

"I'm sorry," he said, so softly that I only understood him by reading his lips. I suspected that apology was harder for him than his actual punishment.

I doubted I'd completely won him over, but I believed the apology was sincere, so I nodded at him in acceptance. He held my gaze a moment longer, then knelt before the block without having to be prompted. Holding on to the block with both hands, he laid his neck in the notch. Logan bent over and brushed Jamaal's braids to the side, baring his neck. Then he grabbed the sword.

Maggie reached over and took my sweaty hand, giving it a reassuring squeeze, for which I was absurdly grateful.

"When you're ready," Logan said to Jamaal, "let go of the block and put your hands to your sides."

Logan held the sword in both hands, poised to strike, while Jamaal took a deep breath. The moment Jamaal's hands moved, I shut my eyes tightly. Anderson had insisted I be present for this, but he couldn't force me to actually *watch*.

I heard the whistle of the blade as it sliced through the air, then the wet thunk as it made contact, then the soft, sympathetic gasps of the onlookers. They might not be as squeamish as me about it, and they might have seen worse horrors during their long lives, but they weren't completely hardened. That made me feel better even as the wind carried the scent of blood to my nose.

"It's over," Maggie whispered to me. She was still holding my hand, a very welcome anchor.

"Good," I said, but I didn't open my eyes. I knew without a doubt that I would hurl if I did.

The light behind my closed eyelids grew dimmer, and at first I was afraid I was about to pass out. Then I realized someone was dousing the torches.

"I'll stay with him until he revives," Logan was saying, and I heard the gathered *Liberi* starting to stir.

I was tempted to let Maggie lead me out of the clearing without ever opening my eyes, but at the last moment, morbid curiosity got the better of me. Still sure the sight was going to make me hurl, I opened my eyes.

There was a lot of blood, though with the torches doused that blood was black enough I could pretend it was just pools of shadow. Logan had laid Jamaal out on his back, placing the head right up against the neck so that I could almost believe the two were attached.

"He'll heal," Maggie reminded me yet again, giving my arm a little pull.

I turned away and followed her back to the house, my stomach unsettled, but so far under control. Despite everything I knew about the *Liberi,* I would have to see Jamaal up and walking around before I could fully believe he could survive beheading.

The moon was just beginning to rise as Maggie and I headed toward the kitchen. If I were following the plan I'd made during the afternoon, I'd immediately get in my car and go visit a couple of properties. Instead, I made a cup of coffee and parked myself in the kitchen. Logan and Jamaal would almost certainly come back this way when Jamaal was healed. Then, once I'd seen with my own two eyes that he was still alive, I'd be able to concentrate on my hunt enough to have a hope of success.

I sat in that kitchen, drinking coffee and waiting, for more than three hours. I don't know how many times I halfway convinced myself to go back out to the clearing and see what was going on, but every time I made it to the back door, I changed my mind. If something had gone wrong, if Jamaal was truly dead against all expectations, I didn't want to know about it until I absolutely had to. There comes a point when you just can't deal with any more shocks, and I had passed that point a long time ago.

I was so wired on caffeine that I jumped and spilled my coffee when I heard the back door open. Lucky for me, the coffee had gone cold as I held it and stared off into space, so I didn't burn myself. I put the mug down on the table, then dried my wet hand on the leg of my jeans as I stood up and listened to the approaching footsteps.

Logan went by first, the sword belted to his side, though I'd seen no sign of the scabbard earlier. He gave me an unfathomable look as he passed by, not stopping for a friendly conversation. He'd voted to expel Jamaal, but I got the feeling he resented me for putting him in the role of executioner—though maybe that was just my own guilt speaking.

Jamaal did not look good, though he looked far better than he had the last time I'd seen him. A bloody, bruised scar circled his neck where his head had somehow reattached itself to his body, and there was dried blood caked in his hair and on his shirt. More dried blood mixed with dirt speckled his face, and behind that blood his skin was unnaturally pale.

He came to a stop when he saw me, swaying on his feet and grabbing onto the doorjamb to steady himself. I took a couple of steps forward. Maybe I was a fool to dismiss him as a threat because of his current condition, but it was obvious from the tightness at the corners of his eyes that he was still in pain, and I knew from personal experience how weak the supernatural healing made you.

"Do you need a hand?" I asked him, because even if I didn't feel threatened at the moment, I didn't think touching him without his permission was the best idea in the world.

His eyes widened at the suggestion, and he swayed a little more. I hoped he wasn't about to fall down, because I knew for a fact I wasn't strong enough to get him back up if he did.

"Thanks," he said, and he didn't even sound sarcastic. "I think I need a rest before I tackle the stairs."

Why Logan wasn't helping him was anyone's guess, since it was clear he was still in bad shape. Maybe he was in Logan's doghouse, though why Logan should get mad on my account or even on Steph's, I didn't know. I'd had only the briefest interactions with him since we'd met, and as far as I knew, he'd never even set eyes on Steph.

Doing my best to ignore the blood, I draped Jamaal's arm over my shoulders and supported him to the nearest chair. He was built of solid muscle, and the operation would have been a heck of a lot easier if I were bigger and stronger—like, say, Logan. However, I managed to get him into the chair without either of us going down in a heap. He closed his eyes and breathed hard from the exertion. He'd probably have been better off lying out in the clearing for a little longer, though I supposed that would have been cold and unpleasant.

"Would you like a cup of coffee?" I asked. "I made way more than I should drink."

He opened his eyes, frowning in puzzlement. "Why are you trying to help me? You of all people . . ."

What could I say? To properly explain, I'd have to lay out my life's history, and I wasn't about to do that. Instead, I shrugged in what I hoped looked like a casual manner.

"I'm not the type to hold a grudge. If you'd intended Steph harm, that would be one thing, but I know you didn't believe me."

"I intended *you* harm." His expression was almost challenging, although I heard no hint of threat in his voice. It occurred to me that he wasn't very used to people being nice to him or forgiving him and that he was looking for some hidden motive.

"Well, I took out your eye, and you just got your head chopped off, so I think that makes us even. Now do you want some coffee or not?"

He opened his mouth to say something, then shook his head like he'd changed his mind. "Yes. Thanks. Black."

I poured him a mug of the now rather stale coffee, then set it on the table in front of him. That should have been the end of our conversation. After all, I had a plan for the evening, and through the kitchen window I could see the moon, almost full, gleaming in the clear night sky. It was a perfect night for me to go hunting if the moon would indeed help me in some way. Yet I couldn't just walk out and leave Jamaal sitting here by himself. Not in the condition he was in. I wasn't sure how he would make it downstairs without falling and breaking his neck— again. So I pulled out a chair and joined him at the table.

Jamaal raised an eyebrow at me, and despite the dried blood and the unnatural pallor of his face, I noticed again how amazingly attractive he was when he wasn't scowling or frothing at the mouth. He'd be devastating if he ever smiled, which I suspected he hadn't done often even before Emmitt's death.

"I'm going to ask Anderson to . . . give you a stay of execution, for lack of a better term." The words came out of my mouth without any conscious thought behind them, so that I was almost as startled by them as Jamaal was. I avoided his gaze, staring instead at the coffee I had no intention of drinking. "You've been through enough already." I wasn't just thinking about tonight's ordeal, either.

"Don't bother."

I looked up again, unable to interpret the tone of his voice. The words sounded brusque, but he wasn't giving me the evil eye.

"It wouldn't do any good," he continued. "He's not going to reverse his decision. He can't without looking weak."

I snorted. "No one who's known him for more than five seconds would think he's weak."

I might have been imagining things, but I think one corner of Jamaal's mouth twitched a bit, as if he'd been considering the possibility of trying on a small smile for size.

"All right, weak was the wrong word. But he's already given me a second chance by not banishing me. If he went any easier on me, it would set a bad precedent. I'll take my medicine, and I won't complain about it. I might not have known your sister would get hurt, but I *did* know Anderson had forbidden me to hurt you, and I did it anyway. I'm not a victim."

He had a point, but considering how many times I'd lashed out at people in my life, I wasn't in any position to throw stones. "I'm so sorry about Emmitt," I blurted, then tensed for Jamaal's inevitable hostility.

There was a glint of anger in his eyes, and the muscles of his jaw worked, but he didn't leap across the table at me. That was an impressive amount of progress, as far as I was concerned.

"I know you still don't really believe me," I said, figuring I might as well spit out the whole apology while Jamaal was weakened enough not to attack me, "but I swear to you, it was an accident. I'm not a killer." The idea was so ridiculous it was all I could do not to laugh. Then I remembered my earlier insistence that Alexis had to die, and it wasn't so funny anymore. "Did you know that when I shot Blake, I actually apologized to him before I ran?"

This time, the twitch in Jamaal's lips was more obvious. Not quite enough to be a real smile, but a hint that he did know how. "He did mention that."

"Well, does that sound like the act of a cold-blooded killer to you?"

He sipped his coffee, thinking about it. "If you're actually one of Konstantin's pets, then it would all be part of your act. Even talking to me now, trying to disarm me—it's all the role you've taken on for the mission."

Gone was the fury and malice he'd shown me time and time again, but somehow his words stung more delivered calmly and at a reasonable volume. Stupid to have hurt feelings over it, I know. What he said was completely true, and he had no reason not to believe I was Konstantin's spy.

"I'm going to find Emma," I told him. My resolve strengthened, and I glanced out the kitchen window at the moon. I wasn't sure how much time I had before it disappeared from view, but the more time I spent here sitting around, the less time I'd have to look for Emma while its light lasted.

"I hope you do, but that won't really prove anything—except that Konstantin's desperate enough to get a spy inside that he's willing to give up Emma."

My shoulders slumped. "So what you're saying is there's no way you're ever going to believe me, no matter what I do." It shouldn't matter so much. *I* knew I hadn't killed Emmitt on purpose. What did it matter if Jamaal thought the worst of me? And yet, it *did* matter to me. His suspicions had never bothered me when he was acting like a raving lunatic, but they were a lot harder to take now, when for the first time he seemed completely rational. Either I'm pathetically needy and desperate for approval, or I was just making the logical assumption that my life would be a lot simpler and more pleasant if Jamaal weren't seeing everything I did from behind a veil of suspicion. I tried to convince myself it was the latter.

"Only time will tell," he answered. "But I promise I won't act against you again without proof."

I had the uncomfortable suspicion that his definition of proof and my own weren't quite the same. However, he was making what was for him a big concession, and that had to be a step in the right direction.

I sighed. "Finish up your coffee. Then I'll help you get downstairs."

"I don't need your help."

I pushed back my chair with a huff of exasperation. "Fine. Be that way. Just try not to crack your skull open when your legs give out and you fall down the stairs."

"I'll do my best," he promised gravely. If I didn't know better, I'd have sworn he was teasing me.

Leaving him to his overblown sense of male pride, I headed up to my room to grab the list of properties I planned to explore tonight.

TWENTY-THREE

The moon was one night short of being full, but it was large and bright enough that I could see pretty well even without the aid of streetlights. The first property on my list was a gated monstrosity at least as large as Anderson's mansion. It belonged to Konstantin, and he'd obviously modeled the thing on a palace. I'd have stopped to take a closer look, but even this late at night, the place was brightly lit and well-guarded. When I'd been by during the daytime, there'd been just enough traffic on the street that I could drive past multiple times without fearing I'd be noticed, but the same could not be said now.

I drove by without slowing down, though I kept my eye out for any neon signs saying "Emma is here" that the moon's light might reveal. There were none. I was pretty sure my gut instinct said this was not where Emma was buried. But it was hard to know if that was really my gut speaking, or if it was influenced by my rational mind, which said there was no way in hell I was going to be able to sneak in there and find the grave even if it was the right place.

My next likely candidate was another mansion in Chevy Chase, this one belonging to Alexis. It wasn't quite on the scale of Anderson's or Konstantin's homes, but it was still huge, the grounds vast enough to hold an entire graveyard's worth of bodies. The place even had a large man-made—I assumed— pond in the backyard.

An ornate gate blocked the driveway, but unlike Konstantin's place, there was no wall or fence to keep out people on foot. That didn't mean the grounds were unprotected. The security cameras were well hidden, but I had too much experience with surveillance not to spot them. Again, I drove by without stopping. The cameras might be set up on motion sensors, only photographing people who tried to pass across the borders of the property, but if any faced the road recording a continuous feed, I didn't want to be captured on them acting in any way suspicious.

It was as I was driving away that I felt my first gut-level hunch, one that told me Emma was on that property somewhere. The sensation was so strong, it took some willpower not to slam on the brakes. My pulse sped up, and my palms started to sweat.

Was this a real hunch? Or did some part of me want Emma to be on Alexis's property so I could really stick it to him by sneaking her out from under his nose?

I let out a little growl of frustration. I had no way of knowing for sure.

I checked out the next three properties on my list, trying my best to listen to my instincts without consciously influencing them. Although all of the other properties would have been considerably easier to explore than Alexis's, I didn't feel any sudden piques of interest. My pulse remained steady, and if I'd had to venture a guess, I'd have said Emma wasn't at any of them.

The moon had disappeared behind a bank of clouds by the time I drove by Alexis's mansion the second time. I still had the vague feeling that it was the right place, but there was no quickening of my pulse this time, and I felt no instinctive reluctance to drive by without stopping. Either my reaction the first time had been a fluke, or it had been strengthened by the light of the moon.

Unsure whether or not I'd made any progress, I headed back to Anderson's and vowed to check it out again tomorrow night.

The next day, I spent many hours digging up every scrap of information I could find on Alexis's home: survey maps, floor plans, work permits, going as far back as I could find. I was even able to find out some details about the security setup, having identified the security company involved. They wouldn't tell me anything about the specific setup at Alexis's home, of course—I didn't even ask, or I would have immediately flagged myself as a suspicious character. Instead, I described a fictional property that bore a non-coincidental resemblance to Alexis's and asked for suggestions on how they would help me set up security.

Based on what I learned, and on the information I was able to dig up—illegally, I must admit—on Alexis's financial transactions, I made an educated guess as to which security measures he had in place. It seemed likely that the cameras I'd spotted in the trees were indeed motion-activated. There was probably a security center somewhere in the house, complete with a guard who monitored the cameras. However, it was unlikely that triggering the cameras would trip any kind of alarm. The area around Alexis's home was heavily wooded, and thus full of deer. If an alarm sounded every time a deer passed a camera, it would get old fast.

So, there was definitely security on the grounds, but it wasn't exactly impenetrable. The house itself was likely another story, but if I needed to get in *there* to dig Emma up, I'd have a whole new set of problems.

That evening, Jamaal was executed again. It was a hanging this time, much less gory than the beheading. I'd been relieved when I first saw the noose, thinking that this would be an easier death to witness, but I'd been wrong. It was less gruesome—but it took Jamaal longer to die, and I found his suffering bothered me more than the gore.

Once again, Logan stayed out in the clearing, waiting for Jamaal to revive. And once again, I found myself unable to leave the house on my quest until I'd confirmed that Jamaal was alive.

The one bright spot was that it took Jamaal less time to heal the damage from being hanged, and he and Logan returned to the house less than an hour after the execution. Jamaal was just as exhausted, however, and when I offered him a cup of coffee, he gladly accepted. His eyes were sunken, his cheeks hollow, as he wrapped his hands around the mug and sipped. Physically, he was healing, but I feared the ordeal was putting scars on his soul. That is to say, *more* scars—I knew without having to be told that he had plenty of them already.

"If I didn't know any better," he said, "I'd think you were worried about me."

I forced something approximating a wry grin. "I've been told I'm a bleeding heart. There's some truth in the accusation."

He cocked his head, the movement causing the beads to rattle and click. "You know I still suspect you."

"Yeah, I know. I also know that it wouldn't take much to 'prove' to you that I'm Konstantin's bitch. I still think you've suffered more than enough already."

For the first time, he smiled. It wasn't a big smile, but he didn't try to fight the expression off, either. And I was right. Despite the haunted eyes and hollow cheeks, the smile was devastating. My hormones woke from their long sleep and danced a jig at the sight, and I suppressed a groan. Jamaal was *not* a man I should be attracted to, no matter how tasty he looked. He thought I was a spy, a traitor who had murdered his friend. He'd threatened me and attacked me, and because of him my sister had been brutalized. Not to mention that he was a descendant of a death goddess and borderline crazy. No smile, no matter how devastating, could erase any of that.

"You really are a bleeding heart, aren't you?" he asked.

"Either that, or I play one on T.V."

The smile made another cameo appearance, but faded even more quickly. "You might want to skip tomorrow night's . . . festivities, then. If you can."

"Why?" I held my breath, already knowing I wouldn't like the answer.

"Logan's going to choose something heinous for the grand finale."

As far as I was concerned, what I'd seen so far was more than heinous enough. Then again, I wasn't descended from some Germanic war god, like Logan was.

"Why?" I asked again. "This whole punishment is barbaric enough as it is. Why would he want to make it worse?"

"Because it's not just about punishing me for disobeying Anderson's orders. It's about giving me a way to prove that I'm committed in spite of what I've done. The more I have to go through to win the privilege of staying, the more Anderson— and all the rest—will believe I'm determined to control myself, which I've done a shitty job of doing since Emmitt . . ." His voice faded as grief clouded his eyes.

Impulsively, I reached out and laid my hand over his, wishing I could bring Emmitt back.

During the last couple of days, Jamaal and I seemed to have reached a truce, but that truce only went so far. Jamaal glared and I jerked my hand away, my cheeks heating with a blush.

"Sorry," I mumbled, wishing the floor would swallow me. What had come over me? Just because we weren't currently at war with each other didn't mean we were friends. I pushed my chair away from the table, suddenly desperate to flee the room.

"Do you need any help getting downstairs?" I asked without looking at him.

"No."

It was the answer I'd expected, and I left the kitchen at a pace just short of a run.

For tonight's excursion, I dressed all in black, because I'd be getting out of my car and skulking around, not just driving by. The more inconspicuous I could make myself, the better.

The full moon rode the sky like a beacon, only the occasional thin cloud dimming its light. If my powers were moon-based at all, tonight they would be at their peak, and I had to take advantage of them as best I could. I drove straight to Alexis's home, the instinct to search there too strong to deny.

Of course, I couldn't just pull up in front and leave my car in full view while I went exploring on foot, so I drove around until I found a church with a convenient parking lot. My car looked uncomfortably conspicuous in the otherwise empty lot, and I had to walk the better part of a mile to get back to Alexis's house, but it was the best I could do.

I'd packed a bunch of odds and ends that might be useful—including my gun and my cell phone—in a light black backpack, which I slung over my shoulders as I began the trek that I still worried was a waste of time. The temperature was on its way down to freezing. I wished I'd worn something warmer than lightweight black fleece, and I walked at a pace just short of a jog to keep my teeth from chattering.

It was a long, tense, freezing walk. On foot in a ritzy neighborhood, dressed all in black and carrying a gun in my backpack, I didn't dare let anyone see me, so anytime I caught sight of headlights in the distance, I took cover.

By the time I reached the fringes of Alexis's property, I was sweaty beneath my fleece, although my cheeks stung and burned from the cold wind and I shivered with chills. I was struck again by the certainty that Emma was here somewhere, the feeling stronger than ever. Unfortunately, "somewhere" wasn't going to do me much good. We couldn't dig up the whole place searching for her, so I was going to have to narrow it down.

Crouching in the darkness, I opened my backpack and pulled out a smooth black rock, small enough to fit in the palm of my hand, but heavy enough to be an effective weapon. Despite the clear sky, the wind whistled briskly through the trees, taking the wind chill down to arctic levels—and giving me a little cover. I waited for a particularly energetic gust of wind, then slung my stone at the nearest security camera.

My aim was, of course, dead-on, though I'd packed extra rocks in my backpack just in case. The blow from the rock didn't break the camera—that was likely to bring someone out to investigate—but it bent the mounting enough to point the camera away from my intended path, creating a blind spot. If someone had been watching at the moment my stone hit, they might still come to investigate—but they would more likely think the wind was responsible and not want to venture out into the cold.

Taking a deep breath for courage, I slipped past the camera and onto Alexis's property.

TWENTY-FOUR

My instincts were still insisting that Emma was nearby. Unfortunately, I wasn't having much luck convincing those instincts to tell me *where*.

At first, I stuck to the woods that bounded Alexis's property, not because I felt it likely Emma was buried there, where roots would have made digging difficult, but because it was easier to stay hidden. I traipsed through those woods for at least forty-five minutes, having no idea what I was looking for but hoping to God I'd recognize it when I saw it.

No luck. If Emma was buried in the woods, I lacked the power to find her.

I turned my attention to the gardens and lawns that surrounded the house on all sides. There weren't any lights on in the house, so it was likely no one would see me if I ventured out from the cover of the trees. Still, I hesitated to do it. I'd seen what Alexis had done to Steph, and he'd been interrupted before he could finish. If he caught me trespassing on his property . . . He might still technically have an agreement with Anderson, but I doubted that would protect me.

I squatted behind a bush at the very edge of the tree line, trying to work up the courage to break cover. The cloud cover was growing thicker as the temperature continued to drop. There were moments when the moon disappeared from view, and I worried that soon the patchy clouds would turn into a heavy overcast. If I had any moon-driven powers, and if those powers depended on actually being able to see the moonlight, they'd better hurry up and make themselves known to me.

I was gnawing my lip indecisively when a flicker of movement off to my right made me jump and gasp. I was frantically trying to unzip my backpack before I'd even finished turning toward the sound, cursing myself for not having the gun in my hand already. Then I saw the doe picking her way through the underbrush and almost laughed myself silly.

My heart was racing, my breath coming short and steaming in the frosty air. I sat down on the cold ground, putting a hand to my heart, waiting for the flood of adrenaline to fade.

Braver than I, the doe ventured out of the woods and onto the outskirts of the manicured lawn. She paused briefly to look at the house, as if assuring herself that the coast was clear, then set off toward the man-made pond at a brisk, elegant trot. Still waiting for my heart rate to return to something resembling normal, I watched her progress and felt reassured by the lack of alarms, blaring lights, or barking dogs. My fear of venturing out from the woods was just a side effect of stretched-taut nerves.

The doe reached the shore of the pond, and stood poised there for a long moment. Her head turned in my direction, until I could have sworn she was looking me straight in the eye. The light of the moon limned her with silver, giving her an ethereal look. I shivered as I remembered that Artemis was often depicted with a deer by her side. Was the animal even real?

The doe quit staring at me and bent her head to drink from the pond. And suddenly, for no reason I could point a finger at, I knew. Emma was in the pond. Not buried, as Konstantin had claimed, but drowned. Tossing her into the water, weighted down with chains, required a lot less effort than digging a grave and burying her. I wondered if the magic of the *Liberi* caused her to revive on a regular basis, and then drown again. I shuddered away from the thought, which was too horrible to contemplate.

All right—I finally had a strong hunch where Emma was. It was based on absolutely zero empirical evidence, and no matter how strong my hunch, I wouldn't be shocked to find out it was wrong. However, the only way to confirm I was right was to take a dip in the pond. The prospect was far from inviting. The water would be freezing, and while the pond was relatively small and probably not very deep, it would take a significant amount of swimming to check the whole thing. All the while out in the open and defenseless against attack.

Slowly, carefully, I edged back into the full cover of the woods. If Emma really was in that pond, I would need help getting her out. I was less certain of her location than I'd have liked to be, but I figured now was a good time to call Anderson and share my theory. Obviously, he knew more about the *Liberi* and their powers than I did. If my evidence was enough to convince him that Emma was in the pond, then I'd feel a lot more confident that I wasn't just imagining things. And if I wasn't just imagining things, then it was time to call in the cavalry and get Emma out of here.

About forty minutes later, I was so numb from cold I felt like I might have frozen in place. That's when Anderson appeared suddenly and without warning at my side. I about had a heart attack, and a strangled scream escaped my throat as I backed hastily away and tripped over an exposed tree root, landing on my butt.

Like me, he was dressed all in black, with a black knit hat pulled low over his forehead. Hard to spot in the dark, for sure, but I should have seen *something*.

He grinned down at me, apparently enjoying the spectacle I'd made of myself. "It's just me."

I closed my eyes and sucked in a deep breath, searching for calm. How had he just appeared out of thin air like that? Emmitt and Jamaal had both pulled similar stunts, and I'd assumed it was an ability unique to *Liberi* who had death magic. Then again, no one seemed to know who Anderson's divine ancestor was, so perhaps he was himself a descendant of a death god, though apparently an obscure one if no one recognized his glyph.

I opened my eyes and glared up at him. "You're lucky I managed to swallow that scream," I told him. "This expedition could have been over before it started, all because you felt like being a comedian." Probably no one would have heard me if I'd screamed—I'd told Anderson to meet me in the woods at the property line, right near the realigned camera—but it was the principle of the thing.

Still grinning, he reached out a hand to help me up. "I didn't mean to startle you. I kind of forgot I was in stealth mode until it was too late."

I brushed dead leaves and pine needles from the seat of my pants. I wasn't sure I believed him, but I didn't suppose it much mattered. I glanced into the woods behind him, but saw no other lurking *Liberi*.

"You didn't bring any backup?" I asked incredulously. When he'd put enough faith in my hunch to agree to come himself, I'd assumed he'd bring at least a couple of his other people in case this turned into a fight.

"It's easier to be sneaky with just two of us," he responded, and I knew at once he was lying, maybe just because it was such a lame explanation.

I gave him a hard look. "What aren't you telling me?"

The look Anderson gave me in return was just as hard. "Things you don't need to know," he said, and took a step forward as if he thought the conversation was over.

I grabbed his arm. "Hey, if I'm putting my butt on the line for you, I deserve full disclosure before I go charging in there." The sneaking about I'd been doing so far had no doubt been dangerous, but not half so dangerous as an actual attempt to extract Emma from the water. Assuming she was even there.

Anderson twitched his arm out of my grip. "Come help me, or go back to the house. It's your choice." He plunged forward again without a backward glance.

Common sense told me to get the heck out of there. I couldn't begin to guess what Anderson was hiding, but chances were it was going to come back and bite me in the butt. That's just the way my life works.

But common sense and I haven't been on speaking terms for a while now, so instead of trekking back to the car and heading for safety, I followed Anderson deeper into the woods. When I caught up to him, I adjusted our course so we'd come out as close to the pond as possible.

We paused for a while when we came to the edge of the woods, both peering into the heavy darkness left by the moon's disappearance. Still no lights on in the house. It would be pretty funny, in a sick sort of way, if after all this fearful skulking around, it turned out that Alexis wasn't even home.

"Any idea where to start looking?" Anderson asked me as he sat on the ground and started unlacing his boots.

"What are you doing?"

"I don't plan to swim in my hiking boots." He pulled off one boot, along with the sock, then started working on the other one.

"That water has got to be freezing!" I protested, and I meant it literally. Even in the darkness, I could see the thin crust of ice that was forming along the shore.

"You think I can get her out of the water without getting wet?" Off came the second boot, followed by his utilitarian black jacket. "The clothes won't keep me warm if they're wet, and I'd rather have something dry to put on when I get out."

The thought of setting even a toe in that water made my teeth chatter, but of course he was right. And unlike a normal human being, he wouldn't die of hypothermia.

"Of course, I'm not exactly looking forward to it," he continued, pulling his sweatshirt off over his head, "so if you can give me a general idea where to look, I'd appreciate it."

I know I've said before that Anderson is rather unprepossessing, but seeing his nicely muscled chest and sculpted shoulders made me rethink the assessment. Then he slipped out of his jeans, leaving himself naked except for a pair of black briefs that clung very attractively in all the right places. I decided I hadn't just been wrong, I'd been *dead* wrong. Without the camouflage of his scruffy, unflattering wardrobe, he was very nice to look at indeed.

Which was *so* not what I needed to be noticing right now.

The surprising view had momentarily distracted me, and I all but smacked myself in the head to get my brain working again and remember what he'd asked me. I glanced at the pond, trying to listen to my gut in case it had a message for me, but there was nothing. The clouds had thickened enough to hide the moon, and even the certainty that Emma was in there had faded with its light. I was going to be completely mortified if I made Anderson swim around in that frigid water for nothing.

"Maybe if you go in where I saw the deer?" I suggested doubtfully. The second thoughts were pounding at me now, telling me this was the stupidest idea I'd ever had. I only came looking for Emma on Alexis's property because I wanted him to be the one who had her, and I was making an awful lot out of the fact that I saw a deer take a drink from the pond. It was probably a popular watering hole for the local herds, and what I'd seen had been nothing remotely supernatural.

"As good a guess as any," Anderson said, already beginning to shiver in the cold. "Show me where."

What confidence I'd had was now completely shot, and I wanted to tell Anderson to forget it, that I'd been wrong and we should just get out of here and go somewhere warm and safe. But I knew he wouldn't listen to me even if I said it. If there was a chance he would find his Emma in that pond, then he'd take it, no matter how slim the chance might be, or how unreliable the source.

I visualized watching the deer cross the lawn to the pond, homing in on the spot she'd paused to take her drink, then hesitantly stepped out from the cover of the woods. My entire body was tense, expecting against all reason that Alexis was going to jump out from behind a bush somewhere and attack. I did my best to fight the feeling off as I led Anderson to the spot where I'd seen the deer.

I'd have felt a lot surer of myself if there were some nice, clear hoofprints in the mud, but of course there were none to be seen. Had I imagined the deer? Or had it been a supernatural creature, one that didn't leave prints?

I gestured at the general area, giving Anderson a helpless shrug, feeling like a fool.

"All right," he said, stepping to the edge of the pond. I felt a little better about the possibly imaginary deer when I saw that Anderson wasn't leaving footprints in the mud, either. As he eased his way into the water, wincing at the cold, I reached out and touched the ground, finding it frozen solid. I should have guessed as much. The film of ice around the water's edge had visibly spread since we'd first peeked out of the woods.

Anderson took a series of quick, deep breaths, preparing himself for the shock of cold. Then he dove forward into the icy water and disappeared beneath its surface.

Twenty-five

I stood on the shore of the pond, chilled down to my bones in sympathy for Anderson as I watched the ripples from his dive glide over the glassy-smooth surface. With the full moon hidden, the only light came from the ambient glow of the nearby city. It was enough that I didn't feel completely blind, but I was uncomfortably aware of the blackness of the shadows—shadows that could hide anything.

Figuring a little paranoia might be healthy under the circumstances, I put my backpack down and rooted through it until I found my gun. I pointed the gun at the ground and kept my finger off the trigger, remembering how badly I'd been startled earlier by the deer. It wouldn't do for me to fire blindly out of startled reflex if another deer made an appearance.

Anderson's head broke the water at the center of the pond. Immediately, steam rose from his skin. The shadows hid his expression, and I didn't dare call out to him. He dove again after a few quick breaths, his feet flashing up into the air as he went straight down.

Did that mean he'd found her? If he was still looking, he should be swimming forward, not straight down. Right? I held my breath in anticipation. It was all I could do not to cross my fingers like a superstitious child.

He stayed down a long time, long enough for me to worry that something had gone wrong. For all I knew, the Olympians had pet monsters that lived in the bottoms of ponds. I had yet to fully embrace the magic I'd already witnessed, and I'd been slow to ponder what my newfound knowledge of the supernatural meant to the rest of my narrow view of the world. I shifted uneasily from foot to foot, hoping like hell he would hurry up and surface before I felt obligated to go in after him.

Moments later, he bobbed to the surface once more, sucking in a great gasp of air. I opened my mouth to call out to him, too curious now to worry about who else might hear me, but before a sound left my throat, I was blinded by a bolt of lightning, traveling horizontally across the lawn.

The lightning hit the surface of the pond, and I heard Anderson's strangled cry of pain. The residual energy of the bolt lifted me off my feet and tossed me onto my back. The gun fell from my fingers as I hit the ground, and a clap of thunder resonated so loud it sent a spike of pain through my head.

Woozy, blind, and deaf, I retained just enough brain cells to know holding still was a bad idea. I rolled over until I got my feet under me, then broke into a stumbling run, having no idea where I was going. I could have run straight into the icy water, but, for once, luck was on my side, and I managed to stay on the smooth, grassy lawn.

My hair rose on end, and I instinctively dove forward just in time. The next lightning bolt struck the ground just a few yards away. I clapped my hands over my ears to dull the roar of the thunder as I squeezed my eyes tightly shut. I was close enough to the point of impact that the electricity in the air made my heart beat erratically, but at least it *was* beating.

Once again, I forced myself to my feet. Even through my closed lids, the flash had been hell on my night vision. However, I could see just well enough to point myself toward the trees before I started running again.

A third bolt incinerated a tree seconds after I made it into the cover of the woods. The concussion knocked me down to my hands and knees, but I was up and running again in a fraction of a second. There were no further bolts as I zigzagged through the trees, slowing my pace just enough to keep from tripping over roots and sprawling on my face.

My ears popped and my vision started to clear—not that I could see much in the darkness. But the return of my physical senses signaled the return of my higher reasoning as well. If *I* couldn't see in this darkness, then probably my enemies couldn't, either. However, they *could* hear me crashing headlong through the underbrush. My flight was making me more conspicuous rather than less so.

I forced myself to slow down, sucking in one calming breath after another. I hadn't caught even a glimpse of our attacker, but since Alexis was a descendant of Zeus, it seemed a logical conclusion that he was the one who'd thrown the lightning bolts. And, while the bolt in the water wouldn't have killed Anderson—at least, not permanently—it would certainly have disabled him for a while.

Anderson's "treaty" with the Olympians obviously wasn't anything close to bulletproof. Perhaps Alexis had only been taking advantage of a perceived loophole when he attacked Steph, and the treaty itself was still nominally in place. Maybe that treaty meant Alexis would fish Anderson out of the water, then let him go. But though I'd been forced to retreat, there was no way I was going to abandon Anderson and hope for the best.

Of course, I wasn't sure what use I was to Anderson in the current situation. My gun lay abandoned on the lawn somewhere, and though I'd have loved to call for help—for the backup Anderson had failed to bring with him, the idiot!—my cell phone was in the backpack at the edge of the pond.

I stopped for a moment to think, listening intently for any sounds of pursuit. The only sound I heard was the wind whistling through the branches above. No doubt Alexis thought I'd done the sensible thing and run for my life.

It was hard to get my bearings in the depths of the darkened woods, but I'd always had a pretty good sense of direction. I relied on that sense of direction now as I attempted to steer myself back toward the security camera I'd knocked out of position earlier. I managed to find it, then groped around on the ground until I found the rock I'd thrown at it. As weapons went, it wasn't much, but it was heavy enough to do some damage if I threw it just right.

Heading back through the trees toward the pond, I hoped I wasn't making the world's biggest mistake.

The situation was pretty damn grim. Alexis, looking smug and superior, stood by the side of the pond. Beside him stood another man—unfamiliar to me, but with a haughty bearing that immediately pegged him as another Olympian. They watched the water as a third man towed an unconscious—or maybe temporarily dead—Anderson toward the shore.

Three men, one rock. I didn't like the odds. I tried to spot my gun in the grass, but either the shadows hid it, or one of the bad guys had picked it up.

The third man labored out of the water, visibly shivering as he dragged Anderson's limp body through the shallows and then up onto dry land. Neither of the *Liberi* looked inclined to help, and I guessed that the third man was a mortal Descendant—a lesser being from the Olympians' point of view.

"Bind him," Alexis commanded.

Panting with exertion, Alexis's flunky turned Anderson over onto his stomach, then dragged his hands behind his back and secured them with a pair of handcuffs he drew from his sopping pants. Unlike Anderson, he'd gone into the water fully clothed. I suspected he was regretting it now as the wind gusted over his wet skin.

"M-may I t-take him now, my lord?" the Descendant stammered, hunching his shoulders and crossing his arms over his chest as if that would keep him warm.

My lord? Talk about delusions of grandeur. Unfortunately, the question made me realize the treaty was truly out the window. I had no doubt the Descendant was asking for Alexis's permission to kill Anderson and steal his immortality.

"Not yet, Peter," Alexis said in a tone of almost affectionate condescension. "I'd like to have a few words with him first. Why don't you run back to the house and put on some dry clothes? He'll still be here when you get back."

Peter got to his feet and actually *bowed* to Alexis. I rolled my eyes, amazed at Alexis's arrogance even as I tried to figure out how to take advantage of the slightly improved odds. I wondered if Konstantin, the self-proclaimed king, knew Alexis was having people bow to him and call him "my lord." I would have thought Konstantin the type to reserve such accolades for himself alone.

Peter trotted off to the house, leaving Anderson lying on his stomach in the grass. I couldn't tell whether he was breathing or not. I'd like the odds a whole lot better if he were conscious. I didn't know what his capabilities were—other than that Hand of Doom thing, which I didn't figure he could pull off while in handcuffs—but as long as he was just lying there, any heroics I tried would be useless. Even if I managed to take out both *Liberi* with my one stone, I wasn't Maggie, and I wouldn't be able to carry Anderson to safety.

I wished like hell I could figure out a way to take advantage of Peter's absence, but with Anderson out cold, there was nothing I could do.

"You really mean to do it?" the second *Liberi* asked as soon as Peter was out of earshot.

Alexis nodded. "I was happy to bide my time, but if the fool is going to deliver himself to me with a pretty bow tied around him, I'm not going to refuse the gift."

The other guy looked uncomfortable, shifting from foot to foot. "What about Konstantin? He won't be happy."

Alexis dismissed Konstantin with a negligent wave. "He can hardly complain about me eliminating his greatest enemy."

"If he wanted Anderson dead, he would be dead by now. There must be a reason he hasn't killed him yet—"

"Enough! If you're feeling squeamish, you can tuck your tail between your legs and go running back to your master. I won't hold it against you, as long as you keep your mouth shut. And you will keep your mouth shut, won't you, Dean?" This last was said in a menacing croon designed to turn blood to ice.

"O-of course," Dean stammered. "I mean, I'm not going anywhere. I'm on your side, always."

On Alexis's side of *what,* I wondered? Was there dissension within the ranks of the Olympians? I *had* sensed some undercurrents between Konstantin and Alexis when I'd met them at the Sofitel, but I'd assumed much of that was playacting, meant to emphasize how big and powerful Konstantin was.

Anderson coughed loudly, and everyone jumped—including me—though we'd all been expecting it. He turned over onto his side and coughed some more, painful, racking spasms that brought up gouts of water and made him gag. But at least he was alive, and awake. I hefted my stone, but until Anderson had quit coughing, I doubted he would be in any shape to take out whichever Olympian I didn't hit.

I decided that as soon as Anderson was able to breathe without retching, I'd take out Alexis. I had no idea which divine ancestor Dean was descended from, or what powers he might have, but I *did* know Alexis could throw lightning bolts, and those were a dangerous long-distance weapon. I had to hope that whatever Dean's powers were, they weren't much use in a fight.

"It never occurred to you that there would be extra security on your lady wife once you took a descendant of Artemis into your household?" Alexis mocked, though I wasn't sure Anderson could hear him over all the coughing. "I never took you for a fool, but then women do tend to have a negative influence on masculine intelligence."

Still coughing, though not quite as desperately, Anderson managed to push himself up to his knees. I still didn't think he was capable of doing anything really useful like fighting or running.

A flash of movement in the distance caught my eye, and I realized I was running out of time: Peter was coming back. When he got here, he would kill Anderson, and that would be that.

Of course, Peter was only human for the time being. I hefted the rock, wondering if I could put enough oomph into my throw to kill.

The thought shocked me, but only for a moment. I wasn't a killer, but I wasn't some helpless damsel in distress who would stand horrified and useless on the sidelines, either. I knew next to nothing about Peter, but if he was in cahoots with Alexis, then he was a bad guy, period. I wouldn't feel bad about killing him.

At least, that's what I told myself.

"Stay out of this, Nikki!" Anderson suddenly shouted, his voice loud and clear despite all the coughing.

I was so startled I almost dropped my rock. Dean jumped, and Peter started running faster, but Alexis just laughed.

"You think she hung around to try to save your pathetic hide?" Alexis asked through his laughter. "Or is that supposed to make me paranoid?" He looked straight at Anderson, not glancing away for a moment—proving how unthreatened he felt. Of course, his cronies were doing enough looking around;

he didn't have to. I huddled down lower behind the bush I was using for cover.

Did Anderson know I was here somehow? Had that been an actual order? Or was Alexis right, and he'd just been trying to distract the opposition?

The moment of indecision cost me, and by the time I made up my mind to ignore Anderson's command—if it even *was* a command—it was too late. Peter had drawn a gun—*my* gun, I suspected—and was pointing it at Anderson. If I managed to clock him with my rock, the impact might cause him to pull the trigger. I didn't dare risk it.

Feeling a little like that useless damsel in distress after all, I remained crouched behind the bush, hoping Anderson had some kind of a miracle plan up his sleeve, because I was plum out of ideas.

TWENTY-SIX

Anderson spat a couple of times, then shook his head in an effort to get his wet hair out of his eyes. He should have looked like a helpless victim, kneeling there on the ground in his underwear with his hands cuffed behind his back and a gun pointed at his head. Instead, he looked poised and unruffled.

"Have you ever wondered why Konstantin made a deal with me?" he asked Alexis, and despite the dire situation, a small grin tugged at the corner of his mouth.

Alexis looked nonplussed, both at the question and the casual tone, but he answered quickly enough. "Because it was not worth our effort to squash you and your little friends like you deserve." He sounded very sure of himself, but both of his accomplices were visibly worried.

Anderson's grin broadened. "Really? Why don't you give

your boss a call right now? You've got me helpless, after all, and if you have your pet kill me and steal my immortality, my followers would most likely disperse. So call Konstantin and ask him if he wants you to kill me."

Alexis snorted. "You trespassed on my property. I'm within my rights to kill you, and I don't need to ask anyone's permission."

Anderson shrugged. "Fine. Don't ask him. If ignorance is bliss, you must be in heaven right now."

Alexis landed a crushing punch on Anderson's nose, though he had to bend over a bit to do it. I winced at the crunching sound of cartilage giving way. Blood spurted from Anderson's nose, and he crumpled to the ground. His muscles remained tense, however, so I knew he wasn't unconscious.

Alexis bent and wiped the back of his hand on the grass, cleaning off the blood I supposed. Then he stood up straight and resumed his arrogant, cross-armed pose, towering over his fallen foe.

"You and your people have been a thorn in my side for some time now," Alexis said. "A quick death would be too easy for you." He pulled back his foot and delivered a brutal kick to Anderson's belly. Anderson grunted and curled himself around the pain.

Just how slow a death did Alexis have in mind? Enough that I had time to run for help?

I dismissed the thought with only the briefest consideration. With my car all the way back at the church, and the mansion at least a half-hour's drive away, I couldn't risk it. But the slow death comment gave me hope. Whatever torture Alexis planned, it would probably mean some relaxing of Peter's guard. The Descendant still had the gun pointed and ready, but I didn't think he was quite as poised to shoot as he had been when he'd first arrived on the scene. Maybe if Alexis was going to deliver a beating, he'd get a little careless and place himself between his flunky and Anderson. And wouldn't it be a terrible shame if I hit Peter with the rock and he ended up shooting the wrong guy?

"I'm sure you're not enjoying this," Alexis said. He was panting with eagerness, getting his rocks off on the pain he was inflicting. He delivered another kick before continuing. Unfortunately, Peter still had a clear line of fire. "But I suspect it will hurt you more to hear about all the fun I've had with your dear wife since she's been my guest here."

Anderson froze, his sudden stillness overcoming even the reflexive writhing. I closed my eyes for a moment in an attempt to stave off my sympathetic horror. Behind my closed eyelids, I couldn't help seeing the image of Steph, the damage she'd taken, and the pain she'd endured after less than an hour in Alexis's clutches.

Emma had been Alexis's prisoner for the better part of ten years, and he might not have kept her in the water all that time.

Alexis laughed, enjoying the pain and horror Anderson couldn't hide. "Once a year, on the anniversary of her capture, we fish her out, and Konstantin and I share her. Even after all this time, she still cries for you when we—"

Anderson let out a roar, like nothing I'd ever heard before. So loud my bones and my teeth rattled with it, and so savage it froze Alexis and his cronies in their tracks. Three sets of eyes widened to almost comic proportions, stunned by the fury of that roar.

And then Anderson moved, his pain forgotten as he lurched to his knees.

The sudden movement broke all of us out of our stupor. I knew from the terror on Peter's face that he was totally unnerved and that he was going to shoot. I also knew that my thrown rock would be too late to stop him. I leapt to my feet and hurled it anyway, putting all my strength behind it and aiming for his head.

The gun fired. I watched in horror as Anderson's head snapped back, blood spurting from the back as the bullet passed all the way through. His eyes glazed over, and his body started listing just as my rock caved in the side of Peter's skull.

There was another moment of disordered shock as everyone looked around, trying to make sense of what had happened. Anderson and Peter lay on the grass, both staring sightlessly into the night.

I cursed myself for waiting as long as I had to throw the damned rock. Sure, I'd been worried hitting him with the rock would make Peter reflexively fire the gun; however, I'd known for a fact he was going to fire it on purpose eventually, so the smart thing would have been to take a chance that the blow wouldn't make him pull the trigger or that his shot would miss. I'd wanted a better opportunity, hoped for a sure thing.

And because of that hesitation, Anderson was dead, and the Olympians now had a new *Liberi* to add to their stable.

At least, they would have him soon, once Peter's wound healed enough for him to revive. The rock had done an impressive job on his skull, and that kind of an injury would take time to heal. Not that that helped me a whole hell of a lot.

Alexis's searching eyes found me, and his lips twisted into an expression somewhere between a grin and a sneer. Now would have been a good time for me to run for my life, but I stood there frozen by his gaze, horrified by my failure.

"I was just starting to have fun," Alexis said with a mock pout. "But then *you'll* be more fun to play with anyway. I'll show you everything I did to your sister, and everything I *would* have done if that interfering faggot hadn't showed up and spoiled everything."

I'd never asked Blake how he'd managed to run Alexis off that night, but now I had a good guess. The air crackled with electricity, raising the little hairs on my arms. I could have turned tail and run, but with Alexis so close, I didn't see how he could miss if he threw a lightning bolt at me. I was superstitiously reluctant to turn my back on him.

Dean squatted beside Peter's limp body, frowning down at him. "Umm, Alexis?"

"What?" Alexis snapped, obviously annoyed to have his gloating interrupted.

"He doesn't seem to be healing."

"What?" Alexis said, and this time he sounded more surprised than angry. He turned to look at Peter's body.

I'd have taken advantage of his distraction to run like hell, only I took one last glance at Anderson first. His eyes, instead of staring sightlessly at the sky, were focused on the two *Liberi*. As I watched, a smile curled his lips, the expression so sinister as to be almost evil.

Anderson reached out with one leg, hooking it around Dean's ankle and yanking him off his feet. With a cry of surprise, Dean fell, and Anderson rolled until he was straddling him. His hands were still cuffed behind his back, but Anderson leaned back and tucked those hands just under the waistband of Dean's pants, making contact with his bare skin.

Dean let out a shriek of pain, his back arching as he tried to buck Anderson off of him. But Anderson held on tight, bracing himself with his legs and using his grip on Dean's waistband as an anchor.

When Anderson had used his Hand of Doom against Jamaal, Jamaal had passed out after only a few seconds, and I expected the same thing to happen now. The surprise and his friend's screams had momentarily kept Alexis from attacking, but surely a lightning bolt would be on its way any moment.

Figuring that even in the handcuffs, Anderson had a better shot of taking out Alexis than I did, I decided to take one for the team. With an incoherent battle cry, I launched myself at Alexis. If he was busy fighting with me, he couldn't electrocute Anderson. Surely Dean would be unconscious any second now, and then Anderson could turn his attention to the greater enemy.

Dean was still shrieking, his voice high and thin with

agony. If he weren't already starting to go hoarse, Alexis might not even have heard my own cry.

Alexis whirled toward me, and I knew the lightning bolt was coming. I'd semi-resolved myself to taking it, but at the last moment I threw myself to the side. The quick dodge kept me from taking a direct hit, but even a near miss with that kind of power was enough to stun me.

I hit the ground with a thump, too disoriented to soften my fall. My limbs felt like jelly, and my head hammered and rang with pain. I wanted to just lie there, maybe slip into soothing unconsciousness so I wouldn't have to hear Dean's piteous screaming anymore.

I blinked away the afterimage of the lightning, expecting another blast at any moment but unable to muster the strength or coordination to get up. I looked over my shoulder, thinking maybe Alexis was going to strike at Anderson now that he'd temporarily disabled me.

Alexis was indeed staring at Anderson, but he showed no sign of tossing a lightning bolt. Instead, he stood there in slack-jawed horror, his face a mask of fear. Muscles still weak and quivering, I forced myself to sit up and see what had put that look of terror on Alexis's face.

Dean's body was glowing cherry-red as Anderson continued to straddle him, teeth bared in a truly savage snarl. A thin, keening wail rose from Dean's throat, but the sound was growing thinner by the second as the glow intensified. Anderson was glowing, too, his skin radiating a white light that made me squint.

"You're next," he growled at Alexis, the snarl turning into a smile that was no less savage.

Alexis looked like he was about to wet his pants. I know I would have if Anderson had looked at me like that. Of course, I'm pretty sure that in spite of my fear, if I'd been in Alexis's shoes I'd have mustered the courage to throw one more lightning bolt in an attempt to save my friend from agony. But

Alexis always chose to look out for number one, so instead of trying to help Dean, the cowardly bastard turned tail and ran.

Anderson turned to me, no longer looking anything like the unprepossessing normal man I'd first met. He seemed to have grown in size behind that white glow, muscles bulking up as he put on what I'd guess was another six inches or more in height. His blah-brown hair was now snow white and shoulder length, and his medium-brown eyes were like twin white stars in his face.

"Stop him!" he ordered me, his voice resonating differently in that suddenly deeper, broader chest.

I wasn't in any shape to chase after bad guys, but I wasn't crazy enough to defy an order given by a crazed immortal.

I forced myself to my feet, considering my options as Alexis fled toward the house. Fear had given his feet wings, and even at my best, I wouldn't have been able to run him down when he had this much of a head start. If he made it through the house and to a car, there would be no stopping him.

It was only a slight detour for me to dart to the shore of the pond and grab my backpack before I sprinted after Alexis, but in that time he'd put even more distance between us. I ran as fast as I could, one hand digging blindly in the backpack until my fingers found another rock.

Puffing with exertion, I drew that rock out of my backpack. Alexis was almost to the back door. If he got inside the house I'd never get a shot at him. So even though I was still a good fifty yards away, and it was so dark I could only make out his shape because he was moving, I pitched the rock with every ounce of strength I could muster.

Alexis's hand closed on the doorknob, and he twisted it while banging into the door with his shoulder. He took about half a step inside before the rock made solid contact with the back of his head.

I was too far away and too weak to do the same kind of damage I'd done to Peter, supernatural powers or not. But the blow was hard enough to drop Alexis to his hands and knees. He didn't lose consciousness, but he was clearly woozy, his body swaying as he tried to regain his feet.

My own knees gave out then, and I collapsed onto the grass. As I lay there panting, I dug through my pack for another rock, pushing myself up into a sitting position. Even with the power of Artemis, I wasn't sure I could hit Alexis again from this distance, especially not while sitting down, but I was willing to give it a try.

It turned out I didn't have to. A glowing white pillar of fire—Anderson—ran by me at an easy lope that seemed to cover about ten yards per stride. Alexis screamed in terror when he saw what was coming for him. He lurched to his feet, still visibly unsteady, and stumbled through the doorway. He tried to slam the door behind him, but Anderson had already closed the distance.

I turned my head and covered my ears when Alexis began to scream.

TWENTY-SEVEN

Covering my ears didn't help, at least not enough. I didn't care *what* Alexis had done—I couldn't bear to hear a human being suffer like that.

Sobbing with the effort, I got to my feet once more and, still covering my ears, ran back toward the pond, putting more distance between myself and the house in hopes the sound would be muffled. I made it all the way back to the edge of the water before my legs refused to carry me anymore and I had to sit down. The screams were fainter now, but I could still hear them, and I knew the sound would haunt my sleep for years to come.

Peter lay where we had left him, his head still caved in from the impact of my rock. There was no evidence of any healing whatsoever, so he'd clearly failed in his quest to become *Liberi*. I didn't see how, though. He'd shot Anderson in the freaking head. I'd seen the bullet come out the other side, seen the life drain from Anderson's eyes. Anderson had died, I was sure of it.

Maybe Peter hadn't really been a Descendant after all, though I wasn't sure how one could make a mistake about that. The glyphs were pretty clear indicators.

And then there was Dean.

Actually, there *wasn't* Dean. Where Dean had lain, there was a shirt, a pair of jeans, and a pair of sneakers, all empty. The air smelled of sulfur and ash, although as far as I could tell there wasn't even a speck of ash or dust to mark where the *Liberi* had once been.

He was dead. And not the kind of dead a *Liberi* could get up and walk away from. He was an immortal being who could only be killed by a mortal Descendant. And yet Anderson—clearly *not* a mortal—had killed him.

Footsteps approached me from behind, but I didn't turn to look. Alexis's screams had finally stopped a couple of minutes ago, so I guessed Anderson was through with him. There was no eerie white glow lighting the night now, but that didn't stop the chill of fear that traveled up and down my spine. I'd been coming to think of Anderson as a friend, but after the savagery I'd witnessed tonight, I couldn't force myself to look at him.

In my peripheral vision, I saw him come up beside me and then sit on the grass, just out of arm's reach. Even just seeing him out of the corner of my eye, I couldn't help noticing he'd lost the handcuffs and the underwear somewhere along the line. Likely when he'd morphed into that humanoid pillar of fire.

"They're dead, aren't they?" I asked in a choked whisper when the silence became too heavy.

"Yes."

"Permanently."

"Yes."

I shook my head, trying not to remember the sounds of their screams. I couldn't be sorry they were dead—especially Alexis, though for all I knew Dean was just as bad—but their suffering sickened me. Worse, I wasn't a hundred percent sure I wasn't about to face the same fate. It didn't take a rocket scientist to realize I'd witnessed something I shouldn't have. Anderson seemed to be a nice guy most of the time, but even before tonight, I'd seen ample evidence of the ruthlessness his genial manner hid.

Trembling, I wrapped my arms around my knees. "Are you going to kill me, too?"

He turned his head to face me, and I reluctantly met his eyes. "Are you going to tell anyone what you saw tonight?" he countered.

I shook my head, unable to trust my voice. How could he possibly believe my denial, though? What kind of idiot would admit they were planning to run around blabbing in this situation?

His expression was grave, though not especially menacing. "You know what fate awaits you if you talk. And the same fate awaits anyone you talk *to*. I trust that will motivate you to keep quiet."

There was another long stretch of silence, but silence gave me too much room to think, and that was the last thing I wanted to do right now, so I hurried to fill it.

"You aren't *Liberi,* are you?" I asked.

One corner of Anderson's mouth tipped up, though I wasn't sure what he found funny. "No, I'm not *Liberi.*"

"Then what are you? If you don't mind my asking . . ."

I thought at first he wasn't going to answer. Then he shrugged, perhaps deciding it wasn't necessary to be coy when I knew too much already.

"I am the bastard child of Thanatos and Alecto." I gave him what I was sure was a blank look. "The Greek god of death and one of the Erinyes, or Furies," he explained. "I am Death and Vengeance, rolled into one."

I swallowed hard. "So what you're saying is . . ." My throat tightened, and I considered the possibility of panicking. "What you're saying is you're not *Liberi,* you're an actual . . . god?"

He gave me a small smile. "Is that really so hard to believe after all that you've seen?"

I stammered like an idiot, making his smile broaden and bringing a mischievous twinkle to his eye. The expression further widened the chasm between the Anderson I knew and the terrifying creature I'd seen him turn into.

"There are a few of us left on this earth," Anderson said. "We were abandoned here by those who thought themselves our betters. We keep our existence a closely guarded secret."

"But Konstantin knows who you really are, right? That's why he made a deal with you?"

Anderson nodded. "Yes. He saw me kill one of his people, back when we were at war. He escaped, but immediately abducted Emma so that if I killed him, I'd never be able to find her and I'd doom her to an eternity of suffering. That was when we made our deal. He's made sure to abide by it, knowing that as long as he didn't provoke me unbearably, I would let him live in hopes that he would one day lead me to Emma."

"And no one else knows who you are. Konstantin has kept your secret."

"To tell anyone who and what I am would be to acknowledge that he isn't the most powerful being to walk the Earth, something his ego will never allow."

A number of facts lined up in my mind, and something clicked. "That's why Konstantin was so desperate to recruit me, right? Not because he wanted me to hunt Descendants— or not *just* because of that, anyway—but because he didn't want me to help you find Emma."

Anderson nodded.

"And you didn't bring any of the others tonight because

you knew you were going to end up killing *Liberi,* and you didn't want any witnesses."

Another nod. "I am as anxious to keep my identity a secret as Konstantin, only for different reasons. I had no choice but to risk letting *you* find out, but I did have a choice with the others." He shrugged.

There was more to it than that, I knew. I didn't really matter to him, so if I saw something I shouldn't and he had to kill me to silence me, it wouldn't break his heart, not like it would have if he'd had to make the same decision with one of his own people. I was still an outsider, an interloper, and I probably always would be. I told myself I was used to it and that it didn't hurt a bit.

I turned to stare at the pond. "Is she in there?"

Something sparked in his eye, an expression that held no hint of mischief and screamed of fury. "She's there. If you've settled down enough that I can trust you not to bolt, I'll go get her out and we can all go home. And then Konstantin and I are going to have a long talk."

I suppressed a shudder. Right now, I was really, really glad I wasn't Konstantin.

"Then go and get her," I said. "I want to get out of here."

Without another word, Anderson rose gracefully to his feet. And wouldn't you know it, despite everything I'd learned about him that night, despite all the fear and awe and horror, I couldn't help taking a moment to admire his naked backside as he walked to the water and once more plunged in.

It took the better part of forever to get Emma out of the water. She was chained and weighted down, and god or not, Anderson didn't have the strength to break the chains that bound her. It occurred to me that Alexis might have been planning to haul her out and maul her in front of Anderson as part of the slow, torturous death he'd had in mind, so I reluctantly went back to the house. Shuddering the whole time and trying desperately not to think, I searched through Alexis's empty clothes until I found a ring of keys. I brought these to Anderson, and sure enough, one of them was the key to the shackles. Anderson brought Emma's body to shore and laid her on the grass.

She was naked, naturally. Her skin was ivory pale (or corpse white). Her hip-length black hair and her rosy lips gave her the look of a sickly Snow White, and I knew that alive and healthy she would be a stunning beauty. Which I supposed was only appropriate for the wife of a god.

"Does she know?" I asked Anderson as he knelt beside the body, brushing his wife's hair from her face as we waited for her to revive.

He spared me only a brief glance. "No. And it's going to stay that way."

I raised my hands in a gesture of surrender. No way in hell I was going to mess with him, not with everything I knew, although I kind of thought his wife had a right to know exactly who and what she was married to. Still, that was their problem, not mine.

Naked and wet in the frigid air, his teeth chattering, Anderson was almost blue with cold. I fetched his clothes from where he'd discarded them in the woods, but for the time being, at least, he ignored them, all his attention focused on Emma. She wouldn't be in much better shape when she came to, and I figured we were past the time for stealth by now. Even so, I stayed near Anderson, giving him ample chance to veto my decision as I called the mansion. I got Logan, and asked him and Maggie to come help us. I provided zero details beyond the address and the need to bring something warm to wrap Emma up in.

It was at least twenty minutes before Emma suddenly sucked in a breath, then started coughing. Anderson turned her onto her side and supported her head as she expelled the pond water from her lungs.

Embarrassed by their mutual nudity and wanting to give them time to get reacquainted without an audience, I wandered off into the woods before Emma finished retching. I sat heavily on the ground as soon as I was out of sight, drawing my knees up and resting my forehead on my folded arms.

I'd seen too much pain and misery in the past few days, endured too much fear. I couldn't contain it anymore, and I finally let it all go at once. Muffling the sounds with my arms, I cried for everything Steph had suffered at Alexis's hands; for the multiple deaths Jamaal was suffering in punishment for his disobedience; for all the abuse Emma must have suffered over the years she'd been Konstantin and Alexis's prisoner; for the normal life I'd once taken for granted; and for the uncertain future, which I had no doubt would expose me to even more life-altering traumas.

Twenty-eight

I let Anderson do all the explaining when the cavalry arrived. I tried to make myself concentrate on the answers, thinking it was a good idea if I actually paid attention to the "official" story, but I was a little too shocky to manage it. Certainly I knew Anderson made no mention of Alexis's demise, or that of his crony, Dean. We'd weighted Peter's body down in the chains that had once held Emma, then dumped him in the pond, where hopefully he would never be found, at least not by any human authorities. We'd disposed of the empty clothes, as well. No one except Konstantin could possibly guess what had actually happened here tonight.

Emma was alive and conscious, but that's about the best you could say for her. Her eyes had a glazed, shell-shocked expression, and she didn't react to anything anyone said to her. Anderson cradled her in his arms, and while she didn't resist, she didn't cuddle up to him, either. For now, at least, there seemed to be no one home. My heart broke for both of them, and if

I hadn't already cried my eyes dry in the woods, I probably would have done it again on the ride home.

As far as I could tell, Emma was no better the next day, although she would move around and eat and drink if prompted. She wouldn't make eye contact with anyone, and forget about talking or changing her facial expression. Still, Anderson seemed confident she would recover, if perhaps not all the way. I didn't know if that was the wisdom of the ages speaking, or just wishful thinking, but I certainly wasn't going to argue with him or try to take away his sense of hope.

I'd really hoped that Emma's presence would inspire Anderson to commute Jamaal's sentence, but when I tentatively made the suggestion, he silenced me with one cold look. Before I'd seen his true form out at Alexis's mansion, I might have tried to argue or cajole him out of it, but there was no pretending he didn't scare the crap out of me now.

"What really happened last night?" Maggie asked me when we were alone. "It's obvious Anderson didn't give us the whole story."

I would have loved to have told her, to unburden myself and talk the situation through with another human being. But of course, I couldn't, not without risking my own life and hers.

"Don't ask," was all I said, though I could see that the way I'd shut her out hurt her.

Not being able to tell Steph the truth was even worse. According to Anderson's version of events, we had run Alexis off, but there was no mention of his slow and painful death. Blake was still sticking to Steph like glue, and I didn't dare even hint at what had happened to Alexis when Blake might hear me. I trusted Steph to keep a secret, but not Blake.

Eventually, I managed to get her alone for all of about five minutes. I was worried enough about Anderson's threat that I dropped my voice to a bare whisper even though we were alone.

"Alexis is dead," I told her. "I can't share details, and if anyone gets a hint that I told you, we'll both join him in the grave. But I thought you should know."

Steph's eyes misted with tears. Of the two of us, I'd been by far the most bloodthirsty, so I was a little surprised when she whispered back, "I hope it hurt."

I shuddered, remembering Alexis's screams. "It did," I assured her, then hugged her tightly as she burst into tears.

When sunset rolled around, I seriously considered finding somewhere in the house to hide so I could avoid having to witness Jamaal's third and final execution. I was scared to death of defying Anderson, but I honestly wasn't sure my psyche could survive one more horror.

In the end, though, I pulled on my big girl panties and headed out to the clearing with the rest of Anderson's *Liberi*—minus Emma, thank God, because even hard-assed Anderson had *some* compassion, at least for his own wife. I figured Jamaal was being punished in part because of me, and therefore it was my moral duty to stand witness. In hindsight, I think I was still fighting a boatload of guilt over having killed Emmitt and started Jamaal down the self-destructive path he'd chosen.

What courage I'd managed to muster completely failed me when I stepped out from between the trees and into the clearing, however. Jamaal had warned me that Logan would choose something "heinous" for the grand finale, as he termed it, and he hadn't been kidding.

In the center of the clearing, illuminated by the light of many torches, was a wooden stake, driven into the ground and surrounded by firewood and kindling.

"No fucking way," I said, coming to such an abrupt halt that Maggie bumped into me from behind and almost knocked me over.

There were winces and gasps of sympathy from the other assembled *Liberi,* but no one else reacted as violently as I did. I whirled on them, my outrage reaching epic proportions.

"We are *not* going to just stand here and watch while . . ." I couldn't even say the words, but Maggie was frantically shushing me anyway.

"You're going to do exactly that," Anderson told me coldly as he stepped into the clearing, followed by Logan and Jamaal. Jamaal staggered when he saw what was awaiting him, but he regained his composure and his courage in a heartbeat, visibly steeling himself for the ordeal.

Earlier in the day, I'd been unable to shake the vision of Anderson in his true form, an avenging god of death with pitiless eyes. Memories of Alexis's and Dean's screams had silenced me better than any gag ever could. But this was too much. Jamaal's actions had been misguided, but not truly evil. He hadn't meant to harm anyone but me, and he'd thought he had good cause. He didn't deserve this torment—and I didn't deserve to have to watch it.

I took a belligerent step in Anderson's direction and opened my mouth to tell him exactly what I thought of him, ignoring the steely threat in his eyes.

"Shut up, Nikki!" Jamaal snapped at me, surprising me into silence. "It's my choice whether to submit to this or not, and I choose to submit."

I wanted to argue, but he had a point. He could walk away if he wanted to, high though the cost might be. But he wasn't going to walk away. "Fine. Be a martyr if you want to. But I am *not* watching this."

I didn't wait for Anderson's reply, instead turning and plunging into the woods, running full speed toward the house, hoping I could get inside and as far away from the clearing as possible before the screaming started. If Anderson insisted on punishing me for my act of defiance, I'd deal with it when the time came. I just couldn't bear to see or hear any more suffering.

I wasn't thinking when I ran, but once I entered the house, I found myself pounding down the stairs toward the basement instead of heading up to my room. I didn't analyze my instincts, just went with them, and soon found myself in the cell I'd been locked in the very first night I'd set foot in the mansion. Slamming the door behind me, I threw myself onto the narrow cot and pulled the pillow over my head.

I lay there for a long time, listening to the thrum of my pulse and the harsh rasp of my breath, my body so tight my muscles ached. Even when I was sure the execution was over and done with, I couldn't relax a single muscle. I figured I might take the whole rest of the night to pull myself together. I was sure I'd have as much time as I needed, because no one would think to look for me here. But I was wrong.

There was a soft knock on the door. I ignored it, not remotely ready to face anyone just now. The door opened despite my lack of invitation, and I did a double take when I saw Jamaal step into the room.

I sat up abruptly, shoving the pillow aside. I didn't know how much time had passed, but I was sure it wasn't enough for Jamaal to have healed from being burned to death.

He closed the door behind him and leaned against it. "He didn't go through with it," he told me. "They tied me to the stake and he had Logan bring a torch over, but he never lit the fire."

My shoulders sagged in relief, although I wanted to punch Anderson's lights out for putting us all through that. The buildup had been bad enough that even failing to light the pyre didn't lessen the horror.

Jamaal pushed away from the door and sat beside me on the cot. Not so close as to be intimate, but not giving off his usual keep your distance vibes, either.

"The point of the whole exercise was for me to prove myself willing to submit," Jamaal said softly, staring at the floor. "There is nothing I wouldn't face to avoid going back to the way I lived before Anderson found me and brought me here. I was so upset about Emmitt that I lost sight of all the good things I still had. I'd forgotten how important being part of Anderson's crew was to me. The punishment sucked, but it also woke me up. So don't, uh, feel bad about all this shit, okay? I'm in a better place than I was before."

I looked over at him, and it was all I could do not to smile at the patent discomfort on his face. I didn't know if it was because he was unused to speaking words of comfort, or because he didn't like speaking to me so civilly, but whatever it was, it made him adorably awkward. I suppressed an urge to reach out and touch him, having learned last night that such overtures would not be welcomed despite our truce.

"Thanks for coming to talk to me," I said, giving him a tentative smile. "I'm glad to know he didn't go through with it. And I'm sorry—"

He cut me off with an abrupt hand gesture. "No. No apologies. Even if you're Konstantin's spy and you killed Emmitt on purpose, you aren't responsible for what happened to me. I made my own decisions, and I'm enough of an adult to own up to that."

I sighed. "I wish I could convince you I don't work for Konstantin."

He cracked a smile that reminded me for the zillionth time just how mouthwateringly gorgeous he was. "If it makes you feel any better, I'm less convinced now than I was a couple days ago. You *did* find Emma, after all." The smile faded into a thoughtful expression. "And Anderson is no fool. He trusts you for a reason. That's good enough for me for the time being."

I rolled my eyes at him. "Wow, what a ringing endorsement."

He smiled again—I think that made three times in two days, which might be a record for him. "Ask anyone—coming from me, that *is* a ringing endorsement."

He stood up, and I felt obliged to stand, too, if only because I didn't want to have to crane my neck to look at him.

"Now if you're finished sulking in the basement," he said, "Anderson's called a meeting for about thirty minutes from now to discuss our future relations with the Olympians now that we have Emma back. You don't want to miss it."

He turned his back and skedaddled out of the room before I could tell him what I thought of his "sulking" comment.

When I'd come down to the basement, I'd been halfway thinking I needed to make myself disappear. How could I consider working for a terrifying god of death and vengeance who could kill immortals with a touch and had no qualms about burning one of his own people to death in punishment for disobedience?

Jamaal's words, however, gave me serious pause. Not only had Anderson not followed through on his most dire threat, but Jamaal was clearly feeling better. Before, he'd been like a wounded animal, snarling and biting without any rational thought. "Borderline crazy," I'd labeled him, and I suspected it was the truth. Now, he seemed human. Still in pain, and still a dangerous man, but not plunging off the deep end anymore. It made me wonder: how much of Anderson's "punishment" had truly been punishment? And how much had been a demonstration of a particularly harsh version of "tough love"?

I wasn't yet convinced that staying with Anderson and his merry band was the best way for me to deal with my uncertain future. They were likely soon to be at open war with the Olympians, and that spelled more ordeals and more trauma for me if I stayed with them.

But maybe, just maybe, if Anderson could take an alienated loner like Jamaal and make him into something like a member of the "family," he could do the same for me.

And that was something I'd gladly brave the terrifying future to achieve.

DEADLY
DESCENDANT

PROLOGUE

There's nothing like breaking things to lift a girl's spirits when she's had a lousy day. I'd been having a lot of lousy days lately.

I hefted a fat ballpoint pen, wondering if it was heavy enough to break one of the bottles I'd lined up on the opposite side of the clearing. Only one way to find out.

I sighted at a little eight-ounce Coke bottle, then pulled back my arm and threw the pen at it with all the strength I could muster. Pens aren't exactly aerodynamic, so my weapon's flight path was erratic at best. But seeing as I was a descendant of Artemis, goddess of the hunt, I had infallible aim. The pen tinked against the Coke bottle, making it waver on the fallen log I'd dragged into the clearing to hold my targets. Waver but not fall or break. Having infallible aim didn't mean I had the pitching arm of a Major League Baseball player.

Regular throwing practice was definitely making my arm stronger—when I'd first started, I never would have hit the bottle from this distance—but I was out here to break things, not just prove I could hit them. I bent over and dug into the tote bag I'd stuffed full of small, throwable household items. I pulled out a satisfyingly heavy ceramic coaster. Not exactly something you'd think of as a deadly weapon, but I was betting it would do the trick.

Instead of throwing overhand, this time I threw sidearm, thinking the coaster would fly more like a Frisbee. It wasn't the prettiest throw in the world, but it was accurate and hard. The bottle shattered into a satisfying spray of glass fragments, the force of the hit strong enough to break the coaster in two. Much more satisfying than the pen toss. If I'd been aiming at a person, I'd have done significant damage.

"I thought a petty thief had robbed the house, but now I see you were just gathering ammunition."

The voice came from behind me, and I couldn't help a little squeal of surprise as I whirled around to find Anderson Kane watching me.

Anderson was the leader of a small band of *Liberi*—immortal descendants of the ancient gods—who held to the lofty ideal that the *Liberi* should use their supernatural powers to help make the world a better place. I was the newest and most reluctant member of that band. We all lived together in Anderson's enormous mansion, although I had yet to acknowledge the place as home. I wasn't planning to give up my condo anytime soon, and I tried to spend the night there, in my own bed, at least once a week.

Anderson was also a god—not just the descendant of a god like the rest of his people but a real god, son of Thanatos and Alecto. Death and Vengeance, to their friends. He was also the only being in the universe—that I knew of, at least—who could destroy a *Liberi*'s seed of immortality. Mortal descendants of the gods could *steal* a seed by killing a *Liberi*, but only Anderson could actually *destroy* it, as I'd learned when I'd seen him reduce two *Liberi* to nothing more than a pile of empty clothes. I was one of only two people who knew his secret identity, and I hadn't been able to look at him the same way since I'd found out.

"Do you know how hard it is for me to find any time to myself in this place?" I grumbled at him, because even though he intimidated the hell out of me, I tried not to show it.

Anderson glanced at his watch. "I saw you storm out here about a half hour ago. I figured I'd given you enough time to do whatever brooding you needed to do."

I clamped my jaws shut to keep from saying anything I might regret. Anderson looked like such a normal, unprepossessing guy, everything about him "medium." Medium height, medium build, medium brown hair . . . You get the picture.

But I'd seen him without his human disguise, and I knew beyond a doubt that I didn't want to piss him off.

"I'm not brooding," I ground out. "I'm doing target practice."

"Yes, I can see that. But I've noticed a strong correlation between you doing target practice and you being out of sorts about something. So tell me what's wrong."

The way he phrased that—like a command, not a question—rubbed me the wrong way, but then, just about everything was rubbing me the wrong way this afternoon.

"Nothing that matters to you," I said, sounding a little more sullen than I'd have liked. Have I mentioned it had been a really lousy day?

Anderson gave me one of his reproving looks. He was really good at them, and I decided I'd get rid of him sooner if I just told him what was eating me.

"There was a fire at my office building," I said, kicking at a patch of crabgrass. I was still nominally a private investigator. It said so on the door to my office. I'd had to put my work on hiatus when I'd first become *Liberi,* but now I was trying to resume at least part of my normal life. Which involved making money to live on. I might be getting free room and board at Anderson's mansion, but I was still paying rent and utilities on my condo, not to mention making car payments. I'd managed to work two whole jobs before today's setback. No, not setback, disaster.

"Some idiot left his space heater running when he went home for the night. Between the smoke damage and the dousing from the sprinkler system, my office is pretty much DOA," I continued. Insurance would reimburse me for the damages but not for the lost business or for the cost of the temporary office space I was going to have to find.

I kicked at the crabgrass again. Not that long ago, I'd been in a horrendous car accident. Well, it was an accident on my part, at least. Emmitt Cartwright, one of Anderson's *Liberi,* had strolled right into the middle of an ice-slicked road. He knew I was a mortal Descendant and therefore one of the only people in the world who could kill him. He'd used me to commit suicide, and by killing him, I'd inadvertently stolen his seed of immortality and turned life as I knew it on its ear.

The ripple effect of that accident was still causing me unexpected headaches. For example, I'd practically emptied my savings account to make the down payment on my new car, the old one having been totaled. Normally, that wouldn't have been a hardship, but now that I no longer had any money coming in, it was a different story. It sure looked like I was going to have to do something I'd vowed never to do: dip into my trust fund.

My adoptive parents had set up trust funds for me and their daughter, Steph, when we were kids. Steph had no qualms about living on that money, but I had steadfastly refused to touch it. It felt too much like charity, and as much as I loved them, I could never quite get over the feeling that I wasn't their "real" daughter. It was all right for their real daughter to use their money but not for me. Neurotic, maybe, but there you have it.

"Do you need some money?" Anderson asked.

"I'll be fine," I said, and it was true. I was going to have to swallow my pride, and I was going to feel like a hypocrite for touching that trust fund, but I wasn't facing financial ruin. All I had to do was get over my stupid hang-up. "I don't need charity."

There was a spark of something that might have been anger in Anderson's eyes, and I reminded myself who I was talking to. This was not someone I wanted to pick a fight with.

"I wasn't offering you charity," he said. "I was offering you a job."

That took me entirely by surprise. "Huh?"

He smiled faintly at the face I must have made. "I was trying to give you more time to acclimate before springing this on you, but it seems Fate had a different idea. One of the things I and my people do is help other *Liberi* and their families who are trying to escape the Olympians."

The Olympians are a group of *Liberi* descended from

Greek gods. They do some truly awful things, slaughtering whole families of Descendants to protect their own immortality. Occasionally, they spare a small child and raise it as one of their own, indoctrinating it to their values of superiority, privilege, and cruelty. They had a whole flock of Descendant toadies, all vying for the privilege of being given a sacrificial *Liberi* from whom to steal the seed of immortality. Whenever the Olympians stumbled on *Liberi* who weren't descended from Greek gods or who refused to accept the natural order of things as dictated by the Olympians, they gave those *Liberi* to their pet Descendants to kill, and a new Olympian was born.

"Not everyone we help wants to join us," Anderson continued, then smiled ruefully. "And sometimes I'm not inclined to issue an invitation."

I frowned. "Then how is it you help them, exactly? Financially?"

He nodded. "That's one thing. But most important, we help them go into hiding, make sure the Olympians can never find them."

"You mean like a *Liberi* witness protection program?"

He grinned. "Exactly." The grin faded. "We've been doing this for years, and we've helped a lot of people. I think we do a damn good job, but we're not pros at this, and we've lost a couple of people."

"So what is it you want me to do?"

"I want you to go over the records for everyone we've hidden. See if you find any flaws in their cover, and then help us move them again with better cover if necessary. I'll pay you a retainer for as long as it takes to get all of the covers examined and patched."

The clanging sound in my head was the peal of warning bells. I had already been sucked into Anderson's merry band more deeply than I could ever have imagined. I was living in the freaking mansion, for Pete's sake! I'd spent too much time in foster care as a kid to allow myself to depend on anyone too much.

The idea of fitting in somewhere, of being part of a family, of *belonging,* was my Holy Grail. But the Holy Grail wasn't real, and I knew better than to seek it. The last thing I needed was to let Anderson get even more hooks into me than he already had.

"Thanks for the offer," I said, "but I'd rather go it on my own. I haven't spent all this time building up my business just to abandon it at the first sign of trouble."

Anderson probably heard the falseness in my words. It wasn't commitment to my own business that made me refuse, but that was the most convenient excuse I could come up with off the cuff. Of course, I should have known better than to think Anderson would take no for an answer.

"Perhaps I wasn't completely clear about what I was asking," Anderson said. "People have gotten killed because we didn't do a good enough job of hiding them. I'm asking you to help me protect people who will be murdered—or worse—if their covers are blown. Surely, saving lives is more important than maintaining your independence."

Ah, the guilt trip. It was a highly effective tactic against me, and yet . . .

"Wait a minute. You want me to *examine your records* to see if these people are well enough hidden?"

"Yes."

Anderson was not an idiot, and I was sure he knew exactly what I was getting at. However, he didn't budge, giving me a look of polite, bland inquiry. Making me put it into words.

"Why the hell would you keep records on people you're trying to make disappear? It's like burying your treasure and then spray-painting a giant X on the spot."

"Only if the Olympians got hold of those records, and of course, we're very careful with them."

"But why?"

"You know why."

Of course I did. Anderson was capable of being a nice guy, but he was also a ruthless and manipulative son of a bitch when it served his purpose. "You want to make sure you can find them if you ever need them for something."

Hiding these *Liberi* fugitives gave Anderson a huge amount of power over them. If he needed something, and they refused him, he could hand them over to the Olympians. I didn't know if even he was ruthless enough to do such a thing, but it would make for a compelling threat.

"Nikki, you might not like how I go about things, but I am trying to keep these people safe, and I could sure use your help."

And I needed the money, unless I dipped into the trust fund. Which was the lesser of two evils: tapping the trust fund or letting Anderson draw me ever deeper into his world?

I was already being forced to live in the mansion because of the treaty Anderson had crafted with the Olympians. The Olympians had agreed that Anderson's *Liberi* and their families would be off-limits, and living in the mansion was what made someone "Anderson's *Liberi*." If I didn't live in the mansion, the Olympians would be free to continue their efforts to recruit me—efforts that included tactics like raping my sister. The Olympians had justified the attack by saying that Steph didn't count as family because we weren't blood relatives. Anderson had killed the bastard who hurt Steph, and Konstantin—the self-styled "king" of the Olympians—had sent a specious apology along with a promise to leave my adoptive family alone as long as I was one of Anderson's *Liberi*.

"Did you set the fire at my office to twist my arm into accepting this offer?" I asked, wondering at my ability to see Anderson as one of the good guys and yet still suspect him of something like that.

"No," he said, completely unoffended by the accusation. "You'll do it because you want to save lives, not because you need the money."

Anderson hadn't known me all that long, but he already had me pegged. If there weren't lives at stake, I'd have chosen taking money from the trust fund as the lesser of two evils in the end. I was already forced to depend on Anderson for room and board, thanks to his stupid treaty with the Olympians. To be forced to depend on him for my salary, too, was something I'd have greatly preferred to avoid.

But seriously, money aside, how could I justify using my abilities to track down deadbeat dads and people who skipped out on their bills when people's lives were potentially at risk? I knew I was being manipulated. But I also knew I couldn't live with myself if people got killed because of my selfish desire not to be subsumed.

"I want my old life back," I said sourly.

Anderson just gave me that knowing look of his.

ONE

Early January is not the best time to enjoy the outdoors in Arlington, but Anderson and his bitchy wife, Emma, were having a screaming argument in the house, and outside seemed the best place to be to avoid hearing it. I closed the front door behind me, and the shouting voices were muffled down to a low buzz. The winter air bit at my cheeks, and I stuffed my hands into the pockets of my jacket to keep them warm. Definitely not my favorite kind of weather, but the silence was sweet and soothing.

Figuring that I could handle the cold for a while, I sat on the picturesque porch swing and tried to pretend my life was my own. The illusion was hard to uphold when I lived in the mansion and spent my days working for Anderson, examining the covers he had built for the *Liberi* he had hidden.

He'd actually done a surprisingly good job, in large part thanks to Leo, our resident descendant of Hermes, who had become a computer genius in order to better keep his finger on the pulse of the financial world. I hadn't found too many blatant holes in the covers so far, though I'd patched many small ones and still had a long way to go before I was finished.

My feet had gone numb, and I was beginning to think it was time to go in, when I noticed an unfamiliar car navigating the long driveway. I shivered in the freezing air as I watched the car approach, wondering who it could be. We didn't exactly get a lot of visitors at the mansion. That was sort of the point of the place. Whoever this was, someone was expecting them, since they had to be buzzed through the front gate.

I heard the door open behind me and turned to find Anderson stepping out to join me on the porch.

"Back inside, Nikki," he said, jerking his thumb at the house. "We're meeting in the formal living room."

I swallowed to contain my instinctive retort. I wasn't fond of being ordered around. A few weeks ago, when I'd thought Anderson was "just" a *Liberi,* I probably would have told him so. I wasn't a timid person, but I found I couldn't look at Anderson anymore without picturing him as the pillar of white fire he had turned into when he'd shed his disguise, and that image was more than enough to discourage my smart mouth.

I stifled my urge to protest and ducked back inside the mansion as Anderson waited on the porch for our mysterious visitors. The warm air flushed my cheeks, and they were probably red enough to look sunburned. Guess I'd been outside longer than I'd realized.

I made my way to the formal living room. I think the last time I'd set foot in there had been when Maggie gave me the grand tour of the house the night I'd moved in. It really was a *formal* living room, and Anderson's *Liberi* were a decidedly informal bunch.

The sofa and many of the chairs were already filled with other members of Anderson's household, with the notable exception of Emma. I guessed that meant her fight with Anderson was over—or at least on temporary hiatus. It was well nigh impossible to win a fight with Anderson, and Emma didn't take well to losing. Often, she flounced off in a huff afterward; other times, she'd go completely nonresponsive, staring off into space. She'd been Konstantin's prisoner for about a decade, until I'd found her and rescued her (with Anderson's help). When we'd first brought her back to the mansion, she'd been the next best thing to catatonic, and sometimes I harbored the guilty thought that I'd liked her better that way.

The woman was disturbed, no doubt about it, and there was only so much slack I was willing to cut her for the trauma she'd been through. I couldn't help wondering if some—if not all—of her "episodes" were faked, meant to guilt Anderson into being more agreeable. Sometimes it seemed to work. Other times, not so much.

I sat on a chair that, judging by the hardness of its seat and the carved knobs that dug into my back, was meant to be more ornamental than functional and leaned over toward Maggie. She was the closest thing I had to a friend among the *Liberi*.

"Any idea what's up?" I asked her.

She shrugged. "We have visitors, and I'm guessing it's Olympians, because Anderson gave us his 'my house, my rules' speech."

I made what I was sure was an ugly face. Anderson trotted out that phrase whenever he made an unpopular decision—like, for instance, when he invited me to live in the mansion. I was pretty sure that if it came down to a vote, I would be out on my ear. They were a close-knit bunch, Anderson's *Liberi,* and I was very much on the outside looking in.

"Sorry I missed it," I muttered, and Maggie laughed. She was a descendant of Zeus through Heracles, and she had the super strength to prove it. She was also by far the nicest of any of the *Liberi* I'd met. "Why would an Olympian be coming here?" I asked. I wouldn't quite say we were at war with the Olympians, but it was close. I suspected I knew what Anderson and Emma had been fighting about—her hatred for Konstantin and the Olympians was truly epic.

"I'm guessing we're about to find out," she said, jerking her chin toward the front, where Anderson was leading three people—two men flanking one woman—into the living room.

The woman was petite and fine-boned, like me, but that was where the resemblance ended. Her ash-blond hair was cut in a stylish bob, and though she wasn't classically beautiful, she was striking. I'd guess her age at around thirty—if she weren't *Liberi,* which meant she could be a thousand years old for all I knew. Her posture was regally straight, with an aristocratic tilt to her chin that said she thought she was better than everyone around her. But then, she was an Olympian, and feeling superior to all non-Olympians was one of the membership requirements. The navy-blue skirt suit she wore looked like it cost about as much as your average compact car.

Beside the woman was a guy, maybe early twenties, with coarse-looking black curls and olive skin. He wasn't movie-star handsome, but he was roguishly cute, with a hint of dimples. He didn't have the woman's haughty demeanor, and he was dressed casually in jeans, a button-down shirt, and a slightly weathered sportcoat.

The other man had the look of hired muscle. Broad-shouldered, with buzz-cut hair and a square face, he was obviously wary of everyone in the room. The iridescent glyph on the side of his neck proclaimed him to be more than strictly human, but if I had to guess, I'd say he was a mortal Descendant, not a *Liberi* himself. At least, not yet.

Anderson invited the woman to sit in an armchair. When she crossed her legs, she made sure to flash the red soles of her Louboutins. Apparently, she wanted everyone to know that she was rich, because acting superior wasn't obnoxious enough. There weren't enough chairs for everyone, so our other two guests stood, the *Liberi* beside the woman's chair, the Descendant behind, looking menacing. As a Descendant, he could do what no one else could: kill a *Liberi,* thereby stealing his or her immortality and becoming *Liberi* himself. Well, no one else but

Anderson, but that was far from common knowledge. His eyes suggested he was sizing us all up.

Across from me, Blake leaned forward and glared at the woman. He was a descendant of Eros and had once been a reluctant Olympian himself, until Anderson had offered him an alternative.

"You wouldn't be here if Anderson hadn't given you safe passage," he said. "Bringing your goon with you is an insult."

There was a glimmer of amusement in the woman's eyes. I doubted the insult had been unintentional, and Blake was giving her exactly the reaction she wanted. The goon didn't seem to mind being talked about that way, and the other guy deepened his dimples by smiling.

"How do you know the goon isn't mine?" he asked. His voice was pleasantly deep and mellow. "You could be taking Phoebe to task for something that is entirely my fault."

Blake looked back and forth between the two men and shook his head. "He's not your type, Cyrus." There was noticeably less hostility in his voice when he addressed Cyrus.

Cyrus laughed, looking over his shoulder and giving the goon a visual once-over. "Too true," he said, turning back to Blake. He leaned a hip against Phoebe's chair and propped his elbow on the top of it, his casual demeanor a striking contrast to the goon's menace and Phoebe's stiffness.

"This is supposed to be a peaceful meeting, Blake," Anderson chided. "Don't start a fight." He gave Blake a quelling look. Blake crossed his arms over his chest and leaned back in his seat.

Anderson turned his attention back to the two *Liberi*. "I believe you know everyone here except Nikki," he said, gesturing to me. "Nikki, this is Cyrus, Konstantin's son."

I might have blinked a bit in surprise, though now that I knew he was Konstantin's son, I could see the faint resemblance. Cyrus was much better-looking and didn't immediately set my nerves on edge as Konstantin had the one time I'd met him. His smile looked genuinely friendly, but looks can be deceiving.

"And this is Phoebe," Anderson continued.

"Also known as the Oracle," Blake said, and my eyes widened.

Blake had told me about the Oracle once before. She was a descendant of Apollo, and she had visions of the future. According to Blake, her visions were usually impossible to interpret until after the fact. It was thanks to some vision of hers that the Olympians had found out about me in the first place, and that automatically made her not one of my favorite people.

Phoebe looked me up and down, her lip faintly curled with disdain. Apparently, she wasn't impressed by what she saw. I can be sensitive about my looks sometimes, but I'd been looked down on by better snobs than Phoebe, and her disdain didn't bother me.

Phoebe dismissed me with a little sniff, turning her attention back to Anderson. "Let's not pretend a courtesy we don't feel," she said. "You don't like us, we don't like you, but at the moment, that's beside the point."

"Speak for yourself!" Cyrus said. "I like everybody." His visual once-over had been just as assessing as Phoebe's had been, but far less unpleasant. I was certain he wasn't a nice guy—otherwise, he wouldn't be an Olympian—but he put up a better front than any other Olympian I had met.

Phoebe gave him an annoyed glance. "We're here on business, remember?"

"I see no reason that should prevent us from being civil."

Either they were doing a good cop/bad cop routine, or Phoebe and Cyrus didn't much like each other. I put my money on the latter. The animosity between them seemed genuine.

"Why don't you tell us why you're here?" Anderson asked. I was sure he already knew, or he wouldn't have let the Olympians set foot in his territory.

Phoebe uncrossed her legs—I wondered if she'd crossed them in the first place just so she'd have the excuse to flash her Louboutins—and got down to business. "I had a vision."

"I'm shocked, *shocked* to hear that," Blake stage-whispered.

Phoebe spared him a curl of her lip, then pretended to ignore him. Cyrus sucked in his cheeks as if he was trying not to laugh.

"One that concerns both the Olympians and you people." There was a wealth of derision in the way she said that last part, and more than one of Anderson's *Liberi* stiffened at the insult. A quelling look from Anderson forestalled any interruption, and Phoebe continued.

"If you've been reading the papers, you may have noticed that there have been a string of rather bizarre deaths in the area over the past three weeks."

Once upon a time, I'd been pretty good at keeping up with the news. Being up-to-date on current events struck me as a job requirement for a private investigator, but I'd been so distracted by my new life that I'd been slack about it lately.

"You're talking about the wild dog attacks, right?" asked Jack. He was a descendant of Loki, and making trouble was his religion. I wouldn't have expected him to be up on current affairs—that smacked almost of responsibility, a concept he usually disdained.

Phoebe inclined her head without speaking. Perhaps she didn't want to answer questions from "us people."

Jack let out an exaggerated sigh and rolled his eyes heavenward. "You've found me out!" he cried, jumping to his feet. "My evil plan is foiled!"

The air around him shimmered, and moments later, he disappeared, replaced by a massive black dog that looked like a cross between an Irish wolfhound and a pit bull. It barked loudly enough to rattle my teeth, then let out a fierce growl and bit the air.

It seemed I was the only one taken aback by Jack's little stunt. I'd had no idea he could do that. I made a mental note to look up Loki on the Internet when this meeting was over. Honestly, I should have spent some time researching everyone's divine ancestors by now, but I was still trying to adjust to my new reality. I had enough trouble worrying about my own ancestor and abilities without looking into others', at least for now. Maybe that was self-centered of me, but it helped protect my sanity.

Anderson shook his head in long-suffering patience. "Jack, sit. Stay. And shut up, while you're at it."

Jack gave him a doggie grin, complete with lolling tongue, then jumped back onto his chair, changing back into his human form in midair. I must have been staring at him in open amazement, because he turned to me and winked. I looked away quickly.

Phoebe was sneering again, and Cyrus's eyes twinkled with humor. He seemed to think pretty much everything was funny—rather like Jack, come to think of it. It made him seem less dangerous, and I realized that was the point. With his dimpled cheeks, Cyrus wouldn't be that good at overt menace, so camouflaging it to lull everyone into a false sense of security was probably a calculated strategy.

I put my speculation aside for the moment and looked at Phoebe. "What do wild dog attacks have to do with the *Liberi*?"

"They're not really wild dog attacks," she said, her every word dripping with condescension. Evidently, she didn't have a very high opinion of my intelligence.

"Yeah, I figured you wouldn't be here talking to us if they were," I said. "I was just trying to move this conversation along."

Phoebe glanced sidelong at Anderson, as if expecting him to chastise me for speaking out of turn. There was a moment of uncomfortable silence, and then Phoebe continued.

"In my vision, I saw a man with a jackal's head being dragged through an institutional-looking hallway under armed military escort. I believe that means there's a *Liberi* behind these attacks and that he's descended from Anubis."

The sum total of my knowledge about Anubis was that he was an Egyptian god with a jackal's head. Despite everything I'd seen and been through already, I always felt a little shock of incredulity when hearing about someone being descended from a god. A mental *Yeah, right* was still my natural reaction, although I'd feel stupid about it two seconds later.

"If I'm right," Phoebe continued, "we have to stop him before the mortals track him down. If the government gets its hands on a *Liberi* . . . Well, it would be bad. For all of us."

Blake snorted. "Notice how the fact that there's a *Liberi* out there killing people is completely irrelevant to this discussion. If the Olympians weren't worried about their own hides, they'd just sit back and enjoy the show."

"I don't see any sign that *you're* out there hunting the killer already," she retorted.

"Oh, we were supposed to know already that these wild dog attacks are actually the work of a *Liberi*?" He raised his eyebrows at her in a mockery of polite inquiry.

"You know now," Cyrus interjected, surprising me by taking the heat off of Phoebe. Not that I thought she appreciated it. "We don't have to have great and noble intentions, do we?"

"Maybe you ought to try it sometime," Blake said. The words were antagonistic, and yet there wasn't the same rancor in his voice when he spoke to Cyrus as there was when he spoke to Phoebe.

Cyrus shrugged. "I don't think it would suit me. To tell you the truth, I'm not sure it suits *you* all that well, either."

It wasn't Blake's fault he'd been an Olympian—before Anderson came along, the choice was join the Olympians or die—but I'd often thought his moral compass was a little short of due north. With his casual words, Cyrus seemed to have finally hit a nerve, and Blake clenched his jaw so hard I could see his bones outlined against his cheeks.

"So," Anderson put in before tensions could escalate, "do you have any idea what this *Liberi*'s powers are? How is he killing these people? And why is he doing it, especially here, of all places?"

Here in the *Liberi* capital of the world, he meant. Because the Olympians were headquartered here, the D.C. area had the highest number of *Liberi* per capita of anywhere in the world, by a wide margin. It was like the killer was just *daring* the Olympians to come after him and "harvest" his immortality.

"We're not sure how he's doing it," Phoebe answered. "Our best guess is that he can control anything canine and that when he wants to kill, he just summons all the stray dogs in the area and commands them to maul his victim. As for why . . ." She shook her head. "Either he doesn't know the kind of danger he's putting himself in, or he's just plain crazy. Serial killers don't necessarily need reasons—at least, not reasons that make sense to ordinary folk."

Phoebe turned to fix her eyes on me. "We will, of course, do our best to help find this *Liberi* and stop him. However, now that you have a descendant of Artemis in your fold, you probably are better equipped for the hunt than we are."

Although she was looking straight at me, she was obviously talking to Anderson. That didn't stop me from answering.

"You left out one strong possibility for why Dogboy would be wreaking havoc in D.C.," I said. "Like he knows perfectly well that this is the Olympian headquarters, and he has a major grudge against Olympians. I mean, I can't imagine why, since you guys are all sweetness and light and everything, but I think the possibility bears examining."

The look Phoebe gave me was positively chilling—I seem to have a talent for pissing off Olympians.

"I can't imagine why someone who has a grudge against us would attack a bunch of mortals," she said. "That would be more likely to hurt *you* than *us*." She flashed Anderson a sly smile. "Perhaps it's someone who has a grudge against *you*? You have been around a while, and I'm sure you've made some enemies in your day."

I'd seen ample proof that Anderson had a temper, and a scary one at that, but he showed no sign that Phoebe's insinuations had gotten under his skin.

"I'm not aware of any descendant of Anubis who might wish me ill," he said mildly, "though I suppose it's possible. I have, as you said, been around for a while. But then, so has Konstantin."

She conceded the point with a shrug. "I don't think it much matters why the killer is in D.C. He has to be stopped, before the mortals get their hands on him and our existence is exposed."

The overwhelming concern for human life was touching, to say the least. But despite her selfish motivations, she was right, and this guy had to be stopped. Assuming anything she'd told us was the truth, though I couldn't imagine what she'd have to gain by making this up.

Cyrus suddenly stood up straight for the first time, his gaze focused somewhere behind my left shoulder. I couldn't resist glancing behind me to see what he was looking at.

Emma stood in the hallway, just outside the living room. Her glossy black hair hung loose around her shoulders, making her skin look even paler and more delicate than usual. The ruby-red lipstick heightened the effect even more, though I already knew she wasn't as delicate as she looked.

Cyrus had stopped smiling, his expression turning solemn as he met Emma's gaze. Out of the corner of my eye, I saw Anderson stiffen ever so slightly, and I knew why. Konstantin and Alexis, his then right-hand man, had raped Emma while she was their prisoner. Anderson couldn't help wondering if any of the other Olympians had participated. Emma, apparently, refused to talk about it.

I think Cyrus saw and understood the speculation in Anderson's eyes, too, and he gave Emma a courtly half bow.

"What my father did to you was unnecessarily cruel," he said, and he sounded sincere enough. "He'll never apologize for it himself, so I'll do it on his behalf."

Phoebe made a sound of annoyance. "Oh, stop posturing, Cyrus. I never heard you complaining during the years she was our 'guest.'"

Emma stood silent and motionless in the hall; then she shivered and crossed her arms over her chest. I couldn't imagine the hell she'd gone through, and for the moment, I forgot her frequent bitchy spells and just felt sorry for her.

"I'd have complained if I'd thought it would make a difference," Cyrus said. His words seemed directed to Emma rather than Phoebe.

"Because you're such an all-around nice guy?" Blake needled. His tone made the barb sound almost friendly, like there was no real rancor behind it. If I had to guess, I'd say Blake actually *liked* Cyrus, despite the antagonistic potshots he'd been taking.

Cyrus finally pried his gaze away from Emma and glanced at Blake, his expression solemn. "Because I'm not my father."

Phoebe rolled her eyes and rose to her feet. "I think we're done here."

"I agree," Anderson said tightly. This talk of Emma's ordeal had clearly gotten to him. He stood up, his attention torn between Emma, who was now silently crying, and the Olympians, who were technically his guests—and whom he didn't trust for a moment.

"I'll show them to the door," Blake offered.

Anderson nodded his approval, then quickly crossed to Emma and gathered her into his arms.

TWO

After briefly accepting Anderson's hug, Emma pulled away and gave him a quavering smile. She looked frail and broken, quite unlike the battle-ax I knew she was capable of being.

"Why don't you come sit down?" he asked her gently. "I'll fill you in on what you've missed."

But Emma shook her head. "I think I need to lie down for a little while."

Call me a cynic—or an insensitive bitch—but no matter how sorry I felt for Emma, I couldn't help being annoyed at what seemed a blatant attempt at manipulation. The pathetic way she was looking at him said she wanted him to come with her and comfort her. I didn't know how much of our meeting with the Olympians she'd overheard, but she had to know that we'd been discussing something important. There was no other reason Anderson would have let the Olympians cross his threshold. And yet she wasn't even interested enough to find out what was going on before she tried to draw him away.

Anderson stroked a tear from her cheek. "Are you sure? Maybe—"

"I'm sure," Emma interrupted. There was a slight edge in her voice, like she was really put out that Anderson might think there were more important things in the world than cuddling her when she cried. She put her nose in the air and made a tastefully dramatic exit just as Blake returned from seeing the Olympians out.

"You're not seriously considering teaming up with the Olympians, are you?" Blake asked Anderson the moment Emma was out of sight.

Anderson glanced at him but didn't say anything as he took his time crossing the room and sitting down. He was generally pretty easygoing and wasn't the type to bark out orders. Not the kind of guy who screams "alpha male" with every word he speaks and every move he makes. And yet he was an alpha male through and through, and I don't think he much liked Blake's tone.

Anderson sat back in his chair, making himself comfortable before he deigned to answer the question. "We're certainly not 'teaming up' with them. However, it's possible that just this once, their interests and ours are in line."

"If anything Phoebe said was true," Blake countered.

"Well, the part about the dog attacks was true," Jack said. "And you have to admit, that's not something you'd expect in the heart of the city. And the victims were all adult men. It's a rare pack of wild dogs that would attack an adult male."

"Since when have you become an expert in dog behavior?" Blake countered.

Jack grinned. "Wasn't it just this morning you called me a son of a bitch?"

I winced and groaned. "Ugh. That's bad even for you."

"Honey, I save my A material for people who are capable of appreciating my genius."

I knew he'd called me "honey" with the express purpose of irritating me, but that didn't stop the surge of indignation. I'd have dazzled him with my own witty repartee, except Jack was sitting there grinning at me, ready to pounce on my response. He loved being the center of attention, and I didn't want to play into his hands.

Lucky for me, Anderson intervened before I lost my ability to contain my retort. "Let's stay on topic, people. When Phoebe called me to request this meeting, I did a little fact checking, and there have indeed been three fatal dog attacks recently. Jack's right that it's all pretty bizarre. What kind of wild dog pack is randomly going to maul three adult men, all in different parts of the city, and with absolutely no witnesses?"

"No witnesses to the attacks," Jack added, "and no reported sightings of a pack of dogs large enough to do it."

We all chewed that one over for a while. It wasn't so ridiculous to think the attacks might be supernatural in nature. Once you allowed yourself to admit that the supernatural exists at all, of course.

"Just because a *Liberi* is probably behind the attacks doesn't mean anything else Phoebe said was true," Blake argued. "Like her explanation of why the Olympians care about someone who kills people."

"It's plausible that they would be concerned about the risk of exposure," Anderson said. "It's also plausible that there's something else behind their request for help."

"Like they're going to use this hunt to try to trap Nikki and force her to work for them," Blake suggested.

Konstantin had tried to recruit me for the Olympians when I'd first become *Liberi*. His recruitment techniques included such compelling persuasions as having his right-hand man kidnap and rape my sister—a fate I could supposedly have saved her from if only I'd agreed to join them. Of course, since it was their mission in life to wipe out every mortal Descendant in the world except for the chosen few they indoctrinated, if I'd joined them, they'd have made me hunt for who knows how many innocent men, women, and children whom they would slaughter. File that under "Not Gonna Happen."

"I'm not suggesting we go blundering into anything blindly," Anderson said. "I'd like us to start out by just doing a little more research." He turned to Leo, who was sneaking glances at a handheld every few seconds. Guess he was afraid the stock market would pull a fast one on him if he didn't keep an eye on it. "See if you can get hold of the actual police reports. There might be information they haven't shared with the public that will help us figure out whether the attacks are supernatural or not."

"Sure thing, boss," Leo said. I'd known he was good with computers, but the confidence with which he agreed to go searching for police reports said he was hacker-level good.

"And Nikki," Anderson continued, "see what you can find out about the victims. See if you can find any link between them and the Olympians."

That was something I could do, something my years as a private investigator had prepared me for. Hunting for a supernatural serial killer, on the other hand, was so far outside my comfort zone it might as well have been brain surgery. I hoped to God we'd find out there was nothing supernatural whatsoever about these attacks so that I could get off the hook. It was a selfish attitude, no doubt about it, but I figured after the hell I'd been through lately, I was entitled to a little selfishness.

I stopped by the kitchen before going up to my suite. I needed a healthy dose of coffee before I got to work. By the time I'd brewed a pot, doctored it to my liking, and gotten to my suite, Leo had already emailed me several articles about the dog attacks, along with the police report on the first one.

I skimmed the news articles, although I seriously doubted they'd have a lot of important information compared with what I would find in the police reports. Maybe I was just stalling because I wasn't looking forward to cracking open files that would have photos of dead, mauled bodies. I was a P.I., not a cop, and I was embarrassingly squeamish. I'd thrown up when we had to dissect a frog in high school, and even *thinking* about looking at the photos was making me a little queasy.

According to online reports, the attacks had each occurred on a Friday night, one attack per week over the last three weeks. The first had been in Anacostia, and the victim had been so badly mauled he had yet to be identified.

The second attack had occurred in Trinidad. The victim, Eddie Van Buren, was an unemployed former banker who'd been found near the National Arboretum. According to the article, Van Buren had been forty-three when he died, though the accompanying photo showed a man who couldn't be more than twenty-five. In the photo, he was handsome and athletic-looking, and I had to wonder if they'd chosen to use the old photo because falling on hard times had stolen his good looks.

The third attack had occurred in Ledroit Park, and the victim was Calvin Hodge, a criminal attorney. The picture in the paper showed a smiling middle-aged man with a neat black beard and a power suit.

It was impossible to imagine that a pack of wild dogs could cover that much territory in the heart of D.C. without being spotted by someone. It was also impossible that they would randomly decide to attack lone male victims on Friday nights exactly one week apart. The reporter who wrote the third article parroted the police's assertions that, despite the improbability of it all, these killings were all the result of wild dog attacks, but I could almost feel the reporter's skepticism.

Either the perpetrator was a serial killer who owned a pack of attack dogs, or Phoebe was right and there was a *Liberi* behind it. I had to put my money on option number two, no matter how much I didn't like it.

By the time I'd finished skimming the articles, copies of all three police reports were in my in-box. Leo worked fast. And I didn't want to know how he'd managed to get hold of confidential police reports within the space of an hour.

I chugged down the rest of my coffee before it got cold, staring at my in-box, trying to work up the courage to open the first file. I gave myself a mental kick in the ass, took a deep breath, and double-clicked on the first attachment. There were several pages of notes, but I skipped immediately to the photos, knowing I wouldn't be able to concentrate on the text until I'd gotten this part over with.

I managed to get through the first shot by almost convincing myself I was looking at special effects from some cheesy horror movie. I was less convinced when I peeked at the second one, and the third one made everything too real. I had to bolt to the bathroom, where I emptied out my coffee and my lunch. By the time I was finished, I was sweaty and shaking, my stomach still rumbling unhappily. I splashed cold water on my face and tried to keep my breathing slow and steady.

"Some kick-ass supernatural huntress *you* turned out to be," I muttered to my reflection.

The last thing in the world I wanted to do was go back to my computer and look at those photos again. What were the chances I'd spot something the police hadn't and that whatever I spotted would lead me to the killer? Even given my own brand-new supernatural abilities, those odds were pretty slim. But I knew I had to look. If it turned out there was something I should have seen and someone else died horribly because I'd been too much of a wimp to look at a few nasty photos, I'd never be able to live with myself.

It took several more tries before I could force myself to look at the photos for more than half a second at a time. My imagination was going to have a field day with these images if I let it.

"Mind over matter," I kept repeating to myself under my breath, then gripped the arms of my chair and forced myself to look.

It wasn't hard to tell why victim number one hadn't been identified yet. Saying he'd been "mauled" was an understatement. *Shredded* was more like it. The crime scene was under an overpass, and there was blood everywhere. Blood painted the sidewalk and the street, dripped down the walls on both sides, and spotted the ceiling. Bits and pieces of him were scattered willy-nilly, and I wouldn't have known these were human remains if it weren't for the head—skull, actually—that rested on its neck on the sidewalk, like it was rising out of the ground. Close-ups showed obvious teeth marks on the exposed bone.

I tried very hard to distance myself from what I was seeing, to look at it with dispassionate eyes and search for clues to who might have done this and where he might have gone, but I couldn't get past the horror. I hoped to God the poor man had been dead before most of the carnage occurred. I told myself he had to have been, otherwise someone would have heard the screams and seen something. Of course, residents of tough neighborhoods like Anacostia knew investigating sounds of violence was seriously bad for your health, as was volunteering information to the police.

Still shuddering in revulsion, I forced myself to look through all of the photos. If there was important evidence there, I failed to see it.

I combed over the written report, hoping I'd have an easier

time coping with that. And I did, until I got to the part that said the victim's internal organs were missing. The report theorized that the victim had been killed by a pack of feral dogs and that the dogs had eaten the viscera.

Nausea roiled in my empty stomach, and my skin was clammy with sweat as I tried not to let my imagination paint too clear a picture of what the poor victim had been through. And what his family would go through, if and when the body was ever identified. The idea of having your loved one not only killed but eaten . . . I shuddered.

"I'm not cut out to be a cop," I muttered under my breath. There was a reason I'd chosen to be a private investigator instead of entering law enforcement. Numerous reasons, actually, but being exposed to violence on this level topped the list.

The next two reports were just as awful, the victims brutalized beyond recognition. By the time the third victim was found, the police were sure they were hunting a human suspect who used dogs as his deadly weapon, though they hadn't shared this conclusion with the press.

I spent several hours going over the police reports, and while they gave me a clearer picture of what had happened, I couldn't say they brought me any closer to finding the killer.

I closed down the files at around five o'clock, and as if he had a sixth sense, Anderson showed up on my doorstep at approximately 5:01.

"Ready to wrap up the case yet?" he asked me with a wry smile.

I was already jittery from my day's work. Being alone in a room with Anderson was not high on my list of things I wanted to do at the moment. Someday I would have to find a way to get over being creeped out by the knowledge that he was a freaking god, but I wasn't there yet.

I pushed back my chair and stood up, stretching out my stiff muscles and putting a little more distance between us as Anderson came to rest a hip on my desk.

"Not quite," I responded, hoping I didn't sound nervous. "You know, looking at crime-scene photos and police reports isn't exactly the same as chatting up nosy neighbors to see if they've seen the deadbeat dad around lately." I waved my hand vaguely at the computer. "This is not my area of expertise."

"Not yet," he agreed amiably. "But expertise or not, you're more likely to find the killer than the police are. They're going to be limited by their insistence on rational explanations."

I acknowledged that with a shrug. Since the police were convinced the killer had a pack of attack dogs, they were sure he was traveling in some kind of van or truck—a perfectly rational conclusion but one that could potentially skew their investigation. I didn't know exactly what the killer was doing, but I doubted it was what the police were thinking.

"What have you found?"

I moved to the other side of the room, Anderson following me. *There's no reason to be nervous around him,* I told myself. He was still the same guy he'd been before I learned his secret. True, I had seen him kill a couple of people, and that was bound to make me uncomfortable. But I'd known all along he had a ruthless streak, and it had never made me this edgy before.

I sat stiffly on the sofa, hoping Anderson would take the love seat. Of course, he didn't get my mental hint, instead taking a seat on the other end of the sofa and turning to face me.

He looked so unprepossessing it was hard to reconcile that image with what I knew was inside him. His medium brown hair was perpetually in need of a cut, his cheeks were perpetually peppered with five o'clock shadow—the kind that looks scruffy, not the kind that looks sexy—and he really needed to start buying no-iron shirts.

I cleared my throat, trying to focus on the here and now, not think about Anderson as a towering pillar of white light loping off in pursuit of his prey.

"The police are very confused," I said. "These definitely look like dog attacks. The bites indicate at least five or six medium-sized dogs. There are some paw prints here and there, though not as many as there should be with that many dogs, and the crime-scene techs haven't been able to find any dog hair, which is totally bizarre."

"Maybe the dogs were wearing gloves," Anderson suggested, completely deadpan.

The comment surprised a quick laugh out of me. "Or at least hairnets. Maybe the men were attacked by dogs in the food-service industry. That ought to narrow down the suspect pool."

Anderson smiled. "There. Now, that's more like the Nikki I know."

The comment killed my amusement. I guess I hadn't been acting as normal around him as I'd hoped. There was a long moment of awkward silence. I knew better than to race to fill that silence, but I couldn't help myself.

"What do you want me to say?" I asked. "I can't pretend I didn't see what I saw."

"But you don't have to tiptoe around me like I'm a keg of dynamite just waiting to blow. I'm dangerous to the bad guys, not to you."

I met his eyes in a challenging stare, too irritated by his statement to be cautious. "Are you forgetting that you threatened to kill me?"

He waved that off carelessly. "I had to give you incentive not to tell anyone about me. It's certainly not a threat I have any expectation of carrying out."

Oh, yeah, that made it *so* much better. "Look, I'll try to act more normal, but you're going to have to give me some time. I've had to absorb a hell of a lot of shocks in the last few weeks, and there's only so much I can take."

There was no mistaking the remorse that flashed through Anderson's eyes then. "Of course. I'm being an ass. Sorry."

All at once, he seemed more human to me than he had ever since I'd learned his true identity, and the knot in my gut loosened ever so slightly. I acknowledged his apology with a nod, then moved on.

"I guess my next logical course of action is to go examine the crime scenes myself," I said, thinking on the fly. "I didn't get anything out of looking at the photos, but maybe an idea will come to me when I'm on-site."

Anderson looked doubtful. "You really think there'll be any evidence left?"

"Probably not. But I'm not looking for evidence so much as clues. And if there's anything I've learned about my power, it's that I don't much understand how it works." My supernatural aim was something I could wrap my brain around, something I could pinpoint and control. My knack for finding people was much more elusive and hard to tap consciously. "Maybe looking at the crime scenes will give me nothing, but it can't hurt to try."

Anderson nodded. "Makes sense. But take Jamaal with you when you go. There's always a chance this is some kind of weird Olympian setup we don't understand. I don't want you going anywhere alone for the time being."

I was perfectly happy to take backup, but . . . "I'll take someone with me but not Jamaal."

Jamaal was a descendant of Kali, and he had some severe anger-management issues, especially where I was concerned. Not that I could blame him. I *had* killed his best friend, Emmitt, in a car accident. He probably didn't think I was an Olympian spy anymore, and he seemed to have accepted that I hadn't killed Emmitt on purpose, but I was still far from his favorite person.

"No, you'll take Jamaal," Anderson said firmly. "If you need the backup, you'll want someone who's good in a fight. Jamaal and Logan are the best for that, but Logan might draw unwanted attention in Anacostia."

"And Jamaal won't?" I asked incredulously. Sure, Jamaal was black, but he wouldn't exactly fit in with the gang-banger crowd.

"Maybe. But he looks a lot more intimidating."

Which I had to concede was true. Logan looked like an ordinary guy, despite being descended from a war god. Jamaal, on the other hand, looked like the kind of guy who could kill you with both hands tied behind his back. In fact, I was pretty sure he could. But I still didn't like the idea of us spending so much time together, especially not without a referee.

Anderson met my mutinous gaze and smiled. "Think of it as a team-building exercise."

I'd have argued more, except I was sure this was an order, not a request. I didn't like taking orders, but Anderson was now officially my boss, so I didn't suppose I had much choice in the matter.

"You should give me hazard pay for this," I grumbled, and I meant for traveling with Jamaal, not hunting the killer.

"That can be arranged," Anderson said, though I'd meant it as a joke. "Chasing serial killers is definitely not in the job description I gave you."

I had a feeling that over time, I'd end up working on more and more stuff that wasn't in the job description if I let Anderson keep pushing me. But there was no way I was going to push back under the circumstances; I was just going to have to bite the bullet.

THREE

I found Jamaal out on the front porch, smoking one of those foul-smelling clove cigarettes he was so fond of. Anderson wouldn't let him light up in the house. I'm not a big fan of smoking, even if you were immortal and didn't have to worry about lung cancer, but I *am* a big fan of anything that helps keep Jamaal from going psycho, so as far as I was concerned, he could smoke five packs a day if it helped calm him. Still, my nose wrinkled whenever I caught the scent, and I tried to stay upwind.

"I'm going to go check out the crime scenes," I told him as the wind shifted and the cloud of smoke followed me like a homing pigeon. I waved my hand in front of my face and stepped to the side. "Anderson wants you to go with me in case the Olympians are lying in wait or something."

I refrained from rolling my eyes. Honestly, I didn't think this was an Olympian setup. If they'd wanted me that bad, they could have jumped me anytime in the last several weeks. I'd been cautious ever since I'd been dragged into the world of the *Liberi,* but it wasn't like I had a bodyguard with me twenty-four/seven. Besides, one of the main reasons they'd wanted to "recruit" me had been to keep me from helping Anderson rescue Emma, and that horse had left the barn long ago.

Jamaal made a face and shook his head, the beads in his hair rattling and clicking. "You mean he wants us to make nice with each other," he said, stubbing out his cigarette in the ashtray he carried around with him.

The wind shifted again, and the cloud of smoke from Jamaal's last puff blew straight into my face, making my eyes burn. I stepped away, holding my breath until I was in the clear.

"That's how I interpreted it," I agreed. I didn't much enjoy the prospect of being shut up in a car with Jamaal. He'd dialed back on the hostility a lot, but I knew it was still there, lurking. He was learning to live with me, but I didn't think he'd ever forgive me for being the instrument of Emmitt's death.

Jamaal didn't look much happier with the situation than I was, but he'd learned his lesson about defying Anderson's orders, and he wasn't about to do it again anytime soon. He finished stubbing out his cigarette with a little more force than necessary, then laid the ashtray down on a low, glass-topped table.

"Fine. Let's go."

He headed down the stairs toward the garage, which was a

separate outbuilding just past the circular drive. With his long legs and huge stride, he was practically halfway there before I even got moving. I hurried to catch up.

"Hold on a sec," I said. "I don't have my purse."

He didn't slow down. "What do you need a purse for? We're just going to look around, right?"

"Car keys, driver's license, wallet. You know. Stuff."

He reached into his front pocket and pulled out a set of keys. "I'm driving, so you don't need any of that shit."

Ah, the joys of living with supernatural alpha males.

"No, *I'm* driving," I said, still trailing along behind him. "I'm the one who knows where we're going, remember?"

He came to a stop so abruptly I almost crashed into him. "So give me directions," he said, glowering down at me. He had a very effective glower, and I had to fight my instinctive urge to take a step back. "I'm not cramming myself into that clown car you drive."

After I'd wrecked my last car, I'd decided to splurge and buy myself the Mini I'd been lusting over for a couple of years. I'd always driven sedate, nondescript sedans before—much more practical for my job than the zippy little Mini—but after the fistful of traumas I'd suffered, I'd decided to reward myself.

"Bullshit," I said. "You're just one of those guys who has a problem letting a woman drive."

I thought I saw the corner of his mouth twitch, like he might have been considering a smile, but Jamaal's smiles are as rare as four-leaf clovers. He hit the button on his key fob to open the garage door, then selected a key and held it out to me.

"Can you drive a stick?" he asked.

I had a feeling he already knew the answer. After all, I'd committed the ultimate sacrilege of getting my Mini with an automatic transmission. I was tempted to lie just to call his bluff—I wondered if he'd have a change of heart as soon as he learned I'd actually take him up on his offer—but decided to let it go.

"Fine," I grumbled, reaching for the passenger door of Jamaal's sleek black Saab. "You drive."

He nodded in satisfaction as he slid in behind the wheel.

About thirty minutes later, we arrived at the first crime scene in Anacostia. Naturally, it was dark by the time we got there. Anacostia is a neighborhood I'd avoid if possible during the daytime and categorically refuse to set foot in once the sun was down. I might not be eager to spend a whole lot of time in Jamaal's company, but I was reluctantly grateful to have him along as we walked from the dilapidated parking lot at Anacostia Park to the underpass where victim number one had met his demise.

There weren't a whole lot of people around, but those who *were* around stared at me like I was a zoo animal. Like, say, a dik-dik wandering through the lion enclosure.

The murder had occurred three weeks ago, so I wasn't expecting to find anything. I stood where our John Doe had been killed, hoping to spot an important clue, and tried not to remember the crime-scene photos.

If the killer had been looking for the perfect place to kill someone in complete privacy in the heart of D.C., he'd done a good job of it. The road curved as it went through the underpass, limiting the line of sight, and the concrete walls would block sound effectively. Not that there seemed to be any houses or businesses within hearing distance right here by the park.

"See anything significant?" Jamaal asked me, and I had to shake my head. "Then can we get out of here? It reeks."

There was a certain eau-de-men's-room scent in the air. I looked around a little more, taking note of a couple of drains at the edge of the road, but nothing leapt out and yelled "Clue!" at me. I wished I had some idea of what I was doing. I was used to feeling like a more-than-competent professional, and this being-clueless crap sucked.

We made our way back to the parking lot, which was just around the bend in the road, and I silently cursed my mercurial power. I had no idea if I'd actually seen anything significant in that underpass, and I had to trust my subconscious to have absorbed whatever information might be there and disgorge it later, when and if it was relevant. Personally, I was a big fan of sure things, and anything subconscious was *not* a sure thing.

The parking lot had been practically deserted when we parked there, but, like chum in the water, Jamaal's Saab had drawn some local predators. A handful of teenage punks, the oldest of whom was maybe sixteen, were circling the car, checking it out with greedy eyes. We'd probably been gone no more than ten minutes, but I got the feeling we were lucky the car was still there and in one piece.

When Jamaal and I stepped into view, the kids lost interest in the car and fixated on me. I'm short and fine-boned, and my delicate features make me look like an easy victim. The oldest of the kids straightened up from his slouch, his eyes locked on me in a way that made my skin crawl. I was afraid things were going to get ugly, and I wished I'd insisted on going back into the mansion for my purse, because I could have stuck a gun in it.

Beside me, Jamaal came to a stop, turning to glare at my admirers. There were five of them, and I pegged them as gang-bangers, probably armed despite their tender age. I worried that Jamaal's challenging stare would pique their leader's alpha-male instincts, but apparently, the kid was smarter than he looked. He only held Jamaal's gaze for about five seconds before something he saw there warned him off. I might have been imagining things, but I could have sworn the kid shuddered as he looked away. If he did, he recovered his composure quickly.

With a careless shrug, he beckoned to his pals and strutted down the sidewalk away from us. I turned to compliment Jamaal on his intimidation techniques, but the words died in my throat when I saw his face.

Jamaal is a naturally intimidating guy, and I'd been on

the receiving end of more than one of his death glares. He'd seemed to have backed off from the edge a bit lately—ever since Anderson had threatened to kick him out of the house if he didn't reel it in—but I saw now that the rage was still very much there. His chocolate-brown eyes were practically giving off sparks, and his lips had pulled back from his teeth in a feral snarl. He was leaning forward ever so slightly, his fists clenched at his sides, his breath coming in shallow pants. Now I knew why the kids had backed down so quickly: he looked like a maddened killer about to go on a rampage.

Anderson had told me once that Jamaal possessed some kind of death magic. Magic that would allow him to kill someone without even touching them. Magic that *wanted* to be used, that ate at Jamaal's self-control. I knew without a doubt that Jamaal was struggling for control right now, that the magic inside him wanted to be released, and that those gang-bangers could very well end up dead—even though they'd chosen to walk away—if I couldn't get Jamaal to cool it.

Unfortunately, I'd never had much luck in the past with cooling his ire, and I was afraid anything I said right now would draw his attention—and his death magic—to me. Of course, I was immortal, and the gang-bangers were not, so I had to risk it.

"Hey. We've got two more crime scenes to investigate," I said gently. "I don't know about you, but I've had enough of this neighborhood. What say we move on?"

For a moment, I thought he hadn't even heard me. Then he blinked and shook his head sharply, like he was waking up from a dream. His fists unclenched, and he drew in a deep breath. He reached into his pocket and pulled out a cigarette and a lighter. His hands shook a little as he lit the cigarette and took a hasty drag. Wordlessly, he glanced down at me, and I read the question in his eyes.

I held up my hands. "Don't worry. I'm not going to tell Anderson you almost lost it."

He cocked his head, his brows drawing together in puzzlement. "Why not?"

Good question. I'd kept my mouth shut about one of Jamaal's little incidents before, and it had come back to bite both of us in the ass. You'd think I'd have learned my lesson. Except . . .

"Because you *didn't* lose it," I said. "Almost only counts in horseshoes and hand grenades, you know?"

He gave a short bark of something that vaguely resembled laughter before taking another long drag on his cigarette. "Some might argue I *am* a hand grenade," he said under his breath as he turned from me and unlocked the car, rounding the hood and heading for the driver's side. I hoped he would put out the cigarette before he got in, but I wasn't going to make an issue of it. He probably needed its calming effects more than I needed fresh air.

"More like an atom bomb," I replied, even though he'd clearly signaled the conversation was over and I knew his sense of humor wasn't exactly well honed.

He gave me a quelling look over the top of the car, but though he didn't laugh, he also didn't fly into a rage. For Jamaal, I figured that was a major breakthrough.

The scene of the second attack was a lot less unpleasant than the stinking underpass in Anacostia, though I doubted the victim had appreciated the upgrade. The neighborhood itself wasn't such great shakes, but the victim had been killed right against the fence that separated the neighborhood from the National Arboretum, an oasis of stately trees and well-manicured lawns. I wondered if he'd been trying to jump the fence to escape his attackers.

There were some houses across the street from the crime scene, their vinyl awnings and bent chain-link fences declaring them less than prime real estate. It was possible there was enough distance between the houses and the fence to keep anyone inside from hearing a disturbance late at night, at least if they were heavy sleepers. Possible but not likely. The cops had canvassed the neighborhood and gotten nothing, and I doubted I'd have any better success, even with Jamaal at my side.

There was still nothing that jumped out at me and yelled "I'm a clue!" so I had Jamaal take me to the third, most recent crime scene.

The third murder had taken place on the grounds of the McMillan Reservoir, which was, of course, closed for the night when we arrived. Jamaal parked on the street with a lovely view of a cemetery, and we walked to the barbed-wire-topped fence that surrounded a series of huge, empty fields, featuring regular circular depressions in the grass. I had no idea what the fields were about, but I made a wild guess that the rows of circular concrete structures that separated them were water towers of some sort. Our victim had been found just beside one of those vine-covered towers.

The crime-scene techs had found what they suspected was blood on the barbed wire atop the fence, so it looked like this victim had tried to escape by jumping a fence just like victim number two. Fat lot of good it had done him. The police were really scratching their heads over how the dogs had managed to follow him, since there were no breaks in the fence or tunnels underneath, and the gate was clear on the other side.

Come to think of it, I was scratching my head over that one, too.

"How did the dogs get past the fence?" I mused under my breath.

"Like this, I'll bet," Jamaal said. He took a quick glance around to make sure there were no witnesses, then walked through the fence like it was no more substantial than smoke. I touched the chain links, but for me, they were solid metal.

"How did you do that?" I asked, amazed. I was pretty sure I'd seen Jamaal walk through a locked door before, but we hadn't been on speaking terms at the time, so I hadn't ever asked him about it.

"It's a common ability among descendants of death gods. There's no way to keep Death out."

"Right," I said, nodding. "And Anubis is a death god."

As soon as the words left my mouth, I whirled around, turning my back to the fence and facing the street.

"Wait a second. He's a descendant of Anubis . . . a death god . . . and there's a cemetery right on the other side of that street." Something went *click* in my head. "And didn't we pass a cemetery right before we got to the last crime scene?"

Jamaal nodded. "Mount Olivet, yeah."

There were a lot of cemeteries in the area, so it could have been a total coincidence. But then again, maybe not. I frowned as I thought about the scene in Anacostia.

"There weren't any cemeteries that I saw around the first crime scene," I said.

"The Congressional Cemetery is right across the river," Jamaal said.

"You sure know your cemeteries."

"Descendant of a death goddess, remember?"

Out of the corner of my eye, I saw a police car cruising down the street. It slowed as it went past us, and I figured we looked kind of suspicious loitering by the fence.

"Let's head back," I said to Jamaal, starting toward the car. "I think I've learned all I'm going to for now."

The police cruiser picked up its pace as soon as Jamaal and I crossed the street.

When we arrived back at the mansion after our excursion, we saw a white Mazda parked in the circular drive.

"That's your sister's car, isn't it?" Jamaal asked as he pulled into the garage.

"Yep."

Things were a little bit . . . strange between Steph and me these days. We'd always been close, ever since her parents had taken me in as a rebellious eleven-year-old troublemaker, but our relationship seemed to be undergoing an adjustment period since I'd become a *Liberi*. I'd always loved Steph, but it was becoming abundantly clear that I'd never had a whole lot of respect for her. She was the rich and beautiful socialite who lived the easy life, and I was the street-smart ugly duckling who understood how the world "really" worked. At least, that's how I used to see us.

Steph had gotten hurt—badly—because of me, and I was finally beginning to see just how strong a person she really was. But I'd been treating her like a child in need of protection for a long time, and I was having a hard time backing off and treating her like the responsible adult she was. Which meant I couldn't hide my disapproval of her relationship—whatever the hell it was—with Blake. That disapproval rubbed her the wrong way, big-time.

Jamaal stayed outside to smoke another cigarette, and I cautiously entered the house, hoping not to run into Steph and Blake. It was amazing how hard a time I had not editorializing whenever I saw them together.

Seriously, though, who could blame me? Blake was a descendant of Eros, and he had the power to arouse an overwhelming and unnatural lust in anyone, male or female, whenever he felt like it. I knew he wasn't doing that to Steph, but it made me uneasy that he *could*. And then there was that other major downside to their relationship: according to Blake, he was such a supernaturally good lover that if he slept with a woman more than once, she'd never be satisfied with another man for the rest of her life. On the surface, it sounded like a ridiculous boast, and yet I knew he was dead serious.

Blake had enough of a conscience to keep out of Steph's bed—so far—but he *was* a guy, and I had a hard time believing he would go very long without sex. Which meant that someday, he was either going to misplace his conscience and sleep with Steph, or he was going to break her heart. Neither alternative was acceptable to me, but no matter how logically I argued with Steph, she refused to stop seeing him. Maybe she thought the sexual limitations were convenient. After what she'd been through at Alexis's hands, maybe a relationship with no sex was all she could handle.

I made it up to my suite without encountering anyone and breathed a sigh of relief as I opened my door and stepped into my sitting room. Living in a house with eight other people didn't leave me with as much alone time as I was used to.

My first clue that something was up should have been that the lights were already on. I always turned them off when I left the room. But I was a little slow on the uptake, lost in thought, and I took a couple of steps in before I realized I wasn't going to get that blessed alone time after all.

Steph was curled up on my couch, drinking a cup of coffee, and apparently waiting for me. I almost jumped out of my skin when I caught sight of her, but I managed to keep things down to a soft gasp and an adrenaline spike.

"Have fun on your date with Jamaal?" she asked with a little smile.

"If you call walking around a stinky underpass in Anacostia a date," I said, sitting down beside Steph and wondering what was up.

She laughed and took a sip of her coffee. "I've seen Jamaal, remember?"

My cheeks heated just a little, because yeah, I had to admit, Jamaal was a thing of beauty, and I would have had to be dead not to have noticed. But he's beautiful in the way that a leopard is beautiful—nice to look at, but you're a hell of a lot better off if there are some sturdy steel bars between you.

"Just because he's a hottie doesn't mean investigating crime scenes with him is romantic or anything. In case you haven't noticed, the guy's a psycho."

Steph had never seen Jamaal in action, but she knew about his previous vendetta against me, and she knew just how violent that vendetta had been. It should have been enough to quell even the slightest hint of attraction in me, but I had a long history of being attracted to the wrong men.

"Nikki . . ." Steph said in a warning tone, and I realized I might be protesting just a little too much.

"There's nothing going on between me and Jamaal," I said in what I hoped was a calm voice. "I'm not a moron."

Steph laughed. "You are where men are concerned."

"Says the woman who's dating a descendant of Eros."

That killed her amusement in a heartbeat. "Don't start."

I held up my hands in a gesture of surrender. "I'm not trying to start anything. Now, why don't you tell me why you're lying in wait for me? I know it's not because you want to talk about relationships."

Steph scrutinized me. She's two years older than me, which means she thinks she's older and wiser. Sometimes she can't resist dispensing advice, and I was afraid this was going to be one of those times.

I was more relieved than I liked to admit when she sighed and shook her head. "Actually," she said, reaching for a brief-case on the floor, "in a way, this *is* a bit about relationships. Just not the romantic kind."

"Huh?"

Steph popped open the briefcase, withdrew a manila folder, and handed it to me.

"What's this?" I asked, taking it cautiously from her hand, as if expecting it to bite.

"Your adoption papers," she said, and I quickly dropped the folder onto the coffee table.

Despite being a private investigator, I'd never had any interest in trying to locate my birth mother. The woman had abandoned me in a church when I was four, and I wanted nothing to do with her or with the baby brother she'd been carrying in her arms the last time I saw her. I knew my adoptive parents, the Glasses, had a whole bunch of paperwork they'd kept for me, in case I ever changed my mind, but I'd never even given a passing thought to asking for it.

"What are *you* doing with my adoption papers?" I asked.

The Glasses were still on their around-the-world cruise and would be for another six weeks, so I knew they hadn't given the folder to Steph.

She gave me a chiding look that told me she thought I was being intentionally dense. Maybe I was.

"There's this thing called a key. You put it in the door, and, voilà, it opens. I thought you might try out this incredible invention yourself and get the file now that the mystery of your origins has become so much more interesting, but I got tired of waiting for you to make your move."

I looked at her askance. She knew perfectly well I had no intention of tracking down my birth mother. I didn't really think what I'd learned about myself changed anything. I wanted nothing to do with my birth mother. Even if I *wanted* to find her, I wasn't sure it was possible. She'd done a damned thorough job of abandoning me. The police were never even able to find out my last name, and all I could tell them was that my mom and I had been traveling by bus for a long time before she'd taken me to the church and left me there. It wasn't like she'd purposely put me up for adoption with a nice, neat paper trail.

"I'm really not interested," I told Steph, grabbing the folder and trying to give it back to her.

"Yes, you are," she said with total conviction. "It's possible you got your divine blood through your mother, isn't it?"

The thought had already occurred to me. I'd even had a dream about the day she'd abandoned me, and in that dream, she'd suddenly developed a glyph on her forehead. But that had to be wishful thinking on my part. It was nice to think that my mom might have been a Descendant and might have been in trouble with the Olympians. If that were the case, I could tell myself she'd abandoned me in an attempt to sever our connection and protect me in case the Olympians caught up with her. But I'm not what you'd call a Pollyanna. It made a nice fantasy, but I was a big believer in Occam's Razor, and the simplest explanation for her abandonment was that she hadn't wanted me. I preferred to keep my faint hope that she'd abandoned me for a noble reason, and if I went looking for her and found her, I would most likely destroy that pleasant fantasy forever.

"It's possible, but I don't care," I said, still trying to get Steph to take the folder back. Of course, she wouldn't.

"I know you *do* care," she said gently. "You don't think I can see how badly you want to know why she left you?"

With a grunt of frustration, I threw the folder onto the coffee table. "I *don't* want to know," I insisted. "I want there to be a lovely, happy ending, where I go searching for her and find her and discover that she left me for my own good. But that isn't likely, and if she abandoned me because she didn't want me, then I'd really rather not know. So stop pushing me."

"I can't force you to do anything with the information," Steph said. "You can look for her or not. It's up to you. But I think you're wrong. I think you're the kind of person who'd rather know the truth than be left with a mystery. I know you've never been interested in looking for her before, but I think a big part of that was because you didn't think you had any hope of finding her. Well, now you do."

Maybe she was right, but I'd had enough crisis in my life lately. I didn't want to add to it by starting down this road, one that could so easily lead to a heaping helping of pain.

"I've got a lot of other stuff on my plate," I said. "I don't have time for any personal crap."

Steph gave me a long-suffering look. "Okay. Fine. Hang out in Denial Land a little longer. Eventually, curiosity is going to get the better of you, and you'll go looking for those answers. When you're ready, the file will be waiting for you."

She stood up, pointedly leaving the folder on my coffee

table. I hurried to stand up, too, afraid she was angry with me again, but there was no anger in her eyes, only a hint of pity, which was just as bad, if not worse.

"I love you, you know?" she said. "And I know getting there sucked for you, but I'm glad you became part of our family. I hope you know that."

My throat felt suspiciously tight, and I found myself giving Steph a hug.

I'm not the most demonstrative person in the world, and I could feel her little start of surprise. But she hugged me back and seemed to accept that hug as a suitable alternative to the words that I couldn't force out of my throat.

When Steph was gone, I sat on my couch for longer than I care to admit, staring at the folder.

Did I want to find my birth mother? I'd told Steph categorically no, but I knew deep down inside that she was right, that there was a part of me that had always longed to know the truth. Even if it turned out to be painful and ugly.

But maybe now wasn't a good time to go poking around. I already had a supernatural murder case on my plate. One seemingly impossible task at a time seemed like enough.

I left the folder on the coffee table right where it was, the temptation out in the open and staring me in the face, daring me to go searching. I ignored it, instead popping open my laptop and looking for more information on the two identified murder victims.

It was hard not to keep glancing over at it from time to time, though.

Four

A few more hours of research on the two identified victims gave me approximately squat.

Different backgrounds, different ages, different socioeconomic status. The only thing I could find in common between them was that they were both white males, which was about all the police had been able to say about the first victim, anyway. It wasn't exactly a lot to go on, and I had the uneasy suspicion there would have to be another victim before I'd be able to make heads or tails of the case. If I ever could. A pillar of confidence I was not.

Tired and frustrated, I headed down to the kitchen to brew a pot of coffee. My plan was to ingest large quantities of caffeine and then continue researching the victims' lives until I found something or my vision went blurry, whichever came first.

My plans took an unexpected detour when I stepped into the kitchen and discovered I wasn't alone. Anderson was sitting at the table in the breakfast nook, sipping from a cup of something hot and steaming. A quick glance at the coffee maker told me his beverage of choice was probably tea.

Before Anderson and I had had our little talk, I might have peeked into the room, seen him sitting there, and then beaten a hasty retreat. I was tempted even now to just grab a bottle of water from the fridge, but that smacked too much of cowardice. Besides, I was eventually going to have to get over my discomfort around him, seeing as I was living in the same house with him and he was my boss.

Anderson raised his mug to me in a silent salute, and I nodded. Then I began the ritual of making coffee, hyperaware that Anderson was nearby. I kept sneaking glances at him, and what I saw almost made me forget the whole god-of-death-and-vengeance thing.

He looked . . . sad. Almost lost. And I took a wild guess about just what the cause might be.

I doctored a cup of coffee, trying to talk myself out of starting a conversation with Anderson. Whatever was wrong was none of my business. Especially if it had something to do with Emma. Anderson wasn't my friend, not in any real sense of the word, so I had no moral obligation to try to make him feel better.

Logical arguments had no effect, and once my coffee was ready, I found myself walking toward the kitchen table instead of heading back to my suite and my work. I sat across from Anderson but didn't quite know what to say.

"Making any progress on the case?" he asked, then took a sip of his tea.

I shrugged. "Not a whole lot. The best lead I've got is that the murders seem to be happening close to cemeteries."

"I'll wager that's more than the police have."

He was no doubt right. Normal people wouldn't pick up on the proximity to cemeteries because they'd never dream it was significant. At least, not now—a few more murders with the same pattern might change that.

"It's more than nothing," I agreed, "but not as much as I'd hoped for."

Anderson nodded. "And how did you and Jamaal get along?"

Okay. I'd sat down to talk to Anderson because he looked like he needed a little human contact, but that didn't mean I wanted to have a deep, personal conversation, especially about myself. Or about Jamaal, for that matter. I remembered how Jamaal had almost lost it when those gang-bangers had challenged him, and I knew that Anderson would expect me to tell him what had happened. That didn't mean I was about to do it.

"We're both still alive, and no body parts are missing," I

said with a hint of a grin. Maybe if I kept it light, we'd quickly move on to another subject, and I'd stop feeling uncomfortable. "It's an improvement."

I decided that only a moron would ask Anderson probing questions; I then decided that sometimes I *was* a moron, like right now. As a bonus, it would be a handy change of subject.

"Did you and Emma have a fight?" I asked. I was pretty sure I already knew the answer, because only Emma seemed able to put that particular shade of misery on his face. Blake had once described Emma as "high-maintenance." From what I'd seen, that was a charitable assessment.

Anderson smiled faintly. "Is it that obvious?"

I didn't bother to answer. "Are you okay?" I asked instead.

He shrugged. "We're going through a rough patch. It's not the first time. And I can hardly blame her after what she's been through."

Thanks to Konstantin, Emma had spent the better part of ten years chained at the bottom of a pond, unable to free herself but also unable to escape through death. If that wasn't an ordeal that would warp a person beyond recognition, I didn't know what was.

"Give her some time," I said, though I didn't for a moment think time was going to fix whatever was going on between the two of them. "She's doing a lot better now than she was when we first brought her home."

Being a raging bitch was better than being catatonic, right?

Anderson nodded. "She's doing better, but the scars . . ." His voice trailed off, and he looked haunted. "She's always been volatile, but she's a powder keg right now. One wrong word, and . . ."

Yeah, that about summed it up. But from what I'd gathered from the rest of the *Liberi,* that wasn't anything new for her.

"Maybe you need to learn not to speak," I suggested.

Anderson's smile was faint but nice to see.

The smile disappeared moments later, when Emma bulled into the room. Her eyes scanned the kitchen—obviously looking for Anderson—but when she saw me sitting there, she did a double take, like it was a total shock that the two of them might not be alone in the room. Maybe she forgot there were eight people living in the mansion besides herself.

Emma was disgustingly beautiful, with glossy black hair that would have done a shampoo-commercial actress proud and the figure and face to go with it. She was kind of like Steph, in that she instantly brought out my inner insecurities, making me feel plain and dowdy in comparison.

The look she gave me was anything but friendly as she stalked over to the coffee pot and helped herself to a cup, her movements jerky with anger. Apparently, she was eager to resume her fight with Anderson, and I was in the way.

I wanted to get up and flee the room, but the pleading look Anderson shot me kept me rooted to my chair. I knew without being told that he was hoping my presence would curb Emma's enthusiasm for their fight, but I also knew it wasn't going to work. Emma had never shown any sign that it bothered her to fight in front of the rest of us.

Why did I stay anyway? I guess I'm a glutton for punishment.

Emma brought her cup of coffee to the table, fixing me with a glare that made me shiver inside. There was a spark of madness in her gaze, and I really didn't want it to remain fixed on me.

"I see you're consoling my dear husband after our little quarrel," Emma said with a curl of her lip. "How kind of you."

Yikes. Guess I should have run when I had the chance. I held up my cup of coffee and tried to look nonchalant.

"I'm just drinking a cup of coffee. My laptop and I needed a little time apart." I decided that it wasn't too late to get out from between the happy couple, so I pushed my chair back from the table.

Emma was still staring daggers at me. Her expression reminded me a little too much of how Jamaal had looked when he'd lost his mind in rage, and I wondered exactly how unstable she was. I'd thought of her as annoying ever since she'd started talking again, but I'd never considered her dangerous.

The look in her eyes now said that had been a mistake.

"Nikki has every right to be here," Anderson said quietly, and I tried not to wince. I was now officially stuck in the middle, and I wanted to kick myself for not getting out when the getting was good.

"I'm going to go back to work now," I announced, eyeing the doorway longingly. Unfortunately, Emma had positioned herself in front of it, and considering the sparks in her eyes, I didn't think getting close to her was a good idea.

"Oh, no," Emma said with a hard smile. "Please don't let me interrupt your little tête-à-tête. I know you and my husband get along *famously*."

Double yikes. If I didn't know better, I could have sworn she sounded jealous. But why the hell would a woman like her be jealous of someone like me? It wasn't like there was anything going on between Anderson and me. I liked him and all, but there was nothing romantic about it.

Anderson heaved a sigh. "Please, Emma. Don't be childish."

She snorted. "Says the man who runs away from conflict as if it might kill him."

I took a couple of steps toward the door, hoping maybe Emma would move out of the way and let me go. She stood her ground, and I came to an indecisive stop.

"We've had a year's worth of conflict in the past week alone," Anderson countered, sounding tired. "Leave it be for a while, why don't you?"

"Leave it be?" she cried, her voice rising. "How can you possibly ask me to leave it be? Especially when you run straight into the arms of your new girlfriend here."

O-kay. Crazy as it seemed, I'd have to say that really was jealousy in Emma's voice. Which made no sense.

"Listen," I said, hoping I didn't sound as desperately uncomfortable as I was, "I'm going to get out of your hair. You two hash things out in private, okay?"

Neither one of them looked at me, locked in their own staring match. I'd had enough, so despite my reluctance to go anywhere near Emma when she looked like she was about to explode, I walked toward the doorway, giving her as wide a berth as I could.

Just as I thought I was home free and that she would let me pass unmolested, Emma reached out and grabbed the top of my arm in a brutally tight grip, yanking me toward her so hard that half my coffee sloshed out of the mug onto the floor.

"You listen here," she growled at me, baring her teeth.

"Emma!" Anderson said sharply, and I heard the sound of his chair scraping hastily back. "What are you doing?"

Emma gave me a little shake. "You stay away from my husband. Am I making myself perfectly clear?"

Yeah, she was making it perfectly clear that she was insane. Why did the nut cases always seem to focus on me?

I fought the urge to wince at the tightness of her grip. Maybe humoring the crazy would have been my best move, but I didn't think things through before I spoke.

"Your husband is my boss," I said in what I thought was an admirably calm voice. "Are you really going to fly into a rage every time I speak to him? Because you have to know there's nothing going on between us."

Her grip on my arm became even tighter, which I hadn't thought was possible, and this time, I couldn't suppress a gasp of pain.

"Emma," Anderson said. "Let go of her. *Now.* You can fight with me all you want, but leave my people out of it."

I had a feeling he was only making things worse by sticking up for me, and the blackness I saw in Emma's eyes confirmed it. I was beginning to wish we'd left her at the bottom of that pond, though I felt guilty for the thought the moment it crossed my mind.

"Stay away from him," Emma repeated, then let go of my arm and shoved me out the door.

FIVE

Predictably, Emma's and Anderson's raised voices echoed down the hall as I made my escape. The whole incident had completely creeped me out.

Why the hell was Emma jealous of me? I could think of no logical reason, and no matter how closely I scrutinized my own actions, I couldn't think of anything I'd done that could give Emma the impression I was after her husband.

But what really had me worried was that her hostility toward me seemed to be escalating. If I wasn't doing anything to fan the flames—and I was sure I wasn't—I worried that nothing I *did* do or say would calm them. I didn't get the feeling that Anderson's people were huge fans of Emma, but she was Anderson's wife and had been with them way longer than I had. Life in the mansion could get very, very difficult for me if I couldn't find some way to patch things up.

With those cheerful thoughts in mind, I retreated to my suite to work on the clearer, more manageable task of catching a serial killer. However, fatigue was making me loopy, and my brain seemed determined to obsess over the situation with Emma. I wasn't getting anything useful done, so I forced myself to turn off the computer and crawl into bed.

Eventually, I drifted off to sleep. I slept late enough that there was no one in the kitchen when I cautiously poked my head in the next morning. Someone had cleaned up the coffee

I'd spilled. I'd bet anything it wasn't Emma. I hurried through making a fresh pot of coffee, wanting to get out of the kitchen quickly. This was one of those times when I really missed living in my condo. It was like the tension of the argument had soaked into the walls, and I was glad to escape back to my room. Maybe I should buy myself a coffee maker to keep in the suite.

When the caffeine hit my system and woke up my still-sluggish brain cells, I realized I'd really needed that sleep. It seemed my subconscious mind had been hard at work mulling over the issue of how to catch the killer while I was sleeping, and I now had the inklings of a plan. Maybe not the safest or sanest plan in the world but a plan nonetheless.

My first impulse was to go haring off on my own the moment I had some idea what to do. For most of my adult life, I'd been an independent operator, doing what I wanted, when I wanted. That was one of the big perks of starting my own business and not joining someone else's P.I. firm.

I wasn't an independent operator anymore. I was part of a team—a concept I was still getting used to—and I had a boss to answer to. I knew better than to think Anderson would be okay with me making unilateral plans of action. Not only that, but for once in my life, I had some serious backup available, which was a nice luxury. Nonetheless, it chafed a bit, because talking to Anderson before acting smacked of asking permission, something I'd never been too good at.

I found Anderson ensconced in his study, the one room in his wing of the mansion that the rest of us *Liberi* were actually allowed to enter without special dispensation. He was sitting at his desk, his brow furrowed as he stared at a piece of paper in front of him. I had a feeling he wasn't really seeing that paper, that he was actually lost in thought, but he didn't jump when I rapped on the door. He merely turned his chair toward me and raised his eyebrows in inquiry.

I made a show of looking up and down the hall before stepping cautiously into the room. "Is Emma around?" I asked. "Do I need to get us a chaperone?"

As attempts at humor go, it wasn't my best. The corners of Anderson's mouth tightened, and he dropped his gaze like he was embarrassed.

"I'm really sorry about that," he said softly, and I wanted to kick myself for being a smartass. Marital troubles weren't funny, not to the people involved. As a private investigator, I'd seen more than ample evidence of the fact.

I sighed and invited myself in, dropping into one of the chairs in front of Anderson's desk like a good little employee.

"You don't have to apologize," I assured him. "I'm sorry about the dumb joke. Sometimes I joke when I'm uncomfortable."

Anderson leaned back in his chair. "I'm sorry that Emma and I have made you uncomfortable. What the Olympians did to her seems to have brought out every insecurity she's ever had. She's having a hard time coping, and I'm not making things any easier by fighting with her."

I didn't think Anderson had anything to apologize for. From what I could tell, he was acting perfectly reasonable. It was Emma who was the loose cannon, but even with my low relationship IQ, I knew better than to say that.

"She wants me to declare war on the Olympians," Anderson said. "She can hardly think of anything but revenge."

"To tell you the truth, I've been kind of expecting you to declare war myself. I thought the only reason you weren't fighting them was that they had Emma."

He shook his head. "That was just one reason. I hate Konstantin, and I hate the Olympians, and I hate everything they stand for."

Was it my imagination, or were there literal sparks coming from his eyes?

"But there are a lot more of them than there are of us," Anderson continued. "And with their stable of brainwashed Descendants, they have far more deadly weapons than we do. If I start a war, then it's highly likely all my people will end up dead. It's not a chance I'm willing to take. Now, if I could get Konstantin somewhere nice and private where there were no witnesses, that would be another matter altogether."

His smile was fierce and chilling, and I was glad that menace was not directed at me. Then the smile faded and the menace with it. "I know Emma understands my reasons deep down, and I know she'll come to her senses as her psyche heals. But for now, she's not thinking straight."

Personally, I didn't think Emma was the one who wasn't thinking straight. I'm no shrink, but I felt pretty convinced that her trauma had caused permanent damage, that she would never go back to being the wife Anderson remembered. Assuming that wife had ever existed in the first place.

"But you didn't come here to talk about me and Emma," Anderson said. "What can I do for you?"

"I have an idea for how we might—and I emphasize *might*—catch our killer."

"I'm intrigued. Tell me more."

"You know how I told you last night the murders all occurred near cemeteries?"

He nodded.

"They've also all occurred on Friday nights."

"Hmm," Anderson said, his eyes narrowing. "I'm beginning to see where you might be going with this." And based on the way he was looking at me, he didn't like it.

Still, I forged on. "Seeing as this is Friday, I have a strong suspicion our killer will strike again tonight and that the attack will be somewhere near a cemetery."

Anderson nodded. "Probably true. But do you know how many cemeteries there are in the area?"

"A shitload," I agreed. "But when you look at a map, you can see that each attack occurred north of the attack before." I had brought my big map of the D.C. area with me, and I unfolded it on Anderson's desk, the sites of the three murders numbered and circled. They formed more of a triangle than a straight line, but I still felt there was a definite direction of movement. A pattern I could exploit.

"I've highlighted the cemeteries in yellow," I pointed out, "and I think if his pattern holds true, he'll hit near the Rock Creek Cemetery tonight." I pointed helpfully at the cemetery in question.

Anderson looked skeptical. "That seems like an awful lot of conjecture."

I couldn't help grinning. "Conjecture seems to be a big part of my power." My gut was telling me this wasn't all in my head, that there really was a pattern to the murders. I couldn't say I completely trusted my gut, but it had certainly steered me in the right direction many times before.

"Even if you're right, Rock Creek is huge. And if you have to include anything within walking distance in your search, the chances of you running into the killer are really low."

I grabbed the map and started wrestling it back into its tidy brochure size. "My chances are better if I go hang around the cemetery than if I sit here doing nothing. I checked the weather and the lunar calendar, and I should have plenty of moon action tonight." My powers were stronger in the moonlight, though it was difficult to pinpoint exactly what effect the moonlight had. The best explanation I had was that it made my hunches stronger and more accurate.

Anderson looked anything but convinced, and I couldn't say I blamed him. If I were an ordinary human being, or even an ordinary *Liberi,* my chances of finding the killer with so little information would be almost nil. But I wasn't an ordinary human being, not anymore.

"Look, it may still be a long shot," I said, "but what do we have to lose by trying?"

Anderson thought about it a little more, then came to a decision. "All right. We'll go stake out the cemetery tonight."

"We?" I'd known he wouldn't let me go alone, and with his ability to kill *Liberi,* Anderson seemed like a logical choice to go with me, but something about the way he said it told me he didn't mean just him and me. "Who's *we?*"

"All of us," Anderson said, and my jaw dropped. "We can cover a lot more ground if we all go together and then split up."

"But I'm the only one who's got a realistic shot at finding him. Maybe."

"Your shot at finding him doesn't get any worse if the rest of us are there looking, too, and our chances of actually *catching* him are a lot better. We don't know what he can do, and I'm not sure what it'll take to subdue him."

It was then that I realized the very important question I had so far failed to ask, had failed even to contemplate. "What are we going to do with him if and when we catch him?"

Anderson was the only one of us who could actually kill a *Liberi,* but I knew without asking that he wouldn't do it. For reasons I didn't understand—and was too fond of being alive to want to delve into—Anderson didn't want anyone to know who and what he actually was. Even Emma didn't know, and I doubted her finding out the truth would make their marriage any smoother. What Anderson saw in her—other than beauty—was beyond me.

"First, we'll question him and see how much of what the Olympians told us was the truth. There's nothing he can say to excuse what he's done, but if the Olympians are hiding something, I think it's important we find out what it is."

I had to agree, though given the ferocity of the killer's attacks, I wasn't sure how much reliable information we could get out of him. He seemed several eggs short of a dozen to me.

"Okay, so we question him," I said. "If we can. Then what?"

Anderson looked at me warily, and I knew I wasn't going to like whatever was coming next. "Then we hand him over to the Olympians."

I was right: I didn't like it.

"No way in hell I'm handing *anyone* over to those sons of bitches," I said in what I hoped was a calm voice.

I thought my statement might piss Anderson off, but there was no sign of it.

"What do you suggest we do instead?"

And that, of course, was the problem. Dogboy couldn't be allowed to run around ripping innocent bystanders to shreds, and Anderson wouldn't tip his hand by killing him.

"We can lock him up," I said weakly, though I already knew the suggestion sucked. We had some rooms in the basement that were basically prison cells, but it wasn't like we were equipped to be the killer's eternal prison guards.

"It's really hard to keep a death-god descendant locked up. Most of them can walk through walls and doors."

I sighed. "And fences," I murmured, remembering Jamaal's demonstration at the reservoir.

"If we can't contain him, then we have to kill him. And we're not equipped to do that."

He gave me a meaningful look, and I swallowed my desire to argue. "So we hand him over to the Olympians, and they have one of their pet Descendants kill him, and now they have a new *Liberi* under their thumb."

"I'll admit it's not an ideal solution," Anderson said. "But it's the best we've got."

Anger burned in my chest, and I fought to hold it back. That *wasn't* the best solution we had, and we both knew it. Death-by-Anderson was not a pleasant fate, and I hated the thought of putting anyone through it, but better that than to hand the Olympians a new *Liberi* on a silver platter. Not to mention that from what I'd heard, the Olympians weren't exactly into clean kills themselves.

"Why won't you—"

"Do not go there!" Anderson warned, and the steel in his voice told me in no uncertain terms that it wasn't open to discussion.

I bit my tongue, but it was hard. Generally, I liked Anderson. When I was able to see him as something other than my boss or a god, he seemed like a genuinely nice guy, and I respected his mission to make the world a better place. If it weren't for him, every descendant of a Greek deity in this mansion—me, Maggie, Blake, Emma, and Leo—would have been forced either to join the Olympians or forfeit our immortality to one of the Olympians' pet Descendants. Those descended from other pantheons—Jack, Jamaal, and Logan—would have been killed, their immortality "harvested" for someone the Olympians considered more worthy. And let's not even talk about all the hidden *Liberi* and their Descendant families Anderson had helped.

Anderson was one of the good guys, but right now, I thought he was being a coward.

I didn't say that out loud, of course, but I didn't make any particular effort to keep my opinion from showing on my face.

Anderson and I stared at each other in a silent battle of wills. Ordinarily, I'd bet on myself anytime, but to my shame, I looked away first. I could never unlearn what I'd found out about him, and I wasn't sure I'd ever be able to stand up to him the way I thought I should again.

SIX

We headed out toward the Rock Creek Cemetery at about ten o'clock. To my surprise, when Anderson had said we were all going, he'd really meant all. Even Emma joined us, though it was clear she'd rather have stayed home and let us do all the work. She had little interest in fighting evil—unless that evil was Konstantin.

It was way earlier than any of the previous attacks had occurred, but there was always hope—however faint—that we might be able to find and capture Dogboy before he struck. Anderson had assigned us to teams of two, with Leo, our immortal accountant and nonfighter, tacked on to one of the teams as a third wheel. I'd argued against him coming, but he was another warm body, and it was theoretically possible he could be helpful. Maybe he could capture our killer and bore him to death with talk of managed futures.

Anderson teamed me up with Jamaal again, but I didn't mind quite so much. Jamaal had been perfectly civil to me on our mission the day before; and besides, if you have to prowl a cemetery in the middle of the night, having a super-intimidating death-goddess descendant by your side is the way to go.

As Anderson had said, the Rock Creek Cemetery was huge. As if that wasn't enough death to choke anyone, there was also the National Cemetery right across from its southeastern border. Both cemeteries were surrounded by spiky iron fences, but it wouldn't be particularly hard for a determined trespasser to get over them.

Each team was assigned a section to patrol. Something about the stretch of Rock Creek Road that ran between the two cemeteries called to me, so Jamaal and I took that as the focus of our surveillance. We'd determined that my supernatural aim made me the most likely to take the killer down without too much of a struggle, so my .38 Special was tucked in my coat pocket. It was about as creepy a section of road as I could imagine, with the National Cemetery and its regular pattern of small rectangular headstones on one side and the Rock Creek Cemetery with its more varied headstones and mausoleums on the other. The streetlights made a feeble attempt to light the darkness, but there were enough pools of deep shadow to make *anyone* uncomfortable.

The night wasn't particularly cold, although there was a chill wind that made me long for a cup of hot chocolate in front of a crackling fire. Jamaal wasn't much of a talker, so our first hour of surveillance went by with nary a word between us to break the eerie silence. There was occasional traffic on the street, but the later it got, the longer the gaps between cars, and the sense of isolation made the hairs on the back of my neck stand up. We weren't actually *in* a cemetery, but my lizard brain didn't much appreciate the distinction.

After the first hour, Jamaal broke out the clove cigarettes. He smoked with quiet intensity. Usually, the cigarettes seemed to be good at helping take the edge off, but he still seemed kind of agitated when he stubbed the butt out. I wasn't entirely surprised to see him light another about five minutes later.

"What do you think the significance of the cemeteries is?" I asked Jamaal when I couldn't stand the silence anymore. "Why does the killer attack near them?"

He blew out a steady stream of smoke before answering. "They may call to him. Maybe he feels most at home among the dead."

"Could it have anything to do with his death magic? I mean, do you think it's, I don't know, powered by the cemeteries or something?"

He shook his head, making the beads at the ends of his braids click and rattle. "I don't know any more about this guy or how his power works than you do." There was an edge to his voice, like maybe my questions were getting on his nerves. He took another deep drag on his cigarette. "I'm descended from Kali, not Anubis."

"Yeah, but they're both death gods, and—"

"And death gods all look the same to you?"

I came to an abrupt halt and stared at him. Was he really suggesting there was something racist about my questions? I noticed the fingers of his free hand were twitching slightly. I didn't think that meant anything good.

I held up my hands innocently. "Whoa. Remember, I've only been a *Liberi* for a few weeks," I said, keeping my voice calm instead of snapping at him as I was tempted to do. "I don't know as much about the gods or about magic as the rest of you, and I never will if I don't ask questions. I didn't mean to offend you, if that's what I did."

Jamaal's eyes glittered in the darkness, and my pulse began a slow and steady rise. If he was going to lose his grip on his temper, I was in deep shit. We were smack dab in the middle of the stretch of road between the two cemeteries, with no possibility of anyone hearing if I yelled for help. Not that I *would* yell for help against Jamaal if it was possible civilians might come to my aid.

Before I had a chance to get too worked up, Jamaal closed his eyes and sucked in a deep breath. He held it for a moment, then let it out slowly. When his eyes opened again, his hand had stopped twitching, and he no longer looked like he was irrationally pissed off at me.

"Sorry," he said softly, hanging his head. "I'm getting the feeling hanging around the cemeteries for so long isn't such a great idea for me. It's making me . . . edgy." He took one last long draw on his cigarette, then used the glowing butt to light another.

I was pretty sure he was feeling ashamed of his weakness, but I had to wonder how much of it was his fault. Did being around so many dead people make his death magic long to come out and play? He had trouble controlling it under the best of circumstances.

I took my life in my hands and decided to try a little humor to lighten the mood. "And this is different from the norm how, exactly?"

He gave me a rueful smile, and my pulse blipped from something other than fear. Jamaal with a smile on his face was enough to make any red-blooded woman swoon.

"I'm sure there's room for one more grave in there," he said, jerking his thumb toward the Rock Creek Cemetery.

I blinked. "Wait a minute. Did you just make a joke?" Jamaal had the sense of humor of an angry bear.

"Who says I was joking? Now, let's keep moving. And save the Q and A for sometime I'm not surrounded by the dead."

We resumed our pattern, walking up one side of the road, then crossing when we got to the end and taking the other side on the way back. The moon was close enough to full to give us some light, but the place still felt oppressively dark. And Jamaal's body language was getting progressively more tense. Despite his chain-smoking, I saw no sign that the clove cigarettes were helping the situation.

"Are you okay?" I asked tentatively, afraid the question would set him off.

His Adam's apple bobbed, and he rattled his beads again. "I'm sick of all this useless wandering around. I want to *do* something."

No doubt about it, he wasn't in as much control as he had been just a few minutes ago. If I didn't think it would make him blow up, I'd have suggested he head back to the car and take a break for a while. There was a light sheen of sweat on his face despite the bracing wind, and he'd picked up his pace, covering so much ground with his long strides I could barely keep up. I could practically feel the . . . *something* . . . within him that was struggling to burst out.

"We should be *hunting* the killer," Jamaal continued, "not just hoping to stumble on him by pure luck."

"We're hunting the best we can with so little information to go on," I reminded him. "And there's a luck factor to—"

"Goddammit, Nikki! Shut up!" He was panting now, both hands clenched into fists. He looked as feral as he had the day before during our brief confrontation with the kids.

I'd have obliged him, except I'd been quiet for most of our watch, and that hadn't stopped his control from decaying.

"How can I help?" I asked instead. He was as twitchy as an addict desperate for a fix, and I suspected he was about as unpredictable. He was also infinitely more dangerous.

A growl rose from his throat. "You can't."

And then he disappeared into thin air.

I had a sense of motion off to my left, and though I looked in that direction, I couldn't see anything. I heard Jamaal's braids rattling, and I used the sound to track his motion as he either leapt over or went straight through the fence and into the cemetery.

"Jamaal!" I called, but he didn't answer, and the sound of clicking braids faded. "Dammit!"

I didn't know where he was going. Maybe even *he* didn't know where he was going. With my subconscious tracking skills, I could probably follow him, but I wasn't exactly sure I wanted to catch him. Whatever progress he'd made toward becoming sane and rational seemed to have fled him completely, and the effect had obviously grown worse the longer we'd been near the cemeteries. I hoped to God it would fade once we got him out of here. Assuming we could.

I might not have known where Jamaal was or where he was going, but what I did know was that I was standing in the dark all alone with a cemetery on both sides of me. Immortal or not, this was *not* a situation in which I felt even remotely comfortable. I dug my phone out of my coat pocket. I hated to tattle on Jamaal and tell Anderson he'd wigged out on me, but I didn't see that I had much choice.

I'd just turned on the phone when I heard the sound of running feet behind me. My first thought was that it was Jamaal coming back, and I wasn't sure if that was a good thing or a bad thing. I shoved the phone back into my pocket, wanting both hands free to defend myself if Jamaal had gone completely berserk, but when I whirled around, the running figure I saw was not Jamaal.

He was approaching from Allison Street, which led to one of the residential areas near the cemeteries, and he was running full speed, arms pumping like mad, coattails flapping behind him. He tried to turn the other way on Rock Creek Church—away from the cemeteries—but something spooked him, and he let out a strangled cry. Then he was running between the cemeteries. Straight toward me.

I got a quick look at him when he passed under one of the streetlights. A tall, well-built white male with dark hair and a matching beard and mustache. His eyes were wide with terror, and I knew he was running for his life. I even had a guess what he was running from, only there was no one else in sight. No dogs, either. Just this one guy, running.

I reached into my other coat pocket, drawing out the extremely illegal concealed weapon I was carrying. Too bad I didn't see anything to shoot at. I took a step toward our would-be victim, thinking I was going to feel like an idiot if he was just some asshole on a bad drug trip.

"Where are they?" I called to him, making sure not to point my gun straight at him.

His eyes went even wider, and I had the feeling he hadn't even seen me until I'd spoken.

"Help me!" he cried desperately as he pumped his legs even harder. Then he came to an abrupt stop, practically falling on his ass as he ground his shoes into the grassy earth that bounded the cemetery.

Just like I saw nothing to explain why he was running, I saw nothing to explain why he'd stopped. Until he screamed, that is.

A shadowy shape coalesced out of the darkness, leaping through the air. The shape was little more than a blot in the darkness until it crashed into the victim, when it became a medium-sized dog that looked like a small wolf. A coyote, maybe. It clamped its jaws around the guy's arm, and even a solid blow to its muzzle didn't dislodge it.

Another shape flew through the air at him, and I fired at it. The creature went insubstantial again in midair, and my bullet passed harmlessly through where it had been. The other, however, had a firm grip on the victim's arm, snarling and shaking its head as he screamed in pain and terror.

I took aim at the creature . . . coyote . . . whatever the hell it was. Despite knowing my aim was infallible, I hesitated before pulling the trigger, afraid to shoot at something that was so close to the victim, but I figured I didn't have much of a choice. I couldn't see any more of them coming, but I *knew* they were there, that we would soon be overwhelmed.

I squeezed the trigger, and this time, the coyote stayed nice and solid. The bullet hit it square in the head, and the man was finally able to shake it off his arm. The coyote landed limply on the pavement, but I saw no sign of blood except for that on its muzzle.

The man climbed to his feet, breath sawing in and out of his lungs as blood soaked the arm of his coat. I hurried to help him, knowing he had to be in dire pain. I kept a careful eye on the coyote as I slipped past it. Its eyes were closed, its tongue extended through bloodied teeth.

It wasn't a coyote, I realized. It was a jackal.

I couldn't remember ever seeing one in person before, but I'd watched enough nature shows to know one when I saw it. I supposed it made sense for a descendant of a jackal-headed god to have a pack of them at his beck and call.

By the time I reached the man and put my arm around his waist to help support him, the jackal had become insubstantial again, just a vaguely dog-shaped shadow against the grass.

"What the hell?" the dazed victim murmured as the shadow lost its shape and dissipated into the darkness of the night.

I didn't have time to contemplate the latest dose of weirdness before something slammed into the guy's back, knocking him to the ground despite my arm around him. When he fell, there was a jackal on his back, its jaws clamped on his shoulder. I pointed the gun, but even with supernatural aim, I had no shot. Anything that hit the jackal would hit the man, too.

Another jackal coalesced out of the air in midleap, landing at the victim's feet and grabbing hold of an ankle. The one on the guy's back could have torn his throat out by now if it wanted to, but it settled for sinking its fangs into the flesh of his shoulder. His screams were swallowed by the emptiness of the night and the silence of the dead.

Two more jackals appeared and dove at the victim, jaws snapping and releasing as the first two maintained their grip, holding the victim down so the rest of the pack could attack with impunity. I still had no shot at the one on the guy's back, but I took aim at the one holding his leg. My bullet hit it square in the head, knocking it back, but it was a Pyrrhic victory, because another immediately took its place. Shooting the jackals was like chopping the heads off the Hydra, so I whirled around, looking for the *Liberi* who controlled them.

He was standing about twenty yards away, leaning against a lamppost, watching the action. He looked like a homeless dude, with lank, greasy hair, filthy sweats, and tattered Windbreaker. He was so skinny it was a wonder the light breeze didn't blow him away. His breath steamed in the night air as he stared at the jackal I'd just killed, his expression one of rage, madness, and, it appeared, raw grief.

I took aim at his head. Because he was *Liberi,* I couldn't kill him. However, I could incapacitate him, and hopefully if he lost consciousness, the jackals would go *poof.*

The jackal I'd shot disappeared, and the *Liberi*'s eyes snapped to mine. The feral smile that shaped his lips gave me about half a second's warning, but it wasn't enough. I tried to dodge and shoot at the same time, but the jackal slammed into me so hard even my supernatural aim couldn't compensate.

The gun fired into the ground as the jackal grabbed hold of my arm with crushingly strong jaws. White-hot pain drew a scream from my throat, but I kept my head enough to transfer the gun to my left hand. Gritting my teeth as my eyes watered and I fought desperately to stay on my feet, I fired at the jackal from point-blank range. It let go, but another one was instantly on me.

I knew the jackals couldn't kill me. I was *Liberi,* immortal. I'd seen Jamaal recover from being decapitated. None of that logic did anything to quell the primal panic that coursed through my blood as I fell.

Another jackal came at me, its jaw clamping down on my left wrist, shaking me until the gun fell from my limp fingers. I slammed my other fist into the side of its head. My body was fighting on autopilot, the pain and terror overwhelming conscious thought. The jackals were everywhere, winking in and out of their solid forms as they darted in for attacks.

I was sure I was about to find out exactly what it felt like for a *Liberi* to die. The magic of the *Liberi* meant that I would revive, but logic is no match for panic. The jackals were going to rip me into bloody shreds, devour me, and they were going to take their time about it.

But all at once, they disappeared.

I lifted my head and saw their master give me a mocking salute before he, too, faded into the night.

Seconds later, a collection of shadows drew together, and Jamaal emerged from their depths. It looked for a moment like he was going to take off in pursuit of the killer, but it was pretty damn hard to follow someone who was invisible. And as big and powerful as Jamaal is, I don't know if he'd have had any better success against the phantom jackals than I had.

I was bleeding from bites on both of my arms and one of my legs. I was pretty sure I'd broken a finger or two punching a jackal in its hard skull. It would all heal in a matter of hours, but goddamn, did it ever hurt.

The poor man I'd been trying to help was in considerably worse shape. He lay facedown on the grass, blood seeping from about a dozen wounds. I could tell he was still alive, because his back occasionally rose and fell with a breath, but I didn't think he would stay alive much longer if he didn't get immediate medical attention.

I forced myself into a sitting position, the pain almost making me black out, then scooted nearer to the victim. I got a better look at him and wished I hadn't. There was a lot of blood, and so many wounds I didn't know which one I should try to put pressure on first. I glanced up at Jamaal, meaning to snap at him to get over here and help me, but the words died in my throat when I saw him.

He was not himself. Literally. I mean, yes, it was *Jamaal* standing there, but not the Jamaal I knew. The small crescent-moon glyph in the center of his forehead was glowing with a golden light, as were his eyes. His expression was of a man in a trance, seeing nothing of the world around him. He took one slow step toward the bleeding man, then another. His hand rose as if guided by an invisible puppet string, reaching out toward the victim.

I hadn't the faintest idea what to do or say. Jamaal wasn't easy to reason with even when he wasn't out of his mind, and I wasn't sure he knew I was there at the moment, his attention entirely focused on the victim. I wanted to at least put myself between the two, but my own pain was making me light-headed and wobbly.

The victim's eyes flew open suddenly, but, as with Jamaal, there was no sign of human intelligence in them. Jamaal's reaching hand tightened, fingers curling into a fist. He was still about five feet away from the victim, not within touching range, but I knew he was doing *something*. Something not good.

The victim's eyes stayed open, but even so, I could see the moment his life slipped away. I couldn't have told you what was different about him. His eyes were no more vacant than they had been from the moment he'd first opened them, but he was dead.

I looked at Jamaal in horror. The glow in his eyes and his glyph faded, and for one moment, I saw an expression of clarity on his face, like he'd come back from wherever he'd been. Then his eyes rolled up into his head, and his knees went out from under him.

SEVEN

I wanted to sit there on the grass and take some time to gather myself, try to make sense of what I'd seen. But I was badly wounded, sitting by the side of the road with one dead man and another unconscious one, and I didn't have the luxury. It was dark, but not dark enough to hide the carnage if someone drove by, and though traffic was sparse, it wasn't nonexistent. I suspected we were far enough away from the residential area that no one had heard the shots, but I couldn't be sure of that.

With shaking hands, I pulled out my cell phone and speed-dialed Anderson. He answered on the first ring.

"Have you found him? We heard gunfire." He was slightly out of breath, and I realized he was running. I cursed the cemetery for being so big, for forcing us to spread out so much.

"N-need help," I managed to stammer out, my whole body now racked with shivers. I didn't know if I was reacting to my own wounds or if I was having a well-deserved panic attack, but I was having trouble getting words out of my mouth and breath into my lungs.

"Nikki? Are you okay? What happened?"

I tried to spit out an explanation, I really did. But what came out was a gasp, followed by something that sounded suspiciously like a sob. My throat was so tight I could barely breathe, and I was shaking so hard it was a miracle I hadn't dropped the phone.

"We're coming, Nikki," Anderson said. "Hang on. Are you still on Rock Creek Church?"

I managed a hiccuped affirmative that, amazingly, he was able to understand.

"Just hang on. We'll be there soon."

He hung up on me, which was just as well, considering I was practically incapable of speech.

I'd always thought of myself as something of a tough chick. I'd spent years in foster care, getting passed from one family to another like an unwanted present that kept getting regifted. I'd been a loner, a rebel, a troublemaker. But becoming *Liberi* had taught me in a very short time just how far I was from being the tough chick I'd imagined. Girls like me weren't supposed to sit by the side of the road and have hysterics after a fight. No matter how horrifying the attack. No matter that they were bleeding from multiple and very painful wounds. No matter that the guy they'd tried to save was dead or that one of the good guys had killed him while in some kind of altered state.

In the distance, a pair of headlights approached, and I knew there was no way whoever was in that car was going to miss the carnage. The strip of grass we were on wasn't wide enough for us to huddle outside the range of the headlights, and there was nothing to hide behind—even if I could have moved both the dead guy and Jamaal. Not to mention the splatters of blood everywhere.

I was coming close to panic again, frozen where I was, my brain trying to think of what to do and coming up empty. That was when a large black dog came galloping through the cemetery, leapt over the iron fence like it was only an inch high, and landed on the grass beside me. Another burst of adrenaline flooded my system, but before I had a chance to react, the dog shimmered, and suddenly, it was Jack kneeling there in the grass beside me—stark naked, though I was too fuzzy-minded to take much note of it.

The headlights were coming closer, and we were sitting ducks, nowhere to hide. Without a word, Jack grabbed my arm, his hand fortunately not landing on one of the bite wounds, jerking me to the ground beside the dead guy. I tried to voice a protest, but Jack ignored me, forcing my hand against the dead guy's mauled shoulder and holding it there with an iron grip while reaching for Jamaal with his other hand.

I tried to pull away, shuddering with revulsion, but Jack turned and hissed at me. "Hold still! Just until the car passes."

I didn't want to. My hand was sticky with the dead guy's blood, and my stomach wanted to rebel at the thought of what I was touching. The car was slowing down as it approached us, and I figured adding a naked guy to this scenario wasn't doing much to improve the visuals. I cringed when the headlights hit us, hoping the driver would go shrieking off in terror at warp speed, giving us time to do . . . something . . . before he called the cops. Instead, the car cruised slowly past us. I had the brief impression of a man's face, taking a good look at us through the driver's-side window, then turning to face front with a grimace.

The car picked up speed as it passed, but there was no squeal of tires as the driver put pedal to metal, and it didn't look to me like he was going more than a little faster than the speed limit.

Jack let go of me, and I jerked away from the dead guy. My head swam at the sudden movement, and I closed my eyes to avoid passing out.

"What the hell was that about?" I snarled at Jack.

"What good is a trickster if he has no illusion magic?" Jack responded, sounding smug. Apparently, the blood and gore didn't bother him nearly as much as they did me.

I forced my eyes open, and though my head still swam, it wasn't quite as bad. Jack was sitting on the bloody grass between the victim and Jamaal, showing no sign of self-consciousness. I kept my eyes pinned on his face as I realized something.

"I've seen you change forms before. You don't have to be naked to do it." When he'd changed in the living room, his clothes had changed right along with him.

He grinned at me and stretched out his legs to give me a better view. "I don't technically have to, but it's more fun this way. You should see the look on your face."

If my gun had been in easy reach, I might have shot him.

"Some poor bastard just got mauled to death by jackals, Jamaal is lying there unconscious, I'm bleeding, and you think this is a good time to yank my chain?"

He met my eyes as the humor left his. It was the first time in my memory I could remember seeing Jack look serious. His expression was strangely chilling, maybe only because it looked wrong on a face that was always smiling.

"I'm a descendant of Loki," he said in a tone that suggested I'd ticked him off. "Deal with it."

Loki, who was a trickster and who didn't much care about the feelings of those around him.

"That may be true," I said. "But that doesn't mean you *are* Loki. You could show a little compassion every once in a while."

The grin was back. "Why would I want to do a silly thing like that?"

I guessed appealing to his better nature was a lost cause. Which I should have known before I opened my mouth. Tricksters aren't known for being nice. I shook my head.

"You're an asshole," I told Jack, who was not the least bothered by it.

Down the street a bit, I could see a couple of people turn the corner at a run. They were far enough away that I couldn't tell who they were yet. I supposed I should be grateful that Jack had gotten there as quickly as he had. If I'd been in trouble, the others would have been too late to help me. Assuming Jack wouldn't have sat on the sidelines eating popcorn if I *had* been in trouble.

"Put some damn clothes on," I snapped at him, only to realize that in the brief moment I'd looked away, he'd somehow managed to clothe himself.

The rest of the *Liberi* converged on us in the next couple of minutes. I was still light-headed and woozy, and the bite wounds hurt like a son of a bitch. I didn't feel like reliving what had just happened multiple times, so I waited until everyone was there before I gave them the play-by-play.

I debated whether to tell everyone about how Jamaal had

wigged out and then ended up killing the victim, but he was still lying there unconscious, and I figured I had to explain. I hoped I wasn't condemning Jamaal to a fate worse than death by telling Anderson what had happened. But I knew it hadn't really been Jamaal who killed the victim; it had been his death magic, which had taken him over completely, possessed him like a demon. I hoped Anderson would understand that.

There was silence among the gathered *Liberi* as they contemplated everything I'd said. Anderson knelt by Jamaal's side and lightly tapped his cheeks, trying to wake him up, but he was still out cold. Another car passed by, and Jack did his thing, reaching down to touch me and the dead guy and Jamaal. I noticed more than one *Liberi* grimace and look away, and, as before, the car went right on by the bloody murder scene without stopping.

"Do I want to know what you're making people see?" I asked Jack.

"No," several people answered at once, and I realized that I was probably the only one who hadn't seen the illusion. I bit my tongue to resist asking him why I couldn't see it. I wasn't particularly in the mood to start up a conversation with him.

"We'd better get back to the house," Anderson said, standing up and brushing dead grass off the knees of his jeans. Somehow he'd managed not to get any blood on him. "The killer isn't going to come back here tonight."

"What about Jamaal?" I asked.

Anderson gave me a neutral look. "I'm not making any decisions until he wakes up and gives me his side of the story. Maybe he had a good reason for what he did."

But Anderson hadn't seen him, hadn't seen the absolute lack of humanity in his face. I wondered if Jamaal would even remember anything when he woke up—assuming the death magic hadn't pushed him over the edge permanently.

Anderson moved around to Jamaal's feet and squatted, glancing up at Logan. "Help me carry him, will you?"

I didn't know how much Jamaal weighed, except that it was

a lot. It probably would be easier to use a fireman's carry, but
we had a considerable walk to get to where we'd parked, and
I figured the guys were going to have to take turns, so maybe
two at a time would be more efficient in the end.

Logan was just starting to bend down when Maggie
grabbed his shoulder and tugged him back.

"I can carry him," she said, then bent and slid one arm under
Jamaal's shoulders and one under his knees, lifting him like he
weighed no more than a toddler. "See? Light as a feather."

Maggie had told me once that although the guys all knew
about her supernatural strength, testosterone poisoning made
them really uncomfortable with letting her carry stuff. I could
see she was right by the way the guys shifted uncomfortably on
their feet. Maggie smiled tightly, and I knew it bothered her
that they were threatened by her strength.

I forced myself to stand up, though it seemed to take a massive amount of effort, and putting weight on my wounded leg
made a reluctant whimper rise in my throat.

"I guess I should carry *you* instead," Anderson said, and
before I had a chance to protest, he'd swept me off my feet. I
instinctively put an arm around his neck to hold on.

"I can walk," I insisted like an idiot.

"Yeah, if we don't mind it taking three hours to get back to
the cars," Anderson retorted.

In my peripheral vision, I saw Jack bend down and feel
around the dead guy's pocket until he found a wallet, which he
promptly transferred into his own back pocket.

"You're stealing his wallet?" I asked, my voice a little shrill
with my indignation.

Jack shrugged. "It'll have ID and credit cards, which might
help us find out more about him and maybe figure out why he
was targeted."

I didn't think that had anything to do with it. He could
have just glanced at the ID to find out who the poor guy was,
then left it at the scene.

Anderson turned away before I had a chance to tell Jack what an asshole he was—for the second time in the last ten minutes—and we started down the road toward where we'd parked.

"The best way to handle Jack is not to engage with him," Anderson told me.

Jack said something under his breath that I think it was good I couldn't hear.

Anderson carried me gently, but I felt every footstep reverberate through my body, bringing stabs of pain from my wounds. I gritted my teeth and held on, trying not to make any undignified noises or start crying.

Emma was watching me with narrowed eyes, and I realized she wasn't at all happy about Anderson carrying me. It made me want to snuggle in closer to him just to piss her off, but I hurt too much to indulge in mind games. Instead, I closed my eyes and prayed for my supernatural healing to hurry up and do its job.

I think I passed out for part of the trip back to the cars, because we seemed to get there faster than I expected. Obviously, neither Jamaal nor I was in any shape to drive, so we had to shuffle passengers and drivers around a bit. I ended up stretched across the backseat of Anderson's car, which I didn't think was the smartest seating arrangement in the world, seeing as Emma was still glaring daggers at me. Anderson must have noticed—she had a few daggers in her arsenal to spare for him, too—but he ignored it.

I *know* I passed out for a while during the car ride, and based on the stony silence and bitter expressions I woke up to, it was probably just as well. Anderson was staring straight ahead, all his concentration fixed on the road in front of him, while Emma stared out the side window, her arms crossed over her chest. I hoped it wasn't me they'd been fighting about. I thought they had enough issues without Emma's irrational jealousy thrown into the mix.

The ride was long enough that I expected to be feeling somewhat better by the time we arrived back at the mansion, but everything still hurt, and I was still weak. In fact, I seemed to be even weaker, although that was probably because I'd let myself forget just how miserable I'd felt the last time I tried to stand.

Anderson wound up carrying me again, and I could tell Emma was just thrilled about it. Here I was, making friends and influencing people without even having to *do* anything.

Jamaal was still pretty out of it, although he was technically conscious. Maggie's arm was around him, and he leaned on her heavily as he walked. I really wanted to know what the hell had happened back there in the cemetery, but I knew I wasn't getting an explanation anytime soon. Jamaal looked like a stiff wind would knock him down, and he was shivering even though it wasn't all that cold. By the time we got through the front door to the main stairway, he was completely spent, and Maggie had to carry him up the stairs. That he didn't protest showed just how out of it he was.

Anderson took me up to my own room. I didn't want him to lay me on my nice, clean bed when I was covered in blood, so I directed him to take me to the bathroom so I could get cleaned up first. When he put me down, I had to grab hold of the sink to keep from falling.

"I feel like shit," I grumbled, wishing my supernatural healing would do its thing a little faster.

Anderson's brow furrowed as he looked at me. "You're looking rather pale."

He had to help me get my ruined coat off, and that's when we first got a close look at one of the bites. My stomach lurched, and I had to tighten my grip on the sink to stay upright.

The jackals' fangs had left a series of deep puncture wounds, and they didn't appear to have healed at all, even though it had probably been almost an hour since the attack. The flesh around the punctures was red and swollen, and if

I hadn't known better, I would have sworn I had a raging infection.

"Why isn't it healing?" I asked Anderson, wondering if I shouldn't have just skipped the cleanup and collapsed into bed.

"I don't know," Anderson said grimly. He reached up and touched my forehead, and I realized for the first time that I was sweating. Anderson looked even more grim. "Feels like you have a fever, too."

"But that's impossible. Isn't it?"

"I would have thought so." There was no missing the worry in his eyes, and that didn't do much to comfort me. "Let's get the wounds cleaned up and put you to bed. Maybe there's some irritant in the jackals' saliva that's keeping you from healing."

An "irritant" probably wouldn't have given me a fever, but I felt too awful to argue.

"I'm going to need some help," I said, though I knew it was obvious that I wasn't up to cleaning and dressing the wounds myself. "I think Emma and I would both be happier if you sent Maggie in to help me instead of doing it yourself."

Anger flashed in Anderson's eyes. "Emma wouldn't be so shallow as to be jealous of you in the state you're in."

Ah, denial. I'd seen the way she'd looked at me while he was carrying me, and I knew without a doubt that she was, indeed, jealous. Ridiculous it might be, but then, feelings often were. But that was not an argument for right now.

"Then forget about Emma," I said. "*I'm* not much of an exhibitionist, so I'd really rather Maggie help me than you. No offense."

"None taken," Anderson said, though I wasn't sure that was true. He reached over and closed the lid of the toilet, then helped me traverse the few feet between it and the sink so I could sit down. Instead of leaving me there and going to get Maggie, he actually called her on his cell phone. The idea that he was worried enough not to leave me alone for the five minutes it would take to go find her was not at all comforting.

My head started to throb, as if the wounds themselves didn't hurt enough. When Maggie arrived, Anderson had a whispered conversation with her right outside the bathroom door. I couldn't hear a word they said, but I didn't think it boded well for me.

Things got a little fuzzy then, so I only vaguely remember Maggie helping me out of my clothes and cleaning my wounds. She had to use water at first, because the *Liberi* didn't have things like alcohol or peroxide sitting around—who needed them when your body repaired itself in a matter of hours?— but somebody must have been sent out to raid a drugstore, because the peroxide came eventually.

By the time I was laid out in bed, my wounds all bandaged, I was sweating and shivering at the same time, and all my joints ached. I'd never been this sick in my life, and I spent some time complaining to myself about how life wasn't fair. Here I was immortal, invulnerable, and I was sick and hurting and scared I was going to die anyway.

My sleep that night was sporadic at best, interspersed with nightmares that would have made me sit up and scream if I'd had the energy.

Eight

I was no better in the morning. In fact, if anything, I was worse.

I was burning up and freezing cold by turns, aching down to my bones while the bite wounds continued to throb. I made the mistake of checking under one of the bandages, and the sight brought bile into the back of my throat.

Not only were the wounds not closed, they were seeping with pus, the redness and swelling spreading. When Maggie came in to check on me and change the bandages, it hurt so much I couldn't stop myself from crying like a baby. And the worst part was there was no sign cleaning the wounds or changing the bandages was doing any good.

Whatever was wrong with me, I knew it was bad when Anderson brought Steph in to visit me. I was sure he'd brought her because he thought I was going to die, and based on how much she cried despite efforts to put on a brave face, she thought the same. She sat by the side of my bed, holding my hand as I drifted in and out of sleep.

I wasn't even vaguely inclined to eat anything, and though Maggie had left a glass of water by my bedside when she'd put me to bed last night, it was still full. Steph urged me to drink, and I knew she was right and I ought to. Considering how much the fever was making me sweat, I had to be pretty dehydrated. With her holding my head up off the pillow, I lifted the glass to my lips, but I couldn't muster the will to swallow.

"It's no use," I told Steph, handing her back the glass. "I'll just puke it back up if I drink it."

In actuality, it wasn't that I felt nauseated. I just didn't want to drink. I couldn't have explained why if you'd asked me, but just the thought of taking a sip made my throat close up.

I have some vague memory of Steph trying again to get me to drink, more determined this time. I think I ended up shoving her away, making her spill the water all over herself, but I wasn't sure if that was real or just one of the nasty dreams I kept having.

The next time I woke up, Steph was gone. I was as miserable as ever, and I tried to turn over in the vain hope that I could find a more comfortable position. That was when I discovered the restraints fastened to my wrists and ankles.

Another nightmare, I told myself as I tugged weakly at the restraints. The movement made all the aches and pains flare up, and I discovered the skin around the restraints was red and raw, as if I'd been struggling against them. If I had, I didn't remember. But the fact that it hurt so much told me this wasn't a nightmare after all.

I tried to call out for help, but my mouth and throat were so dry I couldn't get any sound out. Instead, I closed my eyes and willed myself back into unconsciousness.

When I woke up again, it was dark out. There was a nightlight on in my room—someone must have brought it in from the bathroom. It took me a moment or two to assess my situation, to realize I was still deathly ill and in restraints, but when I did, panic seized me, and I started struggling as if my life depended on it.

My rational mind knew I couldn't fight free, that fighting the restraints was only causing me more pain, but I couldn't help it. I had to get loose, had to be free. I couldn't stand being in that bed for another moment, never mind that I wouldn't be able to walk two steps without collapsing.

"Nikki, please calm down," Anderson's soft voice said from beside my bed, but I couldn't seem to stop myself from thrashing.

I tried to talk, but it came out as an incoherent screech.

"She's probably delusional just now," said a voice I didn't recognize.

The sound of an unfamiliar voice reached my panicky core in a way that Anderson's soothing had not, and I stopped struggling as I strained my eyes in the darkness to see who was there. Someone turned on the bedside lamp, and when I got over being blinded, I blinked a few times and saw a stranger hovering over me.

She was a plump brunette with a round face and hard blue eyes, maybe around forty. An iridescent caduceus glyph marked her cheek, and I gathered that meant she was some kind of healer. I didn't think any kind of healer was going to do me much good. Whatever was wrong with me was impossible, so it was hard to believe someone could magically cure it.

"Why am I tied up?" I croaked.

"Because you've been hallucinating," the healer said, sitting down on the side of my bed. "You tried to get out of bed a few times, and it didn't go so well."

I didn't remember any of that, but Anderson wasn't con-tradicting her, so I guessed it was true. I didn't want her there, didn't want a stranger so close to me, especially not when I was so vulnerable. I glanced over her shoulder at Anderson, who was standing with his arms crossed over his chest and a tight, unhappy expression on his face.

"Get her away from me," I said, scooting over as much as the restraints would allow. The panic tried to rise again, but I fought it with everything I had. I didn't need any more raw spots on my wrists and ankles.

"Nikki, this is Erin," he said, ignoring my polite request, surprise, surprise. "She's a descendant of Apollo . . . and she's a healer."

I recognized her from the files I'd been examining for An-derson before hunting a serial killer became my top priority. I made a mental note to myself to put her file at the top of my list, seeing as she'd compromised her cover identity by coming here.

Erin reached for me, and I let out a screech of warning, thrashing wildly, my heart pounding and my breaths coming in gasps. I was conscious of everything I was doing, but it felt like my body was not my own, like the sickness was driving me. I wanted to stop thrashing around, if only because of how much it hurt, but everything within me rebelled at the thought of this woman touching me.

I won't repeat the names I called her as she inexorably planted her hands on both sides of my face, holding me down with the weight of her forearms on my chest. The touch of her fingers on my skin made me scream, and I think I even tried to bite her.

Anything to get her off me.

But between the restraints and the weakness, I was no match for her, and she held me with little difficulty as her hands began to glow white.

That glow sent me into another paroxysm of sheer, unadul-terated panic. My throat was hoarse from screaming, and if I'd been any stronger, I'd probably have broken bones in my wrists and ankles in my attempts to escape.

Erin said nothing as she sat there with her glowing hands on my face, her eyes closed. I was vaguely aware of Anderson saying soothing things, but I couldn't make out the words, and I was incapable of being soothed, anyway.

Eventually, the glow died down, and Erin dropped her hands from my face.

"Well?" Anderson asked before she had a chance to speak.

"She has rabies," Erin said simply, the words sucking all of the air out of my lungs.

One of my foster mothers had had a rabies scare when she'd been bitten by a stray dog. She'd gotten the preventive treatment and was just fine, but everyone in that family had learned more about rabies than we ever wanted to know. Like that it was fatal once the symptoms started to show.

"Can't be." I gasped. "Not long enough." The words didn't make much sense, but Erin seemed to know what I was trying to say.

"If you were a mortal who'd been bitten by a rabid animal, no, you wouldn't be showing symptoms yet. But this isn't normal rabies—that wouldn't affect a *Liberi*. There's something different about this strain. I've never seen anything like it, but if I had to guess, I'd say the virus itself is supernatural in nature."

"What can we do?" Anderson asked, beating me to the question.

Erin gave us both an apologetic look. "Even in humans, rabies isn't curable at this stage. There's nothing I can do for her."

"There has to be something!" Anderson insisted, and I'd have been touched by the depth of his concern if I weren't fighting the realization that I was going to die.

"I'm sorry," Erin said. "There's nothing."

"If I die from this," I whispered, "do I get to come back?" A *Liberi* could come back from death by decapitation. Surely a little rabies wouldn't keep me down . . .

Erin shook her head. "Let's hope not. Your body will still be infected when you die, so even if it heals the damage, you won't be in any better shape."

I shuddered and had to fight a scream. It would be like what Emma had gone through for ten years in the water—coming to life only to find yourself back in the same situation that had killed you in the first place, a fate worse than death.

"What if we killed the virus?" Anderson asked, and I could tell by the look on his face that he had an idea, but I wasn't getting my hopes up. "If she could come back to a body that was virus-free, she'd be fine, right?"

Erin nodded cautiously. "I suppose so. But I don't know how you'd go about killing the virus. *I* can't do it, and there's no medicine on earth that can do it either."

"What if after she . . . dies . . . we burn the body?"

I must have made some kind of panicked noise, because Anderson nudged Erin out of the way and sat beside me, taking my hand and giving it a firm squeeze.

"You can come back from that," he assured me in a soothing croon. "If your body is entirely destroyed, then you'll just generate a new one. I know *Liberi* who have done it. The immortal seed isn't a physical object, isn't something that can be destroyed, and it's the seed that brings us back when we die."

"It might work," Erin said. "Burning the body would kill the virus cells. If your body has to regenerate from scratch, there's no reason it would regenerate the virus, too. At least, no reason that I can think of. But having never seen anything like this before, I can't make any promises."

Anderson reached out and brushed my hair out of the tear tracks on my cheek. "It's the best chance we have."

"I don't like this plan," I whispered. A sudden chill seized me, and I shivered so hard I practically bit my tongue. My eyes were burning fiercely, but there wasn't enough moisture in my body to produce any more tears.

"I don't much like it, either," Anderson replied, fingers

absently stroking my hair like he thought the gesture could soothe me. It couldn't. Nothing could.

"We can just let nature take its course, if you prefer," Erin said, not sounding as sympathetic as Anderson. "Die, come back, be miserable, then die again, lather, rinse, repeat."

Anderson glared at her. There was something about the way they looked at each other, some kind of invisible sparks, that told me they'd been a couple once. I'd seen enough love-gone-sour looks in my days as a P.I. to recognize it when I saw it.

"Your work is done here, I think," he said. "You can go."

Erin laughed. "What do you think I am? Your servant?"

"No. I think you're a healer who's outlived her usefulness in this situation."

Erin's eyes narrowed. "Don't think this gets you out of anything. You owe me, whether I could cure her or not. I took an enormous risk coming here, and—"

"Yes, yes, I owe you," Anderson said impatiently. "That was the deal. Now, please go instead of terrorizing your patient just to get to me."

She laughed hard at that one, shaking her head. "You have an inflated opinion of your importance to me." She dabbed at imaginary tears of mirth in her eyes, and then her expression hardened. "You mean nothing to me," she said, an obvious lie. "And you'll pay handsomely for this visit."

"Get out."

Still looking mighty pleased with herself, she turned and headed out the door, not looking back.

"Your taste in women sucks," I told Anderson. Maybe not the most sensitive observation in the world, but it was true.

Anderson gave me a small smile, one that looked pretty damned forced to my eyes. "She came by her hard feelings honestly. I left her for Emma many years ago."

Boy, Emma must have been overjoyed that Anderson had called his old girlfriend to come take care of his new girlfriend, or whatever the hell she thought I was. She was probably going to throw a party when she found out I was going to die.

"Her bedside manner could use some work," Anderson said, "but she *did* come out of hiding to help you. It was a big risk for her."

Somehow I didn't think Erin had taken that big risk out of the goodness of her heart. Anderson had made it perfectly clear when he hired me to look over his records that he wanted to keep track of the people he'd helped—even though keeping track of them was detrimental to their covers—so he could press them into service as needed. I seriously doubted Anderson had given Erin much of a choice when he'd requested her help.

"If she hadn't identified the virus, we'd have had no idea what to do to help you."

I swallowed hard, which was quite a feat with my parched mouth and throat. "Letting me die and burning my body isn't exactly the kind of help I was hoping for."

"I know."

Anderson was still stroking my hair, and I was beginning to find the gesture a bit irritating. My skin felt overly sensitive, and even the light brush of his fingers felt like the scrape of sandpaper. I could only imagine what Emma would think if she saw.

I turned my head away from his touch, hoping that would make him stop. Instead, he reached out and cupped my other cheek, turning my face back toward him. I was too weak to resist as he held both hands to my face and leaned down to plant a kiss on my forehead. I was too stunned to say anything, but I hoped that kiss meant he was about to let go of me and give me some space.

"I'm sorry," he whispered against my skin.

I didn't comprehend what he was about to do until the very last instant, which I'm sure was what he intended. Just as the metaphorical light bulb went on over my head, Anderson's hands tightened around my head. I felt him begin to wrench my head around, and then there was nothing.

I had a vague feeling that time had passed when I next regained consciousness, but I didn't know how much, and I couldn't even have said what made me feel that way. I tried to open my eyes, but nothing seemed to happen. I was in complete and utter darkness, and though my brain was sending signals to my eyes that they should blink a few times in case there really was some light somewhere and I just needed to clear them, I couldn't actually feel my eyes doing anything.

I tried to suck in a deep breath to calm myself, but that didn't work, either. My body remained in absolute stillness, and I couldn't even feel the beating of my heart. I tried again for the deep breath, but it was no use.

I felt like I had a body—you know, like you know your foot is there even when it's not moving or touching anything. But I seemed to be utterly paralyzed, my heart not beating, my lungs not working, my limbs ignoring my increasingly frantic orders to move.

I'm dead, I told myself, remembering the feel of Anderson's hands on my face. He must have thought giving me a quick death was a mercy compared with whatever the mutant disease had planned for me.

My nonexistent lungs demanded oxygen, but no amount of trying would persuade my body to take in air. Terror coursed through my blood, though with no heartbeat, it seemed that should be impossible. I shouldn't have been able to feel any of this, but telling myself that didn't stave off the desperate need to breathe. I was suffocating, and there was nothing I could do about it.

But I was already dead, wasn't I? That meant I *couldn't* suffocate. Anderson was probably even now planning the bonfire in which he would burn my earthly body. God, I *hoped* he was doing it now. The sooner he burned the body, the sooner the magic of the *Liberi* would cause it to regenerate.

Unless all of that had been a comforting fiction, meant to give me hope when no hope was left.

I'd thought the symptoms of the illness had made me miserable, but that was a walk in the park compared with being dead. Maggie had told me once that dying was a horrible experience, even for the *Liberi* who knew they would come back.

She was right. More than right.

There was nothing to see, nothing to hear, nothing to smell. Nothing to feel, except for that frantic need to breathe, like a fish gasping in the bottom of a boat. Only I couldn't even gasp.

At first, I kept mentally talking to myself, trying to keep myself calm, or at least as calm as possible. As miserable as I was, this was temporary. This, too, shall pass and all that.

That worked for a while, though I couldn't have told you how long, because I had no sense of time. I was still terrified, would have screamed and thrashed and cried if I could have, but I wasn't out of my mind. Not yet.

But there was only so long I could hold on before the panic took on a life of its own.

Suffocating. Paralyzed. Alone.

What if Anderson and Erin were wrong? What if I couldn't come back from this? What if what I was feeling now was all there was, all there would ever be, until the end of time? I couldn't escape death by dying, so there was no reason to believe this would ever end.

Time passed, and every second felt like a year. A year of unadulterated terror.

This was hell, I eventually decided.

This was my punishment for all my years of youthful rebellion, for all the times I'd been an ungrateful bitch to those who'd tried to take care of me.

With no way to move, no way to make any sound, no way

to cry, there was no outlet for the terror, and it just festered inside me, growing more and more powerful, until fear was all I knew.

I was going slowly mad, screaming endlessly inside, praying for an end I was convinced would never come.

NINE

I jackknifed into a sitting position, dragging in a breath so huge it was a wonder my lungs didn't explode. I immediately sucked in another, the air rasping through my throat.

My heart was back online, that was for sure, my pulse racing, adrenaline flooding my system as my hands rose to my throat and I tried to take about three breaths at once.

"Easy," said a feminine voice, and in a moment, Maggie was sitting on the bed beside me, holding my wrists, keeping them away from my throat. I think I'd been about to tear open my trachea to get the air in faster. "You're back now, and it's going to be all right."

I was not convinced. I didn't know how long I'd been dead, but it had felt like forever and a day. I had so much residual panic stored up it was a wonder I stayed conscious.

I burst into tears, frantic sobs that made my chest hurt and my nose clog up. Maggie put her arms around me, rocking me and murmuring soothing nonsense like I was a baby in need of comfort. It shows just what bad shape I was in that it never even occurred to me to object.

It took a long time before rational thought returned. I gently extricated myself from Maggie's hug, then fell back limply onto the bed, utterly exhausted.

I felt like I was in recovery from the world's worst case of flu, and I was frankly surprised I'd been able to scrape up enough energy to sit up in the first place. Amazing what existential panic can do. I closed my eyes and concentrated on breathing, loving the feel of oxygen flowing into my lungs even though my throat and chest hurt from my previous attempts to hyperventilate.

The good news was that there were no aches and pains in my joints and no throbbing in my arms and legs where I'd been bitten.

"It worked," I said in a small voice, barely able to comprehend what had just happened. I'd died. My body had been burned. And yet here I was, alive again.

"It did," Maggie confirmed, and I opened my eyes to see that hers were all shiny.

"Why are you crying?"

She smiled through the tears. "Because we didn't know if it would or not." She reached up and dabbed at her eyes. "When you're immortal, you get used to thinking that your immortal friends will never die. It's one of the perks, especially when you've outlived anyone you ever knew from your mortal days." There was a wealth of sadness in those words. I couldn't imagine what it was like to see everyone you loved die. One day, I, too, would know the feeling, but I shoved the thought aside.

"I didn't like the idea of losing you," Maggie concluded.

I was touched by her care, which brought a few tears to my eyes, too. We hadn't known each other for very long, but I had the distinct impression she'd been starved for female company before I came along.

"How long have I been . . . gone?"

"Four days."

My heart gave a thud in my chest. "Four days? Jamaal came back in a few hours!"

"Jamaal didn't have to generate a whole new body from scratch. It's time-consuming. Now, stop asking questions and get a little rest. When the others find out you're back, they're going to storm the room and won't give you a moment of peace. Especially Steph."

I didn't want to rest, not after what I'd been through. But I was running on fumes, the supernatural effort to come back to life having stolen every drop of my energy. The power of suggestion was too much, and I found my eyes drifting closed despite myself.

Maggie wasn't wrong about the storming-my-room thing. It seemed like practically everyone in the house came by to welcome me back. The whole thing felt pretty surreal. I mean, I'd only known these people a handful of weeks, and I didn't think most of them liked me all that much. Why should they, when they'd all been together for years, and I'd only come into their midst by killing one of their friends? Maybe they were just freaked out by the idea of a mutated supernatural rabies virus so powerful it could kill *Liberi* and they wanted to assure themselves I was still alive.

Steph, naturally, was beside herself. She'd always been more comfortable with tears than I was, and she cried plenty of them when she came to see me.

"I couldn't believe you would come back," she told me. "No matter how much everyone assured me you would, it seemed impossible."

I probably would have felt the same way in her shoes, despite having personally seen Jamaal come back from the dead twice. That didn't make me squirm any less at the tears. I never knew quite what to do with them.

"What was it like, being dead?" she asked. "Were you . . . aware?"

I fought down a shudder. I'd have given anything not to have been aware. But Steph's question told me that no one had mentioned to her how unpleasant dying was. If she didn't know, I saw no reason to enlighten her. Not to mention that the last thing in the world I wanted to do was talk about it.

Another shudder rippled through me as I wondered if I'd experienced death as regular humans did. Would my sister and my adoptive parents find themselves in the same state someday, with no hope of it ever ending? The Glasses were Christians, their faith low-key but there nonetheless. They believed in the afterlife, but if what I'd experienced was the true afterlife, I wouldn't wish it on my worst enemy.

It was a thought too terrible to contemplate, and I added it to my ever-expanding list of taboo subjects. I shook my head at Steph, silently lying to her. I would never, ever tell her what had happened to me when I'd died. If I had indeed experienced the fate that awaited all mortals, I didn't want Steph to know anything about it. Not until she had to.

By the time Anderson came to see me, it was nearly dinnertime, and I'd been wondering to myself if he was too chicken to face me after having killed me. He'd done the right thing, and I knew that. I'd have died anyway, and who knew how long the disease would have made me suffer before putting me out of my misery?

Actually, *not* putting me out of my misery, just condemning me to a whole other level of misery. I'd still have been dead, still would have had to spend four days in Limbo, or wherever the hell I'd been. But it would have been nice if the choice had been mine, rather than his.

I still wasn't close to full strength, but I'd at least found the energy to get up and take a shower. I hadn't bothered getting dressed, though, so I was sitting around in plaid flannel pajama bottoms with a utilitarian camisole when Anderson came in. My hair was still wet from the shower—blow-drying it would have taken way more energy than I had—and I glanced down at the cami to make sure there weren't any embarrassingly re-vealing wet spots. Either that, or I was glancing down to avoid Anderson's eyes—take your pick.

I was sitting cross-legged on the bed, feeling bone-tired, as if I'd just finished running a marathon. I would have lain down, except I was afraid I might fall asleep again. Besides, I didn't much like the idea of closing my eyes and triggering memories of the smothering darkness. Hell, if I had my way, I'd never sleep again.

Anderson came to sit on the edge of the bed, resting his back against one of the massive wooden posts. "How are you feeling?"

I found my courage and looked up to meet his eyes. There was an uncomfortable amount of understanding and compassion in his gaze, and it pissed me off. He didn't get to be Mr. Nice Guy after he'd broken my freaking neck.

"Like someone who's been dead for four days," I said with a stubborn lift of my chin. Even saying the words sent a chill through me, and I fought off memory as fiercely as I could. I was going to have to come to terms with what I'd been through someday, but I planned to put that off for as long as possible.

Anderson didn't flinch from the anger in my voice. "There wasn't any other way to save you."

"You could have warned me!" I snapped. "Or, hell, I don't know, *asked* me before making a unilateral decision."

He cocked his head. "Would your decision have been different from mine?"

"That's not the point!"

"I didn't think knowing about it in advance was going to make it any easier. I did what I thought was best for you at the moment." His calm, reasonable voice scraped against my nerves, though it was silly of me to expect wailing and gnashing of teeth.

My first instinct was to lay into him some more, but I took a deep breath and went in search of my self-control. I knew Anderson too well to think I'd convince him what he'd done was wrong. To tell you the truth, I wasn't entirely sure *I* was convinced it was wrong—just that I didn't like it.

"How's Jamaal?" I asked instead, hoping Anderson would let me change the subject. Jamaal was the only one who hadn't come to see me, and I hoped that didn't mean Anderson had evicted him for his lack of self-control at the cemetery.

"He's . . . struggling."

"Meaning what?"

"Meaning I never should have sent him to spend several hours in a cemetery." Anderson might not have felt particularly guilty about breaking my neck, but the look on his face said that this he felt guilty about. "It gave the death magic too much power, until Jamaal couldn't control it, no matter how hard he tried."

I was still mad at Anderson for what he'd done, but I didn't see that he had any reason to feel bad about sending Jamaal to the cemetery with me. "Did you know that was going to happen?"

Anderson shook his head. "I've never known that to happen before, but Jamaal is the only descendant of Kali I've ever spent any significant time with."

"If you didn't know he'd react that way, then you couldn't have known it was a bad idea to send him to the cemetery. If you're going to beat yourself up about something, at least do it about something you could have changed. Like, say, breaking my neck."

He gave me a reproachful look but failed to pick up the gauntlet I'd thrown down again. "I *should* have known. Should have at least considered the possibility. He was stabilizing, but now . . ." His voice trailed off, and the look in his eyes was troubled.

I sighed. "If you're going to toss blame around, toss some my way. I noticed that Jamaal was acting strange, but I didn't do anything. Hell, throw some blame Jamaal's way, too, because he *knew* something was wrong long before his control snapped. He could have fessed up and gotten out of there before things went to hell."

A small smile played around the corners of Anderson's mouth. "Oh, I'm not taking all the blame, don't worry. I'm not holding you responsible, because you aren't experienced enough to have guessed what his loss of control meant. Also, you never in a million years would have been able to talk him into leaving. He *is* an alpha male, you know."

"I've noticed."

"You're right that Jamaal should have recognized he was having a problem and how dangerous the problem was. He's been spending his time in the basement ever since, though I'm inclined to release him now that you're back with us."

In one of the makeshift prison cells, he meant. Not that those cells could hold Jamaal, unless he allowed himself to be held. At least Anderson hadn't imposed a more draconian penalty, as he had the last time Jamaal had lost it.

I wasn't able to stifle a yawn. Amazing what dying and then coming back to life can do for your energy level.

"You should get some more rest," Anderson said as he rose to his feet. "You'll feel much better tomorrow, as long as you don't overtax yourself tonight."

"What about the case?"

Anderson had already turned for the door on the assumption that the conversation was over, but I wasn't about to let him go that easily.

"We can talk some more tomorrow," he said.

"What have you found out about the victim? I assume you had Leo do some digging while I was gone."

He turned back toward me with a quelling look. "We'll talk about it tomorrow."

"Today is Wednesday, right?"

He nodded cautiously, as if afraid of agreeing with me.

"That means we have two days before the killer strikes again. We don't have time to wait until I'm all better."

"You're in no shape to work right now."

Another yawn forced its way up my throat, no matter how hard I tried to stop it. Not the best way to convince Anderson I was fit for duty.

I could have argued with him some more, could have tried to insist he let me work. But in the end, I didn't need his permission. The data I needed was no doubt either on my laptop or at least available from it. All I needed was for Anderson to go away, and then I could do what I pleased.

"Fine," I said with a huff, pulling back the covers and sliding into bed. "I'll sleep. But I'm getting to work the moment the sun rises tomorrow, so make sure Leo sends me anything he's dug up."

Anderson raised an eyebrow. I doubt he was used to being given orders. But he didn't call me on it, instead issuing a murmured "good night" and slipping out of the room. I suspected he might be hovering outside the bedroom door waiting to make sure I did as I was told, so I lay down and turned off the light. I even closed my eyes, in case he did a Columbo and came back into the room for "one more thing." And that was a mistake.

When I next awoke, it was after midnight. Someone had left a plastic-wrapped sandwich, a bag of chips, and a bottle of water on my bedside table. I guessed that was my dinner, though whoever had left it probably hadn't counted on it sitting there that long before I got to it. I was ravenous, and I couldn't die of food poisoning, so I stuffed down the sandwich and the bag of chips in about sixty seconds.

I opened the bottle of water and washed down the remaining salty goodness of the chips, then slid out of bed and gave a tentative stretch. I still felt weak, and despite the six hours or so of sleep I'd just gotten, I had the feeling if I let myself fall back into bed, I'd be out for the rest of the night. Still, I felt a whole lot better than I had for a while, and I was all too aware of the clock ticking. If I couldn't track down the killer before Friday night, someone else was going to die horribly.

What we were going to do if and when I tracked down the killer was a whole other question. How do you capture someone who's immortal and has a pack of rabid phantom jackals at his beck and call? Sure, I was back from the dead, but I was not at all up for another face-to-face with those damn jackals.

I told myself not to think about that part, then made my way into my sitting room. I debated going downstairs to get a cup of coffee while my laptop was booting up but decided against it. I was definitely still pretty washed out, and while I was sure I could make it down the stairs, making it back up afterward might be a challenge.

Despite his distaste for being given orders by a worker bee like me, Anderson had obviously talked to Leo, because there were a bunch of new emails waiting in my in-box. The first one I opened purported to be about the latest victim, and though I honestly wasn't sure what I could hope to learn, my instincts told me it was important.

My mind wasn't exactly firing on all cylinders. I had read all the way through Leo's dossier, learning more than I wanted to know about the victim's life, before something finally struck me. I minimized the email so that only the victim's picture was visible, then fished through the rest of my emails and brought up pictures of the previous two identified victims.

One of them was lean and athletic-looking, and had olive skin with dark hair and a beard and mustache. Just like the latest victim. The other was clean-shaven, although he did have olive skin. I also remembered that he was the one whose picture in the newspaper was obviously at least a decade out of date.

I searched Google for a more recent photo and found one in no time. And wouldn't you know it, he had the black beard and mustache, too. He wasn't as athletic-looking as the other two, but he was certainly lean—to the point of looking unhealthy.

I only had three victims to go on, since the first was still unidentified, but the resemblance couldn't be a coincidence. Lean, dark hair, olive skin, beard and mustache . . . all three bore more than a passing resemblance to Konstantin.

And that meant Phoebe was lying when she told us the Olympians had no idea why the killer was hunting in D.C.

The attacks were personal—and aimed at Konstantin.

And that meant Konstantin knew damn well who the killer was.

Ten

I sat back in my chair and stared at the three photos on my computer screen, wondering if I could be making something out of nothing.

No, I didn't think so.

Who was this guy? What did he have against Konstantin? And why had Phoebe and Cyrus lied about it? The obvious conclusion was that they were hiding something—no doubt on Konstantin's orders—but I had no clue what.

I didn't have answers to any of these questions, and I knew that the next logical step was to have a heart-to-heart with Konstantin. Maybe now that the jig was up, he'd be more forthcoming about what was going on. He might not care how many people Dogboy killed, but he *did* want him stopped. I couldn't help wondering if Phoebe's "vision" had been any more truthful than anything else she'd told us. Was Konstantin really trying to keep the killer from being captured by the government, or was he just using us to clean up his mess?

I wanted to question Konstantin right away, but I knew better than to think that was an option. I wasn't getting an interview with him at nearly two in the morning. Not that I believed I was capable of getting the truth out of Konstantin, anyway. I had no leverage over him, no way to make him talk to me if he didn't want to—which I already knew he wouldn't.

Anderson, however, might be able to manage it. He planned

to kill Konstantin someday, and they both knew it. Unless Konstantin was clinically insane, he had to be at least somewhat afraid of Anderson, even if he'd never admit it.

I briefly debated venturing into Anderson's wing to wake him up and get him on it right away, but there was no point in it. Anderson wasn't going to be able to get hold of Konstantin at this hour any more than I could. Besides, waking Anderson meant waking Emma, and that struck me as a bad idea.

I knew I should go back to bed and get some more sleep. I was far from fully recovered. But as drained as my body felt, I no longer felt sleepy, and I was afraid that if I lay down and closed my eyes without instantly falling asleep, I'd end up lying there remembering the suffocating darkness of death.

Even letting my mind brush against the memory made me shudder.

I didn't think there was much else I could do to help the case along at this point, but I needed to keep my mind occupied. I decided to brave the rigors of the stairs after all. Despite the old-fashioned formality of the mansion, there was a fairly comfortable den/media room on the first floor, and I figured I could either find something bearable to watch on cable or I could pop in a movie. Something mindless enough not to require much energy but engaging enough to absorb my attention and keep me from thinking.

I stopped by the kitchen first to make some coffee, then found myself having to sit down to rest before I could manage the trek from the kitchen to the den. Anderson had told me I should feel much better tomorrow, but at my current rate of recovery, I doubted I'd be at a hundred percent. Of course, my refusal to crawl back into bed and sleep the rest of the night probably wasn't helping, but there was no way I was climbing all the way back to my room on the third floor now.

Carrying a travel mug of coffee, because with my shaky legs I was afraid I'd spill with a regular mug, I made my slow and steady way to the den. I didn't bother turning lights on as

I went, so I noticed the flickering glow emanating from the den as soon as I stepped into the hallway. There was a faint murmur of voices in the background, but it was the TV, rather than a bunch of people. Either someone had forgotten to turn the TV off before going to bed, or I wasn't the only one up at this ungodly hour.

I was doing exactly what Anderson had warned me not to do: overtaxing myself. My legs felt like overcooked spaghetti, and there was no way they were carrying me back up to my room, no matter how much I didn't want company. Putting my hand against the wall for a little extra support, I continued down the hall until I could see into the den.

The den was about as masculine as you could imagine, with a pool table dominating one half of the room while a huge flat-screen TV with all the fixings dominated the other. A dartboard hung on one wall—well away from the precious TV—and the furniture was dark wood and leather. The only obviously feminine touch in the room was on the built-in bookshelves, where Maggie kept her collection of romance novels. In a relatively good-natured battle of wills, Maggie liked to pull out the books with the most lurid covers—classics from the seventies and eighties were a favorite—and prop them on the shelves facing out. Whenever she left the room, someone always tucked the books back into their places, spines out.

The guys had been remiss in their duties, because there was a nice collection of covers facing out, including a couple of more modern erotic romances, which featured naked guys discreetly blocking their best features from view. It made me smile. Maybe she'd finally worn the guys down. Or maybe everyone had better things to do than fight the battle of the sexes.

I didn't see anyone in the room at first. The program on the TV was a nature show about penguins, but the sound was so low I couldn't make out what the narrator was saying.

Fighting the fatigue, which was getting worse with each step I took, I set my sights on the couch, planning to collapse there. It wasn't until I'd put my hand on the back of the couch and started to move around it that I realized I wasn't alone after all.

Jamaal was slouched so low the top of his head hadn't shown over the back of the couch. Considering he was about six foot three, that was a lot of slouching. He was wearing a wifebeater and a pair of faded jeans, his bare feet propped on the coffee table. He was facing the TV, but there was a blank look in his eyes that said he wasn't actually watching it. He was spaced out enough that he didn't even seem to have heard me enter.

"Jamaal?" I said softly, hoping I wouldn't startle him. Startling a man who can crush you like an ant isn't good for your health.

He blinked as if coming back to himself, then turned his head slightly toward me. He made a soft grunting sound, put his feet on the floor, and pushed himself up into a normal seated position. If I'd been sitting like that, my back would have been hurting, but he seemed fine.

"What are you doing up?" he asked, his voice gravelly like he'd been sleeping. That was when I noticed the whiskey bottle on the floor by the side of the couch. I didn't know how much had been in it when he started, but it was almost empty now.

"I was going to ask you the same thing," I said, then let myself collapse onto the far seat of the couch before I ended up doing it involuntarily. My head spun for a moment, and I had to close my eyes. I was still holding the travel mug of coffee, but I didn't feel particularly inclined to drink it.

"You should be sleeping," Jamaal said, ignoring my question entirely. "I know how . . . draining it is to die."

I shivered and opened my eyes, to hell with the dizziness. Seeing the room spinning around me was better than seeing the darkness behind my eyes, a darkness that reminded me too much of the complete sensory deprivation of death.

Jamaal had three times surrendered himself to death to win

back the right to stay in the mansion after Anderson had kicked him out. Perhaps the first time, he hadn't known exactly what he was getting himself into, but he knew after that—and he'd done it anyway. I didn't think I could ever voluntarily allow myself to die again. Not that the first time had been particularly voluntary.

"How could you . . . ?" The words died in my throat as horror threatened to choke me. I wanted to burn the memories from my head, but I was stuck with them, and I wasn't entirely sure they weren't going to drive me mad. "You knew what it was going to be like, and yet . . ."

Jeez, I couldn't even get a full sentence out. I'd come down here hoping *not* to think about death. I guess it was just my bad luck that Jamaal was the one I bumped into.

"It'll get better," Jamaal said, and maybe I was already crazy, but I could have sworn I heard something like compassion in his voice. "I've found that the memory fades with time. It feels almost like a bad dream now."

I nodded and swallowed hard, hoping like hell he was right. I'd barely brushed on the subject, and yet my pulse was racing, my skin clammy. If I wasn't careful, this was going to devolve into a full-scale panic attack.

There was a rustling sound, accompanied by the telltale clicking of beads, and to my shock, I realized that Jamaal was scooting closer to me on the couch. His proximity did an admirable job of distracting me from the panic. He took the travel mug from my unresisting fingers, popped the lid off, and poured in most of the remaining whiskey. Then he put the lid back on and handed it to me.

"Booze makes it all better?" I asked with a nervous laugh. He was still sitting intimately close. I could smell the faint hint of whiskey on his breath, along with the faded remnants of clove cigarettes.

"No. But sometimes it helps."

I didn't know what to say to that, so instead, I took a sip.

The coffee was only lukewarm by then, and the whiskey was pretty overpowering, but I didn't care. Beside me, Jamaal raised the bottle to his lips and drained the last little bit. He didn't strike me as being particularly drunk. Just . . . mellow. Which is not a word I'd ever have associated with him before.

"I'm sorry," he said, staring at the empty bottle like it was the most fascinating thing in the world. "I fucked up. Again." He let out a sigh and set the bottle down on the coffee table. Then he didn't quite seem to know what to do with his hands. "If I hadn't lost my shit, I'd have been there when the jackals attacked. Maybe you wouldn't have gotten bit."

I took another sip of coffee, mulling over his words. "I think if you'd been there, we'd both have ended up with mutant rabies. It's not like either of us would have known how important it was to avoid being bitten."

He shrugged. "I dunno. I think if I'd been there, it would have been me they went after. No offense, but you don't look like much of a threat."

I reached out and patted his knee before I thought about it. "Yeah, well, I don't think I'd want to be around you if you came down with super-rabies," I said as my cheeks heated with a blush. I was not the touchy-feely sort, but this was not the first time I'd found myself touching Jamaal when I shouldn't.

He gave a snort of something that resembled laughter, blessedly ignoring my faux-pas. The hint of laughter faded between one breath and the next.

"I still shouldn't have run off like that."

I wasn't about to disagree, despite my doubts about how useful he'd have been.

"Why *did* you run off?"

He shook his head, the gesture accompanied by the almost musical clicking of his beads. "I knew I was losing it. I didn't trust myself not to . . ." Another shake of his head. "I don't know what I thought I might do, just that it would be bad. I meant to run back toward the cars, but somehow that wasn't what I ended up doing. I went right into the heart of the cemetery, where the call of the magic was even stronger."

I could hear a wealth of remorse and self-loathing in his voice. He'd done some pretty shitty things to me in the past, things I could easily hold against him even though I felt a little too much kinship with him to condemn him. But this I was pretty sure wasn't his fault.

"Why did you come back?"

"I heard the gunshots. I meant to come back and help you, maybe save whoever the killer was after."

"And ended up killing the victim instead." Despite all of my empathy for him, there was still a hint of accusation in my voice. I knew he hadn't exactly been present when he killed the guy, but still . . .

"He would have been dead in a few minutes anyway," Jamaal said.

"You don't know that. Modern medicine can do miraculous things."

"I *do* know that," he said more firmly. "Believe me, Nikki, I know death when I see it. Comes with the territory. The poor bastard wouldn't have lived long enough for modern medicine to reach him. Look what happened to you."

"So that makes it all right for you to kill him?" I asked with a definite edge in my voice. He'd sounded pretty damned guilty about having abandoned me, but it didn't seem like he felt bad about having killed a guy. Maybe I was being judgmental, but it seemed to me he should feel at least a little sorry.

"I wasn't in control. I couldn't have stopped myself if I tried."

"But you didn't try, did you?"

"No." He met my eyes, and there was both a challenge and a plea in his gaze. I noticed irrelevantly that he had absurdly long, thick lashes. "When it gets to a certain point, trying to stop it just makes things worse. I was already well past that point."

I felt tempted to poke at him some more but managed to shut myself up. He wasn't showing a lot of overt remorse, but he wasn't sitting here at two in the morning drinking whiskey and staring at a nature show because of his callous indifference to what he'd done. I remembered Anderson telling me that he was "struggling," and I had to admit, he didn't look like himself. Despite the alcohol, there was a tightness to his jaw and an almost haunted look in his eyes. I very much doubted he liked the feeling of being out of control, and I couldn't blame him.

I wondered what he'd been like before he'd become *Liberi* and realized with a bit of a jolt that I knew next to nothing about him, despite having lived in the same house with him for a few weeks. I didn't know how he'd become *Liberi*—he had to have killed someone to do it, and I had no idea who or whether he'd known what he was doing. I didn't even know how old he was. Anderson had made a comment once about how Jamaal had only had "a couple of decades" to learn to control his death magic, but I had to wonder how good a sense of time Anderson had, seeing as he'd been around for thousands of years.

"So that's my sob story," Jamaal said into a silence that was becoming uncomfortable. He seemed to have muted the TV without me even noticing. "Now, why don't you tell me why you're down here talking to me instead of in your room fast asleep?"

"Let me get this straight. You're actually initiating conversation with me? Has hell frozen over?" Just because he didn't seem to hate my guts anymore didn't mean we were friends, and Jamaal was far from the talkative type. There was something of a dreamlike feeling to this whole conversation, and if I didn't feel so physically and emotionally drained, I might have thought I really was up in my bed fast asleep. But there was nothing dreamlike about my exhaustion.

Jamaal ignored my half-assed teasing. "Remember, I know exactly how shitty you feel right now. You should be sleeping it off, so I figure you're down here because something's wrong."

"Why do you care?" I asked, sounding pretty peevish even to my own ears. Getting bitten by jackals, killed, and brought back to life didn't put me in the perkiest of moods.

Jamaal once would have met my flare of temper with one of his own. I'm sure I would have deserved it if he'd done the same now, but he didn't.

"Because you're likely the only one who can lead us to this guy so we can stop him. Unless we spooked him last Friday, which I doubt, he'll be up to his old tricks again in about forty-eight hours. And if you push yourself too hard and are falling over with fatigue, you're not going to do anyone any good."

His words stung a little with their cold logic. It didn't make a whole lot of sense, but I wished Jamaal cared about *me,* not about my special abilities. I guess it was a hint of neediness, left over from my years of foster care. I was luckier than the average foster kid, having found a permanent home at the age of eleven, but the warmth and love I'd found with the Glasses couldn't completely undo the damage from the foster-care merry-go-round.

I grimaced and rubbed my eyes, tired down to the marrow of my bones. Yeah, coming downstairs had been a stupid decision. I could feel how my body was fighting me, telling me to stop being a moron and get some sleep. But I knew that the moment I closed my eyes, my mind would take me back to the darkness, and I wasn't brave enough to face it.

When I stopped rubbing my eyes, I was embarrassed to find that my fingertips were wet. God, I was such a wuss.

"You'll fall asleep faster than you think," Jamaal said, his voice conspicuously gentle, something I wouldn't have thought him capable of.

I blinked a couple of times, still trying to fight off tears. "Huh?"

"You're down here drinking coffee because you're afraid to close your eyes, right?" I didn't want to admit the truth, but Jamaal wasn't waiting for my confirmation, anyway. "That's how

I felt the first time. But your body will take over, and you'll fall asleep before you can make yourself too miserable."

I hoped he was telling the truth, rather than a comforting lie. "I guess I'll have to find out whether it works the same for me. It's not like I can stay awake forever."

I was not looking forward to dragging myself back upstairs and was halfway tempted to simply curl up on the sofa. Instead, I put down my barely touched spiked coffee and used the arm of the sofa to help lever myself up to my feet.

I got so light-headed I almost fell back down, and I realized I might end up sleeping on the couch after all. I honestly didn't think I could make it to the third floor without collapsing. But Jamaal shocked the hell out of me by rising to his feet and sweeping me off mine.

I gave an undignified bleat as my feet left the floor. "What are you doing?" I gasped.

He carried me like I weighed about twenty pounds. "What does it look like I'm doing?"

I didn't know what to do with my right arm, which was positioned awkwardly between our bodies. I should have put it around Jamaal's neck, but that felt way too intimate.

"You don't need to carry me," I said weakly as he made his way to the grand staircase in the foyer.

Jamaal ignored my words, which he had to know were more wishful thinking than fact. I'd have been lucky to make it to the base of the stairs on my own, much less to actually climb them.

Tentatively, I slipped my arm around his neck, because it just felt too awkward not to, like I was afraid to touch him or something. The beads at the ends of his braids tickled my arm, and I was hyperaware of the warmth of his body, the beat of his heart. He'd hated my guts for most of the time he'd known me, and any sane woman would have locked her libido in a safe and then buried the safe, but I couldn't help the highly inappropriate little flutter in my belly.

It didn't matter that he sometimes bore a disturbing resemblance to a raving lunatic; Jamaal was hot, hot, hot. And there was something about him that called to me, that always had, even when he'd been half-mad with hatred. Something that told me that he and I were a lot alike, that we'd both gotten a raw deal in life, that we both felt terribly alone, and that we lashed out at those around us because that felt safer than letting someone get close.

In short, we were both totally screwed up.

There was no particular tenderness in the way Jamaal carried me. He was just helping me because it was the practical thing to do. I'd certainly seen no sign that he'd ever noticed me as a woman. But that didn't stop my pulse from tripping or my skin from tingling.

Steph had once told me she thought my tendency to fall for inappropriate or unavailable men had something to do with my quite understandable fear of abandonment. As long as I fell for men I knew from the beginning could never work out, I never had to risk having someone walk out on me unexpectedly. She made this diagnosis on the basis of having been a psych major in college, but though I always told her she was seeing things that didn't exist, I had the secret suspicion that she was right. And if I ended up pining for Jamaal, it would just be more of the same.

He carried me all the way to my bedroom in silence, not setting me down until we'd reached the bed. I felt almost unbearably awkward, having no idea what to say to him at a moment like this.

I finally settled for a mumbled thanks as I tucked my legs under the covers and lay down with a sigh of relief. Instead of leaving, Jamaal sat on the edge of my bed.

"Go ahead and close your eyes," he said, looking at his clasped hands, rather than at me.

I wondered what was going on, why he hadn't left yet, but my eyelids had grown heavy, and asking questions seemed like too much effort. Despite a shiver of dread, my eyes slid closed.

The moment my eyes closed, the darkness descended on me, pressing on my chest, smothering me, making my pulse race.

"Just focus on the sound of my voice," Jamaal said, so softly I had to strain to hear him.

And then he started to sing just as softly.

His voice was a rich, low baritone, so warm I wanted to wrap myself up in it. I didn't recognize the language he was singing in or the melody, but if I'd had to guess, I'd have said the song was a lullaby of some sort. It had a lilting, soothing quality that wrapped me in a cocoon of warmth and somnolence.

There was no room in my head for anything but the sweet sound of Jamaal's voice, no room for thoughts of death and darkness. I focused on that sound, losing myself to it, letting my muscles relax one by one.

When sleep pressed around the edges of my consciousness, I wanted to hold it off just a little while, wanted to preserve this moment when I felt so serene and peaceful. But my exhausted body had other ideas, and I faded away before the song was finished.

It echoed in my dreams that night, keeping the nightmares at bay.

Eleven

When I next awakened, the sun was high in the sky, the light pouring through my windows telling me I'd slept until almost noon. I yawned and stretched, then pushed myself into a sitting position and waited to see if the effort made me dizzy.

When a minute passed without any hint that I might be about to collapse, I slid out of bed and cautiously stood up. My head felt fine, and there was no telltale quivering in my knees.

I showered and dressed and even blow-dried my hair, and still I felt pretty much normal. Maybe a little weak but not enough to interfere with my day. Sleep had obviously done me a world of good.

I smiled when I remembered the sound of Jamaal's voice singing me to sleep, feeling somewhat bemused by the gesture. Clearly, there were sides of him other than the bitter, angry, dangerous man I thought I knew. Sides I had no business being intrigued by, I warned myself.

Whatever redeeming qualities he had, Jamaal was bad news.

My mood faltered as I made my way down the stairs toward the kitchen in search of a late breakfast. Sleeping till almost noon might have done wonders for my physical woes, but it meant there were now only about thirty-six hours before the killer was likely to strike again. I had to tell Anderson what I'd found out about the victims and their resemblance to Konstantin and then hope that Anderson could pry the killer's identity from his archenemy's lips. And that learning the killer's identity would help us find him. Oh, yeah, and that we could actually *stop* him if we *did* find him.

"One step at a time," I muttered to myself, picking up my pace as the sense of urgency increased. I'd have skipped breakfast entirely, except I was hungry enough to eat a whole elephant, and I feared if I ignored my body's needs, I'd end up weak and sick and useless again.

The scent of what I guessed was pizza wafted on the air as I neared the kitchen, and I figured that meant some of Anderson's *Liberi* were having lunch. However, when I stepped into the kitchen, there was only one *Liberi* in sight: Emma.

She sat at the kitchen table, a slice of pepperoni pizza drooping in her hand, her eyes glazed and vacant. I expected her to blink and come to herself the moment I came into view, but she didn't. I took a couple of tentative steps closer, but she still didn't blink or move.

"Emma?" I queried, just in case she was lost in thought and hadn't noticed me, but she didn't react. She might be present in body, but her mind was taking a break, wandering off to wherever it went when she entered this fugue state. It had been happening less and less often as she continued to recover from her ordeal as Konstantin's prisoner, but obviously, she still had a ways to go.

Most of the time, I couldn't stand her. She was jealous and possessive, bossy as hell, and sulky when she didn't get her way. But when I saw her like this, I still felt a twinge of pity. No matter how much of a bitch she was and no matter how miserable she made Anderson, she didn't deserve what had happened to her.

Not that I thought for a moment she'd appreciate my compassion.

The pizza box was still laid out on the kitchen counter, so I helped myself to a slice. It was ice-cold, fresh from the fridge, and if Emma hadn't been sitting there, I'd probably have nuked it. However, I preferred to be gone when she snapped out of it, so I merely grabbed a paper towel to serve as a napkin and munched on the cold pizza—breakfast of champions!—as I made a quick getaway.

It showed how little I wanted to face Emma that I left the kitchen without even getting any coffee.

Still stuffing my face, I headed back upstairs, hoping Anderson would be in his study. I got lucky for once and found him right where I wanted him. Unfortunately, the sight of his usually pristine workspace brought me to a jerking halt.

Papers and books lay strewn on the floor, along with a smattering of pens, a stapler, and enough paper clips to supply a high school or two. One of his guest chairs was lying on its side, and broken glass from an overturned lamp peppered the carpet.

Anderson sat at his desk, his head bowed as his fingers pinched the bridge of his nose. Everything except his computer had been swept off the desk, but based on how scattered it all was—and on the damage to the chair and the lamp—I didn't think it was Anderson who'd done the sweeping.

Putting this scene together with Emma sitting vacantly in the kitchen, I figured the two of them had just had one of their epic battles. Ordinarily, I'd have had the good sense to retreat, but the urgency was still riding me. I rolled the stale pizza crust in the paper towel and cleared my throat.

Anderson slowly raised his head. I tried not to gasp when I saw the angry red furrows that crossed his cheek, but I was too shocked to mask my reaction entirely. He frowned and looked around the room as if noticing the damage for the first time.

"This isn't a good time, Nikki," he said, sounding as exhausted as I'd felt the day before.

"Yeah, I can see that. But I'm afraid this can't wait."

He muttered something I presumed was a curse under his breath, then shoved himself to his feet, practically sending his desk chair rolling into the wall. With swift, jerky movements, he circled his desk and picked up the fallen guest chair, setting it upright with enough of a bang he was lucky it didn't break. Then he stalked back behind his desk and sat down, clasping his hands in front of him and spearing me with a look that made me want to tuck my tail between my legs and run.

"What is it?" he snapped impatiently when I hesitated.

I didn't like finding myself caught in the crossfire of a domestic dispute, and the awkwardness had made me hesitant at first. However, I can only be tactful so long when someone's being an asshole.

"If whatever you and Emma are fighting about is more important than catching the killer, then tell me to go away. Otherwise, I'd appreciate a little more common courtesy and a little less misplaced hostility."

He glared at me a moment longer; then the tension suddenly drained out of his shoulders, and he laughed weakly. "I think I liked it better when you were intimidated by me."

I snorted as I pulled back the chair and sat down. "Yeah, I'll bet." If he thought my snappish response meant he no longer intimidated me, then I was happy to nurture the illusion.

"I apologize for my manners. It's been a lousy morning."

I swept the room with a quick look. "No kidding?"

He frowned at my attempt at humor. "Keep the commentary to yourself."

I pondered the possibility of telling him that Emma was sitting in the kitchen having an out-of-body experience but rejected the idea because it smacked of getting in the middle again. But Anderson interpreted my silence as a different kind of commentary altogether.

"Don't judge her," he said as he reached up to rub the healing scratches on his cheek. "She's having a really hard time re-adjusting to normal life, and I'm afraid I'm not making it any easier for her. Every time she does something out of character, I get furious at what those Olympian bastards did to her. Then she thinks I'm angry with *her,* and . . . she doesn't take it well. None of this is her fault, and I wish I knew how to help her."

Maybe I was reading into the situation, but it seemed to me Anderson was trying to convince *himself* more than me. Emma had suffered atrociously, but I didn't think her suffering justified all of her behavior. No matter *what* she'd been through, surely she bore some responsibility for her actions. But Anderson was never going to see it that way, and he was perfectly happy to make excuses for her.

"Now, what did you need? You said it was important."

I told him about the similarities among our killer's victims and watched the shift in his face as the harried husband became the leader of a band of *Liberi* once more.

"That son of a bitch," Anderson said when I was done, shaking his head in disgust. Then he sighed. "Well, we suspected Phoebe wasn't telling us everything, so I guess I shouldn't be surprised."

"Do you think Konstantin will tell us the whole truth now that we've partially figured it out?"

Anderson laughed. "You don't know him very well."

"And I don't want to. But if he can tell us who the killer is . . ."

"He won't. It's just not his way."

"But—"

"Phoebe, on the other hand, I might be able to talk into being practical."

My mouth snapped closed on the protest I'd been about to raise. Of our two Olympian visitors, I would have thought Cyrus was the more likely to give us straight answers. "Not Cyrus?"

Anderson shook his head. "There's a reason Alexis was Konstantin's right-hand man instead of Cyrus. I don't know how many of his own children Konstantin has killed over the years, but it's a lot. He can't ever bring himself to trust them, no matter how loyal they are. He wouldn't share any sensitive secrets with Cyrus."

I probably shouldn't have been surprised that a man who had no qualms about slaughtering whole families would be willing to kill his own kids. It would forever be beyond my comprehension how someone could be so cold-blooded.

"And you really think *Phoebe* knows something?"

"She's in love with him. Has been for decades, God only knows why. He treats her like garbage. But if anyone knows what he's hiding, it'll be her. And since I presume he's sicced us on the killer because he knows he's in danger, Phoebe might decide she has to confide in us for his own good."

There was more uncertainty in this scenario than I felt comfortable with, especially when the clock was ticking so loudly in my mind.

"I'm going to invite her back to the house for a debriefing this afternoon," Anderson said. "I'll want you there, and I'll want Blake."

I raised an eyebrow. "Me I understand, but why Blake?"

Anderson's smile was cold enough to make me shiver. "Because Phoebe won't set foot in this house without her goon, and I need someone who can keep the goon occupied from a distance if things get antagonistic."

My nose crinkled with distaste as I figured out what Anderson meant. "You're going to ask Blake to seduce the goon?" I knew that Blake didn't have any qualms about using his power against men, despite his clear preference for women, nor was he hesitant to use sex as a weapon, but still . . .

"When you're fighting Olympians, sometimes you have to get dirty."

"We're supposed to be the good guys, remember?" I said with more than a hint of disgust in my voice. I'd probably have been okay with just conking the goon on the head but not with subjecting him to what amounted to rape, even if it never went that far.

For a moment, I thought Anderson was going to bite my head off for being a wuss. There was certainly a dangerous spark in his eye. But the spark faded quickly enough, and he reached up to scrub a hand through his already unkempt hair.

"It'll be a last resort," he promised me. "Only if we can't get Phoebe to talk without . . . shaking her up. In which case, we have to make sure the goon doesn't kill anyone."

Anderson may have reined in his anger, but my own blood pressure was starting to rise. "You mean only if you decide she needs to be tortured?" None of this was what I had in mind when I pictured the "good guys."

"If you don't like it, then suggest something better. I don't know how else to get the information we need, unless I can guilt her into talking for Konstantin's own good, which I'd say is about a fifty-fifty shot. So, what would you have me do instead?"

Of course, he had me on that one. I didn't know whether anything Phoebe told us could possibly lead us to the killer before he struck again, but I was pretty damn sure we weren't going to find him if we didn't get more info. I'd been able to predict which cemetery he'd show up at last time, but if he realized that running into another *Liberi* out for a casual stroll in the cemetery at night was more than a freaky coincidence, he might change his pattern.

No matter how hard I looked, I couldn't find a moral high ground. If we weren't willing to press Phoebe for details, then we were most likely condemning some other poor bastard to die a horrible death, to put his family through untold misery. I could only imagine what it felt like to have a loved one not only killed but torn to shreds and partially eaten, as the previous victims had been.

"Time's a-wasting, Nikki," Anderson said. "Let's hear your suggestion."

But I couldn't come up with one. "I hate this," I said instead, feeling sick to my stomach.

"Let's not sweat it too much yet. It's possible Phoebe will cooperate, and then none of this will matter."

But it *would* matter, whether it came to pass or not. Because I knew that given the choice, I was willing to stand by and let the evil happen, and that revelation scared the ever-living crap out of me. I *liked* being a bleeding heart. It proved that my difficult childhood hadn't destroyed my ability to empathize with others and that empathy made me feel less isolated. My willingness to go along with Anderson's plan suggested that I might be starting down the road to losing that empathy, and I didn't like what that said about me or what it portended for the future.

I offered to help Anderson clean up the mess in his office, but he declined, which was probably just as well. My feelings were a bit too jumbled to survive prolonged contact with him, at least for the moment.

I really wanted a cup of coffee but wasn't willing to risk running into Emma, so I went back to my room instead. I didn't have any plans for what to do with the rest of my day as

I waited for word from Anderson that Phoebe was on her way, but when I stepped into my sitting room, I found myself glancing over toward the coffee table, where the manila folder containing my adoption records had been sitting unopened since Steph had brought it to me.

My intention wasn't to start delving into my past. But I did a double take when I saw that the folder was lying open on the table. I knew for a fact that *I* hadn't opened it. Steph had probably done it when I was ill, hoping to draw me to it.

Mouth dry, I approached the table cautiously, as if I thought the folder were about to fly up and bite me.

There was a substantial stack of papers in the file, and the one on top appeared to be a chronological list of all of the families I'd fostered with. I told myself to shut the file and have done with it, but instead, I found myself sitting down and picking up the list. There were two more sheets stapled to the first, and I was amazed to see how many different homes I'd had in the seven years before the Glasses had taken me in. I'd never bothered to count before.

Two and a quarter pages of names and addresses. Some of the families I'd stayed with so briefly that I didn't even remember the names, couldn't conjure up a picture of my foster parents' faces. In the beginning, I'd gotten my hopes up each time I was moved that *this* would be my permanent home, that I would find the stability and love I so desperately craved. Then the disappointments mounted up, and all hints of optimism faded.

I'd brought it on myself, of course. After my mother's abandonment, I'd become a total hellion, bound and determined to make everyone else as miserable as I was. I'd lied, I'd cheated at school, I'd shoplifted—if it got me into trouble, I did it. And then, each time a family gave up on me, I felt validated in my conviction that no one loved me, that every home was temporary, that security and stability were myths.

Maybe I *should* start researching my past, if only to find all of the foster parents I'd tormented and apologize for the hell

I'd put them through. Sure, there were some apathetic losers in the bunch, ones who returned me like defective merchandise and didn't give a shit about anything but their own inconvenience, but I was sure I'd driven some of my foster mothers into tears of despair. Despair they didn't deserve.

How the Glasses had seen past all that I had no idea. If I'd been in their shoes, I'd have sent me away in a heartbeat. But they were better people than I, and I loved them so much for what they'd done for me that my throat ached with it.

My body had gone on automatic pilot the moment I'd set eyes on the folder, and I hadn't even bothered to close my door. When someone knocked softly on it, I jumped and hastily slammed the folder closed, as if I'd been looking at porn or something. When I looked up to see Jamaal standing in my doorway, I felt something akin to panic stir in my chest. I couldn't deal with him right now, not when seeing the history of my childhood had scraped my nerves raw.

He came in without waiting for an invitation, closing the door behind him. I meant to tell him to go away and leave me alone, but I couldn't seem to force myself to talk.

Jamaal didn't say anything as he dropped into the love seat. At least he was leaving the sofa to me, giving me some space. But something about the way he looked at me was too knowing.

"You looked at this, didn't you?" I asked as I dropped the folder back onto the coffee table, wishing I'd never laid eyes on the damn thing.

He'd changed the beads at the ends of his braids, I noticed. They'd been white last night, but today they were all in shades of brown and amber. A bright white T-shirt—so new it still had fold lines on it—made his skin look darker than usual. There was an artful tear across one knee of his jeans, and he wore unlaced combat boots.

"It was lying here open," he said, no hint of apology in his voice. "I was curious."

"It was none of your business!" I said between gritted teeth, surprising myself as much as Jamaal.

He tilted his head like a curious dog. "I really didn't mean anything by it. I thought it might be your file on the case when I first saw it."

I sucked in a deep breath and told myself to get a grip. There was no reason to be ashamed of my background, and there was certainly no reason for me to snarl at Jamaal. Not after he'd been so nice to me last night.

"What are you doing here?" I asked, too stubborn to apologize.

"Checking on you."

"As you can see, I'm fine. And why do you need to check on me, anyway? You hate my guts."

God, could I sound any more like a whiny child? But knowing he'd seen the file had catapulted me straight into ultradefensive mode, and I wished he'd just go away.

"I do?" he asked with another of those head tilts.

It was true he hadn't been acting like he hated me anymore. His feelings for me had certainly run to hatred when I'd first come to the mansion, but the more he came to accept that I wasn't an Olympian spy—and the more control he gained over himself—the milder his opinion had seemed. That didn't mean he *liked* me, though. He'd certainly never been anything remotely like friendly toward me before.

"Just leave me alone, okay? I'm not feeling real chatty right now."

He settled deeper into the love seat, studying me. I refused to let myself squirm under his gaze.

"I spent almost fifteen years trying to track down my parents," he said, and something inside me shifted.

The knot that had been steadily tightening in my stomach relaxed. Not all the way but enough that I could take a full breath, that I could let go of some of the almost unbearable tension.

Jamaal wasn't looking at me anymore. He was tugging at a loose string at the torn knee of his jeans, studying it with the intensity of a surgeon at work, which told me just how uncomfortable his own admission had made him.

I spoke carefully, afraid I'd spook him. "Did you find them?"

He shook his head, still fidgeting with the string. "I found my father's grave, but I never did find my mother."

A lump formed in my throat. His voice was perfectly calm and level, but I heard the pain in it nonetheless. I'd always felt a certain amount of kinship with Jamaal, had never been able to condemn him for the things he'd done. I'd sometimes worried that I was seeing similarities that didn't exist, that I was making excuses for him based on my own experiences, when his own actually bore no resemblance to mine. But now I wondered if some hidden part of me had known all along that Jamaal and I had a lot in common.

"I'm sorry," I said, though the words were lame and useless.

One corner of his mouth tipped up in a bitter smile. "I'm not. If I'd found them, I probably would have killed them, and I'd have regretted it eventually . . ." he said. "Guess that sounds terrible. But it took me years to get the death magic even slightly under control. When I was searching for my parents, I didn't know how to fight it yet, and it didn't take much to set me off."

I tried my best not to be judgmental. I had no idea what Jamaal had been through, had no idea what it felt like to have this malevolent force residing within me, eating at my self-control. Still, as angry as I was at my mother for abandoning me, I couldn't imagine *killing* her if I ever found her.

"And you think your parents would have set you off?" I asked, because the question seemed relatively neutral.

"My father, almost certainly. My mother . . ." He thought about that a moment, then let out a grunt of disgust. "She'd have started defending my father, and that might well have pissed me off more than I could handle. I shouldn't have started looking for them in the first place."

Obviously, he hadn't been abandoned as a small child. He knew his parents—enough to despise them.

I'd been lost in my own funk when Jamaal had appeared in my doorway, but curiosity was quickly getting the better of me, kicking my family woes to the background as I tried to figure out how to keep Jamaal talking. Talking wasn't generally one of his strong suits.

"How did you get separated from them?" I asked, hoping the question wasn't too direct.

Jamaal's eyes met mine and locked on. "I'll tell you, if you tell me what happened to you."

The quid pro quo surprised me a bit. He made it sound like I was secretive about my past, which I wasn't. Sure, I'd gotten a little touchy about him looking at the file, but that was because I didn't like having my privacy invaded. And because looking at the file myself had put me on edge.

Of course, while I might not make a big secret of my past, I didn't exactly volunteer information about it, either. Everyone in this house knew I was adopted, but that was about it.

Maybe I made a big secret of it after all and had just never noticed. I wasn't always a pillar of self-awareness.

"My mother abandoned me in a church when I was four," I said. "I don't know who my father was or why he wasn't in our lives. And my mom made damned sure no one would be able to identify me or tie me to her when she dumped me." It was about as bare-bones a version of the story as I could tell, but as the words left my mouth, I realized that I had never told even that much before.

My usual response to questions about my childhood? I'd say I was adopted and then change the subject. So this was progress for me.

I thought Jamaal might press for details, but he settled for giving me a knowing look. Then he fulfilled his part of the bargain, doing a much more thorough job of it.

"My mother was a slave," he said, and I stared at him in

shock. Obviously, he'd been dealing with his death magic for longer than the "couple of decades" Anderson had said. "My father was a white man. Her *owner*." He bared his teeth at the word, and I couldn't blame him.

"My father was married to a woman named Matilda, and she couldn't have children. When I was born, Matilda had no idea I was her husband's son, and I became the child she'd always wanted but could never have. She and my father both doted on me, spoiled me way more than my mother could. They treated me like a member of the family, not a slave. I honestly didn't understand that I *was* a slave. I loved them, and I thought they loved me.

"Then, when I was eight, Matilda found out her husband was my father. I think he confessed in a moment of guilt. She totally lost it. Couldn't stand the sight of me or my mother anymore. She told my father he had to choose between us and her. And he chose her.

"My father sold my mother and me, and our lives went straight to hell. Neither one of us realized how good we'd had it at my father's house. We'd been blissfully ignorant of what life was like for the average slave.

"I was sold again when I was ten, separated from my mother. I never saw her again. And I have no idea what happened to her. But I bet she died still making excuses for my father, for what he did to us. She never once blamed him for giving in to Matilda's demands. And the stupid bitch felt *sorry* for Matilda!"

There was anger on Jamaal's face—fury, even. But even more prominent was the deep, abiding hurt. He'd been betrayed by everyone he loved. Even his mother's sympathy for Matilda was a betrayal, since it was Matilda who'd caused them to be sent away.

I had no idea what to say. Jamaal's story made my own hellish childhood seem practically ideal. Was it any surprise that he and anger were such great friends? He'd probably have been a powder keg even without the addition of the death magic.

There was a long, awkward silence as I floundered for something to say. Maybe if it had been someone other than Jamaal sitting there, I might even have been able to find something. But let's face it, he was capable of scrambling my wits at the best of times, and this wasn't the best of times. Still, I had to say *something,* couldn't just sit there like a moron.

"I can't even imagine . . ." I started, but couldn't figure out where to go from there.

What was the matter with me? I wasn't the type to get all tongue-tied like this.

But you're also not the type to have personal conversations, I reminded myself. Steph had told me once that I tended to avoid intimacy, and I didn't think she was off base.

I cleared my throat. "I can't for the life of me think of anything to say," I told him, deciding to settle for complete honesty. "Why did you decide to tell me this?"

His shoulders rose in a hint of a shrug. "I was wrong about you. I know you're not an Olympian, and I know you didn't kill Emmitt on purpose. I treated you like shit, and then I left you alone to face a madman with a pack of rabid jackals. I owe you more than a little. If you need any help tracking down your birth mother . . ."

The offer made my eyes sting even as my emotional barriers flung themselves into place. "You don't have to do penance."

"Maybe I'm just using your search as a way to relive my own, preferably with a different outcome."

"I haven't even decided for sure whether I want to go looking or not."

Jamaal pushed himself to his feet, and I suspected he was giving me a condescending look, though I didn't have the courage to check.

"Well, when you decide to go looking, let me know."

He said that like he was sure he knew which decision I was going to make. I didn't like him making assumptions and might have told him so, except he was already on his way to the door.

"By the way," he said before he left, "you're the only one I've told. Everyone else thinks I'm only about fifty. I don't want sympathy or pity, and Anderson won't be happy if he finds out how much I haven't told him, so I hope you'll keep a lid on it."

I was too choked up—and too confused by everything I was feeling—to do more than nod.

TWELVE

Phoebe waited until it was almost dark before she finally hauled her ass over to the mansion to talk to Anderson. He asked Blake and me to wait in his study, because he'd suggested to Phoebe on the phone that he would be meeting with her alone. I guess the rest of us hadn't made a very favorable impression the last time she'd dropped by.

Blake and I had both sat in chairs against the wall on the near side of the room, where the open door would block Phoebe's view until she was fully inside. The choice was not coincidental. Her eyes widened in surprise when she saw us, but she wasn't the only one with a surprise in store for her.

Phoebe's goon—whom no one had ever bothered to introduce—we had expected, but Blake was obviously as surprised as I was when Cyrus followed the goon in.

Blake raised his eyebrows. "Who invited *you*?"

The words were confrontational, but his tone didn't quite match.

Cyrus grinned. "I invited myself," he said as Anderson closed the study door behind him. Cyrus's grin faded. "Though perhaps that was a miscalculation."

Phoebe turned to Anderson with a narrow-eyed stare that was probably meant to be intimidating. It's hard for petite blondes to be intimidating.

"What are *they* doing here?" Phoebe asked with a curl of her lip. "You told me—"

"I know what I told you," Anderson interrupted. "But we really need to sit down and have a serious conversation. One that involves you telling the truth."

Phoebe bristled, and it looked for all the world like she was genuinely offended. "I don't know what you're talking about. And if you haven't invited me here to share intel, then this conversation is over."

"Oh, we'll share intel. Nikki, will you do the honors?" he asked without taking his eyes off of Phoebe. I hoped Blake was ready to step in at a moment's notice, because the tension in the room had risen to dangerous levels in no time flat. Phoebe was steaming, the goon looked ready to leap into action, and Cyrus looked tense and wary. Interestingly, his attention was mostly focused on Blake, and I had a feeling Cyrus knew exactly why Blake was in the room.

I grabbed the photos I'd printed of the three victims who'd been identified, then held them up one at a time so that Phoebe could see them. I could tell she didn't want to give up her staring match with Anderson, but curiosity got the better of her. She tried to hide her reaction, but the sudden tension in her shoulders told me that she grasped immediately the significance of the photos. And the sudden, sharp look Cyrus gave her suggested that Anderson had been right, and Cyrus didn't know whatever it was his father was hiding.

"These are three of the four victims of 'wild dog attacks,'" I said, sure I had their full attention. "You might notice there are certain similarities in their appearance."

"As in, they all look kind of like Konstantin," Anderson finished for me with more than a touch of steel in his voice.

Phoebe blinked a couple of times, and I could almost see the thoughts flitting through her head. Should she pretend ignorance? Stonewall? Make up a total fabrication that would throw us off the trail?

Apparently, she liked option D best: retreat.

"We're done here," she said, striding toward the door, although Anderson stood in her way.

Anderson didn't move. Phoebe's goon smiled, like he was really looking forward to a little action. He reached into his jacket, where, no doubt, he had a shoulder holster.

"Don't!" Cyrus warned, reaching out to grab the goon's arm, but he was too late.

Blake did his thing, and suddenly both men froze, their eyes locking on each other as their pupils went dark and unfocused. Phoebe turned to bark an order at them, but then she saw the looks on their faces and quickly whirled on Blake.

"Stop that!" she commanded, but there was a hint of fear in her voice that stole all the power from her command.

Blake grinned like he was having a great time. "Make me."

"Real mature," I couldn't help grumbling under my breath. So far, Blake was being relatively restrained. The lust was plain to see, but it wasn't so strong that Cyrus and the goon couldn't resist it. Yet. But resisting it took all of their concentration, making it impossible for them to make any hostile moves.

Phoebe turned back to Anderson, her eyes flashing with fury, which I suspected was a cover for more fear. I had yet to meet anyone who wasn't freaked out by Blake's power, and she was obviously no exception.

"Call him off!"

Anderson just laughed at her as he stepped around her and relieved her goon of his gun.

I could tell Phoebe was thinking of making a run for the door while Anderson was busy, so I moved over to block her way. It looked like she was considering going through me, but she thought better of it and settled for growling. "Get out of my way."

"You came to us for help because you knew Konstantin was in trouble," Anderson said to Phoebe's back. "Helping Konstantin isn't high on my list of priorities, but presumably, it is on yours. I'm willing to do everything in my power to stop this killer, *despite* the fact that it will help Konstantin. But to do that, I need to know the truth. Even if Konstantin doesn't want you to tell me, you know it's in his best interests."

For a moment, there was a hint of uncertainty on Phoebe's face, and I thought Anderson might have found the perfect persuasion. Then the steel returned to her eyes.

Phoebe turned back toward Anderson, and there was not a drop of give in her voice. "I've told you everything I know, and I don't appreciate the strong-arm tactics."

Anderson laughed. "Lady, I haven't even *begun* the strong-arm tactics yet." The look on his face hardened. "I've got three questions for you," he said, counting them off on his fingers. "One: who is the killer? Two: what does he have against Konstantin? And three: why did Konstantin *really* ask for our help?"

Phoebe sneered at him. "First: I don't know. Second: I don't know. And third: I already told you."

Anderson clucked his tongue. "Are you sure that's your best answer? Because things could get ugly here if you don't start telling the truth."

"Surely I must be mistaken," Phoebe said, drawing herself up to her full height. "You couldn't possibly be threatening me."

He laughed again. "Really? Because I'm pretty sure that's what I'm doing." The humor bled from his face, replaced by something cold and implacable. "You lied to me. Gave me incomplete information so that I'd throw my people into danger without knowing the risks. That pisses me off."

"Konstantin—"

"Can come talk to me in person if my tactics bother him. Now, start talking, whether to save Konstantin's ass or your own, I don't care which."

Phoebe's face had paled, and though she was trying to put on a brave front, she wasn't doing a very convincing job of it. "You wouldn't dare," she said, but it sounded more like a question than a statement.

Anderson bared his teeth in a savage grin. "Which would be more fun, do you think? Having a three-way with Cyrus and your talking ape?" We all looked at the goon, who was sweating with the effort of resisting Blake's magic. Cyrus was sweating, too, and he managed to look furious and seriously horny at the same time. On some silent command from Blake, their attention turned from each other to Phoebe. "Or talking to the hand?"

Anderson held his palm up for display, and a strangled gasp of dismay left Phoebe's throat. I guess she'd seen Anderson's Hand of Doom in action before. I couldn't blame her for wanting no part of it.

"Or you could just tell the truth," Anderson continued with a careless shrug, lowering his hand. "Your choice."

To say Phoebe didn't like it was an understatement. Angry color rose to her pale cheeks, and she practically vibrated with fury. But she knew she'd been beat.

"You'll pay for this someday," she growled from between clenched teeth.

"Skip the whole saving-face thing, and just answer my questions. Who the hell is this *Liberi* you've set us on?"

Phoebe's shoulders slumped in defeat. "His name is Justin Kerner. He's a descendant of Anubis, just like I told you."

Anderson gave a little snort. "That was the one part of your story I believed. What does this Justin Kerner have against our friend Konstantin?"

Phoebe hesitated, reluctant to part with the truth, but all Anderson had to do was wiggle the fingers of his right hand to get her talking again.

"There's a . . . bad seed. We believe it was handed down from the goddess Lyssa to one of her daughters."

Anderson glanced over his shoulder at me. "The goddess of madness," he explained, correctly guessing that the name was unfamiliar to me. "She's often associated with rabies." He turned back to Phoebe, who'd stalled out again.

"We think Lyssa infected the seed with her madness when she gave it to her daughter. Rumor has it that anyone who's possessed that seed has eventually gone mad."

"And what does any of this have to do with Konstantin?"

Phoebe swallowed hard and avoided all of our gazes. "We captured a *Liberi* who seemed to be insane. We didn't know if it had something to do with Lyssa's seed or if he was just a madman in his own right. We wanted to harvest the seed if it was any good, but we didn't want to risk one of our own people in case it turned out the rumors were true."

Anderson shook his head in disgust. "So you captured a non-Greek Descendant and forced him to kill your madman and take on the seed."

Phoebe nodded. "We figured we'd see how Kerner reacted to the seed. If he stayed sane, then we'd harvest the seed for one of our own. If he didn't . . ."

"Finish the story, Phoebe. What was your plan for if he went crazy, as he obviously did?"

"If Lyssa's seed showed evidence of being infected, then we needed it neutralized. We were afraid an insane *Liberi* would be an exposure risk. Obviously, we couldn't destroy the seed. So we figured the only way to neutralize it was to keep it contained."

"Oh, spit it out, already!" Blake snapped. "You buried him, didn't you?"

Blake's moment of impatience was almost enough to get us all in trouble, because Cyrus and the goon blinked and snapped out of the daze he'd had them in. The goon tried reaching behind him, where he probably had another weapon concealed, and Cyrus turned to glare at Blake, but that was all they had time to do before Blake put them under again. Blake gave Cyrus a shrug and a half smile that looked almost apologetic.

Anderson relieved the goon of a second gun, then speared Phoebe with a cold glare. "Is that what you did, Phoebe? You buried the man alive, knowing he'd be trapped in there, unable to die, forever?"

It's what Konstantin had said he'd done to Emma, although he'd actually chained her in the bottom of a pond instead. I shuddered and tried very, very hard not to think about what such a fate would be like.

"There was no other way to contain him!" Phoebe snapped.

"How did you manage to bury him without his jackals tearing you to shreds?" I asked.

"He hadn't figured out how to use his death magic yet. It takes time for a new *Liberi* to learn what he can do. Surely you know that yourself."

That I did. I suspected it might be years, even decades, before I fully understood my powers and was able to use them to the fullest extent.

"So if you buried him," Anderson interrupted before I could ask another question, "then how did he get out?"

Phoebe shifted her weight from foot to foot like a guilty child. "He figured out how to create the jackals while he was buried. We never thought he'd be . . . conscious enough to do anything."

I shuddered again as I put myself in poor Justin Kerner's shoes. He must have died of suffocation over and over and over, each time being brought back to life by his seed of immortality, only to die again within minutes. That would be horror enough to drive a sane person over the edge, but for someone who was already crazy . . .

"The jackals eventually dug him out," Phoebe continued. "If he'd just run, we might not have known he'd escaped for years, if ever. But he holds Konstantin personally responsible for everything, and he wants revenge more than he wants safety."

Anderson nodded. "Your vision warned you that Kerner would get to Konstantin someday and that the jackals' bites would be fatal even to *Liberi*."

"Not just Konstantin," Phoebe said. "When he's finished taunting us with his mortal kills, he'll start coming after the rest of us. He'll come for Konstantin eventually, but not until he's decimated the Olympians first." Her brow furrowed suddenly. "How did you know the bites were fatal? Did you lose someone?"

"No," Anderson said. "We're all safe and accounted for, no thanks to you and the bounty of information you shared."

I hoped my poker face was working, because Anderson's failure to mention just what he'd had to do to cure me bugged the hell out of me. The only reason not to tell Phoebe what had happened to me was that he didn't want the Olympians to know how to save themselves if they got bitten. I wasn't a big fan of the Olympians, but I wasn't exactly into the "kill them all and let God sort them out" philosophy. Still, I managed to bite my tongue. I might argue Anderson's decision, but not in front of the enemy.

I got the distinct impression Phoebe wasn't satisfied with his answer, but she wasn't in any position to press him, and she knew it.

"What it all comes down to," Anderson continued, "is that you came here spewing lies simply because you wanted me and my people to protect Konstantin." The curl of his lip said just how appealing he found that prospect. "There is no higher purpose to be served, no risk that Kerner's actions might expose the *Liberi* to the government."

Phoebe swallowed hard. "Maybe not. But are you willing to let an untold number of innocent victims die horrible deaths just so you can get back at Konstantin? Because if you are, you'll have to give up any claim to the moral high ground."

"Oh, I intend to stop Justin Kerner, mark my words. But I'm *not* doing it for Konstantin's benefit, and I'm *not* handing Kerner over to you when I've got him. Obviously, the Olympians are incapable of keeping him contained."

Phoebe's jaw dropped open, like she couldn't believe anyone would say anything so outrageous about such pinnacles of perfection as herself and her comrades. "We—"

"Will stay out of my way. I will clean up your mess because it's for the greater good, but you have no say in the how of it. And if I find out you're withholding any more information, I will hold *you* personally responsible. Understand?"

Mingled fear and anger played across Phoebe's face. "You don't dare hurt me," she said. "The truce . . ."

Anderson's smile was fierce and chilling. "Right now, Konstantin needs me. Do you think he'd risk having me withdraw my help for *your* sake? He can always find another pretty trophy to warm his bed. He can't find another descendant of Artemis to do his hunting for him."

Phoebe's gaze flicked to me briefly, and I knew her general dislike of me because of my allegiance to Anderson had now become something much more personal. Konstantin would choose me over her—not for any sexual reason but for self-preservation—and she would never forgive me for it.

Great. I'd managed to make yet another enemy without even having to say anything. *Thanks a lot, Anderson,* I thought, grinding my teeth to keep from saying it out loud.

"Now that we've got that all straightened out," Anderson said, "is there anything else you'd like to tell us about Justin Kerner and what he can do?"

Phoebe hesitated, but in the end, she knew she was beat. "He draws power from the dead. No doubt, you've noticed that his kills take place near cemeteries. If you can get him far enough away from such large concentrations of dead, the jackals might not be so virulent, or he might not be able to create so many. It took him years to dig his way free, and we presume it's because he didn't have access to the dead where we were keeping him."

I could think of another reason that was perfectly plausible: that he needed concentration to control the jackals, and it was hard to concentrate when you were repeatedly suffocating to death.

"That's all I can tell you," Phoebe finished. "When he took on Lyssa's seed, he fell to the madness within weeks, so we didn't exactly have time to test him out and see what he could do before we had to subdue him."

Anderson stared at her intently for a few seconds, trying to intimidate her into talking more. When she didn't, he shrugged. He emptied out the guns he'd taken from the goon, then put them back into their concealed holsters.

"You promise your ape will be on his best behavior when Blake releases him?" he asked.

"Yes," she replied, though it looked like the promise physically hurt her.

"And I'm sure Cyrus won't do anything rash," Anderson added, but he looked to *Blake* for confirmation, not to Phoebe. Blake nodded, and his sexual magic evaporated. Phoebe's goon gasped in a deep breath and took several panicked steps backward, almost tripping over his feet in his haste to get away from Cyrus. He regained some of his composure almost immediately, stopping his retreat, but his face was pale and sweaty, and he couldn't seem to look anyone in the eye.

Cyrus's reaction was less dramatic. He blinked a couple of times, then fixed Blake with a heated look. "I'll pay you back for that someday," he said. His facial expression screamed of anger, but there was a completely different undercurrent in his voice. Unless I completely missed my guess, that threat had been as erotic as it had been angry, and I was almost certain that Blake and Cyrus had some kind of history with each other.

"I'm sure you will," was Blake's understated reply.

Phoebe gave Anderson one last withering look before turning on her heel and striding for the door. This time, I got out of her way.

"I'll show you out," Blake said. His offer had nothing to do with courtesy—he was just making sure the Olympians actually left. And didn't do any mischief on their way out.

I should have followed them, should have given myself

time to ponder and digest everything I'd learned from this conversation before saying word one to Anderson.

Even as I told myself that, I found myself closing the door and turning to face him. When I met his eyes, I found not Anderson the laid-back man who was friendly and easy to talk to but Anderson the god in disguise. He was still in his human form, showing no overt hint of the dangerous and powerful being within, but there was a weightiness to his gaze that told me he had no interest in hearing my opinion.

Getting the hell out of the room was probably a good idea when he had that look on his face. But I've never been all that good with authority—as most of my foster parents would be happy to tell you—and I refused to be intimidated.

All right, that's a lie. I *was* intimidated. But if Anderson wanted a good little toady who never argued his decisions, then he might as well kick me out, because that wasn't me.

"Tell me you're not seriously considering burying Kerner alive for all of eternity," I said.

I hadn't thought his expression could get any more forbidding, but I'd been wrong. "Burying him would be pointless," he said in a monotone that still managed to convey plenty of authority. "The jackals would just dig him out again." He frowned, the expression making him look almost human again for a moment. "Perhaps we'll need to encase him in concrete. Or steel. Then we can bury him somewhere far away from the dead so he'll have as little power as possible."

"Don't bullshit me. You're missing the point on purpose."

"He has to be contained." The humanity was gone again. I wondered if he was doing that to make himself more forbidding, or if he just had to cut himself off from his humanity in order to be such an ass.

"No, he has to be killed," I said. "And you can do it." As painful as death at Anderson's hands would be, it had to be the lesser evil compared with being buried alive for eternity.

"Perhaps I haven't made myself clear. My ability and my

origins are top secret. A secret that only you and Konstantin have survived learning. When I find a way to get to Konstantin without witnesses, I will kill him. If you don't keep your mouth shut, I will have to kill you, too."

I was shocked by how much his words hurt. It wasn't anything I didn't know, wasn't anything he hadn't told me before. But in the past, it hadn't been so . . . blunt. Or so cold. Anderson was my friend, at least sort of, and though I'd been under no illusions that I was as dear to him as the rest of his people, who'd been with him for decades, I'd thought he would be at least a little reluctant to kill me.

Apparently, I'd been wrong, and to my shame, my eyes prickled with tears, and my chest felt heavy with loss. Loss I had no right to feel, because I was still an outsider, would *always* be an outsider, and I knew it. You can't lose something you don't have in the first place.

The ice in Anderson's expression thawed, and he reached out to put his hands on my shoulders. I took an instinctive step back, but he followed and trapped me against the door. His hands squeezed the tight muscles in my shoulders, and I knew the gesture was meant to be comforting. But his last words were still echoing through my head, and it was an effort for me to hold still and not try to jerk out of his grasp.

"It's nothing personal, Nikki," he said gently. "I have good reasons for keeping this secret so . . . . aggressively. I'm sorry to have to resort to threats, but I don't know how else to be sure you'll keep quiet."

My throat was tight, but I managed to get words out anyway. "You could try telling me the good reasons. Because from where I'm sitting, it all looks very selfish."

"I'm afraid you're going to have to trust me." His eyes met mine, and I found myself trapped by his gaze. Usually, those eyes were a perfectly ordinary shade of brown, but right now, there was a hint of white light coming from the centers of his pupils. "I've taken a huge risk in letting you live. Konstantin I know well and understand. I know he will not reveal my secret because he fears that if others know, it will diminish his power. You I can't predict as comfortably. I can't know that you won't someday get angry and blurt something out." He raised his hand to my cheek, stroking the backs of his fingers over my skin as he continued to meet my gaze with those unsettling, inhuman eyes.

"You're alive because I care about you," he continued. "I'm taking this massive risk because I like you too much to hurt you." The light in his eyes grew a little brighter. "But I need you highly motivated to keep my secret, and so my threat will always be there, and I may at times feel it necessary to remind you. It doesn't mean I don't care."

"Right," I responded in a hoarse whisper.

I knew he was telling the truth as he saw it. It even made a sort of sense, in a coldly logical way. Anderson was, after all, a god. He'd never been human, and to expect him to have human values might not be very fair of me. That didn't stop me from expecting it, however.

Anderson gave a soft sigh, dropping his hands back to his sides and giving me a little space. The light in his eyes slowly faded until he was fully back in his unprepossessing human guise. The look in those eyes spoke of hurt and loneliness. It might have struck me as funny that he found my inability to accept his justification for threatening to kill me hurtful, except nothing was going to strike me as funny under the circumstances.

I didn't know what to say to him. Maybe there just wasn't anything else to say, at least not at the moment. But if we managed to capture Kerner, I had a feeling I wouldn't be able to stop myself from opening my big mouth again.

I settled for shaking my head and making a graceful retreat. Now that I had a name for our killer, I had a lot of research to do. Work was always a powerful balm for pain and fear, for keeping emotions at bay while the mind was busy being productive and logical. The problem with using work as a balm was that it was like taking aspirin for a brain tumor. It might mask the symptoms for a while, but it didn't cure what was ailing you.

I had a nasty feeling I was going to be in a world of hurt when the emotional aspirin wore off.

Thirteen

I wasn't entirely shocked when my search on Justin Kerner didn't yield any exciting results. I found out he'd been an army brat, spent much of his childhood traveling from place to place, never setting down roots. He'd continued the trend as an adult, working as a consultant, going wherever the jobs took him. In fact, he traveled so often that it took almost two months for anyone to notice when he went missing from his home in Alexandria five years ago. He'd only moved in a few weeks before and hadn't even bothered to introduce himself to his neighbors.

He was still officially listed as missing, and the police had made zero progress in finding him. They weren't convinced that there was foul play involved.

What this all meant for me was that Kerner didn't have any ties I could exploit in my search for his whereabouts. No wife, no kids, no girlfriend, not even a real friend of any kind, as far as I could tell. No permanent home that might draw him back or sentimental locations he might want to revisit when he wasn't busy killing people. His parents were both dead—his father having met his end in a car accident very close to the time Kerner disappeared—and he had no other living family I could find. No doubt, the Olympians had been thorough in their attempt to wipe out this non-Greek line.

I slept on what little information I had, hoping I'd be able to make something of it in the morning, but no dice. When the Olympians had gotten their claws into him, Justin Kerner had left his old life in the dust, and it didn't look like he had much of anything to look back on. That meant his past wasn't going to help me catch him. Which left trying to anticipate his next move as my only option.

I unfolded my huge map of D.C. and its surrounding area, laying it on my desk. I'd already marked the murder sites on it, and I'd highlighted every cemetery I could find. Until the attack at Rock Creek, Kerner had been going on a generally northerly path, but to continue that pattern, he'd have to go outside the D.C. limits. Now that we knew for sure he was making a statement to Konstantin with the murders, I was fairly certain he wasn't going to keep going north.

There were two cemeteries within the D.C. limits to the south of Anacostia, the site of the first kill, and one that was southwest of Rock Creek, where he'd struck last. When I looked at my numbered dots on the map and if I eliminated any cemeteries not within the D.C. limits, it seemed like the Oak Hill Cemetery, in Georgetown, would be the next logical site in his path if he was planning to circle back to the beginning.

Had he realized what meeting a fellow *Liberi* at the cemetery had meant? Did he think it was just a strange coincidence, or did he know I'd been there waiting for him?

If he thought I was just a bystander who got in his way, then there would be no reason for him to change his pattern, and I could feel fairly certain he'd make an appearance at Oak Hill. If he realized my presence at Rock Creek was part of a bungled ambush attempt, then he might be too wary to stick to his pattern. Then again, he might think I was dead, and our "ambush" hadn't exactly been successful enough to strike fear in his heart.

And that's when the anomaly of his pattern finally struck me.

His first kill had been the southernmost of all of them, and yet there were two other cemeteries on my map within the

D.C. limits and farther south. So why hadn't Kerner started with one of them if he was planning to do a grand tour of the cemeteries?

There was no record of Kerner owning any property in the area—the house he'd been living in when he disappeared had been a rental—and when I'd seen him, he'd immediately struck me as a homeless guy. He had to be living *somewhere* when he wasn't out hunting, and his pattern suggested to me that that somewhere was near one of those southern cemeteries, that he was avoiding them because he didn't want to crap in his own backyard. If he was avoiding them and if he was restricting himself to cemeteries within the D.C. limits, then Oak Hill had to be his next target. Unless he decided to go to one of his previous locations, of course.

I folded the map with a huff of exasperation. There were far too many ifs in this scenario. Even so, I had a hunch that Kerner would be at Oak Hill tonight. The big problem with my hunches was that it was really hard to tell the difference between a hunch that was fueled by my supernatural abilities and one that was fueled by wishful thinking. Was the fact that I could think of a logical reason for Kerner to be at Oak Hill and couldn't think of a logical reason for him to be at one of the others influencing my gut reaction?

A straightforward power, complete with step-by-step instructions on how to use it, would have been real nice.

Anderson held a strategy meeting in his office in the afternoon. I did my best to explain to everyone why I thought Kerner would show up at Oak Hill, although the argument sounded even flimsier spoken out loud than it had in my head. I saw more than one skeptical look directed my way, and there was what felt to me like an uncomfortable silence when I finished speaking.

"She was right about Emma," Jamaal said, breaking the silence. "I don't think the reasoning here is any more outlandish than that was."

"The guy is crazy, not stupid," Blake argued. "Why would he risk sticking to his pattern? Even if he doesn't think it's *likely* we're hunting him, he must have some idea it's a possibility. I mean, what were the chances that a *Liberi* just happened to be wandering around the cemetery at night and just happened to run into him?"

"I think the more important question is what good does it do us to assume Nikki is wrong?" Anderson put in. "If she's wrong, then we have no idea where he'll be, and we can't do anything to stop him. But if she's right, we might be able to get the drop on him before anyone else gets killed. I'd say that's a very good reason to act on the assumption that she's right."

No one could counter that argument, and though it wasn't exactly what I'd call a vote of confidence, it did make me feel better. We might be deluding ourselves, but at least now we felt like we had a chance of finding Kerner. Never mind what we would do with him if we actually did.

"Nikki," Anderson continued, "if you see Kerner, ignore the jackals and just shoot *him*. Got it?"

Of course, that was what I should have done last time, but I'd been too disoriented by the jackals' attack to think about looking for their master—until it was too late. I nodded.

"We'll divide into pairs like we did last time," Anderson said. Then he turned a regretful face to Jamaal. "I'm afraid you're going to have to sit this one out, though."

Jamaal clearly didn't like it, but he had to know it was coming after last week's performance. He nodded tightly, lips pressed together and hands clenched.

"So who gets to be my partner for the night instead?" I asked. I had a brief fantasy of going to the cemetery with Anderson at my side, capturing Kerner, and then persuading Anderson to kill him without anyone being the wiser, but of course, Anderson was partnering with Emma, and it was better for everyone that way.

"You're still the most likely of us to find Kerner," Anderson said. "And the most likely to be able to take him out if you do. I'd like Logan to go with you." His focus turned to Logan. Logan was probably tied with Leo in the category of people I lived in the same house with and knew least, but I *did* know he was the descendant of a war god and therefore pretty handy in a fight.

"You might want to bring a sword," Anderson instructed Logan. "If you do find Kerner, it'll be up to you to keep the jackals at bay."

"Sword's a little close-range for that," Logan said skeptically.

Anderson raised an eyebrow. "You were thinking maybe an automatic weapon? One gunshot might be dismissed as a backfiring car, but there will be more than one jackal. We got lucky last week in that Nikki ran into Kerner far enough away from houses that no one heard the shots, but we might not have that luxury this time. Unless you have a silencer somewhere in your arsenal?"

Logan looked chagrined. "Never thought I needed one. Guess I'll be polishing the rust off my sword. It's been a while since I've fought with one."

The statement made me wonder just how old Logan was. It had been a while since *anyone* had done any serious sword-fighting, but I got the feeling he'd done a fair amount of it in his life.

"Let's hope it's like riding a bicycle, then," Anderson said.

There was a little more logistical discussion after that, and then we all went our separate ways to prepare. I was still a little less than my best after being dead for most of a week, so I took a nap. I was pleasantly surprised to discover that Jamaal was right, and the horror of closing my eyes had faded to almost nothing.

When the time came, we paired up for our hunt. I'd thought Logan, as a war-god descendant, might be the kind of manly man who would insist on driving, but when I said I wanted to take the Mini, he didn't make a fuss. That won him a couple of brownie points in my book.

It was more than a little unnerving to see the long, sleek sword Logan stashed in the backseat as we got ready to go. He handled it with the careless ease of long familiarity, and he patted it almost affectionately when he put it down.

Among all of the other difficulties of tonight's venture would be avoiding the attention of the police. Logan was going to look a little conspicuous walking around with a sword, although he swore his trench coat would keep it hidden until it was needed. And I was once again carrying an illegal firearm within the D.C. city limits, which could turn out very bad for me if I got caught. Not as bad as things would turn out if I got caught unarmed, however, so I was more than willing to continue tempting fate.

The Oak Hill Cemetery was in Georgetown, and even at this time of night, we couldn't find enough parking for all of our cars together. I'd have preferred to have a central rallying point, but since we were going to split into four teams, I supposed it didn't matter.

I parked on Q Street at the southeast tip of the cemetery. Oak Hill was vaguely triangular in shape, with two sides of the triangle bordering residential areas. The longest side of the triangle ran parallel to the Rock Creek and Potomac Parkway and the scenic Rock Creek Trails. If Kerner was hitting this cemetery tonight, then it stood to reason he'd make an appearance in one of the residential areas, where there was more prey to choose from. I, however, was putting my money on the scenic route. There wouldn't exactly be a lot of joggers or bicyclists out at this hour, but Kerner liked his privacy, and the isolation of that trail might be a draw.

Logan climbed into the backseat and strapped on his sword as covertly as he could. When he emerged, I could still see the tip of the scabbard poking out from under the tail of his coat. We were just going to have to hope that wasn't enough to draw attention.

The other three teams were staking out the residential

areas and the numerous side streets, while Logan and I got the trail all to ourselves.

We walked back and forth, eyes peeled, nerves buzzing, for a couple of hours, but we didn't see anything suspicious, nor did any of the others. Then, at a little after two, Anderson called.

At first, I hoped that meant he'd spotted our quarry, but that turned out to be wishful thinking.

"What's up?" I asked.

"Leo's been keeping an ear on the police scanner, just in case. There was just a report of someone seeing a pack of dogs in Fort Totten Park."

"That's near the Rock Creek Cemetery," I said with an internal groan, even as I started hurrying back toward the car, gesturing for Logan to follow. I'd *known* my reasoning was flimsy, but I'd definitely gotten my hopes up that it would turn out to be sound.

"Yes," Anderson agreed, and the jostling sounds I heard told me he was moving fast, no doubt heading for his own car. "I doubt we'll be able to get there fast enough to do any good . . ."

"But we have to try," I finished for him.

"Exactly."

I picked up my pace to a brisk jog as I told Logan about the police report. We dove into the car, and I pulled out with an embarrassing shriek of tires.

"If the jackals have been spotted," Logan said, holding on to the oh-shit bar, "we're already too late."

"I know," I answered, hoping I wasn't being unfairly snappish. I gave the car a little more gas, though I didn't dare go too fast, or I'd attract police attention. I could just see trying to explain to the nice officer why there was a sword in the backseat and why I was carrying an illegal concealed firearm.

Logan and I rode in silence for a few minutes as I worked to contain my impatience and not run any red lights or stop signs. And then a thought hit me.

"Weird that Kerner would let someone see his jackals and

live to tell the tale," I said. "They're invisible unless they're in use, as far as I can tell."

"Maybe it really is just a pack of stray dogs," Logan suggested.

My foot eased on the gas pedal as something inside me shouted that this wasn't right. "Maybe. Or maybe it's some kind of trap. He knows we're out looking for him, and he's decided to lure us somewhere where he feels he has the advantage."

I slowed even more. The car behind me honked in indignation, then roared past me. The driver was probably giving me the finger, but I was too distracted to care. My gut was clenching with dread. I came to a stop as yet another theory popped into my head, one that resonated strangely.

"Or it's a diversion," I said. "He's luring us away from where he really means to strike."

I was halfway into the U-turn before I even realized I'd made a decision. I hit the gas, creating another scorched-rubber screech.

My heart was hammering with adrenaline now, and I was certain that we'd just been duped. Someone was going to die because I fell for the trick and ignored what my gut had been telling me from the very beginning.

"How could he lure us to Rock Creek with his jackals and still make an attack at Oak Hill?" Logan asked, bracing himself against the dashboard. I bet he'd think twice before getting into the Mini with me again. "I'm not sure how far there is between the two exactly, but it's a few miles at least."

He was right, and I had to admit I was puzzled. But something inside me was telling me Oak Hill was still the target, and as badly as I understood how my power worked, I felt certain my reluctance to leave the area was driven by more than a suspicion.

"I don't know how he created the diversion, but it doesn't matter. Like you said, if he's at Rock Creek, we'll get there too late to do any good. If he's at Oak Hill, we *might* get back in time to stop him."

Logan glanced at the dashboard clock doubtfully, and I wasn't that much more confident. We'd wasted a buttload of time rushing off after the red herring—if that's what it was—and instinct told me he would already have selected his victim by the time he created the diversion.

My former parking space was still available, so at least I didn't have to circle the block searching for a new one, but we'd been gone at least fifteen minutes, and I had a sinking feeling that we were too late.

I held on to the remnants of hope as I parked. I got out and hurried around the car to the sidewalk as Logan leaned in to retrieve his sword once more. When he stood up, his eyes suddenly widened at something he saw behind me. I started to turn but not in time.

A pair of furred bodies sailed through the air, impossibly high off the ground for such small creatures. They both slammed into Logan's chest.

His sword was still in its scabbard when he hit the ground. I fumbled for the gun in my shoulder holster, then froze when a voice spoke over the snarls of the jackals.

"Move, and they'll tear his throat out."

I looked around, trying to spot the source of the voice, but the only human form I saw was Logan. He lay on his back on the sidewalk, a jackal's jaws at his throat, teeth pricking his skin. There was no sign of blood yet, and we now knew how to cure the supernatural rabies, but I wouldn't put anyone through that if it wasn't absolutely necessary.

A second jackal stood on Logan's chest, its ears flattened to its skull, its teeth bared as it snarled directly into his face. I could almost feel its fierce desire to attack, but so far, at least, Kerner was holding it back.

I stood absolutely still, my heart pounding in my throat as I frantically searched for a way out of this mess. But I already knew the only way to stop the jackals was to stop Kerner, and it's hard to stop a guy you can't even see. Especially when you're standing stock still and hoping he won't order his jackal to tear out someone's throat.

"What do you want?" I asked. This was a calculated ambush, and I'd walked right into it, even parking in the same space I'd left from.

"Start by slowly putting your hands in the air," he said. For a psycho who was infected with rabid insanity, he sounded awfully calm.

I was finally able to pinpoint the sound of his voice, and I realized he was hiding behind a parked SUV. Even if I managed to pull my gun, I'd have no shot. My aim might be ridiculously good, but I wasn't carrying armor-piercing rounds.

Licking my lips and trying to stay calm, I did as he ordered, splaying my hands to show him I had no weapons. Out of the corner of my eye, I saw that three more jackals had joined the first two, menacing Logan. The three newcomers circled him restlessly, snarling and growling, every nuance of their body language showing how badly they wanted to attack. Even more disturbing, they had streaks of blood on their coats, and their muzzles were wet and red with it. I hoped Kerner's hands were steady on the reins.

Kerner stepped out from behind the SUV. He couldn't have seen me comply with his command, so I supposed the jackals were working as his eyes and ears in addition to being his attack dogs.

"What do you want?" I asked again as Kerner came closer and I could get a better look at him. And, unfortunately, a better smell. He was dressed in a filthy trench coat and too-long jeans. The cuffs of those jeans dragged on the ground and had collected a revolting crust of . . . whatever. And the smell wafting from him was rotting garbage, outhouse, and unwashed body.

I must have wrinkled my nose unintentionally, because Kerner stopped and made a point of sniffing the air. Then he shrugged.

"My apologies," he said, smiling at me like we were having

a pleasant conversation. "I'm so used to it I can't smell it anymore. I'll try to stay upwind."

This was not what I was expecting. His voice was calm and level, his words perfectly rational. There was no manic gleam in his eyes, no insane laughter or gleeful rubbing together of hands.

"You obviously want to talk to me," I said as my mind kept trying to figure out what the hell was going on. "So go ahead and talk."

"I would like you to stop interfering," Kerner said.

I blinked at him. "You ambushed me to tell me that? Hate to tell you this, but I could figure that out on my own." I braced myself, thinking maybe a show of attitude might bring out the screeching maniac I'd been expecting, but Kerner just smiled.

"I've pissed you and your friends off by killing civilians. I'll only get to kill the real Konstantin once, and that's a great pity. He deserves so much more after what he did to me. You have no idea . . ." Kerner shuddered, and I couldn't help a moment of pity as I thought about what he'd been through—and what he'd be going through for all eternity if we captured him and I couldn't persuade Anderson to do the right thing.

Kerner was a sadistic serial killer, but he hadn't been before the Olympians had screwed him up, and somewhere beneath the madness of Lyssa's seed was a scared, damaged human being. A scared, damaged human being I couldn't afford to feel sorry for, I reminded myself. A lot of serial killers have sob stories, but they're still monsters.

Kerner shook off the horror of his ordeal at Konstantin's hands. "But never mind my sad story. While I won't deny I enjoyed killing Konstantin in effigy, I have moved on to worthier prey. My quarrel is with Konstantin and his pack of gutless, soulless cronies, not civilians."

All right. This guy was crazy after all. "Let me get this straight. You want us to leave you alone so you can have your jackals rip various and sundry Olympians into shreds. Is that the gist of it?"

He furrowed his brow as if thinking, then nodded. "Yes, that's the gist of it. Once the world is rid of Olympians, it will be a much better place. And I love the irony of it all, that they used me as their lab rat to test Lyssa's seed and that in doing so, they created the one and only being who could destroy them."

Except for Anderson, of course, but Kerner didn't know about that.

"I wouldn't call it irony so much as poetic justice," I said. And if Kerner hadn't already killed four innocent victims, I might even have believed it.

Kerner looked delighted with what he must have taken as my agreement. "Exactly. And I think it only fair that Konstantin watch the ones he cares for die one by one, knowing he'll face the same fate himself, just as he made me watch as he slaughtered my family." He made a face. "Not that Konstantin truly cares about anyone but himself."

My research had turned up very little family for Kerner. His father had died in a supposed car accident near the time Kerner went missing, and I had no trouble believing Konstantin had killed him in front of Kerner's eyes. That didn't exactly sound like watching his loved ones die "one by one," but maybe Kerner thought it made him sound more sympathetic.

I nodded. "Like I said, poetic justice. But I'm still kind of getting stuck on the killing-innocent-bystanders thing."

Kerner stuck out his lower lip in a twisted pout. "I already told you I've moved on. I only meant to take out Olympians, but then I bumped into that first guy. He thought I was some panhandler harassing him for money." For the first time, there was a hint of a manic gleam in Kerner's eyes, one that said he wasn't as sane and rational as he pretended. "He was a condescending asshole, and he looked so much like Konstantin . . . then he got spooked and started running away, just begging me to chase him." He shrugged. "I probably would have been able to contain myself if the stupid shit hadn't started running."

"So it's all his fault he's dead?"

Kerner's eyes flashed with anger, but his voice remained level. "When it was over, I felt more like my old self than I had since I was forced to take Lyssa's seed, and I realized I could get my revenge on Konstantin and stop being so . . ." He made a circular motion beside his head with his finger. ". . . at the same time. Two birds with one stone."

"And that makes it okay for you to kill people just because they have the bad luck to resemble Konstantin?"

The jackals snarled their disapproval of my tone, and I reminded myself that antagonizing a crazy man who commands a pack of rabid jackals wasn't the brightest idea.

"I keep telling you, I'm finished with that," Kerner growled. His voice had deepened, and he sounded strangely like his jackals. "It was fun while it lasted, but I know now that it was stupid and unnecessary."

I glanced at the jackals and once again saw the blood on their coats. They had killed already tonight, and it sounded as if their victim had been an Olympian. Better than a civilian, but still . . . it was an awful way to die.

"Who?" I asked, not sure why I wanted to know.

Kerner smirked. "Someone whose loss Konstantin might actually regret a little. A pretty little blonde, descendant of Apollo. The Olympians call—*called*—her the Oracle."

I fought to suppress my reaction. Phoebe had no redeeming qualities that I could tell. And yet it freaked me out enough to learn that complete strangers had been torn to shreds, partially eaten. Learning that something like that had happened to someone I *knew* . . . My stomach gave an unhappy lurch.

"There is one less Olympian to blight the earth tonight," Kerner concluded with obvious pride.

I swallowed hard to keep my gorge down. "But she'll come back," I said. The body would somehow mend itself, regenerate the missing organs, and come back to life in the throes of the supernatural rabies.

"No, she won't," Kerner said with a smug smile. "Konstantin made the biggest mistake of his life when he chose me to host Lyssa's seed. The madness *infected* the seed—which means it operates on a metaphysical level as well as a physical one. Pair it with death magic, and you have something that can destroy a *Liberi,* body and soul." His voice was replete with satisfaction, then he frowned at me. "But *you* didn't die," he said speculatively. "I thought at first it was because my jackals didn't eat your heart—did you know the heart was the seat of the soul?—but the Oracle expired before they'd managed to do more than nick her heart. I felt her seed snuff out, right here." He patted the center of his chest. "Even without having directly contacted your heart, the infection should have worked its way there eventually. I wonder why it didn't."

I tried really hard not to picture a jackal tearing my heart from my chest and devouring it, but my stomach heaved anyway. I had no intention of letting Kerner in on the secret of how I'd survived. "No idea," I mumbled.

The physical effects of his death magic were somehow mirrored on a metaphysical level. So much so that when the infection reached the heart, the body and the seed of immortality were both destroyed. If Anderson hadn't broken my neck, if he'd let the super-rabies run its course, I would have died. And *stayed* dead.

Anderson had saved my life by killing me.

But that was a paradox to ponder at another time. I still had to get Logan and myself out of this mess, preferably without either of us being bitten.

I could tell Kerner was still curious about my continued existence, but he didn't press me on it. "All I'm asking is that you stay out of it until Konstantin is dead," he said. "I'm through with the civilians, and I have no quarrel with you or your friends."

"No? Then why did your damn dogs bite me?" Once again, I was failing to humor the crazy person, and the jackals growled their displeasure. I checked on Logan out of the corner of my eye. He was lying very still, eyes closed, and he looked very Zen about having a rabid jackal's fangs pricking the skin of his throat.

"That was unintentional," Kerner said with an edge in his voice that said he was getting tired of my attitude. "For future reference, you might want to avoid shooting my jackals. They're a manifestation of my death magic, and if you take one out, the magic comes back to me. The rebound effect makes me a little cranky." He gave me a teeth-baring smile that was closer to a snarl.

"I'm not a fool, and my mind is still reasonably intact, at least when I have a recent kill under my belt. I understand why you feel the need to stop me. I'm just asking you to put it off for a while."

He averted his eyes and ran a hand through his lank, greasy hair. "I know I'll end up in the ground again eventually. I'm just one guy, and you're all out to get me. But I can't ever die." He met my gaze again, and I saw a shimmer of tears in his eyes. "I can't ever be released from the horrors of the prison you will put me in. And if I have to go to that prison knowing that Konstantin still walks the earth, then I will be spending eternity in hell."

His Adam's apple bobbed as he swallowed hard. "I'm begging you to let me have my revenge before you condemn me. Give me the one thing that will make my eternity bearable."

Bleeding-heart alert—I was standing there facing a psycho who'd killed innocent people just because they vaguely resembled Konstantin, and I was feeling sorry for him. Not to mention the vengeful side of me that was overcome with glee at the idea of Konstantin getting killed by a man who was one of his victims.

Of course, it wasn't like I was in any position to stop Kerner at the moment. Not unless I didn't mind letting Logan get savaged. Sure, he'd probably live through it if they didn't tear out his heart, but it would seriously suck. And while I'm a good shot, I'm not a quick-draw expert. With the gun still in my pocket, in all likelihood, the jackals could make short work of both Logan and me before I got a shot on Kerner.

"I'm attempting to show you a sign of good faith," Kerner said with a little edge in his voice. I guess he was getting tired of my hemming and hawing. "I could have killed both of you before you even knew I was here."

"Yeah, thanks for not doing that. But you're asking me to stand by and let you kill people. I have a hard time saying yes to that." And I had a hard time believing that Kerner would *believe* me if I said yes. So what was he really after?

"All right," Kerner said, and there was now an angry glitter in his eyes. "Let me be more blunt: I'm hunting the Olympians now. Keep out of my business until I've finished with Konstantin, and the Olympians will be the only ones who get hurt. But if I see you or any of your friends near me again, civilians are going back on the menu. I've been controlling the death magic, only letting it loose for one kill a week, but the death toll if you don't keep your nose out of my business will be considerably higher. Are we clear?"

Funny how I felt a lot less sorry for him all of a sudden. "Crystal," I grated out.

He smiled, looking very pleased with himself all of a sudden. "I knew we could work this out. And if you or your friend make any attempt to follow me, I'll take that as a sign that you're rejecting our agreement. If that's the case, check out the local news tomorrow to see how many people I chose to punish for your mistake."

He winked out of sight before I could answer, as did all the jackals. I could tell he was still nearby, because I could smell his rancid stink. Logan lay still on the sidewalk, his breaths shallow, as if the jackal's jaws were still around his throat.

"Is the jackal still there?" I asked, because it was abundantly clear that just because I couldn't see it didn't mean it was gone.

Logan just blinked at me, which I figured was answer

enough. I wouldn't want to talk if I had a jackal's teeth at my throat, either.

Kerner's stink was fading, which told me he was leaving, though he was still completely invisible. I had no idea which way he was going, and I wasn't about to move until I was positive he was gone.

As positive as it was possible to be with an invisible man, anyway.

After maybe three minutes, Logan finally sucked in a deep breath and slowly sat up. We both tensed for an attack, but none came.

Kerner and his jackals were gone. Maybe.

Fourteen

Later that night—or, more accurately, later that morning—we regrouped in the kitchen at the mansion. We were all tired and dejected from the failed hunt. I started a pot of coffee brewing, then did my best to recount everything Kerner had said, word for word, with Logan filling in a few details I had missed.

The coffee maker's death rattle announced it was finished brewing, and those of us who were so inclined filled our mugs. Logan got a bottle of Jack Daniel's from the cabinet over the sink, and Maggie boiled water for tea. When everyone had their beverage of choice, we gathered around the table in the breakfast nook. There weren't enough chairs for everyone, so Jack hopped up onto the counter, and Jamaal, who had waited up for us, stood leaning against the wall. Emma stood practically in the doorway and looked like she was bored and wanted to slip away while we weren't looking.

Jamaal's knee was bouncing, which worried me. He'd seemed relatively calm in the week since he'd unleashed his death magic, but I didn't think the fidgets were a good sign. Kerner said the killings had calmed his death magic, and his one-per-week schedule seemed to suggest the calming effects lasted for about seven days. Which might mean Jamaal was creeping back toward his usual dangerous edge. Then again, he *was* drinking coffee, so maybe he just had a caffeine buzz going.

"If Kerner was in Georgetown killing Phoebe," Jamaal said, "then how did he create the diversion at Fort Totten Park?"

No one had an answer to that.

"If it was a diversion engineered by Kerner," I said, thinking out loud, "then either he has an accomplice with a bunch of dogs, or his jackals can cover a hell of a lot of territory without him being nearby." That was not a thought that put me in my happy place.

"Or he can travel between cemeteries a lot faster than human beings can," Anderson suggested. We all turned to him with varying expressions of inquiry.

"I've known some death-god descendants who've been able to use cemeteries as gateways to the Underworld," he continued. "When they leave the Underworld, they can reenter our world anywhere there's a cemetery or burial ground. They need to draw power from the dead to open the gateway. It's a rare power, but it does exist. And I suspect our man has it."

"You're telling me he can teleport from cemetery to cemetery whenever he wants?" I asked. I wondered if this was something Anderson could do himself. After all, he was Death's son.

"Something like that. It would explain how he's getting around."

"So what do we do now?" Logan asked. "How do we stop Kerner without getting a bunch of innocent people killed?"

"We don't."

Everyone turned to look at Emma, who rarely participated in these little staff meetings of ours. I didn't get the feeling she cared about much of anything, and she certainly wasn't eager to talk to anyone except Anderson. Though she yelled at him more than she talked to him.

"Emma . . ." Anderson said in a warning tone, which she completely ignored.

"If he wants to take out the Olympians, I say more power to him."

Anderson looked pained. "I'll admit, they're not good people, but—"

"But nothing!" she snapped, eyes flashing. "Anything Kerner does to them, they deserve. And I quite like the idea of Konstantin watching as his people get savaged one by one, knowing what's coming and unable to stop it."

She was dead serious and had a fanatical gleam in her eyes that reminded me a little of Kerner. She'd moved away from the doorway, finally interested enough in the subject matter to join in. As far as I could tell, the only thing she truly cared about was getting her revenge.

"We'll talk about this later," Anderson said with quiet authority, but Emma wasn't finished.

"No, we'll talk about it now! It's past time you get off your ass and avenge me! You don't want to go to war with the Olympians because you like your status quo so much? Fine. But if there's another *Liberi* out there willing and able to go get that pound of flesh, then you're damn well not going to stop him!"

Everyone in the room must have overheard snippets of this argument before. It wasn't like Anderson and Emma were quiet when they fought. But they'd usually at least made a show of keeping it private.

Emma stalked through the assembled chairs toward Anderson. The anger that radiated from her was palpable, and I don't know about the rest of Anderson's people, but *I* wanted to get the hell out of the room before things went any further. But I don't think any of us wanted to draw Anderson's attention or Emma's ire, so we sat still and silent, unwilling witnesses to what could soon become something truly ugly.

Anderson rose slowly as Emma approached, his full attention on her. "Konstantin deserves to suffer for what he did to you," he said. "But not like this. Not when innocent lives are at stake."

Emma snorted and tossed her hair. "Innocent lives! There's no such thing as an innocent Olympian. The only way more innocents get hurt is if you insist on playing the fucking hero and Kerner decides to make you pay."

"You don't know that."

Considering Emma was in complete battle-ax mode, Anderson was remaining impressively calm. In fact, he looked more sad than angry.

"He may mean what he said," Anderson continued, "or he may not. Either way, I don't trust him, and if you were thinking straight, you wouldn't, either."

I thought for a moment Emma was going to hit him. She looked that pissed.

"I'm thinking perfectly straight," she said in a low growl that reminded me of an angry cat. "Even if there turns out to be some collateral damage, it would be worth it if Konstantin dies."

Anderson gaped at her like he couldn't believe she'd just said that. Maybe whatever she'd been through at Konstantin's hands had warped her beyond recognition, because I had a hard time believing Anderson had married someone this cold and vindictive. I hated Konstantin for what had been done to my sister on his orders, but it would never have occurred to me to let innocent people suffer in order to hurt him.

"You can't mean that," Anderson said weakly.

"Yes, I can." She lowered her voice, attempting to sound calm and reasonable. It would have worked better if there weren't so much insanity and hatred in her eyes. "I don't understand why you're so dead set against it. If you don't care enough about what he did to me, then surely you care about all the hundreds of others he's hurt and killed in his lifetime. If he dies, it will save untold innocent lives. You know that."

She was probably right. Konstantin and his Olympians were a scourge, wiping out whole families of Descendants and taking whatever they wanted without a thought. But there was no great conviction to her argument, no sign that the saving of innocent lives meant anything to her whatsoever. She was merely looking for the angle that would convince Anderson to do what she wanted.

"Everyone out," Anderson said without taking his eyes off Emma. "I need to have a private conversation with my wife."

The haste with which the rest of us jumped to our feet and stampeded toward the door might have been funny in other circumstances.

Despite the coffee, I was dead tired. I could hear Emma's and Anderson's shouting voices behind me, and I suddenly realized I had had all I could take of them, of this house, and of my new and not improved life. For the last two weeks, I'd lived and breathed the *Liberi* and their troubles. I had not once stopped by my condo, nor had I even thought about spending the night there. I was letting myself get drawn in more and more deeply, letting the life I had once known slip through my fingers.

While the rest of the *Liberi* trooped upstairs to get some sleep, I found myself heading out the front door. I might have thought someone would try to stop me or at least ask me where the hell I was going at oh-dark-thirty, but either they were in too much of a hurry to get out of earshot of the argument, or they didn't give a damn. I assumed the latter and felt sour about it.

I let out a breath of relief as I drove through the front gates and pointed my car toward Chevy Chase. I wasn't free of the *Liberi,* not by a long shot, and I still had a lot to do in the fight to stop Kerner. In a few hours, I would be back at the mansion, hard at work. But maybe for a precious few hours, I could take a mental vacation from the turmoil.

The air in my condo felt stale when I let myself in, but I

was pretty sure that was just my imagination. I walked from room to room, reacquainting myself with my things, waiting for the tightness in my shoulders to ease, waiting for my body to acknowledge that I was home.

Maybe I was just too tired and stressed to relax, but being surrounded by my own things in my own home didn't have the soothing effect I'd hoped for. The apartment felt cold and empty, oppressively quiet, and although it wasn't unwelcoming, it didn't feel like *mine* anymore. It reminded me of spending the night in my old bedroom at my adoptive parents' house: I still felt emotional ties to the place, the bond formed from years of memories, but that was all in the past. I was just a visitor now.

More disturbed than I'd have liked to admit by the direction of my thoughts, I slipped between the sheets of my no-longer-familiar bed and tried to sleep. It took me far longer than it should have.

I hadn't kept the kitchen stocked, so when I woke up in the morning, I had to go out for breakfast if I wanted anything to eat. I wanted to stay longer, to give myself an extended time-out, but staying in my apartment wasn't giving me the kind of boost I'd been hoping for. Just the opposite, in fact. There was a hollow feeling in the pit of my stomach, and I feared the life I was trying to cling to had passed me by forever.

I left the apartment as soon as I was showered and dressed. I drove through McDonald's for an elegant breakfast, then headed back to the mansion. I parked in the garage and walked to the front porch, where I found Jamaal lighting one cigarette from the butt of another.

It was none of my business if Jamaal was chain-smoking, but I found my footsteps slowing as I climbed the front steps and ventured onto the porch. He stared at me with neutral eyes while he took a deep drag on the fresh cigarette, holding the smoke in his lungs before letting it slowly out. It was then that I realized he wasn't smoking one of his usual clove cigarettes.

"You're smoking pot?" I asked, surprised. It was something I'd never seen him do before.

He shrugged and took another drag, then held the joint out to me.

For all my rebellious ways, I'd never been into drugs. Of course, if the Glasses hadn't taken me in when they had, I'm sure I'd have headed down that road as a teenager. Luckily for me, the Glasses had cured me of the need to act out in self-destructive ways.

"Um, no, thanks." I boosted myself up onto the rail that surrounded the porch, trying to read Jamaal's face without being too obvious about it. "Everything okay?"

He laughed a cloud of smoke. "You're kidding, right?"

"You know what I mean. You seem to be getting edgy again." And there was a reason he'd graduated from cigarettes to joints.

He took another drag, then stubbed out the joint, putting the remains in a little tin, which he then slipped into his jeans pocket.

"This is normal for me," he said, but he didn't look happy about it. "Releasing the death magic made it better for a little while, but I can feel it building up again. Just like always."

"But it wasn't like this when Emmitt was around," I said tentatively, always afraid to bring up his friend's death. The death *I'd* caused. Emmitt had possessed some death magic of his own, and he'd been teaching Jamaal how to control it, apparently with some success.

Jamaal moved over to the porch swing, dropping into it like he was bone-tired. Maybe he was.

"It was better then," Jamaal admitted. "We'd kind of . . . vent the death magic together. Send it at each other to ease the pressure inside."

I shivered. "You sent death magic at each other? Wasn't that kind of dangerous?"

He shrugged. "It wasn't like we could do each other any

permanent harm. And our magics tended to cancel each other out." His eyes had a faraway look to them, and there was a faint smile on his lips.

Guilt niggled at me for the umpteenth time. If only I'd listened to my common sense that night, or if only I hadn't gone so fast on that icy road, Emmitt would still be alive today. I'd still be mortal, with no idea that the *Liberi* even existed.

"Why can't you just do the same thing with someone else?" I asked. "It's not like you can kill another *Liberi*."

"Yes, I can. Emmitt's magic canceled mine out, but it would kill any other *Liberi*. They wouldn't stay dead for long, but people seem strangely reluctant to try it. Would you like to volunteer?"

"You know, that sounded almost like a joke. If you're not careful, I may start suspecting you have a sense of humor buried somewhere deep down inside."

"Who says I was joking?"

His voice was completely deadpan, and his face revealed nothing, so I don't know what it was about him that told me he was kidding. It was something, though, because no shiver of fear passed through me, despite the very real reasons I had to be afraid of Jamaal.

I didn't respond, instead thinking about the mysteries of death magic. Was it something specific to being a descendant of Anubis that allowed Kerner to channel his death magic into phantom jackals the way he did? Obviously, the *jackals* were specific to Anubis, but . . .

"Isn't there any other way you can vent the death magic? Kerner thinks creating the jackals is helping him keep in control. At least, as in control as a psycho can be."

"I can't make it manifest itself physically, if that's what you're asking."

"Have you ever tried?"

He blinked at me like the thought had never occurred to him. "No, but—"

"Then how do you know you can't? My powers didn't come with an instruction manual, so I see no reason to assume yours did."

He dismissed my question with a shake of his head. "If we believe anything Phoebe told us, Kerner hasn't been *Liberi* a tenth as long as I have. If I had a power like that, I would have figured it out by now."

I swung my feet between the balusters like a little girl, hoping the small movement would both help me stay warm and help me follow my own train of thought.

"But you haven't *needed* to figure it out. Kerner had been buried alive. He had a desperate need to do something to get himself out. You know what they say about necessity being the mother of invention."

Jamaal arched an eyebrow. "Are you suggesting you'd like to bury me somewhere and see if I can make my magic dig me out?"

"Why are you being willfully obtuse about this? If you're so unhappy about the effects of your magic, maybe you should try *doing* something about it instead of just whining."

Jamaal rose slowly to his feet, eyes locked on me with simmering fury. I'd been treating him like a regular guy, allowing myself to forget just how terrifying he could be when he was angry. And how easy it was to set him off.

I held my hands up in a gesture of surrender. "Sorry. I didn't mean to be so abrasive. I'm just trying to help."

The apology did nothing to appease him. "I don't need your help. I don't *want* your help."

So much for any sense of calm the joint might have given him. A smart woman would have retreated in the face of Jamaal's Mr. Hyde, but no one's ever accused me of being smart where men are concerned.

"You need to smoke like five packs a day to keep from completely wigging out, and you gave in to the death magic last week at the cemetery. I'd say that means you need help."

I slid off the railing and straightened to my full, but decidedly inadequate, height as Jamaal stalked closer. There was too much white showing around his eyes, and his pupils were little black pinpricks in a sea of chocolate brown. His nostrils flared like those of a predator who'd scented his prey. All very bad signs. Signs I chose to ignore as I held my ground.

"Are you really going to give in to it this easily?" I asked as my heart drummed frantically and my sense of self-preservation begged me to shut the hell up. "You've fought it for so long. And you've gone through so much to keep from being turned out of the house. Don't fuck it all up just because someone tries to help you."

Jamaal blinked in surprise, and I almost smiled. Amazing how much more effect an F-bomb has if you don't make a habit of using them. He stared at me a little more, and I watched the anger fade from his eyes until he took a deep breath and lowered his head.

"Why would you want to help me?" he asked so softly I could barely hear him. "You have every reason in the world to hate me."

There was a wealth of pain and loneliness in his words. He was not someone who was used to forgiveness. I'd explained to him numerous times by now that I'd forgiven him for his actions when I'd first become *Liberi,* but there was no sign he'd believed me.

I stepped a little closer to him. My feminine instinct was to reach out and touch him, give him a little human contact to anchor him in the now. But I knew he didn't like to be touched, especially by me, so I resisted the urge.

"You know I don't hate you," I said, picking my words carefully. "You and I are too much alike."

Amusement lit his eyes, and his lips twitched with a smile. "Yeah, we have a lot in common."

He meant that sarcastically, but he was right.

"You saw my file, saw how many foster families I went

through. I didn't get bounced around like that because I was Miss Sweetness and Light. I spent years lashing out at people. I remember what that need felt like, remember what it was like to try to keep it buried and have it explode out of me at the least provocation. If the Glasses hadn't seen past all that crap and adopted me, I don't know where I'd be today. In jail is as good a guess as any.

"I got lucky, Jamaal. That's the only reason I don't have serious anger-management issues anymore. Maybe it's my turn to see past someone else's crap now."

Chocolate-brown eyes met mine, warmer than I'd ever seen them, and I thought maybe I was getting through to him. Then, before I had a chance to get my hopes up, his expression clouded.

"You were just a kid when that shit happened," he said. "And you didn't have death magic beating down your barriers. I'm glad you were able to get help, but it's too late for me."

He started to turn from me, and I knew he was planning to retreat to the house without another word. I couldn't let him do that, couldn't let our conversation end on such a hopeless note. So I reached out and grabbed his arm.

He whirled on me, braids lashing through the air like whips. I stood my ground, refusing to let go as he glared down at me for daring to touch him. His biceps were as hard as marble, well defined, and almost completely devoid of fat. He could have broken my grip easily, and the fact that he didn't gave me the courage to hold on.

"It's not too late unless you want it to be," I said.

"You don't know what the fuck you're talking about, so shut the fuck up."

F-bombs from Jamaal were a dime a dozen, so I wasn't particularly surprised by his response. I also couldn't help noticing he still hadn't tried to pull his arm from my grip. There was a battle going on inside him, a battle between the part of him that wanted to avoid all human contact to prevent being hurt and the part that was desperate not to be alone anymore. It was a battle with which I was intimately familiar.

"I know exactly what I'm talking about, and you know it," I countered. "I know exactly what it's like to be abandoned by someone I love, and I know exactly what it's like to build up that suit of emotional armor so—"

Jamaal jerked his arm, the motion making me stumble forward, right into his chest. I expected him to shove me away, so what he did next shocked me.

His free hand plunged into my hair, grabbing a handful and pulling my head back. I started to gasp out a protest, but before a sound escaped me, his mouth crashed down on mine.

He smelled of cloves and smoke, with a sweet overtone of pot. His braids tickled my face and throat, and his lips . . .

This was not a soft kiss, not a kiss inspired by tender emotions and affection. This was rage and pain, loneliness and frustration, and, most of all, fear. His lips pressed against mine so hard I half expected them to fuse. My mouth was open from my interrupted protest, and he thrust his tongue inside.

I won't lie and claim I wasn't a bit turned on. There was no question I was attracted to Jamaal, had been even when he'd hated me and wanted to kill me. He was beautiful and exotic and dangerous, all of which made him sexy as sin. Desire stirred in my belly as his tongue brushed against mine. I wanted to shut off my brain and return the kiss, press my body up against his. I wanted to take him upstairs and get him out of his clothes, see if his body was as beautiful as his face.

But this was wrong on so many levels. Jamaal and I didn't even like each other, and I'd never seen any sign before now that he shared my attraction. He was violent and dangerously unstable, and he was kissing me because he wanted to shut me up—although I had to wonder why he hadn't just pulled free and slammed into the house.

I tried to pull away from the kiss, but Jamaal wouldn't let me. His hand was still buried in my hair, strands wrapped around his fingers as he tasted the inside of my mouth. I put my hands on his chest and pushed, but I might as well have tried to move a tank. He pressed me closer to his chest, close enough that I could feel the impressive bulge in his pants. He might be doing this just to make a point, but he wasn't completely unmoved by it.

His scent filled my head, blurred my mind. His taste threatened to overwhelm me, and his touch threatened to make me forget why I should be stopping him. But I'm nothing if not stubborn, and I held on to my reason with desperate strength. This was not a battle I could allow him to win.

I pressed my teeth gently against his tongue in warning. Of course, he ignored the warning. I pressed a little harder, silently begging him not to make me hurt him, but he was well beyond being warned off.

Wincing in anticipation, I bit down hard enough to draw blood.

Jamaal's mouth jerked away from mine, his hand in my hair tightening to painful levels before he suddenly let go. His chest was heaving with his breath, and his eyes were dilated with lust. If he weren't using this to cover up a whole lot of other, less savory emotions, I might have found the expression on his face smoking hot.

I opened my mouth to force out an apology for biting him but swallowed it before any words escaped. He'd deserved it and was lucky I hadn't done anything worse.

"Leave me alone," he said hoarsely, shoving on my shoulders so hard I almost fell on my butt. "I don't need your interference."

Instead of seeking refuge in the house, Jamaal ran past me, jumped down the porch steps, and sprinted toward the garage. I guess he was afraid that if he ran into the house, I'd follow him.

FIFTEEN

Even though Jamaal had shut me down in no uncertain terms, I decided to do a little research on Kali, to see if there was an animal associated with her that perhaps Jamaal could try to use to make his death magic take physical form. I'd already seen evidence that animals associated with the gods had real significance when it came to *Liberi*. I couldn't be sure the doe that had led me to find Emma had been supernatural in nature, but it seemed a bit of a stretch for it to be a coincidence that Artemis is often pictured with a deer by her side. It all seemed a little whimsical and perhaps not at all useful, especially if Jamaal refused to try anything, but arming myself with knowledge couldn't hurt.

Let me tell you, Kali is one hell of a scary goddess, and I wouldn't want to meet her in a dark alley. She isn't evil—despite some of the really nasty cults that had sprung up in her name—and most of the stories about her involve her killing demons, not people. Still, when you've got a goddess who's often depicted standing on a dead body and wearing amputated body parts for jewelry, it's hard to feel much in the way of warm fuzzies. I did notice that she was often associated with tigers. Perhaps Jamaal already knew that, but I decided that the next time I saw him, I'd try to work the fact into the conversation. Assuming the embarrassment of what had happened this morning didn't make conversation impossible.

I was trying to figure out what to do next when the lights suddenly went out.

It was broad daylight, and while the windows in my sitting room were a little small for my taste, they let in plenty of light. However, when the lights went out, my room was suddenly pitch dark, like someone had switched off the sun.

My adrenaline spiked as I reached up to rub my eyes, not believing what I was seeing. Or, more accurately, what I *wasn't* seeing. But rubbing my eyes didn't suddenly make everything better. No matter how much I blinked, the room remained dark.

The hairs on the back of my neck rose, and my breathing shallowed. I'm not afraid of the dark, but this was something else entirely, and it reminded me far too much of being dead. I forced myself to take a deep breath, forced myself to acknowledge that I had a body and that it was following my orders. I wasn't dead, no matter how much the empty blackness made me feel like it.

Slowly, I rose from my chair as I mentally mapped out the room and tried to keep myself oriented. If I was careful, I should be able to make it to the door and out without falling over anything.

As I stood there hesitating, wondering if the whole house was draped in this unnatural darkness, I heard the faint sound of my door swinging open. No light poured in from outside, and I wondered if I'd suddenly gone blind. Maybe it was some lingering effect of the super-rabies. I grabbed the back of my chair, needing an anchor as panic skittered around the edges of my mind.

The door clicked shut. I was no longer alone in the room.

I closed my eyes and tried to pretend that was the only reason I couldn't see. I could still try a run for the door, but I had no idea who'd just come in, and whoever they were, they could well be in my way. Besides, the fact that I hadn't seen any light from outside when the door opened made the prospect less appealing.

"Who's there?" I asked, but I wasn't surprised when there was no answer.

I was seriously creeped out, my skin crawling, but I was also getting just a tad pissed off. Especially as a suspicion crept into my mind about just who might be behind the unnatural darkness.

Who in this household didn't like me *and* was a descendant of Nyx, the Greek goddess of night?

My fingers began exploring the surface of my desk, looking for something that would make a useful thrown weapon. Something other than my laptop, which I'd never dream of risking.

The most weighty thing I found was my empty coffee mug, and I hefted it experimentally. It wasn't exactly a lethal weapon, but it was all I had. Plus, I'd once taken out Jamaal's eye with a thrown shoe, so ordinary objects could be more dangerous than they looked when I wielded them.

My blood rushed in my ears, the only thing I could hear in the hushed silence of the room. I closed my eyes again, straining my ears for the slightest hint of movement, anything that would help me target the intruder.

There! Something that sounded like the brush of a shoe over carpet.

With a grin that was probably a less-than-attractive expression, I heaved the coffee mug in the direction of the sound, letting my body make the toss on autopilot. I might not understand how my supernatural tracking abilities worked as well as I'd like, but I *did* understand my miraculous aim.

There was a distinctive thump as the coffee mug hit its target, followed by a cry of pain and surprise. Another thump, sounding like a body hitting the floor. And then the lights came back.

I had to blink in the sudden brightness, but it hadn't been dark long enough for my eyes to adjust fully, so I wasn't blinded for long.

Emma was sprawled inelegantly on my floor, and I could practically see the stars and chirping birds circling as she blinked and shook her head. A thin trail of blood snaked down her face from her temple, and I might have felt bad about it if she hadn't been sneaking into my room to terrorize me. My coffee mug lay in pieces on the carpet around her.

I took a couple of steps to my right and grabbed the hardback book that was sitting on a nearby chair, in case Emma decided to object to my treatment and go ballistic. I hadn't hit her hard enough with the coffee mug to knock her out, but the book felt heavy enough to cave in the side of her head.

"How nice of you to come pay me a visit," I said, hefting the book dramatically in case she didn't get the hint.

She shook off the lingering effects of the blow to the head and glared up at me. She pushed herself into a sitting position.

"If you're going to stand up," I said, "do it real, real slow." I held up the book for emphasis.

The look she leveled on me then was pure malevolence. "I'll make you pay for this."

"For *what*?" I cried in exasperation. "You're the one who attacked *me*." Though I supposed, strictly speaking, making the room go dark wasn't exactly an attack. I was sure she'd had more on her mind than just a little optical illusion.

Moving at a normal pace, as if the book in my hand didn't worry her for a moment, she stood up, touching the blood on her face. "I did *nothing* to you," she snarled, staring at the blood on her fingers. "And you drew my blood."

"Oh, cut the crap, Emma. I don't know exactly what you were planning on doing, but I know it wasn't anything good."

She wiped her bloody hand on her shirt, leaving a crimson smear. Scalp wounds bleed like a son of a bitch, even when they aren't deep.

"I came here to apologize, and this is how you treat me?"

My mouth dropped open in shock as for half a second, I thought she meant what she said—no matter how loudly her actions contradicted her. Then I saw the sly smile on her lips and realized she was already crafting her own version of this story. A version that would make *me* look like the aggressor. Once again, she wiped blood from her face and then smeared it on her shirt, making her look like she'd just left a war zone. The small wound on her forehead might fade before she tattled on me, but the blood on her shirt would not.

The bitch had played me.

I shook my head, hating that I'd stepped right into her trap. Anderson should know me well enough to know I wouldn't just pitch something at Emma's head for no reason; however, he had an obvious blind spot where Emma was concerned. If she told him I'd attacked her, there was a chance he'd believe her, no matter how outlandish the claim. If he believed her, things could go very badly for me.

"What the hell, Emma?" I asked as my stomach dropped to my toes. "If it hadn't been for me, you'd still be down at the bottom of that pond." I'd long ago given up on the romantic idea that she might be grateful to me for her rescue, but for her to hate me so much . . .

"Oh, thank you sooo much," she said, oozing sarcasm. "I'm so glad I get to be around and watch you throw yourself at my husband while talking him out of avenging me. I will owe you for all eternity, and you can treat me like your bitch whenever you want."

Throwing myself at Anderson? I couldn't think of a single thing I'd done that any halfway reasonable person would even think of labeling "throwing myself" at him. And did she honestly think *I* could talk Anderson out of *anything*? As for treating Emma like my bitch, I'd done my best to keep my distance from her from the very beginning. I barely spoke to her at all, if I could help it.

Obviously, the woman was delusional. But knowing that didn't help me.

"You need professional help," I told her. "You're being completely paranoid and irrational. And whatever problems you and Anderson are having, you should be working it out yourselves, not dragging me into the middle of it."

The cut on Emma's forehead had stopped bleeding and was probably well on its way to healing completely. But the streaks of blood on her shirt would look very damning if Anderson was prepared to take her story at face value.

If she heard a word I said, she didn't acknowledge it. Instead, her eyes filled with cunning, suggesting that as crazy as she was, she still had enough wits about her to be dangerous.

"I won't tell Anderson what you did to me," she said. "On one condition."

I did *not* like the sound of that. Nor did I like her self-satisfied tone and gloating expression. It told me she was sure she'd won.

I wished I could be sure Anderson would be rational, would realize I wasn't the type of person who would just attack his wife out of nowhere. Maybe he would, but *maybe* wasn't good enough, not with a man who had threatened to kill me on more than one occasion. And even if he did believe me, he might decide this was evidence that Emma and I couldn't live in the same house together, and I was damn sure *she* wasn't the one who would be asked to leave.

"What condition?" I asked through gritted teeth.

"Make no effort to catch Justin Kerner until after Konstantin is dead. Lead everyone on a merry chase, pretend you're trying your hardest. But stay away from him. Do we have a deal? Or should I go speak to Anderson right now?"

I seriously considered throwing the book at her in hopes that another blow to the head would jar some sense loose. I didn't do it, but I'm sure my face conveyed the message of how much I wanted to.

"All I'm asking for is *justice,*" Emma said earnestly. "Konstantin deserves to die. And Kerner has sworn he'll stop killing civilians. It's like the gods themselves dropped a solution to the Olympian problem straight into our laps!" Her voice was steadily rising with her excitement, but she seemed to notice and pull back. She was nuts, but not so nuts as to not realize how nuts she was making herself sound.

"Anderson refuses to declare war on the Olympians because he's afraid some of his people might get hurt if he does," she continued more calmly. "But if we just let Kerner take care of things himself, there won't have to be a war. I don't know why Anderson refuses to see that."

There was a certain amount of logic to what Emma was saying. If I could be certain Kerner would only kill Konstantin, I might even have agreed with her. I'm not the bloodthirsty sort as a rule, but I did want Konstantin dead. Maybe the rest of the Olympians deserved it as much as he did. But no matter what, my conscience couldn't swallow the idea of standing idly by while who knows how many people got torn apart by phantom jackals. I just didn't have it in me to let that happen when I could possibly stop it.

Emma didn't like my hesitation. She plucked at her bloody shirt. "I'm asking you to do the right thing," she said while fixing me with a cold glare. "But if you refuse, I'll tell Anderson you attacked me. Believe me, I'll make it very convincing. After all, I'm his wife . . . and you're just some stray he picked up from the street."

I tried not to let her see that she'd scored, but I must have flinched or something, because she smirked. "Oh, yes. Anderson *will* toss you back out on the street without a single regret, and you and your sister will both lose his protection. How long do you think the two of you will last before Konstantin finds you?"

Dammit, she'd just scored again. I felt the blood draining from my cheeks and could do nothing to stop it. Emma's eyes practically glowed with satisfaction.

"Do you want me to describe in graphic detail what Konstantin likes to do with pretty female captives?" Her lip curled. "*You* he wouldn't touch, but I bet he'd make you watch while he—"

"Shut up!" I shouted, trembling with rage. Steph had already suffered terribly because of me. My conscience would hate me for letting a crazed serial killer continue his reign of terror, but I refused to put Steph at risk again.

"Okay, fine, you win," I growled. "I'll lay off Kerner until

Konstantin is dead. But someday, this is all going to come back and bite you in the ass. And I'll be there to see it."

Emma smiled at me, so smug in her triumph that I wanted to slap her.

"I'm glad we could come to an understanding," she said, then frowned down at the bloody shirt. "I guess I'll have to go change my shirt. But don't worry; I'll keep it nice and safe somewhere, in case I should ever need it."

She waited for my response, but when there was none forthcoming, she sighed in satisfaction and sauntered out of my room.

I'm not a big drinker, but after what had just happened, I felt that a little alcohol was in order. I found an open bottle of Chardonnay in the fridge downstairs and brought the whole bottle and a wineglass back up to my suite. I hadn't even eaten lunch yet, but that didn't stop me from pouring a glass immediately.

What was I going to do about Emma? Sure, I was caving to her demands, and that would appease her for the moment. However, I had just established my willingness to be bullied, and that was a terrible precedent to set. Not to mention that my reaction to the threat to Steph had amply demonstrated where my weak spot was.

I finished my glass of wine and immediately poured another.

Emma's threat was a declaration of war.

For now, she was content to bully me, but as long as she misguidedly saw me as a rival for Anderson's affections, she was going to hate me. And I had no illusions that her hatred wouldn't turn into an all-out campaign to get me kicked out of the house. And hell, if that didn't work for her, I had no doubt the threats would escalate. Steph was an obvious, easy target, and I was under no illusion that Emma would hesitate to hurt an innocent bystander. And that meant it was time to start planning for the worst.

From the beginning, I'd told myself that my stay at Anderson's mansion was temporary. When he'd first offered me shelter, I'd figured my choices were to move in—thereby obtaining protection not only for myself but also for my adoptive family—or to leave everything I knew and loved behind and go into hiding in hopes the Olympians would leave my family alone as long as I wasn't around. I hadn't wanted to lose my job, my home, my family, or my way of life, so I'd chosen to accept Anderson's protection.

Finding Emma was supposed to have cemented my position within Anderson's *Liberi*. It was supposed to be the proof of my sincerity, the proof that I was not a secret Olympian spy.

And it might ultimately turn out to be my downfall instead.

Grim reality was staring me right in the face. I was never meant to be part of Anderson's team, not for the long haul. Believing he and the rest of his *Liberi* could give me the home and the sense of belonging I'd lacked all my life had been a nice fantasy, but it was time to wake up. I would stand on the sidelines and let Kerner continue his reign of terror against the Olympians, and that would keep Emma out of my hair for a while. When Konstantin was dead, I would resume my hunt in earnest, and I would stop Kerner from ever killing again.

But the only way to protect Steph in the long run was for me to get out of her life.

I doubted the Olympians would pick on her if I was gone, but even if they did . . . I felt sure Anderson and his people would look out for her. Especially Blake, who I thought really did care about her.

To make her safe, I had to give up everything that was important in my life, including her, including my parents . . . and including the *Liberi,* the only people in the world I would not outlive. I would be alone, in the most fundamental of ways, always keeping secrets, always on the run. At least, when I'd been bouncing around between foster homes, I'd been able to hope for the future, for the day when I would be an adult with the power to control my own destiny and create my own home. If I fled from the *Liberi,* there would be no hope to cling to.

But Emma was a threat I couldn't protect Steph from. Not when Anderson refused to see her for what she really was. A threat from the outside I might have had a chance against, but not this. I owed Steph and her parents way too much to reward them by subjecting them to this kind of risk. So no matter how much it hurt, no matter how terrifying my future might be, I had to leave.

Sixteen

My resolve to let Kerner have his way with the Olympians lasted almost forty-eight hours. Right up to the time I found out he'd abandoned his once-a-week schedule and made another kill already.

I'd spent most of my time since Emma had confronted me sitting at my computer in my room, avoiding all human contact. I didn't want to get any more attached to Anderson's *Liberi* than I already was, not when I was planning my escape. Instead of trying to make any progress on finding Kerner, I'd been working on picking a new home and planning the new identity I was going to have to adopt. My work as a P.I. had given me plenty of experience finding people who didn't want to be found, so I knew what traps to avoid, but it was still going to be damned hard. I was going to have to swallow my scruples and dip into my trust fund, because I was going to need the cash. I would have to find a new job—there was only so long the cash would hold me unless I wanted to carry suitcases of it—and it would have to be one where I could get paid under the table. And I'd have to find somewhere to live, with a landlord who wouldn't start asking questions when I paid my rent in cash. All in all, it was a daunting, depressing prospect.

It wasn't until after dinner that I decided to check up on the day's news to give myself a break from all of the questions and anxieties that pinged back and forth in my brain. The first screaming headline I read rocked me back in my chair: CAPITAL MAULER STRIKES AGAIN.

I wondered when the press had started referring to Kerner as the Capital Mauler. Perhaps as soon as the police had admitted that the killings were not the result of wild dogs.

A prominent lobbyist had been mauled in his home sometime after midnight, along with his wife and their live-in maid. Police were called to the scene after neighbors were awakened by the screams, but no one saw anything. They wouldn't, of course, since Kerner could make himself and his jackals invisible.

I was willing to bet that both the lobbyist and his wife had been Olympians. However, the maid couldn't have been, because there was no way in hell an Olympian would be willing to do menial labor. The poor woman must have gotten in the way.

Goddammit. I wanted to punch my computer screen. So much for Kerner's vow that he wouldn't target civilians anymore. Though perhaps from his point of view, he *was* keeping his promise. It was possible the maid would have lived if she hadn't somehow gotten in Kerner's way, that he hadn't actively targeted her.

Not that the distinction meant squat to the maid, or her family, or me. Yet another innocent bystander was dead. Maybe I couldn't have prevented last night's attack—after all, I'd had no reason to think the next attack would come so soon—but if I spent any more time wringing my hands and worrying about Emma, then the next death definitely *would* be on me. And I couldn't have that.

Trying to contain my rage, I stomped out of my room and headed for Anderson's office. The door was open when I arrived, but he wasn't inside. Which was probably just as well, because I didn't know what to say.

No matter what, I had to stay on Anderson's good side, or I'd never be able to stop Kerner. I might be able to *find* the crazy son of a bitch on my own, but I didn't think I could single-handedly defeat him. Which meant I needed Anderson to keep trusting me, something he likely wouldn't do if I started slinging accusations at his wife. Especially not after she started slinging her own back.

Crap. I couldn't bring Anderson in on this. The moment I started flapping my gums, Emma would bring out her accusations. And if I got lucky and Anderson didn't believe her, then I would have to worry that she'd retaliate against me by hurting Steph.

No, whatever I ended up doing, I was going to have to keep Anderson out of it. I might have hoped that Emma would take pity on the maid who'd died and change her mind about stopping Kerner, but I didn't bother trying to fool myself. As long as Kerner was a deadly weapon aimed at Konstantin, she wouldn't care who else got hurt along the way.

I took a few deep breaths to calm myself, then left Anderson's office. I'd felt fairly muddled until the moment I learned of the maid's death, but now everything was coming clear in my mind.

I couldn't let Kerner run free, no matter what horrendous threats both he and Emma had made. And I couldn't take Kerner down alone, no matter how much simpler it would have been if I could. Which meant I needed an ally. Someone who would understand my dilemma and be willing to go behind Anderson's back to help me.

My first thought was Maggie. She was my best friend among Anderson's *Liberi,* and her super-strength might come in handy. Asking Maggie would have felt safe and comfortable, but it took only a moment's thought for me to realize it would be anything but.

I hadn't known her—or anyone in this house—for all that long, but I knew she was not a rule breaker. She regarded Anderson's word as law, and if I brought this to her, she would insist we tell Anderson everything. Maybe there was an off chance I could persuade her not to spill the beans once I shot my mouth off, but there was no way she'd risk Anderson's wrath by helping me.

In the end, there was only one person I believed might see things my way and might be willing and able to help me. If I was wrong about this, I was massively screwed. So I crossed my fingers and prayed that I wasn't wrong.

Jamaal wasn't in his suite. Or if he was in, he wasn't answering the door. The next most logical place to look for him was on the front porch, but he wasn't there, either.

Somehow the whole day had slipped away from me, and the sun had gone down. The temperature had dropped, and I went back inside to grab a jacket. It wasn't until I was slipping the jacket on that I wondered why I was going back outside when Jamaal clearly wasn't there. I hadn't seen him since he'd stormed off after kissing me. For all I knew, he'd never come back to the house.

I decided to treat my impulse to put on a coat as if it were one of my hunches and headed out to the garage to see if Jamaal's car was there. Sure enough, the black Saab was inside.

If he were anyone else, I would have checked inside the house first, maybe looked in the kitchen or the den, but my instincts were telling me he wasn't there. I let those instincts guide me and wandered around to the back of the house.

There was a nicely manicured lawn in the back, but Jamaal wasn't there. From the lawn, I could look through the kitchen windows and confirm my hunch that he wasn't inside.

Shivering and wishing I'd gone with a heavier jacket, I crossed the lawn and headed into the woods. The last time I'd been out this way at night, I'd been carrying a lantern to light the path, but tonight I had to rely on the moonlight. Luckily, the night was clear, the moon just past full, and I could see well enough to pick my way through the trees toward the clearing about a hundred yards from the woods' edge.

It was in that clearing that Jamaal had twice been executed, once by beheading and once by hanging. It was also in that clearing that he'd voluntarily allowed himself to be tied to a stake with kindling at his feet, willing to suffer the torment of burning if that was what it took to convince Anderson of his commitment to controlling himself.

Anderson had never ordered the fire lit, had been satisfied that Jamaal was willing to do whatever it took to avoid being kicked out. Logically, the clearing should be the last place I expected to find Jamaal. If I'd been in his shoes, I would have forever associated the clearing with pain and death. But Jamaal was not me.

I kept going until I finally broke through the trees and into the clearing.

The silver-blue moonlight revealed Jamaal's tall, imposing form as he stood in the center of the clearing. He was facing me, but his eyes were closed, his face a picture of concentration. His muscles were taut with tension, and despite the cold, there was a faint sheen of perspiration on his brow.

I stopped at the edge of the clearing and just watched him stand there, fighting whatever personal demons were troubling him. If he was in the process of trying to curb his death magic, I had a feeling it would be a very bad idea to interrupt him.

On the other hand, I felt like a voyeur for standing there and watching him like that. Especially when I couldn't resist drinking in his masculine beauty. As long as his eyes were closed, I could finally drink my fill without worrying about the consequences.

Moonlight and shadows accentuated his high cheekbones and sensuous mouth, and his stark white T-shirt fit tightly across his muscled chest. If I'd been wearing a top that light,

I'd have been freezing, but he showed no sign of being cold. His breath frosted the night, but the sweat on his brow shone in defiance.

As I watched, Jamaal began trembling with strain, and I bit my lip in worry.

I didn't know exactly what he was doing, but I suspected the trembling and sweating was not a good sign. I took a careful step backward, thinking that now might be a good time to make myself scarce. I'd seen Jamaal out of control before, and I never wanted to see it again.

I should have retreated, but something inside me held me rooted in place. Jamaal's trembling increased, his chest heaving with heavy pants. Then his legs seemed to give out under him, and he dropped to his knees.

"Jamaal!" I cried in alarm, and I found myself running toward him instead of away.

Even on his knees, he was swaying, and he propped himself up with his hands, his head bowed to his chest. I scrambled to a stop beside him, my body working on autopilot as I knelt and put a hand on his shoulder.

Heat seemed to radiate from his body, and I almost snatched my hand away in surprise. He was burning up.

"Jamaal, are you okay?" I asked, wondering if I should be running back to the house to get help. "What's happening?"

He made no effort to jerk away from my touch, and I took that as a bad sign. Or maybe I should have considered it a good sign, in that he wasn't going berserk and attacking me, which was what I might have expected him to do if he'd just lost a battle against his death magic. I moved even closer to him, sliding my arm around his shoulders in hopes that I could help keep him upright. If he collapsed, I wouldn't be able to get him back up again.

Sweat soaked his thin cotton T, but even in the few moments I'd been by his side, the intense heat of his body had begun to recede. He was still breathing hard, and his muscles quivered beneath my touch, but I hoped his cooling off meant that whatever it was had passed.

"Do you need me to get help?" I asked, and he shook his head. It was the first sign he'd given that he even knew I was there. His teeth started chattering. I hastily unzipped my jacket and threw it over his shoulders. It was probably too small to be much help.

Jamaal had recovered enough to give me a withering look at the gesture, but I ignored it. As long as I didn't know what was wrong with him, I thought the chances were good he needed the warmth more than I did.

"What happened?" I asked again.

He took a shaky breath and raised his head. The sweat had cooled on his brow, but his eyes seemed to have sunk deeper into his head, and he looked exhausted. He glanced at me quickly, then looked away. I thought that meant he wasn't going to talk, but he surprised me. In more ways than one.

"You were right," he said, with a grimace that said it physically pained him to admit it. "What you said the other day about channeling the death magic."

My feet were falling asleep, so I shifted so that I was sitting on the ground instead of kneeling on it. I gave Jamaal a slight smile. "I know I was right. But which point are you conceding? I think I made a bunch of them."

Jamaal didn't smile back. But then, his sense of humor never had been exactly well honed.

"Take it easy," I said, still smiling despite the chill of his stare. "I'm just trying to lighten the mood." He seemed to be inching his way back toward normal, and I couldn't see that as anything but a positive sign. "Tell me what happened." Third time was the charm, right?

"I just tried to channel the death magic. Tried to make it manifest like Kerner does. Only I have no idea how to do it."

Considering how violently he'd rejected the idea when I'd suggested it, I was pretty surprised he'd even tried it.

"Well, *something* happened," I said. "Aside from the fact that you collapsed, you were burning up when I first touched you. Is that normal for you when you use death magic?" I remembered how he'd collapsed after killing Kerner's last human victim. Obviously, the death magic had some serious side effects.

Jamaal slipped my jacket off his shoulders and dumped it in my lap.

"I'm not cold anymore," he said when I opened my mouth to protest. "And to answer your question, no, that isn't normal. It exhausts me when I unleash it, but that feels different." He touched his chest, then made a face and pulled the damp cotton away from his skin. "It doesn't make me sweat like this."

And it probably didn't make him into a human radiator, either.

"So maybe that's a sign that you're on the right track," I suggested. "If it were an exercise in futility, it probably wouldn't have had any effect on you at all, right?"

Jamaal might not be cold anymore—though I suspected that was a bit of alpha-male posturing—but *I* sure was, so I slipped my jacket back on. It was still warm from his body, and I hugged it around me to chase off the lingering chill.

Jamaal shrugged. "That's one way of looking at it." He reached into his jeans pocket and pulled out his tin of cigarettes and a book of matches. His hands shook slightly as he flipped the tin open and selected a half-smoked joint.

"But I'm guessing from the fact that you're skipping the cloves and going straight to the pot that it didn't relieve the pressure at all."

Jamaal lit up and drew in a deep drag, closing his eyes as he allowed the smoke to linger in his lungs. He blew it out slowly, and some of the tension in his shoulders eased.

"Nope," he said, offering the joint to me.

I declined with a shake of my head, and he took another drag.

"I'm sorry," I said, wishing I had something more productive to say.

"I'll try it again later, when I don't feel like I've been run over by a truck. You're right that *something* happened." He met my eyes, and for the first time since he'd snapped out of it, his gaze held. "I've never *tried* to use the death magic before. It's always been something to fight against, something to suppress. Even when Emmitt and I were venting, it was more like I was letting the magic go than I was actually trying to *use* it."

He was scared of it, I realized, though I was smart enough not to say it. No one else I knew, except for Anderson, had so destructive a power. If I could kill someone without even touching them, and I didn't know exactly how my power worked, you can bet I wouldn't go around experimenting with it, either. It would be like going into a nuclear submarine and pressing a random button just to see what it did.

Jamaal cocked his head at me. "What are you doing out here, anyway?"

"Looking for you."

The wariness in his expression was almost insulting. "Why?"

I took a moment to rethink my decision to confide in Jamaal. Spending more time with him than absolutely necessary was dangerous to both my physical and my mental health. Not to mention that he still looked kind of out of it.

I couldn't tell whether that was the voice of wisdom talking or just cowardice. Either way, I couldn't stop Kerner by myself, and though I couldn't say I trusted Jamaal unreservedly, I thought he was the most likely of Anderson's *Liberi* to help me without telling Anderson. Besides, I'd already determined that once I'd stopped Kerner, I was going to have to bite the bullet and leave to protect myself and Steph from Emma's malice. So even if I found myself getting more attached to Jamaal, it wouldn't matter, because I'd be gone.

Crossing my fingers, hoping I wasn't making a big mistake, I told Jamaal about Emma's ambush.

"You should tell Anderson," was Jamaal's prompt response. "If you tell him what happened, she won't have anything to blackmail you with."

I hadn't been expecting that response from Jamaal, so I hesitated a moment before I responded. "But even if I tell him what happened, Emma will just give him her side of the story afterward. Which one of us do you think he'll believe?"

Scorn lit Jamaal's eyes. "Any fool can see that Emma is out of her fucking mind. She was always a drama queen, but she's gone completely around the bend."

"Yeah, any fool can see that. But can Anderson? He's in love with her, and love does funny things to people's perceptions."

"He's too smart to fall for such blatant manipulation," Jamaal retorted, but there was doubt in his voice.

"I don't think smart has anything to do with it. He blames himself for what she went through, and he's going to put up with a hell of a lot of shit from her he wouldn't take from the rest of us."

Jamaal chewed that one over for a bit. I figured the fact that he hadn't dismissed my argument out of hand was a good sign, though he wasn't jumping up and down with enthusiasm at the idea of keeping secrets from Anderson.

A wisp of chilly air made me shiver, even my jacket, and I couldn't imagine how Jamaal could be ng there in his short-sleeved T-shirt without seeming to e that it was freezing out. My teeth were starting to chaversation inside

"Do you think we could continue thr warmth. "You somewhere?" I asked as I hugged mvinter." may not have noticed, but it's the midis eyes. "You're the

I thought I saw a hint of amusememember? You could one who came out here looking frhouse." have just waited until I came ba

I gave an indelicate snort. "Yeah, because I was really in the mood to sit around twiddling my thumbs waiting for you. Can we go back to the house now, or would you rather sit out here and freeze your tail feathers off some more?"

I rose to my feet and brushed off the seat of my pants, then offered Jamaal my hand to help him up. I wasn't at all surprised when he didn't take it. Nor was I surprised when he got to his feet and swayed dizzily. Even knowing that he wouldn't appreciate my help, I couldn't stop myself from reaching out to steady him. His biceps twitched under my hand, and I couldn't tell if that was from tension or from the aftereffects of death magic.

He pulled away from me, but for once, there was no rancor in the gesture.

"All right, you win," he said. "Let's go back to the house."

I bit my tongue to keep from offering him any more help, even though he still looked unsteady on his feet. I already knew the answer would be an abrupt refusal. Instead, I settled for walking intimately close to him, ready to help prop him up if gravity started winning the battle of wills. Based on the way the corners of his mouth tugged downward, I guessed he knew exactly what I was doing. The fact that he didn't snap at me for hovering told me that somewhere behind the testosterone, he knew he might end up having to lean on me whether he wanted to or no

Jamaal footsteps steadied as we neared the house. We entered through the back door near the kitchen, and I was severely tempted to take a detour for some coffee or hot chocolate. But Jamaal was being relatively accommodating at the moment, and didn't want to risk any interruptions.

Even though he seemed to be doing much better by the time we were I kept hovering, sure the stairs were going to get the better a. We hadn't discussed exactly where in the house we were to continue our conversation, but I'd assumed we would on the third floor. my suite, which was, unfortunately,

Jamaal seemed to handle the stairs just fine, but when we got to the second-floor landing, he veered off toward his own suite instead of tackling the next flight. He didn't gesture for me to follow, but I did so anyway.

I'd never seen his suite before, and I have to admit to a great deal of feminine curiosity about it. I imagined his rooms being cold and austere, with a bare minimum of furniture and decoration. He just didn't seem the type to live in luxury or to care about appearances. But when he pushed open his door and I got a glimpse of his sitting room, I was immediately slapped upside the head with the realization of how little I knew Jamaal.

Most of the mansion's walls were painted a generic shade of ivory meant to be ignored. Jamaal's walls were painted a rich, golden tan that immediately lent warmth to the room. Burgundy drapes and a burgundy futon sofa added to the warmth. A small but elegant cherry-wood dining set was tucked into one corner, and the wall beside the door was covered in floor-to-ceiling bookcases. Those bookcases held mostly large, coffee-table-type books, some of them displayed face out so that their covers served as further decor. If those books were any indication, Jamaal had a connoisseur's taste in art, particularly Eastern art. Several of the proudly displayed books were catalogs from museum exhibits, though it was hard for me to imagine someone like Jamaal strolling through a museum.

I took all of this in with one quick glance before my eyes found the true focal point of the room.

It was a small, square painting set in a plain gold frame, showcased by a discreet museum-style light set into the wall above it. A figure I recognized from my research as the goddess Kali stood on the body of a naked man against a background of metallic gold. She was painted in a blue so dark it was almost black. Unlike many of the other depictions I'd seen of her, she was adorned not in severed body parts but in lotus blossoms and pearls, although, rather disturbingly, she also had a couple of hooded cobras twining around her torso.

I stepped closer to the painting and saw that there was a little wear and tear around the edges, proving that this was the real thing, not a print or a reproduction. It was beautiful, in a creepy kind of way.

"How old is it?" I asked Jamaal without looking away from the painting. On closer inspection, I noticed that there were little bits of iridescent blue-green paint decorating Kali's jewelry, and I figured the painting couldn't be that old after all if the artist had access to iridescent paint.

"Late sixteen hundreds or thereabouts."

I blinked in surprise, then looked over my shoulder at Jamaal, who had come up close behind me while I was focused on the painting. "Really?" He nodded. "Then what's the iridescent stuff?"

"It's actually little pieces of beetle wings."

"Oh."

Strange how one little painting could throw me for so much of a loop. I'd have thought it was some kind of family heirloom, except considering what Jamaal had told me of his background, I knew he didn't have any family heirlooms. Had he bought a work of fine art, or had it been a gift? And if it was a gift, who was it from?

I dragged my attention away from the painting and faced Jamaal. If I hadn't known better, I would have sworn he was embarrassed at having revealed this unexpected aspect of his personality. He averted his eyes and plucked at his T-shirt.

"I'm going to put on a fresh shirt. Be right back."

He disappeared into the bedroom without awaiting a response, leaving me with inappropriate images in my head. I couldn't help picturing him dragging that T-shirt off over his head. From the fit of his clothes and the cut of his biceps, I knew he would look spectacular without a shirt on. My hormones were more than happy to provide me with a mental image.

Jamaal hadn't closed the bedroom door, and despite my best intentions and a stern lecture from my common sense, I found myself drifting across the sitting room. I angled toward the bookcase, but the moment my vantage point allowed me to, I glanced through the bedroom door.

Like the sitting room, Jamaal's bedroom was decorated with a distinctly Eastern flavor in warm, inviting colors. A platform bed covered with a plush mahogany-colored bedspread dominated the room, which was so painfully neat it was hard to believe a single guy resided in it.

Jamaal was bending over to open the bottom drawer of his cherry-wood dresser when my eyes found him, and the sight was enough to steal my breath away. His jeans clung lovingly to his butt and thighs, and I decided the rear view was just as mouthwatering as the front view.

And then he stood up straight, a black and red football jersey in his hand, and I got a look at his naked back.

It shouldn't have come as such a shock to me, not after what he'd told me about his childhood. He'd been a *slave,* and though his father had apparently treated him "well," he'd admitted he'd had a hard life after Daddy Dearest kicked him out to appease the little missus. I just somehow hadn't allowed myself to think about what that kind of hard life might entail.

Ridged scar tissue riddled his back from his shoulders all the way to the waistband of his jeans, and I suspected it continued on below. I couldn't even imagine what kind of pain Jamaal had endured when those wounds were inflicted. Obviously, he hadn't been *Liberi* yet, or there wouldn't be scars, and I realized that although he'd told me about his childhood, I had no idea when and how he'd become *Liberi.*

The scars marred what would otherwise have been a perfect back. With his broad shoulders and narrow waist, Jamaal was a work of art in his clothes, but shirtless, he was even more stunning. I'd never seen someone who wasn't bulked up like a weightlifter and yet had had such perfect definition in his back muscles. Even with the scar tissue, I could see the ripple and play of those muscles as Jamaal stuck his arms into his shirt and pulled the neck opening over his head.

I stood there like an idiot, entranced by what I was seeing, as the shirt slid down his back and hid both his scars and his beauty. In fact, I was so entranced that I think somehow he sensed me staring, because he suddenly whirled around.

I was busted.

SEVENTEEN

I could have turned and pretended to be looking at the books on his shelf. He probably wouldn't have been fooled, but I didn't even bother to try. As long as he knew—or at least strongly suspected—that I'd been looking, I didn't want to do anything that might suggest I was repulsed by what I'd seen. Jamaal wasn't what I'd call the shy, sensitive type, but instinct told me those scars represented a serious chink in his armor.

Something dark and dangerous lurked in Jamaal's eyes as they locked with mine and he stalked toward me. His expression spoke of rage, of pain, and of something else, something I couldn't identify. I wanted to back away from what I saw in his eyes, but again, my instincts insisted doing so would be a mistake, would hurt him even more than he'd been hurt already. For all of the angry words he'd flung at me, for all of the times I'd seen him practically out of his mind with fury, I knew that at his core, he was a fragile and damaged human being. And I didn't want to be the one to make that damage irreparable.

Jamaal's lips curled away from his teeth in a feral snarl. "Get a good look?" He was still coming closer, and my pulse drummed in my throat. "Want a close-up?"

He lifted the front of his shirt, and I practically swallowed my tongue in my effort to keep from gasping. The scars weren't restricted to his back; their pale ridged lines sliced through his sculpted pecs and six-pack abs. It looked like he'd been through a paper shredder, and the sight of that devastation made my throat ache.

Without conscious thought, my hand reached for him, fingers wanting to trace his savaged skin as if I could somehow erase the marks. Jamaal's eyes widened in what looked like fear, and he dropped his shirt down and took a hasty step back before I could touch him.

I kept staring at his chest, even though the travesty of those scars was now covered. In my peripheral vision, I was aware of the way he was looking at me, a combination of hostility, scorn, and challenge on his face, but my vision was starting to blur with tears.

"Sometimes I really hate people," I murmured hoarsely, then cleared my throat as if that could dislodge the lump that had formed there.

Jamaal let out his breath with a loud whoosh, like the air rushing from a punctured tire. I seemed to have passed some kind of test, a test I hadn't realized I was taking, and Jamaal backed away from the edge, his intense glare replaced by an ironic half smile.

"You and me both," he said. He crossed his arms over his chest as if trying to build a thicker shield to keep those scars hidden.

"Did you kill whoever did that to you?" I blurted without thinking.

He laughed bitterly. "I was a slave, remember? If I'd killed anyone, I wouldn't be around today, believe me."

"But you killed someone eventually, or you wouldn't have become *Liberi*." He had to have taken his immortality from *someone,* and it would have been poetic justice if that someone was the sadistic bastard who'd tortured him.

Jamaal moved away from me, but he didn't go far, instead dropping down onto the futon sofa. I wanted to press him for information but managed to control my curiosity. His body language suggested he might continue talking, and I didn't want to say anything that might discourage him.

"It happened during the Civil War," he said. "My master at the time was neither particularly kind nor particularly cruel, but I hated him anyway. I pretty much hated everybody, black or white."

Considering what had been done to him, I could hardly blame him.

"Our plantation was attacked by a bunch of Union soldiers. And believe me, just because they were fighting on the side of the angels didn't make the men themselves angels. These guys were more like a rioting mob than an organized troop of soldiers. My master surrendered without a fight, and they shot him down in cold blood anyway.

"When the soldiers first came, I was thrilled to see them. I figured my life as a slave was over, and I could join the Union army and get my revenge on the people who'd oppressed me. I was angry enough that I probably could have looked the other way even after they'd killed an unarmed man, but then they started going after his family. They raped his wife, and they made his daughter run so they could chase her down. She was only twelve."

"I hate people," I muttered again.

Jamaal ignored me. "I didn't have much of a conscience left at the time. It had mostly been beaten out of me. But I couldn't just stand by while they raped a little girl, so I got my master's gun and started shooting the men who were chasing her.

"It was suicidal. I was just one man, and there were at least a dozen soldiers. I couldn't save the poor kid, but I figured at least I could go out trying to do a good deed." He shook his head. "Maybe at that point, I just wanted to die. I'd seen these soldiers as my salvation, and then to find out they weren't really any better than the people who'd tormented me most of my life . . ." He fell silent, his eyes clouded with memories of his haunted past.

"Did you save her?" I prompted, although everything about his body language told me the answer was no.

He shook his head. "I shot three of the soldiers before they got me, but like I said, I was badly outnumbered. I must have taken twenty or thirty bullets by the time it was all over. I should have been dead, but apparently, one of those three men I'd shot was *Liberi*. I woke up hours later, covered in blood, to see the plantation burned to the ground, still smoldering. There were bodies everywhere. The soldiers had slaughtered everyone, even the slaves they were supposedly there to free. That was probably because of me."

I made a sound of indignation on his behalf, but he shushed me before I could voice the objection.

"They were war-maddened thugs who got a kick out of raping and murdering civilians. By killing some of them, I gave the rest of them the excuse to view the slaves as the enemy. All because I was disillusioned and decided it was time to die." He gave a bitter laugh. "Kind of funny that I tried to commit suicide by soldier and wound up becoming immortal because of it."

"Hilarious."

My heart ached for everything he had been through. He'd been broken—or at least severely damaged—even before he became *Liberi* and had to deal with death magic that had a mind of its own.

"Did you have any idea what was going on?" I asked. "Had you ever heard of the *Liberi*?" As confusing as my own transition had been, at least I'd been surrounded by *Liberi* who could explain to me what was happening. I'd thought they were completely delusional, of course, but at least they'd provided me with some explanation.

What would it be like to awaken after being shot twenty or

more times and have no idea why you weren't dead? I shuddered. I thought about the time when he had actually been dead, when he must have thought the airless dark was his own personal Hell. To go through that, having no reason to believe it would ever end, was unimaginable.

"Nope," Jamaal said. "I had no clue what was going on. Thought I'd gone crazy, actually. I thought I'd make it better by blowing my own brains out, but I woke up again after that. It wasn't until after the war was over that I ended up meeting another *Liberi*. He was a descendant of Odin, and he kind of taught me the ropes—including telling me about the Olympians and emphasizing how important it was to avoid them.

"Problem was, the bastard was bat-shit crazy and hated the world even more than I did. I lost myself under his influence for a very long time, and I did some very bad shit, let the death magic have its way with me. Until Anderson found me and convinced me it didn't have to be that way."

And then I came along, killed his best friend, who'd been helping him keep the death magic tamed, and put everything that was good in his life at risk.

My mind took me back to that fateful night, replaying a picture of that dark, sleet-slicked driveway, of my struggles to keep the car in control. A figure appeared out of nowhere, only a couple of feet in front of my car, no time to stop or swerve. My headlights illuminated his face as he raised his head and smiled at me in the instant before I slammed into him.

I shook my head violently to stop the playback in my head. I wished there were some way I could expunge those images from my brain for good. I'd relived them more than enough already.

"It wasn't your fault," Jamaal said gruffly, and I guessed my face had told him exactly what I was thinking about.

I swallowed hard, trying to keep my emotions under control. Jamaal was making a huge concession by admitting that, though I supposed he'd stopped blaming me long before. Now, if only *I* could stop blaming me.

"I know that," I forced out through my tight throat. "He set me up, and he basically did it to himself. But I had to make a couple of bad decisions for his plan to work, and I can't help wishing I'd made different ones."

When Emmitt had called and asked me for help, I'd agreed because I'd wanted an excuse to cut my bad date short. My gut had told me from the very beginning that there was something hinky going on, but I'd ignored it. That was Bad Decision Number One. Bad Decision Number Two—also known as Worst Decision Ever—was to go looking for Emmitt when he failed to show up at the rendezvous. Driving through those gates and onto private property was against the law, even if Emmitt had left them enticingly open, and I'd known that. I should have—

"But you know that if you'd made different decisions, Emmitt would have found some other way. The goddamned bastard had made up his mind and didn't care what anyone else wanted."

It was the first time I'd heard Jamaal express any anger toward Emmitt for what he'd done. Personally, I'd thought a number of times that I'd like to go back in time and kill Emmitt all over again for being so selfish. He had to have known how devastated Jamaal would be, and he had to have known, or at least have had an inkling of, what I would be put through thanks to his decision. But he hadn't cared enough about anyone to trouble himself about the consequences.

"Why didn't he talk to anyone?" Jamaal asked, the pain in his voice so deep I wanted to draw him into my arms. "If he felt so fucking bad he wanted to die, why didn't he say something, let us try to help him?" His voice was turning hoarse like he was crying, although his eyes were dry. "Hell, why didn't we just *know,* without him having to tell us anything? Why didn't *I* just know? We vented the death magic practically every day, and the days we didn't vent, he was teaching me to meditate to help calm my temper. How could I spend that much time with him and not realize he was fucking suicidal?"

Jamaal was on his feet and pacing before I could answer. There was so much fury in him he could barely contain himself, and I half expected him to start smashing up the room. But at the heart of that fury was pain. And, apparently, guilt. He was furious at Emmitt for killing himself, but he was equally furious with himself for not seeing how depressed his friend and mentor had been.

"*No one* realized," I said gently. "He was obviously very careful to hide it." I stood up, moving slowly because I knew Jamaal was on a hair trigger. "You can't blame yourself."

He was in my face between one blink and the next, hands gripping my biceps as he leaned down and snarled at me. "The fuck I can't!"

I should have been scared of him at that moment. He was so furious I half expected to see sparks flying off him, and I'd had firsthand experience with how savage he could be when his temper snapped. I should have said something noncommittally soothing, appeasing the dangerous madman. Instead, I found my own temper rising to meet his head-on.

"Oh, get over yourself!" I snapped, making no attempt to escape his bruising grip. "First, you decide I'm the one and only person to blame for Emmitt's death, and now you've decided it's all your fault and you're using it as an excuse to act like an asshole. Why don't you just grow up and deal with it like everyone else has to?"

As soon as the words left my mouth, I wondered if I was doing the equivalent of lighting a match while wading in a pool of gasoline. I held my breath and waited for the explosion.

Jamaal stood frozen in speechless shock. His hands still gripped my arms, but they weren't squeezing as hard, and his eyes went comically wide, like he couldn't believe I'd just said that. To tell you the truth, *I* couldn't believe it.

When he didn't immediately go ballistic, I forced myself

to let go of the breath I'd been holding. Yelling at him had been cruel when I knew how wounded he was, and I felt like a mean-spirited bitch for doing it.

"I'm sorry," I said, shaking my head in amazement at myself. "I didn't mean that."

Jamaal's shoulders relaxed, and the rage drained from his eyes. I didn't think the bleakness that replaced it was much better. "Yes, you did. And you were right. I just . . . I can't seem to keep a lid on it. All this shit keeps bubbling out, no matter how hard I try to keep it together."

He finally seemed to realize he was touching me, and his hands quickly opened and dropped to his sides. He sank back onto the sofa, his head in his hands.

"I don't know what to do," he said, and I could barely hear him because he was talking to the floor.

I joined him on the sofa and put my arm around his shoulders. Maybe he didn't like to be touched—especially by me—but I just couldn't help myself.

"You'll figure it out," I told him as I ran my hand up and down his back. "Either you'll figure out how to make it manifest and vent it that way, or you'll figure out how to keep it leashed. I have confidence in you."

Don't ask me where all these words of encouragement were coming from. I'd lost my rose-colored glasses long ago. Jamaal had all the signs of being a ticking time bomb, and logic said that that bomb would eventually go off. I did not want to be around when that happened, and I had no reason to believe Jamaal could control himself indefinitely.

So why was I telling him I had confidence in him? And, even more mystifying, why was that actually the truth?

Jamaal raised his head and met my eyes. He started to say something—something scathing, judging by the look on his face—but he stopped himself.

"Why?" he asked, still holding my gaze. "Why would you have confidence in someone like me? I'm a total fuck-up."

"Beats me," I responded, coaxing a hint of a smile out of him. My heart did a little flip at the sight of that smile. I swear, if that man actually let the smile take over his face, he'd stop traffic.

And just like that, all of the angry energy that had been zipping around the room changed into something entirely different.

EIGHTEEN

I'd been attracted to Jamaal practically from the first moment I'd laid eyes on him. It was an attraction that was purely physical, but that didn't make it any less real. Until recently, I hadn't had any evidence that he'd shared even one iota of that attraction.

Okay, yeah, he'd kissed me that one time, but that hadn't been a *real* kiss, so it didn't count.

The way he was looking at me right now *did* count. His luscious dark-chocolate eyes practically smoldered—with something other than rage, for once—and he seemed to be holding his breath, like he was stunned into immobility by a sudden bolt of desire. No, wait, that was me.

I leaned in to him just slightly, unable to stop myself. His scent of cloves and smoke, which had once made my nose wrinkle, now evoked an erotic cologne, making my pulse soar. His lips were so lush and sensual, made even more so by the elegant lines of his face, with its high cheekbones and artistic curves.

I told myself to back off, to get off the couch and run if that was what it took to snap myself out of the fog that was overtaking me. I reminded myself of all the reasons even trying to be friends with Jamaal was a bad idea, never mind trying to be anything more. I even tried reminding myself of the awful night when Jamaal had ambushed me, preventing me from getting to Steph and saving her from Alexis's clutches.

That memory was almost enough to kill the arousal, because, let's face it, it had been one of the worst nights of my life. Not because of the beating Jamaal had delivered—that hadn't been any fun, but I'd been too hopped up on adrenaline and fear to be much affected by it—but because of what had happened to my sister because of it.

I should hate Jamaal for getting in my way, even though he'd had legitimate reasons at the time to think I was a traitor. A guy beating me up was not something I should be able to forgive and forget, even granted my history of being attracted to inappropriate men.

None of that mattered as our eyes remained locked and he slowly lowered his head.

I breathed in his scent as his braids clickity-clacked with his movements, my eyes half-closed and my lips parted. A little voice in the back of my head was still trying to talk me out of it, but it was no more than background noise, easily ignored.

When his lips touched mine, my nice, sane inner voice, the much-vaunted voice of reason, abandoned me completely.

Who'd have thought a broody, angry man, a death-goddess descendant with a badly damaged soul, could kiss like an erotic dream come true?

His kiss of the other day had been all aggression and dominance, with neither tenderness nor subtlety behind it. This, however, was something different altogether.

Those full, sensual lips of his brushed over mine lightly, teasingly, drawing a little sound of need from somewhere deep inside me. My hands found their way around his neck and locked on, prepared to fight for what my body wanted if he came to his senses and backed off.

That, however, was not a valid concern.

Jamaal put his arms around me and drew me closer as his lips continued their delicate exploration. I had no objection whatsoever to getting closer, having yearned to get to know his body better for quite some time. My hands slid down from his neck to his back, exploring the muscles that rippled beneath his shirt as I returned his kiss and tried to be patient.

I didn't have to try for very long, because Jamaal was apparently as impatient as I. He deepened the kiss, his tongue sliding into my mouth for a delicate taste.

Seeing as he was a smoker, his tongue should have tasted like an ashtray to me, a flavor I would tolerate as the inevitable price for the pleasure of his kiss. Apparently, my brain never got that memo, and a hungry, raw sound rose from my throat.

I wanted to get closer still, so I squirmed until Jamaal's grip loosened enough to let me move; then I straddled him on the sofa. His hands slid down my back until they cupped my ass, and I groaned at the touch. Then, as I settled myself on his lap, I felt the significant bulge in his pants, growing bigger and harder by the moment.

Oh. My. God. I'd thought I was hot before. But that oh-so-tangible evidence of Jamaal's desire seemed to set my very nerves on fire.

I buried my hands in his hair as I opened myself completely to his kiss, my rational mind consumed by my desire. I played with the coarse braids, explored the intricate beading, all the while pressing myself more firmly against him. Without my even noticing, my hips started to rock, and he rose to meet me.

My hands couldn't get enough of him, eager to touch bare skin. I started to pluck at the bottom of his shirt, but he distracted me by shifting in his seat so he could lay me on my back on the sofa. His body came to rest between my legs, sending a flush of heat and hunger through me.

My hands slid down Jamaal's back. The football jersey was thin enough that I could feel the ridges of the worst of his scars. His weight shifted on top of me, the movement dislodging my hands. I made a little sound of protest, until I realized he was just making room for his own hands to explore.

His fingers trailed from my throat down my collarbone to the little V of skin revealed by my button-down shirt.

Our eyes met as he began opening the buttons one by one. The heat in his eyes made me wish we were already naked in his bed.

He only made it through two buttons before he impatiently thrust his hand inside, cupping my breast. I gave a soft cry of pleasure, raising my head and demanding his kiss. He obliged me as he worked his hand under my bra. The brush of his fingers over my nipple fanned my hunger even higher. I hadn't thought that was possible.

I reveled in the sensation of skin on skin, but I wanted more, *much* more. One of my arms was trapped between my body and the back of the sofa, but my other hand was free. I smoothed that hand down Jamaal's back once more. I couldn't reach the hem of his shirt, so I just grabbed a handful of fabric and pulled up until the small of his back was revealed. Finally, bare skin.

I let go of the jersey and touched my hand to his back.

And the moment my fingers made contact with bare skin, Jamaal went stiff, and not in a good way.

He broke the kiss and jerked away from me, jumping to his feet so fast it would have been comical in another situation. One where I wasn't lying there on the sofa so desperate for the touch of his hands that I practically wailed. My nipples ached, and there was that low, insistent buzz of hunger in my belly, a hunger that could only be satisfied in one way.

But though I was still all achy and desperate, Jamaal had clearly lost the mood. His back was turned to me, and I forced myself up into a sitting position in hopes I could at least get a glimpse of his face.

What I saw there dampened the fire inside me.

Jamaal's eyes were too wide, white showing all around the

irises, and there was a glazed look to them. This wasn't the way he looked when he was about to go Incredible Hulk, but I still got the impression that the Jamaal I knew had left the building. I wouldn't have believed it if I hadn't seen it with my own two eyes, but it sure as hell looked to me like he was afraid.

But of what?

"Jamaal?" I asked tentatively. "Are you all right?"

Stupid question; I could see that he wasn't, though I had no idea what was wrong.

Stupid question it might have been, but at least it seemed to draw him back from wherever he'd disappeared to. He blinked a couple of times, and his eyes cleared. He glanced quickly in my direction, then averted his eyes and slid his hands into his pockets. His shoulders hunched a bit, and he turned away from me.

I took a deep breath to compose myself, then stood up and went to him, putting a hand on his shoulder but not making any more intimate gesture. His muscles quivered under my touch, like he was fighting the urge to pull away. I'd have been hurt, except I didn't think whatever was going on had much to do with me.

"Tell me what's wrong," I urged him, though I honestly didn't know if a man like him was capable of sharing anything that might resemble intimate details. Even the things he'd told me about his past had been lacking real depth, like he was giving me the Cliffs Notes version.

"It's not you," he said hoarsely, and if it had been someone other than him, I might not have been able to resist making some wisecrack about the famous cliché. "I just . . ." But he couldn't seem to finish his own sentence, falling instead into a brooding silence.

I might not be a genius where relationships are concerned, but I could put two and two together with the best of them.

Jamaal's back was riddled with scars. He'd pulled away abruptly the moment I had touched those scars skin-to-skin. Ergo whatever was wrong had something to do with the scars.

Was he self-conscious about them? He certainly had seemed to get prickly about me having seen them, but I didn't think it was self-consciousness that had made him run away from me as abruptly as he had. This was something more visceral than self-consciousness.

Should I press him about it? Or should I just figure he'd tell me in his own good time?

I honestly don't think of myself as a particularly pushy person. Sometimes I'm almost embarrassingly ready to ignore the elephant in the room and skip out on potential conflict. But with Jamaal, I was having a damn hard time finding my emotional balance, and I found myself incapable of letting it go.

"You don't like when someone touches your scars," I said.

Jamaal moved away from me, his body language screaming of tension. "Just leave it alone," he said tightly. "We have more important things to talk about, like—"

"Not right this second we don't." Yes, I did still have a sense of perspective. I knew figuring out a plan to stop Kerner was more important than having a Dr. Phil moment. I also knew neither of our minds would be fully in the game if we were both distracted by what had been left unsaid between us.

"Tell me what that was all about," I insisted.

Jamaal's eyes flashed, telling me he didn't appreciate how I'd made that into an order. Not that I was in any position to give orders.

"It's none of your business," he grated.

"You can't honestly believe that. Not under these circumstances."

His glower became even fiercer. "I believe you need to back the hell off. We shouldn't have let things get that far, anyway."

He was sealing the cracks in his emotional armor with alarming speed, and there was nothing I could do to stop him. Maybe what had caused him to back off had nothing to do with me touching the scars; maybe he'd just been scared he was letting me get too close.

Curiosity, desire, and common sense battled within me, but common sense won out. I could see that Jamaal had fortified his defenses against me, and any further attempts I made to breach them would only make him dig in his heels more firmly.

It wasn't easy to let it go, but I managed somehow.

"Fine. We won't talk about it. Yet. But someday, when this whole mess with Kerner is over, you and I are going to have a long talk." My stomach knotted up as I remembered that when this mess was over, I would be hitting the road and wouldn't be having any long talks with anyone.

Secure in his victory, Jamaal visibly eased back from the edge. He arched an eyebrow at me. "You think so?"

I nodded briskly and hoped my face hadn't given away my sudden burst of gloom. "Yep."

The arousal of our little make-out session hadn't fully faded yet, but I did the best I could to shove it to the background of my mind. Later, I'd probably regret letting things go as far as they had, and I'd be grateful that Jamaal had put on the brakes, but for now, I had to battle my own frustration.

Rebuttoning my shirt, I plopped back down onto the futon. I really wanted to go back to my own suite to pull myself together and lick my wounds—possibly even to do a little sulking—but I'd sought Jamaal out for a reason, and sex wasn't it.

"All right, then," I said with a sigh of resignation. "Let's talk strategy."

Nineteen

Not surprisingly, it was a little hard to change gears back into problem-solving mode. Especially when Jamaal was brooding and I was suffering from an acute case of sexual frustration. I knew Jamaal still wanted to tell Anderson about Emma's threat, but, at least for the time being, he was willing to respect my desire to keep Anderson out of the loop.

From hours of staring at my map, I had determined approximately where Kerner spent his days—or at least, I had a theory about where he spent his days. That didn't necessarily mean I was right, and even if I was, I didn't know which of the likely cemeteries Kerner actually hung out in. The fact that Kerner was most likely hiding in a cemetery made Jamaal into a less-than-optimal ally, but I had no other choice but to use him as my co-conspirator.

"I won't go apeshit the moment I set foot in a cemetery," he assured me. "It took a couple of hours for me to lose control that first time. We'll just have to make sure we don't need that much time to track Kerner down."

I bit my tongue to avoid pointing out that my power wasn't as predictable as that. He already knew.

"So what do we do if we find him?" I asked. "I'd really rather not be a jackal's chew toy again. That wasn't fun."

"If the jackals are a manifestation of Kerner's death magic, then it's possible they wouldn't be able to hurt me; Emmitt's magic couldn't." He frowned. "At least, it couldn't when I countered it with my own. I'm not sure if I'd have to target Kerner or the jackals."

Whichever one he didn't direct his death magic at would be all over me. Assuming his death magic had any effect at all. Which sounded like a pretty big, scary if.

"I could act as a diversion," Jamaal continued. "Draw off Kerner's jackals while you take him out with a shot to the head. It wouldn't kill him permanently, of course, but if you can knock him out of commission, that'll take care of the jackals, and we can . . . do what we need to do."

I found it interesting that Jamaal was unwilling to put into words exactly what it was we needed to do to keep Kerner contained. I couldn't blame him, and I still hoped that somehow I'd be able to persuade Anderson to do the right thing. Which was almost certainly wishful thinking on my part, because Anderson was not an easy man to persuade, and he obviously felt very, very strongly about keeping his damn secret.

"But if you're wrong about the death magic . . ." I said.

Jamaal shrugged. "If I'm wrong, then I get mauled. I'll still be a distraction, and we know how to 'cure' the rabies. I'd rather not go through that, but I'm willing to if that's what it takes."

I have to admit, I was impressed at the nonchalance with which he offered himself up. No, he didn't act like he was all eager or anything, but he was willing to put himself through hell—a hell he'd personally experienced before, so he knew exactly what he was getting into—to stop a bad guy. I like to think that I'd have been able to do the same thing, take one for the team if it were necessary, but I wasn't so sure. I'm not a total wimp or anything, but I've never thought of myself as particularly brave, either.

"All of this assumes we can even find him," I said, not at all secure in my ability to do so. All I had was a hunch that he was in one of two places. The cemeteries were relatively small, compared with, say Rock Creek, but if Kerner realized I was there, he could lead us on a merry chase, and we might never catch up to him. At least, not until the proximity to the dead pushed Jamaal over the edge.

"Maybe we need him to find us instead," Jamaal suggested.

That might be the way it happened, whether we wanted it to or not. After having warned me off, Kerner would probably turn out to be a little grumpy if he saw me poking around. Maybe he would come out of hiding to show his displeasure. But I didn't know if we could count on it. He was crazy but not stupid. If he saw us looking for him, he'd know we were rejecting his deal, and he might play hide-and-seek with us, then go find some innocent victim on whom to take out his frustrations.

"Maybe isn't good enough," I said. "We need to draw him out for sure, or we'll get people killed."

What would draw Kerner out of hiding?

The first thing that came to my mind was Konstantin. Kerner's plan was to torment and terrify Konstantin by taking out his Olympians one by one, but it was Konstantin himself he hated most, and he might not be able to resist the temptation if he thought Konstantin was within his reach. Of course, there was the small problem that in order to use Konstantin to draw Kerner out, we'd have to get hold of him. Somehow I didn't think that would be so easy.

"Do you think there's some way we can trick Konstantin into meeting us at one of the cemeteries?" I asked, thinking out loud. "If we could jump him, we could use him as bait." And wouldn't it be a shame if we used him as bait and then didn't manage to stop Kerner until Konstantin was dead?

I felt a brief twinge of shame for thinking like Emma, but all I had to do was remind myself what had happened to Steph on Konstantin's orders, and I didn't feel bad about it anymore. If we could kill Konstantin *and* capture Kerner, it would be an entirely satisfying mission.

Jamaal gave me an incredulous look that told me just how impressed he was with my idea.

"That was a joke, right?" he asked. "Konstantin would smell this rat from a mile away. And even if we could trick him out into the open, there's no way he'd come without backup. There's a reason he's been the leader of the Olympians for so long, and it's not because he's an easy target."

I gave him a dirty look. "Come up with a better idea. Then you can criticize all you like."

We mulled things over for a few minutes, both lost in thought. I could see the moment an idea struck Jamaal by the way his eyes suddenly sharpened with interest.

"You've got something?" I asked.

Jamaal frowned thoughtfully. "Yeah. I think. But you'd have to be willing to let someone else in on the plan. You willing to do that?"

I didn't like that idea one bit. The more people who knew, the more likely someone was going to blab to Anderson, and that could be a disaster.

"Depends how good your idea is," I answered cautiously. "And who the someone is."

"Getting hold of Konstantin would be the next best thing to impossible. But getting hold of someone who could *impersonate* Konstantin would be doable."

I had to think about it a second before I got it. "Jack," I finally said. I still hadn't taken the time to look up Loki on the Internet, but clearly Jack possessed strong illusion magic. And he could change into a dog. It wasn't much of a stretch to imagine he could disguise himself as Konstantin.

Jamaal made a face—he couldn't seem to help expressing distaste when Jack's name came up—but he nodded. "He can create an illusion that no one would be able to see through."

The idea had merit, I had to admit. "So we have Jack disguise himself as Konstantin, then we drag him out to the cemeteries and parade him around until Kerner makes an appearance." A few more things clicked into place in my mind, and I found myself liking the idea more and more.

"We can pretend we grabbed Konstantin to hand him over so that Kerner won't kill any more innocents on his way to his main goal. Maybe we can have Jack make his illusion look like Konstantin is in rough shape, extra vulnerable."

Jamaal shrugged. "I suspect if Kerner gets a look at Konstantin, his brain will short-circuit, and he won't bother worrying that it's too good to be true. Some temptations are strong enough to make people forget to be cautious."

He had a point, but I suspected we were getting just a bit ahead of ourselves. It sounded like Jack might be an extremely useful ally if we were going to take Kerner down, but . . .

"Are we really willing to make a plan that relies on Jack?"

I didn't feel like I had much of a read on Jack. Being part

of Anderson's crew made him automatically one of the good guys—I trusted Anderson's judgment where anyone but Emma was concerned. But his trickster heritage made him unpredictable. Would he think it was more "fun" to rat Jamaal and me out to Anderson, thereby getting us into trouble he might find entertaining to watch? Not to mention the fact that he and Jamaal weren't exactly the best of friends.

Jamaal made a dismissive sound. "The little shit will get a kick out of going behind Anderson's back."

Was I crazy, or was there a hint of gruff affection beneath Jamaal's expressed disdain? He made such a habit of snarling it was hard to take it very seriously or personally, but I'd always assumed his animosity toward Jack was real and heartfelt.

"That isn't exactly what I'd call a rousing endorsement," I pointed out.

"Come up with a plan that doesn't require illusion magic, then."

"You're not being very helpful," I grumbled.

Jamaal didn't bother with a response, which was just as well. He was right, and for the plan we'd come up with, we'd need Jack's help. I still didn't like it. I was used to working alone, and it had taken some adjustment to get used to thinking of myself as part of a team. I didn't like having to trust other people, especially someone as mercurial as Jack.

There was that, and there was also the fact that even if our plan worked out perfectly, Anderson would be furious with us. Then, if Emma threw a little more gasoline on the fire by trotting out her accusations against me, I could find myself in big trouble. There were makeshift prison cells in the basement of the mansion—Anderson's version of the preschooler's "time-out"—and I didn't want to think about what would happen to Steph if I found myself locked up in one. Emma would have a field day. And that was the best-case scenario! If our plans failed, it would be much, much worse.

If I'd been able to think of another plan, even if I'd just had an inkling of one, I'd have seized it. But I had nothing, and I wanted to stop Kerner before he killed again.

"All right," I said reluctantly. "Jack's in. Assuming he agrees to join us, that is."

"Oh, he'll join us, all right," Jamaal said with complete confidence.

I gave him an inquiring raise of the eyebrows.

"Sneaking around? Doing something recklessly dangerous? That is so his cup of tea. He'll be all for it."

"Great," I answered while trying to silence my internal alarm bells. Either my gut was trying to tell me that this plan sucked, or I was suffering an acute bout of paranoia. I wished like hell I knew which one.

TWENTY

After reaching our decision, Jamaal and I sought out Jack—who was surprised to see us, to say the least—and laid it all out for him.

Jamaal was right, and Jack was more than eager to participate. I would have liked to have gone running out to the cemetery right that moment and get the whole mess over with, but I managed to put a lid on my eagerness.

The phases of the moon seemed to have an effect on my hunting abilities, and though the moon was near full tonight, it was cloudy out. If I had more moonlight, I'd have a better chance of tracking Kerner down, and the clouds were supposed to clear during the day.

I discussed timing with Jack and Jamaal, and we all agreed it would be best to wait until the next night to implement our plan. We needed to stack the odds in our favor as much as possible.

Not surprisingly, I couldn't sleep that night. Let's face it, I was scared. There were so many things that could go wrong with our plan. And even if everything went perfectly, I knew I had to make myself disappear before Emma realized I was reneging on our "deal." The only reason I was still hanging around was that I needed to stop Kerner first.

In the wee hours of the night, I packed my bag, taking only the essentials, and snuck through the darkened house out to the garage while no one was around to see me. I stashed the bag in the trunk of my car. Tomorrow night, regardless of what happened with Kerner, I would make my escape.

I didn't think I could bear to say good-bye, but I couldn't just disappear without a word. I spent the rest of the night composing letters of farewell to those who mattered most to me: Steph, my adoptive parents, Anderson—who needed to hear the truth, even if he refused to believe it—and, yes, Jamaal. I even wrote a short note for Blake, asking him to take good care of Steph.

It was a good thing I composed those letters on my laptop, because if I had been writing by hand, I'd have smudged the ink with my tears. You never appreciate what you have as much as you do when you've lost it. I wished I could hug the Glasses one more time before I disappeared from their lives completely—thanks to their cruise, it had been weeks since I'd seen them. More than anything, I wished I could hold on to the fantasy of being part of Anderson's team, of living with fellow immortals who knew my secrets and would remain constant as the years, decades, and centuries passed. I had tried to keep myself aloof from them, and I had failed miserably.

As the long, slow hours of the night crept by, I couldn't help wondering if the best-case scenario wasn't for the jackals to get me. But I wasn't Emmitt, to think only of myself and my own needs. If I went on the run tomorrow, it would hurt Steph and our parents—and maybe some of the *Liberi*—pretty badly, but at least they'd know I was alive. And maybe in their own minds, they could imagine a better and brighter future for me than the one I knew was coming.

As consolations go, it wasn't much.

We met on the front porch at a little after nine the next night, going out one at a time so that no one would see the three of us leaving together and wonder what we were up to. I was the last to arrive, because I'd waited until the last possible moment to print out my farewell letters, seal them, and leave them on my desk. Seeing those envelopes neatly lined up on my desk had made everything seem much more real. My heart was already aching with loss, and I hoped like hell Steph would one day forgive me for leaving her like this. I was pretty sure she would understand, but understanding isn't the same as forgiving.

I wondered if this was how my mother had felt when she'd walked out of that church without me. Had she had a good reason? Had she hoped I'd forgive her someday?

I shook the thought off. This wasn't the same thing. Steph wasn't a child, and I wasn't disappearing without a word. *Yeah, like leaving a typewritten note is going to make it all better.*

Jeez, I was a maudlin bundle of nerves tonight, but who could blame me under the circumstances? When I stepped out onto the porch and found Jamaal smoking a joint, I was almost tempted to ask him to give me a puff. But somehow I didn't think adding drugs to my anxiety and sleep deprivation was going to be an improvement.

While my stomach was tight with dread and Jamaal was smoking the joint because he needed it to help him stay calm, Jack seemed more excited than nervous. He watched Jamaal smoking with a hint of amusement in his eyes.

"You gonna share that?" he asked hopefully. Jamaal gave him a withering look, and Jack pouted.

"You're bad enough sober," I said, to save Jamaal the trouble of responding. "I don't want to be around you if you're stoned."

Jack grinned at me. Sometimes I swear I thought his face had frozen that way. "But it doesn't bother you to be around a stoned death-goddess descendant?"

"I'm not getting stoned," Jamaal snapped, playing right into Jack's game as usual. Amazing how easily Jack was able to provoke him. And that he'd lived to tell about it. "I'm just trying to keep the death magic quiet."

"Riiiight," Jack drawled. "And you read *Playboy* for the articles."

"Guys," I interrupted before Jamaal could react, "let's not start this, okay?" I glared at Jack, though I'd never seen any evidence that glares affected him. "If you set Jamaal off before we even get in the car, you'll have screwed up our plan at step one, because it'll be noisy, and someone will wonder what the hell we're up to."

Jack's eyes twinkled with mischief, and Jamaal grumbled something under his breath that I was perfectly glad not to have heard. I ignored them both and headed out to the garage, glancing over my shoulder at the lighted windows behind me, hoping no one would see us. But who sits around looking out windows at night?

We made it to the garage without incident and without anyone from the house seeming to notice us. The moment we were inside the garage, Jack started in on the troublemaking again, reminding me of all the reasons why I'd hesitated to include him in the plan.

"I'm driving," he announced, pulling a rabbit's-foot key fob out of his jeans pocket.

"No," Jamaal and I replied in concert.

I'd ridden in a car Jack was driving once, and I had no desire to repeat the experience. Besides, my bag was in the trunk of *my* car, and I intended to drive myself. I knew Jamaal wouldn't want to get into the Mini, so that meant we'd have to take two cars—which was perfect, because I didn't want to leave Jamaal and Jack stranded when I made my getaway from the cemetery.

"I'm never getting in a car you're driving again," I said. "At least, not without a blindfold and Valium."

"That can be arranged," Jack answered, undaunted. "Jamaal's stoned, and you're going to need all your concentration for the hunt."

"I am *not* stoned," Jamaal gritted out. "Stop being such an asshole."

"I'm driving," I declared. I unlocked the Mini and reached for the door. "If you have a problem with that," I said over my shoulder to Jamaal, "then you can drive your own car, and we can do rock, paper, scissors to figure out who gets stuck with Jack."

To my surprise, Jamaal opened the passenger door like he was fine with the idea of riding with me. It meant I was going to have to strand them at the cemetery after all, but I wasn't going to renege now that I'd already offered.

Jamaal started folding the seat forward to let Jack into the backseat, then paused with a thoughtful look on his face.

"We shouldn't take the chance that Kerner might see Jack riding around in the backseat while we're looking for a place to park. We should have our cover all ready to go by the time we get there." He turned and looked at Jack, his expression almost gleeful. "You should ride in the trunk and be in your Konstantin disguise by the time we open it to get you out."

Crap. This was not a contingency I'd planned for. I didn't want the guys to know I was planning to bolt. Maybe they wouldn't try to stop me—I doubted Jack cared one way or another, and with the dangerous undercurrents that ran between us, Jamaal might be just as happy to see me go. But even if they didn't try to stop me, I knew they wouldn't let me go quietly and without fuss.

"You won't give me a hit, *and* you're going to make me ride in the trunk?" Jack said. "Man, you two are cold."

Jamaal surprised me by holding the joint out to Jack, which made Jack laugh.

"No, thanks," he said. "Never touch the stuff."

Jamaal took one last drag, then stubbed out the half-smoked joint and put it away. He blew his smoke directly into Jack's face. Jack laughed again but not until after he stopped coughing.

"My trunk is too small for Jack to ride in," I said, trying to sound casual. "Maybe you guys should take the Saab, and I can meet you there."

Jack's form shimmered, and seconds later, there was a fluffy white miniature poodle, complete with a pink bow and painted toenails, sitting where he had been. The poodle made an impossibly long leap and landed on the passenger seat, then put its paws on the dashboard and panted eagerly, tail wagging furiously, looking for all the world like a real dog excited for a car ride.

Jamaal rolled his eyes. "Size isn't an issue," he informed me unnecessarily as he grabbed the poodle by the scruff of its neck and lifted it off the seat. He held the poodle up to his face and glared at it. "This is not a laughing matter, so quit with the hilarity."

The poodle nodded solemnly, then flicked out its long, almost froglike pink tongue and licked Jamaal's face. Jamaal made a choking sound and tossed the poodle away from him hard enough to make me wince in sympathy. Jack resumed his human form before he slammed into the wall of the garage. He let out a soft "oof" and slid to the floor on his butt, but it didn't seem to put a damper on his sense of humor.

"You should have seen your face!" he said, laughing at Jamaal as he picked himself up off the floor. "Priceless! If only I'd had a camera."

"Whose idea was it to bring Jack?" Jamaal asked me with

a look of chagrin. He wiped at his face where Jack had licked him but showed no sign that he might be losing control of his temper. Which was pretty impressive, considering *I* might have lost my temper in his shoes.

"Yours," I reminded him, then smiled, realizing he'd just made something approximating a joke.

He scowled but with less ferocity than usual. "Pop the trunk."

And here I'd been hoping Jack's prank might miraculously make Jamaal forget about his brilliant idea for deception. I tried to think of a good excuse not to put Jack in the trunk, but I came up empty. Either I had to let the guys see that I was ready to bolt, or I would have to change my mind about taking my own car. The latter meant I'd have to come back to the mansion later, and I didn't think that was a good idea.

While I was still hemming and hawing, looking for a third option, my trunk popped open of its own volition. I leapt out of the car with a startled gasp and saw Jack peering curiously into the trunk.

"How did you . . . ?" I let the words trail off as I realized my car keys were no longer in my hand. I tried to remember what I'd done with them after I'd opened the locks, but I couldn't recall. Not that it mattered—one way or another, Jack had relieved me of them and opened the trunk.

"What's all this?" Jack inquired, blinking at me innocently.

Jamaal peeked over Jack's shoulder and made a low growling sound. So much for my clandestine getaway. I fought the urge to hang my head. I hadn't done anything wrong.

"Emma's going to take this as a formal declaration of war when she finds out," I explained. "I can't be around when that happens. If she were just going to come after me, that would be one thing, but she's threatened Steph."

Jamaal's face was hard and cold. "And you think the rest of us are just going to sit idly by and let Emma hurt your sister?"

"What are you going to do to stop her?" I asked, shaking my head in exasperation. "Are you going to put her under twenty-four-hour surveillance? Lock her in the basement? Besides, I'm getting you two into enough trouble with Anderson as it is. I've got enough crap eating away at my conscience already. It's better for everyone if I just get out of here as soon as this is all over."

Jack shrugged like it didn't matter to him one way or another—which it probably didn't. "Suit yourself," he said, then reached into the trunk and pulled out my suitcase, lugging it to the backseat and shoving it in. "We'll call Anderson to come pick us up—and help us get Kerner permanently contained—after you've blown his brains out and taken off."

Jamaal just stood there looking at me reproachfully. The needy little girl in me wanted him to argue with me, wanted him to show some evidence that he wanted me to stay. Even if that evidence was him yelling at me for being a coward. But all I was getting from him, apparently, was the evil eye. And that wasn't anywhere near enough to persuade me.

Since no one seemed inclined to say anything more, I got back into the car and fussed with the rearview mirror, though its angle was just fine. The trunk slammed shut, presumably with Jack inside, and Jamaal slid the passenger seat as far back as he could get it before climbing inside. He didn't look at me, and I couldn't read the expression on his face. Which was probably just as well.

Blowing out a breath and telling myself I'd worry about my future later, after I'd survived the night's mission, I started the car and headed out.

The Hebrew Cemetery was the closest of the likely candidates for Kerner's home base, so I drove there first. Neither Jamaal nor I spoke for the entire ride. It wasn't a companionable silence. I'd have broken it if I could have thought of something to say.

The moon was conveniently high in the sky, and there was nothing more than the occasional wispy cloud to block its light. The perfect night for a hunt. As I neared the cemetery, I tried to listen to my instincts and get a feel for whether Kerner was there or not, but I felt nothing. No surge of excitement, no quickening of my heartbeat, no conviction that this was the place. I drove around the block, circling the cemetery, just to be sure, but there was nothing. Either Kerner wasn't here, or my powers weren't going to lead me to him.

Jamaal still hadn't spoken to me, and he made no comment when I veered away from the Hebrew Cemetery and started wending my way toward our next destination, a pair of cemeteries to the northwest. I suppose he figured out that my radar hadn't picked up anything without having to ask me about it.

The silence had taken on a life of its own, and I squirmed with discomfort. I wished I knew what Jamaal was thinking.

Did he think I was a coward for running? Was he pissed off at me for trying to sneak away without telling him good-bye? Was he regretting the fact that we could no longer explore whatever it was that was going on between us? Or was he glad I would finally be out of his life because of all the ways I'd screwed him up?

I mentally growled at myself to keep my head in the game. What Jamaal was feeling, what *I* was feeling, was irrelevant at the moment. All that mattered was finding and catching Kerner. When that was over, I could wallow to my heart's content.

Jamaal cleared his throat, and I jumped, realizing I'd spaced out a bit while getting a head start on the wallowing. I looked around, disoriented and not sure where I was.

"Is there a reason you turned onto Suitland?" Jamaal asked.

I glanced at the street sign as I came to a stop at an intersection. Sure enough, I had somehow ended up on Suitland Road when I was supposed to be on Alabama Avenue. There was no traffic, so I could easily make a U-turn, but I felt a strange reluctance to do it.

I started the car rolling forward into the intersection and was about halfway into the U-turn when it occurred to me I might have made that wrong turn for a reason. I mentally pictured my map of D.C. and its environs, with all of the cemeteries marked with little stickers.

Just across the D.C. limits into Maryland, there was a cluster of three cemeteries, and Suitland Road led directly to those cemeteries. I didn't think it was a coincidence that I'd turned down Suitland while I was spaced out.

I made my U-turn into a clumsy circle and kept going down Suitland. It felt right.

"I think Kerner is in one of the cemeteries on the other side of the D.C. border," I told Jamaal when he gave me a strange look. He nodded but didn't say anything, still giving me the silent treatment.

I drove until the cemeteries came into view, then found a conveniently dark parking space off one of the side streets. We might not want Kerner to see Jack riding around in the backseat, but we also didn't want civilians seeing us dragging our Konstantin lookalike from the trunk of the car. The pool of shadow formed by a burned-out streetlight was perfect for our purposes.

I looked at Jamaal and swallowed hard as my palms began to sweat with nerves.

"I guess this is it," I said, and I hoped I didn't sound as scared as I was. It was one thing to plan a confrontation with Kerner and his jackals from the safety of the mansion, quite another to actually walk out into a darkened cemetery as bait for a crazed serial killer.

Jamaal nodded sharply at me without making eye contact. "Let's do it," he said, and stepped out of the car.

I took a deep breath for courage, then popped the trunk and stepped out onto the sidewalk.

Despite knowing what to expect, I still did a double take when I looked in the trunk and saw Konstantin's body wedged in there. Jack had apparently decided Konstantin would have needed a lot of subduing, because his disguise included an impressive array of swollen, angry-looking bruises, as well as handcuffs, rope, and even some duct tape. Not only that, but he lay still in the trunk with his eyes closed, as if unconscious. Or dead.

I looked at Jack's disguise more closely and saw what looked like a bullet wound in the middle of his chest.

"Jeez," I muttered, "isn't this a bit of overkill?"

"Konstantin wouldn't go down without a fight," Jamaal reminded me, his voice just as low as mine. "It would take a lot to subdue him."

Jamaal checked up and down the street, looking for potential witnesses, but there was no one around. Then he leaned down and hefted Jack out of the trunk, throwing the supposedly unconscious/dead man over his shoulder. I noticed Jack had left a large bloodstain on the trunk's upholstery from his phony bullet wound.

"That blood better not be there when we come back," I said, and though he didn't move, I could swear I heard a little snort of amusement from Jack.

I slammed the trunk closed, then checked to make sure my gun was easily accessible. I'd stashed it in my coat pocket, not having a holster for it. A situation I should probably remedy if I was going to be trotting around D.C. carrying a concealed firearm on a regular basis.

Of course, I *wouldn't* be doing that, I reminded myself, because I was leaving as soon as we'd accomplished our mission.

The fence around the cemetery was purely ornamental, so low we could step right over it. I managed to trip anyway and almost went sprawling on the grass. My cheeks heated with embarrassment—not the most auspicious start ever—and I stared straight ahead so I didn't have to see Jack laughing at me.

"Which way?" Jamaal asked.

I didn't feel sure of anything, but I felt slightly more inclined to go to my right than my left, so I went with it. Jamaal, with Jack still draped limply over his shoulder, followed me as we wove our way through the headstones. The light of the moon was just enough to keep us from tripping and stumbling over the various obstacles.

We made it all the way to the fence on the opposite side of the cemetery without any sign of Kerner, and my senses were blurred and confused from thinking too hard. Probably the only reason I'd managed to bring us to this cemetery in the first place was that I'd distracted myself enough with my brooding that my body was able to follow subconscious signals.

Spacing out involuntarily is pretty easy, especially when you're stressed and sleep-deprived. Doing it on purpose, however, proved to be impossible. I tried to let my conscious mind drift, but I was too aware of the creepiness of walking through a cemetery at night and of the fear of facing Kerner and his jackals again.

I picked a direction at random and started walking again, reminding myself that our plan was for Kerner to find us, not the other way around. For all I knew, he was watching us right now, trying to figure out what we were up to.

"Kerner?" I called into the night. My voice was too soft to carry—it's hard to get yourself to shout in a cemetery—so I tried again. "Justin Kerner. We've brought you a present."

I waved my hand at Jamaal and his fake Konstantin. If Kerner could hear me, he wasn't answering.

"I guess we keep walking," I decided, and Jamaal fell into step beside me.

Our haphazard path took us all the way to the fence once again, and I had a sinking feeling that Kerner wasn't going to bite. Either he knew this was a trick, or he had more self-control than we'd thought and wasn't willing to give up his slow revenge for the quick kill.

Jamaal and I turned around, preparing to plunge back into the heart of the cemetery, but we both came to an abrupt halt when we saw that we were not alone. A figure stood in the shadow of a tree, his features hidden by darkness.

I started to draw my gun, but when the figure stepped forward out of the shadow, the moonlight revealed that it wasn't Justin Kerner.

It was Anderson.

And boy, did he ever look pissed.

Twenty-one

What the hell was Anderson doing here? I was certain no one had seen us leave the house, and even if I'd been wrong about that, surely I would have noticed if someone had been following us the whole way. I wondered for a moment if Kerner was a shape-shifter of some sort—like Jack—and could make himself look like Anderson, but I quickly dismissed the idea. He wouldn't know Anderson well enough to match that uniquely pissed-off body language.

Jamaal slung Jack's body off his shoulder. He probably expected Jack to shift back into his real form and join us to face the music, but Jack just allowed himself to fall limply to the grass, still in his Konstantin disguise.

Anderson stalked to within a few feet of us, his eyes fixed on me the whole time like he knew this was all my idea. I had to fight the urge to hang my head in shame. I was only doing what I had to do to catch Kerner—without putting myself or my sister in Emma's sights. There was nothing to be ashamed of in that.

"How did you find us?" I asked when the pressure of silence became too much.

"I got a phone call from your accomplice," Anderson grated, "saying you were going to kidnap Konstantin and try to hand him over to Kerner. Without having discussed your Lone Ranger plan with me or the rest of the team."

Confusion struck me speechless, and I shared a puzzled look with Jamaal. If someone had told Anderson what we were up to, then he'd know we hadn't really kidnapped Konstantin.

Anderson glared down at our faux Konstantin, and I suddenly understood. He might be so angry he was thinking of whipping out his Hand of Doom, but Anderson wasn't going to blow our cover story just in case it was working and Kerner was nearby.

"Jack called you," I said in a flat voice, careful not to look at Jack as I spoke and give anything away. Obviously, putting him in the trunk where we couldn't see him had been a bad idea. "Why would he do a thing like that?"

"Perhaps because he thought you two are acting like idiots," Anderson snapped. He turned his glare to Jamaal. "I can understand why Nikki would do this under the circumstances, but what's your excuse?"

If I didn't know what I knew about Anderson, I would have found it almost comical to see a big, intimidating guy like Jamaal shrink from the rage of a much smaller, unprepossessing man. I don't think Jamaal was *afraid* of Anderson, per se, but he definitely held him in considerable respect.

"Maybe this isn't the right time or place to talk about it," Jamaal suggested.

I couldn't have agreed with him more. As angry as Anderson was right now, he was at least keeping his cool enough to maintain our cover. I didn't know exactly what Jack had told him, but I suspected hearing the details would send his temper into overdrive.

Anderson, apparently, didn't give a damn about any of these concerns, and I felt a shiver of unease when I saw just a momentary hint of white light in the center of his eyes, gone before I could be sure it was there. Jamaal might be able to dismiss that as some kind of optical illusion, but I knew I'd just seen a hint of the being who resided beneath Anderson's mild-mannered human facade. A being—a *god*—I wanted to stay as far away from as possible.

"I want to know what the two of you thought I would do if you'd brought this to me instead of going behind my back," Anderson said, flexing his right hand.

Surely he wasn't going to use his Hand of Doom on us. Not here, at least. Not if he thought Kerner might actually fall for our trick, which he must, or he wouldn't be keeping our cover.

"I wasn't worried about what *you* would do," I told him, fighting a cowardly urge to step backward and out of range of his hand. "It was Emma I was worried about."

The little growling sound Anderson made in the back of his throat told me just how much that distinction meant to him. He started reaching for me, and I couldn't fight my instinctive retreat.

Anderson opened his mouth to say something, but his words were drowned out by a sudden chorus of feral growls.

Kerner's jackals appeared out of nowhere, surrounding us. There were eight of them that I could see, although there could have been others that were still invisible or hidden by tombstones or trees. I swiveled my head around but saw no sign of Kerner. I slipped my hand into my coat pocket, grabbing the gun, although I didn't draw it. As long as Kerner was out of sight, I had to pretend I was here in good faith.

The jackals circled us, growling and snarling, the circle growing tighter and tighter, but at least they weren't attacking. Not yet.

Beside me, Jamaal was standing with his eyes squeezed shut, and there was a thin sheen of sweat on his face. I couldn't understand why—even if Jamaal was afraid, he was the kind of alpha male who'd never dream of showing it. I reached out to him, but before my hand made contact, I felt the heat that radiated from his body and realized what he was doing.

"You're trying to do that *now*?" I asked incredulously. I was all for using every weapon at our disposal, but unless Jamaal had been practicing when I wasn't looking, a physical manifestation of his death magic was not on the menu. And if he failed, he'd be so weak and exhausted he'd be useless in a fight, which this was bound to come down to.

Jamaal, naturally, ignored me.

Anderson had, at least momentarily, forgotten his anger and was scanning the cemetery past the jackals, no doubt trying, like I was, to spot Kerner. I didn't think it was a coincidence that Kerner's jackals had pinned us in an area with lots of trees for cover.

One of the circling jackals broke from the pack and began stiff-leggedly approaching our faux Konstantin. I wasn't sure Jack's disguise would hold up to close examination. Did the jackals have a sense of smell? And if so, would they be able to tell the blood wasn't real?

I withdrew my gun from my coat pocket and pointed it at the jackal.

"Tell your dog to keep its distance!" I yelled.

The jackals growled more loudly, and I took a slow, deep breath to try to calm myself, but it was hard. The jackals weren't that big, but there were a lot of them, and I already had more than enough firsthand knowledge of their ferocity. Never mind the extremely unpleasant consequences of being bitten.

"If you're here to deliver Konstantin into my hands, then why do you want my jackal to stay away?" Kerner's voice called, and sure enough, it was coming from behind a tree. He might be crazy, but he wasn't an idiot.

He had a good point, but right now, he had all of the advantages on his side. I couldn't see him, we were surrounded by his jackals, and we were on his home turf. I needed to keep him talking until we could somehow tip the scales to our advantage.

"Because I want some assurances before we hand him over," I said, improvising. Anderson looked at me with a raised eyebrow, then frowned at Jamaal, who was starting to breathe hard in his efforts to manifest his death magic.

Kerner laughed, and it sounded like he'd lost a few more

inches of his sanity since we'd last spoken. Either that, or he was just embracing his cackling-villain role.

"You think you have any option *other* than handing him over?" Kerner asked, then laughed again.

I still couldn't see him, dammit! I wondered if I could make a trick shot and get my bullet to ricochet off one of the tombstones. I'd never tried anything like that before, so I didn't know just what the limitations of my supernatural aim were. Of course, if I tried that stunt and it didn't work, the jig was up. Kerner would bolt, and we'd be hard-pressed ever to track him down again. Somehow, I had to get him out from behind that tree.

I was trying to think of something to say that might tempt him to be incautious, but before I came up with anything, Kerner's jackal took a flying leap at Jack. My finger squeezed reflexively on the trigger, and the jackal went down with a very realistic yelp. I reminded myself that it was a phantom, not a real animal.

Kerner roared in rage but stayed behind the tree.

"I warned you not to do that!" he yelled, and then all of the jackals charged us at once.

Jack jumped to his feet, his form changing in midair until he was himself again, only this time clad in chain mail. In his hands, he held a baseball bat, which he swung at one of the on-coming jackals, making solid contact.

Hoping the sound of gunfire wouldn't bring any civilians running, I started shooting jackals right and left. Anderson disappeared from sight, but I knew he was still there because one of the jackals suddenly went flying backward with a yelp for no apparent reason.

Realizing I had a bit of an opening, I tried to scramble sideways so that I'd have a clear shot at Kerner—or at least at the spot where I thought Kerner was standing. It was only when I'd moved away a bit that I noticed Jamaal had fallen to his knees, his eyes still closed despite the chaos around him.

"Jamaal!" I screamed as I saw two jackals leaping at him. Jamaal didn't react.

I shot one of the jackals, but I wasn't fast enough to get both of them, at least not before one of them latched on.

I winced in anticipation even as I moved my hand to try to belatedly target the second jackal, but before I could steady my aim, Jack slammed into Jamaal from the side, knocking the bigger man to the ground. And leaving himself completely vulnerable.

The leaping jackal landed on Jack's back, its jaws snapping at the hand that held the baseball bat. Jack screamed and dropped the bat. I pulled the trigger and hit the jackal square in the head, but the damage had already been done. Jack was bitten, and that meant he had some serious hell to go through. Assuming he survived this, that is.

It was damned hard to turn away when my friends were in danger, but I knew my best chance of defending them lay in finding a clear shot at Kerner. Gun held out in front of me in hands that shook despite my best efforts, I continued moving away from the battle so I could get a look at the shadowed area behind the tree.

I got to where I had an angle, but there was no sign of Kerner. Either he had moved, or he was invisible. I suspected the former, because if he was invisible, he wouldn't have needed to hide in the first place. I shot at the empty space behind the tree, just in case, but there was no telltale cry of pain.

As soon as I fired off that shot, I cursed myself for stupidity. I'd been shooting at the jackals as if I had unlimited ammo, but my gun only held six bullets at a time. My shot into empty air was number six.

With my supernatural aim, six shots would usually be more than enough, but with Kerner's ability to re-create the jackals after I "killed" them, ammo was definitely an issue. I should have ignored the jackals from the beginning, just as Jamaal and I had planned, and gone straight for Kerner.

I had stuffed a handful of extra cartridges into my pocket, but it's kind of hard to reload a revolver during a fight, especially when ninety-nine percent of your experience with guns came from the firing range. My hands shook with adrenaline, and the various growls, snarls, and screams from the battle kept ratcheting the sense of urgency up and up and up. I was so rattled that I dropped the first cartridge when I fumbled it from my pocket.

With a curse, I bent to grab the cartridge, trying to move as fast as possible without rushing. Rushing was what made me drop the cartridge in the first place.

A deep-throated roar split the night, and I was so startled I almost dropped the cartridge again. Unable to resist the temptation, I spared a glance for the battle between my friends and the jackals.

Anderson was still nowhere to be seen, but that was only because he was using his death-god stealth. Jack was on his knees, cradling his bloody right hand to his body while he swung out seemingly at random with his baseball bat. And Jamaal sat on the ground with his eyes closed, not moving despite numerous bleeding wounds. But none of that was what stunned me into near immobility.

An enormous tiger ripped a jackal open from shoulder to hip with a casual-looking swat of its skillet-sized paw. The tiger roared again, and if the jackals had been real animals, they would have fled the scene with their tails tucked between their legs. But these were a crazy man's phantom constructions, and they didn't have the good sense to flee.

I forced my eyes away from the battle as I finally got a firm grip on the cartridge, and that was when I caught sight of Kerner, slipping through the trees away from the battle at a pace just short of a full-out run. I didn't dare lose sight of him, so I leapt to my feet in pursuit, even though it would be even harder to get the gun reloaded in the dark while running. A semiautomatic with an easy-to-change clip would have come in real handy.

Kerner glanced over his shoulder and saw me, and I thought for sure he was going to manifest another jackal just for me. Instead, he picked up speed, running toward a deeper patch of darkness amid another small stand of trees.

Just looking at that deeper darkness made the hairs on the back of my neck stand up. It was *too* dark. I remembered Anderson telling us that some death-god descendants could open up entrances to the Underworld in cemeteries and that Kerner was one of them. If he made it into that darkness, he could re-emerge anywhere, at any cemetery he wished, and who knew how many people he would kill in retaliation for my attempted trickery?

I wasn't skillful enough to reload while running, and if I stopped running, Kerner would make it through that portal before I could finish and shoot. So I forgot about trying to reload and instead pumped my arms to give myself more speed, putting everything I had into an all-out sprint.

I was closing the distance between us at a good pace, but even so, I knew I wouldn't make it. He had too much of a head start. If only I hadn't fired that last bullet!

Hopeless though it was, I kept running. Kerner glanced over his shoulder in the moment before he hit the patch of blackness, and even in the dark, I saw his snarling smile of victory. As a last resort, I tried heaving my gun at him. I'd crushed a *Liberi*'s skull with a thrown rock once, but the gun wasn't as heavy as the rock, and though my aim was perfect, I'd waited too long. The gun struck Kerner in the temple, knocking him back—right into the portal.

My rational mind insisted it was time to wave the white flag. I was running headlong, and Kerner was even now disappearing into the darkness. If I didn't stop, either I'd find myself following him into the damned Underworld—assuming that was possible—or, more likely, I'd end up crashing headlong into a tree or a monument or something that was hidden behind the portal.

But this whole thing had been my idea, and even though I had accomplices, I held myself fully responsible for the result. If the result ended up being both Jack and Jamaal getting the super-rabies and having to go through the terrifying cure while Kerner escaped and killed a bunch of innocent people to punish me, I would never, ever forgive myself.

So I didn't listen to my rational mind. I kept sprinting even as Kerner disappeared into the blackness and the portal started shrinking in on itself. And when it became clear the portal would be gone in a fraction of a second, I threw myself forward, diving for the darkness like it was home plate.

TWENTY-TWO

My stomach crawled up into my chest as my arms and legs flailed through empty, black air.

I let out a breathless scream as I fell into what could very well turn out to be a bottomless pit. There was not a hint of light anywhere, nothing but complete blackness. I would have been completely disoriented if it weren't for the sickening falling sensation that let me know in no uncertain terms which way was down.

I couldn't help flashing back to the empty darkness of death, momentarily terrified that I had just plunged headlong into it, but there had been no falling sensation in death. And I hadn't been able to breathe or move my limbs, both of which I was doing just fine.

I wasn't dead. Not yet, at least. But assuming I wasn't going to fall forever, I might well be when I hit the ground, especially if I hit headfirst.

I'm not an acrobat, and the only time I ever went skydiving, I did it in tandem, where I didn't have to try to control anything. Still, I tried my best to orient myself and twist in the air until my feet were pointing vaguely downward, just in time to burst through the blackness into a lighter darkness. One that allowed me to see the rock floor rushing up to meet me.

My feet hit the floor with teeth-rattling force, and I rolled with the impact. My ankle twisted painfully, and I banged my hip so hard I was surprised I didn't break it. When I came to a breathless stop, I was pleasantly surprised to find I *still* wasn't dead. In fact, although I ached from head to toe and no doubt had a host of bruises to go with my twisted ankle, I was pretty sure I hadn't even broken any bones.

For a moment, I could do nothing but lie there on my back where I'd come to rest, staring at the black nothingness from which I'd emerged. Then I reminded myself that Kerner had come through before me, and I groaningly forced myself into a sitting position.

I was in what looked like a tunnel of some sort, although the walls disappeared within about seven feet into the blackness above. If I hadn't just fallen through that blackness, I would have said the tunnel was dark, but there was just enough ambient light for me to see the roughly hewn walls and the uneven floor. Don't ask me where that ambient light was coming from, though, because though I looked in all directions, I could see no source.

I'd obviously clocked Kerner pretty good with my gun, because even in the dark, I could see the smear of blood on the floor where he'd landed. There was another, hand-shaped smear on one wall, and a few drops on the floor marked which way he had gone.

I didn't have time to explore or absorb my surroundings. I had to catch up to Kerner before he disappeared back into the mortal world at some unknown location.

What I was going to do with him when I caught up to him

was anyone's guess, as I was now officially unarmed. I glanced around on the off chance the gun had come through the portal with Kerner, but I didn't see it.

I started following the trail of blood, moving cautiously despite the sense of urgency that hammered at me. It was dark enough that I could only see a few yards ahead of me, and I had no idea what might be lurking in these tunnels.

The air was uncomfortably warm and smelled stale. I hoped there was enough oxygen. Then I wondered how the hell I was going to get out of here, but I shoved the thought aside. I would worry about that after I'd taken care of Kerner. And no, I still didn't have a plan for how I was going to do that.

I patted down my pockets in search of a weapon, anything heavy enough to take Kerner down with a really good throw, but the best I could come up with was my keys. Even throwing them as hard as I could and with perfect aim, I doubted I could kill Kerner with them or even knock him out. But it was all I had, and I wasn't going to accomplish anything by sitting around in the dark twiddling my thumbs.

The tunnel broadened as I followed it, but there were no branches. I could have stayed on Kerner's tail even without the helpful blood trail. But with every step I took, I became more and more convinced I'd done something unutterably stupid by diving into that portal.

I was unarmed and in unfamiliar territory. If Kerner caught sight of me, all he had to do was conjure a single jackal, and I had no way to defend myself. Who did I think I was to pit myself single-handedly against a supernatural serial killer? In the Underworld, no less, a place I wasn't sure I could escape from if I didn't have Kerner around to create one of his portals.

My mouth was dry, my skin clammy despite the heat, which seemed to be growing more oppressive by the second. Was I imagining things, or was there a hint of sulfur in the stale air? What *was* the Underworld, anyway? Was it Hell?

I blew out a steadying breath and continued forward until a soft growl emanated from the darkness in front of me. I came to an abrupt stop, hardly daring to breathe, as I strained my eyes, trying to see farther down the tunnel. Was there a patch of deeper darkness up ahead, darkness that might be the shadowed form of a jackal?

The beat of my heart seemed unnaturally loud in the echoing silence of the tunnel. A bead of sweat rolled down the center of my back.

There was a scraping sound from up ahead, like claws scratching across stone, and the deeper pool of shadow moved. Enough that I could tell it was approximately jackal-shaped.

"You tried to trick me," Kerner's voice rasped from far enough down the tunnel that I couldn't even see him as a shadow. "I thought we had an agreement."

There was another growl, and I realized there was more than one jackal hiding just beyond the edge of the weak light. I was going to be torn apart, just like Phoebe had been. Unless I could find some way to talk Kerner out of it. But how do you reason with a madman?

"I thought so, too," I said, and I was proud of myself for not letting my voice quaver. "Then you killed that poor maid just because she was in the wrong place at the wrong time."

"She worked for an Olympian," Kerner argued with no hint of remorse. "She lived in his house. That makes her not a civilian."

"I don't see it that way."

"That's too bad."

I didn't get the feeling our conversation was increasing my chances of survival. The problem was, I didn't know what would. I could try throwing my keys, using Kerner's voice to target him, but I didn't know if that would work, and if it didn't, I could be sure the jackals would come for me immediately. Anything that bought me just a little more time was worth it.

I took a couple of cautious steps forward. There was no point in retreating—I couldn't outrun jackals. Maybe if I could get closer to Kerner, I could figure out a way to stop him.

"Let's talk about this," I said in my best therapist voice. The jackals voiced their displeasure, and I stopped immediately.

"There's nothing to talk about!" Kerner snapped. And yet the jackals still hadn't attacked me. There had to be a reason for that.

"Maybe we can make another deal." My mind raced as I tried to think of what Kerner might want from me. And almost immediately, I came up with the answer.

Kerner wanted from me what *everyone* wanted from me.

"I could make it a lot easier for you to find all of the Olympians. And Konstantin, when the time comes." He didn't say anything, and I took that as a sign of encouragement. "I'm a descendant of Artemis." I was pretty sure he already knew that, but it didn't hurt to make certain. "I'm really good at hunting. It's why I've been able to find you as many times as I have."

There was more movement beyond the reach of the light, and I caught a hint of Kerner's foul reek blending with the sulfur smell of the air. He was moving closer, though he was still careful to stay out of sight.

"Why should I believe you'd help me?" Kerner asked. "You came with your friends to kill me. Not even kill me—to bury me alive for all eternity."

The jackals snarled and snapped, a couple of them stepping to the edge of the light so I could see the long, sharp fangs they bared. I swallowed hard.

"I'm descended from Artemis, not a death god," I said, hoping my voice sounded level and reasonable. "I wasn't really thinking about what I was doing when I followed you here, but I'm pretty sure I can't get out without your help. That's a pretty powerful incentive for me to help you, if you'll let me."

He thought about that for a long moment. "It's incentive for you to help me until you get out. Then you'll just turn on me.

Like you did this time." The edge in his voice grew sharper, and I knew that I had to redirect him before his rage took over.

"I came after you this time because I considered that you'd already broken our agreement. I understand now that we were working off of different definitions of the word 'civilian.' It was a misunderstanding, not a breech of faith."

I found my own argument a bit of a stretch, but Kerner's silence suggested he was thinking about it. I decided my best strategy was to shut up and let him think.

"Follow me," he finally said, "but don't get any closer."

The jackals retreated into the darkness, and I heard the echoing sound of Kerner's footsteps. He hadn't indicated one way or another what he thought of my proposal, and I was not at all happy with the prospect of following him into more un-known territory. But what choice did I have?

I followed Kerner through the tunnel for what I'd guess was a couple hundred yards, timing my footsteps to his, getting growled at by jackals if he thought I was getting too close.

"Where are you taking me?" I asked once, but he didn't answer.

I kept my eyes peeled the whole way, looking for some-thing, *anything,* I could use for a weapon. But there was noth-ing any more lethal that the keys I held clenched in my fist. If I could get Kerner into good enough light, I could try aiming for his eye. The keys weren't the most efficient throwing weapon in the world, but they could do an impressive amount of dam-age to something as vulnerable as an eyeball.

There was light coming from the tunnel up ahead. Dim gray light that wasn't particularly inviting, but who was I to be picky? As we approached the light, Kerner's form—and those of his jackals—was silhouetted. I could toss the keys and hit him in the back of the head—except I was too far away to get much oomph on the throw. I needed a more vulnerable target than the back of his head, and I needed to be closer so the keys would hit hard enough to do damage.

The jackals were quite determined that I wasn't to get closer.

The tunnel eventually opened out into an enormous cavern. And when I say enormous, I'm talking big enough to hold a small city. Which apparently it did. I came to a stop at the tunnel's opening and stared at what I saw laid out in front of me.

For as far as I could see, white marble buildings rose from the gray stone floor of the cavern, some of them so tall they flirted with the blackness of the ceiling—a ceiling that was considerably higher in the cavern than it had been in the tunnels.

The city was laid out in an orderly grid pattern, with one main road about three times as broad as any other leading up to something that reminded me very much of the Acropolis—only not in ruins. I shivered, even though the air was still uncomfortably warm. Some of the buildings were small and simple, little more than rectangular boxes with windows, but the larger, more elaborate buildings were adorned with columns and carved with bas-relief. In the dimness of the light, the carvings were nothing more than formless collections of shadow.

Nothing moved in the silent white marble city. Nothing except Kerner and his jackals, that is. The buildings looked like homes and temples and courthouses, but in the silence and stillness, they seemed more like elaborate mausoleums.

Uncommonly courteous for a crazed serial killer, Kerner gave me a moment to stand there and look around in awe before he started forward again. He didn't say anything to me, but I knew I was supposed to follow. The city gave me a serious case of the creeps, but I forced myself onward anyway.

Kerner led the way to the main street, turning down it and continuing on toward the big temple-like structure at its end. He was keeping me about thirty yards behind him, but the oppressive silence made his every footfall sound like a drumbeat in my ears. Or maybe that was just the beating of my heart. Empty windows stared down at me like malevolent eyes, and though the city felt dead, I kept expecting something to jump out at me from the shadows. It didn't help when I got close enough to one of the more elaborate buildings to make out the details of the bas-relief. It looked like the kind of thing you would see carved into the top of your average Greek or Roman ruin, with rows of figures in action. Except the figures were all skeletons.

Maybe it was just my imagination, maybe it was the dim gray light that gave everything an ominous look, or maybe it was just because I knew this was the Underworld, but I had a powerful sense that I didn't belong here, that the city wanted me gone. How an empty city could *want* anything is anybody's guess.

Every step I took involved a battle with my fight-or-flight instinct, which was all in favor of flight. Licking my dry lips with my dry tongue, I took a deep breath of sulfurous air and kept alert for any hint of something that I could use as a weapon. The city looked so ancient that it should be in ruins, but there were no convenient hunks of rock sitting by the side of the road.

At the base of the temple was a pair of circular stone pits in the floor, looking for all the world like empty swimming pools, though I doubted that's what they were. They were about eight feet deep, their walls polished so smooth that the stone gleamed. As I neared those pits, Kerner had to go partway up the stairs leading to the temple's entrance to keep his distance.

"Stop there!" he commanded when I was a couple of yards from the pits. His jackals stood at the base of the stairs and growled at me in case I didn't get the hint.

Kerner turned around, and for the first time, I got a good look at him. Blood coated the left side of his face and neck and stained his already filthy coat. My gun had hit him right above the left eyebrow, and the damage it had done was more than a bloody scalp wound. I was surprised Kerner wasn't staggering around with a concussion. Then again, with the insanity he'd inherited from Lyssa's seed, his brain didn't exactly function like normal in the first place.

"I will accept your deal," Kerner announced from his perch on the stairs.

"Um, great," I said, though I knew it wasn't going to be as simple as all that. Kerner had led me here for a reason, and it wasn't just because he'd look impressive pontificating from the temple stairs.

"But I need a guarantee," Kerner continued.

I already didn't like it. "What kind of guarantee?"

Kerner smiled at me, an expression that couldn't help but look sinister on his bloody face. "I want you to hop into one of those cisterns. Either one, it doesn't matter. Then I'm going to go fetch a hostage or two. I'll put the hostages in the other cistern, and then I'll get you out, and we can go hunting together. Unless you want the hostages to die a slow and miserable death here in the Underworld, you'll need to keep me alive so I can free them for you."

No, I definitely didn't like this plan. I jumped when a jackal growled from behind me.

"Choose a cistern," Kerner commanded as I backed away from the jackal that menaced me.

The good news was that the cisterns would make the perfect place for me to contain Kerner once I'd subdued him—assuming he couldn't just create a portal back to the world above anywhere he pleased, but if he could do that, I was screwed no matter what I did. Now all I had to do was figure out how to get him into one of them. Maybe if I did as he asked, he would come closer to gloat at me.

I kept backing away from the jackal, looking back and forth between the two cisterns while keeping an eye on Kerner out of my peripheral vision. He was still too far away for me to hurt him with my keys, but he wasn't trying to maintain his distance anymore, and every step I took closer to the cisterns was a step closer to Kerner.

No matter what, I couldn't follow his instructions and jump into the cistern. If I did that, even if he came close enough for me to hit him afterward, he would just heal, and I wouldn't be able to get him into the cistern because I'd be stuck in it myself.

"I'm losing patience," Kerner said, and I realized what I had to do.

I was too far away to get a good shot at Kerner's head, and the jackals would attack me the moment I made a hostile move. They could run a hell of a lot faster than I could, but if I caught Kerner by surprise . . .

I took a deep breath, my hand spasming on the keys I still held, hard enough that I was sure I'd have key-shaped marks on my palms. This might be the craziest, most suicidal plan in the history of the universe. Even in the best-case scenario, I would be stuck in the Underworld forever. A frightened little corner of my mind suggested I go along with Kerner's plan and figure out how to rescue the hostages after I'd gotten out of there and taken care of Kerner.

But I couldn't do that. If I let Kerner get away, a lot of people would die for my cowardice. Maybe I'd find a way to rescue whatever hostages he brought, but I couldn't forget that in Kerner's mind, I'd violated our first agreement. When we'd made the agreement, he'd warned me he would kill innocents if I broke it, and I had no doubt he was still planning to do so. If I let him go now, he would return to the Underworld later with his hostages and with proof of how many innocents he'd killed to punish me.

It was now or never.

I hung my head as if in defeat, but I was really just trying to hide my face, making sure Kerner could read nothing in my expression that might give me away. I took a couple of hesitant steps forward, turning my body like I was going to head for one of the cisterns.

Then I charged Kerner.

TWENTY-THREE

Kerner and his jackals were so taken aback that for a moment, they didn't react. I let out a battle cry as I picked up as much speed as I could within a few steps.

Kerner recovered from his moment of shock, and suddenly, his jackals all leapt into action at once.

Hard though it was, I ignored the jackals, pulling back my right arm for a throw. I was still a bit farther away than I'd have liked, but at least I had the momentum of my brief sprint behind me as I hurled my keys at Kerner with every drop of strength I could muster, aiming not at his eye but at his wounded temple.

I put so much into the throw that I lost my balance, landing on the stone floor on my hands and knees. It turned out to be a lucky break, as a jackal sailed right through where I would have been if I'd kept my feet. I lashed out at one of the onrushing jackals with one foot, knowing it was a lost cause. A single bite was all they would need to kill me—assuming I never found my way out of the Underworld, which was a frighteningly good assumption.

A choked scream from above told me my keys had hit their mark, and the jackal I'd been trying to kick suddenly disappeared, my foot going through empty air. I looked up in time to see Kerner put both hands to his wounded head as fresh blood welled between his fingers. He staggered woozily and lost his footing on the stairs, tumbling down them and hitting his head numerous times on the way. When he reached the bottom of the stairs, he lay still.

I stayed on my hands and knees for a moment, hardly daring to believe I wasn't buried under a blanket of jackals. A vicious, fang-filled blanket. But I saw no sign of them, and Kerner wasn't moving.

Slowly, I rose to my feet and approached his body. A pool of blood was forming on the stone beneath his head. I wasn't sure whether he was unconscious or dead, but even if he was dead, it would only be temporary.

I didn't understand how Kerner's power worked. Could he create a portal anywhere in the Underworld he wanted to? Or were there certain places—like the tunnel we'd fallen into from the cemetery—that led back to the world above? I had to hope for the latter, or even trapping Kerner in one of the cisterns wouldn't keep him from escaping once he came back to life. Unless I were willing to stay by his side and pound his head into hamburger every time it came close to healing. I had the disturbing thought that if I really was trapped down here till the end of time, I wouldn't have anything better to do. Though I supposed I would starve to death or die of dehydration periodically, which might give Kerner the time he needed to heal and escape.

Kerner reeked, and I didn't want to touch him, but I did it anyway, bending down and feeling for a pulse. There was none. Even if the blow from my keys hadn't been enough to kill him, the fall down the marble stairs had done the trick. Now all I had to do was drag him to the cistern and hope he couldn't just form a portal and escape.

Along with being disgustingly filthy, Kerner was also malnourished and as thin as a rail, but he still weighed more than I did. Dragging his dead weight—pardon the pun—toward the cistern was harder than I thought it would be, and I had to stop every couple of feet to suck air into my lungs. I was physically and emotionally exhausted, and fear hovered around the edges of my mind as I tried not to contemplate my bleak future. I wanted to sit down, hug my knees to my chest, and let loose with a fit of hysteria. Then maybe fall asleep and wake up later to find this was all a bad dream.

All of which I promised myself I'd do once I'd gotten Kerner into the blasted cistern. Gritting my teeth in determination, I bent down and grabbed Kerner's ankles to pull him another few feet closer to the cistern, which I could have sworn was moving farther away every time I turned my back.

"Need some help with that?"

The unexpected voice made me screech with alarm, and my clumsy attempt to whirl around was made even clumsier by my unfortunate mistake of putting my foot down on the edge of Kerner's leg. I fell awkwardly, getting blood and filth on me as I landed partway on Kerner's body.

I scrambled away, adrenaline still whipping me into a frenzy even as my rational mind realized it recognized that voice.

When I stopped my panicky retreat, I looked up to find Anderson standing a few yards away, his arms crossed over his chest as he regarded me with amusement. I closed my eyes and tried to calm my racing heart.

I'd allowed myself to forget that Anderson was a death god. I'd wondered once before whether he had the ability to travel into the Underworld. Now I had my answer.

I took a deep breath and let it out slowly. When I opened my eyes, Anderson was bending over me, offering me a hand up. I accepted his help, but he didn't let go once I was on my feet. He'd been smiling at me when I first caught sight of him, but he wasn't smiling now. I guess he was still mad that I'd gone behind his back.

"You could have gotten yourself, Jamaal, and Jack all killed tonight," he said, his hand tightening on mine enough to make my bones ache.

I swallowed hard, hoping he wasn't going to do the Hand of Doom thing. I'd have tried to pull away, but I knew it was pointless.

"I couldn't just let him keep killing people," I said. "And I couldn't let Emma know what I was doing. I couldn't risk Steph."

Anderson closed his eyes, but not before I saw the flash of pain in them. He let go of my hand, and I rubbed at my sore knuckles.

"She wouldn't have hurt Steph," Anderson said, but his voice held a trace of doubt. "Emma's not like that."

"Maybe she wasn't like that before the Olympians got to her. But she is now."

"Why didn't you come to me?"

"Is that a trick question?" Anderson scowled at me, and I held up my hands in surrender. "Because I didn't think you'd believe me. You want the old Emma back so much you refuse to see what she's become."

Anderson shook his head, either in denial or in disgust, I wasn't sure which. My heart ached way more than any of my physical injuries.

"I have a bag packed in my car," I said, forcing words through my tight throat. "I'll be out of your hair as soon as you get me out of here. Maybe if I'm not around, Emma will start to stabilize."

I didn't believe my own words, but it felt right to say them. "You *are* planning to get me out of here, right?"

Anderson sighed. "Of course."

I couldn't help hoping that he would ask me to stay, that he would somehow keep a leash on Emma and make sure that both Steph and I were safe from her malice. But I wasn't shocked when he merely squatted by Kerner's side and touched the dead man's throat. I thought he was checking for a pulse. Until his hand started to glow.

I took a couple of hasty steps back, primal fear urging me to run. I'd seen what Anderson could do with that glowing hand, and I didn't want to see it again.

I turned my back and squeezed my eyes closed as the light in the cavern brightened. I remembered the screams of agony from the men I'd seen Anderson kill before, and my entire body was taut with horrified anticipation. Only Kerner was already dead, so there were no screams. No sounds at all, except for the pounding of my pulse.

When the light dimmed, I turned around. Anderson was

still squatting, but instead of a dead body at his feet, there was only Kerner's empty clothes. His body had been entirely consumed by Anderson's magic, leaving not even a trace of him behind.

Anderson dusted off his hands and rose to his feet, eyes averted. "Come on," he said, still without looking at me. "Let's get out of here."

I nodded my agreement, then gingerly picked up my bloodied keys from where they had landed on the steps. There were already bloodstains on my coat, so I used it to wipe off as much of the blood as I could before shoving the keys back into my pocket. I fell into step with Anderson as he led me back down the main road. The deserted city still gave me the creepy feeling that I was being watched by malevolent eyes, but it didn't seem to disturb Anderson in the least.

"What is this place?" I asked, hoping that breaking the silence would help me shake off the heebie-jeebies.

Anderson slanted a glance at me. "It's the City of the Dead. Well, one of them, anyway."

That didn't exactly tell me much. "Does that mean there are dead people hanging around here?"

But Anderson shook his head. "The city has been deserted for a long, long time. Ever since the gods abandoned Earth. The same is true, at least for the most part, of the entire Underworld."

I resisted the urge to ask him what he meant by "for the most part." I was pretty sure I didn't want to know.

Anderson led me back to the tunnel from which I'd come, and we left the City of the Dead behind. The hair on the back of my neck remained raised until the city disappeared from view. When we were back to the spot where I'd fallen through the portal—I recognized it by the splotch of Kerner's blood that marked the floor—Anderson reached over and took my hand.

"Hold on tight," he warned me. "Whatever you do, don't let go."

He took a step forward, and his foot landed on empty air, about eight inches from the ground. His next step was about eight inches higher than that, and I realized he was climbing stairs I couldn't see. He was also pulling on my hand, so I took a tentative step forward, lowering my foot until I felt something solid below. I glanced down just to be sure, but yes, my foot was resting on empty air.

Blowing out a deep breath, I squeezed Anderson's hand a little tighter and followed him upward into the impenetrable darkness.

Twenty-four

Life in the outside world had not come to a stop while I was in the Underworld, and by the time Anderson and I emerged from the portal into the cemetery, it was deserted.

"Are Jack and Jamaal all right?" I asked, ashamed of myself for not having asked earlier. I remembered Kerner's jackal chomping down on Jack's hand, and I remembered the blood I'd seen on Jamaal. That meant they were far from "all right," but I hoped what I'd seen had been the worst of it, that the jackals hadn't done any more damage when I'd run off in pursuit of Kerner.

Anderson waggled his hand in the universal gesture for so-so. "Jamaal was passed out when I came after you, but his wounds seemed to be healing. Jack was already starting to run a fever, but he'd only been bitten once, so it'll take a while for the infection to put him on his back. I sent them home while I went after you."

"You sent them home when Jamaal was unconscious and

Jack was infected?" Jack was a lunatic driver under the best of circumstances, but with the super-rabies in his system . . .

Anderson shrugged. "It was either that or leave them lying in the graveyard for however long it took me to retrieve you. I thought it was the lesser of two evils."

"And what did you tell Jack when you created a portal to the Underworld?"

Anderson's people all assumed he was *Liberi,* but none of them knew who his divine ancestor was.

"I admitted that I'm descended from a death god," he said. "There was no harm in telling him that much, though I made it clear the discussion was going no further."

"And what are you going to say about Kerner?"

"We trapped him in the Underworld." His expression dared me to contradict him, but I wasn't about to. As long as he'd put Kerner out of his misery, I was happy to let him keep however many secrets he wanted.

I was following Anderson blindly, but when we came to the edge of the cemetery, I blinked and did a quick visual survey. Anderson turned left after stepping over the miniature fence that marked the cemetery's boundary.

"My car is that way," I told him with a jerk of my thumb toward the right. Another perk of my ancestry was an extremely good sense of direction.

Anderson kept walking. "Not anymore it isn't."

I hurried after him, frowning. "What do you mean?"

"I sent the boys home in it." He shot me a look that was almost apologetic. "It was closer than my car, and Jack and I had to carry Jamaal, who is not a featherweight."

I narrowed my eyes at him suspiciously. How convenient that the car with my suitcase in it wasn't there and that I would therefore have to go back to the mansion after all. Then I shook my head.

"Wait a minute. How did you guys get keys to my car?" Jack had managed to pick my pocket earlier that evening, but

I knew for certain the keys had been on my person when I jumped into the portal, seeing as they'd been the weapon I'd used to kill Kerner.

Anderson laughed. "Jack's a trickster, Nikki. Do you really think he doesn't know how to steal a car?"

I bit my tongue to prevent myself from saying anything unwise. Not only had Jack jeopardized our mission by calling Anderson, but he'd also monkeyed with my car. Sure, he'd probably saved all of our lives by ratting us out—even with Anderson's help, the jackals had done some serious damage—but it was the principle of the thing. I'd have loved to entertain myself with fantasies about getting revenge, but I wouldn't be around to carry them out.

The ride back to the mansion showed me just how exhausted I was. Within minutes of climbing into the passenger seat of Anderson's car, I was fast asleep with my head against the window. I'm sure I'd have slept all the way back if we hadn't hit a pothole that made my head bump painfully against said window. I sat up with a start, then promptly yawned so big my jaw made an alarming cracking sound.

"If you're still determined to leave," Anderson said, watching the road studiously, "you should at least wait until morning. You're worn out."

He was right about that, and my body begged me to agree. My eyelids felt like they weighed about ten pounds each, and my mind was all fuzzy around the edges. I wouldn't be the safest driver in the world, and I certainly wouldn't get far.

It was tempting, I won't lie. But I knew that if I spent the night at the mansion in my own bed—I wondered briefly when I had come to think of the bed in the mansion as "my own"—it would be even harder to get myself to leave.

"Please make sure Emma doesn't do anything to Steph when I'm gone," I said. "I know you don't really believe she'll do it, but look out for Steph anyway."

Anderson didn't answer, but the tightening around the corners of his eyes and mouth proved he'd heard me just fine. In the letters I'd left at the mansion, I'd asked both Anderson and Blake to keep their eyes on Steph and keep her safe, though I still hoped that was an unnecessary precaution, that Emma would have no interest in Steph if I wasn't around to be hurt by whatever she did.

My head was starting to inch back toward the window, my eyes almost closed, when Anderson spoke again.

"Jamaal needs you."

The words startled me enough to wake me up and make me feel almost alert. My throat tightened at the mention of Jamaal's name. There was no denying there was a connection between us, whether we wanted there to be or not. And despite his failure to ask me not to leave, I knew it would hurt him when I did, that some little part of him would see my departure as just one more abandonment. But he had the rest of Anderson's *Liberi* to help him through the tough times, and he'd figured out how to manifest his death magic in a way that might help him control it.

"He'll be fine," I said tightly, not truly believing my own words.

Anderson made a little snorting sound that bore no resemblance to agreement, but that was all he had to say on the subject.

I figured that despite the ungodly hour, there would be people up and about at the mansion, since Jack's and Jamaal's return would have caused a stir even if Anderson's departure hadn't. But I hadn't expected to see practically every window lit, nor had I expected the porch lights to be blazing. From the way Anderson stiffened beside me, I knew he hadn't expected that, either.

As we made our way down the long driveway, our headlights picked up an unfamiliar car parked in the circular drive. Anderson stepped on the gas a little harder. I tried to muster some alarm, but I was too exhausted, and my body seemed to have run out of adrenaline.

Instead of turning off toward the garage, Anderson pulled up beside the mysterious car, and that was when I saw a very unexpected tableau.

Emma, dressed in an elegant mink coat and stiletto heels, was sitting on the porch swing, a large suitcase at her side and a smile on her face that didn't match the fury in her eyes. Lounging against one of the columns that supported the porch stood Cyrus, holding a knife to Blake's throat. Blood trickled from a small cut on Blake's throat and also from a split and bleeding lip. Even so, he seemed remarkably . . . relaxed in Cyrus's grip. Of course, Cyrus couldn't kill him, but I doubted Blake would enjoy having his throat slashed.

Anderson was out of the car and at the base of the porch steps before I'd even managed to open my door.

"What the hell is going on here?" he demanded, looking back and forth between Cyrus and Emma.

Emma rose lazily to her feet as I fumbled my way out of the car, swaying from exhaustion. Anderson was right, I realized—there was no way I was making my great escape right now. I couldn't kill *myself* if I fell asleep at the wheel, but I could kill someone else, and I didn't want to take that chance.

Emma gave me a quick glance and a curl of her lip before fixing her eyes on Anderson.

"What's going on is I'm leaving you," Emma declared, raising her chin proudly.

Anderson tried to keep his face expressionless, but there was no missing the pain that punched through him at Emma's declaration. And there was no missing Emma's pleasure at his reaction. He hid his pain quickly, turning an icy look toward Cyrus.

"And what's *your* story?" he asked in a tone that would have made a wise man take a hasty step backward.

Cyrus smiled and adjusted his grip on Blake, pulling the other man tighter against him in something that looked almost like a lover's embrace—or at least it would have, without the knife. Blake rolled his eyes.

"Blake objected to the idea of my leaving with your wife," Cyrus said. "I figured I'd better control him before he had me performing unnatural acts with my car."

Anderson slowly climbed the stairs to the porch, eyes fixed on Cyrus.

"We have an agreement with Konstantin," Anderson grated. "Trust me, you don't want to break it."

"It only applies if I try to remove someone by force, but Emma's the one who called *me*. Isn't that right, my dear?"

I half expected Anderson to forget his whole disguise and go on a rampage when Emma smiled and nodded.

"You can't mean that!" Anderson said, his voice just below a shout. "You wanted me to let that monster roam free just so he could kill Konstantin, and now you're going to run off and become one of his Olympians?"

"Perhaps I should clarify," Cyrus said before Emma could answer. "My father is not in charge anymore. *I* am."

A whole slew of expressions crossed Anderson's face all at once, foremost of which was shock.

Cyrus smirked. "My father made a grave error in judgment that could have resulted in the death of every single Olympian in the world. You don't seriously think we're all going to keep following him after that."

"So you killed him."

Cyrus shook his head. "He's not an idiot. He saw the writing on the wall and went on the run. Took a few of his best friends with him."

"But not you?" Anderson taunted. "His only son? *Living* son, that is?"

The look on Cyrus's face didn't change. Anderson's taunt had missed its mark. "I'm not an idiot, either," he said, and there was a hint of sadness in his voice. "I know I've never been one of his nearest and dearest."

"I'm sure you cry about that every night," Blake muttered under his breath. "You think you could put the knife away now?"

Cyrus looked at Anderson. "I'm not here for any nefarious purpose," he said. "I'm just giving Emma a ride, if she wants it. If you'll tell Blake not to try any of his tricks, I'll put the knife away."

Anderson looked like he was grinding his teeth, but he gave a brief nod. Cyrus lifted the knife from Blake's throat and retracted the blade. Blake pushed away from him but without any obvious rancor. Then he turned and gave Cyrus a dirty look, which seemed like a pretty mild reaction to me, considering the blood that spotted his throat and face. Cyrus reached out and swept his thumb over the blood beneath Blake's swollen lip, smiling enigmatically.

"Sorry about that," he murmured.

I'm sure I wasn't the only one who noticed the bulge in Cyrus's tight pants, and I didn't think it was Blake's lust aura that was causing it. If I'd had any doubts before that they'd once been lovers, I was certain now.

Cyrus made his switchblade disappear—up his sleeve, I think, though I didn't see him do it—then headed for the stairs, brushing past Anderson.

"I'll wait in the car," he said, then stopped a moment. "And I will uphold my father's agreement with you," he added to Anderson. "I see no reason why your people and mine need to be at war with one another."

Anderson sighed. "No, of course you wouldn't."

Cyrus turned to Emma. "Join me when you're ready." He descended the last few steps and then got into his car, starting the engine.

Anderson had a brief staring match with Emma, but he lost, his eyes dropping to the floor as his shoulders hunched with pain. I wanted to be anywhere but here, but I'd have to walk past both of them to get away, and that wasn't going to happen.

"Send her away," Emma said, pointing at me without taking her eyes off Anderson. "If she goes, I'll stay."

I opened my mouth to tell Emma I was going anyway, but Anderson silenced me with a look. The expression on his face hardened.

"If you'd rather be an Olympian than stay here with me, then I won't stop you."

Fury blazed in Emma's eyes—fury that she aimed equally at Anderson and me. But it would be a lot easier for her to hurt me than to hurt Anderson, so I knew I would bear the brunt of it should she decide to exact revenge.

"If you're an Olympian, then you have to abide by the Olympians' treaty," I said, unable to keep my mouth shut when I could so clearly read the threat in her eyes. "My sister and I are both off-limits to you."

Emma made a sound that reminded me of a snarling jackal, and I doubted the Olympians' treaty would keep me safe from her wrath. Not when it was so very, very personal. She reached into her mink coat and pulled out a handful of envelopes, dropping them haphazardly to the floor. I saw the names handprinted on the fronts of those envelopes—and I also saw that they were open. Emma had been snooping in my room while I was gone, which explained why she was packed and ready to go. She knew I was breaking our agreement, and she wasn't as confident as she'd pretended to be. Better to leave Anderson in a huff than face the possibility that he might believe me over her.

It also meant that Emma had known I was already planning to leave when she demanded Anderson kick me out.

"The treaty won't protect you—or your family—unless you're living in the mansion," Emma said. "If you think I'm going to let bygones be bygones just because you've left town, you're sadly mistaken. *Please* leave town. Give me the opening I need. I know word of what I do will reach you one way or another, and I'll enjoy fantasizing about your reaction even if I can't see it."

Anderson looked at her like she was an alien. Maybe he was finally really seeing her for what she'd become. He looked so lost my heart ached for him, even as Emma's threat sent a bolt of terror through me.

Anderson was back to trying to hide his feelings, and his face was almost completely blank when he reached out to pick up Emma's suitcase.

"I'll carry this for you," he said, lugging it toward Cyrus's idling car.

I'm sure Emma had been expecting Anderson to protest more, to try harder to get her to stay. Hell, I'd been expecting it, too. But maybe Anderson had finally woken up to what she'd become.

With a last venomous look at me, she stomped down the stairs and got into the car without a backward glance. The trunk popped open, and Anderson hefted her suitcase inside, then slammed it closed. Cyrus tapped the horn a couple of times in a pseudo-friendly farewell, then worked his way past Anderson's car and onto the driveway.

Blake and I stood and watched the lights receding while Anderson stalked into the house and slammed the door behind him.

I was so exhausted I had to steady myself on the railing to get up the steps to the porch, and I wanted to follow Anderson into the house and retreat to my bedroom with every fiber of my being. And if Blake weren't dating my sister, I'd have done just that.

"Does Steph know about you and Cyrus?" I asked him.

It looked for a moment like Blake was going to deny there was anything between the two of them, but he must have seen from the look on my face that it would never work. He reached up and dabbed away the blood on his throat, and I saw that the wound had been so small it had already healed.

"She knows," Blake said. "Not about Cyrus specifically, but . . . She knows I've been with men, if that's what you're really asking. Not that it's any of your business."

"It's my business if it's something that's going to hurt Steph in the long run. And it's pretty obvious there's still something going on between you and Cyrus. I don't want you breaking Steph's heart over *anyone,* much less an Olympian scumbag."

"He's not—" Blake started indignantly, then his cheeks reddened as he realized how his instant defense sounded. He sighed. "Cyrus isn't a bad sort as long as he's not trying to impress Konstantin, but the only thing left between us is a bunch of regret. When I left the Olympians to join Anderson, I couldn't get Cyrus to come with me."

"But if he had, you two would still be together?"

Blake shook his head. "I'm not gay. Being descended from Eros gives me a lot more flexibility than your average straight guy, but I still have a strong preference for women. It's just . . ." He rubbed his eyes like this conversation was making him tired. "I can't sleep with a woman more than once. I can never have a real relationship with anyone, even Steph. I mean, there's only so long she's going to put up with me. But I don't have the same effect on men."

For the first time ever, I really thought about what it would be like to be in Blake's shoes. If he slept with a woman more than once, she would never be satisfied by a normal lover again. Which was fine, I suppose, if they were both willing to bet her future happiness that they would be together for the rest of her life, but even a starry-eyed optimist would have trouble gambling on that.

"So you can sleep with a guy multiple times without ruining his sex life forevermore?"

Blake nodded. "If I ever want a sexual relationship that lasts more than one night, it has to be with a guy, even if I'm not naturally wired that way. So even if Cyrus had left the Olympians with me, it wouldn't have lasted. Friends-with-benefits gets old when one of you wants more and the other can't give it."

"And Steph knows all this?"

"Cyrus would have dumped me eventually when he got

tired of sex without love, and Steph is going to dump me when she gets tired of love without sex." He looked me square in the eye for the first time since we'd started talking. "It would be nice if you could cut me some slack every once in a while, let me enjoy what I have with Steph for the short time I have it without constantly having to defend myself to you."

I felt sorry for him, I really did. Living with his peculiar set of powers couldn't be easy. But as much compassion as I might have for him, the fact remained that he was not good for Steph. His conscience had so far kept him out of her bed, but I wasn't sure the loneliness inside him was going to give him the strength to let her go in the long run. Which would be all well and good if he and Steph were ready to commit to each other for the rest of Steph's life, but building that kind of relationship would take time. Time they might not have if Blake got too lonely to resist temptation.

And so I did the one thing I could to plant a seed of doubt in Blake's mind, doubt that he really would spend the rest of his life alone if he didn't forget his conscience and bind a woman to him.

"You're still in love with Cyrus," I told him, and I wasn't sure I was making that up. There had been a definite vibe between them every time I'd seen them together, and I didn't think it was all on Cyrus's side, despite what Blake thought.

"I was never in love with him," Blake countered, perhaps a little too fast. "I like him on the rare occasions when he's not acting like an Olympian, but it can never be more than that."

Maybe I was actually doing Blake a favor in my effort to protect Steph. Looking in from the outside, it seemed pretty clear to me that there was something more than friends-with-benefits going on between Blake and Cyrus. And if Blake had hopes that he could build a lasting relationship with someone other than Steph, he'd have a lot easier time letting her go.

"That's not what it looked like from where I stand," I said. "If you could have seen—"

Suddenly snarling, Blake gave my shoulder a push, hard enough to make me stagger but not fall down.

"You don't know what the hell you're talking about!" he spat. "Even if I could fall in love with a man, it wouldn't be Cyrus, not after the things he's done."

To my shock, there was a sheen of tears in Blake's eyes as he turned away from me and stormed through the front door, leaving me standing on the porch in a state of exhausted confusion. And curiosity.

Deciding it was past time for my brain to shut down for the night, I followed Blake's example and entered the house. Blake was nowhere to be seen, which was just as well. I was so tired I didn't want to tackle the stairs and instead spent the remainder of the night—actually, early morning—on the sofa in the den.

EPILOGUE

It's going to take quite a while to sort through all of the fallout from my hunt for Justin Kerner, and I know I'm going to be spending a lot of time second-guessing my decisions.

Jack was infected with the super-rabies and had to go through the same draconian cure that I had. When he revived afterward, there was a shadow in his eyes that didn't belong there, not in eyes that usually sparkled with mischief. As mercurial and capricious as he seemed, he'd been the true hero of that night, making the decision to call Anderson and tell all while we were en route and then jumping to Jamaal's defense when Jamaal zoned out. If it hadn't been for his actions and decisions, we might very well not have lived through that night.

Although Jamaal had been bitten more times than Jack, the bites healed normally, and he showed no signs that he'd been infected. He suspected that this had something to do with his death magic. He can create the tiger now at will, although he has difficulty controlling it—as Logan discovered one time when he interrupted one of Jamaal's self-training sessions. Jamaal reeled the tiger in before it tore Logan's throat out, but just barely. On the plus side, Jamaal's moods are evening out, and he no longer smokes like a chimney in a vain attempt to keep calm.

Leaving town is no longer an option, not with Emma's threat hanging over my head. I can't leave the Glasses and Steph vulnerable to her malice, especially not when she's got the Olympians backing her. Sometimes I feel a kind of guilty gratitude that Fate provided me with a reason to stay.

Konstantin and his cronies are still out there, in hiding somewhere. Right now, Anderson is too devastated about losing Emma to think about what that means, but I know that one day soon, he'll realize that he's now free to attack Konstantin without having to start a war with the Olympians and risk losing his people. How long will it be before he asks me to go on a new manhunt? Hunting Kerner to stop his killing spree was one thing, but hunting a man down for personal vengeance is another. I'm not sure how my conscience will swallow that when the time comes.

And then there are the Olympians themselves. To all appearances, Cyrus is by far a lesser evil than Konstantin. According to Blake, he will put a stop to the most egregious of the Olympians' actions—like killing Descendant children—but that doesn't make him one of the good guys. He still believes in the basic Olympian philosophy, which is that they are the pinnacle of creation and can do whatever they please, unfettered by the morality of mere humans. Blake has warned me to be very careful with Cyrus, who he's sure will want to recruit me as an Olympian just as his father had—but who will do so in a more subtle and insidious manner.

Personally, I'm not worried that Cyrus is going to sweet-talk me into joining him. I don't care how subtle or charming he can be; he's the enemy, and my mind is very clear about that. I just hope that once he realizes I can't be persuaded, he doesn't decide he needs to employ tactics like his father's to change my mind.

My heart—or maybe just my innate pessimism—tells me that eventually, I'm going to be forced to make myself disappear. Even if I somehow manage to make peace with Emma so I don't have to worry about her hurting my family, my power is unique and useful enough that I can't see the Olympians ever giving up hope of getting their claws into me. Hell, even a revenge-crazed madman like Kerner had wanted to bend me to his will. If I stayed out in the open long enough, someone would eventually find a way to crack me, and that was something I could never allow to happen.

But for now, for however long I can, I will stay here with my fellow *Liberi* and bask in the feeling that I almost kind of belong.

For me, that's a big step in the right direction.

PROS
AND CONS

ONE

Playing hide-and-seek is fun when you're a kid. At least, it had always looked like fun to me when the other kids played it. Since my mom had abandoned me in a church when I was four, I'd been shuffled through so many foster homes I never had a chance to make a lot of friends, and the other kids weren't that eager to play with me. I couldn't blame them; considering the attitude I'd had on me, *I* wouldn't have wanted to play with me, either.

Playing hide-and-seek as an adult isn't as much fun, but I was on a mission.

The longer I could dodge Anderson Kane, the leader of our merry band of *Liberi*—immortal descendants of the ancient gods—the longer I could avoid the confrontation I knew was coming. The one where he asked me to hunt his nemesis, Konstantin, who until recently had been the self-styled "king" of the Olympians, a rival group of *Liberi*. I was all for using my power as a descendant of Artemis to serve the common good, and it was hard to argue that the world wouldn't be a better place without Konstantin in it. But revenge killings just aren't my thing. If the best I could do was delay the confrontation, then so be it.

Living in the same mansion with Anderson made it hard for me to avoid him, so I made it my personal mission to be out of the house as much as possible. Which was why I was meeting a potential client at a D.C. coffee bar despite having officially put my business as a private investigator on hiatus. I insisted on thinking of it as temporary, but I knew deep down it could well turn out to be permanent.

Heather Fellowes had not been deterred by the message on my answering machine, which informed callers that I was not accepting new clients for the foreseeable future. She'd left a total of three pleading messages, and since I needed an excuse to get out of the house anyway, I decided I would take her case.

Tracking people down had always been my specialty, even before I'd become a *Liberi* and gained supernatural hunting skills. Skills that were terribly hard to pin down and that I didn't come close to understanding, unfortunately. And since Ms. Fellowes was looking for the father of her child-to-be, it was a cause that was near and dear to my heart, what with my own parentless childhood.

The coffee bar Ms. Fellowes had selected for our meeting was apparently *the* place to be at ten o'clock on a Monday morning. There were people at every table, and the line at the counter was so long people had to scooch over to let me in the door. The roar of the espresso machine coupled with the voices of too many people in too little space made for a noise level that would discourage all but the most determined eavesdroppers.

In short, it was the perfect place to discuss sensitive matters, now that I no longer had my own private office.

All I knew about Ms. Fellowes was that she was a redhead, but I spotted her in about two seconds anyway. She was kind of hard to miss, although my immediate impression was that she was trying to blend in. She was wearing jeans and an un-attractive fleece sweatshirt. He hair was twisted into a messy knot at the back of her head, and she wore little or no makeup, but even so, she was beautiful enough to turn more than one male head. She sat at a tiny corner table, guarding the one free chair and scanning the crowd. Looking for me, no doubt, al-though her eyes passed right over me. I doubted I matched her mental image of what a P.I. should look like. She was prob-ably expecting an intimidating tough chick who could beat bad guys into submission. Instead, she got me, Nikki Glass: an ordinary-looking short chick with delicate bone structure that made me look far more fragile than I was. I wouldn't intimi-date anyone.

I shouldered a couple of people aside and made my way toward the table. When Ms. Fellowes saw me coming toward her, her eyes widened in surprise for just a moment before she gave me a tentative smile and rose to her feet.

"Ms. Fellowes?" I asked.

She firmed up her smile and stood a little straighter as she reached out to shake my hand. "Please, call me Heather."

"All right. And you can call me Nikki." Her hand was ice cold, and even a little clammy, when I shook it.

"Do you want some coffee before we get started?" she asked.

I glanced at the line, which hadn't gotten any shorter in the last five seconds. "No, thanks." Heather already had a half-empty cup in front of her.

She looked relieved that I wasn't going to keep her waiting and quickly sat down and grabbed her cup as if it were a security blanket. She seemed nervous and fidgety, which I guess was understandable under the circumstances.

"Tell me what happened," I prompted her. She had, of course, laid out the basics of her case for me over the phone, but I wanted to hear it all again in person, when I might pick up clues from her facial expressions and body language. "Be as detailed and specific as possible, and don't leave anything out, even if it doesn't seem important to you. Okay?"

Heather grimaced and squirmed in her seat. It didn't take a rocket scientist to guess that the reason she'd ignored the message on my machine was that she'd had a hard time finding a P.I. who would take her case.

"Don't worry," I told her as gently as I could. "I know you don't have a lot of details. Just tell me everything you can remember, and we'll start from there." I pulled a pen and a notepad out of my pocketbook.

She nodded and bit her lip, then swirled her coffee around in her cup and took a sip as if fortifying herself. She sighed and put it down, looking me squarely in the face.

"I went to a bar called Top of the Hill on the first Friday night of December," she said. "I don't usually go out to bars alone, but I'd just broken up with my boyfriend, and I wanted to, you know, take my mind off things."

I nodded at her encouragingly. "Go on."

She cleared her throat. "Well, I met this guy, Doug. He was really hot, and he seemed to like me. We flirted, and I drank a little more than I probably should. We really hit it off, and, uh, I invited him back to my place." Her cheeks pinkened. "We drank more when we got there, and I guess I was really plastered. I swear I'm not the type to fall into bed with a guy on the first date."

I held up my hands. "I'm not the morality police," I assured her.

Heather nodded and started playing with her coffee cup again, her eyes downcast. "When I woke up in the morning, he was gone," she said sadly. "He didn't leave a note or anything. I never got a phone number. Hell, we never even got around to telling each other our last names. I guess we both knew from the beginning that it was a one-night stand. I'm usually really good about using protection, but like I said, I was pretty plastered." She reached down and laid her hand on her belly self-consciously.

It was less than a month since she'd had her little fling, so it sure hadn't taken Heather long to figure out she was knocked up.

"I don't know what I'm going to do," she said in a small, plaintive voice as her eyes shone behind a film of tears. "I can't afford to be a single mom, but the only other option I'd even *consider* is to give my baby up for adoption." Her voice hitched, and she had to take a moment to collect herself before continuing. "Obviously, I don't know a whole lot about Doug. Not even his last name. But he's the father of my baby, and I believe he should have some say in what happens to it."

I leaned back in my chair and eyed her with what I had no

doubt was an expression of skepticism. She sounded sincere, and the expression on her face was one of imploring innocence. Maybe she was telling me nothing but the truth, and she wanted to find Doug out of some sense of moral responsibility. However, I was familiar with Top of the Hill, and it's a decidedly upscale joint. The kind of place where you can't throw a dart without hitting a millionaire. (Well, *I* could, thanks to supernatural aiming skills, but you get my drift.) I suspected Heather wanted to find Doug in hopes that he would be her sugar daddy, but it wasn't my job to make judgments on her motive. If I found Doug for her, and he ended up making generous child-support payments, that was his business.

"So," I said, sidestepping the issue of the white lie I felt fairly certain she was telling me, "what else can you tell me about Doug? The more information you can give me, the more likely I'll be able to find him."

There was a hint of panic in Heather's eyes, and I suspected this was the point where the other private investigators she'd tried to hire had balked. "I can give you a description," she said, "but not much else. We were flirting, not sharing life stories."

No wonder her case had been turned down. How do you track down a man with nothing but a physical description and a first name? A name that could be fake, for all I knew. He wouldn't be the first man to use a phony name when trolling a bar.

"Go ahead and give me the description," I prompted her. "I assume you can tell me more than 'he's hot.'" I gave her a smile and a wink, trying to put her at ease. She forced a returning smile, but she didn't seem any more relaxed. She looked almost scared, like she'd just confessed to some terrible crime and was waiting for the cops to haul her away. It made me wonder about her background. Had she been raised in a really conservative environment? Was she afraid I was going to start stoning her or something?

Heather swallowed hard. "He was about six feet tall. Short

dark hair with a little gray at the temples. Brown eyes." She shook her head. "I know it's not much to go on, but—"

"I knew that from the beginning. How old was he? Approximately?"

"I'd say around forty."

I nodded and scribbled a few notes in my notebook. If Heather was more than twenty-five, I'd be shocked. Forty seemed a little old for her, especially for a one-night stand, but what did I know? "How was he dressed?"

Heather frowned slightly, like that was an odd question. What I was really trying to figure out was whether Doug was the typical Top of the Hill patron. I didn't want to ask flat-out if he looked rich, because Heather might be insulted by the implications of the question.

"He was well dressed," she said, a slight narrowing of her eyes telling me she'd seen through to my real question. "Tailored slacks, a Ralph Lauren shirt. And he had a really nice coat. I think it might have been cashmere."

Bingo. The fact that she'd noticed and remembered these particular details was more evidence that she was looking for a sugar daddy. I found that way more distasteful than her irresponsible one-night stand. I don't get women who want to depend on a man for their livelihood. However, if I only took cases from clients I respected and admired, I'd have been out of business long ago.

"Is there anything else you can remember about him?" I asked. "Was he wearing any jewelry?"

"You mean like a wedding ring?" she asked with a touch of frost, her expression suddenly forbidding.

I shrugged, not wanting to make a big deal out of the issue. "A wedding ring, a class ring, a watch . . . anything."

My matter-of-fact tone—and my refusal to apologize for the implications of my questions—seemed to disarm her, and her expression thawed. She was still awfully fidgety, her fingers moving restlessly from her coffee cup to the plastic stirrer that lay discarded on the table to the extra Splenda packet beside the cup.

"No ring," she told me. "And there wasn't a mark on his ring finger or anything. I wasn't drunk yet when we first met, so I checked." She drew herself up a little straighter in her chair. "I'm not a home wrecker."

I could have told her that I didn't care if she was, but I doubted it would help. She had a chip on her shoulder about this whole affair—no pun intended—and I didn't feel like trying to put her at ease anymore. Instead of saying anything, I merely sat there with my pen poised above my notebook and waited. There were a couple beats of silence. Then Heather realized she wasn't going to get a rise out of me and continued.

"He was wearing a Rolex. A real one, not a knockoff. I swear, that's all I can remember."

Before I'd become *Liberi,* I'd have had severe doubts that I could handle a case like this. When I'd talked to Heather on the phone, she'd told me she'd already asked around about him at the bar and no one had seen him before or since. Other than stopping by Top of the Hill and asking the same questions myself, there wouldn't have been much I could do. Searching for Doug on so little information would have seemed like a waste of my time and Heather's money.

However, now that my powers had awakened, anything was possible.

I would go to Top of the Hill and ask around, and even if no one could give me any information about Doug, it was possible I'd be struck with some kind of hunch or notice some small detail that no normal person would.

I can't say I had high hopes that I'd be able to track down the father of Heather's baby—my powers were way too mercurial for me to put a whole lot of confidence in them—but I did what no other P.I. had been willing to do: I took the case.

Two

Top of the Hill is located in Capitol Hill—hence the name. The decor is classy—or pretentious, depending on your point of view—the clientele upscale, and the drink prices outrageous. I'd been there before a couple of times but only because my adoptive family sometimes ran in elevated circles. I've never had much patience with elevated circles or the people within them.

I hoped I wasn't wearing my attitude on my sleeve when I stepped through the door the following Tuesday night.

Like every bar I've ever set foot in, the place was dimly lit, so my first impression when I stepped through the door was that I'd entered a cave. Tuesday isn't what I generally think of as a happening night at most bars, but Top of the Hill was crowded, the VIPs and wannabes flocking to the place in droves.

Unlike many trendy places, Top of the Hill wasn't designed to lure in twenty-somethings. The club reeked of power and money—things we twenty-somethings don't generally have a lot of—and I'd guess the median age of the patrons was in the mid-thirties. Most of the men had at least some gray at their temples, and many of the women would have had wrinkles if they weren't dipping into the Botox. It struck me that Heather would have looked out of place here, too young and unpolished. Why had she chosen this particular bar to drown her sorrows in after a nasty breakup? If it'd been me, I'd have been looking for somewhere . . . *fun*.

I made my way through the crowd toward the bar, looking all around me as I walked, searching for something that would ping my subconscious radar. Whatever mysterious hunting powers I'd inherited from Artemis functioned on a strictly unconscious level. The harder I tried to look for clues, the less likely I was to actually find them. I'd been overthinking things for as long as I could remember—a hard habit to break.

The music playing was something jazzy and instrumental, and the buzz of conversation was subdued for a bar. People were drinking, but at first blush, at least, no one seemed to be drunk. It made the place seem even stuffier than it was, and I felt like I was intruding on some country-club cocktail party rather than a public watering hole.

If the main room, with its decor of mahogany, crystal, and marble, wasn't exalted enough for you, there were a couple of semiprivate alcoves that, judging by the velvet ropes and bouncers around them, were the VIP areas. There was a crowd of younger folk in one of those alcoves, their voices louder than anyone else's. They'd probably be getting louder as the drinks flowed, and I wondered if that area might be more like a quarantine.

In keeping with the generally staid and stodgy theme of the club, the bartender was in his forties and wore a crisp white shirt that just *dared* drinks to spill on him. He moved with brisk efficiency, not being unfriendly to his customers but not hanging around to chat, either. I ordered a margarita I didn't really want and tried not to wince at the price.

The bartender, whose name tag declared him to be Mike, gave me a polite smile as he served my drink, but he was quick to move on to his next order. He was also the only one on duty behind the bar, and he was clearly overworked. Getting him to hold still for a conversation might be a challenge.

I drank about half of my margarita and fended off two unwanted advances as I angled for a better opportunity to get Mike the bartender to talk. I was just running out of patience when he was finally joined by a second bartender so he could slow down and take a breath. I then got his attention by spilling the rest of my drink. Let's just pretend I did it on purpose.

"I was wondering if I could ask you something," I said, slipping him a more-than-generous tip as he cleaned up the spill.

His eyebrows rose, and he made eye contact briefly before he continued wiping down the bar. "What can I do for you?" he asked.

"I have a friend who met a man here early last month," I said. "She was hoping to get in touch with him, but she only ever got his first name, so—"

The bartender rolled his eyes, and a look of disgust crossed his face. "Is your 'friend' named Heather Fellowes, by any chance?"

Not the most promising start to our conversation. "Actually, yes, she is. I take it you know her."

He tossed the bar rag aside with a little more force than necessary. "Unfortunately. And I've told her ten thousand times, I don't know the guy."

Heather had mentioned that she'd asked around at the bar, but it sounded like she'd made a nuisance of herself. Nothing better than a client who plays amateur detective before hiring you and thereby pisses off anyone who might help.

"I'm sorry to bother you," I said with a smile, hoping to take the edge off his annoyance. "I didn't realize she'd already talked to you."

"Hmph," he snorted, and started to walk away.

I continued on as if I hadn't noticed he was through with our conversation. "I realize you don't know the guy yourself, but might there be someone else who does? Maybe one of the waitresses?"

He looked like he was tempted to keep walking—Heather must have made quite a nuisance of herself—but he relented with a sigh.

"Look," he said in what I'm sure he thought was a reasonable tone, "I remember seeing her with the guy. But she never leaves the bar without some rich older man on her arm, and they all kind of blur together. I doubt I'd be able to pick him out of a lineup, and the same goes for the rest of the staff."

I raised an eyebrow. "So she's a regular here?" That, Heather had *not* mentioned.

His glance darted left and right, like he was looking for an excuse to blow me off. "I'll take another margarita," I told him, pulling a twenty out of my purse. Good thing I'd stopped at the cash machine on the way.

At my unsubtle suggestion that another big tip was on its way, Mike decided the other bartender could handle the heavy lifting and stopped looking like he was going to bolt.

"I wouldn't say she's a regular," he said. "But she's been in here more than once." I might have been imagining things, but I thought there was a hint of pink in his cheeks. "She makes quite an impression, you know?"

I imagined Heather would be a knockout with some makeup and nice clothes. The frumpy look she'd affected the other morning had probably been intended to disarm me.

"I can imagine," I said, sharing a conspiratorial smile. "So she's been here before and left with other men, huh?"

He nodded. "Not that I'm one to judge or anything. But yeah. She's a sucker for the geezers."

The geezer on the stool next to me must have heard that during a lull in his own conversation. The bartender didn't see the dirty look the guy flung his way, and it was just as well. I didn't want him to start editing himself and clam up.

"And Doug was one of those 'geezers'?"

"Nah," the bartender said. "He was younger than her usual fare. But I'm sure he looked like a good catch, if you know what I mean. I don't know why she's so worked up about him, though. It's not like she can't have just about any guy she wants with a snap of her fingers."

So Heather hadn't told him why she was looking for Doug. Not surprising, I suppose. She hadn't seemed comfortable sharing the secret even with me. Certainly she wouldn't be willing to confide in someone who already thought she was some kind of bimbo.

"Who waited on them that night?" I asked, but it seemed Mike had had enough of my questions, no doubt thanks to Heather's previous badgering.

"Take a look around you," he said, grabbing for a clean dishrag. "This is what this place is like on a slow weekday night. On a Friday or Saturday, we'll have twice as many, easy. If you think there's anyone working here who pays that much attention to a customer who isn't a celebrity or a politician, you're nuts. I don't know who the guy was, and no one else does, either. Tell her better luck next time for me. Now, if you'll excuse me, I've got to get back to work."

I had no choice but to let him go. If he hadn't already had his back up, I might have been able to coax some more details out of him, but clearly that wasn't the case tonight.

It was looking like Top of the Hill was a dead end, and finding someone there who knew the identity of Heather's mystery man had been my best hope of tracking him down. I was beginning to think the other P.I.s who'd turned down the case had been right. If the future of an innocent child weren't at stake, I might have decided it was just as well. I try not to be judgmental, but the portrait Mike had painted of Heather wasn't what I'd call a flattering one. My suspicion that she was looking for a sugar daddy was even stronger now, and I couldn't help wondering if this was the first time she'd "forgotten" to use protection.

But whether I liked Heather or not, whether I trusted her motives or not, her baby's future might depend on my ability to track down this Doug person. There would probably be no trouble finding a loving couple to adopt an infant—it wouldn't be like trying to find a home for a troubled four-year-old, I insisted to myself—but having spent so much of my time in the foster-care system, I didn't want to risk sending another child there because of my failure.

Maybe I was letting it get too personal. It was just a case, after all, and the only reason I'd taken it in the first place was to give me an excuse to stay away from the mansion for long periods of time. Even I couldn't be expected to succeed on *every* hunt.

And yet I found myself reluctant to call it a night and go back to the mansion, so I sipped at my margarita and kept scanning the club, looking for something I might have missed, some opportunity that no one but me would recognize.

Like I've said, my power is annoyingly nebulous, and it usually doesn't come out if I'm concentrating too hard. I was way too keyed up to do a good job of picking up subconscious clues, and all I saw was a crowd of rich, powerful people, drinking and mingling.

If it weren't for the margarita nibbling away at the edges of my concentration, I probably never would have noticed the flashes.

The party I'd glimpsed earlier in the VIP area was gaining momentum as the night wore on and the drinks kept coming. The ambient noise level grew progressively louder as those in the main room had to raise their voices to be heard over the partyers. The rousing, painfully off-key rendition of "Happy Birthday" they shouted out had me wishing for earplugs and might well have chased me out of the bar if my eye hadn't suddenly been drawn to the flashing of the cameras as people took photos of the birthday boy.

There was nothing remotely remarkable about people taking pictures, especially not at a party. And yet, beneath the soft buzz of my drink, I felt an odd sort of compulsion in my gut, a need to take another look.

Why would flashing cameras draw my attention like that? The alcohol made my brain a little slower to catch up, but I practically smacked myself in the forehead when it did.

What if that VIP area was rented out to private parties on a regular basis? And what if there had been a party there on the night Heather met Doug? And what if someone at that party had taken pictures? Pictures that just happened to have Heather and Doug in the background?

It sounds like one hell of a stretch, I know. The chances seemed slim that anyone would have caught an image of Doug, and even slimmer that having a picture of him would in any way help me find him. But those flashes had pinged something on my subconscious radar, and I was trying to learn to listen to those pings more faithfully. Besides, it wasn't like I had anything else to go on.

Abandoning my drink, I went off in search of someone who might be able to tell me if anyone had been holding a private party on the first Friday night in December.

THREE

Usually, I'm very good at coaxing information out of people, even stuff they shouldn't share with me. If I weren't any good at that, I'd have had to shut down my business about five minutes after opening. But that Tuesday night, my skills deserted me. I tried talking to Mike the bartender again, this time about the VIP area, thinking he might still have a soft spot for me and my big tips, but he was having none of it. I got just a tad rude at the end, which is why the manager came over and suggested I leave.

It was an ignominious ending to a tedious evening, and I was feeling both surly and a bit embarrassed as I entered my suite at the mansion well after midnight. At least the excursion had served its primary purpose and kept me out of the house when Anderson was most likely to be looking for me.

The only information that I'd been able to get out of Mike before he lost patience with my questions was that the VIP lounge was booked by private parties virtually every night of the week, and the waiting list to book it for a Friday or Saturday night was several months long. I'd pissed him off before I even got around to asking him if I could see who had booked the lounge on the night in question, and after the way I'd botched things tonight, my chances of getting someone at Top of the Hill to talk to me seemed slim at best.

Luckily, I was not the only *Liberi* who worked for Anderson, and I had a house mate who might well make cooperation by the Top of the Hill staff unnecessary.

Leo Huff is a descendant of Hermes, the Greek god of commerce. He's an absolute genius with finance, and his work with stock markets around the world is enough to finance all nine people living in the mansion and then some. Above and beyond his financial wizardry, however, he's also an all-around computer expert and hacker. The guy had accessed police files for me in the past, and I had no doubt he could get into Top of the Hill's computer system. Assuming they kept their bookings on a computer somewhere—which was a damn good assumption, because who actually writes these things down these days?—Leo ought to be able to find out everything I needed to know.

His light was off when I returned to the mansion, so I didn't knock on his door for fear of waking him. Besides, he seemed more comfortable with email communication—he was so focused on his computers and the stock markets that sometimes the rest of us had to remind him to take a break and eat. I wrote him a succinct email, telling him exactly what I wanted to know and sending a link to the bar's website, in case it would help.

I slept in on Wednesday morning—which for me means I woke up at sunrise instead of before. It was early enough that I didn't expect anyone else to be up yet, so I was pleasantly surprised when I settled in on my couch with my laptop and a cup of coffee, meaning to scan my favorite news sites, and discovered I had a response from Leo.

The man is a freaking genius. Not only did he confirm that the lounge had been booked for a bachelorette party on the night in question, but he also had sent me a guest list, complete with names, addresses, and phone numbers.

It was way more than I had asked for, but then it had never occurred to me to ask for a guest list. The club probably needed it so the bouncers could keep out interlopers, but all they would need for that were names. I suspected that Leo had, in that incredibly thorough way of his, looked up each name on the list individually so he could give me contact information. If I could think of a way to repay the favor, I'd have done it in a heartbeat, but I had not yet come close to understanding Leo. I'd just have to owe him one.

Now all I had to do was come up with a way to persuade complete strangers to show me pictures from their party. Telling the truth wasn't an option. Not only would it violate Heather's privacy, but it would also sound terribly far-fetched. I wasn't even sure I could explain to *myself* why finding a photograph with Doug in the background might be important. It felt vaguely ridiculous in the cold light of day; however, one thing I'd learned about my powers is that they're stronger at night, when the moon is out. (As well as being a goddess of the hunt, Artemis is also a moon goddess.) Seeing the flashing cameras had felt important to me last night, and that probably meant it was.

No one was likely to believe I was looking at their photos in search of a complete stranger, so I immediately knew I was going to have to claim I knew Doug. When I reminded myself that the event that night had been a bachelorette party, I knew exactly what pretext I could use to persuade the attendees to let me look at their photos.

I debated whether to do my first round of investigations via the phone or in person. Phone calls would be a hell of a lot faster and more efficient; however, people were more likely to say no to an anonymous voice on the phone. My physical appearance screamed "harmless," and I suspected people would be more likely to feel sorry for me when I spun out my tale if they were forced to look at me while I did. So door-to-door it was.

It made for a long and grueling day behind the wheel. Most of the women from the party had full-time jobs and therefore weren't home. I should have waited until evening to get started, but driving around and knocking on doors all day fulfilled my primary purpose of making myself unavailable to Anderson.

I did find one woman at home who had taken pictures that night, but though she was happy to let me look at them when she heard my story, I saw no sign of Heather or a man who might fit Doug's description. On the upside, she was able to tell me the names of several others who had definitely been taking pictures, so at least she narrowed my search for me.

I had spent more hours than I wanted to count on my day's errand, with little to nothing to show for it. On top of that, I ended up stuck in rush-hour traffic, which would try the patience of the most Zen person in the universe. So I was not in the best of moods when I rang the bell at the Georgetown town house of Katie Radcliff, one of the women I'd been assured had been taking a lot of pictures at the party.

I probably would have been wiser to stop somewhere and have a nice cup of coffee, decompress a bit after the traffic nightmare and my long day. Putting on my friendly, charming face was harder than it should have been, and I hoped I had enough energy for the acting job I was going to have to do.

The peephole darkened, though I hadn't heard any footsteps coming to the door. I lifted my chin a little and tried a tentative smile, projecting an image of small, harmless female. There was a pause and then a barely audible sigh. The door opened.

My immediate thought when I first caught sight of Katie Radcliff was "lawyer." She wore a charcoal-gray skirt suit with a dusty-rose silk blouse. Her hair, which hung loose around her shoulders despite the top part being plastered to her skull by hairspray, rippled with the distinctive kinks of a braid that has been recently undone. On the floor at her feet were a pair of sensible but expensive black pumps and a crumpled pair of pantyhose.

"Can I help you?" she asked, eyeing me warily as if suspecting I was going to try to sell her something.

I gave her another tentative smile and hoped I'd been wrong in my guess that she was a lawyer. Somehow, I didn't see an attorney being overly willing to share personal photos with me. "I hope so," I said, then bit my lip as if nervous. "Caitlin Paulus thought you might be able to." I figured dropping one of her friends' names might take the edge off of her wariness, and I was right. After all, no door-to-door salesman or Jehovah's Witness would know the name of one of her friends.

Katie shivered and opened the door wider. "Oh. Um, please come in," she said. "It's freezing out there."

I was happy to come in from the cold and considered the invitation a good sign. "Thanks," I said as I stepped inside.

Katie closed the door, then turned to me with a look of polite inquiry. "Now, what can I do for you, Ms. . . . ?"

"Glass," I answered, figuring there was no need for a phony name. It wasn't like I was doing anything illegal, after all. "But you can call me Nikki."

She inclined her head. "What can I do for you, Nikki?"

I fidgeted nervously and averted my eyes, slipping into character. I don't know if it was the power suit or something about her facial expression, but my instincts told me Katie was a protective sort, so I tried to make myself seem fragile. "Umm," I hedged, "it's a bit embarrassing and kind of personal." If I could have willed myself to blush, I would have.

In the distance, a kettle started whistling furiously. "I was just going to make a cup of tea," Katie said. "Would you like some?"

A quick glance at her face told me her curiosity was piqued, just as Caitlin's had been. I'm not a big fan of tea, but I'm also not one to pass up an opportunity that plops down onto my lap. "I'd love one, if you wouldn't mind."

"Not at all," she said, smiling warmly. "Come on."

Katie led me to a state-of-the-art kitchen that looked like something you would see in a model home. A pot rack displayed a selection of copper pots hanging over the center island, and a plain white teapot whistled away on the top of the high-tech gas stove. There wasn't a spot or a smudge on anything except the refrigerator, and I doubted Katie turned that stove on for anything more taxing than boiling water. No kitchen that people actually use is that pristine.

Katie pulled a pair of mismatched mugs from one of the cabinets, along with a variety box of herbal teas. I was happy to see mint as one of the choices—mint tea doesn't really taste like tea, and that was a point in its favor. I noticed Katie picked chamomile, and I wondered if that meant she'd had a rough day.

There were a couple of bar stools tucked under the far side of the granite counter, and that's where Katie and I took our cups of tea.

"So what is this embarrassing and personal situation I might be able to help you with?" she asked as we sat. There was a hint of amusement in her tone, but her face was open and friendly.

"This is going to sound a little strange, but bear with me for a moment." I cleared my throat and took a tongue-searing sip of tea, still playing up my nerves. "I have reason to believe my husband is cheating on me." I rubbed at the ring finger of my left hand, as if missing the wedding ring that should have been there.

Katie blinked. "I'm sorry to hear that," she said. Her smile had turned into a puzzled frown, and I imagined she was mystified by the concept that she could help in this particular situation.

"A friend of mine was at this bar called Top of the Hill last month," I continued, "and she told me she saw my husband there with some redhead hanging all over him. If I could get proof of that, it'll be a big help to me in the divorce."

Her eyes widened just a bit in recognition when she heard the name of the bar. I wondered if she was mentally making the connection between her attendance at the bachelorette party and my imaginary cheating snake of a husband. Even if she was, I doubted she could guess what I was going to ask.

"I must admit," she said, tilting her head to the side, "I'm really curious about how I could possibly be of help to you."

"You were at Top of the Hill on the same night my friend spotted my husband," I said.

"I see. And how do you know that?"

I fidgeted with my cup, suddenly feeling a little bad for my subterfuge. I'd only known Katie for about two seconds, but she was warm and friendly, and I liked her. I usually don't mind lying in the line of duty, but this felt more like I was taking advantage of her. It was too late to back out now, and my discomfort over the lie probably made my act even more convincing.

"I hired a private investigator to try to track my husband's movements. The P.I. found out about the party and got a look at the guest list."

Katie's eyes narrowed at the invasion of her privacy, and I figured Top of the Hill was going to get at least one angry phone call tonight. I couldn't feel too bad for them. After all, Leo *had* managed to hack their files . . . never mind that he was good enough to access much more private files than that.

"I'm sorry about that," I hastened to say, wincing. "He went further than I asked him to go. But he said he heard there was a party there that night and that there were a lot of people taking pictures."

The light bulb went on over Katie's head, and she was intrigued enough to forget her annoyance. "Ah. You think your husband might be in one of those pictures."

I shrugged and smiled at her sheepishly. "It's possible. I looked at the photos Caitlin took, and I didn't see him, but she told me *you* took a lot. So I was wondering . . ." I let my voice trail off and looked plaintive.

Katie nodded slowly as she thought things over. I was hoping the opportunity to nail a scumbag husband would be tempting enough that she wouldn't try to delve too deeply into my story. I could improvise more details if I had to, but the simpler I kept things, the better. I also prayed she wasn't the lawyer I'd guessed her to be when I first laid eyes on her, because then she'd be all worried about possible litigation if she provided a photo that nailed said scumbag husband. I'd have said Katie was too friendly to be a lawyer, but that would be a gross generalization.

Finally, she released a breath and shrugged. "What could it hurt?" she asked, and it was exactly the attitude I'd been hoping for. She was, after all, showing me pictures that had been taken in a public setting, not anything private.

She slipped off the bar stool. "Wait here," she told me, and I was happy to oblige.

She came back to the kitchen a couple of minutes later, carrying a digital camera. She'd ditched the suit jacket and run a brush through her hair so that it no longer lay so stiffly against her head. I suspected if I hadn't been waiting for her, she'd have done away with the work clothes altogether and slipped into something more comfortable.

"I don't have any prints," she told me apologetically as she turned on the camera. "I keep meaning to print some, but . . ." She shrugged.

"That's okay," I told her, although finding a picture of Doug and Heather on the camera's tiny screen was going to be a challenge. It would have been easier to look at them on a computer, but maybe she hadn't bothered to download them. If my first examination didn't yield any results, I'd ask her if she would be willing to do that so I could see the photos at a larger size, but it wouldn't hurt to glance through them on the camera.

Katie scrolled to the first of the photos from the party, then handed the camera to me and let me scroll through.

I swear she must have taken five hundred pictures that

night, or at least that was what it felt like as I scrolled through photo after photo of people I didn't know and didn't care about. She was a decent photographer, her subjects filling up most of the screen and not providing a whole lot of background. However, every once in a while, there was a shot from a little larger distance, with more people in the background, and those were the ones I scrutinized heavily, looking for Heather.

I was nearing the end of the photos, my eyes ready to cross from squinting at the tiny lighted screen for too long, when I finally found what I was looking for. In the background of a picture of the bride-to-be opening presents was a tall, stunning redhead. She was barely recognizable as the Heather Fellowes I'd met at the coffee bar. Her hair had been curled and coiffed to perfection, her face could be on an ad for expensive makeup, and the short cocktail dress she wore clung to her every curve and revealed legs a mile long. She was the epitome of the drop-dead-gorgeous single woman hunting for a mate, and I saw what Mike the bartender had meant when he said she could have any man she wanted with a snap of her fingers.

Standing beside Heather, with his arm around her waist and his hand curled around her hip possessively, was a handsome forty-something man who could only be Doug.

"Hey, you've found something?" Katie asked, sounding excited.

I'd felt a thrill of triumph when I'd spotted Heather, but since I was supposedly finding proof that my husband was cheating on me, I tried to look devastated instead of elated. I swallowed hard and nodded.

"That's him," I said, barely whispering.

Katie looked at the picture and winced in sympathy. Heather was a jealous wife's worst nightmare, the kind of woman who would make just about anyone other than a supermodel feel plain and dumpy by comparison.

"I'm sorry," Katie said softly, giving me a gentle pat on the shoulder. "But at least you have some good evidence you can use to nail his ass."

I smiled more broadly than I probably should have in my supposedly devastated state of mind, but I couldn't help it. I liked this woman and wished I hadn't had to tell her so many lies.

"Can I trouble you to email this photo to me?" I asked.

FOUR

I ate dinner in Georgetown, then headed over to the condo I'd refused to give up even though I'd moved into Anderson's mansion. Little by little, my possessions were migrating to the mansion, making it more and more into a home and giving my beloved condo an empty, neglected look. I didn't know if I would ever move back in, but I was determined to at least keep the place clean and in good repair. I managed to kill a couple of hours puttering around before heading back to the mansion.

It was after ten by the time I got there, and I slipped up to my third-floor suite as quickly and quietly as possible. Someone was in the media room watching an action movie with the volume turned up so high the floor vibrated with every explosion, which made a stealthy entrance easy. It looked like I'd managed to avoid Anderson for one more day. I wasn't sure how long I'd be able to keep it up.

The first thing I did after arriving in my suite was to check my email. Sure enough, Katie had sent me the photograph. I downloaded it, then opened it up as big as I could on my relatively small laptop screen, centering the image on Heather and Doug. I cropped that part out and enlarged it even more, and that was when I caught Heather in her first bald-faced lie. It was Doug's left hand that rested on her hip, and I could plainly see that he was wearing a wedding ring.

I leaned back in my chair and scowled at the photo. It was far from the first time I'd ever had a client lie to me, and it wasn't like I hadn't already been harboring some doubts about Heather; however, I most definitely did not like the portrait of her that was beginning to emerge: a femme fatale who trolls upscale bars and leaves with rich older men without regard to their marital status. Maybe she just had a thing for older men, and their wealth had nothing to do with it. But the fact that she'd lied about Doug not being married bothered me. It was possible she did it because she was embarrassed, or she thought I'd be judgmental about it and refuse to take her case. But instinct told me there was more to it than that.

I decided to stick my nose where it most likely didn't belong and did some background research on Heather Fellowes.

As it turned out, Doug's marital status wasn't the only thing Heather had lied to me about.

Heather was twenty-four and lived in a three-bedroom house in a nice neighborhood in Bethesda. A high school dropout, she'd worked at a dizzying array of crap jobs ever since, from housecleaning to waitressing to retail. A couple of those jobs paid a bit more than minimum wage, but they certainly wouldn't provide enough income to buy a house. Figuring it was possible she had financial support from her family, I looked into them, too. Her father had been absent from her life since before she was born, and her mother worked as a housekeeper. There were no rich aunts, uncles, or grandparents I could find, so there seemed to be no legitimate way Heather could afford that house.

A beautiful woman who lived above her means, frequented a posh bar, and made a habit of leaving with rich older men. I couldn't help wondering if money changed hands during these one-night stands of hers, although it seemed to me a pro would *not* get careless about protection as she claimed to have done. Then again, the human capacity to act like idiots sometimes astounds me.

One thing I knew for sure: Heather had lied to me. I wasn't taking another step in the search for Doug until I'd pried the truth out of her.

I figured my next conversation with Heather wouldn't be the kind we'd want to have in public, so I decided to drop in on her unexpectedly at her house on Thursday evening. I'd had to fight off the momentary urge just to call and tell her I was dropping the case. I hadn't liked her all that much in the first place, and the lies and omissions really pissed me off. However, every instinct was telling me there was more to this case than met the eye. Heather seemed desperate to find Doug. I remembered thinking that she seemed scared when I first met her, and that didn't make sense if she was just looking for a sugar daddy. Something wasn't adding up.

When I pulled into the driveway of her house, I was once again struck by the incongruity between her chosen profession—if you could call her parade of crappy jobs a profession—and her standard of living. She wasn't exactly living high off the hog, her house being of moderate size and sporting a postage-stamp-sized lawn, but with her income, she should have been living in some cheap, small apartment in a less-than-ideal neighborhood, maybe with a roommate or two to help foot the bills.

I parked in the driveway, then went to the front door and rang the bell.

The Heather who answered the door was an interesting compromise between the ordinary Jane who'd met me at the coffee bar and the femme fatale from the photograph. She was dressed casually in skinny jeans and a baby-blue hoodie, but her makeup looked like it had been done professionally, as did her hair. From the neck up, she looked like she was ready for a fashion shoot. She blinked her sooty, mascaraed eyelashes in evident surprise at finding me on her doorstep.

"Nikki!" she said. "I wasn't expecting you."

I bit back a caustic remark. "I know," I said with admirable restraint. "But we need to talk. Like, now."

Another dramatic blink, but although batting her eyelashes might win her points with her gentleman callers, it didn't work on me. She wasn't as innocent as she'd have liked me to believe.

"Did you find Doug?" she asked. There was no true hint of hope in her voice. I wasn't yelling at her or being openly rude—yet—but I was sure she'd noticed the stiffness of my body language. She knew I wasn't there with good news.

"May I come in?" I asked, instead of answering.

"Of course." She opened the door wider and smiled at me, but the expression was false, and her voice was tight. She might not know exactly what had brought me to her doorstep, but she wasn't exactly clueless, either.

The interior of Heather's house wouldn't have looked out of place in the home of a corporate mover and shaker. I took in the expensive furniture, the art on the walls, and the Bose home-theater equipment as she guided me to the living room and invited me to take a seat on her plush leather sofa. The lamp on the end table nearest me looked suspiciously like a genuine Tiffany, although I supposed it could be a high-quality knockoff.

Heather sat on the other end of the sofa and folded her hands in her lap. She tried the wide-eyed-innocent look again, but the way her teeth worried at her lower lip was yet more evidence that she suspected the jig was up.

"So . . . what brings you?" she asked with another false smile.

Wordlessly, I pulled the photo I'd printed out of my pocketbook and handed it to her. Her jaw dropped open, and a small, startled gasp escaped her.

"How did you get this?"

"It's a long story." I wasn't in the mood to dazzle her with tales of my brilliance.

"So *have* you found Doug?" she asked as she tried to hand the photo back to me. She didn't seem to know *what* to think now. On the one hand, here I was showing her concrete evidence of progress; on the other hand, I was wearing my surly mood on my sleeve.

I didn't take the picture back. "Why don't you look a little more closely."

She did as I instructed, her brow furrowing as she inspected the photo, but she didn't catch on to what was bothering me.

"Look at his hand on your hip," I told her with thinly veiled annoyance.

A soft little "oh" escaped her lips when she finally understood. She licked her lips and averted her gaze. This time, when she handed the photo back, I took it.

"You told me he wasn't wearing a ring," I said, just to hammer home the point.

She winced and flashed me a look that was half-guilty, half-sheepish. But there was something else behind it, something that looked like alarm, maybe even fear.

"I'm sorry," she said. "I was ashamed of myself for hooking up with a married man. I didn't want you to know." Her hands were still folded in her lap, but I could see the tension in her fingers. Her knuckles were turning white with how hard she was clenching those fingers together.

I'll admit, I can see why someone might want to conceal the fact that she'd had a one-night stand with a man she knew was married. But this same woman had admitted she'd had a one-night stand with some guy she'd met in a bar when she was drunk, and she'd admitted she was pregnant. Something about this whole scenario wasn't right, and I was determined to find out what it was.

"I don't work for clients who lie to me," I lied, just to see how she would respond. "Good luck finding someone else to take this case." I started to rise, and Heather leapt to her feet so fast she practically knocked the coffee table over. Her face had drained of color, and her eyes were wide with what looked an awful lot like fear.

"Oh, *please* don't quit," she begged, grabbing hold of my arm. Even through the fabric of my sleeve, I could feel how cold her hand was. "I'm sorry I lied to you. I was afraid you'd turn me down if you knew, and I didn't think it would hurt to keep that one little detail to myself."

One little detail, my ass. Her face was still a bloodless white, and there was a sheen of perspiration on her upper lip. If Doug's marital status was the only little detail she'd left out, I was Captain Kangaroo.

"What are you so afraid of, Heather?" I asked. I was frankly mystified by her reactions, by her apparent desperation.

Heather let go of my arm and forced a laugh that, rather than making her seem more at ease, as she wanted, made her seem that much more nervous. "You're my best hope of finding Doug," she said, talking a little too fast. "No one else would even take the case, and you not only took it but somehow found a photo of him. I couldn't bear it if you dropped the case because of a stupid white lie."

If this was her bid to make me think she wasn't afraid, it had exactly the opposite effect. She practically vibrated with fear and desperation. I didn't know why she wanted to find Doug, but it wasn't because she wanted to find the father of her child-to-be. It wasn't even because she wanted a sugar daddy. I have to admit, as pissed as I was, I was also intrigued.

"If you want me to keep looking for Doug, then you're going to have to tell me the truth, the whole truth, and nothing but the truth," I warned her. "Whatever it is you're hiding may be the one big clue I need to track him down."

"I've told you the whole truth," she protested weakly.

I shrugged. "Fine. If that's the way you want to play it." I turned for the door but wasn't surprised when Heather grabbed my arm again.

"Wait!" she cried. "Please!"

There was a shimmer of tears in her eyes, and I felt the tremor in the hand on my arm. Heather wasn't just afraid; she was *terrified*.

"Tell me the truth," I said implacably. I couldn't help feeling sorry for her when she was so scared, but I wasn't about to let it show in my voice.

She licked her lips, and I saw there was almost no lipstick left on them. "If I tell you something confidentially, can I be sure you won't repeat it to anyone?"

The question connected a few dots for me, whether she meant it to or not. "You mean if you tell me you've done something illegal, will I go to the police?"

She winced and nodded. "You have to promise not to."

Actually, under the circumstances, I didn't have to make any promises whatsoever. Any idiot could see she wasn't in a strong bargaining position, and if I threatened to walk away again, she'd start talking. But she was obviously in some kind of trouble, and I was beginning to feel a bit like a bully.

"Unless you tell me you murdered somebody, I promise not to go to the police," I said, relenting. Heather's face lit with hope, and I held up my hand to keep her from getting carried away by it. "Now, if the police were to question me for some reason, there's nothing like attorney-client privilege protecting our conversation, and I'm not about to lie for you."

For a moment, I thought she was going to argue, but she thought better of it. Eyes still swimming with tears that so far she had not let fall, she nodded and sank back down onto the sofa.

"All right," she whispered, as I, too, returned to my seat. "I'll tell you the whole, ugly story." She clasped her hands together in her lap again, and she stared at those hands instead of looking at me as she began haltingly.

"I grew up really poor," she said, and I refrained from telling her I already knew that. "My father left my mother when she was pregnant with me, and she had a real hard time as a single mom. She did her best, and she worked real hard, but . . ." She gave a shrug that was supposed to look careless. "Whatever. It's the past. But I just . . . wanted you to have some idea where I was coming from."

Heather risked a look at me, and I tried to look encouraging despite my natural inclination to cry foul. Growing up poor was not an excuse for whatever it was she was going to confess. It was nothing but a rationalization.

She unfolded her hands and wiped them on her jeans. "Men have been hitting on me since I was about fifteen. It was kind of flattering sometimes, but it got old fast, and some of the men were just gross. Married guys, arrogant pricks, men old enough to be my father—or even my *grand*father—all thought I was fair game."

If she thought I was going to feel sorry for her because she was pretty, she was sorely mistaken. My adoptive sister, Steph, is drop-dead gorgeous and rich to boot. Men hit on her for all the wrong reasons all the time. Yeah, it's annoying, but as hardships go, it's not exactly tragic.

Heather cleared her throat. She began fidgeting with a loose thread on the seam of her jeans, then seemed to notice herself doing it and hurried to clasp her hands together again. No doubt about it, she was a nervous fidgeter.

"A couple of years ago, I decided I was going to stop being annoyed about it and use it to my advantage." Her voice died out, and one of the tears she'd been suppressing finally leaked from the corner of her eye. She swiped it away with annoyance, but she didn't start talking again.

"You started accepting money for your services," I said, hoping to make the confession a bit easier for her.

Heather's eyes widened, and she recoiled. "No! I'm not a prostitute!" Her cheeks reddened with embarrassment.

I held up my hands. "I wouldn't judge you if you were," I said, wishing I'd kept my mouth shut. "But please, go ahead and tell me how you took advantage of the guys who hit on you."

She looked like she wanted to protest her innocence some more. I imagined most women who weren't hookers would be mortally offended by my suggestion, but Heather struck me as being more defensive than most, almost desperately so. She might not get paid for sleeping with these men, but something about her interactions with them felt to her like a form of prostitution, one she wished mightily to deny.

She let out her breath—and her protests—on a whoosh of air, then raised her chin. The tension in her neck and shoulders told me how unhappy she was about admitting whatever she was about to say.

"I figured if married men were so all-fired eager to cheat on their wives just because they saw an attractive woman, then they deserved to be punished for it."

"Uh-oh," I said under my breath as the puzzle pieces snapped together in my brain. "You've been blackmailing them," I said, swiveling my head to look pointedly at her expensive theater system, at the art, at the lamp that may or may not have been genuine Tiffany. "And somehow, this time it's gone terribly wrong."

Heather squirmed in her seat and grimaced. "You could say that," she murmured.

"Tell me what happened."

She huffed out a deep sigh. "The men I pick are always super-rich, and I always ask for a small amount of money. I want it to be way easier for them to pay me off than to make a big deal about things. They get angry, and they sometimes make threats, but in the end, they always pay."

"Why do I get the feeling there's an exception to that rule?"

Heather ignored my interruption. "Early last year, I hooked up with this guy named Wayne Fowler. He seemed like just my type. Expensive suit, flashy watch, designer shoes . . . and a wedding band. We, uh, hit it off, and I took him back to the hotel room I'd rented for the night. I like to pretend I'm from out of town—it makes it easier for the men to tell themselves their wives will never find out. I had set up a hidden video camera and recorded everything. Then, the next day, I called him." She shivered suddenly and wrapped her arms around herself. Her eyes glazed over as she temporarily lost herself in the memory.

"I'd made so many phone calls like that before . . . I thought I was prepared for anything, but . . ." She shivered again, shaking her head and dragging herself back into the present. "I told you other guys made threats when I contacted them, but they were threatening to call the police, and I never really believed they would do it. For them, it wasn't worth taking the risk of their wives finding out. But for Wayne . . . it's not the police he threatened me with." She swallowed hard. "He told me in detail everything he would do to me if that video was ever made public. And he meant every word he said, Nikki, I *know* he did."

Her face was pale, and her hands were shaking ever so slightly. Whether Wayne Fowler meant to follow through on any of his threats or not, *Heather* was convinced he would. However . . . "What does this have to do with Doug?"

"Wayne told me the only reason he didn't kill me then and there was that the video might come out once I was dead. He told me I'd better hope nothing ever happened to that video, or he'd have the green light to do whatever he wanted." She wiped her still-shaking hands on her jeans. "When I got off the phone with him, I got real paranoid. I backed up the video files online, but I was afraid Wayne might be able to get to the files there, so I made a couple of copies on USB drives and put them in a safe deposit box." As if unable to help herself, she began fidgeting with the string on her jeans again. "A couple of days later, I came home to find my place completely trashed. Wayne—or someone he hired—went through my house with a fine-tooth comb looking for that video. They destroyed the memory card from my camera. Then they destroyed the computer. And they deleted my online backup files, too. I'm probably really lucky they didn't hang around to wait for me, or maybe I'd have been dead before I could tell Wayne I still had a copy."

Obviously, Heather had done a terrible job choosing her mark. The death threats might have been hyperbole, but the destruction in her house suggested maybe not. It sounded like Wayne was one dangerous dude, and I could see why Heather was sacred. However, I *still* didn't know where Doug came into the equation.

"Months went by with nothing else happening," Heather continued. "I put the safe deposit key in a locket, which I wear twenty-four/seven, just to keep it safe." She pulled a heart-shaped locket out from under her hoodie to show me. "I had to spend a lot of money to repair the damage Wayne's goons did. And I'd never be able to afford the mortgage on this house without some supplemental income. I figured running into Wayne was a once-in-a-lifetime thing, so I started . . . going out again."

I didn't know whether to admire her courage or roll my eyes at her stupidity. You'd think she'd have learned her lesson, and keeping the nice house with all the nice stuff wouldn't do her much good if some guy she picked up turned out to be another Wayne.

"Then, on that day in December, I met Doug at Top of the Hill. He seemed *perfect,* and I even sort of liked him. When I took him back to the hotel room, I was thinking to myself that maybe just this once, I'd let him slide and not use the video. We'd had a couple of drinks at the bar, and we had a couple more back at the hotel. And then . . . nothing." She shook her head. "I woke up the next morning with a hangover from hell. I could tell Doug and I had had sex, but I didn't remember it. I tried checking my video camera, but it seemed we'd knocked it over during the night, and all my footage was of the bottom of the dresser. I spent most of the morning in bed at the hotel, feeling sick as a dog. Eventually, I went to check out, and when I did, I found out my wallet was gone.

"At first, I was pissed off, thinking I'd dropped it or lost it when I was drunk. Then I started really thinking about what had happened the night before and how sick I felt after. I'd never had a blackout like that before, and I'm not a moron. I'm not about to let myself get that drunk when I'm with a guy I just met that night.

"I think he slipped me a roofie, then went through my purse while I was out. He stole my wallet, which was bad. I figured he was some kind of con man and was going to be disappointed to have only scored about twenty bucks. It was a pain in the ass, but I didn't think it was that big a deal. Until about a week later, when I got an angry call from one of the men I'd blackmailed. He was pissed off because some guy had called and demanded *more* money, even though *I'd* promised him I'd only ask once and that I'd destroy the video." She shook her head in despair. "That's when I finally thought to check my locket and found out the key was gone.

"He took the video, Nikki. He must have hired some chick who looked a little like me and given her the ID from my wallet. She went to the bank and opened the safe deposit box. The one thing that was keeping Wayne from killing me is now gone!"

FIVE

I didn't say anything for a while as I processed everything Heather had told me. She sat beside me on the couch and cried softly, covering her face with her hands. I had no doubt that she was genuinely afraid; however, she wasn't exactly a paragon of honesty. I suspected Heather was the kind of woman who could and would summon tears on demand if she thought they would help her get her way. If she thought they were going to soften my heart and make me feel sorry for her, she was sorely mistaken. The woman was a serial blackmailer, and you could argue that she deserved whatever she got now that one of her schemes had gone wrong.

Okay, maybe *you* could argue that, but *I* couldn't. Sure, she was a crook, and if she hadn't been caught with her hand in the cookie jar, so to speak, she wouldn't be the least bit sorry for what she'd done. She'd made it clear that she thought the men she preyed on deserved what she did to them, although how much of that was true conviction and how much was just an attempt to justify her actions to herself I didn't know. However, despite not being a model citizen, she didn't deserve the death penalty, and if there was a chance that Wayne Fowler was as dangerous as Heather thought, then I couldn't not help her.

"You really believe Fowler will kill you if he finds out you don't have the video anymore?" I asked.

Heather nodded vigorously.

"And there's something that makes you think he isn't behind Doug's little escapade?"

She shook her head. "He doesn't work for Wayne. If he worked for Wayne, I either never would have woken up, or I'd have woken up somewhere awful. Besides, if he worked for Wayne, he wouldn't be trying to blackmail my . . . um . . ." She stalled out, searching for a polite term.

"Your marks," I supplied for her, because there *was* no polite term.

She looked for a moment like she was going to object, then thought better of it and hunched her shoulders. "My marks," she agreed meekly. "Doug's been calling them one by one to demand money. Eventually, he's going to call Wayne, if he hasn't already, and Wayne will know I don't have the video anymore. And then Wayne will kill me, and probably Doug, too."

Doug was one hell of an enterprising guy. In fact, he'd played Heather to perfection. Picked her up (or let her think *she* was picking *him* up) at a rich man's watering hole, slipped her a roofie, stolen the safe deposit key from her locket, and taken over her blackmail. He'd even grabbed her wallet, giving him access to her ID while also distracting her from the theft of his real target.

That had not been a crime of opportunity. Doug had known

exactly who Heather was, what she had done, and what to look for. He was a larger, more sophisticated predator, and Heather had had no chance. Of course, if she was right about Fowler, she and Doug both might fall prey to a predator bigger than either of them. I put a thorough investigation of Wayne Fowler on my to-do list.

"I *have* to find Doug," Heather continued. "I have to warn him about Wayne before he makes the same mistake I did. If it's not too late."

I couldn't resist a little snort of amusement. Unlike her besotted marks, I wasn't blinded by her beauty and wouldn't take anything she said at face value. "If you want me to help you, then I suggest you cut the crap. You aren't looking for Doug because you want to warn him. You're looking for him because you want to steal the video back."

"I would have warned him, too," she told me earnestly.

I wasn't sure if I believed anything from her anymore. "Before or after you told him he was going to be the father of your child?"

Her cheeks flushed pink. "I'm sorry I lied about that, but I didn't know if you'd take the case if you knew the truth. I really need your help."

"Have you considered going to the police?"

Heather's face quickly drained of color. "I'd go to jail. And even if Wayne didn't manage to have me killed while I was there, he'd be waiting when I got out. Google his name. If I'd done that before I tried to blackmail him, I'd have steered clear. I *need* to get that video back. It's my only chance. Please help me. I'll pay double your fee. Triple! Whatever you want."

I held up my hand to stave off her pleas. There had never really been any chance I would wash my hands of her when she could be in mortal danger. "I'll keep looking for Doug, and I won't charge you extra for it."

Her shoulders sagged in relief.

"The good news," I told her, "is that Doug didn't just pick

on you out of nowhere. If he hadn't been specifically targeting you, he'd never have known to look in your locket for the key, nor would he have known where the box was."

"But how could he know any of that anyway? It's not like I go around shouting it out to the world."

"I don't know what exactly brought you to his attention in the first place, but *something* did. He either knew or suspected what you were up to. And chances are he kept a close eye on you long before he struck." I took another look at the smooth, handsome grifter from the photo. Dressed in cheap clothes, without the fancy watch and wedding ring, maybe with a little five o'clock shadow to roughen his jaw, he'd probably be the kind of man Heather would never deign to notice. How long had he stalked her before swooping in to make the kill?

And then it struck me. Just because *Heather* hadn't noticed her stalker didn't mean no one else around her had. Even scruffed up a bit, he'd turn a woman's eye, if she was looking for something other than a rich mark to victimize. No one at Top of the Hill seemed to know who he was, but that didn't necessarily have to be a dead end.

"I'm going to go out on a limb and say Top of the Hill isn't your only hunting ground," I said.

Heather gave me a dirty look, having apparently gotten over any hint of embarrassment over her behavior. "It's not the only place I've met men," she confirmed with a defiant lift of her chin.

"Then I'll need a list of every pickup spot you've trolled for the last six months or so. It's highly likely Doug has been at some of the same places, and it's possible someone at one of them will know who he is."

At this point, I had no clue what I was going to do if and when I found Doug. But I'd cross that bridge when I came to it.

I had been in the car for umpteen hours already, and the thought of driving around to a bunch of bars that were scattered throughout the D.C. metro area was spectacularly unappealing. Heather had cast her net wide, which I supposed made good business sense for a blackmailer but wasn't exactly a picnic for me. I could have been satisfied with my day's work already—I had, after all, gotten a hell of a lot accomplished—but aside from my desire not to hang around at the mansion, I had a nagging sensation that I didn't have all the time in the world. I hadn't had a chance to research Wayne Fowler yet, but I figured for the time being, my best bet was to assume he was as dangerous as Heather thought.

Unlike a police officer, I couldn't just walk into a bar and start asking questions. Not if I wanted anyone to cooperate with me, that is. And so at each stop, I had to buy an expensive drink and leave a big tip, then hang around for a while sipping at the drink to establish myself as a "real" customer. Having learned my lesson at Top of the Hill, I took no more than one or two sips of my drink in any one place, not letting myself get even a hint of a buzz. While alcohol might lower my inhibitions enough to let my subconscious hunches shine through, I couldn't afford to let my tongue get away from me. Besides, I was driving.

I had no luck at the first two bars I tried. No one at either place even recognized Heather, much less Doug. A bartender and a waitress at the third place recognized Heather, and the waitress thought she might have seen Doug around, but she couldn't be sure, and she didn't know his name.

I hit pay dirt at bar number four, a tiny little place called Farraday's. It was upscale, as were all of Heather's hunting grounds, but it didn't have the pretentious decor and stuffy atmosphere of Top of the Hill. The bartender recognized Heather and knew her by name, and though he didn't recognize Doug, he directed me to the bar's owner, who was apparently the kind of hands-on type who spent more time at her establishment than any two of her employees combined.

Linda Farraday was a friendly-looking forty-something

whose body language screamed confidence and competence. There was a sharp intelligence in her eyes that made me swallow the pretext I'd made up about why I was hunting for Doug. So far, I'd made up a different story at each bar, tailoring the story to my audience, but my instincts suggested that Linda might know bullshit when she heard it.

Of course, I couldn't tell her the truth about why I was looking for Doug, either, so after our initial greeting and handshake, I got right to the point.

"I'm a private investigator," I told her, drawing the now much-handled photo print of Doug and Heather from my pocketbook, "and I'm looking for this man. I have reason to believe he's spent some time at this bar."

Linda took the photo from my hand and put on a pair of reading glasses to examine it. I saw immediate recognition in her eyes, though I was pretty sure she was trying to remain impassive and not give anything away.

"Why are you looking for him?" she asked. "Is he in some kind of trouble?"

I quelled my natural desire to manufacture an explanation. "It's a private matter," I told her instead. "I can't violate my client's confidentiality. I hope you understand."

She gave me a shrewd look over the top of her reading glasses, and though I wasn't sure she'd be willing to talk to me without any explanation, I knew I'd made the right decision in not lying.

Linda stared at me another long moment; then she shrugged. "I can't tell you a whole lot. He's only been in here once that I know of, and if he hadn't been such an asshole, I probably wouldn't remember him at all." She peered at the picture again. "He looked a lot scruffier when he was here, and he wore glasses. I thought he looked like a guy I went to school with, so I tried to talk to him." She made a face. "He acted like I was trying to pick him up instead of reconnect with an old classmate. Like I said, an asshole."

"So, *was* he your old classmate?" Something within me resonated, told me I was on the right track. I tried not to look too eager.

She shrugged again. "He said no. Said he never went to Georgetown." She handed the picture back to me. "Maybe I'm just imagining the resemblance. People change a lot in twenty years, and I never really *knew* the guy. Just had a class with him."

My enthusiasm dimmed, but that was just logic talking, throwing doubts on my gut reaction. "What was his name?" I asked. "This classmate of yours?"

Linda scrunched up her face in thought, but eventually she gave up with a regretful sigh. "I don't remember. I'm not sure I ever knew. He and I didn't exactly run in the same crowd, and he probably skipped more classes than he went to." Her lips curled in a small smile. "But he was a treat to the eyes, and I was a teenager. I noticed the hell out of him. Sorry I can't be more help."

But my gut was telling me she'd helped far more than she knew.

Six

I was both mentally and physically exhausted when I got back to the mansion. I don't know how many total miles I ended up driving that day, except that it was a hell of a lot. And although I now had a good, solid lead, my next step in finding the mysterious Doug required a visit to the Georgetown library, which would have to wait until morning.

The fact that Anderson had taped a note to my door telling me we needed to talk didn't exactly soothe me into sleep. It was somehow more personal—and more invasive—than the voice mails he'd left me, which I'd ignored. Of course, he could just let himself into my room and wait for me there if he was really determined to corner me. The notes and messages told me he was trying to give me at least a little bit of space, but I knew it wouldn't last. Eventually, we would have to talk about his mission to get revenge on Konstantin, and I was going to have to find the courage to refuse. I wanted to think he would take my refusal with grace and acceptance, but unlike the rest of us in this house, Anderson wasn't a *Liberi*. He was an actual *god,* although I was the only one who knew it. Read a few mythology texts, and see how accepting the gods tend to be when a mere mortal says no to them.

As a general rule, I'm not too much of a procrastinator, but the longer I could put off the confrontation with Anderson, the happier—and safer—I would be. As long as he was willing to let me dodge him, I was going to take advantage of the opportunity.

I woke up at five on Friday morning, my body stubbornly programmed to get me up by dawn no matter how late I went to bed. I was still bleary-eyed and sleepy after showering and dressing, and it was way too early to head out to the library, so I hunkered down on my sofa with my laptop and my coffee to do a little research on Wayne Fowler. Maybe Fowler wasn't as bad as Heather thought. Maybe he was really an upstanding guy who just happened to be good at putting the fear of God into people who tried to blackmail him.

At first glance, he seemed respectable enough. A wealthy attorney with a posh Chevy Chase address, an old-money wife, and a pair of children. Photos showed a middle-aged man who was fighting off baldness and had expensive taste in clothes. The thinning hair and the slight paunch the clothes couldn't hide gave him a look of jovial harmlessness, but it didn't take long to see that something not so harmless lurked beneath his facade.

Fowler was best known for working high-profile criminal cases, defending drug lords, murderers, and even professional hit men. He had a frighteningly good track record, so much so that there were rumors of jury tampering, witness intimidation, and bribery. Of course, rumors aren't reality, but there were also two cases he'd tried in which key witnesses turned up dead before they had a chance to testify. As if that weren't bad enough, his first wife, with whom he'd had a rocky relationship at best, had been raped and murdered during a home invasion when he was away on business. He had an airtight alibi, but the wife's family insisted he had hired someone to kill her. The police had never been able to find enough evidence to arrest him, but it wasn't because they didn't believe the family. I could totally see why Heather was so scared.

The law had to presume Fowler was innocent until proven otherwise, but that didn't mean *I* had to. There might not be enough evidence to arrest him for any of the crimes he was suspected of committing, but a man doesn't arouse that level of suspicion without there being at least some kernel of truth. Heather was in danger, and I was the only person who had a legitimate chance of helping her.

I headed out of the house not long after sunrise, slipping away before anyone else was up. It was still too early to hit the library, so I took my laptop to a nearby Starbucks and killed time there, drinking more coffee than was strictly good for me.

I was the first visitor in the library that morning, standing at the ready when the doors opened. Reading about Fowler and his history had ramped up my sense of urgency, and I was eager to get to work.

The librarian directed me to the fifth-floor archives, where there was a complete collection of Georgetown yearbooks. I grabbed the books from what I figured were the most likely years that Doug had graduated—assuming Linda had been right when she thought she recognized him. And assuming he had graduated. Then I sat cross-legged in the aisle and started flipping through the photos of the graduating classes, my photo of Doug on the floor in front of me for easy reference.

The job was tedious as all hell, and I grumbled under my

breath in annoyance that the yearbooks hadn't been digitized and made searchable. I examined photo after photo, trying to find a younger version of Doug's face among all those smiling twenty-somethings. A couple of times, I caught sight of faces that might have been familiar, but when I looked at them more closely, I felt certain they weren't Doug. I'd started out with a stack of three yearbooks, and when none of them yielded results, I pulled down four more. I was getting stiff from sitting on the floor but preferred that to having to tromp back and forth from a more comfortable seat.

After four hours of searching photos with meticulous care, I'd still found no sign of Doug, and it was looking like either Linda had been mistaken, or Doug had never graduated. My morning coffee had worn off, my eyes were dry and burning, and my butt was numb because I was *still* sitting on the floor. I stretched and groaned as I stood to put the latest set of yearbooks back on the shelf. It seemed like a dead end, and yet my instincts had led me here for a reason.

Gritting my teeth, I reached for the first yearbook I'd looked at, planning to go through them all again, but as I was flipping through the book to get to the first page of pictures, something else caught my eye: a list of graduates who had declined to send in pictures for the yearbook. I considered smacking myself in the head for not having thought to check those lists sooner. Douglas isn't the most common name in the world, so if I could compile a list of all the Douglases who hadn't been pictured in the yearbooks, I would probably have a manageable number of names to research.

There were no unpictured graduates with the first name Doug or Douglas in the book I was holding. However, there were two people with the surname Douglas, one Lucy and one Elliott. Obviously, Lucy wasn't a candidate, but I figured I might as well take a chance and look for Elliott.

I hadn't thought to bring my laptop into the library with me, but I did have my phone. I looked up Elliott Douglas from

Georgetown on Facebook and was quickly rewarded with some hits, the first of which showed a lovely thumbnail photo of a man who was unquestionably Heather's Doug.

"Gotcha!" I said under my breath, thinking to myself that con men probably shouldn't put up public Facebook profiles but feeling glad that this one had.

I had found Doug—or at least, I now knew his real name. The question still remained: what was I going to do about it?

Elliott Douglas turned out to have a very . . . colorful history. As far as I could tell, he lived a fairly ordinary middle-class life as a kid, and he'd graduated from Georgetown with the always-useful degree in English. It was after college that his life seemed to have taken a turn. I don't know if he'd gone to college planning to live a respectable life forever after, but that's certainly not the plan he came out with.

He started collecting arrests at the tender age of twenty-one, and he seemed to have made a steady career of it. It was always small stuff—shoplifting, passing bad checks, engaging in various commercial endeavors without a license. No history of violence, and his only convictions were for misdemeanors, for which he'd spent a grand total of one week in prison. The arrests had tapered off over time, and it had now been almost ten years since his last one. I doubted it was because he'd turned over a new leaf—he'd just become a better crook, as demonstrated by his slick operation against Heather.

I tracked down his address with no problem, and I decided that I couldn't make an informed decision about how to proceed until I knew whether Douglas had already contacted Fowler. If he hadn't, all I had to do was get the video back before Fowler ever found out Heather was vulnerable. But when is anything ever that easy?

I wasn't sure what Douglas claimed as his profession on his income taxes—I don't think "full-time con man" is an option—but whatever it was, it apparently paid a lot. Either that, or the

FBI was right behind me, trying to figure out how he could afford to live in a pricey Georgetown town house. If you'd told me the CEO of some Fortune 500 company lived there, I wouldn't have been surprised. It seemed our pal Doug wasn't as concerned about keeping a low profile as Heather was.

If Douglas had held a respectable job, my odds of catching him at home on an early Friday afternoon might have been slim. However, I seriously doubted he actually worked for a living. I climbed his front steps, rang the bell, and crossed my fingers.

Moments later, I heard footsteps approaching, so I put on my best harmless smile. The peephole darkened, and I added a little more wattage to my smile. With his history, I suspected Douglas was leery of strangers on his doorstep, but sometimes being petite can be an advantage. I certainly didn't look like most people's image of a cop.

The door opened, and Elliott Douglas stuck his head in the crack, looking me up and down with naked suspicion in his eyes. He was dressed casually, in expensive jeans and a Polo shirt, but there was no doubt that he was Heather's "Doug."

"Can I help you?" he asked, sounding anything but helpful.

"Maybe," I answered him in a chipper tone that did nothing to disarm him. "But it's more likely I'm going to end up helping *you*." I casually wedged my foot in the door as I pulled the battered photo print out of my purse and held it up for him to see. "We need to talk, and it's probably best to do it inside."

His face lost a little color when he saw the photo. I could almost see him weighing his various options, one of which was no doubt to slam the door in my face, regardless of the minor obstacle of my foot.

"If I were going to call the cops on you," I said, "I'd have done it already."

"It's not the cops I'm worried about," he mumbled. "Open your purse. Let me see."

My hopes that he hadn't yet contacted Wayne Fowler lowered a notch. He looked seriously spooked, and I doubted he made a habit of asking visitors on his doorstep to let him inspect their purses.

I hadn't brought my gun with me, not feeling like I was in any particular danger. I opened my purse as Douglas asked, showing him each compartment. Of course, my purse was full of enough crap that I probably *could* have had a gun under there somewhere, and I certainly could have had one concealed on my person. I wasn't eager to have some guy frisk me, so I tried to stave off the request before he made it.

"I'm gathering you've had a chat with one of Heather's gentleman callers recently," I said. "And it looks like he had about the same effect on you as he did on Heather."

"Who are you?"

I gave him what I hoped was a reassuring smile. "I'm Nikki Glass," I said, holding out my hand for him to shake. He still hadn't invited me inside, but he did shake my hand. "Heather hired me to find you. She was hoping I would before you made an unfortunate phone call, but I guess I'm too late."

Once again, I could see Douglas considering his options. As a con man, his natural inclination would be to deny all wrongdoing and try to charm himself out of trouble. But the pallor of his skin and the frightened look in his eyes told me he knew he was in over his head.

"Let me in," I urged him. "Tell me the whole story, and I'll do what I can to keep both you and Heather safe." Not that I was exactly brimming with plans, mind you, but I was hoping something would come to mind.

Douglas let out a deep breath and opened the door wider. "That might be a neat trick, if you can pull it off," he said under his breath.

The first thing I noticed when I set foot inside Douglas's town house was the large suitcase sitting in the foyer.

"Going somewhere?" I asked him with an arch of my eyebrow as he closed the door behind us.

Douglas rubbed his hands together nervously. "I thought getting out of town for a little while might be a good idea."

I couldn't blame him. However, the things I'd learned about Wayne Fowler made me think running away wasn't going to do a hell of a lot of good. He was not the kind of man to forgive and forget a blackmail attempt, and he had the money, power, and connections to pursue his quarry as long and as far as necessary.

"You tried to blackmail someone who's had witnesses under federal protection murdered," I reminded him. "Getting out of town might delay things, but you'll be looking over your shoulder for the rest of your life."

He swallowed hard. "If you have a better idea, I'm all ears."

"I'm still working on it," I told him, though an inkling of a germ of an idea was beginning to take root. "If you tell me everything you know, and I pair that with everything I know from Heather, and everything I learned on my own, I might be able to work something out."

Douglas was unnerved enough that my lukewarm assurances were enough to get him talking.

SEVEN

I spent a good two and a half to three hours interviewing Douglas, though to tell you the truth, nothing I learned from him was terribly useful as anything other than background information. Turned out he had glommed onto Heather when she started blackmailing a guy Douglas was already working some convoluted scam on. Douglas quickly saw a chance to make a big score without having to do a whole lot of work, since Heather had already done the hard part for him. Not only was he a blackmailer, but he was a *lazy* blackmailer.

If Douglas *hadn't* been so lazy, if he'd done more than the most cursory research into Heather's victims, he'd have avoided Wayne Fowler like the plague. I suppose the same could be said of Heather, although at least she'd met him personally. Some of the baddest bad guys out there have the most charming personalities—the better to lull their victims into a false sense of security.

By the time I left Douglas's town house, I knew there were only two ways to keep Fowler from coming after Heather and Douglas. The first and easiest way was to kill him, but I'm not a murderer, so that option was firmly off the table. The second way was to set him up for a long, hard fall. The kind that would put him in prison for the rest of his natural life. The setup, however, was going to be something of a bitch to pull off.

In theory, I could use Heather and Doug as bait to lure Fowler in. Set up some kind of a trap, where I could catch him on camera threatening their lives. Unfortunately, there were numerous problems with the idea. Fowler might not come after Heather and Doug himself. He had people for that kind of thing. And even if he did come in person, he might well shoot first and ask questions later. Catching Heather and Doug's murders on camera wouldn't do them a whole lot of good.

I left Douglas's house after securing his promise that he would give me a little time to work out a permanent solution to his problem before he went on the run. The promise of a con man isn't worth a whole lot, but I had to hope he saw that it was in his own best interests to let me handle things. Besides, in the end, I would probably only need one of them to serve as bait.

I stopped by Heather's to give her an update on the situation, and I assured her that I had a plan in the works to hoist Fowler with his own petard. I didn't mention how nebulous and uninspiring that "plan" was so far. Then I arranged a rendezvous with the member of Anderson's merry band I least wanted to spend any amount of time with.

Jack Gillespie is very possibly the most irritating person on the planet. A fact in which he takes great pride, I might add. He's a descendant of Loki, the Norse trickster god, and he thinks he's a laugh a minute. He isn't.

I trusted Jack about as far as I could throw him, and since my supernatural aim doesn't come with a side order of inhuman strength, that isn't very far. However, he is at least nominally one of the good guys, and his powers as a trickster could be key to putting Fowler away without endangering Heather and Doug.

I'd feared that persuading Jack to help me would require a lot of verbal fancy footwork, because he isn't what you'd call a natural altruist. However, when I called and told him I wanted to ask a favor, he asked only one question.

"Will it be fun?"

"Not to any normal person," I said. Jack's idea of fun included pissing off out-of-control death-god descendants, which in my mind made him certifiably nuts.

"Sounds like it's right up my alley, then," he said, ever predictable. He probably wasn't going to like it when he found out my plan involved *avoiding* mortal danger instead of plunging headfirst into it.

Because Jack couldn't wait until we were actually together to start being annoying, he declared that we would meet to discuss the situation at a combination bar and arcade in downtown D.C. I could have avoided the place if I'd been willing to go back to the mansion, but I feared the chances of Anderson catching me there at this hour were too strong. I, of course, had never been to a combination bar and arcade, but I was able to conjure up a pretty vivid—and, it turned out, depressingly accurate—mental picture of what it would be like.

My first impression when I walked in the door was that the space was far too small for its intended purpose. The bar took up a significant chunk of wall space on one side of the room, and the game cabinets against the other walls were crammed in there so close I wondered if people bumped into each other while playing. My second impression was that if you were going to set up a space where you'd be blasting music while various video games bleep, bing, and honk, you'd be better off not choosing a place with interior brick walls and a tile ceiling. The brick was pretty, but the sound echoed and reverberated through the place with headache-inducing volume. Of course, normal people didn't go to arcades for quiet conversation, so maybe it hadn't been a bad choice after all.

It wasn't hard to spot Jack, who had beaten me there. He was hunched over a flashing, blinging pinball machine, hitting the flippers hard and fast, putting his whole body into the effort. It was an impressive display of dexterity, considering he was holding a bottle of beer by its neck in the fingers of his right hand. He didn't look up as I approached, though I was sure he knew I was there.

"You're going to tilt the machine if you're not careful," I said. The ambient noise was loud enough that I practically had to shout. It was going to be a long evening, if the start of it was any indication.

Jack gave me a sidelong glance. "Oh, ye of little faith," he said, taking a moment to swig from his bottle of beer. The pinball took that opportunity to roll through the gap between his flippers. I hoped that meant the game was over and we could go somewhere quieter to talk, but I should have known better. The machine flashed a "game over" message, but that quickly blinked out and was replaced with "free ball."

"Here, hold this," Jack said, thrusting his beer bottle into my hand. Then he pulled back the plunger and sent his "free ball" into play.

I considered pouring the remains of his beer over his head, but he'd probably find that funny. And the bartender would probably get stuck cleaning it up.

"Really, Jack?" I said instead. "We have more money than everyone else in this place combined, and you're too cheap to just feed a few quarters into the machine?" In a lot of ways, Jack is the most powerful of all of Anderson's *Liberi*. Not because he could cheat a pinball machine, but because of the impressive variety of skills he'd revealed over the short time I'd known him. I was pretty sure he could use his powers in more ways than I had yet seen.

"I'd have had to start back at zero if I did that," he answered, not looking at me this time.

Don't let him draw you in, I reminded myself. Arguing with Jack was a pointless endeavor. I bit my tongue and reminded myself to slip a big tip to the bartender when we left to make up for whatever Jack stole.

"So," Jack said, his eyes still on the ball as it careened wildly. "You said on the phone you needed some help setting up a sting. What can I do for you?"

Silly me. I'd thought Jack would stop playing so we could talk.

He didn't turn his attention from the pinball machine once as I told him all about Heather and Doug and their ill-fated blackmail attempts. His lips twitched a couple of times—I suspected he found the idea of Doug running a scam on Heather, who was running a scam on Fowler, amusing—but that was the only indication that he heard a word I said.

He kept right on playing after I'd finished telling him the whole story, saying not a word. I hoped his mind might twist the same way mine had, because I was pretty sure he'd like any plan better if *he* was the one who came up with it. I waited a good minute or two in hopes that he might be thinking things over, but it became quickly obvious that he wanted to force me to do all the talking. Like maybe contributing something to the conversation himself would be too much trouble.

I get that he's descended from a trickster god, but is it *really* necessary for him to be so annoying *all* the time?

I let out a sigh of resignation. "Well?" I prompted, trying to hide my annoyance because I knew he'd enjoy it. "Do you have any brilliant ideas for how I can get Fowler locked away for good without risking getting Heather or Doug killed?"

He waited a little while longer to answer, bouncing the ball repeatedly off of the same bumper, making the same high-pitched dinging noise over and over again until I wanted to do something much more violent with the beer bottle I was holding than simply pouring it over his head. Then, as if he hadn't been focused on the game with such intensity for the past fifteen minutes or so, he took his hands off the buttons and stood up straight, letting the ball roll through and ending his game.

"Why ask for ideas when you already have a plan?" he inquired with one of his cocky smirks.

So much for my attempt to make him think the plan was his idea. I was just going to have to hope he thought it would be fun anyway. *Here goes nothing,* I thought, resisting the urge to cross my fingers.

"My first thought was to use Heather and Doug as bait and try to lure Fowler into doing something incriminating that I could catch on video."

Jack snorted and rolled his eyes. "Oh, brilliant!" he said. "Because this Fowler guy is likely to come after Tweedledum and Tweedledumber personally. It's not like he might, you know, send one of his hit-man buddies to take care of the problem for him."

I gritted my teeth. "I said that was my first thought. Generally, when someone tells you something was their first thought, it means they came up with something better."

"Then maybe they should have skipped right to the something-better part. Just sayin'."

I was letting him get to me, and I knew better. Although if I somehow, miraculously, *didn't* let him get to me, odds were he'd just try harder, so maybe giving in early and often was the key to maintaining my sanity.

"Did you know your ears get red when you're pissed off?" Jack asked, really enjoying himself at my expense.

"Fascinating. My heart rate and blood pressure go up, too. And I start fantasizing about slow and painful ways to kill people. So, now that we've got all that out of the way, how would you like to play the role of Wayne Fowler in the sting I just described?"

One of Jack's gifts from his divine ancestor is the ability to shape-shift. I'd seen him turn into a huge black hellhound, a fluffy white poodle, and a perfect doppelgänger of Konstantin. I doubted he would have any trouble duplicating Fowler.

"Hmm," Jack said, rubbing his chin as he mulled it over. "Not bad. Saves you from having to persuade Fowler to show up in person. And reduces the chances of anyone getting killed."

"We can also be sure you'll say something incriminating enough to put Fowler away."

Jack looked doubtful. "Might be hard to get him put away on words alone. Would you mind if Doug got roughed up a bit? If I physically attack him, it'll be much more convincing to a jury. You can spring out of hiding to save the day before it gets ugly. And don't worry, I won't touch your paying client."

I stared at him long and hard. His logic made perfect sense, but with Jack, I always had the sense that there were layers upon layers of motives. Was it really necessary to use violence, or was Jack merely making the suggestion because he thought it would be more entertaining and dramatic?

"You don't want to set up this elaborate sting and then have him convince a jury he didn't really *mean* it when he threatened to dismember your client," Jack wheedled when I hesitated.

Dammit, he was right. We had to catch Fowler in action, not just talking.

"Fine," I agreed grudgingly. "Just remember, he's human and breakable."

"I'll be very gentle with him," Jack promised with an earnestness I'd have been a fool to believe. "I'll have to pay Fowler a quick visit so I can impersonate him."

I decided not to think about just what kind of mischief Jack might get into during this visit. What I didn't know couldn't hurt me, right? Besides, I had other things to worry about.

"And *I'm* going to have to persuade Doug and Heather to show up for a meeting with a guy they're sure wants to kill them." I had a feeling that was going to be a daunting challenge. Especially when my plan ultimately required they reveal to the police that they'd been attempting to blackmail Fowler. I wondered if I could leave that part out somehow when I explained what I wanted them to do.

"Remind them they might wake up dead someday if they don't put Fowler away," Jack said. "From what you've told me, neither one of them is as smart as they think they are, so you might be able to convince them they could get immunity in return for testifying against him. The authorities already have a hard-on for the guy, so it might sound believable."

Yeah, if Doug and Heather forgot that the authorities would already have a viable witness in me, plus video evidence that probably made *any* witness testimony a bonus rather than a necessity.

Jack must have seen my doubt. "Desperate people don't think things through, and these two are desperate. But let's not give them a lot of time to consider other options. We should do it tonight, after we're sure Fowler has turned in and won't have a good alibi to confuse things."

Despite all my misgivings, I agreed. Having pulled a similar switcheroo with Jack before, I should have known better than to think he'd told me everything that was going on in that twisted mind of his.

EIGHT

Time was of the essence, so Jack and I set up our sting for just after midnight the very same night. Talking Douglas and Heather into playing the bait was every bit as difficult as I'd thought it would be. I told them I'd called Fowler and arranged for them to turn over the video in return for a promise that he would let bygones be bygones. Since no one in their right mind would believe Fowler would actually go for such a deal, I acknowledged that Fowler was more likely to show up with the intention of killing them once he got hold of the video.

Not having enough money to fund herself if she tried to run away and create a new life where Fowler couldn't find her, Heather was desperate enough to take the risk, even if it meant having to confess to her blackmail. Douglas was another matter. He was scared, but he was also an arrogant bastard who thought he was smarter than everyone else, that he was such a good crook he could disappear himself so thoroughly that even Fowler couldn't find him. Of course, I don't know if he'd have been quite so confident if he didn't also believe I could pull off my sting without him. He figured he'd let me and Heather take all the risk. If everything went as planned, he'd be off the hook without any consequences, and if it didn't, he'd go to his Plan B and make a run for it.

He was right that I could have done the sting without him. All I needed was someone to play the helpless victim so Jack could incriminate Fowler both on video and with eyewitnesses. But I wasn't about to let Douglas off so easy. I wanted to save both his life and Heather's, but I also wanted them to pay for their crimes. Maybe they would learn a valuable lesson from this whole nightmare and turn over a new leaf when they got out of jail. So I might have played a little bit dirty. I might have been wearing a wire myself when I talked to Douglas about the plan, and I might have manipulated him into making a number of confessions that could get him in trouble if the police ever got hold of the recording. If that put me in some kind of moral gray area, well . . . I was okay with that.

I arranged for our meeting to take place on a wooded running trail that would see little or no foot traffic late at night. The last thing I wanted was innocent—or not-so-innocent—

bystanders getting in the way and screwing things up. Besides, Heather and Douglas would expect Fowler to meet them somewhere spooky, and a running trail in the middle of the night definitely fit the bill. The spot was just isolated enough to give us a modicum of privacy but not so much that we couldn't park nearby. Best of all, it was outside the D.C. city limits, so I could legally carry my .38 Special. Not that I intended to *use* it, mind you, but it was an important prop for when we sprang the "trap" on "Fowler," and since the police would be hearing all about it, I didn't want to find myself up on firearms violations.

I wanted someone to keep an eye on Douglas in case he had second thoughts, so I took him to Heather's house. I was prepared to intervene in the event that feathers started flying. Luckily, Heather was too scared to do more than call Douglas a few unflattering names, and he seemed to be mortally embarrassed by coming face-to-face with her after what he'd done. I suspected he was used to being long gone before his marks ever knew they'd been conned, and that meant he never had to see the damage he'd caused.

I gave Heather strict instructions to call me if Douglas made a break for it so I could sic the cops on him. Then I did a quick drive-by of Fowler's house to make sure he was alibi-free. A peek into his garage showed me his car was there, and the lights were all off in the house. When Jack had stopped by Fowler's office in the afternoon, he'd learned that Fowler's wife and kids were off visiting her mother, so unless he'd brought some other woman home, he was alone in there, probably asleep.

Satisfied that there would be no one who could truthfully say Fowler had been with them all night, I headed out to the rendezvous point nice and early to set up my surveillance cameras.

You never experience true darkness in the heart of a big city, and there was enough ambient light that, after my eyes adjusted, I could walk without tripping over my own feet. The images my cameras would collect would be darker than opti-mal, but since Jack knew he was being recorded, he'd make sure to position himself in the best light so that the jury would have no trouble identifying Fowler when the prosecution showed them the video. And to make sure we got a good, in-criminating view of his face, I had an industrial-strength flash-light with me that I would shine right at him when we sprang the trap.

When I was sure all my equipment was ready, I hunkered down behind a clump of bushes to wait. I almost laughed to think how perplexed the real Fowler would be when he saw the video from tonight. He would think he was either insane or sleepwalking, or maybe even both.

Heather and Douglas, both wired for sound, showed up right on time. Whatever anger Heather might have felt over being conned, she seemed to have gotten over it. I noticed she was clinging to Douglas's hand as if it were a lifeline. I felt a little bad for terrifying her so badly, but it wasn't like I could tell her she wouldn't have to face the real Fowler tonight.

While Heather looked scared to death, Douglas looked grim and determined. I'd made it very clear that his only choice was to show up, and he was making an appearance even though it went against every one of his con man's instincts. He hunched his shoulders against the chill of the January night, and one hand was tucked into the pocket of his brown leather bomber jacket. He made a slight motion as if to pull his other hand free of Heather's grip—it was pretty nippy out, and he wasn't wearing gloves—but she held on tight, and he relented.

The three of us waited in nervous silence, our breath steam-ing, our extremities freezing. Jack was late, which, considering his determination to be annoying, wasn't much of a surprise. Douglas and Heather became progressively edgier as every minute ticked by. Douglas finally wrested his hand free of Heather's and shoved it into his pocket while she wrapped her arms around herself and shivered. I entertained myself with visions of murder, wishing I had come up with something, *anything,* that didn't involve relying on Jack.

It was almost fifteen minutes after the scheduled rendez-vous, and I was beginning to worry that Douglas and Heather were going to lose their nerve and bolt, when finally a figure appeared at the other end of the trail. He was wearing a dark, full-length coat and a hat tipped over his eyes, and I worried for a moment that he was some stranger stumbling into the middle of our sting. After all, Jack should be trying to make himself as recognizable as possible, not obscuring his face with a hat. Then again, this is Jack we're talking about, and expecting him to be practical was like expecting the sun to set in the east.

Heather and Douglas both noticed Jack at the same time, going visibly tense and stiff as he made his ponderous way toward us, each slow footfall echoing in the quiet of the night. One thing I'll give him: Jack has a flair for the dramatic. His approach was ominous enough to send a chill down my spine. Heather and Douglas were both visibly breathing faster.

He was almost on top of us before Jack finally raised his head enough to let the light hit his face. *Fowler's* face, that is. I'd never seen the man himself in person, but I'd seen enough pictures to know that Jack had managed a convincing likeness.

"Where's the video?" Jack/Fowler growled.

Heather and Douglas looked at each other nervously.

"We don't have it on us right this minute," Douglas said, just as we'd planned. His refusal to turn over the video immediately was supposed to be our fake Fowler's opportunity to start making threats. He would then attack Douglas and try to choke him to death, at which point I would burst out of hiding with my gun drawn and save the day. We'd have video, audio, and eyewitness evidence that Fowler had both threatened and attempted murder. We'd stage an escape so that Jack could shift back into his real form, and then we'd send the police after Fowler.

That was the script I'd written, and for the record, I still think it was a damn good one. We'd have kept the entire transaction entirely within our control, and no one would have been in any danger. Unfortunately, neither Douglas nor Jack seemed inclined to follow my carefully constructed script.

"That's too bad," the fake Fowler said, drawing an enormous handgun from his coat pocket.

Heather took one look at that gun and, quite sensibly, screamed and started running away as fast as her feet could carry her.

"Oh, no, you don't!" Jack shouted, adding a maniacal laugh that if you ask me was over the top. He then fired off three quick shots in Heather's direction. None of them hit her, thank goodness, and she leapt off the path and into the trees, using them for cover.

While Jack was busy shooting at Heather, Douglas ducked for cover behind the nearest tree. Unfortunately, unlike Heather, he didn't run away. For the first time since he'd arrived at the rendezvous, he took his hand out of his jacket pocket, and I saw that he, too, had brought a gun. I had thought of him as a con man and therefore not particularly dangerous. Obviously, I had miscalculated.

"Look out!" I yelled, breaking cover and cursing both men under my breath. Douglas couldn't kill Jack, but our carefully laid-out trap was going to fail if Jack ended up with a gunshot wound. The fact that the real Fowler had no such wound would make it a lot easier for his defense attorney to convince a jury that the man they saw in the grainy nighttime video was not Wayne Fowler, no matter how close the resemblance.

Jack fired off another shot in Heather's direction, then, at my shouted warning, dropped to the ground just as Douglas fired.

"Douglas!" I shouted. "No! Stay behind the tree. Let me take care of this!" I held my gun up so that Douglas could see I had the situation under control. Maybe if Douglas had brought his gun for self-defense, he'd have listened. But it seemed he'd

never truly been on board with my plan and had come prepared to eliminate the Fowler problem in the most final way
possible.

Douglas ignored me and took aim at Jack again. Jack
lurched to his feet and dove toward a clump of bushes on the
far side of the trail just as Douglas fired. The bullet ricocheted
off the pavement about a millimeter from Jack's head.

Jack fired a couple of shots from behind the bushes, then
shifted position so he had a tree between him and Douglas. In
the distance, I heard sirens wailing. We weren't so far off the
beaten path that people wouldn't hear the gunshots. Because
the boys with guns hadn't screwed everything up enough already, and we needed to have the police breathing down our
necks. I glared at Jack, who crouched behind the trunk of his
tree and grinned like an idiot.

Across the path, Douglas was visibly trying to decide between finishing his shootout with "Fowler" and getting the hell
out of Dodge before the police arrived. Jack helped him along
by firing at him yet again, the bullet slamming into the tree
behind Douglas and taking out a fist-sized chunk. At which
point, Douglas decided Heather had made the smart choice
when she ran for it. He plunged into the woods, bobbing and
weaving through the trees, his body hunched over to make a
smaller target. The sirens were much closer now, and I could
see the flashing lights even through the cover of the trees. I
gave Douglas at best a fifty-fifty shot of making it to his car
without being arrested.

Our own chances, however, might not be as good.

Still grinning like a maniac, Jack threw his gun to the
ground between us, getting down on his knees and putting his
hands behind his head.

"Damn," he said, with mock regret. "You got me."

I gaped at him. "What are you doing? We have to get out
of here. Now!"

"I suggest you drop the gun and do exactly what the nice

officers say when they get here," Jack said. "Don't forget to tell them about your video cameras. And remind them that Heather and Douglas were wired for sound."

"You can't let them arrest you!"

Jack raised his eyebrows. "Why not?"

Was this just another one of his jokes? Any moment now, he was going to jump to his feet and start running. Right?

But he just knelt there placidly.

"You'll ruin the whole thing," I said. How could he not understand that? "They'll put you in jail. And they'll take your fingerprints. And they won't be Fowler's prints."

Jack frowned at me. "They won't?" He gasped dramatically and put his hand to his chest. "Oh, my God! You're right! I didn't think of that!" He rolled his eyes and put both hands back on his head.

My understanding of the situation took a disorienting step to the right. "Wait. You *will* have Fowler's prints?"

Even in the darkness, his eyes twinkled with amusement. "I don't do things by half measures, Nikki. That's why I told you earlier I had to meet Fowler. All I had to do was shake his hand so I could get his prints. Now I'm an *exact* duplicate of Wayne Fowler. And I feel an irresistible urge to clear my conscience. I have been a bad, bad man."

I'd have had a few more choice things to say, except at that moment, the police arrived. I dropped my gun and held my hands up before they got anywhere near me, hoping they weren't the kind to shoot first and ask questions later.

"You'll get out before me," Jack said calmly, as if there weren't a herd of adrenaline-pumped police charging our way. "Go to Fowler's house, and wait for me there. And make sure he doesn't leave before I get there."

"How the hell are you planning to get out?" Even if some judge would grant bail in a case like this, it wouldn't happen *tonight*.

Jack just gave me a droll look as the police converged.

NINE

What could possibly be more fun than spending more than three hours at a police station in the wee hours of the morning after having been hauled in from the scene of a gunfight? Paying taxes and having a root canal come to mind.

I told my story in careful detail, hoping the police had been able to get hold of Douglas and Heather so I could have some extra corroboration. The video from my surveillance cameras was likely enough to lend an aura of truth to my account of what had happened, as was my status as a licensed private investigator, but you never can be too sure when gunfire enters the picture.

I made it out without being arrested, although I was lectured more than once about how I should have called the police instead of trying to take on Fowler myself. There were even some grumblings that I might be charged with obstruction of justice, but that was just bluster and intimidation.

By the time I left the station, all I wanted to do was crawl into bed and sleep for a week. I was sorely tempted to leave Jack to his own devices. If he really needed me to go wait for him at Fowler's house, then he should have filled me in on his version of the plan *before* he implemented it. It would serve him right if he had to try to find a cab at four in the morning.

I fought off the temptation, and after picking up my car, I drove to Wayne Fowler's house and parked at the curb. I wished I knew exactly what Jack was up to, though I had some pretty good guesses. He was a trickster, after all, and I doubted this would be the first time he had to engineer an escape after one of his escapades. My guess was that he was planning to make an escape and lead the police straight to Fowler's doorstep. How they would explain to themselves that the man had fled the police only to come back to his own home and go to sleep I didn't know. However, with who knows how many officers having seen "Fowler" at the station, with the mug shots that were no doubt taken, and with the fingerprints that were apparently going to match Fowler's, there was no way he'd be able to convince anyone that the man who'd been arrested and had confessed wasn't him.

It was nearing five o'clock—and I wished I'd brought a thermos of coffee to help me stay awake—when the lights in Fowler's house went on. I cursed under my breath, wishing Jack would hurry up. Our carefully concocted story was going to get a hell of a lot weirder and a lot less believable if other people saw Fowler going about his normal business while he was supposed to be in the process of escaping arrest. I didn't know how the police would explain the discrepancy—they'd probably say the witnesses were lying or mistaken, but that explanation would wear thinner and thinner the more witnesses there were.

I kept glancing at my watch and looking out my windows and mirrors, hoping to see Jack, but no dice. Minutes passed, one after another, and I got progressively more worried. I didn't know what Fowler was doing up at this hour, but my gut told me he wasn't going to lounge around his house until it was time to go to work. He was up early because he had somewhere to be, and I couldn't afford to let him get there.

On the theory that safe was better than sorry, I rolled my car forward until I was blocking Fowler's driveway. Then I let the air out of one of my front tires and began the rather convoluted process of changing the tire on a Mini. I had to read the directions just to figure out where the spare *was*. But it gave me a good excuse to sit there blocking the driveway for a good long time.

I had just pried the front tire off when Fowler's garage door opened. I looked over my shoulder in time to see him shoving a suitcase into the trunk of his BMW. He slammed the trunk shut, and that was when he saw me blocking him in. I hoped he wasn't the Good Samaritan type who would try to help the damsel in distress fix her flat, because it would be . . . awkward if Jack made an appearance in his disguise while Fowler was around.

I needn't have worried.

Scowling fiercely, Fowler stomped down his driveway toward me. I tried giving him a sheepish smile over my shoulder, but he didn't look any less pissed off. Knowing what I knew about him, I casually picked up the socket wrench I'd used to free the spare tire and rose to my feet. I didn't really think he would physically assault me, but at least I was ready to defend myself if he did.

"You are blocking my driveway," he growled at me, as if there were some chance I hadn't noticed.

I gave him the sheepish smile again. "I'm *so* sorry. I tried to make it to the curb." I bit my lip and batted my eyelashes at him. Maybe if I'd looked like Heather, it would have worked, but Fowler was unmoved.

"I need you to move this car *immediately*! I have a very important meeting, and you're going to make me late."

An important meeting at five in the morning? On a Saturday? And for which he needed a freaking suitcase? Yeah, right.

"I'll be out of your way as soon as possible," I assured him.

"Get that damn car out of my way *now*!"

Playing helpless damsel in distress wasn't getting me anywhere, so I dumped the charade and matched his glare with one of my own.

"What do you expect me to do? Pick the car up and move it? If you'd stop yelling at me and leave me alone, I could fix it a lot faster."

"If you're not out of here in ten minutes, you're going to regret it," he said, and he actually shook his finger in my face. He looked at his watch pointedly. "Ten minutes. Got it?"

Wow, what a prince. I clamped my jaws shut to keep my retort contained, because engaging him in an argument was not what I needed. Instead, I nodded my acknowledgment and turned back to my car, keeping an eye on him in my peripheral vision. He glared at me for another minute, then marched up the driveway and slammed back into his house, where it was probably warm and toasty.

My fingers were numb with cold, but I was too clumsy with gloves on so I had to continue bare-handed. I wanted to move slowly so that I could keep Fowler trapped as long as possible, but I also wanted to be able to make a quick getaway if and when Jack ever showed up. Fowler had left his garage door open, and I could hear him opening and closing the door to his house as he looked out to check on me every minute or so. I got the spare tire on, but since I didn't want Fowler to know I was basically done, I stayed on the pavement, blocking his view of the wheel with my body as I pretended to be hard at work.

The faint sound of sirens in the distance made my heart beat a little faster. What were the chances those sirens were coming this way, with Jack only a little way ahead of them?

Fairly good, I decided as the sound came steadily closer. I hurried to tighten everything up and put my tools and flat tire away. If Jack *wasn't* just ahead of a posse, then I would be out of excuses to keep Fowler at home, but I had to chance it.

The sirens were coming ever closer. I was just closing my trunk when a car careened around the corner, the engine roaring as the driver poured on the gas. I grabbed my keys and jumped into the driver's seat. It was hard to tell how far away the sirens were, but I knew Jack was cutting it ridiculously close. The car he was driving—stolen, no doubt—pulled to a shrieking stop by the curb behind me, and Jack leapt out, still in his Fowler disguise.

I started the engine and put my car in drive. At that moment, Fowler stuck his head out, either to check on my progress again or to see what the disturbance was. Jack kept his back to the house as he jumped into the car beside me, and I couldn't tell if there was enough light for Fowler to see his double.

"Drive!" Jack hollered unnecessarily, hunkering down in the passenger seat and quickly shifting out of his disguise.

The adrenaline of the moment made me want to shove the gas pedal to the floor, but I knew better. If the police saw me tearing away at top speed, they'd probably assume Fowler had stolen another car and give chase. If I drove away sedately, they probably wouldn't come after me.

I glanced out my rearview mirror as I started down the road at a leisurely pace. Fowler took a moment to frown at Jack's car, parked so haphazardly by the curb, then shrugged and got into his own, no doubt planning to go about his regularly scheduled business. I don't think it occurred to him for a moment that the police who came tearing around the corner with lights flashing and sirens blaring were there for him. Why would it?

I turned at the first corner I came to, getting out of sight as quickly as possible, as Jack started laughing maniacally and slapping the dashboard in glee. I considered taking out my gun and shooting him somewhere it would really hurt.

"You couldn't have told me what you were planning?" I asked between gritted teeth. I knew arguing with him was a pointless effort, but I couldn't help it.

"And spoil the surprise?" he responded in mock horror, then laughed again. "I wish I could be there to see the cops pick Fowler up. The look on his face must be priceless."

"Were you this much of a dick before you became a *Liberi*?" According to Anderson, the awakening of a *Liberi*'s powers could change them over time. I had no idea how old Jack was, but I supposed it was in the realm of possibility he'd been a decent human being once upon a time.

"Hey, I helped you save those two losers from themselves, didn't I? I didn't have to do that."

For half a second, I almost conceded the point. Then I remembered who I was talking to. "You did it because you thought it would be fun, not because you were being such an upstanding guy."

Jack's eyes glittered in the light from an oncoming car. "Maybe my life before becoming a *Liberi* wasn't a whole lot of fun," he murmured. "Maybe I lived through shit that should have destroyed me, should have made it impossible for me ever to laugh again." He turned to look at me, his face more serious than I had ever seen it. "Maybe I decided that I deserved to enjoy my new life, and maybe you should stop judging me when you know fuck-all about me."

I felt about two inches tall all of a sudden. I had never made much effort to hide my dislike of Jack and his antics—even if they did occasionally surprise a laugh out of me—and I knew absolutely nothing about his life prior to when we met. I sat in awkward silence, trying to frame an apology, when I felt sure an apology was inadequate.

Suddenly, Jack burst out laughing again, turning to face front and shaking his head. "Man, you are such a sucker! I can't believe you swallowed that crock of shit!"

He sounded genuinely amused, his eyes watery with laughter. I don't know what it was about it that rang false, but something did. He was trying to make it seem like he'd been jerking my chain, but I knew in my gut he hadn't been joking.

"Guess I'm just gullible that way," I said, knowing that despite the curiosity his words had aroused, I had to let it go. He'd been serious for as long as he could manage it, which was about sixty seconds. I could try some probing questions, but chances were any answers I got would be pure fiction.

TEN

Jack's plan went off perfectly. Wayne Fowler was in custody, as were Heather and Douglas. The police had video and audio evidence that Fowler had attempted murder, and they had three eyewitnesses who could testify to what Fowler had done. And, most damning of all, they had his signed confession, which Jack told me he "might have embellished a little." Jack had also considerately started claiming he wasn't the man in the video and hadn't signed the confession even before he made his escape, which I'm sure made Fowler's claim of an impostor sound just that much more ridiculous.

All in all, it was about as satisfactory an ending to the case as I could have hoped for. It was theoretically possible that Fowler could still be a danger to Heather and Douglas even from prison. Evidence certainly suggested he had a long reach, as well as connections in low places. But I figured in his current circumstances, he had many more important things to worry about than getting revenge on two petty crooks. Like how to avoid a lethal injection for the murders he'd "confessed" to. My guess was that he was going to cop some kind of insanity plea, seeing as he had no memory of having made the confession.

But in the end, I underestimated Jack once again.

Three days after his arrest, Wayne Fowler was shot to death by an unknown assailant while returning to prison after his arraignment.

I couldn't help confronting Jack once again.

"What, exactly, did Fowler confess to doing while you were him?" I asked. Sure, it was possible Fowler had lots of enemies who had just happened to get to him after his arrest. Maybe some of his "business associates" were worried about what he might say during his time in the penal system. But the speed with which the murder had occurred screamed of an urgency that formless worry wouldn't explain. Jack had "embellished" more than I'd suspected, and he had gotten Fowler killed.

Jack flashed me a fierce and unrepentant grin. "I might have fingered a few of his best clients for a murder or two. It's true that hit men usually don't like it when their lawyers-cum-clients start pointing a finger at them, but I felt that confession was good for Fowler's soul."

What the hell was I supposed to say to that?

"I told you, I don't do things by half measures," Jack continued. "Evidence suggests Fowler has had witnesses killed before. If he thought Douglas or Heather—or you, for that matter—were going to testify against him, he might have had you killed just on principle. That could have been . . . annoying."

"So you set Fowler up to be murdered to protect me, is that what you're saying?"

"Something like that."

I swallowed hard. He was lying, and he wasn't making any attempt to hide it. "Oh, man. You told Anderson what we were up to," I said with a groan. As a general rule, Jack wasn't a big fan of playing by the rules, nor was he fond of being responsible. But he deferred to Anderson in a very un-trickster-like way, and this wasn't the first time he'd tattled on me. I was probably lucky Anderson hadn't yanked me out of bed one night to yell at me for working behind his back.

I shook my head. "Why? Why would you do that?"

"Because that's the deal I have with Anderson. Sticking it to a scumbag like Fowler was fun, but not worth getting kicked out on my ass for."

"And Anderson told you Fowler had to end up dead before it was all over." Being a god of death and vengeance, Anderson was definitely a hanging judge, although that wasn't why he'd ordered Fowler's death. "He didn't want there to be a trial," I said, thinking aloud. "He didn't want Fowler publicly talking about the mysterious, impossible double who showed up at the station in his place. Like that might somehow clue people in to the existence of the *Liberi*. And he didn't want *me* embroiled in a high-profile trial where I would have to testify."

Jack smirked at me. "Welcome to Andersonville, where the Ten Commandments are . . ." He held up one finger. "Thou shalt not draw attention." He held up a second finger. "Thou shalt not draw attention." He held up a third finger. "Thou shalt not—"

"Okay, I got it," I interrupted, because he probably would sit there and say it all ten times for maximum annoyance value.

"And the last but most important one . . ." Jack continued as though I hadn't said anything. "Thou shalt do as I tell you, or thou shalt be very sorry."

I heard the warning loud and clear.

I'd used Jack to help me protect Heather and Douglas, but even so, I'd allowed myself to forget the one simple fact I could never forget again: my life was no longer entirely my own. I was one of Anderson's *Liberi,* and I would always be subject to his will. Better than being captured by the Olympians, and better than having to live the rest of my immortal life on the run, but still . . .

This wasn't a job I could simply quit if I didn't like the management style. And Anderson wasn't the kind of boss who would let his employees' free will get in the way of what he wanted.

The day of reckoning was coming, no matter how hard I tried to avoid it. Soon, Anderson was going to corner me and order me to do something my conscience would not allow.

And when I denied him the revenge he'd been dreaming of for years, I would see once and for all just what kind of boss he really was. God help me.

ROGUE
DESCENDANT

ONE

"It's time, Nikki," Anderson said.

I made a very undignified squealing sound and almost dropped my towel.

"Goddammit, Anderson!" I snapped, my heart pounding. The sun hadn't risen yet, and I was still bleary-eyed even after my shower. I certainly had *not* been expecting to find anyone waiting for me in my bedroom at this hour, especially when I was pretty certain I'd locked the door to my suite. The adrenaline coursing through my veins did more to wake me up than ten cups of coffee.

"Sorry to startle you," he said with an unrepentant smile.

"Like hell you are," I grumbled, clutching my towel a little more securely around me. I knew Anderson well enough by now to know a deliberate intimidation attempt when I saw one. He was at his rumpled, harmless-looking best, in a wrinkled shirt, wash-faded cords, and tattered sneakers, but he was anything but harmless. He was a real, bona fide *god,* the son of Thanatos, the Greek god of death, and Alecto, one of the Furies.

"If you hadn't been so determined to play hard to get," Anderson said mildly, "we could have done this differently."

I'd have preferred not to do this at all, which was why I'd spent the last two weeks making myself scarce, finding any excuse I could to avoid the confrontation I knew was coming. Gods are notoriously bad at taking no for an answer, but it was the only answer I could give to the request he was going to make.

"This wasn't going to go well no matter *how* we did it," I said. He had to know what my avoidance strategy meant, and I knew he'd come prepared for a fight despite his so-far mild manner.

"I'm sorry to hear that," he replied, a slight edge creeping into his voice. "I would have thought you'd be eager to rid the world of a predator like Konstantin."

Ridding the world of Konstantin, the deposed leader of the Olympians, sounded like a great idea, in theory. He was vulnerable now that he no longer had the might of the Olympians behind him, and with my skills as a descendant of Artemis, the Greek goddess of the hunt, I was the perfect candidate to find him in whatever hole he was hiding in. It was what would happen when I found him that gave me problems.

"This isn't something I want to talk about while wearing a towel," I said.

Anderson's eyes strayed downward as he took a visual tour of my body. I wasn't much to look at with my knobby knees and winter-white skin, but guys don't seem to care about aesthetics much when a woman is wearing nothing but a towel. I gritted my teeth and kept my mouth shut, knowing he was only looking at me like that to unsettle me. I wasn't about to let him do it. At least, that's what I told myself.

"Why don't you go wait in the sitting room while I get some clothes on," I suggested. "Then we can talk."

"All right," he agreed. "You aren't going to try climbing out the window to avoid me, are you?"

I might have been tempted if my rooms weren't on the third floor of the mansion that was home base for all of Anderson's *Liberi*. "I'm not in the mood for a broken leg, so no." Of course, breaking a leg might be more fun than whatever was going to come next.

"Don't take too long," Anderson ordered. He strode out my bedroom door and didn't even bother to close it all the way behind him.

I gave the door the kind of glare I really wanted to give to Anderson himself, then stalked to my closet to get some clothes. I didn't want to do this *ever,* much less at the literal crack of dawn and with no coffee in my system. I usually don't have any qualms about defying authority, but Anderson was a different story. Most of the time he seemed like a pretty nice guy, but I knew what lay under the surface, and I didn't want him angry with me if I could avoid it.

Knowing Anderson's patience had more than reached its limit, I pulled my clothes on hastily and toweled my hair dry. I had to at least run a brush through it a few times to smooth out the tangles before they dried that way, and I swear I could *feel* Anderson's impatience from the other room. I looked at myself in the mirror over the sink and saw a delicate, anxious woman with bedraggled hair and a faded T-shirt.

Don't you dare let him browbeat you, I told myself as I tried to wipe that anxious look off my face. I stood a much better chance of holding my ground if I at least *looked* strong and confident.

"Hurry up, Nikki," Anderson called, and I knew I couldn't afford to stand there and make faces at myself in the mirror any longer.

"Well, here goes nothing," I muttered, and left the relative safety of my bedroom to join Anderson in my sitting room.

I gave him a few mental brownie points for having brewed a pot of coffee while he waited. I'd gotten tired of having to go all the way down to the first floor whenever the craving hit me, so I'd brought my own coffeemaker from my condo, which I hadn't relinquished, despite having taken up residence in the mansion. Anderson was sitting on the armchair beside the couch, and there were two steaming mugs on the coffee table.

"Thanks for making coffee," I said, picking up my mug and inhaling the steam. I didn't look at him as I reluctantly lowered myself onto the couch. I harbored a brief hope that he would let me get some coffee into my system before the fun and games began, but I knew better.

Out of the corner of my eye, I saw him lean forward in his chair. I realized I was holding my breath, and forced myself to let it out and take a sip of coffee. I'd dawdled long enough that it didn't burn my tongue.

"I would have thought you'd be chomping at the bit to hunt down Konstantin the moment he was forced to step down," Anderson said. "I don't understand why you've been avoiding it."

"I'm sure it's hard for someone whose mother was a goddess of vengeance to understand," I said, though I knew there were plenty of others who wouldn't have my moral qualms, either.

"How can you not want his blood after what he did to your sister?"

That made me flinch. Konstantin hadn't hurt Steph himself, but there was no doubt his late second-in-command had acted with his blessing, if not on his direct orders. If you'd asked me when I first found Steph if I wanted Konstantin dead, I'd have answered with a resounding yes. Even now, I would be happy to dance on his grave. But there was a difference between wanting a man dead and taking it upon yourself to make him that way. If I hunted Konstantin and found him, then Anderson, who had even more of a score to settle than I did, would kill him. I'd seen Anderson kill before, and the screams still echoed in my dreams sometimes. Death at Anderson's hand was neither quick nor painless.

I fidgeted with my coffee cup and avoided Anderson's gaze. "I've told you before I'm a bleeding heart. I'm not the kind of person who can cold-bloodedly hunt someone down so you can murder him."

"You had no qualms about hunting Justin Kerner," he retorted.

But he was wrong about that. I'd had plenty of qualms. Kerner was a serial killer, but he was a victim before that. An ordinary man with an ordinary life who'd been captured by the Olympians and used as a lab rat, forced to take on a seed of immortality that the Olympians suspected might be infected with madness. When Kerner had gone mad, they'd buried him, meaning to leave him in the ground, constantly dying and re-viving, till the end of time. He'd been killing civilians. But I'd felt sympathy for him the whole time.

"I hunted Kerner because he had to be stopped before he killed more innocent people," I said, then again met Anderson's eyes. "You want me to hunt Konstantin for revenge. That's an altogether different beast."

"For *justice,*" Anderson corrected sharply. "He can't be tried in a court of law. There is no way to make him account-able for his crimes. Unless we do it ourselves. You know that."

"Yeah, I know. But I'm not a freaking hit man!"

Anderson's gaze was hot enough to burn, and the muscles in his jaw and throat stood out in stark relief. "I'm not asking you to kill him. I'm asking you to *find* him."

Usually, Anderson looks mild mannered and relaxed. The kind of man you'd pass in the street without a second glance. Certainly not someone you'd be afraid of. But that's just his human disguise, and sometimes when he's with me, he lets the disguise slip. Like right now, when pinpricks of white light ap-peared in the center of his pupils.

I won't say I wasn't intimidated. I'd seen what Anderson could do, and though I liked to think of him as something of a friend, I knew he didn't have some of the boundaries human beings do. I was pretty sure he would hurt me if he got mad enough. But I was not a murderer, and I wasn't going to let him turn me into one.

I put my coffee cup down, as if freeing my hands to defend myself would really help. My mouth had gone dry with nerves, and I couldn't bear to meet his eyes and see that glow. It was hard to feel like I was drawing a firm line in the sand while not meet-ing his eyes, but I hoped he'd hear the conviction in my words.

"You sound just like Konstantin," I told him. "Remem-ber? He asked me to hunt 'fugitives' for the Olympians and basically told me I shouldn't feel bad about doing it because I wouldn't be the one actually killing the people I found." In truth, there'd been no *asking* involved. The Olympians were on a mission to destroy all mortal Descendants—the only people capable of killing *Liberi,* at least as far as they knew—and they thought having a descendant of Artemis on their payroll would make their mission a lot easier. I was pretty sure that under the supposedly kinder, gentler leadership of Cyrus, they still had the same goal in mind, and still would love to recruit me by hook or by crook.

"If I hunt someone down knowing that person is going to be killed, then I'm a murderer, whether I do the deed myself or not," I argued. "I'm not a murderer."

"You were willing to hunt Kerner down, and you were *hoping* I would kill him!"

Since the alternative had been to bury him alive for all eternity, yes, I had indeed hoped Anderson would kill him. But as a mercy, not as a punishment. I was pretty sure he was being willfully obtuse, but I restated my point anyway.

"I hunted Kerner because it was the only way to stop him from killing innocents. Not because I hated his guts and wanted revenge."

"And you think Konstantin won't kill innocents if he's allowed to live?"

I understood why Anderson wanted me to do this. Really I did. I could even acknowledge that he had a point. Konstantin had raped, tortured, and killed countless innocents in the centuries he'd been alive, and there was no reason to believe he would mend his ways now. Anderson would probably want to kill him even if Konstantin *hadn't* kidnapped Emma, Anderson's now-estranged wife, and chained her at the bottom of a pond to drown and revive for almost ten years. But we'd both be doing it as revenge for what Konstantin had done to our loved ones, not for any great and noble cause, and that would make me a murderer in my own eyes.

"Whatever I do, I'm going to have to live with it for the rest of my life," I said, and with an impressive effort of will managed to meet Anderson's gaze once more. The glow in his eyes had widened, the anger on his face inhuman in its intensity, but I didn't let myself look away. "Unless you're planning to kill me for saying no to you, I'm likely to have a very, very long life. And a revenge killing is something I don't want to have on my conscience."

"You don't think Steph deserves vengeance?" There was both contempt and surprise in his voice, along with the anger. Yes, there was a good reason I'd been avoiding this conversation.

"She wouldn't want me to do this," I answered. "She didn't even want me to kill Alexis." Not that I was capable of killing a fellow *Liberi* myself, but I'd been trying to dream up a scheme to *get* him killed when Steph put the kibosh on it. "She wanted him dead," I clarified at Anderson's incredulous look. "But she didn't want *me* to be involved." *I want Alexis to pay for what he did,* she'd said, *but not at the price of putting a black mark on your soul.* She was the best big sister I ever could have hoped for.

Anderson slowly rose from his chair. I rose just as slowly, my heart pounding, my breaths shallow. My lizard brain really wanted me to get the hell out of there, away from the dangerous predator that was Anderson, but I forced myself to stay rooted in place.

"I *need* you to do this for me," he said in a low growl that resonated strangely in his chest. He slowly raised his hand, threatening me with what I had dubbed his Hand of Doom. It wasn't glowing, which is what it did when he was about to kill someone, but I didn't much want him to touch me, either. I'd seen him use that hand against Jamaal. He'd been able to make the big, tough death-goddess descendant scream in pain with nothing more than a touch. I did *not* want to know how bad it had to hurt to accomplish that.

"If your plan is to torture me until I agree to do what you want, then you really *are* no better than Konstantin," I said. My voice shook a little, and I was sure my eyes were wide and frightened looking. Under ordinary circumstances, I wouldn't expect him to follow through with his threat, because I believed he was one of the good guys. But he'd never been able to see straight about anything involving Emma, and I was standing between him and his longed-for revenge. It took every scrap of courage I could gather not to run screaming from the room.

We stood there like that—Anderson's eyes glowing, his hand halfway extended toward me while I quaked in my boots—for what felt like forever.

Then Anderson let out a whoosh of breath. His hand fell back to his side, and the glow receded from his eyes. There was still a wealth of tension in his body language and a hint of menace in his facial expression, but at least he looked short of murderous. It seemed like I'd won round one of our game of chicken.

"This isn't over," he told me. "But I guess we have to wait until Konstantin kills someone else before you can feel righteous about hunting him. Don't worry. I doubt it will take long."

He was still so angry I didn't dare move, and I didn't think any response was required. So I stood there like a statue as he stalked out of my sitting room and slammed the door behind him.

Two

Having survived my verbal skirmish with Anderson, I supposed I no longer needed to work so hard at avoiding him. However, I'd already made a couple of appointments for the day to keep myself out of the house, and I saw no reason to break them. Funny how being turned into an immortal huntress and moving into a huge mansion owned by a god didn't make the mundane cares of the world go away. I still had to go to the post office, and go grocery shopping, and get my hair cut. Ah, the glamour of it all.

The problem was the *Liberi* had a way of intruding on even the most mundane aspects of my life. After my haircut, I stopped by my favorite little French bistro to have a leisurely lunch while indulging in some people-watching from my seat in front of the generous picture window.

I'd been expecting to watch strangers, but before I'd even had a chance to place my order, I saw someone I knew crossing the street, headed my way.

Cyrus, the current leader of the Olympians, was Konstantin's son, and you could see the resemblance in his olive-hued skin and coarse black curls. Cyrus, however, gave off the vibe of being an approachable human being, unlike his father, who looked exactly like you'd expect someone who calls himself a king to look. I'd met Cyrus a few times now, and he seemed like a friendly, personable kind of guy. If he weren't an Olympian, I might almost say I liked him. But he *was* an Olympian, and he believed in a world order that was anathema to me.

I hoped that Cyrus just happened to be passing by, his presence nothing but a coincidence. Too bad I don't believe in coincidence.

Cyrus finished crossing the street, obviously not caring about the indignant drivers who were honking at him. He smiled and waved at me through the window and made a beeline for the bistro's door. So much for my plans for a quiet, uncomplicated lunch.

Either assuming he was welcome or not caring if he wasn't, Cyrus plunked himself down on the seat across from me.

"Mind if I join you?" he asked with a charming smile.

"If I told you I minded, would you leave?"

Why I bothered to ask the question, I don't know. Cyrus gave me a mock-reproachful look and helped himself to my menu. I considered getting up and walking away, but as I said, Cyrus is likable enough, and I harbored more than my fair share of curiosity about him. For one thing, I knew he and Steph's . . . Well, I didn't quite know what to call Blake. Boyfriend, I guess, although as far as I knew, they weren't sleeping together. Blake, being a descendant of Eros, is apparently such a supernaturally good lover that any woman he sleeps with more than once will never be satisfied with another man. Anyway, it seemed that Blake's unfortunate ability didn't have the same effect on men, so he and Cyrus had hooked up in the past. Having seen the two of them interact before, I wasn't sure how mutual—or how permanent—the breakup had been. Blake had described their former relationship as "friends with benefits," but I suspected there was more to it than that. If there was any chance Cyrus would play a continuing role in Blake's life, Steph had a right to know, and I figured I could try to work in a pointed question or two.

The waitress came over to take our orders. I guessed Cyrus was staying for lunch, since he ordered a *croque monsieur,* which is a fancy name for a grilled ham and cheese sandwich. I'd gone for a light soup-and-salad combo, resisting the temptation of all that butter and cheese. I felt virtuous and deprived at the same time.

"So to what do I owe the dubious pleasure of your company?" I inquired as soon as the waitress had retreated.

"Dubious pleasure?" He put a hand on his chest as if it hurt. "Why, you wound me." He'd have looked a lot more wounded without the glint of humor in his eyes.

If he weren't the leader of a bunch of rapists and murderers, I might have let myself relax and be charmed. I certainly liked his pleasant, easygoing demeanor a lot better than I'd liked that of any other Olympian I'd met. Which made it even more imperative that I keep reminding myself what he was. It would be easy to become unguarded with him, and that would be a very bad mistake.

"Look, I'm not making a big scene here because I refuse to let you chase me out of my favorite restaurant and because I know I can't get you to leave. That doesn't mean we're friends, and that doesn't mean I actually want you here."

Cyrus's grin faded, but there was no hint that my admittedly rude pronouncement had annoyed him.

"Sorry," he said, and he sounded like he actually meant it. "I'm a dyed-in-the-wool wiseass and I couldn't resist teasing you. But that was overly familiar of me."

Yes, it was. But his admission made me like him better.

"I know we're not friends," he continued, "and considering our . . . differences, I don't suppose we ever will be. But that doesn't mean we have to be enemies."

I frowned at that. "I'm not sure what you're getting at. Assuming you're actually getting at something."

"You're ruining my soliloquy," he said in mock annoyance, then shook his head and made a face. "I told you, dyed-in-the-wool. I'll just issue a blanket apology now and hope it'll cover our entire conversation. Konstantin did his best to beat the wiseassery out of me when I was growing up, but it never took."

It was no surprise to hear that Konstantin physically abused his kid. From what Anderson had told me, Cyrus was Konstantin's only *surviving* child, but there had been others. Others he'd distrusted so much he'd killed them. I'd spent a lot of years in foster homes, and yet I bet I'd had a better, happier childhood than Cyrus had. I found I couldn't help smiling at him, despite my determination to be cautious.

"I'll let you off with a warning," I said. "But if you could get to the point without too much preamble, I'd appreciate it."

He nodded, leaning forward in a way that signaled the fun and games were over and he was being serious. "I'm the first to admit that Konstantin won't win any man-of-the-year contests. He certainly won't win father of the year. But he *is* still my father, and even though he's stepped down and removed himself from the public eye, I still consider him an Olympian. I talked to Anderson last week, and when I got off the phone with him, I had the impression we had both agreed that he would make it clear to his people that my father was not to be harmed."

My years of working as a private investigator had given me

both a good poker face and a nice touch of acting skill. I didn't think my expression gave anything away, though Cyrus was watching me with great intensity. Funny how Anderson had failed to mention this "agreement" this morning when he'd tried to bully me into hunting Konstantin.

"I'm sure Anderson is upstanding and honorable at heart," Cyrus continued without a hint of sarcasm, "but I find myself wondering if his hatred for my father might trump his honor. I wonder if he followed through with his promise to warn his people off. You, particularly, descendant of Artemis that you are."

"If you think Anderson lied to you, then I suggest you take it up with him. No way I'm getting in the middle of that, and I'm not going to confirm or deny what he told us." Cyrus looked like he was about to protest, but I cut him off. "I *will* tell you that I have no intention of hunting your father for revenge. That's just not me. Does that make you feel better?"

He gave me a long, thoughtful stare. Trying to read me, I guessed. I'd told him the truth, even if I hadn't exactly told him everything, and he seemed to read that in my face. He nodded and let out a little sigh.

"Thank you. That does."

He looked honestly relieved, like he'd been worried about Konstantin's safety. I knew there were all sorts of people out there, but I still had trouble understanding how someone could actually *care* about Konstantin. Fearful respect I could understand, but not affection. And yet I didn't think it was fear or respect driving Cyrus right now.

"Anderson told me Konstantin killed all his children before you," I said. "Why would you care so much about his safety? And what makes you think he won't kill you, too, someday?"

Cyrus shrugged. "He's my father, Nikki. I know he's not a nice person, and I know he doesn't have a good history with his children. But he's still the man who raised me, and I think we both learned a lot from what happened with the others. I've made it clear that I have no desire to take his place, and while he doesn't trust me completely, I think he at least for the most part believes me."

"Um, correct me if I'm wrong, but you *have* taken his place. Haven't you?"

He smiled blandly at me, and I understood.

"You've taken his place in name only," I said. I should have known someone like Konstantin would never voluntarily step down. "He's still pulling the strings." I frowned. "And he's okay with your decree that the Olympians not kill Descendant children anymore?"

It had always been the Olympian policy under Konstantin that when they discovered a family of Descendants, they would kill them all, except for children under the age of five, who would be raised to believe in the Olympian ideal—and would later be used as lethal weapons against other *Liberi*. That policy had been the first thing Cyrus had changed when he'd taken over.

Cyrus grinned wryly. "He doesn't love it," he admitted. "But since I don't actually *want* to lead the Olympians, he had to make some concessions to get me to do it."

I didn't for a moment believe Konstantin had abandoned his quest to rid the world of all Descendants and *Liberi* who weren't under his thumb, and in his mind, that meant killing children too old to be controlled. If he was letting Cyrus put a stop to the practice, that meant he thought of his son's rule as nothing but a temporary inconvenience. I didn't like Cyrus's chances of surviving the regime change when Konstantin took back the reins.

"You keep playing with fire and you're going to get burned," I said, and Cyrus laughed like I'd made a particularly funny joke. I thought back on my words, but they were nothing more than a perfectly ordinary cliché, not funny at all. Whatever the joke was, I didn't get it.

Cyrus realized I didn't get it and raised his eyebrows at me. "Playing with fire?" he prompted. "Getting burned?"

Nope, that didn't clear things up a bit.

"You are aware that my father and I are descendants of Helios, the sun god, aren't you?"

Actually, I'd never bothered to ask. For some reason, I'd kind of assumed they were descendants of Zeus because he was king of the gods. I wouldn't have thought Konstantin, who puffed himself up with so much pomp and circumstance, would be the descendant of a god many people had never even heard of.

"I'll take that as a no," Cyrus said. He turned in his chair and tugged down the collar of his shirt so I could see the glyph that marked his skin, right where his neck joined his shoulders. It was an iridescent sun with long, spidery rays. If he wore a shirt with no collar, some of those rays would be visible, though only to other *Liberi*. I myself had a glyph in the middle of my forehead, and no mortal had ever shown any sign that they could see it.

"I'm still kind of new at this game," I reminded Cyrus. "I tend not to think about who a person's descended from unless I can see their glyph. Out of sight, out of mind."

"Understandable," he said, turning back toward me. "I've known what my father was, what *I* was, for all my life. I can't imagine what it must be like to have all this thrust upon you all of a sudden."

There was real sympathy in his words, and I had to give myself another mental slap in the face to remind myself he was one of the bad guys. He was just more subtle and deceptive about it than the rest of the Olympians.

The waitress returned to our table, bringing our food. I tried not to stare at his *croque monsieur* with naked envy, but it was hard when the bread was a perfect toasty brown and glistened with butter. My soup and salad would make a perfectly nice lunch, but Cyrus's looked positively decadent.

To my surprise, Cyrus didn't even bother to glance at his food. Instead, he opened his wallet and pulled out a twenty-dollar bill.

"Lunch is my treat, since I barged in on you so rudely," he said, laying the money on the table and pushing back his chair.

"You're not going to eat?"

He shook his head. "I've said what I needed to say. There's no reason for me to disturb you any further."

Then why did you order food? I wondered, but declined to ask.

"I'm sure they'd be willing to give you a to-go bag. Throwing away a *croque monsieur* is a crime against nature."

Cyrus grinned at me as he stood up. "I saw the way you looked at my food when the waitress brought it. I have a strong suspicion it won't go to waste. It's been a pleasure."

I watched him leave with what I was sure was a puzzled frown on my face. I'd been properly warned off, but I had the nagging suspicion that there'd been more going on during our conversation than met the eye. However, I couldn't figure out what it was. And the *croque monsieur* was getting cold.

Cyrus was right; his food didn't go to waste. It wasn't until I was almost halfway through the sandwich that I realized Cyrus had specifically come to talk to me here, nowhere near where I lived or worked. No one knew where I was. So how had he found me?

The only explanation I could come up with was that he had tracked me by my cell phone somehow. Not something a private citizen would ordinarily be able to do, but the Olympians had so much money to throw around they could buy just about any service known to mankind.

I resisted the urge to dig my phone out of my purse and remove the battery. Cyrus already knew where I was right this moment, so there was no point. But I added a new task to my to-do list: buy a disposable cell phone.

There are some people who can chow down on butter-soaked ham and cheese sandwiches for lunch every day without gaining an ounce. I am not one of them.

Considering the radical changes my life had undergone recently, I'd decided to step up my workout regimen so I'd be in the best possible shape to fight off bad guys, and one of my favorite workouts was running in the woods. My overindulgence at lunch and the relatively mild weather meant this was a good day for a run.

I returned to the mansion and changed into my running clothes—nothing fancy, just a T-shirt and shorts. Sometimes my friend and fellow *Liberi*-in-residence Maggie went running with me, but after my meetings with Anderson and Cyrus, I needed some time to myself, so I didn't go looking for her.

Being a city girl, I have very little concept of how big an acre is, but I knew there were a lot of them on Anderson's property. Even just running up and back along the driveway was not an inconsiderable amount of exercise, but there were also tons of woods. Those weren't conveniently furnished with running trails, though Maggie had told me that during the warmer months, Anderson brought in a tree service on a regular basis to keep the weeds and underbrush tamed. The result was that we had all the beauty of nature, without any of the inconvenience.

I went up and down the driveway once as a warm-up, then plunged into the woods, just deep enough that I couldn't see the cleared land on which the house and its environs stood. Pine needles and leaves crunched pleasantly under my feet, and the air smelled of earth and evergreens. A brilliant red cardinal peeped from its perch on a branch above me, and I was far enough away from the road that I couldn't hear any car sounds. The knot of tension in my gut released as I drank in the peace and solitude.

I was in the zone, my breathing steady, my legs carrying me at a comfortable pace without any conscious control, and I felt like I could run ten miles without being overly winded. I couldn't, of course. Marathon running wasn't one of my supernatural powers. When I came out of the almost trancelike state I was in, I'd be breathing like a racehorse and the muscles in my legs would burn something fierce, but for a few perfect minutes, I was transported.

My footsteps faltered when I heard a sound that most definitely didn't belong out here in the woods of Maryland— a roar that sounded like it came from the throat of a big cat. The sound of that roar brought me back to myself, and I felt the brisk January air burning my throat and lungs as I panted heavily. My legs felt like a pair of tree trunks, rooted to the ground, and I bent over and put my hands on my knees, watching my breath steam as I slowly came to myself.

There was another roar, and I forced myself to stand up straight and look around. I have a very good, possibly supernatural, sense of direction, and even though there were no obvious landmarks around me, just trees, trees, and more trees, I knew exactly where I was.

In the woods behind the house, there was a large, grassy clearing. I wasn't sure what its original purpose had been, but some of Anderson's *Liberi* used it as a sort of practice field, where they could hone their powers without anyone seeing them. I had used the clearing for target practice, trying to learn the limits of my supernatural aim, which seemed to apply equally well to throwing and shooting.

I was currently about fifty yards from the clearing, and with the leafless trees and the lack of underbrush, I wouldn't have to go very far before I'd be able to see whatever was going on there. The feline roar ripped through the air again, and I knew any sensible person would turn tail and run as far away from that sound as possible. But I've rarely been accused of being sensible, so I started forward again, this time at a brisk walk.

I knew who and what was in the clearing, of course. It had to be Jamaal.

A descendant of the Hindu death goddess Kali, Jamaal possessed a terrifying kind of death magic that almost had a will of its own and *wanted* to be used. The death magic had driven him half-mad, though I suspected his temper had always been an issue, even before he'd become *Liberi*. Thanks to some info I'd gathered from serial killer Justin Kerner, Jamaal had learned to channel some of that magic into the form of a tiger. Summoning the great cat seemed to vent the death magic for him, so that he was no longer as volatile as he had once been. However, his control of the tiger was shaky, to say the least, which meant that when I heard the roar, I should have known better than to approach.

Curiosity was more likely to kill *me* than the cat under the circumstances, but I'd had the reluctant hots for Jamaal almost since we first met, and I couldn't resist my urge to investigate.

I eased my way through the trees toward the clearing. I hadn't heard any more roaring, so it was possible Jamaal had put the tiger to rest. I'd only seen the creature once before, during our final battle with Justin Kerner, and I'd been too distracted by my attempts to catch a killer to take a good look.

I caught a flash of movement out of the corner of my eye. I stopped in my tracks and turned slowly, noticing for the first time that the wind was at my back—carrying my scent straight to the clearing. Perhaps the tiger had been aware of me all along and its roars had been warnings I'd foolishly failed to heed.

It was peering at me through the trees, way too close for comfort. It was a beautiful creature, no doubt about it, with pumpkin-orange stripes and a magnificently muscled body. Paws the size of skillets sported claws that could rip a person open with one swipe, and the amber eyes practically glowed with intensity.

I stood still and swallowed hard. I had no doubt the tiger could outrun me in about two strides if it felt so inclined. I stared into those amber eyes, trying to guess what it was going to do. The tiger snarled, showing off an impressive set of teeth, and I quickly dropped my gaze. I knew dogs and primates took eye contact as a form of challenge, but I wasn't sure about tigers. Of course, if this one was the embodiment of Jamaal's rage and death magic, it probably didn't take much to provoke it.

"Jamaal?" I called softly, afraid yelling would spur the tiger into motion. "A little help here?"

I didn't know exactly where he was, but he had to be nearby. I just hoped he hadn't completely lost control of the animal.

The tiger stalked forward, moving with sensuous grace. I scanned the ground in search of a rock I could use as a weapon, while keeping the tiger in my peripheral vision. Even with my powers, I didn't think throwing a rock at it would even slow the tiger down, but anything was better than just standing there and being mauled. As far as I knew, the tiger couldn't do me any lasting harm, but it could hurt me, even kill me, in the short term. The magic of the *Liberi* would bring me back no matter what happened to my body, but I'd died once before and hadn't enjoyed the experience. I wasn't eager for a repeat performance.

"Jamaal?" I called again, louder this time.

The tiger was close enough now that I could probably have reached out and scratched behind its ears. If I had a death wish, that is. I was shaking with the effort of restraining my primal urge to run, but I was sure that was the one thing I could do to make the situation even worse.

"I don't think Sita likes you," Jamaal said from behind me.

I hadn't heard him approach, but then I'd been keeping my attention firmly fixed on the tiger, where it belonged.

"Sita?" I risked a glance over my shoulder, and saw Jamaal standing a few yards away, leaning casually against a tree.

"I thought a name from Indian mythology would suit her best," he said, and even propped against the tree as he was, he swayed a bit on his feet. I realized he wasn't leaning against the tree in an attempt to look casual—he was leaning on it for support. "The wife of the god Rama."

I couldn't have cared less about the origin of the tiger's name. Jamaal's face was gleaming with sweat, and his T-shirt clung wetly to his well-muscled chest. He looked like he was about to collapse at any moment. It was possible Sita would disappear if he passed out. It was also possible she wouldn't, which would be bad.

"The name suits her," I said, rather inanely. She wasn't creeping closer anymore, but she was still giving me the evil eye, and the tip of her tail was twitching. In a house cat, that wasn't a good sign. I didn't know what it meant in a tiger, but I tended to think it was bad. "She's truly magnificent," I continued, "but don't you think it's time for her to go away now?"

Sita's lips pulled back in a snarl, as if she'd understood me and been insulted. Maybe she had.

"Come here, Sita," he called, and she obeyed, though she kept me pinned with her eyes the entire way.

Jamaal pushed away from the tree when Sita was an arm's length away, and I saw his legs trembling. He was pushing himself too hard, and it was dangerous as hell. Sita might not be able to do me permanent harm, but if he passed out and left her to her own devices . . . We didn't have any close neighbors—that was part of the point of the mansion—but the tiger wouldn't have to go very far to find more vulnerable prey.

I bit my tongue to stop myself from editorializing. The last thing I wanted to do was get Jamaal's back up while he had a lethal carnivore under tenuous control. So instead of urging him to hurry the hell up and put Sita away, I stood there and held my breath.

Jamaal reached out toward the tiger with a shaking hand, and she finally dragged her attention away from me. She closed her eyes and pressed her head up against his hand in what looked like an affectionate gesture. She followed that gesture by butting her head against his hip. I couldn't say with any accuracy how big Sita was, but if I had to guess, I'd say she weighed around five hundred pounds, most of it muscle. Her gentle head-butt was too much for Jamaal's shaky legs, and he went down.

"Jamaal!" I cried, instinctively taking a step toward him.

Sita whirled on me with a roar that made my bones vibrate, putting herself between me and Jamaal and crouching menacingly. But she didn't pounce on me, and I had the feeling she was defending Jamaal, rather than attacking me. I wasn't about to argue with her, and I stepped back slowly, trying to give her some space without making her want to chase me.

Luckily, Jamaal had only lost his balance, not passed out. While I stood there with my heart in my throat, he reached up and touched Sita's flank. She gave me one last snarl, then disappeared.

For a couple of minutes, neither one of us moved. Jamaal lay on his back on the ground, his eyes closed as the sweat evaporated from his skin. His breathing was deep and steady, and I might have thought he'd passed out after all if it weren't for his bent knees, which didn't flop to the side as they would if he were unconscious. For myself, I continued to stand still, willing the adrenaline to recede.

Unfortunately, when I didn't have the heady rush of adrenaline keeping me warm, I noticed that I was freezing. I was as sweaty as Jamaal from my run, and I was wearing even less clothing. It was a nice day for January, but it was still January. I shivered and crossed my arms in a vain attempt to keep warm.

"What are you doing here, Nikki?" Jamaal asked without opening his eyes.

"I was running," I answered, although surely he'd figured that out on his own based on how I was dressed. "Did you send Sita out to stalk me, or was that her own idea?" Jamaal wasn't what I'd call the mischievous sort, and I doubted he'd have used Sita to scare me like that, but I didn't much like the idea of a magical tiger with a mind of its own.

For a moment, I thought he wasn't going to answer me, which was answer enough in its own way. Then he opened his eyes and levered himself up into a sitting position with an obvious effort. I almost reached out and offered him a hand, but I knew better by now. Jamaal was not the type to graciously accept help of any kind.

"My guess is she heard you running and decided to investigate the potential threat," he said. "You might have noticed she's a little protective of me." He shook his head as if to clear it, and I noticed that the beads at the ends of his braids were a combination of orange, black, and white.

Jamaal was color coordinating with his tiger? I had to suppress a laugh at the idea, though I wondered if Jamaal was even conscious he'd done it. He had enough beads to wear a different color every day for a year; maybe it was just a coincidence that he'd chosen tiger colors.

"I can't blame her for that," I said, though I'd have been happier if he could teach her the distinction between the good guys and the bad guys. "But maybe you should go a little easy on your practice sessions. You know, stop before you're about to drop from fatigue?"

He gave me a sour look as he laboriously dragged himself to his feet. "Venting the death magic was *your* idea. Don't complain if you don't like the results."

Jamaal's temper was a lot more stable now that he'd learned how to summon Sita, but he was still a pro at being surly. I tried not to take it personally, though I suspected there *was* something personal about it. And maybe it was time we got whatever it was out into the open. Ordinarily, I wouldn't think to initiate a personal conversation when I was standing outside in January in a damp set of running clothes and Jamaal was so shaky on his feet he had to concentrate to stand up, but this might be my only chance to get him alone for a while.

"Are you still pissed at me for trying to leave?" I blurted, wincing a bit in anticipation of his response. At the time, I'd thought leaving was the only way I could protect both myself and Steph. Emma and Anderson had still been trying to make a go of it, and Emma had—for reasons that mystified me to this day—decided that I was after her husband. I'd been sure that Emma and I couldn't coexist in the mansion, and that if it came down to it, Anderson would choose her over me. And so I'd decided I should make myself disappear.

It had seemed like a good idea at the time, though I realized now that deciding to disappear without talking it over with anyone, or even saying good-bye, had been taking the coward's way out. And I was pretty sure I'd hurt Jamaal's feelings, though he'd never admit it.

Jamaal blinked, as if confused by the abrupt change of subject. "What are you talking about?"

I didn't for a moment believe he didn't know. He just didn't want to talk about it. Like most men I knew, he wasn't a big fan of talking about his feelings.

Actually, he wasn't a big fan of talking, period. He was the strong, silent type personified, but I didn't think that was particularly good for him. Even living in the mansion with seven other people, he managed to hold himself aloof, and I thought the isolation, self-imposed though it was, exacerbated his difficulties with the death magic.

"It was wrong of me to try to sneak away like that," I said. "I was afraid that if I let anyone know I was leaving, someone would try to talk me out of it." I'd been equally afraid of how I'd feel if someone *didn't* try to talk me out of it, but I wanted to talk about Jamaal's baggage, not my own. "And I was afraid I wouldn't be able to force myself to leave. I—"

Jamaal shook his head, making his beads click. "Don't make something out of nothing. I don't care whether you stay or go."

I couldn't help flinching at his words, my heart clenching unpleasantly in my chest. I shouldn't have let it get to me. I *knew* he cared, whether he admitted it or not. And yet the words still hurt.

Jamaal sighed and wiped some of the drying sweat from his brow. "Sorry. Didn't mean it like that. Just meant it's your decision, not mine. Now I need a shower and a nap, and you need to get inside before you turn blue."

He didn't wait for my response, turning his back abruptly enough that he almost lost his balance again and heading toward the house with a ground-eating stride. I considered running after him, trying to get him to stop and talk, but I didn't like my chances of success. And yeah, I was still feeling pretty stung.

Trying to act as if none of what had happened had gotten to me, I resumed my run. I doubt I managed more than a couple hundred yards before I gave it up as a lost cause.

THREE

The phone call came at three thirty Saturday morning, startling me out of a deep sleep. For a moment after I opened my eyes, I just lay there and hoped the annoying ringing sound would go away, but of course it didn't. I sat up, groping for the phone and staring blearily at the illuminated numbers on my clock. I'd had a land line installed in my room, but I rarely used it. I picked up the receiver and crossed my fingers it would be a wrong number.

"Hello?" I croaked.

"Don't panic," Steph's voice answered, and it sounded like she'd been crying recently. "I'm all right. No one is hurt."

Well, *that* woke me up in a hurry. I yanked the chain on the bedside lamp, blinding myself with the glare, and rubbed at the crust on my eyes.

"What's wrong?" I asked, panicking despite Steph's orders not to. Anything bad enough for her to call me at this hour was going to suck even if no one was hurt.

Steph sniffled. "It's our house." Steph lived alone, so I could only assume that by "our" house, she meant the house we'd grown up in. My throat tightened. "There was a fire . . ." Her voice faded into more sniffles.

My own eyes burned with sympathetic tears as something cold and hard sank to the pit of my stomach. "How bad?"

Steph's more of a crier than I am, and it took her a while to get her tears under control enough to talk. "The worst," she finally said. "It's gone. Everything's . . . gone."

I tried to absorb the enormity of what had happened, but I couldn't quite wrap my brain around it. Maybe I wasn't fully capable of it. Until I'd moved in with the Glasses at the age of eleven, the concept of a "home" had been alien to me. Homes were just temporary way stations, interchangeable places to sleep. I'd resided in more houses and apartments than I could count. The Glasses' house meant more to me than all the rest of them put together, but I knew instinctively that it didn't mean as much to me as it did to Steph and her parents. After my childhood, I just didn't let myself grow attached to places the way normal people did.

That didn't mean I didn't feel the loss.

I'd spent the happiest years of my life in that house, after I'd finally come to accept that the Glasses were going to keep me no matter how badly I acted out. It was warm and beautiful, decorated with exquisite taste while still managing to look comfortable and inviting. It was the Glasses' history, Steph's childhood, and my safe haven, all rolled into one. I was going to miss it, but my adoptive family was going to *grieve* for it. And I was already grieving for them.

"What happened?" I asked. I wanted to say something comforting and sympathetic to Steph, but I knew better. Steph would expect me to be as devastated and heartsick as she was about the loss of our childhood home. Comforting her when I was supposed to be equally upset would make me sound aloof and distant. I *was* heartsick, but not for reasons she'd understand.

"They don't know yet," Steph said. "The fire's out, but they won't be able to investigate until daylight."

I hoped like hell it had been a freak accident of some sort, but I couldn't help wondering . . . Emma wasn't allowed to hurt me or my family because of the treaty between the Olympians and Anderson. But I doubted that protection applied to our *property*. What also gave me pause was the fact that this wasn't the first fire that had affected me in recent weeks. Earlier this month, the office building I was renting space in had had a fire, one that destroyed my office. It hadn't *started* in my office, and the fire investigator had determined that some idiot had left his space heater on by accident. Maybe it was completely unrelated, but it seemed like quite the coincidence.

"Have you called your folks yet?" I asked.

The Glasses were on an around-the-world cruise and had been gone for two and a half months already. They still had three more weeks left, and I hated the idea of spoiling it for them when there was nothing they could do.

"*Our* folks, Nikki," Steph said sharply.

Oops. I'd forgotten. It was about fourteen years too late, but I was trying to train myself to think of the Glasses as my parents. Despite all the warmth and love they'd shown me, I'd always managed to keep a little bit of distance between us. It wasn't like I was *trying* to do it. It just sort of happened. I didn't feel like I was really their daughter, no matter what the adoption papers said. I think my insistence on referring to them as Steph's parents had been bugging her for a long time, but it was out in the open now.

"Our folks," I repeated meekly. I wasn't sure I'd ever be able to get myself to call them Mom and Dad, but I could at least take a couple of baby steps. "Have you called them yet?"

"No," she said in a small voice, and I knew she was about to cry again. "I don't know how—" She couldn't finish the sentence, her voice breaking in a sob.

"I'll do it," I told her, though it was going to be hell. Who likes breaking that kind of news to people they love? And I *did* love the Glasses, even if I didn't truly think of them as my parents. But I could give them the news without bursting into tears, and I doubted Steph could.

"You don't have to," Steph managed to choke out, but I heard the hope in her voice.

"I'll do it," I repeated. "You shouldn't have to make this phone call more than once."

"And you can stay calm, cool, and collected when you tell them."

I was pretty sure there was a hint of censure in those words, but I chose to ignore it. I was never going to be as open and demonstrative as Steph was, and I refused to apologize for it.

"Why don't you come over when we get off the phone," I suggested. "Neither one of us is going to get any more sleep tonight. We have several industrial-sized tubs of ice cream in the freezer. Maybe you and I can demolish one together."

Steph thought about it briefly, then let out a shuddering sigh. "Okay. I'll be there in about forty minutes."

Dreading what I had to do next, I hung up the phone.

The phone call with the Glasses was every bit as excruciating as I expected. My adoptive mother's heartbroken sobs would haunt me for a long time. I wished I could give her a hug, but she was halfway around the world, and I wouldn't be hugging her anytime soon. At least Mr. Glass was there so she could cry on his shoulder. He's the stereotypical stoic male, and though the news had to have hit him hard, he kept himself together. I hoped that when he and Mrs. Glass were alone together and he didn't feel like he had to put up a brave front for me, he would take comfort from her as well as give it.

"I don't know how soon we'll be able to get home," he said. There was just a hint of hoarseness in his voice, betraying the emotions he was trying to repress. "Even if we get on the next flight, it'll take a couple of days."

"There's no need for you to cut your trip short," I said, and my motives in saying so weren't entirely pure. No, I didn't want them to miss out on whatever exciting destinations were still on their itinerary, but I also hadn't yet figured out what the hell I was going to tell them about what was going on in my life. I'd talked to them a couple of times since I'd become *Liberi,* but I hadn't told them much of anything. How I was going to explain that I was now living in a mansion with seven other people was beyond me. Especially when I insisted on holding on to the condo the Glasses had bought for me. (They'd bought it for me as a gift, but I insisted on paying rent. My baggage made it hard for me to accept money or gifts from them.)

"Steph and I can take care of anything that needs doing until you get back," I continued, crossing my fingers that he'd find my argument sound.

Mr. Glass sighed heavily. "We're not going to be in any mood for sightseeing or even relaxing after this. We might as well come home."

I had to agree that I wouldn't feel much like being on vacation, either. However, that didn't mean I had to concede the point. "I know you're not in the mood, but it might be nice to have something to take your mind off your troubles for a while. As far as I know, there's nothing you have to do that can't wait until you get back." Not that I knew much of anything about what needed to be done. There would be insurance company wrangling for sure, and heaven only knew what would be involved in getting the ruins cleaned up and a new house built. Surely Steph and I could take care of *some* of that on their behalf.

"At least take a little time to think about it," I urged. "If you decide to stay on the cruise, you can always change your mind and come home, but vice versa doesn't work. Steph and I will find you a nice rental so you don't have to stay in a hotel or anything. And we'll start the ball rolling on insurance and stuff. There's no need to make a bad situation worse by losing out on the rest of your cruise."

He let out another heavy sigh. "When did you get so smart?"

I smiled at the affection in his tone. "Guess someone just raised me right."

"All right. Your mother and I will talk it over before we make any hasty decisions. But you call us if there are any updates, or if there's anything we need to do."

"I promise."

"We'll call you tomorrow to let you know what we've decided."

"Okay."

I suspected from the tone of his voice that he was still leaning toward coming home immediately, and I couldn't blame him. Probably I'd have done the same in his shoes. But at least I'd bought a little bit of time.

Of course, if I hadn't been able to figure out how to explain my current circumstances over the course of the last few weeks, a couple of extra days probably weren't going to help all that much.

For those of you who might be tempted, I wouldn't recommend downing a tub of chocolate ice cream at four in the morning, even if you have just learned your childhood home burned to the ground. Steph and I had had help—she'd called Blake while I was on the phone with the Glasses, and he'd met me at the bottom of the stairs when I went to let Steph in. I felt like the third wheel all of a sudden, but that didn't stop me from shoveling down the ice cream until my stomach felt queasy. The sugar high buoyed me for a while, but when the crash came, I decided it was safest to leave Steph and Blake to their own devices. I felt sick enough from overeating without getting myself all worked up about their relationship.

I excused myself and went back to my suite to brood in quiet solitude. I was trying to hold on to hope that the fire had been the result of faulty wiring or some other legitimate accidental cause. I'd brought enough hardship down on my adoptive family since the fateful day my car had slammed into Emmitt Cartwright and killed him, making me a *Liberi*. The last thing I wanted to do was be the cause of more pain and heartache.

I might have lived on in blissful ignorance for at least another few hours if I hadn't decided to check my email.

I wasn't getting a whole lot of email lately, not since I'd

temporarily closed up my business as a private investigator. There was never anything important in my in-box, so mostly when I checked email, it was to delete the spam that had gotten through the filter. I was happily deleting away when my cursor hit a message that chilled my blood.

THIS IS JUST THE BEGINNING, screamed the subject line, and the name in the From column said Konstantin.

Dreading what I would see, I opened the email and held my breath.

Dear Nikki,

I hope this letter finds you well.

Actually, no, I don't. I hope it finds you miserable and guilt stricken.

I've put a lot of time and thought into my current situation. I have been forced to step down as king of the Olympians, a position I've held for several centuries and to which I had become accustomed. I have been exiled from my people, forced to live in hiding for fear that the more predatory amongst them might want to ensure my permanent removal. I have been forced to abandon a magnificent home and watch as my worthless son attempts to destroy from within everything I've built over my long, long life.

All of these indignities I've been forced to face, I can trace back to one person: you.

If you had joined the Olympians when I invited you, none of this would have happened. You and I could have lived harmoniously together, and we could have hunted down Justin Kerner without all the fuss and fireworks. Maybe if I hadn't had to ask for Anderson's help to stop Kerner, we could have captured and neutralized him before he killed Phoebe. Certainly we could have taken care of him quietly, in such a way that no one untrustworthy had to know about my lapse in judgment.

But you *didn't* join us. Instead, you set yourself up in opposition, and you went out of your way to reveal every detail of what had happened. You cost me everything I hold dear, and I plan to pay you back in kind.

This morning's little surprise was nothing more than a warning shot across the bow. I have much, much more in store for you. I know you'll be hunting for me, and maybe you think you'll catch me before I can fully realize my revenge. But I didn't manage to become king of the Olympians and lead them for centuries without having an impressive bag of tricks at hand. I'm betting I can break you before you get to me. And if you think you can invoke your silly little treaty and get Cyrus to control me, you are gravely mistaken. I will do nothing to harm you or your family. Nothing that will officially break the treaty. Hurting you without breaking the treaty will be quite the enjoyable test to my creativity. And believe me, I am highly creative.

Be afraid, Nikki Glass. I am coming for you.

Yours, Konstantin

I read the email twice, hardly believing what I was reading. Konstantin blamed *me* for all his troubles? That was nuts.

I'll admit, I'd certainly had a hand in his downfall. It was I who'd unraveled the mystery and found out why Justin Kerner was hunting the D.C. area. I'd discovered that his death magic combined with the taint of supernatural madness made him capable of killing *Liberi,* and that he wanted to kill them all— starting with Konstantin—for having forced him to take the tainted seed in the first place. I'd uncovered the fact that all of the Olympians could have been killed because Konstantin made a mistake, and that was what caused him to lose power. But that didn't mean it was my *fault*.

I rubbed my eyes, which ached with a combination of weariness and lingering grief over my family's pain. Why did every *Liberi* blame *me* when things went wrong in their lives? Jamaal had originally blamed me for killing Emmitt. Emma blamed me for the dissolution of her marriage, which I believed she was 100 percent responsible for herself. And now Konstantin was blaming me for his own screwup.

I had only met Konstantin once, and though he'd chilled me to the bone with his coldness and malice, I had never once suspected he was *insane*. But a vendetta of this magnitude did not speak of a man of sound mind. Maybe losing his place at the top of the totem pole had cost him his sanity as well as his power.

Whatever the reason, he was one hell of a dangerous enemy. And if he was coming after me, my life was going to get a lot more difficult very soon.

FOUR

It was still oh-God o'clock, and the sun hadn't even begun to peek up over the horizon yet, but I was so wired on stress and chocolate ice cream that I didn't put much consideration into other people's comfort and routine.

I forwarded the threatening email to Leo, our resident computer expert. He was a descendant of Hermes, and had a Midas touch where money was concerned. He'd first started learning about computers so he could keep in constant touch with the stock market, but he'd taken to them like a duck to water, and his hacking skills were sometimes downright scary.

Leo's rooms were down the hall from mine, and after I hit send, I scurried to his door and knocked. I figured the email I just forwarded needed an explanation, and it wasn't until I'd knocked a second time without an answer that I realized what time it was, and that I was probably the only person in the house awake at this hour, other than Blake and Steph, if they were still up. I was badly rattled and wanted to get a start on finding Konstantin *now,* but as urgent as it felt to me, I knew it wasn't reasonable to be waking anybody up before six. Whatever Konstantin had planned for me, it would take days, weeks, maybe even months to develop, and letting Leo get another couple hours of sleep wouldn't endanger anyone.

I was just turning to go back to my room when the door behind me opened.

When I first caught sight of Leo, I was sure I'd rousted him out of bed. He was wearing a fluffy white bathrobe over blue and white striped pajamas. A second glance showed me that his mousy brown hair was slightly damp and his cheeks were freshly shaven. He smelled of drugstore aftershave and Listerine, and I came to the inevitable conclusion that I hadn't woken him up after all. His eyes widened when he saw me.

"Nikki?" he said. "What are you doing here?" He reached into the pocket of his robe and pulled out a pair of wire-rimmed glasses, shoving them onto his face in a gesture that looked almost nervous. I realized I'd never seen him without the glasses before.

I think Leo has a good heart, or he wouldn't be working for Anderson, but he's about as socially awkward an individual as I've ever met. He has an obvious aversion to eye contact, and he always seems a bit nervous and distracted, like only a fraction of his attention is actually focused on whoever he's talking to. I suspect when he heard the knock on his door, he assumed it was Anderson, and finding me there threw him for a bit of a loop. His shoulders hunched as if he were expecting a blow, and his gaze dropped to the floor.

He was nervous with everyone, but more so with me, the newcomer to the house. I wondered if I should have explained what was going on via email instead of coming to his suite, but it was too late now.

"Hi, Leo. I'm sorry to bother you so early in the morning. I hope I didn't wake you." I knew I hadn't, but it seemed like the polite thing to say, and I found Leo's nerves and awkwardness contagious.

"I was awake," he told my left shoulder. "The European markets start opening at four."

Geez, and I'd thought *I* was an early riser. I'd never known anyone else in the house was up at this hour, which I guessed meant Leo didn't venture out of his rooms in the morning. Actually, Leo didn't venture out of his rooms much at all. Sometimes he had to be reminded to step away from his computers and eat. It didn't seem like much of a life to me, but what do I know?

With anyone else, I probably would have tried a little small talk before launching into my request, but I figured Leo wouldn't blame me—hell, he probably wouldn't even notice—if I skipped the social niceties.

"I forwarded you an email," I told him. "It's supposedly from Konstantin. I wonder if you'd be able to trace it or something." I honestly didn't think Konstantin was stupid enough to send me a trail of bread crumbs that would lead right to him, but I figured it would be foolish not to at least check it out. Not to mention that Konstantin was centuries old and might not be as computer literate as a modern man.

"I'll see what I can do."

Leo didn't beckon me to follow as he retreated into his room, but he didn't close the door, either. I assumed that was an invitation to come in, so I stepped inside.

All of the suites Anderson's *Liberi* inhabited consisted of two rooms. For most of us, one of those rooms was the bedroom, and one was some version of a sitting room. I supposed with his fanatical attachment to the stock market and his lack of socialization, a sitting room would have been useless for Leo. Instead, the first room of his two-room suite was what I imagined the inside of a NASA control room might look like, only less tidy.

A huge L-shaped desk took up about half the room, and practically every inch of that desk was covered with computer equipment, bristling with tangled cords and surge protectors. I saw laptops and desktops, Macs and PCs, shiny new machines and old clunkers that looked like they were held together by duct tape. There were monitors sprinkled here and there on the desk, but there was also a bank of them mounted on the wall. Disassembled units spewing spare parts were tucked under the desk and pushed up against the other walls, and a freestanding air conditioner blasted cold air into the room even though it was January.

Leo must have noticed me staring at the air conditioner.

"The computers generate a lot of heat," he explained. "If I didn't keep the air conditioner going, my equipment would overheat."

He plopped down into a rolling chair and used the edge of the desk to pull himself over in front of one of the computers. His fingers moved lightning fast over the keyboard. Whatever he was using as an email reader wasn't anything I'd seen before, and I wondered if it was something Leo had created himself. There were no pretty icons or neatly labeled buttons, and instead of tooling around with a mouse or track pad, Leo was typing into a command window. He paused practically mid-keystroke and glanced over at one of the other monitors. He frowned and wheeled himself over, hit a couple of keys, then returned to the email.

"You're really into multitasking, aren't you?" I murmured.

"Have to be," he answered without turning his attention away from the computers. "Sometimes all the markets are open at the same time. Don't want to miss anything."

I was tempted to ask him what he did for fun, but I already knew the answer. Maybe he wasn't just socially awkward. Maybe he actually bordered on autistic, though he was obviously high functioning. I wondered if he'd always been like that, or if becoming *Liberi* had changed him. Then I wondered how someone as mild mannered and aloof as Leo could have become *Liberi* in the first place. Unless he was one of the original *Liberi*—the *son* of a god, rather than just a descendant of one—he had to have killed someone to become immortal. I had a hard time imagining him doing that.

"I like numbers more than I like people," he said without looking up, as if he could guess the direction of my thoughts. His fingers kept zipping across the keyboard. There was an edge of defensiveness in his voice. "Whenever someone new comes along, they feel sorry for me and try to draw me out, but I'm not like the rest of you. I'm happy like this."

Maybe that was why he was so nervous around me—he was waiting for me to try to "save" him. If he were an ordinary human being, I might have thought him desperately in need of human contact. I might have thought he couldn't possibly be living a good life shut up in his room with his computers all the time. But he wasn't an ordinary human being—he was a *Liberi*. Immortality, and the powers that were awakened in a *Liberi* when he or she became immortal, changed people, made them something other than human. When Leo said he was happy with his life as it was, I believed him.

"I don't feel sorry for you," I said, though maybe that wasn't strictly true. It seemed sad to me that Leo would spend so much of his time so completely alone, but I knew I was imposing my own likes and dislikes on him. "I wouldn't want to live like this, but if it works for you, that's all that matters."

He paused for a moment in his typing, looking over his shoulder at me, though he still didn't meet my eyes. "Thank you."

"No problem."

He turned back to his computer and tapped a few more keys. Then he nodded sagely and spoke without turning around.

"The email was sent from a computer at the FedEx Print and Ship on K Street at 4:02 A.M. The email account was created at 3:46 A.M. and deleted at 4:03. Sending that email is the only activity associated with the account, and the user registered as John Smith."

"Creative," I muttered under my breath. I'd have to swing

by and see if anyone there remembered seeing Konstantin, though even if they did, I didn't think it would be much help. I needed to know where he was *now*, not where he'd been at 4 A.M.

Leo shrugged apologetically. "Sorry that's all I could get."

I almost laughed. "You got everything there was, and in about five minutes. I couldn't have asked for more."

He didn't respond, instead zipping his chair over to another computer and typing at high speed. But even so, I didn't miss the pleased little smile on his lips.

I'm not particularly fond of admitting I'm wrong—who is?—but it seemed like the logical conclusion, given the evidence. Trying to catch Konstantin all by myself would be flat-out stupid, and it wasn't like I could do anything to him if I caught him. Which meant I had to swallow my pride and tell Anderson I'd changed my mind about the hunt.

I was in a foul mood when I stepped into his study after a late breakfast I'd forced myself to eat in an attempt to counteract the ice-cream binge. I desperately wanted to catch Konstantin before his next attack, whatever that would be, but I wasn't overly optimistic about my chances. I didn't have much to go on, and since Konstantin knew he'd have a descendant of Artemis on his tail, he was no doubt going to be extra paranoid and careful about keeping himself hidden.

The icing on my grumpy-pants cake was the sympathy the rest of Anderson's *Liberi* had thrown my way. Blake had apparently spread the word after Steph's visit, and my friends/coworkers had paraded through my suite to offer their condolences. I had to endure a long, motherly hug from Maggie, who was so sweet my misfortune brought a sheen of tears to her eyes; an awkward visit from Logan, who was too much of a manly man to know how to express his sympathies comfortably; and an even more awkward visit from Jack, who, with his trickster heritage, had trouble being serious for more than two minutes in a row.

Only Jamaal failed to put in an appearance, and that hurt me though it probably shouldn't have. He was even less comfortable with expressing feelings than Logan. But I couldn't help taking it as even more evidence that whatever friendship we had started to build together had been destroyed, either by my willingness to leave, or by our tentative foray into romance. I wished I knew which.

Anderson was sitting at his desk when I ventured through the open door of his study. I had the immediate impression he'd been waiting for me, though perhaps that was egocentric of me. He spent a lot of time in his study, and it was always the first place to check when I wanted to look for him.

I didn't know what Anderson generally did all day while he was sitting around in his study, but this morning, he was reading the newspaper. I hadn't read a real, printed newspaper since I was a kid clamoring for the Sunday comics, but Anderson was a bit of a traditionalist. Not surprising for a god who'd been around since the dawn of time, I suppose.

He folded the paper when I came in and laid it down on his desk. His fingertips were stained gray from handling newsprint. He was badly in need of a haircut, and I wished he'd either learn how to iron or start buying no-iron shirts. But looking like an unprepossessing slob is part of his disguise, part of how he hides the enormous power that lies just beneath his surface.

"I'm sorry to hear about your house," he said, beckoning me to one of the chairs in front of his desk. There was no hint of "I told you so" in his voice, and he looked genuinely sorry.

If one more person told me how sorry they were, I was going to scream. *Unless that person is Jamaal,* I mentally amended.

The sympathy—I refused to think of it as pity—sat heavily on my shoulders, and I practically collapsed into the chair. I wanted to maintain some semblance of dignity, but the weight of it all was getting to me, and my throat tightened like I was going to cry.

It was just a house, dammit. A thing, an object. Something that could be rebuilt. It had been empty when it burned down, and no one was hurt. That was all that mattered. I swallowed hard, trying to push the irrational grief back down inside. The Glasses and Steph had a right to grieve over the loss of their home, but it had never really been mine to begin with. So why did I suddenly feel like someone had just died?

Anderson rolled one of his desk drawers open and pulled out a little pop-up box of tissues, setting them on the edge of the desk within easy reach. "Just in case," he said with a small, sad smile.

I was *not* going to cry about this. I was not going to make it that easy for Konstantin to hurt me.

"I'm fine," I said, more to convince myself than to convince Anderson. "And you win: I will hunt Konstantin to the ends of the earth if that's what I have to do to keep him from hurting my family anymore."

I had the brief, unworthy thought that it was convenient for Anderson that the very week when he'd pinned me down and forced me to listen to—and refuse—his request, my adoptive parents' house should burn down and Konstantin should taunt me with that email.

"I knew he'd lash out eventually," Anderson said. "But it never occurred to me that he'd come after *you*. *I'm* his true enemy here, not you."

"Yes," I agreed, "but you're a lot harder to hurt. Plus, he's scared of you, though I don't suppose he'd admit it."

To tell you the truth, despite Anderson's dire predictions, I was actually kind of surprised that Konstantin had decided to go on the warpath. If he'd kept his head down and hadn't bothered anyone, I wouldn't have been motivated to hunt him down for Anderson to kill. Though perhaps he didn't know that. Perhaps he was incapable of understanding my reluctance to commit murder for revenge. Even Anderson hadn't understood, and he had a much firmer grasp of the concept of morality than Konstantin did.

"Good point," Anderson said. "Though I expect he will eventually scrape up his courage. I already want him dead, and he knows that. It's not like provoking me would change anything."

No, but provoking *me* had had a definite effect, spurring me into the hunt. Maybe Konstantin hadn't realized I wasn't planning to hunt him—or maybe someone who really, really wanted Konstantin dead had thought it a good idea to provide me a little motivation.

I stared at Anderson across the desk, wondering if he was ruthless enough to do something like that. He'd wanted his revenge badly enough that he'd neglected to tell anyone that Konstantin was still under the Olympians' protection. But still, burning down my parents' home . . . As ruthless and manipulative as I suspected Anderson could be, I couldn't see him doing something like that to innocent bystanders. However, I didn't have much trouble coming up with another suspect.

"What if someone knew I wasn't going to hunt him for you?" I asked, watching Anderson's face carefully. I suspected I was about to piss him off. "And what if that someone wanted him dead and would get a real kick out of hurting me in the process?"

Anderson froze in his seat, his face going so still he looked like a statue. He didn't breathe or blink, and I had the feeling something dangerous was brewing inside him. I half expected him to leap over the desk and seize me by the throat, and I mentally mapped out my escape route. Then he blinked, and the life returned to his face.

"You mean Emma," he said, as if there could be any doubt who I was talking about. His voice was even and his expression bland, but he had never taken well to accusations about Emma, and I didn't expect that to change now.

"Yeah. She'd love to be able to hurt me without breaking the treaty. And she knows my family is my weak spot. And the only person she hates more than me is Konstantin."

"I understand why you suspect her," Anderson said carefully, then paused.

"But . . . ?"

"She was . . . damaged by what Konstantin and Alexis did to her. I know that for a long time I tried to ignore that damage, and that makes my judgment where she's concerned questionable in your mind. But no matter how damaged she is, she's still the same woman I married, beneath it all. She's joined the Olympians to spite me, but just because she's joined them doesn't mean she *is* one at heart."

I clenched my jaws to hold back my protest. His judgment was more than just questionable where Emma was concerned, and I had absolutely no doubt she was capable of burning down my parents' house if she thought that would get her what she wanted. What I *did* doubt was that any force on earth could make Anderson believe that without some pretty overwhelming evidence to support the theory.

Anderson shook his head, having thoroughly talked himself into discounting my suggestion. "Emma didn't do it," he said firmly. "I told you Konstantin would strike out, and he has. Let's not go looking for complex explanations when a very obvious and simple one exists."

That clanking sound I heard was the doors of his mind slamming shut. I would have argued with him more if I thought there was a chance I could convince him, and if I thought for sure Emma really was the culprit. I was certainly willing to entertain the possibility, but I had to admit that for the moment, Konstantin had to take center stage as the prime suspect.

"I don't have any clue how I'll find him," I said, cursing my annoyingly mercurial power. My ability to find people is based on supernaturally fueled hunches, but it's hard to tell the difference between an honest-to-goodness hunch, wishful thinking, and random stray thoughts. "But I'll get right on it. I still have that list of Olympian properties from when I was searching for Emma. I doubt he'll be on one, but I'll start cruising by them one by one tonight."

For the most part, I didn't truly understand how my powers worked. It would probably take years of trial and error before I had any real confidence in them. But it did seem they worked better in the moonlight, which made sense because Artemis was a moon goddess as well as a huntress.

"The question then becomes, what do we do if I find him?" I gave Anderson a hard look. "I ran into Cyrus the other day, and he informed me that his father is still an Olympian and under their protection. He said he'd talked to you about it and you'd agreed to leave Konstantin alone."

Anderson didn't bother trying to act like he felt guilty about his tacit deception. "I gave him that impression, it's true. And if there's any way we can eliminate Konstantin without Cyrus having to know we're responsible, that's how we'll do it."

I shook my head. "If you kill him and he disappears off the face of the earth, everyone's going to know you were behind it."

"Not true. Only you know what I can do. As far as anyone else is concerned, I can't kill Konstantin unless I have a Descendant around to do my dirty work, and I don't. As long as we leave no evidence that can be traced back to us, Cyrus will have to assume that one of Konstantin's other enemies got to him. An Olympian enemy, because, believe me, those exist."

I did believe him about Konstantin having enemies within the Olympians. There were probably plenty of them who'd chafed under his rule over the years. But I didn't buy the idea that Anderson wouldn't be suspect number one.

"Look," Anderson said, leaning forward and clasping his hands on the desk, "Cyrus isn't going to start a war unless he's certain I've broken our treaty. Unlike Konstantin, he actually values people and would care if someone close to him got killed. It's not something he's going to risk unless he has to."

I reluctantly had to admit that Anderson had a point. I knew Cyrus wasn't as nice a guy as he pretended to be, but he wasn't *evil*. After all, he was protecting his father out of loyalty—misguided though it might be—and that proved he cared about something other than himself. I didn't know who else among the Olympians Cyrus cared about, but I did know he cared about Blake. And Blake could very easily get killed if we went to war.

"So what you're saying is if I find Konstantin, I should keep my mouth shut to everyone else and only tell you. Right?"

Anderson nodded. "Exactly. I don't mind everyone knowing you're hunting him, because no one would believe you weren't, after what happened. But if you find him, that has to be our secret. And I'll take care of what needs to be done."

I still didn't like it, not one bit. But I'd gotten as much concession out of Anderson as I was going to, and I had to be satisfied with it.

FIVE

The rest of the day didn't go a whole lot better than the beginning of it had. Steph called me to say the fire investigator had already declared the incident was arson. Whoever had set it had made no attempt to be subtle or try to hide the crime. Which made sense, considering the whole point of it was for me to know it was the start of Konstantin's path to revenge.

Steph was brisk and businesslike when we talked, telling me the facts without falling apart or betraying any emotion whatsoever. She was in problem-solver mode, and she'd distanced herself from her own pain. Considering how much charity work she did, and how often she ended up in charge of the charity functions she worked on, she was better suited for the job than I was. She'd already been in touch with the insurance company and had even tracked down the builder who'd designed and constructed the house more than twenty years ago.

Not once did Steph hint that she blamed me for what had happened, but I didn't know how she could *not*. I had already brought so much misery into her life. She'd been attacked by Alexis because of me, and now her childhood home had been destroyed. She didn't need me to tell her the fire had something to do with me, not after it was declared arson. Guilt pounded at me relentlessly, and I didn't know what to do with it. Big Sister Steph was the one I leaned on when I needed emotional support, but that wasn't an option this time.

I tried burying myself in work, digging up my previous list of Olympian properties in the D.C. area and then doing some research to see if they'd bought anything else since last I'd checked. Let me tell you, the Olympians own a lot of property, both commercial and residential, and I doubted I'd identified all of it despite my research. They knew how to use shell corporations and offshore bank accounts and out-and-out bribery to hide their assets. And let's not even talk about their worldwide holdings.

My gut told me Konstantin would not have left town, and the fact that he'd sent that email from a local FedEx seemed to support the theory. My ever-present voice of self-doubt pointed out that Konstantin could easily have hired someone to do the dirty work from afar. Maybe he was living like the king he thought himself to be in Monte Carlo or somewhere else far away from here. But if I had to search the whole world for him, I was in deep trouble.

I mapped out a driving route that would take me past many of the Olympian properties that I deemed likely candidates. It would take several nights to do a drive-by on every one, especially if I wanted to actually get some sleep once in a while. For the time being, I was skipping the places that were directly owned by known Olympians, figuring those were just too obvi-ous, but that still left me with a daunting list of possibilities. Yet I had to start somewhere.

I got so caught up in what I was doing that I forgot to eat lunch, and when I finally was satisfied with my itinerary for the first night, the sun was on its way down and I was raven-ous. I ventured downstairs into the kitchen, hoping someone was cooking a communal dinner.

It was something of a frail hope, as only Maggie and Logan did much in the way of cooking, and they usually let everyone know when they were doing it. Anderson made a vat of chili every once in a while, and Jack had once made some kind of stew that no one in the house had been willing to touch. Maybe he'd thought he'd fool me into tasting it, seeing as I was the new person, but I wasn't stupid enough to eat something a trickster prepared.

There were no enticing aromas drifting from the kitchen, and I figured it would be a Lean Cuisine night for me. How-ever, I was in luck after all. There were no enticing smells, but Logan was hard at work on some kind of cold noodle dish. A huge salad bowl filled with noodles in brown sauce sat on the counter, and Logan was shredding a head of bok choy with the ease and quickness of a professional.

"Need a sous chef?" I asked as he tossed the shredded bok choy in with the noodles.

Logan looked at me doubtfully as he sliced a red pepper into ribbons. If it had been me wielding the knife, I'd probably have sliced my own fingers off, even if I *was* looking at what I was doing. He jerked his chin toward the salad bowl.

"You can toss all of that together, if you'd like. I'm almost done with the knife-work."

I was just as happy not to be put to work slicing veggies, as it would take me at least four times as long as it was taking him. The man was almost as fast and efficient as a Cuisinart. He was a descendant of Tyr, a Germanic war god, and apparently his supernatural skills with weapons carried over to the kitchen.

I grabbed the salad tongs and began gingerly tossing the noodles and veggies with the sauce. I was afraid to do it too vigorously, or I'd spill stuff all over the place. Close up, I could smell soy sauce and ginger, and now the aromatic tang of red pepper. Leave it to Logan to make a cold salad into an enticing meal.

Logan finished his chopping and shredding, then nudged me aside to take over tossing the noodles. I don't think he'd really wanted my help in the first place.

I drifted into the breakfast nook, which is like a mini-sunroom with three walls of glass looking out over the back lawn. Sunset tinged the scattered clouds with hints of peach and pink, and the woods beyond the lawn created the illusion that we were miles from civilization.

It was a nice view, until I saw the familiar orange and black stripes through a break in the trees. Moments later, Sita emerged onto the lawn, ambling along like she was taking a leisurely tour. I didn't think it was smart of Jamaal to bring her this close to the house, particularly when she didn't seem to differentiate friend from foe. Then again, I didn't see Jamaal anywhere, so Sita might have decided to go on a walkabout all by herself, which did not speak well of his ability to control her.

"What are you looking at?" Logan asked as he set a couple of bowls of noodles down on the table.

Mutely, I pointed.

"Oh." Logan sounded about as thrilled to see her as I was. There had been an . . . incident with Logan and Sita before and he'd almost gotten mauled before Jamaal was able to reel her in. I think he held a bit of a grudge. "Where the hell is Jamaal?" he muttered, and it was a good question.

If Sita were to leave the edge of the property, that would be bad. I didn't want to think about how the humans around us would react if she toured the neighborhood, nor did I want to think about what Sita would do if she took exception to the reactions.

"We can't just let her wander around loose," I said.

"I know," Logan replied grimly, then headed back into the main part of the kitchen and grabbed the chef's knife he'd been using. "I'll keep the damn cat busy, and you use your mojo to find Jamaal and drag his ass over here to corral her."

This did not sound like the world's greatest plan to me. Logan might be a war-god descendant and really good with a knife, but I doubted he was a match for a full-grown tiger. Especially a supernatural one that might have powers we were as yet unaware of. However, he and I could survive being mauled if it came to that; our human neighbors could not. I hoped Jamaal wasn't passed out somewhere.

Logan strode out the back door with me following close on his heels. Sita caught sight of us immediately and went eerily still. Her lips pulled back in a snarl.

"I am going to kick Jamaal's ass," Logan muttered, then started toward Sita with a resigned sigh.

I began edging my way toward the woods, keeping a wary eye on the tiger. She *should* have been focused on Logan, who was coming directly toward her, but to my dismay, she was looking straight at me.

"Here, kitty, kitty," Logan called, and I had to admit I was impressed with his bravery. He was acting like initiating hand-to-claw fighting with a supernatural tiger was nothing more than an annoying inconvenience.

Sita flicked a glance at Logan, flattening her ears, and I thought our plan, such as it was, was working. I sped up, making sure not to get any closer to her on my way to the woods. Unfortunately, Sita dismissed Logan after that single glance, fixing her gaze on me once more and stalking toward me. I'm no expert at reading tiger body language, but the predatory glide of her movement suggested she wasn't heading over to give me an affectionate head-butt like she'd given Jamaal. I'd thought Jamaal was being a smartass when he said Sita didn't like me, but I was beginning to think he'd meant it literally.

"Oh, come on, you dumb animal," Logan said, moving to put himself between me and the tiger. "She's no threat. *I'm* the one you have to worry about."

Sita roared, and I didn't know if she was pissed off because Logan had gotten between her and her prey, or if she was smarter than your average tiger and was insulted by the "dumb animal" comment. Logan crouched, ready for the tiger's attack, but Sita decided that was a good time to remind us that she wasn't really a tiger and was in fact a supernatural being. Instead of attacking Logan to get him out of the way, she merely leapt over him, her ridiculously powerful haunches lifting her so high that she sailed over the point of Logan's knife as he tried to strike at her.

"Shit!" I yelled succinctly, and though I knew running would only stimulate her predatory instincts, I didn't have a choice.

I bolted for the door as Logan yelled again, trying in vain to distract Sita. I could have sworn I felt the vibration of her footsteps as she thundered after me, but that was probably just my imagination. I knew better than to look over my shoulder, because the last thing I needed was to lose speed.

I made it to the door and shoved it open, skidding over the threshold and practically falling flat on my face. I turned to push the door closed, and saw that Sita was almost upon me. I pushed with all my might, and this time I really did knock myself down. But the door closed before Sita made it through, and for a moment, I lay there on the floor and tried to regain my breath and slow down my frantic heart.

Until Sita gave me another nasty reminder that she wasn't a natural tiger and passed right through the door.

There was nothing I could do to defend myself. I was lying on my back on the floor, gasping for breath, and she was practically on top of me. She roared directly in my face, so close I could feel the heat and dampness of her breath. I closed my eyes and tried to brace myself for the pain I was about to suffer, and the horrifying ordeal of death that would come shortly after.

She roared again, nowhere near as close to my face, and I opened my eyes to see that Logan stood in the doorway and had grabbed her tail with his left hand. That finally got her attention, and she turned to swat at him with one massive paw. He let go of her tail and jumped backward, moving faster than should have been possible, and she just missed him. I could almost see her moment of indecision, as she tried to decide which of us she wanted to kill first.

"Sita, stop it!"

Jamaal's voice was about the most welcome thing I'd ever heard. Sita gave a snarl that sounded almost surly. I didn't want to attract her attention by moving while she was still in easy swatting range, but I didn't much like lying flat on my back on the floor, so I cautiously pushed myself up into a sitting position.

Between Sita and Logan, my vision was well and truly blocked, and I couldn't see Jamaal.

Logan couldn't see Jamaal, either, because he was still focused on Sita, his knife at the ready. "I am going to kick your ass six ways from Sunday," he said with feeling, and he wasn't talking to the tiger.

Sita roared out another challenge, this one directed at Logan, not me.

"No!" Jamaal yelled, and his hand clamped down on Logan's shoulder and pulled him back out of the doorway. "He didn't mean it!" Jamaal said to Sita. "It was a figure of speech."

I blinked at him. He looked terrible, his clothes drenched with sweat, his eyes bloodshot, but at least he wasn't passed out somewhere.

"Does she understand you?" I asked.

Jamaal nodded. "I'm not sure exactly how *much* she understands, but yeah, she definitely understood that."

Yet another reminder that she wasn't a normal tiger. "Well,

maybe you could have a talk with her about the difference between the good guys and the bad guys."

Sita snorted, and flicked her tail across my face. I took that
as an insult, though if she had to hit me with something, I definitely preferred her tail to her paws.

"Enough excitement for one day, sweetheart," Jamaal said,
smiling fondly at the creature that had just almost eaten Logan
and me for dinner. He reached out and scratched behind her
ears. She turned to look at me once more, and I could swear the
expression on her face was *smug*. Then, she disappeared.

Jamaal sagged against the door frame, his head lowering
in obvious exhaustion. He was shivering in the cold, and there
was dirt ground into the knees of his jeans. I was pretty sure
this meant he had collapsed during his practice session with
Sita and that was why she'd been free to wander around the
property on her own.

"Get inside and sit down before you fall down," Logan said
curtly, then gave Jamaal a little shove to get him moving.

Jamaal wasn't up to handling a shove in the back, and he
pitched forward just as I was getting up off the floor. I held
out my hands, both to steady him and to avoid being crushed,
while Logan stepped inside and closed the door behind him
with more force than necessary. I had to admit, he had reason
to be pissed off, but now wasn't the time to express it. I gave
him a dirty look as I looped Jamaal's arm over my shoulders
and braced myself against his not-inconsiderable weight. It
says something about the shape he was in that when he tried to
pull away from me, he couldn't.

"Come on," I said, taking a step toward the breakfast nook,
which was the closest place to find a chair, and hoping Jamaal
would move along with me. After a moment's hesitation, he
did. He was still shivering, and I didn't think his sweat-soaked
shirt was helping the situation.

I helped Jamaal to one of the chairs, which he practically
fell into. Logan was still behind me, and I knew without look-

ing that he was giving Jamaal the evil eye. Jamaal tried to take a deep breath, but he was shivering too hard.

"Will you let me get you a dry shirt?" I asked.

"I'm fine," he said with a shake of his head that rattled his beads. It would have been more convincing if his teeth weren't chattering.

I knew without needing to be told that Jamaal had never taken his shirt off around his fellow *Liberi*. He was more than a little self-conscious about the wealth of scars that riddled his chest and back, a consequence of his mortal life, in which he'd been a slave. He had never told anyone but me about his background, and Anderson and the rest of his *Liberi* were under the impression that Jamaal was only about fifty years old.

"You are *not* fine," Logan snapped, and to my surprise, he pulled off his own long-sleeved tee and threw it at Jamaal. "Put that on!"

Jamaal had never been too good at taking orders, and he gave Logan a snarl that would have done Sita proud. "I'm not wearing your fucking shirt," he said, and threw the shirt back at Logan. Which would have worked better if he weren't weak as a kitten. The shirt fluttered to the floor well short of its goal.

Logan snatched the shirt from the floor and held it out to Jamaal. "Put it on yourself, or I'm putting it on you. You're in no shape to fight me."

Jamaal growled, but Logan was right and he didn't have the strength to put up a fight. He took the shirt with obvious reluctance and went to pull it on over his head.

Logan rolled his eyes. "Take the wet shirt off first, dimwit."

Jamaal froze, a look of near panic on his face. He gave me a pleading look, and it shows just how shaken he was that he was willing to reach out to me for help.

"You think I don't know you have scars?" Logan asked, his voice suddenly gentling.

Jamaal's eyes went even wider, and he gaped at Logan. "How can you know?" he asked.

"I tended your body after the executions, man. I know you have a shitload of scars. You don't want to talk about them, that's fine with me. Just change out of that wet shirt before someone else comes in looking for dinner."

Still shivering, Jamaal reluctantly peeled off his shirt, his shoulders hunched in a protective posture. He pulled Logan's shirt on so fast it was a wonder he didn't rip it, especially since he was at least a size larger than Logan.

"I'm going to run up and get a new shirt," Logan said, "and when I get back down, we're going to talk about what just happened."

"That's what you think," Jamaal muttered under his breath, but Logan hadn't waited to hear his answer and was already on his way out the door.

Jamaal's head was bowed, maybe in exhaustion, maybe in shame. He'd always seemed ashamed of himself when the death magic made his temper crack, but from my point of view, he had nothing to be ashamed of. It wasn't like the death magic was a character flaw; he'd never asked for it. But I knew he wouldn't appreciate it if I voiced the sentiment, especially when he seemed to be studiously avoiding my gaze. I decided acting as if nothing had happened might be the wisest course of action.

"Do you want some coffee?" I asked. "Or some food? Logan made some kind of cold noodle dish that looks delicious."

"I'm sorry Sita went after you," he said, ignoring my question and still not looking at me.

I sighed and pulled out a chair so I could sit closer to his eye level. He met my gaze for about a millisecond before glancing away again.

"Please talk to me," I said. "I can't help thinking Sita's aversion to me may have something to do with how *you* feel about me." It made sense to me that if Jamaal was still pissed at me for my attempted abandonment, Sita would pick up on it and hold it against me.

"I'm not the sharing-my-feelings type." He shoved to his feet, his balance still unsteady.

I reached out to help him, but he neatly avoided my grasp.

"I don't need your help."

"Jamaal—"

"Leave me alone, Nikki."

He turned his back on me and staggered out of the kitchen. I wanted to follow him, to try again, but I knew better. He had shut himself off from me—and from the rest of Anderson's *Liberi*. Everyone was relieved that his temper was so much better controlled these days. So relieved I doubted anyone but me had seen the downside yet. Sure, he was easier to live with this way, but I didn't think the isolation was good for him. Leo might be genuinely happy to live ensconced in his room with his computers and minimal human contact, but Jamaal needed people, whether he liked to admit it or not.

Someone was going to have to chip away at the barriers he'd built around himself. I had a feeling the only someone who'd even be willing to try was me.

Six

My appetite had fled after all the excitement, but I sat down and ate the bowl of noodles Logan had dished out for me anyway. Logan didn't return to the kitchen, and I wondered if he and Jamaal had bumped into each other on the stairway. Logan had seemed pretty determined to give Jamaal a talking-to, and Jamaal had been equally determined to avoid it. I hadn't heard any sounds of battle, so I assumed either it was something else that distracted Logan, or he and Jamaal were talking things out like civilized adults.

I put the rest of the noodles in the fridge, then picked up the soggy shirt Jamaal had considerately left in a heap on the floor. I draped it over the back of one of the chairs to dry, then retrieved my purse and my planned itinerary for the night from my room. I thought long and hard about whether to bring my .38 Special with me. I would be within the D.C. city limits for some of the drive, and it would be illegal to carry a loaded gun when I was. I could have locked the gun in the trunk, unloaded, but that would defeat the purpose of having it with me.

In the end, as I had so many times in recent weeks, I decided to risk carrying it. I was probably in no danger just driving by Olympian properties, but I had too many enemies to feel comfortable going anywhere near them unarmed. I would have to be doubly careful to obey all traffic laws while I was out.

I got into my Mini and started the long and tedious journey. There were scattered clouds in the sky, and the moon was only a crescent when it was visible. I didn't know how much moonlight my powers needed to be juiced up to the max—hell, I wasn't even certain moonlight had any effect. If the moon was covered by clouds when I neared one of the properties of interest, I tried to find a way to hang around inconspicuously until it broke through. I spent a lot of time by the side of the road with my map unfurled as camouflage, but whether the moon was peeking through or not, I didn't feel any special interest in anyplace I passed.

I didn't have a huge amount of time until the moon set at a little before ten, but I was determined to use every glimmer of moonlight I could, methodically going through my itinerary. I was using the Beltway to carry me between locations, and the traffic was for once cooperating without any snarls or major slowdowns. The steady movement, and the sound of my tires on the asphalt, lulled me, and I went into autopilot—that state of mind where you arrive at point B and realize you have no memory of the turns and exits you took on your way from point A.

I came back to myself as I was hanging a right off the exit ramp, and I honestly had no idea what exit I had taken. I glanced at the dashboard clock and knew for sure that wherever I was, it wasn't the exit I'd been aiming for, or I would have been there ten minutes ago. A bolt of adrenaline shot through me, banishing the cobwebs in my brain and making me feel awake and alert again. If I'd just been driving on normal autopilot, I would have gotten off at a familiar exit, but I had to consult my map to figure out where I was, which likely meant that my supernatural hunting sense had taken over.

There were no known Olympian properties anywhere close, and now that I was alert again, I felt no particular pull to go one way or the other. I tried to send myself into autopilot again, but that's hard to do when you're driving unfamiliar streets. I also tried pulling over and closing my eyes, attempting to tuck my conscious mind away so my subconscious could feed me some clues, but it's almost impossible to get your mind to drift on command.

Frustration beat at me. I *knew* I'd been going in the right direction to get to Konstantin when I'd pulled off the Beltway, but now I had nothing. I slapped the steering wheel and uttered a few choice words as I reluctantly turned back toward the Beltway. Whatever had led me here was now refusing to cooperate, and the moon had set for the night.

Playing a long shot, I stopped by the FedEx store Konstantin had used when sending his nasty email. I luckily found an employee who'd been at work at the time Konstantin had been there. When I described Konstantin to her, she shrugged and said she didn't remember seeing anyone meeting that description. However, she also said she could barely remember her own name when she worked the graveyard shift, so I had no way of being sure whether Konstantin had been there or not.

Disappointed but unsurprised by the dead end, I headed back to the mansion.

I slept in on Sunday morning, though I was still up earlier than anyone else in the house—with the exception of Leo. I had developed a morning ritual very similar to the one I had had when I'd been living blissfully alone in my condo. I still missed the place, and I tried to stop by on a regular basis to have some time to myself and to remind myself that I had a home to go back to if and when I could ever extricate myself from these messes with Konstantin and Emma. But every time I left the condo, I found myself taking something else back to the mansion with me, moving in little by little, growing ever deeper roots.

In my condo, my morning ritual was to make a pot of coffee and a couple slices of toast, then sit on the couch in my bathrobe with my laptop on my lap and read, or at least skim, my favorite news sites. Having brought over my toaster and coffeemaker, I was now able to re-create the ritual in my suite, though I'd gotten away from it when I'd been trying so hard to avoid Anderson.

I was enjoying the leisure of my "new normal" when my cell phone rang. My gut clenched in anxiety because I feared it was the Glasses calling to tell me they had decided to come home. But when I picked up the phone, the caller ID said Cyrus Galanos. I knew Cyrus and Konstantin by first name only—very kingly of them—but I suppose it would have been legally inconvenient to go by only one name.

I stared at the phone for a good long time, wondering what he could possibly want and if it would be better to let him go straight to voice mail. But until I got around to getting a disposable phone, he could probably find me and waylay me somewhere if I played hard to get. With a sigh, I answered the phone.

"Hello?" I said, sounding tentative. Showing weakness of any kind probably wasn't the wisest idea, but I doubted he was calling for anything good.

"Hello, Nikki," Cyrus said, his voice warm and friendly as always. "I hope I didn't wake you."

"No, I was up."

"I thought maybe you were sleeping in after your late night."

Oh. That was what this was about. My drive-bys last night

must not have been as subtle as I'd hoped. Taking the Mini had been a mistake. I should have rented a nondescript sedan that no one would notice.

"What, no clever comebacks?" Cyrus mocked, sounding considerably less friendly. "No elegant denials?"

I shook my head. "What do you want, Cyrus?"

"I think I made that quite clear the other day: leave my father alone."

"I'd have been happy to do that, if he'd left *me* alone."

"Huh?"

I did a mental double take, because he sounded genuinely puzzled. I supposed Daddy Dearest hadn't run his little vendetta idea by Cyrus before acting on it.

"He burned down my parents' house, Cyrus," I said, letting my own anger rise to the surface and color my voice. "Then he sent me an email telling me how creative he was going to be in making my life miserable without formally breaking the treaty. If you think I'm just going to sit here and take it—"

"He didn't do it."

There was no hint of doubt or uncertainty in Cyrus's voice, but I had to wonder how well Cyrus really knew his father. He seemed like such a decent guy himself, it was hard to believe he could condone the kinds of things Konstantin did. Maybe his mind just didn't work the same way and he couldn't fully grasp his father's evil.

"He claimed responsibility for it," I argued, despite my own doubts.

"Really. Via *email*. Anyone can write an email. Ask yourself who has the most to gain from threatening you. It sure as hell isn't Konstantin."

"Oh, come on—Anderson wouldn't do that," I said, because there was no doubt in my mind who Cyrus meant. I sounded 100 percent certain, but that was only because I was pretty good at acting. I had mostly convinced myself that Anderson wasn't behind it, but there remained a touch of doubt.

"You've known Anderson, what, a couple of months? I'm telling you he's not the saint he pretends to be. He's a world-class manipulator, and like all old *Liberi,* he's deeply selfish at heart. It's impossible not to be when you've lived for centuries."

I snorted. "And how old are *you?*"

Cyrus laughed. "I'm selfish, too, and I'm not afraid to admit it. Just ask Blake. But my point is that Anderson might seem like he's too good and moral to do something like that, but he isn't. He'll do whatever it takes to get what he wants, and what he wants is you hunting Konstantin."

I'd have been able to put up a better protest if I hadn't had the same thoughts myself. Instead of defending Anderson and perhaps letting Cyrus see the seed of doubt, I changed tactics.

"As far as I'm concerned, the top suspects are Konstantin . . . and Emma. She hates both of us, so she'd be happy to hurt me while pushing me into hunting Konstantin."

There was a moment of silence as Cyrus thought that over, but he soon rejected it. "It's not Emma. It's true that she hates you and my father, but the person she wants to hurt most right now is Anderson. I don't know exactly what happened between the two of them, but it was obviously a very nasty breakup."

It certainly had been. However . . . "Emma blames me for it, though I *still* don't understand why. She may complain about Anderson, but it's *me* she wants to hurt."

"I hate to contradict you, but I can guarantee you it's Anderson she's after. And she's already taken her revenge."

"Huh?" Even not knowing what he was talking about, I felt a chill.

Cyrus sighed. "I believe she's planning to visit to explain later today."

"Explain what? Cyrus, what are you talking about?"

"You'll find out soon enough. Having seen her in action, I know I don't want to get on Emma's bad side, and she wouldn't want me spoiling the surprise."

"Bastard."

"Sorry. I shouldn't have brought it up in the first place. Suffice it to say that she's made it clear to me that you're not her target. And what I said about Konstantin still stands. If you or any of your people harm him, it'll be a declaration of war."

I was too sick with dread to keep talking. "I understand," I said, and hung up the phone.

It was hard to go back to my morning routine when I got off the phone with Cyrus, but I gave it my best shot. I drank my coffee and scrolled listlessly through the news, not really reading anything, just sort of skimming and making a show of it. As if by going through the motions of acting normal, I could actually *be* normal. But it was damn hard not to obsess, both about who was responsible for the fire, and about what hell Emma was going to release on Anderson in the near future.

When something finally *did* capture my full attention, it was an ad, of all things. There was a new exhibition opening at the Sackler Gallery next weekend. I'm not a huge fan of museums—thanks to umpteen million school trips in this museum-filled metropolis, and aided by the necessity of taking every visiting relative and friend of the family on museum tours—and normally, I wouldn't even notice an ad like that, or care what exhibitions were in town. But since I'd set my sights on mending my fences with Jamaal . . .

You wouldn't think to look at him that Jamaal was into museums, not with the testosterone that fairly oozed from his pores. Ask your average manly man if he'd like to go to a museum, and he'll look at you like you suggested he wear a tutu in public. But there was nothing average about Jamaal, and the one and only time I'd been in his suite I'd noticed an impressive collection of museum catalogs displayed on his bookshelves. Not to mention the crowning glory of his sitting room, which was a tiny Indian painting of the goddess Kali, from whom he was descended. It was a bona fide work of fine art, dating from the seventeenth century.

The new exhibition opening at the museum was of Indian art, and I'd bet anything Jamaal would want to go. Maybe I should tell him I was planning a visit and invite him to come along.

Yeah, like Jamaal would make it that easy.

I had about a half hour to make and reject a number of plans to coax Jamaal out of his shell before Emma and her malice drove every other thought out of my head.

SEVEN

The window of my sitting room looks out over the front of the house, so when a candy-apple-red sports car wended its way down the long and twisty driveway, it caught my eye. I'm not enough of a car nut to guess what it was, except that it was probably something Italian and obscenely expensive. No one in this house drove anything so ostentatious, and I made an educated guess that Emma was behind the wheel, dropping by for the visit Cyrus had warned about.

I told myself it was none of my business, and that I should stay up in my suite, as far away from the impending fireworks as possible. But after Cyrus's advance warning, my stomach was tied up in knots wondering what terrible thing Emma had done. Whatever it was, whatever Anderson's faults, I was sure he didn't deserve it, not from her. He'd done everything he could to take care of her after we'd rescued her, had made excuses for her and forgiven her outbursts well past the point of being reasonable. *She* was the one who'd walked out.

My feet carried me to the door before I'd consciously made the decision to go downstairs. I was probably being stupid. My presence was likely to throw gasoline on the fire, and though I considered Anderson a friend, of sorts, we weren't close enough to justify me sticking my nose into his marital difficulties. But of course I kept heading downstairs anyway.

Anderson was waiting in the foyer when I reached the landing above the first floor. He was standing straight and tall, his arms crossed over his chest and his gaze focused on the front door. Emma had to have called him to let him know she was coming, or she'd never have gotten past the front gate. Anderson had changed its code the day after she'd left.

"Go back upstairs, Nikki," Anderson said without looking up.

I stopped on the landing and blinked in surprise. "How did you know it was me?" I wasn't surprised he'd known *someone* was coming, considering we had a few creaky steps, but unless he had eyes in the back of his head . . .

He glanced up over his shoulder at me, and his expression was inscrutable. "Because you're the only private investigator in this house, and the only one nosy enough to try to eavesdrop."

"I wasn't eavesdropping!" I said in outrage, but the doorbell rang, and I no longer had his attention.

I stood hesitating on the landing as Anderson opened the door. It was hard to interpret his words as anything but a direct order, and yet I was reluctant to leave him alone to face Emma. Which was ridiculous, of course. He wasn't a man, he was a *god*. He could probably handle whatever Emma was about to dish out.

I was still debating what to do when Emma swept into the room, followed by another woman I didn't know. Both women wore full-length fur coats, and diamonds sparkled from their earlobes and fingers. Clearly, Emma had embraced the Olympian way of life, where ostentation was considered a good thing.

I decided too late that I had made a foolish decision in coming downstairs. I turned to leave, but Emma had already spotted me.

"Nikki!" she cried in feigned delight, and I had to suppress the instinct to cringe. "How lovely to see you."

Anderson shot me a steely look. "Upstairs. Now."

"Yup, I'm going," I assured him, holding up my hands in surrender.

"Oh, please, *do* stay," Emma said, smiling up at me as malice glittered in her eyes. "What I have to say concerns you, too."

I looked at Anderson for a verdict, and if he had told me to leave, I'd have been out of there.

"Very well," he said. "Come on down."

"Aren't you going to invite us in to somewhere more comfortable?" Emma asked as I descended the last flight of stairs.

"If it weren't so cold out, we'd be having this meeting on the front porch." Surely Anderson was battling a severe case of mixed emotions, but he sure as hell wasn't letting it show in his face or voice. He spoke to Emma as he would speak to any other Olympian, with no pretense of courtesy.

Emma's eyes narrowed at Anderson's response, whether from pain or from anger, I wasn't sure. Maybe both. I didn't understand what gave her the idea that Anderson's interest had strayed to me, but I was sure she actually believed it, and that his imaginary betrayal hurt her. If she weren't such a crazy bitch, I might even have felt a tad sorry for her.

I descended the last few steps, getting a closer look at Emma as she opened her coat. She was as beautiful as ever, but I could tell she'd lost weight. Her cheekbones looked sharper, her eyes almost sunken, and her hair seemed to have lost a little of its luster. She stroked the fur of her coat absently, and I saw that her fingernails were chewed down to nubs, a fact her glossy red nail lacquer accentuated more than it hid.

The smile on her face was cruel, and the glint in her eyes held both confidence and spite, but her body told a different story. She was *not* flourishing as an Olympian, no matter what she wanted Anderson to think. But leaving him to join them had been her choice, and she now had to live with it.

Emma's companion looked far more comfortable in her own skin. She wore a skintight black miniskirt displaying legs about a mile long. Personally, I thought she was too skinny to pull off the look, and her legs looked like matchsticks tucked into expensive designer pumps. A crescent moon glyph glowed on her cheek, and her gray-blue eyes glittered with what looked to me like anticipation.

Shrugging as if Anderson's rebuff meant nothing to her, Emma turned to me. Her gleeful self-assurance might be an act, but her hatred of me was definitely not. "Come meet Christina," she said, beckoning. "You two have a lot in common. She's a descendant of Selene, who's also a moon goddess."

I was sure that was about the *only* thing we had in common. "Charmed," I said with a curl of my lip and went to stand by Anderson.

"I don't remember giving you permission to bring a guest," Anderson said coldly.

The calculating gleam in Emma's eyes sharpened. "Oh, but I just *knew* you'd want to meet Christina."

Christina just stood there smiling, a prop rather than a person.

"Whatever it is you have to say, just say it and get the hell out," Anderson said.

Emma pouted. "You never did have a sense of drama, did you?"

"I'm in no mood for banter. I let you come here because you said it was important, but I'd be happy to throw you and your lovely companion out on your asses. So talk."

The look on Emma's face said she was genuinely disappointed Anderson didn't want to play word games with her. She was purposely drawing out the encounter as much as she could, letting the suspense build. I wondered if Anderson knew she was here to unveil her revenge, or whether he thought something more mundane was going on.

"Fine," Emma said with a resigned sigh. "I'll get to the point." She turned to me. "You remember when Kerner's jackal bit you and you came down with rabies?"

I tried not to shudder at the memory. The supernaturally enhanced rabies would have killed me permanently if it had been allowed to run its course. Instead, Anderson had killed me himself and burned my body, and the seed of immortality had generated a brand-new, virus-free body for me. It was something I'd have loved to forget.

"It rings a bell," I said, hoping I sounded dry and casual despite the chill the reminder had given me. "What does that have to do with anything?" I glanced over at Christina, and the lump of dread in my stomach grew tighter and colder as my mind began rapidly connecting the dots.

"Anderson was so very concerned about you that he called a *Liberi* who had refused to join his merry band and was living in quiet anonymity out in the countryside. He needed a descendant of Apollo to examine you and figure out what was wrong with you, and she was the only one he knew who might actually help."

I started to shake my head, as if I could somehow stop her from finishing her thought.

"What have you done?" Anderson asked in a horrified whisper, but we were both looking at Christina now, and I think we both knew what was coming.

"I never liked Erin," Emma said to him. "And not just because she was your wife before me. She was so bitter about you dumping her it made her quite unpleasant to be around. I'm sure it was the bitterness that made her choose not to live under your roof, where she would be off-limits to Olympians."

Anderson stood frozen in shock and horror beside me. Frankly, I wasn't doing much better myself, and I shared Emma's opinion about Erin's likability.

Emma drank in Anderson's pain, then turned to me with another of her vicious smiles. "I have you to thank for making this so easy for me. I don't know if I could possibly have hunted her down if she hadn't come out of hiding to treat you. When she left, I followed her home so I knew where I could get to her if I ever had a need."

I guess I was supposed to feel guilty about that, but there was no way I was going to accept it as my fault. Although perhaps I should have thought of it when Emma left us to join the Olympians. Maybe I should have anticipated the animosity between Anderson's ex-wives and constructed a new cover identity for Erin.

"I told Cyrus where she was hiding," Emma continued, "and he sent a squad to harvest her seed. Of all the mortal Descendants in our service, Cyrus thought Christina the most deserving of elevation, so he had her do the honors."

By which Emma meant Christina had killed Erin, thereby stealing Erin's seed for herself. She was no longer a Descendant, but had joined the ranks of the *Liberi*. With an act of deliberate murder.

I swallowed hard, horrified by what Emma had done—and by the reminder that Cyrus wasn't really a nice guy, no matter what he liked to pretend. And then I sneaked a peek at Anderson and practically stopped breathing.

He was still firmly in his mortal disguise. There was no white light leaking from his eyes, nor was any glow coming from his hands, and yet he was still incandescent with fury. Enough so that Christina had taken a step backward, and even Emma looked just a touch less sure of herself. She glanced quickly down at his hand, and I knew she was wondering if she'd pushed him too far, if he was actually pissed off enough to use his Hand of Doom against her. Not that she knew what that hand could do if Anderson set his mind to it. Anderson took a step closer to Emma, his hand rising from his side. Her breathing quickened, but she held her ground.

"Do you want to go to war against all of the Olympians?" she asked. "Because if you hurt me, it will break your treaty with Cyrus, and he will destroy you and all of your people.

Except for Nikki, of course." She smiled her malicious smile again. "We'd have other uses for your new girlfriend."

Even in the midst of the crisis, I couldn't help rolling my eyes. Emma was descended from Nyx, the goddess of night, but if there was a goddess of jealousy—and I was sure there was, even if I couldn't name her off the top of my head—I would swear Emma was at least her kissing cousin.

Anderson looked like he was about to choke on his rage. He was a god of vengeance, and it had to be killing him to restrain his need to strike out. I think everyone in the house was damn lucky he was rational enough to care about the consequences of unleashing his inner Fury. "I will not start a war," he said in a low and dangerous voice. "You and your companion may leave this house unscathed. I was a fool not to see this coming and move Erin to a new location."

It took everything I had not to burst out with something scathingly unwise. Even after all the crap Emma had pulled, Anderson was still willing to take some of the blame and put it on his own shoulders.

"But I warn you, Emma," Anderson continued, letting more of his anger creep into his voice, "you had better not try me again. I am better at vengeance than you are, and you would not be the first ex-wife to learn that the hard way."

Being the son of a Fury, Anderson most definitely was an expert in the vengeance business. *I* sure as hell wouldn't want to mess with him. Emma was crazy, but only if she was *stupid* and crazy would she take another shot at Anderson after this warning. There was a sense of . . . portentousness in the air, like Anderson's words might be more than just words. But maybe that was just my imagination running away with me because of what I knew about him.

Emma had lost her gloating smile, and I think that under her calm facade, she was actually afraid of Anderson for the first time. I *know* Christina was afraid, because her face was

ghostly pale and her eyes too wide. I bet she'd have run screaming out the door if Anderson had said boo.

"I've done nothing wrong," Emma said, and I think she actually believed it. "I haven't broken the treaty, and it was your
own fault Erin was vulnerable."

"Get out. Now."

I think Emma would have liked to have hung around and
looked for more chances to gloat. This was probably the end
of her revenge—Cyrus was right, and I couldn't see her settling for burning down empty houses when she had this rabbit
already in her hat—and she wanted to savor it. But she also
knew when Anderson had been pushed as far as it was safe to
push him, and that was the case now.

"Well, it was lovely seeing you both again," Emma said,
then turned her back on Anderson and walked with affected
nonchalance toward the door. Christina, who truly had been
there as nothing but a prop for Emma's revenge, was in such a
hurry to get out she practically bowled Emma over on the way.

The door closed behind them, and seconds later the car
revved its engine and pulled away. Leaving me alone in the
foyer with an enraged god of death and vengeance who might
be on the verge of exploding.

Eight

I was afraid to move. Afraid to even breathe. I felt like I was
standing on a land mine, and one false step would blow me
to smithereens. Should I try to say something sympathetic and
comforting to Anderson? Should I apologize for my role in
Emma's revenge, even while refusing to accept any blame? Or
should I try to slink away without bothering him?

Sometimes it really sucked knowing the truth about him. Even having witnessed his Hand of Doom in action, I doubt I'd have felt this level of dread if I thought he were merely another *Liberi*. But I *did* know the truth, and I wasn't sure what would happen if Anderson reached his breaking point.

"Don't stop breathing on my account," he said. His voice sounded almost normal, but there was still something about him that *felt* dangerous.

"I've seen you lose it before," I replied quietly, thinking about what had happened when we'd trespassed on Alexis's property to rescue Emma from the depths of his pond. Alexis had taunted Anderson with what he and Konstantin had done to Emma while she was in their custody, and Anderson had dispensed with his mortal disguise and turned into a humanoid pillar of fire. "I don't want to see it again."

"I didn't 'lose it,'" he said, sounding affronted.

"I saw you turn into—"

"I know what you saw." He turned and looked me squarely in the face. "I was entirely in control of myself, Nikki. I had always planned to . . ." He looked around, as if just noticing we were standing in the foyer, where anyone could overhear. "What I did then was calculated. Trust me: you don't want to be near me if I ever really do 'lose it.'"

Oh, I trusted him about that all right. I might not know the details of what would happen, but it would be ugly, and there was likely to be collateral damage.

"I'm . . . sorry about Erin," I said, because I couldn't walk away without saying it.

"Me, too." He was almost eerily calm now, his face showing no emotion, his voice flat. "I need to be alone right now."

He turned from me without another word, climbing the stairs, no doubt heading for the east wing, which was his private domain within the mansion. My throat was tight, and my heart hurt for him. I'd had very little contact with Erin, and my memories of the time were a little hazy, but I remembered how she and Anderson had sniped at each other as ex-lovers often do. Yet Anderson had loved her once, and to have Emma bring about her death was a devastating blow. I wished he had someone to turn to, someone to give him support and companionship to help him through.

But Anderson was a god in hiding, and that meant he had to be used to dealing with the hardships of life alone. My heart might ache for him, but there was nothing I could do.

After Emma left, I tried to forget all about her nasty visit. I had enough crap on my plate that it wasn't too hard.

Despite Cyrus's unequivocal warning that I was to back off Konstantin, I had no intention of doing so, especially now that I'd crossed Emma off my suspects list. It was still possible Anderson was behind it, that he'd done it to light a fire under my ass, so to speak, but Konstantin was the more likely suspect. It might have been smarter for him to leave me alone, but being deposed from his position as "king" of the Olympians, he might be angry enough to act on emotion rather than logic.

I wasn't breaking the treaty by merely driving around the city looking for Konstantin, but just in case Cyrus didn't see it that way, I rented a sedan that would blend in with the city's traffic. Last night had revealed the pitfalls of cruising around by myself and trying to follow my instincts. I needed to be able to let my conscious mind drift, which was hard to do—and potentially dangerous—while driving. I'd be much better off if I could get someone else to do the driving for me.

There were only three people in the house I was willing to spend that many hours shut up in a car with. My first choice, naturally, was Jamaal, but he turned me down with some lame excuse about being too tired after having worked so much with Sita during the day. He didn't *look* tired when I cornered him. More like sullen and . . . distant. He was drifting further away, and I might be the only one in the house who saw it happening.

My second choice was Maggie, but I couldn't find her, and

she didn't answer her cell. My third and last choice was Logan, but he informed me he already had plans for the evening. I was tempted to ask him what he was up to—for the most part, Anderson's *Liberi* didn't seem to have much of a social life—but it was none of my business, and he hadn't seemed like he wanted to share.

I tried Maggie one more time, but no dice. She was off the grid, and I was on my own.

That is, I was on my own if I insisted my driver be one of the *Liberi*. I hesitated to ask Steph to do anything that might be even remotely dangerous, but I couldn't see any problem with her driving me around. We'd be in a rented vehicle no one recognized, and I would not make the mistake of loitering around if the moon hid behind the clouds at inconvenient times. No one was going to notice a nondescript car that drove by without stopping or slowing.

My decision to ask Steph was reaffirmed when I got a call from the Glasses. They had decided to come home early after all, although they hadn't been able to get a flight until Wednesday. That meant I could no longer put off trying to come up with a plausible explanation for why I was living in the mansion, and I'd need Steph's help to corroborate it. Driving around with her tonight would give me the opportunity to kill two birds with one stone.

It was getting uncomfortably late by the time I reached the decision to ask Steph to drive me, the sun already starting to set. Moonset wasn't until almost eleven, but a quick check on the weather had shown me rain was heading our way. The skies were still clear, but who knew how long it would last? I stood by my window and watched the sky anxiously as I called Steph. There was no urgent reason why I should have to go out hunting tonight, specifically, except for my fear that Konstantin wasn't going to wait very long before he struck again.

The phone call started off poorly, because Steph was planning to meet Blake for dinner. If the rain weren't moving in,

I'd have said we could go on our hunting expedition afterward, but it didn't look like we were going to have a whole lot of time tonight. Steph reluctantly agreed she could reschedule her date for the next day.

The good news was that since she'd been planning to meet Blake, Steph was already on her way to the mansion when I called, and she arrived about fifteen minutes later. I waited for her on the front porch, my rental car parked along the mansion's circular drive. Steph pulled up behind the rental, and I took a deep breath before starting down the stairs toward her. Silly of me to feel nervous about seeing my own sister, but I was still swimming in guilt about the hell I'd brought on our family, and I knew she wasn't happy with me for interrupting her planned evening with Blake.

Our eyes met over the hood of her car as Steph got out, and maybe I was reading things into her expression that weren't there, but I thought I detected a hint of coolness. I wondered if asking her to do the driving tonight was a bad idea, but it was too late to change my mind now. I dug the keys to the rental out of my coat pocket and took a quick glance at the darkening sky. So far, there were only wispy clouds, and the moon was easily visible. It was a good night for a hunt.

"Thanks for helping me out," I said to Steph as I handed her the keys.

She certainly didn't need to dress up for a date with Blake, who would find her beautiful and alluring even in ratty sweats, but either they'd been planning to go somewhere fancy, or she'd dressed up because she felt like it. Her red wool swing coat covered most of the outfit, but her black pencil skirt and stiletto-heeled pumps gave her away. Not the kind of outfit she'd have worn if she'd known how she'd be spending the next few hours.

I guess my visual assessment of her outfit wasn't terribly subtle, because Steph looked down at herself and chuckled. "I'll be the best-dressed assistant private eye out there."

"I'm sorry—" I started, but Steph cut me off.

"I have even more reason than you to want Konstantin caught," Steph said, all hints of humor banished. "I'm not doing this as some kind of favor."

I knew that was the truth, but that didn't stop me from wanting to apologize. I refrained, because I knew Steph wouldn't appreciate it. "Am I allowed to thank you at least?"

She sighed dramatically. "I suppose so," she said in a tone of long-suffering patience.

My lips twitched with a smile. Maybe I really *had* been imagining the hint of coolness I'd thought I'd seen when she first got out of the car. She seemed like her usual self, full of warmth and good humor.

"Thank you," I said again, and then I gave her an impulsive hug. She was more than just my big sister; she was also my best friend, and a truly nice person at heart. Maybe somewhere deep down inside she was angry about all the chaos I'd brought into her life, but she would be ashamed of those feelings and would do her best not to show them. That was all I could ask for, and maybe more than I deserved.

"All righty then," Steph said when I released her from the hug, "let's get this show on the road."

I smiled at the stupid pun, and Steph and I piled into the rental. I'd thought about planning out an elaborate route that would take us by more Olympian properties, but I hadn't been near any of those properties when I'd spaced out last night, so I saw no reason to keep operating under the hopes that Konstantin was hiding somewhere I could find him by logic.

"So what's the plan?" Steph asked as she adjusted the seat and mirrors, then started the car.

"It's a pretty lame one," I admitted. "But I think we should just get on the Beltway and see what happens."

The Beltway circles all the way around the city, and driving on it is easily tedious enough to put anyone on autopilot. Unless you hit traffic or there's an accident, in which case it's more suited to road rage, but I was going to pretend those possibilities didn't exist.

Steph's sidelong glance told me how enamored she was of my plan, but she didn't argue. "Do you care which way I go when I get to the Beltway?"

"I don't think it matters. Take whichever way seems to be moving fastest. Once we get on the Beltway, I'll need you not to talk to me anymore. Just let me zone out."

"If you're zoned out, how are you going to tell me which way to go?"

I made a face. "I don't know," I admitted. "This is really just an experiment. I have no idea if it'll work. It might be a waste of time."

Steph shrugged. "Okay then. Only one way to find out."

During the ride to the Beltway, Steph and I tried to concoct a plausible story about why I was living in the mansion. Preferably one that didn't cause her parents—*our* parents—to ask too many questions. We didn't have a whole lot of luck. Let's face it, the situation was hard to explain. I could tell the Glasses I was working for Anderson, and they might almost believe that I'd spend a night or two there if I was working late for some reason. However, being there *every* night, as well as me moving an awful lot of my stuff from the condo to the mansion, was a lot harder. I was almost glad when we hit the Beltway and it was time to invoke radio silence, because thinking about it was making my head hurt.

It was full dark when we got to the Beltway, and there wasn't any sign of the upcoming storm yet. The moon's light was bright and clear even with the city lights doing their best to drown it out. I checked with my gut to see if I had any compulsion to go one way or another on the Beltway, but I felt nothing. There seemed to be a lot of brake lights going east, so Steph chose to go west, and I tried to let my mind drift.

As I'd already established numerous times, it's hard to get

your mind to drift on command, especially when a sense of urgency is riding you. I found myself overanalyzing every minute sensation, every stray thought, every person, place, or thing that caught my eye. My mind bounced around like a hyperactive toddler on a sugar high, and the more annoyed I got at myself for not being able to knuckle down and concentrate, the harder it got for me to knuckle down and concentrate. Or *not* concentrate. Whatever.

After a fruitless half hour of driving in silence, I was climbing the walls and squirming in my seat with frustration. And that was when we hit the traffic.

I didn't know whether refraining from talking was necessary, especially since the silence didn't seem to be helping me, but I bit back a couple of curse words as I caught sight of the brake lights ahead and our car slowed first to a crawl, then to a stop. It was six thirty on a Sunday night, but I'd run into traffic snarls on the Beltway at two in the morning, so I wasn't entirely surprised. Irritated, yes, but not surprised.

Steph glanced over at me as the traffic eased forward about six inches before coming to a stop again. "Anything?"

I shook my head and wondered if we should just give up. We weren't getting anywhere—literally or figuratively—and being stuck in stop-and-go traffic is about as much fun as having a root canal.

"Maybe we should just take the next exit and call it a night," I said. To hell with my vow of silence.

Steph gave me a withering older-sister look. "You aren't seriously planning to give up after a half hour on the road, are you?"

We'd actually been on the road almost an hour, because the mansion wasn't particularly close to the Beltway, but I supposed that wasn't really very long in the grand scheme of things. Both Steph and I had understood that this would be a long, tedious night.

I shook my head. "Sorry. That was frustration talking. I can't seem to get my mind to shut up so I can zone out."

Steph shot me a droll smile as she propped her elbow against the window and laid her head down on her hand, waiting for the next opportunity to inch forward. "If anything can make your eyes glaze over, it'll be this traffic. Now hush and get back to work."

I hushed as ordered, and tried once again to let my mind wander. I spent more time than I care to admit mentally cussing out the traffic, wondering what the holdup was. My guess was an accident with rubberneckers, but if I was right, it was far enough away that we couldn't see any flashing lights yet.

Roll forward. Stop. Roll forward. Stop. Roll forward . . .

I can get pretty damned keyed up sometimes, particularly when I've been dipping into the coffee too much, but eventually the monotony of the drive got to me. My mind drifted a couple of times, but I unfortunately *noticed* it drifting, which yanked me back into full alertness. But it took me less time to start drifting, and I figured I was going to either get myself into the zone or fall asleep.

I blinked, and saw that not only were we not stuck in traffic anymore, we weren't even on the Beltway. I shook my head to clear the cobwebs.

I remembered thinking—dreaming?—that I was in a hedge maze, trying to find my way to the center. I'd mumbled to myself each time I got to an intersection and had to decide which way to go. I remembered a sense of urgency pressing on me, telling me to hurry. I'd started out walking, then switched to jogging, then to an all-out run. It was . . . clearer and more coherent than an ordinary dream, but fuzzier than just a flight of imagination. I honestly had no idea if I'd been awake or asleep.

The car came to a stop at a red light, and Steph turned to me with an inquiring raise of her brow. A couple of raindrops spattered on the windshield, and the trees swayed in a gust of wind. I leaned forward, staring up at the sky, but I saw no hint of the moon or of stars. The light turned green, and Steph drove through the intersection, continuing on straight, probably because I hadn't told her to turn.

"Umm . . . Have I been giving you directions?" I asked.

Steph glanced over at me again. More raindrops spattered down, and she was forced to turn on the windshield wipers.

"Yeah," she confirmed. "You've been kind of mumbling to yourself for a while. I thought you'd fallen asleep, only your eyes were open. Don't you remember?"

I rubbed my eyes, but I knew I hadn't been asleep. "I remember daydreaming, or something, about being in a hedge maze."

I ran my hand through my hair in frustration. "Let me guess: the clouds rolled in, and that's when I stopped giving you directions." The rain came down harder as if to emphasize the point that I wouldn't be getting any more moon-fueled hunches tonight.

"Yeah."

I was so frustrated I wanted to kick something. If I'd been able to get into the zone before the rain had started . . .

"We wouldn't have gotten here any faster if you'd started directing me earlier," Steph said, guessing my line of thought. "We were stuck in traffic, remember?"

I made a sound of grudging acceptance. I knew she was right, but it didn't make me any less frustrated. Two nights in a row, I'd been on Konstantin's scent, and two nights in a row, I'd failed to find him. I was not the happiest of campers.

Steph and I drove around the area a little while longer, just to be thorough, but the rain had settled in to stay, and the moon wouldn't be giving me any more help tonight. Our meanderings had taken us deep into the heart of D.C., and the most convenient way to get back to Arlington was to take Independence Avenue to the Arlington Memorial Bridge. I was staring out the rain-speckled side window, brooding about what a total failure this expedition had turned out to be. It wasn't until we passed the Sackler Gallery that I snapped out of my funk and directed my mind toward another of the many problems on my plate.

To be fair, I shouldn't have been thinking of Jamaal as one of my problems. I wasn't his girlfriend, was barely even his friend anymore. And he was a grown man, responsible for his own issues. But I couldn't help wondering if his almost obsessive practice with Sita—and his decreasing ability to keep her controlled and contained—was a sign that his self-imposed isolation wasn't good for him.

The new Indian art exhibit would be opening on Saturday, but I'd already determined that Jamaal would blow me off if I asked him to go see it with me. I needed a stronger temptation, something Jamaal couldn't get on his own. I glanced sidelong at Steph, who was quietly concentrating on driving. Through her extensive charity work, Steph knew practically everybody who was anybody in the D.C. area. Her virtual Rolodex contained a veritable cornucopia of the rich, famous, and powerful.

I didn't know how to bring up the subject gracefully, so I just blurted it out.

"Do you happen to know anyone who's a big muckety-muck at the Sackler Gallery?" I asked.

We conveniently came to a red light, so Steph could turn in her seat and give me a long, puzzled look. "The Sackler? Why? Have you developed a sudden interest in Asian art?"

There was something too knowing in her eyes as she stared at me. My sister's no dummy, and not only was she aware I had the hots for Jamaal—despite my repeated attempts to deny it—but she was also aware that he was the descendant of an Indian goddess. Even if I could have thought of a more innocuous-sounding reason for my interest, I didn't think Steph would buy it, not when the look in her eye said she'd already put two and two together.

The light turned green, and Steph returned her attention

to the road. I let out a breath I hadn't realized I was holding. Steph disapproved of Jamaal almost as much as I disapproved of Blake, so asking for her help might not have been the smartest idea I'd ever had. However, I'd already committed to the course of action.

"There's a new Indian art exhibit opening up next weekend," I said. "I'd like to see if I can draw Jamaal out to go see it, but I know if I ask him, he'll say no. I was thinking maybe you had a contact who could get us in for a private tour, maybe before the exhibit is open to the public. I think he'd have a much harder time saying no to that."

Steph was silent for the next couple of blocks, and I forced myself to be quiet and let her think. If I tried too hard to persuade her, she might come to the conclusion that I was letting myself get too involved. Actually, she probably already thought that, but there was no reason to make it worse.

"Do you really think that's a good idea?" she finally asked me.

I shrugged, trying to look casual. "It wouldn't be that big a deal. Just a trip to a museum. But I think Jamaal needs to get out of his own head for a while."

"That's your professional opinion, eh?"

I bristled, but managed to refrain from making an angry retort. "It's my opinion as a fellow human being." I didn't think telling Steph about Sita's walkabout was going to incline her to see things my way, though it was that more than anything that convinced me Jamaal needed more human contact. "We're not meant to be solitary creatures. Or didn't they teach you that in psych class?" Steph had been a psych major in college, although she'd chosen not to pursue a career.

She raised an eyebrow at me. "No reason to get testy."

"I'm not!" I protested, though I knew I was.

Steph ignored me. "If I have to listen to you telling me Blake isn't good for me, then you have to listen to me telling you that Jamaal is bad news for *any* woman."

I slumped in my seat. I thought I'd been getting better, refraining from editorializing about Blake, but maybe I hadn't. "You *don't* listen to me about Blake," I pointed out.

"That doesn't stop you from sharing your opinion."

"When was the last time I said anything to you about him?" I honestly couldn't remember. I'd bitten my tongue more times than I could count.

"You don't have to say anything to make your opinion clear. All I have to do is take one look at your face when I'm talking about him."

I glanced out the side window to orient myself, hoping we were almost at the mansion so I could escape this conversation. No such luck.

"I'm doing my best to keep my opinions to myself," I said. "That doesn't mean I don't *have* opinions, and I can't just turn them off like a light. Sorry."

Steph's hands had tightened on the wheel, and I hated the tension that radiated from her. She was a genuinely nice, good person, and she deserved to be happy. Ever since I'd become *Liberi,* I'd been dragging her down, and I wished I could make things better. But I *knew* Blake was bad for her. Eventually, they would both get tired of a relationship that didn't include sex, and then one of two things would happen: either Blake would sleep with her, thereby tying her to him for the rest of her life, or he'd dump her, breaking her heart. Neither of these alternatives was acceptable.

"I just want you to stop treating me like a child who's not capable of making her own decisions. I'm twenty-seven years old, and I don't need your guidance."

"What do you want me to do, Steph? Stop caring about you? Stop worrying about you? That isn't reasonable."

"Oh, but it's reasonable for you to ask me not to care that you're falling for Jamaal?"

"I'm not falling for him!" I snapped, which probably cemented her opinion that I was. I took a deep breath to calm my temper. Steph had seen me make a lot of bad relationship decisions over the years, and I couldn't blame her for trying to warn me away from what she saw as just one more. I took a second deep breath just for insurance, then continued in what I hoped was a calmer, more reasonable tone.

"Jamaal is a different story. I live in the same house with him, and unless the Olympians turn over a new leaf and decide to live and let live, I'll be stuck with him for the rest of my life. And in case you've forgotten, I'm immortal." Despite already having come back from the dead once, those words sounded almost laughably absurd. I supposed I'd get used to it someday, but that day sure hadn't come yet. "It's in my own best interests to try to help him, because I have to live with him either way, and he's not good to live with right now."

Everything I said was true, but it wasn't really the reason I wanted to help Jamaal, and we both knew it. Steph tapped her fingernails against the steering wheel, but the gesture seemed more restless than angry. Maybe we were making progress.

"Why does it have to be you who tries to help him?" she asked, and I decided we weren't making progress after all. "Why don't you let Anderson handle it? He's supposed to be in charge, right?"

It was a perfectly reasonable question. Anderson had certainly known Jamaal longer than I had, and Jamaal respected him a hell of a lot more. But I didn't think Anderson or any of his *Liberi* could connect to Jamaal the way I did. Our lives and backgrounds were completely different, and yet there were unmistakable similarities between our emotional landscapes. I knew what it was like to feel isolated, to hold everyone at arm's length and be completely self-sufficient. Anderson could see Jamaal's outward behavior, but he couldn't *understand* it like I could.

Of course, if I told Steph any of that, she'd read a whole lot more into it, and things felt rocky between us already.

"Anderson is too much of a guy to be much help," I said, and it was the truth, even if it wasn't the whole truth. "But he does have money up the wazoo, so maybe he'll have some contacts that can get me into the Sackler. I'll ask him about it tomorrow, and we can pretend we never had this conversation."

There was a long silence, and then Steph shook her head and sighed. "Don't bother. I know one of the trustees, and I can probably arrange something." I started to thank her, but she cut me off. "You can thank me by laying off me and Blake. What we do or don't do is our business, not yours. You've more than done your sisterly duty in trying to warn me, and you need to back the hell off."

I swallowed a protest. I *had* backed the hell off. Hadn't I? But maybe I needed to try harder.

"Okay, fine. It's a deal," I said.

Steph didn't respond.

The rest of the ride passed in silence.

NINE

It was still raining when I woke up on Monday, and a glance at the weather forecast showed me the rain was settling in for a lengthy visit. This did not increase my chances of hunting down Konstantin before he struck again, and I was tempted to drop-kick my computer for giving me the bad news.

I made another pot of coffee instead. Then I stretched out on the sofa in my sitting room with my laptop on my lap to make a show of keeping up to date with the news. I was brooding a little too much to read more than a couple of paragraphs here and there, and those only for the most interesting of stories.

My heart took a nosedive into my stomach when I saw the headline that read ARSON SUSPECTED IN CONDO FIRE THAT LEFT THREE DEAD.

There was no reason to think it had anything to do with me, but the words *arson* and *condo* jumped out at me like monsters at a horror movie.

My throat was tight, my every muscle taut, as I reluctantly clicked on the link to the full story. My breath whooshed out of my lungs when I saw the picture of a burned-out husk of a building. The roof had collapsed, and the brick facade was black as charcoal, but the shape of the building was familiar, as were the rows of granite planters that adorned the circular drive.

Without a doubt, it was *my* building.

Konstantin had struck again, and this time it wasn't an empty building he'd burned.

My eyes were clouded with tears as I took in the horrifying details the article revealed. The fire had occurred around ten last night, while Steph and I had been riding around the Beltway in our fruitless quest. The three dead were a ninety-two-year-old woman who was apparently overcome by the smoke before she'd even gotten out of bed, a twenty-five-year-old single mother whose broken leg had hampered her attempt to escape, and the three-month-old baby she'd been trying to carry to safety.

All dead because of me.

I shook my head violently. No, it was because of Konstantin. I had to remember that, had to keep it front and center in my mind, or I would go crazy. I'd done nothing wrong, nothing I'd had any reason to believe would endanger innocent civilians. Konstantin had always made it clear that he valued humans about as much as he valued insects. It was his contempt and malice that was behind the deaths, not me.

All sound, logical reasons why I shouldn't feel guilty about what had happened. And not one of them did a thing to lessen the guilt that sat heavily on my shoulders.

I read the article about four or five times, under the guise of getting all the details down, but I think I was mostly just flogging myself with them. Maybe if I'd done a better job on one of my aborted hunts, I would have been able to stop Konstantin before he killed innocents. Maybe instead of giving Jamaal a hard time about his obsessive practicing with Sita, I should be practicing my own powers just as obsessively. I'd practiced throwing and shooting because I understood exactly how that worked, but I hadn't done a whole lot with the hunting because it was hard to figure out how to train for something I didn't understand. Maybe if I'd put some serious time and effort into it . . .

Frightening how easy it was for me to find reasons to blame myself, even when I knew that was exactly what Konstantin wanted and that I was playing into his hands.

For a while, I was too busy wallowing to notice the incongruity in last night's fire. But when my mind kept circling back to my failed hunts, something jumped out at me.

The article said the fire had started around ten last night. That was when I'd been dreaming about hedge mazes and directing Steph toward what was presumably Konstantin's location. My powers had cut out the moment the rain set in, but we'd been way across the city from my condo when that had happened.

I unfolded my D.C. metro area map. Steph said we'd been in Maryland when I'd directed her to get off the Beltway, and while I'd had her make quite a few turns as I homed in on the "signal," we'd been traveling in a northwesterly direction at the time my supernatural radar went silent. My condo was northeast of that location, and quite a distance away.

It didn't necessarily mean anything. I couldn't be certain my powers were actually leading me to Konstantin, and even if they were, he probably hired a third party to set the fire for him. He wasn't the type to do his own dirty work if he didn't have to. But that line of thought reminded me of my doubts about Konstantin being the culprit. He had always struck me as coldly calculating, cruel, and dangerous, but not *crazy*.

No, an attack that left three innocent civilians dead pointed more to a mind like Emma's, dangerously unhinged. Maybe

Cyrus and I were both wrong about her. Maybe having Erin killed *hadn't* been the end all, be all of her revenge.

I'd been having a hard enough time tracking down Konstantin when I'd been sure he was behind the fires. Now I had another viable suspect, one who was just as much under the Olympians' protection. And yet, whoever the firebug was, I was going to have to catch them, and catch them soon. Before more innocents died.

I gave myself a few hours to get over the initial shock and horror of what had happened, locking myself in my suite and turning off my phone. If I didn't pull myself together before I talked to anyone, I was going to say something I would later regret. Either that, or I'd burst into tears, which was almost as bad. I didn't know what whoever it was had planned for the next attack, but I was sure the other shoe would drop soon, and it would be worse even than the condo fire. If I was going to stop it from happening, I had to keep my emotions as under control as humanly possible.

Hours of sitting alone in my room and brooding didn't do much to improve how I felt, and I eventually decided no Zen-like state of calm was going to descend on me out of the ether. I didn't have time to sit around anymore anyway.

I didn't like my chances of hunting down Konstantin in the next handful of days, especially not with the rain cutting off the moonlight. That meant my best chance of preventing another attack was through diplomacy. Whether the person behind the attack was Emma or Konstantin, they were both Olympians, and that meant they answered to Cyrus, at least in theory. I'd already seen evidence that Cyrus was not the nice guy he pretended to be, but I believed he genuinely wanted to avoid a war between the Olympians and Anderson's *Liberi*. Maybe he could be persuaded to put a leash on whoever was behind the fires.

It was a long shot, particularly if it really was Konstantin who was behind them. No matter what terms he and Cyrus had come to in order to effect their peaceful regime change, I didn't think there was a chance in hell Konstantin would take orders from his son. Maybe I would just have to hope that Emma was the guilty party and that she would be forced to obey Cyrus.

Of course, I was getting way ahead of myself. First, I had to find a way to convince Cyrus to call off the dogs.

My first inclination was to pick up the phone and call him, but even in my depleted mental state, I knew that wasn't a good idea. I didn't have enough clout to enter into a negotiation with Cyrus myself, and Anderson would *not* appreciate me going behind his back. I'd done it once before, and had the feeling I'd just barely escaped a date with his Hand of Doom.

I printed out the article about the fire, sticking it in a manila folder so I didn't have to see the headline and the photo anymore. Then I ducked into the bathroom to wash my face and put on some makeup, trying to make myself look more normal than I felt. The concealer lightened the dark circles under my eyes, but it didn't make them go away completely, and there wasn't any makeup in the world that could conceal the stark expression in my eyes. I wanted to look calm, strong, and completely reasonable when I pleaded my case to Anderson, but the reflection in the mirror told me I was falling short.

There was nothing to be done about it, so I grabbed the manila folder and marched down to the second floor, hoping Anderson would be in his study. The door was open, but when I stepped inside, Anderson wasn't at his desk. He didn't go out much, so chances were he was in the house, most likely somewhere else in his own private territory in the east wing. The rest of us weren't allowed to venture into the east wing except in case of emergency, and I wasn't sure this would qualify in his book, no matter how urgent it felt to me.

I stepped out into the hallway. "Anderson?" I called, hoping he was within earshot.

A door down the hall opened, and Anderson stuck his head

out. His hair was slicked back from his face with water, and I caught a glimpse of bare shoulder, though he used the door to shield his body from view. If I weren't such an emotional wreck, I might have tried some wisecrack about our mutual propensity for interrupting showers, but I couldn't muster even a hint of humor.

I must have looked even worse than I thought, because Anderson didn't wait for me to speak.

"Just let me throw some clothes on," he said. "I'll be right back."

I nodded, my throat tightening up on me as my mind insisted on flashing me an image of the poor, injured mother trying desperately to get her baby to safety while the building burned around her and smoke stole her breath. I had always been a bit of a bleeding heart, and I had the unfortunate tendency to let other people's misery become my own. I would never have made it as a health-care worker of any kind, being completely unable to hold myself at the distance necessary to maintain sanity. I told myself not to think about the doomed woman, or to imagine what she must have felt in the final minutes of her life, how terrified and utterly devastated she must have been when she'd realized she wasn't getting her baby out.

I made a fist and banged it hard on my thigh, trying to force myself back from the brink. The last thing I wanted to do was start this conversation with tears already running down my cheeks, and my eyes were burning in that familiar, ominous way. At least I could hand the article to Anderson instead of having to tell him what had happened.

Taking as deep a breath as my tight throat would allow, I stepped into Anderson's office and took a seat in front of his desk. I swallowed convulsively, hoping that would loosen my throat—and hoping that Anderson would take his time getting dressed so I could regain my composure.

I was going to be asking Anderson to have a civilized conversation and even negotiate with the man who'd ordered Erin's death, and I was going to have to bring up the possibility that Emma was the one responsible for the fires. No matter how cold Anderson might have acted when Emma had come by to drop her bombshell, I knew he wasn't going to want to accept the possibility that the woman he'd loved and married had set a condo full of people on fire. I had to be in control of my emotions, because Anderson might well lose control of his, and that would be bad.

I no longer felt on the verge of tears when Anderson stepped into his office, but I still wasn't as put together as I'd have liked. Anderson had donned one of his endless collection of wrinkled shirts, and if he'd combed his wet hair at all, it had to have been with his fingers. He dropped into his desk chair looking even more safe and ordinary than usual, and though I knew it was an illusion, I grasped hold of it to help steady myself.

Wordlessly, I tossed the manila folder across the desk, still not trusting myself to talk. Anderson raised an eyebrow at me, but opened the folder and read the article while I averted my eyes to avoid the pictures. I heard the pages flipping as he read, but I didn't look up. An unfortunate, whiny voice in my head kept asking why everyone was so eager to blame me for everything that went wrong in their lives. I tried not to listen to it, because feeling sorry for myself wasn't going to help the situation one bit.

I heard the sound of the papers being tucked back into the folder, then the soft groan of Anderson's chair as he leaned back in it. Safe from the worry of catching another glimpse of the pictures, I raised my head and tried to interpret the look on his face.

The best word I can come up with to describe his expression was *neutral,* and I realized he was making a concerted effort to hide his feelings. He was doing a much better job of it than I was. I hadn't a clue what he was thinking or feeling behind that mask.

"In case you were wondering," I said, though I was sure he'd figured it out already, "that was *my* condo."

"So I gathered. Have you made any progress in your hunt?" he asked, his voice as neutral as his face.

"Depends how you define progress," I said. "I thought I was on his tail last night when the rain came in, but I have no way to be sure." I braced myself for trouble as I took a tentative step into dangerous territory. "I was on his tail right about the time the fire seems to have started, and he was nowhere near my condo."

Anderson kept his neutral mask firmly in place, though I was sure he knew what I was implying. "A man like Konstantin never does his own dirty work. He has people for that kind of thing."

I was certain that was the truth, but I still couldn't shake the uncomfortable suspicion that Emma was the true culprit. She had a much more obvious motive, at least in her own twisted version of reality, but Anderson wasn't going to believe that unless I came up with actual proof, and I didn't have it. At least not yet.

"It doesn't really matter who's behind it," I said, although it did matter, quite a lot. "Whoever it is, it's an Olympian, and Cyrus should be able to put a stop to it."

Anderson shook his head. "I don't care that Cyrus has supposedly taken Konstantin's place at the top. He doesn't have the kind of power that Konstantin does, and there's no way in hell he can control Konstantin's actions. Even if he wanted to."

I mentally cursed Anderson's stubbornness. If he'd only acknowledge the possibility that Emma was behind the fires, he'd probably have set up a meeting with Cyrus already. Cyrus might not be able to stop Konstantin from coming after me, but I'd bet good money he could stop Emma.

"So what you're telling me," I said through gritted teeth, "is that you're content to sit back and do nothing while whoever it is kills babies and old ladies." Anderson's narrowed eyes said he didn't appreciate my tone, but I was pissed enough not to care. "You're not even going to *try* to negotiate with Cyrus."

"I didn't say I wouldn't try." Despite the narrowed eyes, he sounded calm enough. "I was merely pointing out that it's not likely to work. We have no leverage."

No, we didn't have leverage. Not unless Anderson was willing to go to war with the Olympians for my sake, which he wasn't. And to tell you the truth, I was just as happy about that. The Olympians had too much of an advantage in numbers, and they would wipe us all out. Cyrus might not be eager to start that war, but not eager wasn't the same as not willing. Konstantin had laid off Anderson and his *Liberi* because he knew that Anderson was capable of killing him, and that was a risk he wasn't willing to take. Taking that thought to its logical conclusion . . .

"We'd have leverage if you'd let Cyrus know what you are, and what you can do."

I'd tried to broach this subject any number of times since I'd learned Anderson's secret, and he had always shut me down fast and hard. He'd even threatened to kill me—and whoever I told—if I revealed what I knew. I didn't think he was bluffing, but I couldn't for the life of me understand why he wasn't willing to reveal the deadly weapon that could act as a powerful deterrent and give us a leg up on the Olympians. It felt kind of like we had a nuclear bomb but didn't want anyone, not even our own people, to know it.

"I think I've made it perfectly clear that that is not an option," Anderson said in a low and menacing voice. "You'd be wise never to bring it up again."

I felt like grabbing him and shaking him. I couldn't think of a single reason why we shouldn't use his special power to our advantage. He obviously wasn't shy about using it, at least not when nobody but me could see. I'd already seen him kill three *Liberi*.

"I know you want me to shut up about it," I continued. "But letting Cyrus know you have the power to kill him might be the only way to motivate him to—"

"Enough!" Anderson pushed back his chair and practically jumped to his feet. His expression was dangerous enough that I stood, too, and took a couple of hasty steps back.

Anderson stepped around his desk, but instead of coming toward me, he stalked toward the study door and banged it shut, turning a dead-bolt lock I'd never noticed before. He swiveled toward me, and I made sure there was a chair between us. It wouldn't slow him down much, but it was better than nothing.

"What's it going to take to keep you quiet, Nikki?" He took a step toward me, and I took a corresponding step back as he raised his right hand. The Hand of Doom.

My heart was slamming in my chest, my every nerve on red alert, but frankly, I was getting sick to death of being bullied. I wanted to shout out my rage, but I shoved a muzzle and leash on my temper. If I wasn't careful, I could end up dead, or wishing I were dead, in no time flat.

"You could try explaining *why* you're so dead set against anyone knowing," I said.

Anderson blinked like he was startled. I guess he'd expected me to back down in the face of his threat. And why shouldn't he expect that? It's what I'd always done before.

"Innocent people's lives are at stake," I reminded him. "People are getting hurt, getting killed, losing everything they own, all because one of Cyrus's people has some psychotic vendetta against me. I couldn't live with myself if I didn't do everything in my power and explore every possible way to make it stop. Even if it means pissing you off yet again. I don't get why—"

"If I tell you why it's imperative that the truth doesn't get out, will you promise to stop asking questions?"

It was my turn to be startled. I don't know where I was expecting the conversation to go, except that it wasn't here. Anderson was actually backing down? It seemed impossible, and I was immediately wary.

"So after all the huffing and puffing, you're just going to give up and tell me?"

"I'll tell you what could happen if the truth got out. The answer won't satisfy your curiosity, and you'll want to ask me ten million questions in search of more details. You must swear to me that you won't ask even one, no matter how curious you are. Not now, not ever."

Scant seconds ago, I'd been in fight-or-flight mode, sure this conversation was going to end with something ugly. Now I felt like I was going to explode with curiosity. Nothing like telling me I'm not allowed to ask questions to make me desperate to ask questions.

"Or you *could* try taking my word for it," Anderson said. "Giving me the benefit of the doubt, believing that I'm not a shallow, selfish person acting on a whim."

Anderson wasn't human, and he never had been. At times, I was painfully aware that his thought processes weren't always the same as ours. How could a man who'd never been mortal, had never had to face the possibility of his own death, think like everyone else, or understand the specter we all have to live with? Even the *Liberi* could die, no matter how hard it was to kill them, but Anderson couldn't, and there was an inherent otherness that came with his true immortality. But despite that otherness, he *did* have feelings, and I realized for the first time that my insistence on knowing his reasoning had hurt them.

When you read mythology, you see examples aplenty of gods acting shallow and selfish. I mean for Pete's sake, the Trojan War started when a couple of goddesses got offended that a mortal said another goddess was prettier than they were. But I'd seen no sign that Anderson was like that, and I had yet to see him act on a whim. So the question became: did I believe Anderson had a good reason for keeping his secret?

I hadn't known Anderson all that long, admittedly, but I knew him well enough to feel certain the answer was yes. I was dying of curiosity, having been unable to form even a reasonable guess as to why keeping the secret was so important, but did I really want to draw this line in the sand over curiosity?

Anderson was willing to tell me why he wouldn't reveal his identity, but I realized that if I pressed for it, it would change something between us. He would always feel that when it came right down to it, I didn't trust him. Once upon a time, that had been nothing but the truth. It still was, if you threw Emma into the mix. But this particular secret had nothing to do with her.

I swallowed hard, forcing my curiosity back down. I believed Anderson had a good reason, and it wasn't going to kill me not to know what it was.

Maybe Anderson was manipulating me. It was something he was very good at, though I liked to think I was aware whenever he tried to do it. Maybe his feelings weren't really hurt by my lack of faith, and he was just laying the guilt trip on me because he knew it was an effective tactic. But considering the things that had happened with Emma over the last few weeks, I figured Anderson was in enough pain already. No reason for me to add to it.

"All right," I said. "I'll trust you, even though I'm not very good at it. You've earned that."

He smiled at me, the tension easing out of his shoulders. "I appreciate it. More than you know."

If I didn't know better, I could swear he was a little choked up under that smile. I thought about giving him a hug, but decided it would feel awkward, for both of us.

"I'll call Cyrus and see if I can set up a meeting," he said. "I don't have high hopes we can reach a resolution, but we should at least try."

"Thank you." Going in there with such a defeatist attitude wasn't going to help our cause, and I worried that Anderson's refusal to suspect Emma would hamper any negotiations that occurred. But I'd gotten as much out of him as I was going to get.

Anderson stepped aside so I had a clear path to the door, the gesture something between a release and a dismissal.

"Um, sorry I got so pissy," I said, because I couldn't walk out without another word.

"Me, too," he replied, and the twinkle in his eye told me he'd deliberately left it up to interpretation as to whether he was apologizing to me or teasing me.

I shook my head as I reluctantly smiled back. I stepped up to the door and opened the dead bolt.

"If word of my existence reaches the wrong ears," Anderson said softly, "it could mean the death of every man, woman, and child on this earth."

I turned back to him, and I'm sure my expression was one of naked shock.

"When I say I have a good reason, I mean it."

What could I possibly say to that? My cheeks felt cold and bloodless, and my mouth gaped open. My mind could barely encompass what he'd just told me, and I desperately wanted to dismiss it as some kind of hyperbole. A shudder ran through me. When the first shock wore off, I was going to have a million questions—none of which Anderson would answer—but right now I couldn't think of a single thing to say. I opened my mouth a couple of times in hopes that I would magically say *something,* even if it wasn't something intelligent or meaningful, but nothing came out. So instead, I opened the door and hurried out of the room.

TEN

It was still raining later that afternoon when Anderson and I left for our meeting with Cyrus. Anderson had invited Cyrus to the mansion, but Cyrus insisted the meeting be held on neutral ground, so we were meeting him at a coffee bar downtown.

I whipped out my umbrella as Anderson and I walked from the main entrance of the mansion to the outbuilding that held the garage. Anderson didn't bother with an umbrella, stepping out into the steady rain without hesitation. He jogged ahead of me to the garage before I could offer to share my umbrella. I'd have suggested Anderson not make himself look any more disheveled than usual when going to meet Cyrus—I wasn't sure the frumpy look gave off quite the aura of power he would need to convince Cyrus he meant business—but he wouldn't have listened to me.

I followed at a more sedate pace. I was carrying the manila folder with the article about the fire in it, and I'd also tucked in the email from Konstantin.

Anderson was waiting for me behind the wheel of his black Mercedes by the time I reached the garage, the engine already running. His car was more elegant than he was, but in this area of politicians and diplomats, black Mercedes were a dime a dozen, so his car didn't catch the eye any more than Anderson himself did. I took a deep breath as I slid into the passenger seat. I can't say I held out any great hope that we'd get Cyrus to see things our way, and I was more than a little worried about Anderson's temper.

"Are you sure you can have a civilized conversation with Cyrus after what happened to Erin?" I asked as Anderson drove out of the mansion's gates. I figured with his distorted view of Emma, he'd probably shifted a lot of the blame for Erin's death onto Cyrus.

"Yes," Anderson said in his familiar mild voice. "He's an Olympian. He did what Olympians do, and I know it was nothing personal on his part."

I was impressed with his stoicism, and wondered if that meant he was finally going to stop making excuses for Emma.

The rest of the drive passed in silence, except for the annoying squeak of the windshield wipers. The rain was just hard enough to make them necessary, but not enough to keep them silent. The noise grated on me, but that was just because of my generally crappy state of mind. It took a lot of effort to keep myself from dwelling on the deaths that had occurred because of me. I wasn't *responsible,* but I *was* part of the chain of events that had led to them. That was more than enough to have my conscience bothering me.

Cyrus was waiting for us at a corner table when we arrived at the coffee bar. Not surprisingly, he wasn't alone. No self-respecting Olympian would attend a meeting with Anderson and not have a pet Descendant in tow. It always seemed a bit rude to me—kind of like carrying a gun in your hand—but obviously they felt threatened by him, despite being under the impression that he couldn't kill them.

Not being a *Liberi,* Anderson couldn't be killed by the Descendant, so Cyrus's gun would be shooting blanks if it ever came to that. Of course, *I* could be killed by a Descendant, so I gave Cyrus's companion a careful once-over as Anderson and I approached the table.

He wasn't as goonish as most of the Descendants Olympians liked to use as bodyguards, though he wasn't a ninety-pound weakling, either. Blond, good-looking, and stylishly dressed, he reminded me more than a little of Blake. I darted a quick glance at Cyrus, wondering if the resemblance was coincidental.

Cyrus and his companion were standing when we reached the table. With his trademark friendly smile, he greeted us, shaking hands first with Anderson, then with me.

"This is my friend Mark," he said, indicating the Descendant, who offered his hand. "I hope you don't mind him sitting in."

Anderson stared at Mark's extended hand, but made no move to shake it. There was a lightning bolt glyph on the back of Mark's hand, telling us he was a descendant of Zeus. I didn't like leaving him hanging there, but I took my cue from Anderson and didn't offer any pleasantries, either. I guess Anderson found the Descendant's presence as rude as I did.

Still smiling, Cyrus patted Mark's shoulder, and Mark lowered his hand.

"Just a precaution," Cyrus said, sitting back down. "I figured you probably weren't too happy with me right now. I also figured you probably wouldn't do anything stupid in a public place, but one can never be too careful." He reached over and stroked Mark's back like he was petting a dog. "I promise he won't interfere as long as we're just talking. You won't even know he's here."

Anderson was still standing, giving both Cyrus and Mark his best scowl. I'd never had much patience for posturing, so I pulled back my own chair and sat without waiting for Anderson.

"Were you hoping we'd bring Blake so you could make him jealous?" I asked Cyrus.

He grinned and looked over at Mark in a considering manner. "Yes, there is a certain resemblance, isn't there?" Mark looked more uncomfortable now than he had when we'd refused to shake his hand, and I felt momentarily bad for him. Then I reminded myself that he was an Olympian-wannabe, which meant he was not one of the good guys.

Anderson slowly took his seat.

"Would you like to order something before we begin?" Cyrus asked. Both he and Mark had cups of espresso in front of them, though it looked like Mark had barely touched his.

I'd have loved to have a cup of coffee to fidget with, if not to drink, but Anderson wasn't interested.

"This isn't a social call," he said coldly, "and there's no reason to pretend it is."

Cyrus stuck out his lower lip in a pout. "We can talk business without completely skipping the social niceties." He motioned to the barista, holding up two fingers. "Two more shots for my friends, please," he called.

"You know, the polite way to order at a coffee bar is to go up to the register and talk in a normal tone of voice," I said, not willing to be charmed by his genial manner.

Cyrus was hardly chastened by my rebuke. "I'm a regular,

and I tip really, really well. Amazing the kind of service that buys me."

"You don't actually think we're buying your good-ole-boy act, do you?" Anderson asked.

"It's not an act. If you're expecting me to act all stodgy and self-important like my father, you can forget it. That's not my style."

The barista brought over two demitasse cups of steaming, fragrant espresso, putting them before me and Anderson. "Need anything else?" she asked Cyrus with a coquettish smile. She probably thought he would make a great catch with his good looks and his propensity for throwing money around.

"No, thanks, Lacy," he said, and I wondered if he actually remembered her name, or was just reading her name tag. "We're good for now."

She wandered away, disappointed.

"Now, since you're so anxious to get down to business," Cyrus said, "why don't you start talking."

Anderson turned to me, and I told Cyrus about the two fires that had devastated my life over the last week. He listened in silence, and I passed the folder with the news article and the printout of the email across the table to him.

I'm not a big fan of espresso, unless it has a lot of steamed milk in it, but I was too jittery to sit still while Cyrus read, so I took a sip. Anderson hadn't touched his.

Finally, Cyrus finished reading and tucked the papers back into the folder. He shook his head and gave me a look of genuine sympathy.

"I'm sorry you've had to deal with all this," he said. "I'm sure being tossed headfirst into our world is stressful enough without adding this crap to it." He slid the folder back to me with a sharp gesture that spoke of annoyance. "But I can assure you Konstantin isn't behind it."

Anderson snorted. "He claimed responsibility!"

Cyrus rolled his eyes. "As I told Nikki before, an anonymous email isn't proof of anything." He looked at me. "My father hates your guts, I won't lie. But not because he blames you for his troubles. He can be petty, but he's not stupid."

"Oh, so he readily accepts the blame for what happened with Justin Kerner?" Anderson asked with patent disbelief.

Cyrus smiled ruefully. "Of course not. It's the incompetents who didn't bury him deep enough, and Phoebe, whose visions weren't clear enough, and, hell, me because I met with you a couple of times and didn't stop his secret from getting out. There's plenty of blame to go around. And Nikki, he hates you, but you're nowhere near important enough to him to warrant this kind of attention."

I believed every word of what Cyrus was saying. For a while, I'd allowed myself to accept that Konstantin really was behind the fires, but the motive had never quite made sense. Hearing Cyrus shoot down the theory without even momentarily considering it just cemented my opinion.

Anderson, of course, saw things differently. "Did it ever occur to you that his misfortunes might have caused him to become a bit . . . unhinged?"

"No," Cyrus said. "It never did. I've been in regular contact with him, and I can assure you, he's acting like his usual, ornery, domineering self."

"And I'm supposed to take your word on it?"

"Why would I lie?" Cyrus picked up his cup and frowned at the contents. "Mine's gone cold. Are you going to drink that?" He gestured at Anderson's untouched espresso.

"You'd lie because that's what Olympians do."

"There's no reason to be such a dick," Cyrus said, reaching for the espresso without Anderson's go-ahead. "I'm telling you my father isn't behind these particular attacks. I'm not trying to tell you he's a nice person, and I'm not telling you he wouldn't take an opportunity to hurt Nikki if it fell into his lap. But he's not going to go through this elaborate bullshit in a quest for revenge."

"Of course, you also said Emma wouldn't do this," I pointed out, more to give Anderson a moment to cool down than because I thought the point needed to be raised, "and she's the only other person I can imagine wanting to hurt me. You're wrong about someone, either your father or Emma."

"I suppose it's possible," Cyrus conceded with a careless shrug. He took a sip of Anderson's espresso. "But I don't think it's likely, and you didn't ask for this meeting because you wanted to solve the mystery of who's behind the fires, now did you?"

I think Anderson wanted to snap something about there being no mystery, but he refrained. I suspected that somewhere down inside, he *had* to see where the evidence was pointing, even if he wasn't ready to admit it.

"No," he said, wiping the emotion from his face. "I asked for this meeting because I want you to put a stop to it."

Cyrus took another sip of espresso, as nonchalant as ever. "Can't help you there. Property damage isn't covered under our agreement."

"Property damage?" I cried in outrage, pushing my chair back so I could leap to my feet. "Three people were killed, including an *infant,* for Christ's sake. That's murder, not property damage!"

And here I'd been worried about Anderson losing his temper. Mark's hand had disappeared into his pocket, and he was watching me with studied intensity. I assumed his hand was on a weapon, and that he'd be on me in a heartbeat if I made anything that he could construe as a hostile motion toward Cyrus.

"Sit down, Nikki," Anderson said, still calm and unruffled.

"At ease, Mark," Cyrus said in a similar tone of voice.

I wondered if they were going to tell us to heel or fetch as a follow-up. Mark didn't seem to mind being given commands. He took his hand slowly out of his pocket, but he kept his eyes on me. I minded a lot more, but I knew emotional outbursts were counterproductive. I wished I hadn't just lost my temper in front of the enemy, but there was nothing I could do about it now except try not to make it worse. I sat down and tried to relax, though I was practically shaking with rage.

"Sorry," Cyrus said with a grimace. "I should have known you'd be more upset about the casualties than about your property. I'm sure the intent behind the attack was to destroy something that belonged to you, and that doesn't fall under the purview of our agreement. Nor do the incidental deaths that accompanied the damage."

This was exactly the response Anderson had warned me to expect, but that didn't make it go down any easier. Cyrus made such a good show of being a nice guy that no matter how much I reminded myself what he was, I couldn't ever seem to make the knowledge stick.

"So you're okay with your people burning down buildings filled with innocents, and it doesn't bother you in the least when those innocents die."

Cyrus shrugged. "*I* wouldn't do something like that, but I'm not going to get all worked up about it. If I got all worked up every time an Olympian killed somebody, I'd never have survived to adulthood." He leaned forward and gave me an earnest look. "Look, I'm sorry about what's happened. You seem like a good person, and I'd rather not see you get hurt. But unless the treaty is broken, my hands are tied."

"Spoken like a true Olympian," Anderson said sourly.

Cyrus raised an eyebrow. "You expected something different? I'd have thought Blake had told you all about my deficiencies of character."

"*I'm* not the one who expected something different."

"Ah." He gave me that earnest look again as his voice dropped until I could barely hear it over the roar of the espresso machine. "I've stopped the Olympian practice of disposing of Descendant children. You have no idea how far out on a limb I've already gone. I can't go forbidding my people to bother you just because Anderson asks me to."

If he thought I was going to sympathize with his delicate political situation, he was nuts. He was still looking at me, this time expectantly, though I didn't know what he was expecting.

Suddenly, Anderson gave a harsh bark of laughter. I didn't get the joke.

"What?" I asked, looking back and forth between the two of them.

"Let me translate what Cyrus just said," Anderson answered. "It comes down to: what's in it for me?"

I hadn't fully registered Cyrus's words until that moment. He hadn't said he wouldn't stop his people from tormenting me. He said he wouldn't stop them *just because Anderson asked him to*.

"You bastard," I said, scowling at Cyrus.

The insult rolled off him. "I'm not running a charitable organization, Nikki. I like you, but I'm not going to go sticking my neck out for you just because I'm a nice guy. You want my help, you have to make it worth my while."

"You're just a goddamn shakedown artist, aren't you?"

"Do you want to bargain with me or not?"

If it had been Konstantin offering me some kind of a deal, I'd have refused without even exploring the possibility. In fact, if it had been any other Olympian, I probably would have gotten up and walked away. But there was a part of me that still kept insisting there had to be some redeeming qualities to Cyrus. Naive? Maybe.

"All right, I'll play," I said. "What would it take to get you to order your people to leave me alone?"

I realized Cyrus had planned to take us into a negotiation all along, because he didn't even have to think a moment before he named his price.

"Give me an IOU for one hunt, to be cashed in at my convenience."

"No," I said instantly. I knew more innocents would likely die if I couldn't get Emma (or Konstantin, if I was wrong about him) off my back, but I wasn't willing to actively cause someone else's death. I'd just have to find some other way to fix things.

"I understand that you have severe moral qualms about hunting for us," Cyrus said. "How about if I promise that whomever you hunt will not be killed?"

I'd seen how creatively the Olympians could torture someone without killing them. "Not good enough. You'd have to take rape and torture off the menu, too."

Cyrus thought about that a moment, then nodded. "I could do that. We don't *always* have nefarious purposes when we're looking for people."

I glanced at Anderson, wondering if there was some big loophole I was overlooking. I was pretty sure that Cyrus would be getting the better of this deal, but as Anderson had told me, we had no leverage.

"I think Cyrus is about as close to honest as an Olympian can be," Anderson said in answer to my questioning look.

"Gee, thanks," Cyrus said with another of his grins.

"It's up to you whether you're willing to put yourself in his debt," Anderson finished.

It still wasn't exactly a rousing endorsement. The idea of owing Cyrus held no appeal, but if that was what it took to keep the other Olympians off my back, then I'd just have to suck it up. "Just to clarify," I said, "if I promise to hunt someone for you in the future, you will get whoever's been setting the fires to stop?"

Cyrus shook his head. "I can't promise it will stop. If I'm wrong and my father's behind this, he might not listen to me. But I will warn all of my people off, and if anyone acts against you after my warning, then they'll be disobeying my direct orders. I'm not as much of a hard-ass as my father, but I will *not* tolerate disobedience." He leaned forward and looked back and forth between me and Anderson. No charming smiles this time, and the look in his eyes said that he was dead serious. "And let me make this perfectly clear: if you go after my father, all bets are off."

"What if he sets another fire after you warn him off?" I asked.

"Then I'll have to conclude I'm a gullible idiot and declare open season on him. But that's not going to happen, because he's not behind this in the first place."

Anderson leaned back in his chair and didn't say anything. I didn't for a moment think he was going to let Konstantin go for my sake, at least not in the long run. He would have his revenge, one way or another. But he would have to find a new way to convince me to find him if the agreement with Cyrus worked out. That was a problem for another day.

Both Cyrus and I were looking at Anderson expectantly.

"What?" he asked. "I've already agreed to let him be. Do you need me to agree again?"

"Yes, I think I do," Cyrus said, and I think he was as skeptical about Anderson's agreement as I was. After all, he'd already sort of caught me on the hunt after Anderson and I had both agreed to leave Konstantin alone.

"All right," Anderson said. "I'll say it again. Neither I nor any of my people will harm Konstantin as long as he is an Olympian, and as long as he commits no acts of aggression against us. Satisfied?"

"I guess I am." Cyrus didn't sound convinced, and I didn't blame him. "Shall we shake on it?"

A round of handshaking followed. This time, Mark didn't even try to participate.

I returned home from our meeting with Cyrus more than a little unsettled. I couldn't shake the feeling that although Anderson had raised no objection, I had made a tactical error in promising Cyrus a hunt. The fact that I'd specified no violence made me feel marginally better, but I imagined there were any number of ways Cyrus could twist my promise into something I'd later regret.

I was so worried about what I might have gotten myself into that I went looking for Blake, whom I usually preferred to avoid. The door to his suite was ajar when I arrived. I rapped on it as I pushed it open and stuck my head in, but apparently Blake didn't hear me, because he didn't look up. When I saw what he was doing, I wasn't sure whether to laugh or to gape in shock.

He hadn't heard me knock because he was wearing earbuds, his head nodding along to whatever was playing on his iPod. He was sitting on his couch, one leg tucked under him, as he concentrated intensely on the pair of knitting needles he was holding. I couldn't tell what he was making—he only had about four or five inches of fabric so far—but the yarn was a thin, silky-looking crimson, and the little bit he had done was almost lacy. He executed some complex maneuver with the yarn and needles, his forehead creasing with the effort, then came to the end of his row and let out a sigh of what sounded like satisfaction.

If you had asked me what Blake did in his spare time, I'd have put knitting at about 1,001 on the list of possibilities. He wasn't as macho as guys like Jamaal and Logan, but despite his pretty-boy looks and his onetime romance with Cyrus, he'd never given me the impression that he might be the sort to engage in such a stereotypically feminine pursuit.

"What are you making?" I asked, loud enough that Blake could hear me over whatever was playing on his iPod.

He jumped and practically dropped his needles. He'd been concentrating so hard that I doubt there was any way I could have made my presence known without startling him, but I gave him a sheepish smile anyway.

"Sorry," I said, as Blake pulled out the earbuds and laid his knitting carefully on the coffee table. "I knocked, but you didn't hear me."

He eyed me suspiciously from his seat on the couch. I guess my sudden and unexpected appearance in his suite worried him. Maybe he thought I was going to try to warn him away from Steph for the millionth time.

"I'm making a scarf for Steph for Valentine's Day," he said, that wary look still on his face. "I haven't knitted for a long time, so I thought I'd get an early start."

The admission made me strangely uncomfortable. The idea that he was making something for Steph *by hand,* something he expected to take him nearly a month to complete, suggested a deeper attachment than I'd allowed myself to imagine. I'd known Blake was *fond* of Steph, and I'd even had to admit to myself that he genuinely cared about her, but I'd hoped it was something fun and casual. You don't spend a month knitting something for someone if the relationship is casual.

"I wouldn't have taken you for the knitting type," I said. My voice came out a bit tight. I'd promised not to *voice* my disapproval of his relationship with my sister, but that didn't mean I didn't *feel* it.

Blake shrugged. "I grew up with three sisters. I was a rebel, so when my parents told me boys don't knit, I immediately wanted to do it." He grinned. "I learned by unraveling a couple of my sisters' projects so I could figure out how it worked. Strangely enough, they weren't very happy with me when they found the piles of yarn I left behind."

I chuckled, reluctantly charmed. "How old were you?"

"Nine, the first time. Dad took his belt to me something fierce, so next time, I was more sneaky about it and buried the evidence. I'm pretty sure Dad knew it was me, but there was an outside chance the dog had made off with it, and he wasn't going to thrash me unless he was sure."

I imagined blue-eyed, blond-haired Blake had been a pro at looking angelically innocent as a child.

"But you didn't come here to talk about my hobbies," Blake said. "What's up?"

I hesitated, unsure if bringing up his relationship with Cyrus would come across as some kind of subtle rebuke under the circumstances. But it was why I'd come to Blake in the first place, so I straightened my spine and closed the door behind me. Blake hadn't invited me to sit, so I stood awkwardly and put my hands into my pockets so I wouldn't fidget.

"You know Anderson and I went to meet with Cyrus this afternoon, right?"

He nodded, and his suspicious look made a return appearance.

"Cyrus promised to tell all the Olympians to back off me if I promised to owe him a hunt someday." Blake's eyes widened in alarm and surprise, and I hastened to clarify the details of the deal we'd made. "My question is, is Cyrus like Konstantin? Will he try to find some way to make this deal hurt me despite the conditions I set?"

Blake thought about it a moment, and I decided to sit down despite the lack of invitation. I suspect it hadn't even occurred to him to issue one—he'd just assumed I'd make myself comfortable. He wasn't as formal as Anderson or as standoffish as Jamaal.

"Here's the thing to understand about Cyrus," Blake said slowly, thinking over his words carefully before he spoke. "Unlike Konstantin, there's no malice in him. He'd never go out of his way to hurt someone, and he's even capable of being a nice guy, when the spirit strikes him."

"Nice guys don't lead the Olympians!" I protested.

"I said he's *capable* of it. He's not in the least bit malicious, but what he *does* have in common with his daddy is a deep, abiding selfishness. He'll be nice and actually help someone, if it doesn't cost him anything and he's in the mood. But if you're standing between him and something that he wants, all bets are off. So in answer to your question, no, he won't look for a way to make the deal bite you in the ass. But he won't hesitate to exploit a loophole if he finds one and it's to his advantage."

I shook my head. "How the hell did you end up involved with someone like that?" I asked, not really expecting him to answer.

A hint of sadness crossed Blake's face. "I honestly thought I could change him. He was a good friend for a long time, and I've seen sides of him that no one else has seen. He could be a good person, if he wanted to be." Bitterness now colored Blake's voice, the sadness gone. "But I found out the hard way that he has no desire to change. And that's all I have to say on the subject."

From some of the things I'd heard Cyrus say to and about Blake, I got the feeling the desire to change each other had been mutual. Cyrus would have loved to convert Blake into a full-scale Olympian, and the fact that his current boy toy bore such a striking resemblance to Blake made me wonder if he'd ever fully abandoned that hope.

"Did this stuff make you feel better, or worse?" Blake inquired.

Honestly, I had no idea. "Knowledge is power, right?" I said with a shrug that was supposed to look careless, but probably didn't. "I'll just have to hope he finds some inoffensive use for me before anything potentially sticky comes up."

What I didn't say, but I suspect we both knew, was that if something sticky came up, I might balk at it despite it fitting the letter of our agreement. The consequences of balking might turn out to be disastrous—no way would Cyrus take it well if I failed to honor our agreement—but I would just have to cross that bridge when I came to it. And hope I never did.

Eleven

I'd turned my cell phone off during the meeting with Cyrus, and I didn't remember to turn it back on until I was in my suite after talking to Blake. I saw that I'd missed a call from Steph.

With the way my life had been going lately, I couldn't help bracing a bit in fear of bad news, but Steph's perky greeting instantly put me at ease.

"I got your message," I said. "What's up?"

"I called that trustee I know," she answered, and for a moment I didn't know what she was talking about. In all the stress and drama, I'd temporarily forgotten about my plan to draw Jamaal out of his shell.

"Wow. You work fast." I wouldn't have been surprised if she'd dragged her feet about it, considering how much she disapproved of my interest in Jamaal.

She breathed a delicate sigh. "Well, after what happened, I figured you'd be badly in need of an escape."

My heart swelled with love for my sister, who was way better to me than I had any right to expect. "You have enough balls in the air trying to get ready for the big homecoming. I don't want to add to your workload." I knew Steph had already talked to the insurance company multiple times, and that she had rented a furnished condo for the Glasses to stay in while the house was being rebuilt.

"It wasn't that much work. Just a few phone calls."

"Have I ever told you you're amazing?"

I could hear Steph's smile in her voice. "Will you still think I'm amazing if I tell you I've arranged for you to meet with the curator of the exhibit for a private showing at seven o'clock tonight?"

"Tonight?" I asked in a startled squeak.

"Yeah. Sorry for the short notice, but Dr. Prakash is going to be massively busy in the next few weeks, so the only time she could fit you in was today."

When I'd asked Steph if she could set something up, I'd imagined Jamaal and me being shown around during regular business hours by a docent. Not being given a special, after-hours showing with the curator, who was probably already overworked and underpaid.

"I don't want to put her out," I said, hedging.

"It's a done deal," Steph said firmly. "I've done a lot of favors for people who've donated a lot of money and art, and I was past due to call some of them in."

"Yeah, but the curator isn't—"

"She'll be excited to have a chance to show off the exhibit, especially if Jamaal is knowledgeable about art, which I gather he is."

The books in his room gave me the same impression, but I wasn't convinced Dr. Prakash was going to be as thrilled to show us around as Steph thought. If it were me, I'd resent being made to drop everything just because someone with connections wanted a special perk.

"She's already rearranged her schedule to fit you in," Steph said. "Don't you dare try to wriggle out of it. And instead of asking Jamaal if he wants to go, you'd better *tell* him he's going. It would be unspeakably rude to stand her up."

I glanced at my watch and saw that it was already three thirty. I didn't have a whole lot of time to track down Jamaal, convince him this was a good idea, and get to the museum. I wondered if putting me in such an awkward position was part of Steph's plan, if she was giving me extra fuel I could use to help me talk Jamaal into going. She can be a bit devious at times, though always for a good cause.

"I'll get Jamaal out there, one way or another," I promised. I wished I felt more certain that I could deliver, but I would at least do everything in my power. "Thanks so much. You're the best."

"I know. Now get off the phone and go give him the good news."

"Yes, Mom."

I could almost see Steph shaking her head and laughing as she hung up.

I'd have called Jamaal's cell in an effort to locate him, only I wasn't sure he'd answer if he saw my name on caller ID, and he might make himself scarce once he knew I was looking for him.

I headed down the stairs toward his suite, my pulse tripping along even as I rolled my eyes at myself for being nervous.

I'm not a shy person, nor was I as intimidated by Jamaal as I probably should have been, but asking him out on what was essentially a date was well beyond my comfort zone. Especially when I felt sure it was going to turn into a battle of wills.

After a deep, calming breath, I knocked on his door. If he was out in the clearing working with Sita, then I was going to settle in and wait for him. Frankly, if I never saw another tiger for the rest of my life, that would be fine with me. I would never forget the feeling of her breath on my face.

Footsteps told me at once that Jamaal was in, and my pulse picked up even more speed. Damn, I was as nervous as a sixteen-year-old girl asking a boy to the junior prom. I wiped my palms on my pant legs in case they were sweaty, then tried my best to brace myself for the rejection that was sure to come. I might be able to talk him into coming with me, but I'd faint in shock if his first answer wasn't a resounding no.

The door opened, and I was suddenly face-to-face with Jamaal. Well, face to chest. Jamaal is about a foot taller than I am, so I always have to look up to meet his gaze.

His cheekbones looked a little sharper than usual, and I wondered if he had lost weight. But other than that, he looked good enough to eat, as always. He was still wearing the tiger-colored beads in his hair, and he had on torn jeans and a faded T-shirt. The outfit would have looked scruffy on, say, Anderson, but it somehow looked carelessly sexy on Jamaal.

He didn't scowl on seeing me on his doorstep, and I figured that was a good sign. He didn't smile, either, but then he didn't do a whole lot of smiling even at the best of times.

"If you're here to get on my case about what happened with Sita the other day, you can turn around and go back upstairs," he said. The scowl made its appearance after all.

"Really?" I said, crossing my arms over my chest and giving him an exasperated look. "You think I'd come down here and knock on your door to lecture you?" I didn't for a moment believe that was why he thought I was here. He was just trying to establish a sense of distance before we'd even started.

He leaned against the doorjamb. It would be nice if he'd invite me in, but I wasn't surprised he didn't. "I don't suppose we have much else to talk about."

It appeared I was lucky he hadn't slammed the door in my face. Whatever had caused the new friction between us, it wasn't getting better over time.

"Why don't you stop acting like a jerk and let me in?" I'd often found that tact was overrated when dealing with Jamaal.

His scowl darkened. "Like I said, we have nothing to talk about."

The fact that he still hadn't slammed the door in my face made me think some hidden part of him was more interested in talking than he liked to admit.

"Yeah, actually, we do," I countered. "And I promise it won't involve any of that girlie-talking-about-feelings stuff you hate so much."

I thought I saw a flicker of amusement in his eyes before he shut it down. "In that case, we can talk about it right here."

"You hiding a girl in there or something?"

Jamaal gave a grunt of exasperation and stomped into his sitting room, leaving the door open. I guessed that was as much of an invitation as I was getting. I stepped inside and closed the door behind me. Jamaal watched me with suspicious eyes as I invited myself to take a seat on his futon sofa. I might have hoped he would join me, but he remained on his feet, giving off keep-away vibes.

"Did you hear about the new Indian exhibition opening at the Sackler later this week?" I asked, and was rewarded by a look of complete confusion on Jamaal's face. Bet he didn't see that one coming.

"Huh?"

"Sackler. Exhibition. Indian stuff." I nodded my head toward the small Indian painting that was the focal point of Jamaal's sitting room. "Did you hear about it?"

The look on his face told me he was still busily trying to figure out where I was going with this. "Yes," he admitted cautiously, as if he expected the answer to get him into some kind of trouble.

"Well, how would you like a chance to visit with the curator and have her give you a personal guided tour of the exhibition before it even opens?"

Boy, did I ever have his attention now. I saw the spark of greed and excitement in his eye before he managed to hide it under his habitual grumpy face. "Are you claiming you have contacts at the museum?" He sounded skeptical, but I heard the undertone of hope.

"No, but Steph does."

Jamaal shook his head, rattling his beads in a way that had become familiar to me—and strangely endearing. "I don't know what you're trying to talk me into, but the answer is no."

"I'm trying to talk you into getting a sneak peek at the exhibit. That's all."

Another shake of his head. "No way. Offers like that come with strings attached."

Considering Jamaal's life experiences, his attitude and suspicion weren't surprising. "The only string is that I'm going with you." Of course, that might be the kind of string he considered a deal breaker.

His lip lifted in a faint sneer. "You've suddenly developed an interest in Indian art?"

"No, but I've developed an interest in fixing whatever's gone wrong between you and me. I thought maybe if we stopped avoiding each other and spent a little time together, we might figure out how to start acting normal again."

Jamaal rubbed his forehead like he had a headache, then reluctantly came to sit on the couch—as far away from me as he could get. I remembered our little make-out session on this couch with a pang of regret. But asking Jamaal out wasn't about trying to get into his pants—though my libido thought that sounded like an excellent idea—it was about trying to keep him from withdrawing from everyone around him.

"I know you're the kind of woman who wants to fix everyone," Jamaal said. "But it's time for you to stop trying to fix *me*."

"Why? Because you'd prefer to be miserable so you can bitch and whine about it? Of course, you'd only bitch and whine to yourself, because you won't let anyone else near you."

Jamaal's temper would have normally risen to meet mine, but not today. "I've been broken in one way or another for more than a hundred years. What makes you think you can snap your fingers and make it all better?"

"I don't. I'm not completely naive, Jamaal. It took years for my adoptive parents to bring me back from the brink of becoming a juvenile delinquent, and I don't suppose I'll ever be as well adjusted as someone who spent their whole childhood in a good, loving home. But I'm in a lot better shape now than I was when the Glasses took me in.

"I'm not trying to *fix* you. I'm just trying to be a friend."

"You've been a much better friend than I had any right to expect," he said gruffly. "But now, you have to let me be."

"Why?" I demanded. "What's different now?"

"Didn't you promise we weren't going to talk about feelings?"

"I lied."

His lips lifted in the faintest of smiles. "At least you're honest about your dishonesty."

"And I'm not that easy to deflect. We have to live and work together for God only knows how long. We'll do a lot better job of it if you get whatever's bothering you out in the open."

"Haven't you interfered enough with my life already?" he snapped.

His attitude might have pissed me off if that weren't so clearly the reaction he was hoping for. "You think if you're a big enough asshole I'll flounce off in a huff and leave you alone? I'm way more stubborn than that."

He snorted, but the hostility faded and his shoulders slumped. "I've noticed."

Maybe what I needed to do was pull back a bit and stop trying to make him talk. Every emotional guard he had was up and running, and the chances of me slipping past them were low. I wished I could get him to spill whatever his problem was with me, but I didn't have to get him to do it *now*.

"All right," I said. "You don't have to tell me about your feelings. I wish you would, but I understand that it's hard for you." A little condescending, maybe, and I saw the spark of annoyance in Jamaal's eyes before I hurried on. "But please come with me to the museum. It would do you good to spend some time around people for a change, even if one of those people is me."

"Remember what I said about trying to fix me?"

What an exasperating man. But I hadn't expected any less. "My parents' house was burned down, and my condo was burned down with people inside, all because some nutcase has decided I'm responsible for all his or her problems. Did it ever occur to you that maybe *I'm* the one who could use some fixing right now? That maybe I want to go out to the museum as much for my sake as for yours?"

He flashed me a dry smile. "No, it never occurred to me. If you were just looking for a way to forget your troubles for a few hours, I doubt you'd do it by going to a museum."

He had a point. Maybe that argument had been a bit thin. "That's the opportunity that fell in my lap, thanks to Steph. Look, she's already arranged a meeting for us with Dr. Prakash, the curator. We're supposed to meet her at seven tonight."

Jamaal glared at me. "You didn't think it might be a good idea to ask me about it *before* setting something up?"

"If Steph had given me any warning, I'd have asked first. I only brought this up to her yesterday. I never dreamed she'd work this fast."

He looked at me suspiciously.

"She said Dr. Prakash has already rearranged her schedule to fit us in. Surely it won't kill you to spend a couple of hours in my presence, and I *know* you want to see the exhibit."

I could see from the look on his face that he was torn. He really, really didn't want to spend that much time with me. But he also really, really wanted that private look at the exhibit. I decided it was time to rest my case, so I clamped my lips shut and gave him some time to think. If this didn't work, I was going to have to have a talk with Anderson, see if there was something he or his other *Liberi* could do to persuade Jamaal to engage in some more human interaction. They were all glad not to have to tiptoe around his temper anymore, and they might not want to risk making him change back into the powder keg he'd been. His temper had been so volatile he'd almost been kicked out of the house, and he'd had to undergo a tribunal and a brutal punishment to prove how committed he was to trying to control himself.

Thankfully, Jamaal made such a drastic action unnecessary.

"All right," he said softly. "We'll go to the exhibit. But this isn't a date, and it isn't the start of a beautiful friendship. It's best for everybody involved if you and I stay at a safe distance."

"Why?" I asked.

But I wasn't surprised when he didn't answer.

TWELVE

I had no idea what to wear for a private visit with a museum curator, so I decided to dress for comfort and warmth on this wet, gloomy winter night. I paired a teal cowl-neck sweater with soft black cords and water-resistant ankle boots, then examined myself in the mirror. I decided the outfit was dressy enough to be classy, but not so dressy as to look like I'd dressed up for a special occasion.

I met Jamaal in the foyer. He'd gone with what for him was a pretty dressed-up look, wearing black jeans with an orange polo shirt. Tiger colors again, I noted, though I kept the thought to myself. I didn't bother arguing with him about who would drive. He liked to refer to my Mini as "the clown car," and though he fit in it just fine, he liked his black Saab a hell of a lot better. He'd made a concession in agreeing to come with me tonight, so I made my own about transportation.

When we were in the car with the doors shut, I noticed the faint scent of clove cigarettes in the air. Before he'd learned to summon Sita, Jamaal had tried to keep his temper in check by chain-smoking clove cigarettes—or pot, when things got really bad.

"You still smoking?" I asked, though I don't know why I was surprised. People don't just quit without a concerted effort.

"Not as much," he said defensively. "Just because I don't *need* cigarettes anymore doesn't mean I don't like them anymore."

"I didn't mean anything by it. I was just curious." Had he smoked tonight because he needed the extra help to stay calm in my presence? His body language told me he was agitated in a way I hadn't seen for a long time.

We had to come to a brief stop while waiting for the gates at the head of the driveway to open, and Jamaal took that opportunity to roll his neck from side to side. The crackling sound made me wince.

Why was going out with me such an issue for him? If it wasn't about my attempt to leave, and it wasn't about our experiment with romance, I couldn't imagine what it *was* about. The curiosity was killing me, and his continued reticence just made it worse.

"How did you get into art, anyway?" I asked, just to make conversation. "You don't seem much like an art geek to me."

"By 'art geek,' do you mean rich white guy?"

I suspected he was trying to start a fight—maybe so he could use it as an excuse to turn the car around and go back—but I wasn't about to take the bait. "When I think of an art geek, I think of a sensitive beta male," I said calmly. "You don't fit the description."

The comment won me a reluctant laugh, and a little of the tension eased out of his shoulders. "You shouldn't put so much stock in stereotypes," he said, but there was no rancor in his voice.

"I'm sure you're not the only macho man who likes art. You're just the only macho man I *know* who likes art. Or at least who *admits* it."

"Macho man?" He sounded affronted, and there was no hint of a smile on his face, but I was 99 percent sure he was teasing.

"All right, you like 'alpha male' better. I'll keep that in mind for the future."

He made a little growling sound as he shifted gears, giving the Saab a little more gas. If he got pulled over and made us late, I was going to be seriously pissed.

"You going to answer my question, or just brood in silence?"

He shot me a quick look of annoyance. "You must be the most persistent female I've ever met."

I grinned. "Is that supposed to be an insult?"

He shook his head in resignation. "If you must know, I got into art because it's something I would never have dreamed could be a part of my life when I was a kid. I tried every highbrow cultural door that would open for me. I went to the opera and ballet. Learned to play golf. At least, tried to learn. I sucked at it, and it's not a good sport for someone with a temper problem. I went to fancy restaurants to eat foods I couldn't pronounce. And I visited art galleries. The art's the only thing that stuck."

"And you got into the Eastern stuff because you're descended from Kali, right?"

He nodded. "I thought I might collect paintings of her, because being an art collector was about as far from being a slave as it was possible to get. I went to an auction and bought the painting that's in my sitting room, but when I hung it, I decided I'd rather let the art go to museums. I should probably donate the one I have, but . . ."

"You're allowed to do something nice for yourself every once in a while."

He didn't say anything, but I saw the small smile on his lips. Maybe the walls he'd built around himself were starting to show cracks. Tiny ones, to be sure, but I was going to do my damnedest to widen them.

We were to meet Dr. Prakash at one of the side entrances to the museum. Jamaal and I arrived there a little before seven. Standing outside waiting in the rain wasn't my idea of a good time, especially not with the damp chill in the air.

Jamaal, of course, had no umbrella. If we'd just been walking straight from the parking lot and into the building, I'm sure he would have refused to share mine, but even *he* wasn't macho enough to stand around waiting in the rain as the temperature dipped toward its predicted nighttime low of thirty-five.

Sharing the umbrella meant Jamaal had to stand closer to me than he would have liked. I think he was trying not to show his discomfort, but I couldn't help noticing the stiffness of his posture, or the way the fingers on the hand that wasn't holding the umbrella were dancing nervously at his side.

"Do you need a cigarette while we wait?" I asked.

My question must have cued him in to his unconscious hand movements, and his fingers came to a stop. "I'm fine," he said.

I was debating whether to try to push him into telling me what was wrong when the door to the museum swung open.

I hadn't realized I'd built an image of a curator of Indian

art in my head until I set eyes on a woman who looked absolutely nothing like that image. I'd pictured a petite Indian woman of mature years wearing a sari and sporting a red dot on her forehead. The woman who beckoned us into the museum was indeed of Indian descent, but that was about all I'd gotten right.

Dr. Kassandra Prakash was plump without being fat, and if she was over thirty, she was some kind of cosmetics genius. She wore a thoroughly Western wrap dress with ugly sensible shoes, and she had a smile that made her face look pretty despite an oversized nose and black eyebrows that were just short of being a unibrow.

I darted inside, leaving Jamaal to wrestle the umbrella into submission.

"I'm so sorry to leave you waiting in the rain!" Dr. Prakash said earnestly. "I've been indoors all day and never realized it was raining."

"Don't worry about it," I said as Jamaal won his battle with the umbrella and joined me inside. "We just got here. And we can't thank you enough for taking the time—"

"Nonsense," Dr. Prakash interrupted with a cheery smile. "I'm like a proud mama showing off her baby." She held out her hand for me to shake. "I'm Kassandra Prakash, but you can just call me Kassie."

"Nikki Glass," I answered as I shook her hand. I could tell the moment she got her first good look at Jamaal, because her generically friendly smile turned into something with a hint of hubba-hubba behind it.

"And you must be Mr. Jones," she said.

I highly doubted Jamaal had been born with either his current first or last names, and I sometimes wondered why he'd chosen something as dull as "Jones" for his surname. It didn't fit his exotic good looks, but then I don't think Jamaal realizes just how attractive he is.

"Nice to meet you," Jamaal said dutifully as he shook

Kassie's hand. There was a hint of strain behind his smile, and I wondered how long it had been since he'd had a normal, social interaction with someone other than Anderson's *Liberi*. He certainly wasn't used to smiling at people, and I was glad he'd made the effort, even if it did come off a little forced.

If Kassie noticed Jamaal's awkwardness, she didn't acknowledge it, instead leading us through the empty halls of the museum toward the exhibition. She chattered almost nonstop, and I decided Jamaal's lack of social graces probably wasn't going to be much of a handicap tonight. I didn't get the feeling that she was overly enamored of hearing herself talk, just that she was so excited about the exhibit that she couldn't contain herself. I wondered if she was always like this, or if she'd been overdosing on energy drinks to get her through her long and busy day.

I'd imagined this evening's outing as a chance for Jamaal and me to spend some time together and maybe try to ease ourselves back into something resembling a normal relationship. I thought maybe we'd bond a bit over this shared experience. I might even have thought Jamaal would be grateful to me for giving him this opportunity. Instead, I ended up feeling like a third wheel on someone else's date.

Kassie proceeded to give us a guided tour of the exhibit, which consisted mostly of paintings, with some bronzes and some stone carvings for variety. I knew absolutely nothing about Eastern art of any kind, and to tell you the truth, I didn't find the Indian paintings all that interesting to look at. A lot of them were pretty primitive, with stiff figures and wonky proportions. If I'd been on my own, I'd probably have been in and out of the exhibit in fifteen minutes, tops. Jamaal, on the other hand, was enthralled, and within minutes had forgotten all about being his normal surly self. His face was more animated than I'd ever seen it as he hung on Kassie's every word. He was even able to make intelligent conversation and ask intriguing questions whenever Kassie paused to take a breath.

I followed along beside them in silence, feeling inadequate

and uncultured. Kassie tried to include me in the conversation a few times, and I appreciated the effort, but I didn't have much to contribute. Anything I said about the art would either make me look stupid or reveal that I wasn't that impressed with it, and with the two of them geeking out so much, I didn't think bringing in inane small talk would help.

Eventually, they kind of tuned me out. I told myself that tight feeling in my gut was just because of my inability to join the conversation, but I was pretty sure there was a hint of jealousy in there, too. Jamaal spoke more words to Kassie in those couple of hours than he'd spoken to me in the months I'd known him. And he smiled a lot more, too. I'd have loved to see him smiling at *me* like that.

Not that he was flirting, though. I'm not even sure Jamaal knows *how,* and though he was clearly enjoying his conversation with Kassie, his enthusiasm was directed at the paintings, not at her. That didn't stop me from feeling jealous, especially not when Kassie put her hand on his arm here and there. I didn't think *she* was flirting, either, at least not consciously, but it raised my hackles anyway.

I tried to hide my own discomfort, smiling and feigning interest whenever either of them glanced at me. Whether I was enjoying myself or not, I couldn't help feeling like this was good for Jamaal, and that was supposedly the reason I'd invited him out here. When we'd finally seen the last of the exhibit, I thought the ordeal was over, but then Kassie offered to show us the reserve collection—paintings the museum owned but that weren't currently on display. Jamaal's eyes lit up even more, and I had to suppress a groan. For Jamaal's sake, I faked my way again through the next hour or so, trying not to let myself glance at my watch every five minutes.

It was almost ten by the time we escaped—I mean, by the time we regretfully said good-bye and thank you to Kassie. The rain had slowed to a desultory drizzle, but the temperature was close enough to freezing to make the damp night air feel thoroughly unpleasant. Despite the success of my plan to draw Jamaal out, I was in a crappy mood thanks to three hours of feeling like a moron while Jamaal and Kassie bonded over stuff that was over my head. Not to mention that I'd failed to eat dinner before we'd set out, and my stomach was howling in protest. I had planned to ask Jamaal if he wanted to grab a bite to eat when we left the museum, but now I just wanted to get back to the mansion and lick my wounds.

We didn't speak on the walk to the car, and I figured that meant Jamaal was back to his habitual brooding self already. Maybe I shouldn't have bothered trying to draw him out. Maybe it had done no good whatsoever and had just made me miserable instead. Maybe I really should butt out of his life as he'd repeatedly told me to do.

Okay, so maybe just this once, Jamaal wasn't the most broody person in the car.

"Thank you," he said softly as we pulled out of the parking lot.

A lump formed in my throat. I swallowed hard and tried to respond in a normal tone of voice. "You're welcome. I'm glad you had fun."

We drove for a couple more minutes in silence, then Jamaal pulled into an illegal parking spot against the curb. I looked around, trying to spot whatever had inspired Jamaal to pull over, but instead of parking the car, he left the engine running and turned toward me in his seat.

"That might be the nicest thing anyone's ever done for me," he said, meeting my eyes only briefly before looking away. "And I know it must have been painfully boring for you."

"It wasn't—" I started to protest automatically.

Jamaal met my eyes with a look of frank skepticism that killed my protest.

"You did a good job trying to hide it," he assured me. "And I'm an asshole for taking advantage of you and making you wait while I looked at the reserve collection."

"No, you're not. If I didn't want to do it, it was up to me to say no." And as badly as I'd wanted to escape, I couldn't have denied Jamaal the opportunity to see things the public might never see.

He straightened in his seat and leaned his head back into the headrest, closing his eyes. He was bracing himself for something, but I didn't know what. He opened his eyes and huffed out a breath.

"You remember you said once that Sita's attitude toward you might have something to do with how I feel about you?" he asked, looking out the windshield instead of at me.

"Yeah," I said, then held my breath, wondering if somehow, miraculously, he was going to talk about his feelings after all.

"You weren't wrong."

Even though I'd figured all along that Sita's dislike of me was a reflection of Jamaal's own feelings, I still felt a stab of pain. Things had been strained between us lately, but I'd allowed myself to hope that there was still a spark of friendship underneath it all. The ferocity of Sita's attitude toward me suggested maybe that had been wishful thinking.

"Okay," I said. My voice came out a tad raspy, and I cleared my throat.

To my shock, Jamaal reached out and brushed a strand of my hair back behind my ear. The touch sent a shiver through my whole body.

"You weren't wrong about Sita's attitude being related to my feelings," he said. "But you were wrong about what the feelings were. She's *jealous,* Nikki."

My eyes widened and my jaw dropped. "Your phantom tiger is jealous of me?" That might have been one of the most ridiculous things I'd ever heard. And it made me feel almost giddy with relief.

Jamaal graced me with one of his small, wry smiles. "Yeah. She's jealous of *anyone* who might steal any of my attention from her, and you're Public Enemy Number One."

"Oh." I wanted to say something more intelligent and useful, but my brain refused to feed me any words.

"I'm trying to learn to control her better. That's why I've been practicing so much. Right now, I can keep her focused on me and obeying me as long as I'm concentrating my full attention on her. But if I let my concentration waver . . ."

"Or if you practice so hard that you pass out?"

He grimaced. "Yeah. That, too."

"I don't get why you've made this into a state secret. Why wouldn't you just tell me what was going on?" He gave me a long, condescending look, until I answered my own question. "Because you didn't want to admit feeling anything that would make her jealous."

There was another long silence between us. I didn't know what to say to Jamaal's admission, and he didn't seem to have much idea what to say, either.

"I'm glad you told me," I finally said.

"It doesn't change anything. It's going to take everything I have to keep Sita under control the next time I summon her after tonight. It would be best if you weren't even in the house when I do it, just in case I can't stop her from going to look for you."

Trying to manifest his death magic in the form of an animal had been my idea in the first place, and I'd thought it had turned out to be a pretty good one. It was nice not having Jamaal ready to fly off the handle at any moment. Now I was beginning to wonder if an out-of-control phantom tiger was really any better than an out-of-control temper.

"It's an improvement," Jamaal said. Obviously, it was clear what I was thinking. "I *feel* a hell of a lot better. And Sita may be hard to control, but at least I can control when and where I let her out. When I was fighting the death magic instead of cooperating with it, everyone knew I could snap at any moment."

That was a bit of an exaggeration. Sure, his temper had been volatile, and he could be dangerous when his death magic got antsy, but he didn't go off without provocation. Of course, it hadn't taken much to provoke him . . .

"I'm glad you feel better," I said carefully. "But I hope you won't let Sita cut you off completely from the rest of us." Especially me. No matter how much my common sense told me I shouldn't let him get too close.

He shrugged. "I guess we'll see what happens. I've only been working with her a couple of weeks. Maybe my control will get better. And maybe she'll stop seeing everyone else as her competition. But until then, you have to give me my space. I had a great time tonight, but I never should have let you talk me into this. Sita is going to be one angry kitty next time I summon her."

He put the car back in gear and pulled out of the makeshift parking spot. I got the signal loud and clear: our heart-to-heart conversation was over.

I couldn't have told you how I felt about the night's revelations. There was good news and bad news, and I didn't know which was bigger. But at least I no longer thought Jamaal was avoiding me because he was pissed at me. That was a step in the right direction.

THIRTEEN

On Tuesday, I had to meet Steph so we could make the apartment she'd rented for the Glasses as welcoming as possible before they arrived the next day. The place was attractive enough, with good-quality, bland vanilla furniture, but the decoration was sparse, to say the least. Steph thought coming home to a bare-bones apartment was going to make the Glasses feel worse than they already did, so we spent the whole afternoon darting around from store to store buying things like throw pillows and wall hangings, and then spent the evening and well into the night installing our purchases.

The rain was finally starting to clear when I couldn't take decorating anymore and left Steph to finish up alone. The clouds were patchy, and at times I caught quick glimpses of the moon between them. I didn't think it was clear enough for a hunt yet, even if I weren't exhausted and I hadn't agreed to Cyrus's terms. Maybe by tomorrow night . . .

But no. I didn't believe Konstantin was the firebug, and if Cyrus thought for a moment that I'd continued the hunt despite my promise, there would be hell to pay.

Knowing Wednesday probably wasn't going to be any easier on me than Tuesday had been, I collapsed into bed the moment I got home.

The following day dawned bright and clear, not a cloud in the sky. The weather forecast said we'd be venturing up into the low fifties, and after the chilly rain of the last few days, it was going to feel like spring.

The cheerful weather did nothing to calm my rampaging nerves, however. Steph and I had agreed that she would pick up the Glasses at the airport when they arrived around noon. I'd have gone with her, except the Glasses had packed for a three-month trip and would need every spare inch in the car for their baggage. Steph would call when she was leaving the airport, and I'd meet them at the apartment.

I had missed my adoptive parents while they were away, and there was a part of me that was looking forward to seeing them again, whatever the circumstances. I *wasn't* looking forward to seeing their lingering grief over the loss of their house, nor was I looking forward to their worry when Steph told them about the fire at my condo. On paper, they were the owners of the apartment. There was no evidence that the police had linked the two fires—yet—but you could be certain the Glasses' insurance company would take a serious interest in the "coincidence." And, since I was supposedly living in the condo, the Glasses would probably worry I was in some kind of trouble, especially when they factored in the fire at my office building.

What I was dreading the most, however, was the distance I was going to be forced to put between us because of all the things I couldn't tell them.

I remembered what it had been like trying to tap-dance around the truth with Steph before she was dragged in so deeply that I had to tell her my secrets. I may be a good liar, but people who know me really well—like Steph and her parents—tend to see through me. Maybe they had enough crap on their plate that their parental Spidey senses wouldn't start nagging at them right away, but I knew it was only a matter of time before they came to the conclusion I was hiding something from them. I wasn't sure I could face their disappointment and hurt when that happened.

Jamaal was on the porch smoking a clove cigarette when I left the house to go meet the Glasses. I hadn't seen him at all the day before, but considering how little time I'd spent at home, that wasn't a surprise. He held a glass ashtray in one hand. There were three butts and a considerable heap of ashes in it already. I hoped they were old, because if Jamaal had started chain-smoking again, it was not a good sign. I tried to think of a tactful way to ask him about it, but it turned out I didn't have to.

"I didn't get to practice with Sita yesterday," he told me, then took another drag off his cig. "You were out of the house, but I didn't know how long you would be gone."

I shook my head. "So you mean you were serious about not being willing to summon her when I'm nearby."

He nodded as he finished off his cigarette and stubbed it out in the ashtray. "Better safe than sorry. Any idea when you're coming back today?"

I had no clue, actually. However, I didn't think I'd have a

hard time making myself scarce for hours on end if that was what Jamaal needed.

"How about I call you before I come home?" I asked. "If I don't get you, I'll figure you and Sita are still at it and I'll find some way to kill time. I'm sure it won't be hard."

He thought that over for a moment, then nodded his approval. "That'll work."

I started down the porch steps toward the garage, but paused midway down. "You know, you could have called me yesterday and asked me when I was coming back."

His only answer was a shrug. I understood now why he was so determined to keep distance between us, but it didn't really make me feel any better.

The Glasses had beaten me to the apartment. I closed my eyes and sucked in a deep breath as I pulled up next to Steph's car. I hated the anxious knot in my gut, and I hoped like hell I'd be able to cover my discomfort with a convincing veneer of normalcy.

By the time I'd reached the front door of the apartment, I'd put on my happy face. When Mrs. Glass opened the door, I let my cares and worries sink into the background and allowed myself to be swept into the warmth of her hug.

"I missed my girls so much," she said as she tried to hug the breath out of me.

"I missed you, too," I replied, hugging her back just as hard. I glanced over her shoulder at Steph, who was smiling fondly at us. Steph nodded slightly, confirming that she had told her parents about the fire at my condo on the ride from the airport. It was hard to see anything like a silver lining in a fire that had left three innocents dead, but at least it made it easier for me to explain why I was currently "staying with a friend."

"I'm so sorry about everything," I said, my voice suddenly hoarse. "Everything" encompassed a whole lot of things I couldn't talk about, as well as my condolences over the loss of property.

Mrs. Glass only hugged me tighter, holding on until Mr. Glass nudged her aside so he could take her place. He was a little more reserved than she, so my aching ribs survived his hug without greater damage.

"I just made a pot of coffee," Steph said. "Want some?"

"Is water wet?" I retorted.

Mr. Glass released me from his hug, but kept an arm around my shoulders as he guided me to the living room. I saw that Steph had already served her parents coffee and was steeping a cup of tea for herself. The tea was looking a little dark, so I removed the teabag while waiting for Steph to return from the kitchen with my coffee. I'd have told her she didn't have to serve me, except I didn't think the Glasses were going to let me out of their sight quite so soon.

They both had that weary, slumped-shouldered look of people who've been traveling way too long. They'd had to fly in from Hong Kong, and they had to be jet-lagged like nobody's business. Especially Mrs. Glass, who had never been able to sleep on an airplane, even in first class. I hoped that meant that we'd have a pleasant, stress-free visit today and that we'd leave any difficult conversations for a later date.

"So tell me about your trip," I prodded as Steph brought me my cup of coffee. Maybe if I started the ball rolling in the right direction, I could steer the conversation in the direction I wanted. In a perfect world, I'd be able to avoid talking about the fires and what they meant for my continued safety. But it had been a long time since I'd believed in a perfect world.

For a while, my strategy seemed to be working. Mrs. Glass came alive, apparently forgetting her jet lag completely, as she told Steph and me about all the exciting things they'd done and the exotic ports they'd visited. Mr. Glass provided visual aids in the form of photos, which the cruise ship had printed out for him—no doubt at an exorbitant fee. We were all aware of the elephant in the room, but at least we tried to pretend it wasn't there.

The stop-by-stop recounting of the cruise eventually petered out, and that was when the Glasses invited the elephant in the room to join us for coffee. I spent a good fifteen minutes nonchalantly telling them the official version of the story, trying to pretend I genuinely didn't think the fires had anything to do with me. No one called me a liar, but I could see the skepticism on their faces.

"You'd tell us if you were in some kind of trouble, wouldn't you, Nikki?" Mr. Glass asked with fatherly concern.

"Of course," I lied.

"Because I can't help thinking that in your line of work, you might make the kind of enemies who would do something like this."

I had to look away, unable to lie convincingly when he was looking at me like that. The Glasses had never once criticized my choice of career, though I was sure they'd have preferred it if I'd taken a desk job of some sort—or lived off my trust fund and dedicated my life to charity, as Steph had. There had always been an element of danger to my job, and I imagined this wasn't the first time they'd worried about me.

"I'm not in any trouble, at least not that I know of," I said into my cup of coffee. I was acting squirrelly, and I knew it. I just couldn't get myself to stop, too uncomfortable with the direction of the conversation to act normal.

"And what about the rest of us?" he persisted, looking pointedly at his wife and his biological daughter. "Anything we should know about?"

Steph gave an exasperated huff, and I gathered they'd already had this discussion in the car. "It's just a bizarre coincidence, Daddy," she said. "If Nikki thought someone might hurt us, I'm sure she'd tell us."

Steph isn't as good a liar as I am, and I could see her father mentally digging in his heels. I hated the very thought that they might be in danger because of me. I was doing everything I could to protect them, but it wasn't enough.

I received a reprieve from an unexpected source when Mrs. Glass patted her husband's leg. "Now, Ted," she said warningly, "I thought we'd agreed we weren't going to give Nikki the third degree."

My mouth dropped open, though I quickly snapped it shut. If anyone was going to press me for details, I'd have expected it to be my adoptive mother. That was what mothers did, wasn't it?

Mrs. Glass met my gaze with a sad smile. "I'm sure if there's something you're not telling us, it's for a good reason."

My throat squeezed tight, making it impossible for me to answer. There was no hint of reproach in her voice or her eyes. Just loving acceptance and trust. How I'd been lucky enough to be placed with this family when I'd been well on my way to being a lost cause, I'll never know. I swallowed hard, trying to scrape up my voice from wherever it was hiding, but I failed.

"This might be a good time for a change in subject," Steph said. She drained the last few drops of tea from her cup. "You said in the car you had something you wanted to tell us."

Mr. Glass was still looking at me as if he could read my every secret—and he wasn't happy with what he was reading. Mrs. Glass, however, looked suddenly uncomfortable and fidgeted with her empty coffee cup. I shared a quick, puzzled glance with Steph.

"Maybe now isn't a good time—" Mrs. Glass started.

"There never *will* be a good time, May," Mr. Glass said gently, which sent a bolt of adrenaline shooting through my veins.

"What's wrong?" I asked, my voice tight with alarm.

Mrs. Glass was still fidgety, and there was a sheen in her eyes that suggested she was fighting tears, which didn't make me any less alarmed.

"Nothing's wrong," Mr. Glass assured me and Steph, who looked as worried as I felt. "We just have something to tell you." He gave Mrs. Glass a pointed look, but her eyes were now swimming and she shook her head. He sighed. "We're not going to rebuild the house," he said. "Your grandma Rose is getting old, and she's all alone. Your mother and I have been talking for a long time about moving closer to her."

Grandma Rose was Mrs. Glass's mother, and she'd celebrated her seventy-fifth birthday last year, three years after being widowed.

"But Grandma Rose lives in San Francisco!" Steph said in a tone that suggested San Francisco was akin to Timbuktu.

Mrs. Glass rallied her mental forces and cleared her throat. Her eyes were still shiny with tears, but her voice was firm and sure. "We've been talking about it ever since your grandpa passed," she said. "And it feels like the house burning down is almost like a sign from the universe that now is the time."

Mrs. Glass wasn't the only one with shiny eyes now. Steph looked completely stricken. Her whole life, she'd never lived more than a half hour away from her parents. She hadn't even left town to go to college, going to Georgetown because it was close to home. I couldn't imagine what she must be feeling at the moment.

Actually, I wasn't exactly sure what *I* was feeling at the moment. Despite the tears that shone in both Steph's and her mother's eyes, I wasn't feeling inclined to cry myself, nor did I feel the kind of sinking sensation in my stomach I might have expected. My adoptive parents were moving all the way across the country from me. Instead of being able to pop over and see them any day of the week, I would only be able to see them a handful of times a year. They had rescued me from a future that had looked unbearably bleak, and I loved them with all my heart.

And yet at that moment, I felt . . . nothing.

I'd experienced this kind of emotional numbness before. It meant my psyche wasn't ready to deal with my emotions just yet, so it had shut them down entirely.

Even numb as I was, I understood why my emotions had shut down. Despite all the many years I'd lived with the

Glasses; despite the fact that they'd adopted me, and treated me in every way as though I were their biological daughter; despite the fact that even if they were living in San Francisco, I could see them as many times as I was willing to endure the long flight, I couldn't help flashing back to the many times in my childhood when I'd been abandoned. First, my biological mother had abandoned me in a church. Then foster family after foster family had given up on me and sent me away. The small child who lived in my core felt like she was being abandoned yet again, and it was more than I could deal with.

Steph was openly crying now and had moved to the sofa to hug her mother. I should have made a similar gesture, but I sat rooted in my chair, wondering when the dam within me would burst. Mr. Glass shot me a look of undiluted sympathy as he reached over to pat Steph's back, and I knew he understood. At least my less-than-normal reaction to the news wasn't hurting his feelings, and probably wasn't hurting Mrs. Glass's, either. They both knew me well enough to understand my abandonment issues. Maybe that was even part of the reason why they hadn't before now gotten past the stage of *talking* about moving.

My cell phone chirped. After the bombshell the Glasses had just dropped, I probably should have ignored it, but I dug my phone out of my purse anyway, acting more on reflex than considered thought. The caller ID announced the call was from Cyrus.

"I'm sorry," I said to no one in particular, "but I have to take this."

I didn't wait for anyone to acknowledge my words, bolting from my seat in search of privacy.

It wasn't until I was halfway to my rendezvous with Cyrus that I saw the similarity between my current situation and the series of bad choices that had landed me in my new and confusing life in the first place. That time, I'd been on the blind date from hell. I'd gotten a call from Emmitt, asking me to meet him under mysterious circumstances. My gut had been telling me something was wrong, and I'd ignored it, desperate for any excuse to get out of my date. This time, it wasn't a bad date I was running away from, it was the turmoil of my emotions. I had left Steph and her parents with a flurry of excuses, no doubt causing them to worry about me even more. But running away was easier than dealing with the announcement, and I was all for easy.

It could be argued that running off to meet Cyrus without Anderson or any of his other *Liberi* to back me up might be dangerous—and stupid. I didn't think there was any danger that he would hurt me, but he was a devious son of a bitch and could be setting me up for . . . something.

If I'd been able to put my finger on a specific suspicion, I probably would have turned around before I reached the rendezvous. However, I couldn't think of anything Cyrus could do to me in the middle of a public coffee bar, not when the truce between the Olympians and us was still intact. He wouldn't want to piss me off and have me start hunting for Konstantin again.

I drove past the coffee bar, trying to get a look inside before fully committing myself to the meeting, but the cheerfully sunny sky meant all I saw was a reflection of the street with a few shadowy figures moving behind it. I gave a mental shrug, then found myself a parking space. If I was walking into some kind of an ambush, then so be it.

To my surprise and relief, Cyrus was alone this time. At least, he appeared to be. I took a quick visual survey of the rest of the people milling around the coffee bar, and didn't spot anyone with any visible glyphs. Cyrus rose from his table and beckoned to me, like he thought I couldn't find him. I'm sure he knew exactly why I didn't immediately rush to join him. He then shouted an order to the barista—a different one this time, but she seemed just as unflustered by his manner as the previous one—for two espressos.

"I'm not a big espresso fan," I informed him as I approached.

"Make that a latte," he called to the barista, then smiled charmingly at me. "Better?"

Arguing with him over a beverage order seemed like more trouble than it was worth. "Whatever," I said, taking a seat. "I've had a long day already. Can we just cut to the chase without the whole dog and pony show?"

The espresso machine let out a shriek that set my teeth on edge, and Cyrus waited until it went silent before answering.

"No theatrics, I promise."

The barista brought our coffees over. I hadn't been planning to drink mine, but the scent was so enticing I couldn't resist.

"You don't think calling me for an urgent, private meeting is theatrical?" I asked.

He huffed. "Well, I wasn't trying to be, but I guess it was a bit at that. Sorry."

I sipped at my strong, rich coffee, being careful not to burn my tongue. "So what's the big emergency? And why did you need to talk to *me* particularly?"

"I said it was important, not that it was an emergency. But I don't think Anderson will like what I have to say, and I'm trying to spare everyone some drama."

This didn't sound good. I put down the coffee. "What is it?"

"We were speculating the other day about who might be behind the attacks against you. I promised I would warn all my people off, and I did. But I found I was curious myself, so I did a little investigating."

My heart gave a loud ka-thump in my chest. If Cyrus thought Anderson wasn't going to like what he was going to say, then that meant . . .

"It was Emma, wasn't it?"

Cyrus nodded. He pulled a folded sheet of paper from the inside pocket of his jacket. "I stopped by her place and poked around on her computer for a bit while she was out."

I must have looked shocked at his blatant invasion of Emma's privacy, because Cyrus gave me one of his wry grins. "I'm her boss, and she's living in a house that I pay for. I have every right to keep an eye on her, especially when her loyalty's been questionable from the start."

Add one more item to the long list of reasons I never wanted to be an Olympian.

Cyrus slid the paper across to me. "I didn't find anything interesting in her files or browser history. But I did find this in her recycle bin."

I unfolded the paper and saw a screen shot of a computer's recycle bin full of junk files. A number of them with nonsense names had been highlighted, and I could see a bunch of tiled windows that had opened up in WordPad.

"I found seven different versions in her recycle bin," Cyrus continued. "I don't remember exactly what the email you showed me said, but the one on top in that shot is the closest to what I remember."

I had memorized "Konstantin's" email claiming responsibility for the fire at the Glasses' house, and although the one on the screen shot wasn't *exactly* the same, it was close enough. Looked like I'd been right all along to suspect Emma as the author of all my woes. I reread the letter a couple of times as I tried to process what I'd learned. Obviously, Emma was the firebug and was responsible for the fires at the Glasses' house and my condo, but I had to conclude that the fire at my office was every bit as accidental as it had originally seemed. It predated my feud with Emma, and the circumstances were very different. Perhaps what had happened at my office had sparked the whole idea in Emma's head. No pun intended.

"I had a talk with her," Cyrus continued. "She claims she didn't write it and she has no idea how it showed up on her computer."

I gave a little snort of disbelief, and Cyrus's cynical smile said he was with me. The smile faded into a look of grave intensity.

"None of this changes anything in the long run," he told me. "Emma is still an Olympian and under my protection. I have made it abundantly clear that you are off-limits and that I won't tolerate disobedience. I don't expect you to have any more trouble with her. But I thought you should know. I'll leave it up to you whether you want to tell Anderson or not."

I stared at the incriminating paper, shaking my head once more at the irrational depths of Emma's hatred. Anderson wouldn't want to know how low she'd sunk. He had a hard enough time reconciling his image of Emma with the woman who had betrayed Erin to her death just to spite him, but this was even worse. However, this might be something he *needed* to know, whether he wanted to or not.

"Thanks," I said, putting a heavy dose of sarcasm in my voice.

Cyrus smiled. "You can see now why I didn't want him to hear it from me."

I rubbed my eyes, feeling tired and headachy. I didn't exactly want Anderson to hear it from *me,* either.

I wondered if Cyrus thought I was rubbing my eyes to stave off tears, because his voice suddenly went all soft and sympathetic. "I wouldn't take it personally if I were you. Emma's . . . not well."

"No kidding?"

"Her maid tells me she has nightmares every night," Cyrus continued after giving me a reproachful look. "I can see with my own two eyes that she's losing weight. She shouldn't have left Anderson when she did. In retrospect, I can see she was being self-destructive, and I probably served as an enabler."

I'd been so furious at Emma and the things she'd done that I'd never put a moment's thought into what her life might be like now. She was jealous, vindictive, and spiteful as all hell. More than once, I'd thought of her as crazy, but I'd never quite made the jump from "crazy" to "clinically insane." Until now.

"I'm trying to help her," Cyrus said, "but I don't think she's too interested in being helped. I made it very, very clear to her what the consequences of disobeying me would be, but I'm not sure she doesn't have a death wish. I'll try to keep an eye on her, but watch your back, just in case."

My stomach felt sour. I'd be the first to admit I'd disliked Emma from the moment she'd recovered from the catatonic state she'd been in when we first dragged her from the pond. She'd started out being merely annoying with her self-centeredness and bitchy comments, then graduated to being downright mean, consumed by unfounded jealousy and her understandable desire for revenge. She'd stopped having any redeeming features in my mind when she'd threatened Steph. And yet . . .

And yet, I had saved her life. Saved her from an eternity of repeatedly drowning to death. Finding her and rescuing her had been the single greatest victory of my life. I didn't want her to die after all that, didn't want to undo the good I had done.

Of course, I also didn't want her setting another fire.

"You'd better keep more than an eye on her, Cyrus," I said, though I had no ammunition with which to back up my ultimatum.

"I'll do my best."

His assurance didn't exactly fill me with confidence, but then nothing he said would. I picked up the incriminating screen shot. "Can I keep this?"

Cyrus nodded. "Be my guest. And if you tell Anderson and he takes the news as badly as I fear he might, let me remind you that you will always be welcome among the Olympians."

I paused with the paper halfway to my purse as a disturbing thought hit me. "How do I know this isn't all some kind of twisted setup so I'll have a falling-out with Anderson?" I asked. That would certainly explain his reluctance to break the news to Anderson himself. Hell, if I was going to be paranoid, I could even imagine he'd created the screen shots just so he could give me bad news to deliver.

He laughed. "An interesting idea. My father is capable of scheming and manipulation on that level, but I'm not as complicated as he is."

"Yeah, you're just a plain old everyman."

"Well, I didn't say *that*. But I wouldn't make trouble for you with Anderson unless I was sure it would make you join the Olympians. I'm not much of a gambler. Give me the sure thing any day."

Is it weird that Cyrus admitting his own potential for dishonesty made me more inclined to believe him?

What tipped the scales in the end was my absolute conviction that Cyrus wasn't an idiot. He knew that if Anderson kicked me out, I'd make a run for it rather than join the Olympians.

"I'm *never* going to become an Olympian," I told him, just to hammer home the point.

There was a glint in his eye when he smiled at me, and I wondered if making myself into a challenge to be conquered had been a tactical error. "Never is a long time, Nikki. A long, long time."

Fourteen

I wasn't in any hurry to deliver Cyrus's news to Anderson, so I decided to go for a run as soon as I got back to the mansion. As luck would have it, Maggie had the same idea, so I had company. I wasn't exactly feeling sociable, but running with Maggie isn't much of a social occasion for me anyway. She's five eleven to my five two, and she can cover a daunting amount of ground in a single stride. I have to run like my life depends on it to keep up, and I don't usually last all that long or have the breath to do a lot of talking.

On a day like today, running like my life depended on it

was just what I needed. The effort of keeping up the aggressive pace left no room in my mind for inconvenient thoughts and worries. For just a little while, I left my problems behind me and didn't think about anything at all. My muscles burned and protested, my chest heaved with effort, I was sweating buckets despite the chilly temperature, and I adored every painful, oblivious moment of it. I pushed well past my usual limits and didn't even notice I was doing it.

By the time we started our cool-down walk, my legs were shaking with fatigue, and I was really glad I wasn't just an ordinary human being anymore or I'd never have been able to get out of bed the next day. Much of my hair had slipped free of the ponytail I'd tied it in, damp tendrils clinging to my face and neck. Maggie was panting delicately, and her face was glowing a bit with the exertion and a touch of sweat, but her curly auburn hair was pristine in its French braid. She looked like she was just about to *start* a run, while I looked more like someone staggering over the finish line of a marathon. She gave me almost as much of an inferiority complex as Steph did, but she was a good friend anyway.

"So, are you going to tell me what's wrong?" Maggie prompted when I was no longer breathing so hard I couldn't answer.

"Wrong?" I asked, giving her innocent wide eyes. "What makes you think something's wrong?"

"You don't love running enough to push yourself that hard. Not unless you're trying to run away from something that's on your mind."

I grimaced, realizing she was right. There were times when I enjoyed running, but mostly I did it because it was good for me, not because I loved it. And usually I'd quit long before I'd worked myself into such a lather.

I was sick to death of lying and trying to hide my feelings. Or maybe I was just too exhausted, both mentally and physically, to hold it all inside. Instead of pretending nothing was wrong, I told Maggie about my disturbing conversation with Cyrus. My lips were chapped with the cold, but that didn't stop me from chewing on them, making them worse.

"What do you think I should do?" I asked. "Should I tell Anderson?"

I realized I knew her answer before she even spoke. Unlike me, Maggie's first instinct is always to follow the rules. Hiding the truth from Anderson might not be technically breaking any rules, but I suspected it would feel that way to her.

"Of course you should tell him," she said, as if it were the most obvious thing in the world. "He has a right to know. And he would *want* to know."

"But—"

"Besides," she interrupted, "he's likely to find out eventually, and he'll be pissed off that you didn't tell him."

She had a point. I kicked out at a pinecone in frustration, sending it straight into a tree so that it almost ricocheted back at us.

"I just don't get it," I said, restraining the urge to give the pinecone another kick. "Where is Emma getting all this crazy shit from? What have I ever done to give her the slightest hint that I might be after Anderson?"

I'd meant them as rhetorical questions, and wasn't expecting Maggie to answer. And yet there was a kind of waiting quality to her silence. Something that told me she had something to say but was thinking her words over carefully. I came to a stop, shivering in the cold now that I was finally cooling down.

"What is it? What are you thinking?"

Maggie gave me an almost apologetic smile. "I don't think it has anything to do with you or what you've done. I think it's more about Anderson."

I frowned in confusion. "Anderson's never done anything that would give her reason to be jealous, either. Not if she were sane, that is."

Maggie shrugged and turned as if to start heading back toward the house, but I grabbed her arm to stop her. Obviously, she had more to say, even if she was reluctant to say it.

"Come on, Maggie. Help me out here. Is there something going on I don't know about?"

She looked distinctly uncomfortable, but like a true friend, she answered me anyway. "I've known Anderson a long time. I even knew him back when he and Erin were together." She gave me the apologetic smile again. "I can see the way he looks at you when you're not looking, Nikki. It's just like how he used to look at Emma when his relationship with Erin was going south. Emma's a crazy bitch, but she's not making it all up."

I opened and closed my mouth a few times, but I couldn't come up with anything to say. Never once had I picked up that kind of a vibe from Anderson, but now I had to wonder . . . was it because there'd been nothing to pick up, or had I been completely blind to the signals?

I shook my head. "You're wrong," I said. "You *have* to be. I can be clueless sometimes, but not *that* clueless." My voice went up at the end, making my words sound more like a question than a statement of fact.

"Maybe," Maggie said with an unconvincing shrug. "But I bet you anything that Emma's seen the same thing I have, and that's what set her off."

"Guess that means you're *both* nuts," I grumbled. So much for the peaceful oblivion I'd been looking for when I decided to go running.

I was in even less of a mood to deliver bad news to Anderson now than I had been before. How could I look him in the eye after what Maggie had just said? I wouldn't be able to stop myself from overanalyzing every nuance of his behavior, looking for any hint that Maggie was right. If Anderson had the hots for me, I didn't want to know it. I had more than enough complications in my life as it was.

I took a long, hot shower, and by the time I got out, I'd convinced myself I *had* to tell Anderson that Emma was behind the fires, no matter how much I didn't want to. It could turn out to be dangerous for him to underestimate her level of malice, and the sooner he accepted what she had turned into, the safer we would all be.

Dread making my stomach feel twisted and cold, I descended the stairs to the second floor and forced myself toward Anderson's study. The door was open, but when I stepped inside, I found the room empty.

I could have gone looking for him, or I could have tried again later. Instead, I decided to take the coward's way out. Maybe the "right" thing to do would have been to wait until I had a chance to sit down with Anderson and deliver the news in person, but I'd had more than enough confrontation for one day, and I just couldn't face more.

Hoping Anderson wouldn't come back and catch me in the act, I rummaged through his desk for a pen. Then I took the screen shot that Cyrus had given me and scrawled a brief note on it. *I saw Cyrus today, and he gave me this. He says he got it off of Emma's computer. Remember not to shoot the messenger.* I left the paper on the seat of his chair, and then hustled out of there, glad to have escaped without having to face him.

Fifteen

Thursday and Friday passed without me once catching a glimpse of Anderson in the house. I kept expecting him to show up on my doorstep, or call me and demand I come to his study, but he didn't. I might have thought he'd gone off somewhere for a vacation, except when I casually asked Maggie at lunch one day if she'd seen him lately, she told me he was home. I wondered if he had just chosen to ignore the message I'd left him, or whether he was pissed at me for being the bearer of bad tidings and was simply avoiding me.

Another storm was due to roll into town sometime Saturday morning, with a slight chance of snowfall. As usual, it was still dark out when I woke up in the morning, but I could almost *feel* the threat of the approaching storm. I needed to make a grocery run, and it looked like I'd better do it soon if I didn't want to risk having to drive in the snow. The only grocery store I knew of that was open at six in the morning was a good twenty minutes away, but it would be worth it if the snow came.

It started raining as soon as I pulled into the grocery store's parking lot, but it was nothing more than a chill drizzle. No snow yet, but the temperature had dropped ominously. Predictably, the parking lot was almost deserted at this time in the morning, and I hoped that meant the hoarders hadn't hit the shelves yet and bought out all the milk, bread, and eggs as sometimes happens before a snowfall.

It was raining a little harder when I exited the store, and if I hadn't had two paper grocery bags in my arms, I would have put up my umbrella. Instead, I merely hurried a little more, ducking my head to keep the droplets out of my eyes.

The parking lot was still mostly deserted, and though it was somewhere around dawn, the clouds were heavy enough to keep the rising sun from showing through yet. I noticed that even with about a hundred open spaces available throughout the parking lot, some jackass had parked his car so close to mine I'd have to perform contortions to get into the driver's seat.

I'd planned ahead and had put my keys in one hand before scooping a grocery bag into each arm. I popped the trunk, then used my knee to nudge it open enough so I could put the bags in. I heard the sound of a car door closing, and out of the corner of my eye, I saw someone walking around the car beside me.

I shoved my bags into the trunk, planning to ask the driver nicely if he would pull up so I could get into my driver's seat.

I slammed the trunk closed, then turned to the driver beside me. He had opened his own trunk, although I was sure he hadn't gone into the grocery store yet. He turned his head toward me and grinned. I frowned, not knowing what he was so happy about. Until his hand emerged from the trunk and I saw the tire iron in it.

It had taken me way too long to recognize the threat, and though I tried to ward off the blow with my shoulder, the tire iron still connected solidly with my skull, sending a stab of pain through my head. It felt like the parking lot pitched below me, and though I desperately tried to stay on my feet so I could take evasive action, I couldn't do it. The ground rushed up to meet me, and my attacker took another step toward me, raising the tire iron.

My head throbbed, and my brain felt all woozy. I tried screaming for help, though I doubted there was anyone nearby who could hear me.

The lunatic swung at me again, and I rolled violently to the side to avoid the blow. I heard the metallic clank of the weapon striking the pavement, and my attacker's curse at having missed. My stomach didn't like the sudden movement, threatening to toss my breakfast. I wondered if that meant I had a concussion from that first blow.

I didn't have time to bemoan my miseries, not unless I wanted to add more to the list. Swallowing my gorge, I tried to push to my feet. If the world would stop spinning enough for me to stand up, maybe I could run into the store, where there were at least a handful of people who might help me.

The tire iron connected with my back at shoulder blade level, knocking me flat on my face and forcing the air out of my lungs. My reeling mind ordered me to pull myself together and get up, but my body was having none of it. Pain and nausea roiled through me, along with a good dose of fear. No, my attacker couldn't kill me, at least not permanently. However, he could do a whole lot of very unpleasant things to me if I didn't find some way to muster my strength for an escape.

I was still struggling to get up when I heard the scrape of a footstep on the pavement right by my head. I looked around just in time to see my attacker's foot coming for my face.

I blacked out for a while, but either I wasn't as badly hurt as it seemed, or my supernatural healing was working overtime, because I woke up what had to be no more than a few seconds later. Pain screamed through my head, and I wanted to shrivel up and hide in some dark corner until it went away.

I was draped over a hard, bony shoulder, a pair of arms clamped around my legs. I struggled feebly, but the only effect was to let my attacker know I was conscious again. He slung me off his shoulder, and I tried once again to scream for help. I don't think a whole lot of sound made it out of my mouth.

I thumped down on the ground much sooner than I was expecting to, and in my weakened state even that relatively mild impact was almost enough to knock me out again. Like I said, my mind was pretty fuzzy, and it took me an agonizing minute to realize I'd been dumped into the trunk of my attacker's car.

This couldn't be good.

My attacker leaned into the trunk, and I got a good look at his face for the first time. He was no one I knew, and I didn't see any sign of a glyph anywhere on him. I hoped that meant he was just some random human thug who'd seen a delicate-looking woman alone in a darkened parking lot and decided to take advantage of the situation. If that was the case, I might be able to surprise him with my supernatural healing ability and make my escape.

The possibility that he might *not* be some random human, that he might have been after *me* specifically, was not something I cared to contemplate.

I was in no shape to make a flashy getaway from the car in my current condition, and I decided my best chance of escape—at least while my head was still reeling from what I was now sure was a concussion—was to attract attention and get help. I drew in breath to scream, but even that turned out to be more than my body could handle, as the ribs in my back sent a breath-stealing blast of pain through me. Maybe I had some broken ribs to go with the concussion.

My midsection hurt so much I barely even felt it when my attacker punched me and I blacked out again.

When next I woke up, my situation had not improved. My head felt even more woozy, and the car felt like it was pitching and bucking beneath me. I was lying on my stomach, my hands bound behind my back. I heard the distinctive ripping sound of duct tape, and felt something being wound around my ankles. I tried to voice a protest, but there was duct tape over my mouth, too. I swallowed a few times in rapid succession. This would be a really bad time to throw up, no matter how bad the nausea was.

Once again, my struggles served only to let my captor know I was awake.

"Damn, you are one tough bitch," I heard him mutter.

He grabbed me by the hair and slammed my head down against the floor of the trunk. If I hadn't already been hurt, I don't know if the impact of my head against the carpet would have done much, but as it was, it stunned me into semiconsciousness.

In the last few moments of light before the trunk slammed shut, I caught sight of something that struck terror into my heart: lying next to me, on the floor of the trunk beside the roll of duct tape my attacker had thrown in when he was finished with it, was a shovel.

Sixteen

I closed my eyes in the darkness of the trunk and tried not to panic. Panic would steal my ability to think rationally even better than the aftereffects of the concussion would.

It could be just a coincidence that there was a shovel in the trunk with me. Maybe my captor was a gardener, or a handyman or something. It didn't mean he was planning to bury me alive.

Or bury me after killing me, which was just as bad.

My attempts to comfort myself didn't do a whole lot of good, and fear stole my breath. Ever since I'd first heard about what Konstantin had done to Emma, chaining her at the bottom of a lake so that she would revive and die over and over again for all eternity, facing a similar fate had become my worst nightmare. Immortality might have its perks, but making a fate like that possible was one hell of an awful drawback.

Until I had joined the fold, Anderson had been searching for Emma for ten years, unable to locate and rescue her without a descendant of Artemis to help in the hunt. And if my attacker buried me, Anderson wouldn't have a descendant of Artemis to help him find me.

Which meant that no matter what it took, I had to make sure I didn't find myself planted in the ground.

I felt the vibration through my body as my captor started the car, then the lurch as he pulled out of the parking space and a bump when he pulled out of the lot. I didn't know where he was taking me, but I hoped it was a long way away. The more time I had to recover and plan, the better the chances I would be able to get myself out of this nightmare.

At least, that's what I tried to tell myself to keep the panic under control.

I tried wriggling my arms around, seeing if there was any leeway in my bindings, but there wasn't. I tried to fit my body through the circle of my bound arms so at least I could get my hands in front of me, but there wasn't a whole lot of room to maneuver, and my injuries seriously hampered my efforts. I forced myself to lie still for a moment, sucking in deep breaths, reminding myself my life might depend on me staying as calm and rational as possible under the circumstances.

If I wanted to survive this encounter—or at least survive this encounter in a manner that didn't make me wish I hadn't—I *had* to get free. I could try to position myself so I could give my attacker a kick to the face with my bound legs when he opened the trunk, but if I wasn't able to run for it, that would only delay the inevitable. I'd heard that escaping duct tape wasn't all that hard, but I wasn't sure I believed it, and I didn't know any tricky methods to accomplish it. The best I could do was try to wriggle my hands and wrists until the tape either broke or stretched, or until I somehow had enough space to get my hands through.

There wasn't a whole lot of wiggle room at first, that was for sure. I was painfully aware of the passage of time, painfully aware that every second I spent struggling, we were closer to wherever my attacker planned to take me to finish things. Panic kept trying to take over my brain, and though it was cold in the trunk, I was sweating from a combination of exertion and terror.

The sweat worked to my advantage, giving my wrists a little lubrication as I twisted and pulled and writhed, trying to find a way out. I definitely had a little more freedom of movement now than I'd had when I first started, and I seized on to that tiny hint of success to fuel my efforts to keep trying.

Those efforts were complicated by the fact that my attacker was a terrible driver. The car lurched whenever he hit the brakes, and he took every corner just a little too fast. Having no way to brace myself, I was thrown around the trunk like a sack of groceries, and the repeated, jarring impacts weren't doing my head a whole lot of good. It didn't help that the damn shovel was getting tossed around, too. I landed on it—or it landed on me—more than once. I tried to push it out of the way, trying to make sure the metal blade wouldn't come into contact with my head, but there wasn't anywhere to move it to.

I didn't know how much time had passed—it seemed like some weird combination of forever and not long enough—before I started to feel like I had a chance of getting out of the duct tape after all. The car had stopped doing so much starting, stopping, and turning, and I figured that meant we were on a highway somewhere. The steadiness meant that I didn't keep losing my progress every time I was tossed around, and I had slipped one hand up and one hand down so that only the ball of my thumb was holding me in. If I could just get that big part of my thumb out, I would be free, and the shovel would become my best friend. I almost grinned thinking about the look on my attacker's face when he opened the trunk, expecting to see a helpless, bound female, and instead found a heavy metal shovel coming at his face.

My thumb was coming free millimeter by millimeter, and I knew that at any moment now it would slip all the way through the tape, and I would be out.

Suddenly, a car horn blared from way too close.

Even from the trunk, I could hear my attacker's shouted curse as he stomped the brake pedal. Tires shrieked in protest, and I could tell the idiot at the wheel didn't know to pump the brakes, because we were skidding wildly.

I slammed into the side of the trunk, hitting it with my forehead while the shovel thunked into me from behind.

More shrieking tires, more frantic blaring of horns. And then, impact.

I can only guess at exactly what happened next, because the

sound of the impact is the last thing I remember of the accident. I think I took another blow or two to the head, either from the shovel or from the side of the car. It's also possible my head was thrown against the side of the trunk so hard that my neck snapped.

Whatever exactly happened, it killed me.

One moment, I was hurtling around in the trunk of the car; the next, I was nothing but a consciousness in the dark.

Having been dead once before, I knew exactly what was happening this time. I could feel my body, but I think I felt it in the way that an amputee sometimes feels a lost limb. I was aware of its existence, and I felt physical sensations, but I was utterly paralyzed, unable even to breathe, though my nonexistent lungs screamed for oxygen. My similarly nonexistent eyes felt like they were open, but I could see nothing but impenetrable darkness.

As far as I could tell, there was nothing above me, and nothing below me. I felt physical sensations, but only within myself, nothing from outside my body. No sensation of my weight resting on something, no heat or cold or breeze or movement.

Phantom adrenaline flooded my system as my phantom lungs continued their desperate screaming for air. I knew I didn't really need to breathe, knew that my body was right now dead and had no needs whatsoever, but that primal need to flee, to fight, to *survive* was louder and more urgent than any logic. I honestly don't know which is worse: the feeling of suffocation, or the soul-tearing, uncontrollable panic that feeling engenders. There was a very good reason that even the immortal *Liberi* feared death, even when they knew they would come back from it.

The last time I'd died, my body had been completely destroyed, burned to ashes. The seed of immortality meant that I eventually grew a new body, but it had taken days for that to happen, and the time I'd spent in the dark, airless confines of death had felt more like years. I was fairly certain I wouldn't stay dead as long this time. I might have thought that knowledge would make death easier to bear, but it didn't.

I suffered, and it felt like it would go on forever.

I came to to the feeling of someone's fingers sliding off the skin of my neck.

"She's dead," a voice said, sounding like it came from far away.

I sucked in a frantic breath and opened my eyes, but whoever had been feeling for a pulse had already pulled away, and there was enough background noise that no one seemed to hear. Which was probably just as well, because it gave me a little time to gather my wits about me.

I took a moment to appreciate the luxury of breathing, practically hyperventilating in my effort to get as much air as possible into my lungs. The duct tape over my mouth hampered my efforts to fill my lungs, and I lost a few seconds to incoherent panic before I finally calmed down enough to assess my situation.

I was still in the trunk of the car, but I was crumpled awkwardly against one side of it, my head pressed against it, bending my neck at a painful angle. The trunk had been so badly mangled by the crash that I didn't at first realize the car had come to rest on its side. There was no way anyone could have pried the trunk open, but one side of it had buckled enough to create a sizable opening, which was letting in a steady patter of cold rain. I guess whoever had been checking my pulse must have crawled through that opening to get to me. Or perhaps been dangled through by someone holding his legs.

I was probably lucky I'd ended up wedged in like I was; otherwise, I might already be at the morgue. I imagined coming back to life there might have caused some serious issues for everyone involved. I was probably going to startle the hell out of some people even now, and I bet the guy who'd declared me dead was never going to hear the end of it.

The thought might have been amusing, except I had some clue how weird things were going to get when I made it known I was alive. I twisted around so that my neck was no longer in such an awkward position, and twisting like that was enough to show me that any injuries I might have sustained in the accident had already healed. I was utterly exhausted, which I knew was a side effect of the supernatural healing, but otherwise, I doubted I had more than a bruise or two on me. That was going to have a lot of people scratching their heads after I'd been tossed about so violently I'd been declared dead.

But there was no help for it. They knew I was in here, so it wasn't like I had any hope of sneaking away undetected. Even if I weren't still trussed up in duct tape. I was just going to have to feign ignorance and rely on the EMTs to believe they'd witnessed a miracle.

It took a while of kicking at the side of the trunk with my bound legs before someone heard me and came to check it out. There was quite a flurry of activity after that. They pried the trunk open to get me out. I wished they'd just grab me and drag me out through the small opening the EMT had crawled through, but I guess they were too worried about my injuries to manhandle me like that. Not surprisingly, I soon found myself on a gurney being rushed toward a waiting ambulance. I decided not to protest the treatment, because I knew no one would believe me if I said I was fine. I *did* try to protest having my head immobilized, but I couldn't blame them for thinking I had a head injury considering the position I'd been in when they'd first found me.

I had a couple of minutes to take in the scene around me while the EMTs were fussing around, trying to get me strapped onto the gurney and immobilized. The car I'd been in had done its best impression of an accordion, its trunk and hood crumpled to show there'd been solid impact from both ends before it had skidded into a ditch and ended up on its side. Through the shattered windshield, I saw the deflated airbag drooping from the steering wheel, its white fabric spotted with dark blood. Despite the extent of the damage, it was a pretty good-sized car, and I thought it possible my abductor had survived the crash. More's the pity.

There was another, smaller car a little farther up the road, and it looked like it was in even worse shape. I didn't think there was much chance its driver had made it. He or she had probably saved me from a fate worse than death, and I hoped I was wrong about their survival chances.

The ambulance doors closed, cutting off all sight of the wreckage and the flashing lights of an impressive array of emergency vehicles. One of the EMTs gunned the engine of the ambulance, hitting the siren, while the other climbed into the back with me, continuing to try to assess my injuries. I tried to tell the guy I wasn't that badly hurt, but I wasn't surprised he didn't take my word for it. He probably thought I was in shock or delirious or something.

The ride to the hospital didn't take long, but by the time we got there, there was already a lot of head-scratching going on in the back of the ambulance as the EMT failed to find anything wrong with me. I kept repeating that I was okay, except for a little soreness here and there, but he was still sure I had to have some kind of dire injury he had so far missed. I tried to remain calm and patient, knowing he was just doing his job and that there was no reasonable explanation for my condition. I didn't blame him for being confused. I guess toward the end I was getting a little bit testy despite my best efforts, because he gave me a ferocious glare.

"You are *not* all right!" he snapped. "You had no pulse when I first checked you."

I could see why he might find that a cause for concern. "Well, I have one now. And I really want out of this head contraption."

The siren stopped wailing, and the ambulance came to a stop. The EMT took our arrival at the hospital as an excuse to ignore my request, and I knew I was about to go through the whole rigmarole again, because the doctors and nurses of the ER weren't going to believe their eyes, either.

SEVENTEEN

I was right about my reception at the emergency room. I once again had the delightful experience of being ignored when I claimed I was all right, and though I understood why, I couldn't help getting crankier as time went on. I wanted to get the hell out of there. I wanted a little quiet time in which I could try to process everything I'd just gone through. And I was so bone tired, I wanted a little time to sleep it off, too. None of which I was getting.

I put my foot down when they started talking about skull X-rays and an MRI. If they started ordering tests where I'd have to wait my turn to get in and then wait for the results, I was going to be in there all day. I had a right to refuse medical treatment, and I asserted it with a vengeance.

I swear every person in the entire ER tried to talk me out of checking myself out. It felt like I had to repeat myself to about twenty people, everyone from the attending physician to the freaking janitor, before I was finally given some papers to fill out that basically said it wasn't their fault if I died a horrible death due to leaving the hospital against medical advice. If I'd been merely human, they might have scared me so much with their warnings and predictions that I'd have caved.

I was mere moments from escape when the police caught up with me.

For a little while there, I'd almost forgotten that I'd been found bound in duct tape in the trunk of a car. Naturally, the police wanted to know how I'd gotten there. The authorities had caught on to the fact that I was a common denominator between three separate fires—thanks to the Glasses' insurance company, no doubt. I'd never been a direct target, and the first fire had been declared an accident, but it didn't exactly lead them to believe my abduction was a random act by some wandering psycho.

I saw no reason not to tell them the truth about the abduction, with a few errors and omissions. Like how I never mentioned being hit in the head with a tire iron, which would be completely unbelievable when I didn't have any obvious wounds on my head. I knew there was some blood in my hair, because everyone had been looking for its source, but the wound itself was gone. I didn't know how anyone was going to explain away the blood, and frankly, I didn't care.

The policemen shared a couple of significant looks as I told them about my abduction. Maybe they thought I was too shaken up to notice. I knew those looks meant something about my story was striking a false note, but I didn't know what— unless my abductor was still alive and had told all, including the stuff I was leaving out.

"Did the guy who tried to kidnap me survive the crash?" I asked, surprised that I hadn't thought to ask before. Though maybe I'd been too preoccupied trying to get myself out of the hospital to think about anything else.

The cops looked at each other again. Then one of them, a Detective Taylor, answered me.

"A few broken bones, a lot of stitches, and even more bruises, but yeah, the lucky son of a bitch survived. He's got a list of priors longer than my arm, and he was real eager to talk."

Shit. That probably wasn't good for me. The more stuff didn't add up, the more suspicious the cops were going to be, and the more determined they were going to be to get to the truth.

"Are you sure you don't know someone who might have a serious beef with you?" Taylor continued.

I gave him my best baffled face. "I have no idea. I've made enemies because of my job, but I don't know of anyone who would hate me enough to do all this to get back at me."

Taylor gave me a piercing look, no doubt trying to convey the message that he could see right through me. "Think hard."

I made a show of thinking about it, furrowing my brow as if I were racking my brain. Then I shook my head. "I'm sorry, Detective, but I can't think of anyone."

"A woman, maybe?" he prompted, still not satisfied with my answer.

"I assume you have a reason for asking that," I said, hoping my face had shown no reaction. If they had reason to suspect a woman was gunning for me, there was only one logical suspect on my list.

"I told you the guy was eager to talk. Said he was hired over the phone by some woman. Never met her in person, though, and of course never got a name."

I nodded sagely and pretended to think it over some more. Then I raised my hands in a gesture of defeat and shook my head some more. "I still don't have a clue. Sorry."

Taylor gave me his card and asked me to call him if anything came to mind. Neither he nor his partner made much effort to hide the fact that they didn't believe me. I was real glad I was the victim rather than the suspect, or I don't think they would have let me off quite so easily. Even so, I felt their eyes on me as I retreated to the emergency room entrance, where I was able to borrow a cell phone and make a call.

There were lots of people I could have called to come pick me up at the hospital. I could have called Steph, although I wouldn't have wanted to worry her. I could have called Anderson, who, once he heard that an unknown woman had hired some thug to kill me and presumably bury me, would have to finally see

Emma for what she really was. Or I could have called any of my friends at the mansion who would have driven me home without any hints of drama or complication.

So who did I end up calling? Jamaal, of course.

As far as I knew, he was the only one of Anderson's *Liberi* who knew what it was like to die, having gone through the experience at least three times already. So far, I had held myself together through sheer force of will, but once I had a moment of anything resembling privacy, I was going to fall apart, and Jamaal was the only one who would truly understand why.

"Sita's not going to like it," he reminded me when I called.

"I died, Jamaal. I *died*." There was a tremor in my voice, and for a moment I feared I was going to fall apart in front of an audience after all. Not that people in an emergency room waiting area are all that concerned with other people's distress, but it would have been embarrassing to break down in tears in front of them anyway. Especially when I wasn't sure I'd be able to get myself under control anytime this century.

"I'll be there as soon as I can," Jamaal said after a brief hesitation.

He hung up before I could thank him. I closed my eyes and tried to breathe slowly and deeply to calm myself. After my last experience with death, I should have known better.

It wasn't truly dark when I closed my eyes. The fluorescent lighting created a golden red glow behind my closed lids that was nothing like the darkness of death. My adrenal glands didn't appreciate the difference, however, and terror shot through me from head to toe. I gasped and opened my eyes, my heart hammering, my skin clammy with sweat.

"Are you all right, dear?" asked the nice old lady who'd loaned me her phone.

I plastered on what I was sure was a patently false smile. "I'm fine," I told her. "Thanks for letting me use your phone."

Her brow furrowed with concern, and I could see I had one more name I could add to the list of people who hadn't believed me when I'd said I was fine today. Of course, I didn't know her name, so it would be hard to add to the list.

The thought struck me as funny, and I knew that my body was trying to find another outlet for all the turmoil I was holding inside. I had successfully blocked the hysterical tears that wanted to rise up, but the inappropriate laughter almost had its way with me. A sound reminiscent of a bark escaped my lips before I changed it into a fake cough and clamped down even harder on my emotions.

"I'm going to wait for my ride outside," I said, then turned on my heel and practically sprinted for the exit. I knew I was being rude to the little old lady, but if I hadn't gotten myself away from her, I was sure all my walls were going to crack and I would make a fool of myself in front of everyone.

I had kind of forgotten I'd gotten such an early start to my day because of the predicted weather front coming through. One step out of the emergency room doors was all it took to remind me. My kidnapper had removed my coat so he could bind my wrists more easily, and I had no idea where that coat had ended up. My clothes were still slightly damp from the time I'd spent crumpled in the trunk with the rain beating down through the gap the crash had created, and that first blast of cold air practically took my breath away.

The temperature had dropped since I'd last been out, and the rain had changed into a light snow that so far was only sticking in patches here and there. My breath steamed, and I wrapped my arms around myself for warmth. It didn't help, and within seconds, I was shivering.

The smart thing to do would be to go inside and wait where it was warm. However, the biting cold served two purposes: it kept me awake despite the exhaustion that dragged at me, and it made me so uncomfortable there wasn't room in my brain to handle thoughts of death.

I stood shivering in the cold and watched as the snowfall grew heavier, until there was a dusting of white over every exposed surface. So much for the "slight chance" of snow. Exhaustion had made my knees weak, and I was leaning against the side of the building to keep myself upright when I finally saw Jamaal's black Saab turning into the entrance. I pushed away from the wall as he pulled up to the curb, and my legs were so shaky I almost fell. I was in rough shape, and I hoped I wouldn't need Jamaal to help me into the car.

The passenger door sprang open, and I saw that Jamaal had leaned across the seat to open it for me. He was watching me intently as I approached, I think trying to gauge whether I could make it on my own or not. If he hadn't opened the door for me, I don't know if I could have. I collapsed into the passenger seat in a boneless heap, shivering even more violently when the blast of heated air hit me.

Jamaal reached over me to pull the door closed. I'd kind of forgotten that little detail in the blissful glory of sitting down and feeling the warmth of the heater. Despite my fear of the darkness, my eyelids weighed about a ton each, and sleep was pressing in on me from all sides. I was so out of it I'd forgotten about the seat belt, too. I thought about trying to take over as Jamaal buckled me in, but that simple task loomed like a Herculean labor, and I couldn't find the energy to even start.

I was asleep before the car started moving again.

There's no sleep quite so deep and dreamless as that which occurs after a lot of supernatural healing. I didn't wake up when we arrived at the mansion, nor when Jamaal picked me up and carried me through the snow from the garage to the main house, nor when he carried me up to my room on the third floor. When I *did* wake up, it was dark outside. Someone—Jamaal, presumably—had considerately turned my bedside lamp on so that I wouldn't wake up to a dark room. I smiled at that small act of kindness, even as my fuzzy brain realized I didn't remember a thing since collapsing into the seat of Jamaal's car.

My body still felt strangely heavy, and I knew that if I

curled up and tried to sleep some more, I'd probably drift off again. But that effort would require me to lie there with my eyes closed for a while, and I knew from experience I'd have to face panicky memories of being dead.

Deciding I'd rather wait until the exhaustion had a mind of its own again before facing that ordeal, I pushed myself into a sitting position, and that's when I noticed a number of things.

For one, I wasn't wearing my clothes. I glanced down at myself and saw the straps of my bra peeking out from beneath the covers, so at least I wasn't completely naked, but *someone* had undressed me.

Second, I noticed the heavenly scent of coffee. I breathed in deep, wondering if I had the strength to wander into the sitting room and fetch myself a cup.

Then, and only then, did I realize I wasn't alone in the room.

I gave a startled little squeak when I caught sight of the shadowed form sitting quietly in an armchair in the corner. Jamaal leaned forward so that the light from my bedside lamp illuminated his face better. Not that I'd had any doubt who was there once I'd noticed him.

"Coffee?" he asked in a gruff voice, not meeting my eyes.

I wondered if he was the one who'd undressed me, and the thought made my cheeks heat with a blush. "Yes, please," I answered, taking a page from his book and looking away. I felt almost like I was waking up on the dreaded morning after.

Jamaal walked to the sitting room without another word. I wondered if I should scurry out of bed and grab a robe or something, but that seemed both prudish and pointless. I had sheets to cover myself with, after all, and Jamaal was likely the one who'd removed my clothes in the first place.

I had the guilty thought that I wished I'd been awake for that, but I shoved it aside. Now was not the time to indulge in fantasy and wishful thinking.

Jamaal returned with coffee moments later. He handed me

the steaming mug, and I wrapped my hands around it, even though I was no longer chilled to the bone. Then he stood awkwardly by the side of the bed, and I wondered if he was having trouble deciding whether to go back to his chair or sit down beside me.

"How long was I asleep?" I asked, hoping a little normal conversation would help dispel the awkwardness.

"A couple of hours," he answered, then came to a decision and sat hesitantly on the side of my bed.

"Have you been here the whole time?"

He shook his head, making his beads rattle and click, a sound I would forever associate with him. "Maggie and I went to pick up your car before the snow got too bad. You didn't exactly tell me the whole story when you called for a ride, did you?" There was a hint of reproach in his voice, which suggested he'd filled in some of the blanks already one way or another.

I tried to think back to what exactly I'd told him. I'd been nearly out of my mind with exhaustion and stress and leftover fear, and it would have taken more strength than I had to tell him everything that had happened. My memory felt a little hazy, but I'm pretty sure all I'd said was that I was in a car accident and that I'd been temporarily dead.

"I wasn't in any shape for a long explanation at the time," I told him, taking a sip of my coffee. It tasted warm and soothing, and in a little while, I'd be enjoying a caffeine kick that might help me feel less like the walking dead.

"No, I suppose not," Jamaal said drily.

Clearly, he knew something about what had happened. "What have you heard? And where did you hear it?"

He shrugged and pulled at a loose string hanging off the edge of an artful tear in the knee of his jeans. "I figured the police would be called to the scene of an accident as bad as the one you must have been in, so I asked Leo to look up the police reports."

"I don't know that I'm ever going to get used to him being able to do that." I guess that explained how Jamaal had known where my car was to go pick it up.

"They said you were found in the trunk of a car, bound in duct tape. They also said that the first responders had reported you dead."

"Did the reports also say the guy who'd tried to kidnap me confessed he was hired by some unknown woman?"

He nodded. "Yeah. Thanks to Leo, we actually got a look at his full confession. The guy's orders were to kill you and then get you buried within an hour of your death."

I shuddered and hugged the covers closer to me. I had come so very, very close to facing my worst nightmare. If it hadn't been for the accident . . .

All day long, I'd been fighting to keep control of my emotions, to keep them contained inside me where they wouldn't threaten my ability to think rationally. And all at once, I couldn't hold them back another instant. Lord knows I tried, but after the first tears escaped, everything crumbled. I covered my face with my hands and sobbed, letting the aftermath of the terror have its way with me.

I've never been a big fan of crying in front of people, and if I had to name the top-ten people I didn't want to cry in front of, Jamaal would head the list. But there are some things in life you can't control, and this particular burst of emotion was one of them.

Covering my face with my hands didn't seem like enough, so I bent over double, pulling my knees up and burying my face against them as I hugged them. I felt the sheets sliding away from my skin, but I was too distraught to care. I imagined a manly stoic like Jamaal was appalled enough by my outburst not to notice the expanses of skin I inadvertently revealed. These were not delicate, ladylike tears. These were wrenching, noisy, messy sobs.

I expected Jamaal to sit there and look befuddled, or maybe

even to beat a hasty retreat so he didn't have to witness my meltdown. When I felt the tentative touch of his hand on the bare skin of my back, it was almost enough to startle me into silence. However, this meltdown wasn't about to let a sympathetic touch derail it.

Surely *now* Jamaal would retreat, I thought, but he remained beside me, his hand stroking gently up and down my back, more confident now that I hadn't rebuffed him. For his sake—and yeah, okay, for the sake of my own dignity—I tried to get a handle on myself, but it seemed like the harder I fought to suppress the tears, the more determined they were to escape.

Jamaal slid closer to me on the bed. He slipped his arm around me and pulled me against his chest, one hand on my back, one on the back of my head. I resisted for all of about one and a half seconds, then melted against him, clinging to him as if he were a life raft in a stormy sea. He rocked me back and forth like a child, and he made no obvious attempt to get me to stop crying.

His acceptance of my tears, and his strong, silent support, warmed me from the inside out. And that was *before* he started singing to me.

I'd only heard him sing once before, but it was one of those rare moments in my life that I'd have loved to bottle up so I could experience it again. His voice was a lovely unpolished baritone, and the tune had the soothing lilt of a lullaby, though I didn't recognize the language.

There was a part of me that felt faintly ridiculous about cuddling up in a man's arms, being rocked like a baby while he sang me a lullaby. That part of me was drowned out by the part that was touched and moved beyond words. Jamaal was not a man from whom I expected tenderness, and that was hardly surprising in light of the horrors of his life. But it was moments like this when I knew for sure that all the years of abuse he'd endured, and all the torments of trying to control his death magic, had not destroyed the decent human being he was destined to be, no matter how hard they had tried. There was a *reason* I felt such a strong connection to him, a reason I felt the need to reach out to him even when he tried to hold himself aloof.

My tears ran their course, slowing to sniffles and hiccups, but Jamaal didn't let go of me, nor did he stop singing. I took as many deep breaths as I could manage. My head felt swollen and achy, my nose was completely stuffed up, and my chest hurt from the violence of my sobs. And yet for all that, I felt almost . . . peaceful.

Finally, the song ended, and I reluctantly extricated myself from Jamaal's arms, wiping at my eyes with the backs of my hands, unable to look into his face when I felt so raw.

"That was beautiful," I said in a scratchy whisper I could barely recognize as my own voice.

"Matilda used to sing it to me when I was very little," he said. "I should hate it and want to burn it out of my memory, but it's stayed with me all these years."

Matilda had been his owner's wife. She'd been unable to have children of her own, and had treated Jamaal like a surrogate child—right up until the time she found out her husband was Jamaal's father. Then she'd insisted that her husband sell both Jamaal and his mother, and both their lives had gone to hell.

"What language is it?"

Jamaal chuckled, and even brief laughter from him was so rare that I had to look up at his face after all.

"I'm not sure," he admitted. "I think it's Swedish or Finnish or something like that. Matilda's family was from Scandinavia somewhere. I'm sure I'm butchering the pronunciation."

"Whatever language it was, it was beautiful," I told him again, still wiping at my tears.

He shrugged, uncomfortable with the praise. And possibly with the tenderness he'd just shown me. He started plucking at the string on his jeans again. I had a feeling that the discomfort was going to get to be too much for him soon, and he would retreat, leaving me alone to recover. Maybe that would have been the best thing for me, but the last thing I wanted was to be alone.

I reached out and touched the place on his chest where my head had rested. Not surprisingly, his shirt was damp.

"I'm sorry I got your shirt wet," I murmured as I continued to skim my fingers over the wet spot.

"Nikki . . ." There was an unmistakable warning in his voice, but I didn't feel inclined to listen, and despite the warning, he wasn't pulling away.

"It must feel kind of clammy against your skin. Maybe you should take it off."

He shook his head and pulled my hand away from his chest, but he couldn't hide the flare of heat in his eyes. I'm not a ravishing beauty under the best of circumstances, and I didn't want to know how awful I looked after a crying jag like I'd just been through. But I knew Jamaal found me attractive anyway, and I *was* sitting there in front of him wearing nothing but a bra and panties. Mismatched, and not exactly pretty, but I've found men rarely care about such things.

"We've given Sita enough fuel to feed her jealousy already," he said, fingers still wrapped around my hand even as he verbally pushed me away.

I snorted. "Sita can bite me! And probably will, if she gets a chance."

The dirty look Jamaal gave me suggested he didn't find my attempt at a joke all that funny. I guess I didn't, either, because I really didn't look forward to having his psycho tiger even more mad at me than she already was.

"You can't let her run your life, Jamaal."

He tried to stand up, but I anticipated it and grabbed a handful of his shirt. He could have torn away from me easily, but he settled for a halfhearted glare instead.

"The death magic has run my life ever since I first became *Liberi*," he growled at me. "Whether it's contained inside me, or in the form of a tiger, it doesn't matter. It always wins."

He was trying to look and sound fierce and angry, but I could hear the wealth of pain under the facade. Still holding on to my handful of shirt, I got to my knees beside him so my head could be level with his as I looked into his eyes. It would have been more effective if he hadn't turned his face away from me.

"You've always been fighting it solo," I reminded him, then cupped my hand around his face so I could turn him toward me. There was fear in his eyes when he met my gaze, but there was desire, also. "You're not in this fight alone anymore."

"I have to be," he said. I caressed his face, feeling the racing of his pulse beneath my fingertips. "It's too dangerous . . ."

"After what I faced today, I'm not intimidated by a jealous cat." We both knew that wasn't true, of course. Only an idiot wouldn't be afraid of a magical tiger with a grudge. "And besides, I think you're worth fighting for."

Jamaal closed his eyes as if those words hurt, but he leaned forward and rested his forehead against mine, so I guess they didn't.

"I don't want you to get hurt because of me," he whispered, his breath tickling against my skin.

I kissed his temple and felt the shudder of desire that ripped through him. Encouraged, I started kissing my way down the side of his face. One of his hands came to rest on my back, and one on my hip, just above the waistband of my panties. I took that as another positive sign and propped his chin on my palm so that his mouth was at the perfect angle.

His hands clamped down tighter when our lips first touched, and he held himself rigidly still, fighting his desire. But when I ran my tongue along the seam of his lips, he lost all that hard-fought control. A little moan escaped him as his mouth opened for me.

I kissed him hard and thoroughly, and he loved every minute of it. He shifted his grip so that both hands were under my butt, then effortlessly dragged me forward until I was straddling his lap, still on my knees. I pressed myself tightly against him, savoring the scent, the feel, the taste of him. When we'd kissed before, his tongue had been highly flavored by the smoke of his clove cigarettes, and I'd found it surprisingly erotic, perhaps just because clove cigarettes and Jamaal were so closely associated in my mind. I tasted them now, though the flavor was faint because he was smoking so much less.

I played with his braids while I kissed him, enjoying the coarseness of his hair contrasted with the smoothness of the beads. And all the while, I was aware of him hardening beneath me.

My hands slid out of his hair to caress the broad expanse of his back over the thin T-shirt he wore. I desperately wanted to get my hands on bare skin, but the last time we'd tried giving in to our attraction, it had all come to a screeching halt when I'd touched his scars. I didn't want that to happen again, so I forced myself to let Jamaal set the pace.

His hands explored my every curve while staying maddeningly clear of my erogenous zones. I wasn't sure if he was doing it to torture me, or if even now he was fighting what was happening between us, trying to keep the distance I so badly wanted to remove.

I was determined to let Jamaal take the lead, but it was a powerful test of my self-control. Without even meaning to, I was grinding myself against him, and I had to clench my hands into fists to resist the urge to tug at his shirt. His mouth left mine as he trailed kisses down my throat. I arched into them and moaned, wanting him more than I could ever remember wanting anyone in my life.

Jamaal put his hand under my butt again, and I thought we were finally getting somewhere when he lifted me and laid me down on the bed. His body came to rest on top of mine, a warm, solid weight that might have crushed me if he weren't partially supporting himself with his arms.

I thought I might spontaneously combust when he nudged the cup of my bra downward and sucked my nipple into the delicious heat of his mouth. My mind short-circuited with pleasure as my back arched off the bed. I forgot all about letting him set the pace, and about keeping my hands away from his scars. In that pleasure-fogged moment of carelessness, I slid my hands under Jamaal's shirt.

If I'd been thinking rationally—or thinking at all, more like it—I might have expected Jamaal to be so overcome by pleasure that he forgot whatever it was that made him so touchy about the scars. But either he wasn't as lost in the pleasure as I was, or whatever emotional wound those scars triggered was far too deep to be defeated by sensual pleasure.

Whatever the reason, Jamaal's body jerked as though I'd given him an electric shock, and every muscle in his body went tense and rigid. I desperately wanted to hold on to him, but my instincts told me that was a terrible idea, so I kept my hands to myself as he rolled off of me. He came to rest beside me on the bed, lifting his forearm to cover his eyes. His chest rose and fell with panted breaths, but the bulge in his jeans was fading before my eyes.

I had enough sexual frustration coursing through my body to set off an explosion or three, but I swallowed it down as best I could. Whatever Jamaal was going through right now was far more important than my carnal needs. I turned to face him, propping my head on my hand, but I didn't say anything at first, giving him time to gather himself.

"I'm sorry," he said, arm still over his eyes.

"Hey, I blubbered all over you a little while ago and you wouldn't let me apologize for *that*."

He moved his arm so he could give me a look that was both skeptical and strangely tentative. "Not exactly in the same league."

It was hard to shrug in the position I was in, but I gave it a shot. "It's all emotional crap neither one of us is all that comfortable letting others see."

"Still not the same," he said stubbornly.

My heart ached for him, for whatever trauma had happened to him to make him so sensitive about his scars. I wanted to know what was behind it, but I knew I had to tread very delicately or risk scaring him off for good. I reached out and put my hand on his chest—over his shirt, of course—and felt the continued racing of his heart. The one thing I knew I couldn't afford to do was ask him why having me touch the scars freaked him out so much, no matter how badly I wanted to know. He would tell me when and if he was ready, and he didn't need me pushing at him.

"I'm sorry I let myself get carried away," I told him. "I knew better than to touch you like that, and I had every intention of keeping my hands to myself." I smiled at him, trying to convey the message that whatever was wrong, it was no big deal to me. "Maybe next time you should put some handcuffs on me."

He growled and sat up. "There won't *be* a next time," he said, predictably. "I'm too fucked-up, Nikki. I can't do . . . this." He made a vague gesture with his hand, and I didn't know whether his *this* referred to a relationship, or just sex.

"Maybe you can't do it right now," I said as gently as possible, "but I'm more than willing to wait."

"You can't fix me!"

"So you've said. And you're right, I can't. But I can be here for you whenever you decide you want to fix yourself."

"Ain't gonna happen." He had closed down entirely, the expression on his face distant and almost forbidding. If I didn't understand so thoroughly his need to protect himself from the fear and the pain that welled inside him, I might have been hurt at being shut out like that. He slid off the other side of the bed, no longer able to look me in the eye.

I wished there were magic words I could say to make all his pain go away, or at least get him to open up enough to me to let me help him. But for now, he was out of my reach once more, and I blinked away the burning sensation of another bout of tears as he walked out of my room without another word.

Eighteen

After Jamaal left, I felt drained and melancholy. I dragged myself into the shower and stood under the hot spray for way longer than was environmentally correct, washing away the lingering traces of blood, sweat, dirt, and tears that clung to me. I didn't have any plans to go out, having checked out the window and seen the pristine blanket of snow that covered everything in sight. It was still coming down, and only in the direst emergency would I consider trying to drive through it. I wasn't sure why I felt the need to blow-dry my hair and put on makeup, but I did it anyway. Maybe just because it made me feel more normal, though my concealer wasn't up to the challenge of hiding the dark circles under my eyes.

I probably should have left my room in search of Anderson as soon as I was dressed. No doubt Jamaal and Leo had told him what they'd found in the police report and he would expect me to fill in any missing details for him. But I wasn't up to facing him after what I'd been through. Maybe he'd had enough time to absorb the blow, especially after I'd left him that screen shot the other day, but I didn't think it was likely. He had loved Emma so much, and though I suspected she had always been self-absorbed and bitchy, the years she'd spent as Konstantin's prisoner had made Anderson forget her true nature. She had become a paragon in his memory, and I didn't want to see his pain at having that paragon irrevocably destroyed.

I guess that meant my plan was to hole up in my room for the rest of the evening so I could avoid any chance of running into Anderson. Or anyone else, for that matter. My stomach grumbled its disapproval of my plan, reminding me I hadn't eaten all day and my body had burned up tons of energy bringing itself back from the dead. I contemplated a run to the kitchen, but decided I'd dip into the box of granola bars I kept in the filing cabinet in my sitting room instead. Buying myself a filing cabinet had been silly, since most of my paper files had been destroyed by the sprinkler system in my old office, and I rarely kept much in the way of paper files anymore. But it made for a handy pantry, and I grabbed a chocolate bar for dessert while I was at it. It wasn't exactly the healthiest meal I'd ever eaten, but it was damn convenient.

Crunching on my granola bar, I opened up my laptop and went in search of something, *anything,* to keep my mind occupied so I wouldn't keep thinking about what had almost happened to me this afternoon. It was worth a try anyway.

I was just finishing my chocolate bar and trying to resist the urge to go foraging in my filing cabinet again when there was a knock on my door. I had the cowardly urge not to answer. I didn't want to talk to anyone right now, wanted to lose myself in something completely mindless—not that I'd had a whole lot of success with that so far.

"Come in," I finally said with weary acceptance.

The door opened, and Anderson stepped inside. No doubt he would have let himself in whether I'd invited him or not. I closed my laptop and laid it on the coffee table, then stood up, scattering a bunch of granola crumbs all over the place. I brushed at my clothes to dislodge any remaining crumbs, giving the task way more attention than it deserved. It looked like I was going to have to talk about all the things I didn't want to talk about after all, and if I could put it off for a few seconds, I was all for it.

Finally, I was as crumb-free as I was going to be, and I raised my head to look at Anderson. I expected to see pain, anger, and even sorrow, but what I saw on his face was none of the above. Instead, I saw a frozen, almost lifeless calm. I'd seen him run both hot and cold with anger, but I'd never seen anything quite like this before, and there was something so forbidding about it I had to fight the urge to take a step back.

"I came to offer my apologies," he said, and his voice was off-the-charts weird, too. Completely flat and noninflected. Inhuman, almost, though not exactly godlike, either.

"Umm . . ." I couldn't think of what to say. The man who stood in front of me wasn't Anderson, at least not the Anderson I knew.

"I was blind to Emma's faults, and you almost paid an unspeakable price for it."

He was saying the right words, but without any emotion behind them it was hard to tell if he actually meant them or not.

"A-are you all right?" Stupid question, of course, because he was obviously anything but all right. I realized his face was so immobile he wasn't even blinking, like his body was some kind of automaton. Was the Anderson I knew even in there?

His head moved slightly in a sad imitation of a head shake. "No. I am far from 'all right.' I am dangerous in my current condition." There was still no emotion in his voice, like he was reading off cue cards. "I cannot afford to feel anything just yet. I will try to act more like myself when we meet with Cyrus tomorrow."

I shivered, more freaked out than I wanted to admit by the talking husk Anderson had left behind. "We're meeting with Cyrus?"

"One of his Olympians has broken the treaty. We will meet to discuss the consequences."

Not a conversation I particularly wanted to participate in. "Do you really need me—"

"You are the injured party. You are coming."

Not much chance he was going to be flexible about that. "You're not going to kill her, are you?" I didn't know *what* this faux-Anderson was capable of. Maybe in his current state he wouldn't mind letting the world know just who and what he was.

"No."

He turned to leave, and I should have just let him go. But of course I had to open my big mouth again.

"So what exactly are you hoping to accomplish at this meeting?"

After what Emma had tried to do to me, I should have been screaming for her blood. I should have been begging Anderson to kill her. But despite the horrors I'd seen in the last few months, becoming *Liberi* hadn't stopped me from being a bleeding heart. I wanted Emma to pay for what she'd done—and tried to do—and I wanted her not to be able to hurt me again, but I didn't want her to pay with her life. If she were tried in a court of law, she might well get a verdict of not guilty by reason of insanity. Confinement in a mental institution might be the most appropriate sentence, but I was under no illusion that it was an option.

For the first time since he'd set foot in my sitting room, something stirred behind Anderson's eyes. I couldn't have said what it was—the expression was gone almost before I had a chance to notice the change—but it made my heart skip a beat in primal terror. I dropped my gaze to the floor, an instinctive gesture of submission, and held my breath. I didn't like this lifeless talking shell of his, but even that one tiny glimpse of what lay beneath had told me in no uncertain terms that the shell was the lesser of two evils. If and when Anderson unleashed everything he was suppressing, I didn't want to be anywhere near him.

I felt his eyes boring through me for what felt like forever. I kept my own gaze pinned to the floor, and my lungs started to burn with the pressure of holding my breath.

I didn't give in to the need to breathe until Anderson had left the room and closed the door behind him.

I didn't get a whole lot of sleep on Saturday night, despite my exhaustion. When I lay down to try to relax, I kept obsessing about what had almost happened to me. Just thinking about it flooded my system with adrenaline. And to make matters worse, when I closed my eyes I was immediately transported into the memory of the darkness of death.

I knew from previous experience—and from talking with Jamaal about his own experiences—that my fear of the darkness would fade over time. Every night, it would be just a little bit easier. But that didn't help me much on this first night. I wished Jamaal would come up to my room and sing me asleep as he had the first time I'd died, but it wasn't going to happen.

Eventually, exhaustion won out over terror, though it did so not when I was lying comfortably in my bed, but when I was on the couch in the sitting room playing solitaire on my laptop. I remember waking up briefly hours later, when there was a roll of thunder so violent it made the whole house shake. My laptop slid off my lap and onto the floor, but I wasn't awake enough to bother picking it up.

I'd fallen asleep sitting up, and during that brief period of wakefulness, I stretched myself out on the couch, clutching a throw pillow under my head. I had the brief, hazy thought that it was unusual to have violent thunder in the midst of a snowstorm, but the phenomenon wasn't interesting enough to keep me awake. I drifted back into sleep and didn't wake up until the sun had risen.

I was stiff from spending the night on the couch, and I didn't exactly feel well rested. I checked my laptop and found, to my relief, that it had survived the fall. I'd have followed my morning ritual of making coffee in my room while perusing the news, except my stomach was growling at me that my granola-and-candy meal last night had been woefully inadequate.

Though the mansion felt more and more like my home every day, I didn't feel at home enough to go downstairs in my bathrobe, so I showered and dressed before heading down to the kitchen. I'd slept in enough that for once I wasn't the first person up and about, which meant there was already a pot of coffee brewed. I poured myself a cup, then frowned when I noticed someone had left dirty dishes in the sink. There were drawbacks to living in a house with so many other people in it. I put the dirty dishes into the dishwasher, then made myself some scrambled eggs and toast. And cleaned up my own damn mess when I was finished.

I sat down at the kitchen table with my food and coffee, taking a moment to admire the view through the windows. It looked like it had snowed about four inches all told, and the back lawn was a pristine white carpet that glittered in the light of the sun. A dark blot was moving across the snow, and the glare was bright enough I had to squint to make out Jamaal's form as he tromped toward the house. At a guess, I'd say he was coming from the clearing.

I'd have thought after our make-out session yesterday he'd have waited until I was out of the house before summoning Sita again, but apparently not. Maybe he thought the fact that he'd ultimately rebuffed my advances was enough to calm Sita's jealousy. Or maybe I'd ruffled his composure so much he felt he *needed* to vent the death magic immediately, whether he wanted to or not.

I had wolfed down half my eggs and all of my toast by the time Jamaal made it back to the house and into the kitchen. The first bite had proved to me that I was starving, and I'd started shoveling it in as fast as I could chew and swallow. Jamaal nodded at me in greeting before turning his back on me to pour himself a cup of coffee.

Even in that one brief glance, I'd been able to see his turmoil, so when he turned as if to leave with his coffee, I paused between bites to ask, "Did Sita give you a hard time this morning?"

He reluctantly turned back toward me. "No."

If he thought he was going to put me off with one-syllable responses, he had another think coming. There was a haunted, troubled look in his eyes that worried me.

"Then what's wrong?" I asked.

He took a couple of steps closer to me, though he leaned

against the end of the kitchen counter instead of coming all the way into the breakfast nook. "I went to the clearing to practice this morning."

"Yeah, I gathered that." My remaining eggs were getting cold, and my stomach was far from satisfied with what I'd eaten already, so I went ahead and shoved another forkful into my mouth while Jamaal paused to give me a dirty look. "Sorry," I said with my mouth full. Dying had not had a good influence on my table manners. "What happened?"

He shook his head. "Finish your breakfast. I'll show you."

The words sounded ominous, and the expression on his face made them even more so. I wanted to ask him to explain, but he was obviously not in a talking mood, and I didn't want him to get annoyed with me and wander off. I finished my eggs in two big bites, then loaded my dishes into the dishwasher.

"Okay," I said, closing the dishwasher, "time for show-and-tell."

I snatched my parka from the coat closet. Jamaal waited for me impatiently, his edginess making me nervous. What the hell had he seen out in the clearing that had rattled him so much? And was I going to regret going to get a look for myself?

The snow was a little deeper than I'd thought, and I wished I'd run up to my room for boots as my feet sank into it. Of course, I doubt Jamaal would have waited for me. He was agitated enough that he lit a cigarette and puffed on it steadily as we made our way out to the clearing, following the narrow path his shoes had already left in the snow. The air bit into my cheeks, and snow trickled in around the edges of my shoes. I buried my hands in my pockets and shivered.

The first thing I noticed as we approached the clearing was that there were a bunch of trees down. I certainly hadn't thought the storm was violent enough to take down trees, especially not as many as I saw. I glanced at Jamaal, wondering if this was what he wanted to show me, thinking that he could just as easily have *told* me a bunch of trees had fallen.

Jamaal looked grim and kept walking. I followed, and the closer we got to the clearing, the more fallen trees I saw, lying like discarded children's toys among the ones left standing. We had to weave our way around the trees to get to the clearing. Most of the trees were pines, and they were all green and healthy looking.

When we stepped around the last set of branches that were obscuring our view, I finally got a good look at the clearing, and I gasped.

There wasn't a flake of snow anywhere in the clearing, as if someone had come out here and gone to work with a snow blower, doing such a thorough job of it that all you could see was grass. That was weird as hell, but it wasn't what took my breath away.

Mouth gaping open, I continued forward until my feet left the snow, blinking a couple of times as if that might make what I saw go away.

I said there were "a bunch" of trees down. Now that I was in the clearing proper, I could see that there were *dozens* down. Some had been torn up by the roots, and some had snapped in two. Not a single tree that had fronted the clearing was left upright. And the weirdest thing of all? They had all fallen *away* from the clearing. Almost like a bomb had gone off in the center.

Jamaal stood beside me, his arms crossed over his chest as he surveyed the sight. He must have smoked that cigarette in record time, but I had to admit, if I were a smoker, I'd have been diving for the cigs myself.

"What the hell happened here?" I whispered, my words steaming in the brisk air.

Jamaal swallowed hard. "There was a loud noise in the middle of the night. Woke me up and shook the bed under me."

I remembered. "I thought it was thunder," I murmured.

"I did, too, at the time."

I was pretty sure I had at least a clue of what had happened. Or at least *who* had happened. Anderson had made himself into a walking, talking automaton in his effort to contain his fury over what Emma had done. He had promised me he would be more like himself when we met with Cyrus today, and the only way that was possible was if he let out some of that repressed fury. I had the distinct feeling we were looking at the results right now.

Jamaal didn't know what I did about Anderson's origins, but his mind was obviously traveling similar paths.

"No one knows who Anderson is descended from," he said. "I don't know why he's so mysterious about it, but he is. I've never seen him do anything other than that trick with his hand. I have no idea what he's capable of. What I *do* know is that none of the rest of us are capable of this." He indicated the clearing with a sweep of his hand.

I didn't know what Anderson was capable of, either, although I knew more than Jamaal. "If he has a power that lets him do this, I'm just as happy he keep it and any other powers he might have under wraps."

Jamaal grunted something that might have been an agreement.

"You think we should ask him about this?" I asked.

Jamaal gave me a look of disbelief. "You go right ahead. Just tell me when you're going to do it so I can arrange to be in the next county over."

Okay, it had been a dumb question. It didn't take a rocket scientist to know that Anderson would not be open to discussion about whatever had happened out here. And even if he had vented some of his fury last night, he wasn't exactly going to be in a good mood in the foreseeable future. Asking him questions he didn't want to answer would be a poor survival tactic.

"I don't want to be there when he confronts Cyrus," I said. "Not that I have a choice."

I wished he'd at least given himself a couple of days to absorb everything and calm down as much as he could before squaring off with someone who could start a war that could kill every one of Anderson's *Liberi* if he wanted to.

"He'll keep a lid on it," Jamaal assured me, not very convincingly.

"Uh-huh."

I sure as hell hoped he did, despite my skepticism. Because if Anderson let loose whatever it was he'd let loose in this clearing, I didn't think anyone near him, even immortal *Liberi,* would survive.

NINETEEN

As a general rule, Olympians seem to have a taste for palatial homes set on acres of land in the most upscale of neighborhoods. Cyrus, however, lived in an impressive brownstone in Georgetown, perhaps too much of a city boy to enjoy the comforts of a country estate. I had driven by the place before when I'd been investigating Olympian properties, but now I was going to have an up-close-and-personal look at the interior. I wasn't what you'd call thrilled at the prospect.

Because of the sensitive subject matter we'd be discussing, a neutral site with witnesses was deemed unacceptable. Anderson was apparently through with letting Olympians set foot within the borders of his own personal territory, and so we were meeting at Cyrus's house instead. Walking into the lion's den and making accusations didn't seem like the best idea to me, but Anderson hadn't asked my opinion. He seemed closer to normal than he had the day before, able to speak in a natural tone of voice, but I still felt like I was in the presence of a bomb that could go off at the slightest provocation. All I had to do was think of what I'd seen in that clearing, and my desire to question Anderson's decisions melted away.

Anderson didn't have any pet Descendants he could take with him to keep the Olympians honest, but he was wary enough of them not to walk into Cyrus's house completely "unarmed," so Blake had the pleasure of coming with us. He couldn't kill anybody, but he could make it so that all the bad guys were so overcome with lust for each other there wasn't room in their brains for thoughts of attack. I didn't get the feeling Blake was any happier to be going than I was, but he wasn't stupid enough to argue with Anderson's decisions, either.

Thanks to the snow, which showed no sign of melting anytime soon, we had to leave extra early if we hoped to make it to Cyrus's house by our scheduled three o'clock appointment time. Anderson knew that as well as anybody, but he wasn't ready to leave until almost two thirty. There was no question in my mind the delay had been deliberate and that he was making some kind of power play by making Cyrus wait.

I didn't trust Anderson's mood, but when he announced he was driving, I once again didn't feel up to arguing with him. Blake and I shared a doubtful look as we followed him out to the garage; then we both shrugged our acceptance. It wasn't like a car accident would kill us anyway.

The drive was excruciating. All but the main roads were a mess, and there was the usual collection of idiots out who mistakenly thought they knew how to drive in the snow. We did a lot of stopping and starting and threading our way around stranded motorists, then had the always-enjoyable situation of being stuck behind a salt truck.

The ride was made just that much more unpleasant by the tense silence in the car. Anderson was in no mood to make conversation, and his presence was like an oppressive blanket, weighing us down. Blake dealt with the tension by incessantly cracking his knuckles until I turned around and gave him a pointed look. I don't think Anderson even noticed the effect he was having on us.

Parking on the street in Georgetown is a pain in the butt

on any day, but it was well-nigh impossible with the snow. The streets in the heart of the city had been cleared, but that meant there were mountains of dirty snow lining the curbs, blocking off a large percentage of what would ordinarily be parking spaces. Anderson didn't even bother cruising in search of one, instead pulling into a garage.

Blake was out of the car almost before it had come to a full stop. I took my life into my hands and touched Anderson's arm as he was turning the car off.

"Are you going to be all right?" I asked him softly.

He looked at me and blinked a couple of times, as if he didn't quite know what I was talking about. Then he frowned. "I'm in control of myself, if that's what you're asking. I'm still angry, but I'm not going to do anything rash. Come on. I think we've kept Cyrus waiting long enough."

We were back to uncomfortable silence as the three of us walked from the garage to Cyrus's house, now more than a half hour late. Anderson rang the bell, and moments later, the door was opened by a middle-aged man in a stuffy suit. I should have known better than to expect Cyrus to answer his own door. Even having grown up with the ultrarich Glasses, I'd never visited a house that had a butler before, but I guess there's a first time for everything.

"Mr. Galanos has been expecting you," the butler said with just a touch of reproof in his voice. "May I take your coats?"

Anderson hadn't bothered with a coat, making do with a weathered-looking sport jacket. Blake handed over his stylish wool coat, and I handed over my not-so-stylish, but probably much warmer, parka. When the butler laid the coats over his arm, I caught a glimpse of a trident-shaped glyph on the inside of his wrist. I made an educated guess that he was a mortal Descendant whose divine ancestor was Poseidon. I also guessed that since he was middle-aged and working as a butler, he was never going to be given the honor of becoming a *Liberi*.

Coats still draped over his arm, the butler led us to a two-story library that would make any reader drool. I don't know how many books, both modern and antique, were on those floor-to-ceiling bookshelves, but it was a lot. I breathed in deep to take in the comforting scent of ink and paper, even as I mentally rolled my eyes at the rest of the decor. The room would have fit right in as the set of some period drama taking place in one of those British men's clubs the aristocracy was so fond of, all dark colors and manly leather-and-wood furniture. It seemed awfully formal and stodgy for someone like Cyrus.

Cyrus was reclining in a forest-green leather armchair, holding a highball glass filled with something amber colored on the rocks. His pet goon, Mark, had been sitting on the arm of the chair when I first caught sight of him, but he rose to his feet and stood at full bodyguard attention when Anderson, Blake, and I entered the room. He had an enormous, angry-red hickey on his neck, and I had the immediate suspicion that Anderson wasn't the only one who was already playing mind games. Either Anderson had told Cyrus he was bringing Blake, or Cyrus had guessed his old flame would be joining the party.

I stole a quick glance at Blake out of the corner of my eye, but he gave no indication that he'd noticed Mark one way or the other. He and I hung back just a little as Anderson stepped forward.

Smiling, Cyrus put down his drink and rose from his chair. "So nice of you to join us," he said, holding out his hand for Anderson to shake. "I was beginning to worry you'd had an accident. I hear the roads are terrible."

Cyrus had to know that our late arrival was deliberate, but he didn't let it show in either his voice or his face. If I didn't know better, I would have sworn that he actually meant it and had been worried. Anderson paused just long enough for it to be noticeable before he shook Cyrus's hand.

"Sorry to keep you waiting," Anderson said, making no attempt to sound like he meant it. "The weather delayed us."

Cyrus's smile broadened. "No worries. Mark and I managed to keep ourselves entertained while we waited." He reached out to pat Mark's shoulder, and I doubted it was an accident that his hand landed right near the hickey. "You remember Mark, don't you?"

Anderson nodded, but Blake shook his head.

"I don't believe we've met," he said. He sounded ruefully amused. Either he was a good actor, or he wasn't even a smidge jealous. I wondered if he'd noticed that he and Mark resembled one another. He didn't try to shake Mark's hand, and Mark didn't offer.

"Can I get anyone a drink?" Cyrus asked, playing the gracious host.

"Don't be more of an ass about this than you have to be," Blake said. "We're not here to make friendly."

Cyrus sighed dramatically. "When did you become so serious all the time?"

Blake stiffened, and his eyes narrowed. "When you—"

"Blake," Anderson said mildly, but that one word was enough to shut Blake up.

Score one for Team Evil. They'd managed to provoke us, and they hadn't even had to work at it very hard. Blake shut up as ordered.

"Will you sit down, at least?" Cyrus asked. "Or would that be too civilized?"

"We're here because one of your Olympians attacked one of my people," Anderson countered. "I'm not feeling terribly civilized."

Interesting how Emma had suddenly been transformed from Anderson's ex-wife into "one of your Olympians." I wondered if this meant Anderson was officially over her.

Cyrus sighed again. "Understandable, I suppose. Why don't you tell me what happened."

"I already told you on the phone," Anderson snapped. He'd been willing to put up with Cyrus's feigned friendliness the last time we'd talked, but apparently that was not the case today.

"So you did, but I wasn't asking you, I was asking Nikki." He turned an unusually grave look toward me. "I'd like to hear it in your own words."

Anderson raised no objection. I didn't particularly want to talk about my abduction to anyone, much less Cyrus and his pet. I didn't want to relive the memory, and I was also afraid I'd let too much emotion show. Showing Olympians signs of weakness was a recipe for disaster. Not to mention that I didn't like the feeling that I was tattling, and that I was afraid the consequences would be dire. However, it wasn't like I had a whole lot of choice.

I tried to remain as impassive as possible as I recounted the events of the day before. It's hard to keep the emotion out of your voice when you're talking about your own death, and especially about a deranged woman's plan to bury you alive and leave you to suffer eternal torment. I could hear the occasional quaver in my voice, and there was nothing I could do to control it.

Cyrus made sympathetic faces while I spoke, but I couldn't help noticing that Mark seemed to be enjoying the story. There was an eager glint in his eye, and he even licked his lips like a dog looking forward to its meal. I decided Cyrus had creepy taste in men.

There was a long silence after I finished my story. I took a moment to glare at Mark while Cyrus frowned thoughtfully.

"I knew she was unstable when I invited her to join us," Cyrus finally said. "I could hardly blame her after what my father did to her. I thought that perhaps her moods would even out over time."

"That's what I thought, too," Anderson agreed grimly. "But her actions yesterday tell me she has been irrevocably altered. The Emma I knew died years ago when your father raped her and drowned her in that pond."

Anderson was keeping control of himself, but there was no missing the fury behind his words, and something about the look in his eyes raised the hairs on the back of my neck. What-ever it was, Cyrus saw it, too, and his face lost just a little of its color. If he knew what Anderson really was, he'd be curled up in the fetal position.

"I am not my father," Cyrus reminded Anderson. "And you won't have to go medieval on my ass to get me to honor the treaty, if that's what you're thinking." He looked over his shoulder at Mark. "Go fetch our other guest, will you?"

There was a visible flare of excitement in Mark's eyes as he nodded and then hurried from the room. It occurred to me that he might have been present for reasons other than to try to make Blake jealous. Like maybe Cyrus planned to give him Emma's immortality. The fact that Emma was already a "guest" in Cyrus's house did not bode well for her.

Anderson and Cyrus stared at each other, and the tension in the room was so thick it was hard to breathe. I wanted to say something in protest of what I feared would happen, but the atmosphere was so oppressive I couldn't find the courage to speak.

Moments later, we all heard Emma's voice raised in an-noyance. "I'm getting really tired of being jerked around!" she complained, presumably at Mark. "I could have—"

Both her voice and her footsteps faltered when she stepped through the library door and saw our little gathering. Her eyes darted from me, to Anderson, to Cyrus, and she seemed to shrink in on herself. There was something naturally frag-ile looking about her, though perhaps that was just because I knew how badly she had suffered when she'd been Konstan-tin's prisoner. No matter what she'd done—or tried to do—it was hard for me to forget that she'd been a victim.

And maybe, in a way, she still was. I didn't like it when An-derson made excuses for her, and I didn't think she'd ever been a truly nice person. But today, when she hadn't been expect-ing to see Anderson and me and therefore had obviously not bothered to dress to impress, or even put on makeup, I could see more plainly than ever that she was still suffering. Even if she brought some of that suffering on herself. Her face was gaunt, and her clothes hung loosely on her thin frame. Her eyes were red around the edges, as if she'd been crying when Mark had come to get her. I remembered Cyrus telling me she had nightmares every night. Yesterday, I had almost suffered a fate similar to hers, and I wondered if I'd have all my marbles if someone had dug me up ten years from now.

Emma drew herself up and raised her chin in a semblance of dignity, but it wasn't very convincing. She looked tired and scared, and I wished like hell she'd come out of that pond with her mind intact. I suspect her marriage to Anderson would have ended anyway, and it probably wouldn't have been a nice breakup—if there is such a thing—but she might have had a chance at a decent life. But as it was, there was no room in her heart for anything but bitterness, jealousy, resentment, and fear.

"What's going on?" she asked.

"Please do come in, my dear," Cyrus said, gesturing her forward. "We have something very important to discuss." He was smiling his usual pleasant smile, but his voice came out uncharacteristically flat.

I glanced at Anderson, wondering how he was taking all this. He wasn't looking at Emma like the rest of us were, was instead staring straight ahead. His face was a stony mask, and I didn't know what emotions that mask hid.

Emma obviously sensed the dangerous undercurrents in the room. She stood rooted in the doorway and turned a beseeching look on Anderson. When she saw him facing forward, refusing to look at her, she recoiled as if he'd slapped her.

Apparently, she was taking too long to follow Cyrus's orders, because Mark suddenly gave her a shove from behind, propelling her into the room. The shove was so violent that she tripped over the edge of the rug and landed on her hands and knees with a cry of surprise and pain. Neither Anderson nor Cyrus objected to the rough handling.

Emma scrambled to her feet and whirled on Mark. "How *dare* you," she snarled. I suppose she was trying to go on the offensive, but the shrill edge in her voice detracted from the attempt. She had to know the jig was up.

"I'd ask the same question of you," Cyrus said, and Emma reluctantly turned to face him. The little darting glances she sent over her shoulder said that after what had just happened, she didn't like having Mark behind her.

"What are you talking about?"

"Did we not have a discussion the other day in which I *specifically* forbade you from taking any hostile action toward Anderson or any of his *Liberi*?"

Emma blinked as if in surprise. "Yes. And I *specifically* told you I hadn't done anything." Her lip curled in distaste as she looked me up and down. "Whatever that bitch might have told you."

I'd have been more outraged, both by her attitude and her denial, if I didn't fear she was a hairsbreadth away from a death sentence.

Cyrus grunted in exasperation. "And I believed you. Right up until I found those drafts of the letter you wrote in my father's name on your computer."

"Those weren't mine!" There were twin spots of angry color on her pale cheeks now. She certainly could put on a convincing righteous indignation act. "Someone used my computer to write them, but it wasn't me. Maybe you should have a word with your daddy about it."

Cyrus rolled his eyes. "Yes, that makes perfect sense. He broke into your house to use your computer to compose a letter that he then took to a FedEx to email. All because he's batshit crazy enough to blame Nikki for his misfortunes. Strangely, that sounds rather more like you than like him."

"I don't know who wrote it or why. All I know is it wasn't me."

"You hired a hit man to kill Nikki and bury her in the woods where no one would ever find her," Anderson interrupted, the rage in his voice enough to make Emma flinch from it.

"What?" she shrieked, looking back and forth frantically between Anderson and Cyrus.

"You gave Erin to your new friends just to spite me," Anderson continued, taking a step closer to her. He looked intimidating enough that she took a step back. "But that wasn't enough for you, was it? You had to drive the dagger in deeper, so you had to destroy Nikki, too. Just because in your sick, twisted mind you decided she was the reason our marriage fell apart. But it was *you*, Emma. You're the only reason, the only one to blame."

Tears glistened in Emma's eyes. "I loved you," she said in a scratchy whisper. "And you loved me, too. Until *she* came into our lives." She reached out toward him briefly, then snatched her hand back as if to deny the gesture. "I could see from the moment I went back home that she'd already taken you from me. You were perfectly happy to let the monster who . . . who *defiled* me run free because you were too wrapped up in your new love to care."

Sometimes I wondered if Emma inhabited the same reality the rest of us did. Until I came into her life, she'd been chained at the bottom of a pond, continually drowning and coming back to life. How she managed to twist that into her vendetta against me I'll never understand.

"I loved you," Emma repeated. "And you abandoned me."

If Emma's tears affected Anderson in the slightest, he didn't show it. His face was stony and ice cold. "You're the one who did the leaving."

She shook her head. "What good would staying have done?" She was still sniffling, but there was a hard glint in her eye, a reminder of the ugliness that had settled into her soul. She was genuinely hurt by Anderson's perceived desertion, but she was also really, really angry. At him, at me, at Konstantin, at the world in general. "I had no desire to watch another woman parade around my home like she owned the place. Like she owned my *husband*."

I almost interjected a denial, but countering paranoia with logic was a pointless endeavor.

"I'll admit I loved you once," Anderson said. "But I don't love you anymore. You are nothing to me."

Emma gasped in a sob, covering her mouth with her hand as if that could somehow keep the sound contained. She was more than capable of crocodile tears, but that's not what these were. For all the efforts she'd taken to hurt Anderson, both through Erin and through myself, I think there was always a part of her that clung to the hope that she would one day win him back. Maybe she thought that after she eliminated the "competition," he would somehow fall in love with her all over again. She was already living in a dream world anyway, so what did one more delusion matter?

Anderson turned away from Emma and faced Cyrus. "I demand satisfaction."

Those words sent a slash of cold dread through my chest. I'd really been hoping it wouldn't come to this, no matter how obviously the signs had pointed to it. Emma had apparently been hoping the same, hoping his cold rejection of her love would be the only price she had to pay for her attempt to murder me.

"No!" she cried, her face going white. "Anderson, you can't mean that!"

Anderson ignored her. I didn't believe that all his love for her had disappeared so suddenly that no trace remained. What she'd tried to do to me was terrible, but though I knew he cared about me in an abstract sort of way, I wasn't *important* to him. Considering how long he'd been alive—not that I actually knew how old he was, except that he was ancient—the time he'd known me was nothing more than a blink of the eye. *Emma* was important to him, and there was no way her attack against me had changed that. But whatever feelings for her lingered in his heart, he wasn't allowing a hint of them to show.

"Are you sure that's what you want?" Cyrus asked softly. There was what might have been genuine sympathy in his eyes, as if he, too, must be certain that Anderson was in dire pain despite the mask of coldness he hid behind.

"Anderson, please!" Emma begged. Tears were streaming freely down her cheeks now. "I admit I betrayed Erin, but the rest of it wasn't me, I swear it."

"Oh, so you'll only admit to the one crime that Cyrus won't condemn you for?" There was a hint of amusement in Anderson's voice, but that had to be an act. Jesus, I *hoped* it was an act. "How very convenient."

Suddenly, the room went black.

I don't mean the lights went out. I mean it went *black,* as in a total absence of light. I'd seen Emma pull this stunt before, so I knew immediately what it was. She was a descendant of Nyx, the Greek goddess of night, and she had called this darkness to her, no doubt in a desperate attempt to escape. Adrenaline flooded my system as I remembered the darkness of death. I tried to focus on the sensation of breath going in and out of my lungs, proving to myself that I wasn't dead.

I didn't really think about what I did next, just acted out of pure instinct. I knew Anderson was going to lunge at Emma, or at least at Emma's last known position. Now that he'd condemned her, he wasn't going to risk letting her get away.

I stepped into what I calculated would be Anderson's path, and sure enough, he plowed into me. We both went down in a tangle of limbs. I hoped he would think my interference was nothing more than an accident. Having him mad at me in his current state would be a bad, bad thing.

Emma's most immediate threat was no doubt Mark, who'd been between her and the door, but I thought her chances of escape would be slightly higher if I delayed Anderson some more. He tried to get up, and I "accidentally" swept his legs out from under him as I rolled to my feet.

"Sorry!" I said as he went down again, knowing I'd given

Emma as much time as I could afford to. If I tripped Anderson up a third time, there was zero chance he would think it was an accident.

Emma gave a high-pitched shriek that practically shattered my eardrums. There was a thud, and then the light reappeared, blinding after the total darkness. I blinked a couple of times to clear my vision.

Emma had made it about two steps into the hall before Mark had caught her in a tackle. She was flailing wildly and screaming as Mark hauled her to her feet and dragged her back into the library.

A very sane and sensible side of my brain told me there was nothing I could do and that I should stay out of it. Emma was a danger, to me, to Anderson, to the rest of his *Liberi,* and even to my loved ones. Because of her madness, I couldn't say I felt she *deserved* to die, but I could say her death would not be unjust. I could even say I wouldn't be unhappy if she were dead. But I'd drawn my line in the sand when I'd refused to hunt Konstantin for Anderson. I could not condone killing someone for revenge, and that was all that this would be.

Knowing I would be fighting one hell of an uphill battle, I held my chin high and got between Anderson and Emma yet again.

TWENTY

"Can we talk about this a bit?" I asked. I hated how tentative I sounded, but Anderson was really freaking me out. I almost liked the emotionless machine he'd been last night better, though I supposed it was a good thing he'd let some of that out considering the destruction in the clearing.

"There's nothing to talk about," Anderson said, fixing me

with his laserlike stare. "She broke the treaty. And she's proven she can't be trusted."

"Anderson, please," she begged, sobbing. "Please believe me! I didn't do it!"

Anderson might as well have been struck deaf for all the attention he paid her.

"But *I'm* the injured party here," I argued. "And I don't think she needs to die."

"Your opinion is duly noted."

And ignored, obviously. I tried to think up some argument that Anderson might listen to, but Cyrus spoke up before I could.

"Actually, Nikki, you're not the injured party here. *I* am. I gave her a direct order to leave you alone, and she disobeyed me. I can't allow that."

For the first time since I'd met him, there was cold steel in Cyrus's voice. He'd dropped the friendly smile, and there was a predatory sharpness in his eyes. Usually, the only resemblance I saw between him and his father was in their coloring, but the look on his face now suggested they might be more alike than I'd guessed.

Emma seemed to realize there was no reaching Anderson, so she switched her focus to Cyrus.

"I didn't disobey you! I swear to you, I'm being framed. That bitch probably set the whole thing up to try to get me out of the way."

My jaw dropped open. Even now, when I was the only one in the room trying to save her life, Emma was trying to stick it to me. If I'd had any sense, I would have washed my hands of her right there and then. Surely there was a straw that broke the camel's back somewhere in her ravings.

And yet they really *were* ravings. I'd always thought of her irrational behavior like it was some kind of character flaw, but maybe instead of hating her and being angry with her for her behavior, I should have been trying to get her to seek professional help. Maybe if she'd been put on meds shortly after she'd emerged from the pond, she wouldn't be what she was today.

"It's not fair to blame her for being crazy when it was your own father's decade of torture that made her that way," I told Cyrus, deciding it was best to ignore Emma's wild accusation. "You always said you were sorry for what he did to her. Prove it!"

"What caused her to do it is irrelevant. I told her what would happen if she disobeyed me, and she did it anyway. I might have spared her if Anderson were willing to claim her as his own again, but that seems not to be the case." He raised an inquiring eyebrow at Anderson, who shook his head.

I was still scrambling for an argument that might work. I supposed I could try throwing something at Mark and giving Emma another chance to run for it, but I couldn't risk breaking the treaty. If my choices were to let Emma die or to trigger a war we couldn't win between us and the Olympians, I had to let Emma die.

I practically jumped out of my shoes when Blake put his arm around my shoulders, giving them a firm squeeze while whispering in my ear. "There's nothing you can do, Nikki."

"Proceed," Cyrus said to Mark.

Emma started making gasping, gurgling sounds, and I saw that Mark's forearm was across her throat, muscles bulging as he choked her. Emma kicked and flailed, but she was no match against Mark's brute strength.

"*You* could stop it," I hissed at Blake. He could use his power to distract both Cyrus and Mark with uncontrollable lust. That might interfere with their plans, but it wasn't technically breaking the treaty.

"I suspect it would annoy Anderson almost as much as it annoyed me if you tried it," Cyrus said to Blake. I guess my whisper hadn't been as quiet as I'd thought.

"Don't even think about it," Anderson said. He was looking at Emma now, and his face wasn't quite so impassive anymore.

His Adam's apple bobbed a couple of times in quick succession. Emma's lips were turning blue, and her struggles became even more frantic.

"You don't have to do this," I said lamely, my eyes blurring with tears. Yes, I was crying over the impending death of a woman who'd tried to have me buried alive.

"Yes, I do," Cyrus answered, showing no signs that he felt any regret over ordering Emma's death. "You'd better grow a thicker skin if you're going to hang around with *Liberi* for the rest of your life."

If Blake hadn't clamped his arm around my shoulders harder, I might not have been able to resist the temptation to go slug Cyrus. I'd reminded myself time and again that he was one of the bad guys.

After today, I knew I would never forget it again.

Cyrus didn't chortle or rub his hands together with glee as someone like Konstantin might have done, enjoying the suffering of others. But his callous indifference was almost worse. At least if he'd reveled in it, it would have told me the death of a fellow human being actually *meant* something to him.

Emma went limp in Mark's arms. Unlike Cyrus, *he* looked like he was having a great time, but then he was in the process of becoming *Liberi,* stealing Emma's immortality so that he could live forever himself. I guess that could be quite a rush for someone who was raised believing in the Olympian ideal.

Mark didn't let Emma's body fall to the floor until long after she stopped moving.

Before that awful day when my car crashed into Emmitt and changed my life forever, I'd never once seen anyone die. On the way back to our car, I tried to figure out how many people had died in front of me since I'd become *Liberi*. The fact that I had to think about it before I could be sure freaked me out.

There was Emmitt, of course. Then there was Alexis and his two cronies, who had died when Anderson and I rescued

Emma from the pond. There was Justin Kerner, and one of his victims, whom I'd tried unsuccessfully to save. And now there was Emma. That brought the death toll up to seven, if you didn't count the two times I'd seen Jamaal executed. Seven permanent deaths witnessed over the course of two months.

But today's was the worst of all. I'd seen Anderson be ruthless before. I knew he had it in him. He was the son of a Fury, for God's sake. But Emma was his *wife*. Okay, ex-wife, though they hadn't exactly filed for divorce in a court of law. The principle was the same. He had stood there and watched her die when he could have saved her.

I kept having to dab at my eyes as we made the silent walk from Cyrus's house to the garage where we had parked. Anderson was stone-faced, staring straight ahead as he walked. When we reached the car, Anderson pulled the keys out of his jacket pocket and handed them to Blake.

"I'm not fit to drive," he said. His voice was gravelly, and for the first time I noticed the rim of red around his eyes.

It made me feel a little better to know that Anderson was hurting after what he'd done. I don't know if I could have borne it if he'd been as indifferent as he'd pretended to be while we were at Cyrus's. Maybe he'd just been trying to hide his true emotions in front of the enemy.

"It had to be done, boss," Blake said as he took the keys.

A glint of anger flashed in Anderson's eyes. He'd called for Emma's death himself, had stood idly by while Mark killed her, but apparently he didn't like the implication that she'd needed to die. "You never did like her, did you?"

"There are a lot of people I don't like, and only a couple of them I'd like to see die. Emma wasn't one of them. But she wasn't right in the head, and she was getting worse over time instead of better. I just wanted you to know I thought you did the right thing."

Blake gave me a look that held both warning and reproach, probably worried I was going to argue, but what would be the point? I'd made my position clear already. Anderson was obviously suffering—as he had been almost from the moment we'd pulled Emma from the pond and he'd seen what she'd become. I wasn't going to give him an "atta boy" like Blake had, but I wasn't going to kick him while he was down, either.

Anderson nodded a thank-you at Blake, then climbed into the back of the car. The ride home was even longer and more miserable than the ride out had been.

TWENTY-ONE

I felt far from social when we returned to the mansion, so I made a beeline for my suite and locked the door behind me. A long, scalding-hot shower failed to erase my memories, and my mind was stuck on a continuous loop, replaying Emma's death over and over again.

Was there something I could have said or done to save her? Some way to convince Anderson or Cyrus that it wasn't fair to hold an insane woman responsible for her actions?

In some traditions, when you save a person's life, you then become responsible for that person. It was a cruel, capricious universe that made my rescue the first step on Emma's path to destruction. In a fair world, Emma would have come out of that pond sane and healthy. Maybe her marriage to Anderson would have dissolved anyway—from what I'd heard, their marriage had already been on shaky footing when Emma was kidnapped—but she would not have fixated on me, nor would she have run off to join the Olympians to spite Anderson.

It burned me somewhere deep inside that I had rescued Emma only to have her die while Anderson looked on.

Because I wasn't feeling wretched enough already, my mind insisted on dangling my conversation with Maggie in front of me, the conversation during which Maggie had suggested that Emma's jealousy wasn't entirely misplaced. No matter how I looked at it, I still saw no sign that Anderson was interested in me that way, but then maybe I didn't know where to look. Maybe I just didn't know Anderson well enough yet to pick up the cues. And maybe if I *had* picked them up, I'd have been able to find some way to discourage him, and then—

My thoughts were spiraling out of control, and I knew it. Logic told me in no uncertain terms that Emma's death was not my fault. I'd done everything I could to prevent it, and I had absolutely nothing to feel guilty about. But logic was a cold comfort, and despite my attempts to distract myself and stop thinking about it, I was brooding myself into a deep, dark funk.

I tried everything I could think of to occupy my mind with something else, but Emma's death loomed over me like a massive shadow blocking out the light of the sun.

And then, as I sat on my couch with my computer on my lap and clicked from one website to another, looking for my magic potion of forgetfulness, I clicked by the page where I'd seen the ad for the Indian art exhibit at the Sackler, and I remembered the mixture of comfort and passion I'd experienced in Jamaal's arms last night, before he'd pulled away from me yet again.

Jamaal had a way of occupying my mind like nothing else in the world did, and as I closed my eyes and tried to remember every touch and caress, every word, every scent, every sound, the rest of the world seemed to fade away. He was such a hard, angry man, and yet his lips were deliciously soft, his hands gentle. I shivered in remembered pleasure, wishing I had kept my wits about me and not touched his scars.

How would things have worked out if I hadn't made that crucial mistake? If Jamaal were an ordinary man, I knew exactly where things would have led, but Jamaal was anything but ordinary, and there was more than just his scars holding him back.

I was very aware that I was reaching for a distraction, look-ing for an excuse to end my self-imposed isolation, but it oc-curred to me that Jamaal had probably gone back out to the clearing to practice with Sita this afternoon once I was safely out of the house. There was good reason to think she might be a bit cranky today after our aborted attempt at romance. I wondered if there was any chance she would take her anger out on Jamaal if I wasn't around. The thought sent a chill of alarm through me.

Was my sudden concern nothing but a big, fat rationaliza-tion, an excuse to fling myself at Jamaal when he'd made it clear he thought we should maintain our distance? Yes. But I didn't care. I needed a distraction, and Jamaal was the biggest, best distraction I could imagine.

It was a little after eleven at night when I rapped on Ja-maal's door. It didn't occur to me until after I'd knocked that some people like to get a full night's sleep and go to bed at a reasonable hour. I had the vague impression that Jamaal was a night owl, but I didn't have much evidence to support it.

If he didn't answer the door, should I assume he was asleep? Or should I worry that my fears were more than a flimsy ratio-nalization and Sita had hurt him?

Luckily, I didn't have to make that decision, because the door opened, and Jamaal stood there in all his manly glory, looking good enough to eat.

He hadn't been in bed yet, or he wouldn't have gotten to the door so fast, but he had changed into a pair of plaid pajama bottoms topped with a wifebeater. Instinct told me he wore the top to cover his scars, even in his sleep, and the thought made me hurt somewhere deep inside.

"What do you want?" he asked curtly when I just stood there in his doorway staring at him.

If I'd come down just because I was worried Sita might have hurt him, I could turn around and go back to my room now. He was obviously fine. Besides, he was blasting out keep-away vibes so hard I couldn't possibly miss them.

"Did you practice with Sita while I was gone today?" I asked, instead of acting on the unsubtle message.

Jamaal sighed and rubbed his eyes like he was tired. I didn't think he was. I didn't feel like standing in the hall, so I pushed past him into his sitting room. The door to his bedroom was open, and I could see that the covers on his bed had been neatly pulled back. Jamaal was the kind of neat freak who makes his bed every day, so I knew this meant he'd been about to turn in for the night.

"Go to bed, Nikki," Jamaal said, a hint of pleading in his voice.

"Tell me what happened with Sita. Was she pissed off because of last night?"

Jamaal looked like he wanted to strangle me. Once upon a time, I'd have been intimidated by that look, but not anymore. As long as he was in control of himself, he would never hurt me, and he was firmly in control. I crossed my arms and gave him my best stubborn, implacable look.

He closed his sitting room door. It wasn't quite a slam, but it was close.

"Yes, she was pissed off," he said.

"Did she hurt you?" If she had, he was okay now, but that didn't stop my blood pressure from rising at the thought.

He rolled his eyes. "Of course not. But she tried to go looking for you even though I told her you weren't in the house."

That didn't sound good. "Maybe she didn't understand you." I still had trouble wrapping my brain around the idea that Sita understood *anything* people said to her. How the hell did a tiger learn English?

I shook my head at myself. I had to stop thinking of Sita as a tiger. That was the form she took, but that wasn't what she actually was. She was magic, and who knew what her limits were?

"She understood," Jamaal said grimly. "I wasn't sure she wasn't going to pick on someone else to punish me, so I put her away. You have to keep your distance, Nikki. It's not safe to be around me."

I heard the hint of bitterness in my own laugh. "I think *safe* is a thing of my past. In the last couple of months, I've been beaten, bitten, kidnapped, murdered—twice!—and threatened with fates worse than death. I doubt I'll ever feel safe again." I shivered, suddenly chilled by my own recap of what I'd been through. I was lucky I wasn't as insane as Emma by this point.

Jamaal took a step toward me, and I think he was planning to give me a hug, but he stopped himself and clenched his fists at his sides.

"The closest I've come to feeling safe," I continued, and this time I took the step forward, "was last night when I was in your arms. When you kissed me, I forgot the rest of the world existed." I reached out to touch his chest. The fabric of his shirt was thin enough that I could feel the ridges of his scars beneath it. I looked up into his eyes. "I need to forget for a while. Please."

"It's too dangerous," Jamaal said, but he didn't move away from me, and his eyes were dark with desire. "Sita—"

"Is going to have to learn to live with it. And if she can't, then you'll just have to go back to coping with your death magic the old-fashioned way. You managed to do it for a century before her."

His face hardened. "If you can call what I did 'managing.' You remember that long list of bad things that have happened to you? Who was it who *beat* you?"

I'd thought Jamaal had forgiven himself for that. Apparently, I was wrong. "Even when your temper flared, you wouldn't have done that to one of your friends," I said. "You thought I was the enemy. Look, I don't like it when you go off like a powder keg, and I know fighting the death magic made you miserable, but if using Sita to vent it means you have to live your life in complete isolation from the rest of us, then it isn't worth it. I'd rather deal with your temper."

Jamaal shook his head. He opened his mouth to argue, but I reached up and put my fingers on his lips to stop him.

"You deserve to have a life," I told him, caressing the fullness of his lower lip with my thumb as I closed the last remaining distance between us. Almost against his will, he put his arms around me. There was a look very like fear in his eyes, and I was determined to extinguish it. I rose up on my tiptoes and kissed him, and a small sound of need escaped me.

"This is a bad idea, Nikki," he said against my lips, but the sexy rasp in his voice and the way his hands gripped me tighter said he was in as much of a mood to be bad as I was.

I breathed deep, taking in his scent of smoke and cloves and something else I suspected was hair product. And underneath was the scent of *him,* of the man who could chase all other thoughts from my mind with the lightest brush of skin against skin, or even with the faintest hint of a smile. I slid my hands up his chest and looped them around his neck, pulling his head down toward me.

For all his protests, he didn't resist. His lips came down on mine, and there was no longer room in my brain for anything but the taste of him, the feel of him against me. He was rapidly hardening beneath those soft flannel PJs of his, and I wished I were taller so I could grind something other than my belly against him.

Jamaal apparently had a similar thought, because his hands slid down my back to my butt and he boosted me up with casual strength. I groaned into his mouth and wrapped my legs around him, reveling in the feel of him. His tongue stroked mine rhythmically, and I grabbed hold of a double handful of his hair to remind myself not to let my hands wander. It was hard to remember *anything* at the moment, hard to think of anything but how glorious his lips felt as he kissed me.

My heart was already tripping along happily in my chest, but when Jamaal carried me through the sitting room and into his bedroom, I thought it might burst. I wanted him more than

I wanted my next breath, wanted to lose myself in the sensations he sparked in my body, but I knew from past experience that I needed to keep some small section of my brain on-line and functional if I didn't want to scare him off again.

Jamaal laid me down on the crisp white sheets of his bed, pushing the covers farther aside without breaking the kiss. He came to rest on top of me, his lower body held in the cradle of my legs, which I kept wrapped around him. My hands yearned to explore, to tear away the clothing that separated us. I wanted to feel his skin, hot and slick against mine, but I didn't dare make any overtures.

I let go of Jamaal's hair and groped for the headboard. I hadn't paused to examine it when Jamaal had carried me in, but I had a vague impression it was carved of dark wood and had some posts I could hold on to. Maybe if I kept my hands out of the fray entirely, I could keep them from wandering when they shouldn't. I found a couple of handholds and latched on, still kissing him for all I was worth and holding him close with my legs.

I almost howled in protest when he broke the kiss, but he didn't withdraw from me, merely cupped the side of my face in his hand and stared down into my eyes. With his erection pressed up tight against me, there was no missing his desire. Unfortunately, there was no missing the hint of fear in his eyes, either.

"I want you," he whispered, then rolled his hips against me to emphasize his point. I gasped in pleasure and arched my back. "But you know I have . . . issues."

I let go of the headboard long enough to run my fingers down the side of his face in a caress that I hoped was equal parts sensual and comforting. "I know. I don't care about your issues. Tie my hands so I don't get careless, and then have your way with me."

A tremor ran through him, and he closed his eyes.

Shit. I was losing him.

"Don't you dare stop now!" I said, clamping my legs even more firmly around him.

"You deserve better than me."

"*I'll* decide what I deserve." I was somewhat heartened by the fact that despite his words, he was still rock hard against me. There was a part of him trying to withdraw, but it wasn't all of him. "I want you inside me."

He shook his head. "You don't understand. I had an owner once . . . The scars turned her on. She—"

I shut him up with a kiss, gently taking hold of his lip between my teeth when he would have pulled away. Apparently, he found that sexy, because he momentarily forgot his objections and returned my kiss with an intensity that took my breath away.

He was panting heavily when he ended the kiss. "Have to keep my shirt on," he said between breaths.

"Don't care," I said, and realized I was panting with need, too. Actually, I *did* care, but the time to talk to Jamaal about whatever had been done to him to make him so skittish about the scars was not now. I didn't want him thinking about anything that might make him back off yet again, so I channeled my inner porn star. I'm not usually into talking dirty, but for Jamaal I was more than willing to make an exception. "Fuck me. Now!"

It's amazing the effect those two little words can have on a guy. Jamaal forgot all about his excuses and apologies and explanations. He pushed up to his knees so he could get to the fly of my jeans, and he had them open and down before I could even offer to help. I'd have liked to have taken them off entirely, but he seemed in too much of a hurry and I wasn't about to complain.

I groaned when he dropped his pajamas and I got a good look at his erection. I'd known from the feel of him against me that he was, shall we say, well endowed, but naked and ready for action, he was nothing short of magnificent. My fingers itched to reach out and touch him, to stroke the smooth hardness of him, but since I hadn't let him pour out his whole tale of woe, I didn't dare, not knowing what might trigger traumatic memories.

A shiver of need passed through me, along with a tiny twinge of anxiety. I'm no virgin, but my spectacular ability to fall for inappropriate or unavailable men meant I wasn't the most sexually experienced twenty-five-year-old in the world, and Jamaal's size promised an uncomfortable beginning. I hoped it wouldn't hurt so much that I couldn't hide it. The last thing I wanted was for Jamaal to feel even a twinge of guilt.

"Condom," I reminded him as he stretched out above me, having barely remembered in time.

"Not necessary," he assured me. "The lines don't mix."

I took that to mean that descendants of different divinities couldn't have children together, which I stored away as something to ask questions about some other time. Right now, I was more than prepared to take Jamaal's word for it. I spread my legs as wide as I could with my damn jeans and panties restricting the motion. Jamaal didn't take me up on my offer to let him tie my hands, but he did pin my wrists to the pillow above my head. I had no objections.

I arched toward him in anticipation . . .

And felt like I'd been plummeted into a pool of ice-cold water when I heard a feline growl, way too close to me.

Jamaal cursed and shoved me aside, putting himself between me and the five-hundred-pound tiger that had suddenly appeared on the bed beside us. I rolled off the side of the bed, frantically pulling up my pants as I did. Sita growled again, the sound just short of a roar.

"I did *not* summon you!" Jamaal shouted at her.

Staying out of sight might have been my wisest choice, but I couldn't help peeking up over the side of the bed. Jamaal was on his knees, his arms spread wide as if that would block Sita from getting to me. We both knew she could jump right over him if she wanted to. He hadn't bothered to pull his pajamas back up, and I saw that his backside was as scarred as the rest of his torso. He reached out as if to touch Sita—which he seemed to need to do to put her away—but she danced out of reach, baring a very intimidating set of teeth. Her eyes seemed to glow in the darkness of the room, and they locked on me like laser beams.

Jamaal moved to put himself between us again, trying to cut off her line of sight, but I didn't want him getting hurt because of me, and I worried Sita wasn't above taking out her temper on him. The idea that she'd just appeared out of nowhere without being summoned wasn't what you'd call a comfortable one. I wasn't about to cower while Jamaal took the heat for me, so I rose to my feet and glared at the tiger.

"Jamaal has a right to a life, Sita," I said. "You can't keep him entirely to yourself."

"Shut up, Nikki!" Jamaal snapped at me as Sita growled her disapproval. "Just get out of here while you can."

There wasn't much I could do to help, but leaving Jamaal to face an angry tiger by himself didn't seem like such a hot idea. Of course, staying and getting mauled didn't sound so great, either.

I shook my finger at Sita like I was scolding a small child. "If you hurt him, I swear to God I'm—"

Sita interrupted me with a roar that rattled my teeth.

"She won't hurt me," Jamaal said with conviction. "Now get the fuck out of my room."

There were a lot of things I wanted to say just then, but I swallowed them all. Jamaal said he hadn't summoned her, but could I be sure that was entirely true? We'd taken some slapdash steps to avoid triggering his issues, but maybe it hadn't been enough. Maybe we'd avoided the conscious issues, but the unconscious ones were deeper and more insidious. So insidious his subconscious had called for Sita to intervene. Maybe he would have to talk through whatever had happened to him in his slave days before he would be able to let someone get so close again.

Or maybe Sita was as out of control as his temper had been, before he'd learned to summon her.

I knew I couldn't help him. Not right now, anyway. I didn't want to leave him to face Sita's wrath alone, but I suspected my continued presence would just make her more angry.

Mentally promising myself that this was not over, that I was not going to give up on Jamaal no matter how difficult the situation, I slowly backed out of the room.

I was awakened in the night by another blast of thunder. I was surprised to discover that I'd fallen asleep at all, considering how long I had tossed and turned, searching for a solution to the Sita problem—one that didn't involve Jamaal having to shut one or the other of us out of his life. And wondering if he was just one more on the list of unavailable men I was destined to fall for.

I rose from my bed and went to the window, hoping to see that it was pouring down rain, but the sky was clear enough that I could have counted the stars if I'd wanted to. I wondered how big the clearing was going to be when Anderson had finished venting his pain and rage. Hopefully, we'd still have *some* woods left.

I slept only fitfully after that, waking up every forty minutes or so, brooding about Emma, and Jamaal, and my most recent brush with death. By 4 A.M., I was lying in bed debating whether I should try to get some more sleep or just give up and get out of bed. The decision was taken out of my hands when the phone beside my bed rang.

Phones ringing at four in the morning are rarely a good thing. The only person I'd given my land line number to was Steph. The last time she'd called so early, it was because the Glasses' house burned down.

Dread pooled in my stomach as I sat up and turned on the light. I blinked in the glare, trying to see the caller ID before picking up the phone.

My hand was halfway to the phone when my vision cleared enough for me to read the caller ID: Cyrus Galanos.

Twenty-two

I was an emotional wreck when I got off the phone with Cyrus. I spent a few minutes indulging in a crying jag, a little piece of my heart breaking. When the worst of it was over, I went into the bathroom and splashed some cold water on my face. My eyes were red and puffy, and I had shopping bags under them from not sleeping. The hair around my face was wet from the splashes of water, and the hair that wasn't wet was tangled and frizzy. I wanted to get into the shower and put myself back together, but there wasn't time.

I threw on the first pair of jeans I could get my hands on and grabbed a warm, comfortable flannel shirt. Then I dug out my one pair of waterproof boots, nice and fleecy to keep my feet warm in the snow. I braided my hair sloppily as I made my way down the stairs to the second floor. The house was dark and quiet. I glanced at my watch and saw that it was now twenty after four. I'd wasted too much time having my pity party. The moon would set in less than two hours, and I would need every spare second of that time.

Of course, it was possible I wouldn't survive relaying to Anderson what Cyrus had told me when he called. I wished Cyrus had had the guts to tell Anderson himself without using me as his messenger service. After all, Anderson couldn't kill the messenger over the phone.

I hesitated when I reached the hallway leading to Anderson's wing. We were forbidden from going into the east wing past his study, except in case of emergency. This was an emergency, but that didn't exactly make me eager to trespass. Not with the message I bore.

I gave myself a swift kick in the pants and reminded myself once again that I didn't have time for hesitation. I needed to be at my hunting best, and that meant I needed the moon.

Heart throbbing in my chest, I hurried down the hall. I wasn't sure which room was his bedroom, but I made an educated guess that it would be next to the bathroom he'd stuck his head out of the other day. I didn't know how I was going to break the news, and I didn't have time to come up with a carefully worded plan.

I knocked on the door, rapping hard because I assumed Anderson would be fast asleep. "Anderson!" I called, hoping I wasn't shouting so loud I'd wake the entire house. "Wake up! I need to talk to you."

"I'm not asleep," he answered, startling me, and moments later there was a glow of light around the edges of the door and the sound of approaching footsteps.

The door swung open. Anderson was still wearing yesterday's clothes, and a quick glance over his shoulder showed me that his bed was neatly made. I didn't know what he'd been doing sitting around in his room in the dark, but I didn't wonder enough to ask. He looked even more rumpled than usual, his beard bristling with scraggly whiskers he hadn't bothered to shave, his shaggy hair standing up straight in places and lying flat in others. His eyes were bloodshot, and there was a faint scent of stale alcohol clinging to him. That answered my question about what he'd been doing alone and awake in the dark.

"What is it?" he asked, and he didn't sound as alarmed as a knock on the door at this hour of the morning should make him. He just sounded resigned and very, very tired.

I wished like hell I could turn around and leave him to his

grieving. I wished I didn't have to make him feel worse than he already did. Yesterday, I had wanted him to feel bad for what I saw as his cold-bloodedness, but now I wished I could spare him.

I decided to ease my way into the conversation by telling him the easy part first.

"I just got a phone call from Cyrus."

A crease of worry appeared between Anderson's brows. "That was . . . unexpected."

No kidding. "Someone tried to murder him in his sleep."

Anderson no longer looked so weary and apathetic. I didn't know if that would turn out to be a good thing or a bad thing for me, though I supposed even if he'd remained flat and dull-eyed, he would be fully roused and ready to embrace his Fury heritage by the time I was finished.

"Come in," he said, turning his back abruptly and heading toward an armchair in the corner. I reluctantly followed as he sat and grabbed the pair of battered sneakers lying beside the chair. "Cyrus wouldn't call you just to report an attempt on his life," he said, shoving one foot into a sneaker. "Tell me what's going on."

I wanted to sit down. My knees were a little weak and trembly. But Anderson was sitting in the only chair, and sitting on the edge of his bed seemed too familiar and informal. I settled for grabbing one of the bedposts to steady myself, gripping it harder than was strictly necessary. Why the hell was *I* the one who had to have this conversation with Anderson? I swallowed hard.

"The guy who tried to kill Cyrus was a Descendant. One of Konstantin's cronies."

Anderson looked up from tying his sneakers. "You say that like it's some kind of surprise. I told you Konstantin has never trusted his children. I'm frankly surprised Cyrus has lived as long as he has. It might have seemed natural to him to step into his father's shoes, but it was probably the worst possible thing he could have done if he wanted Konstantin to keep him alive. Having his child usurp his 'throne' is one of his biggest fears, which is why he's killed all the others before Cyrus."

"But Cyrus took over in name only," I protested. I'd warned Cyrus myself that Konstantin would turn on him one day, but I still had a hard time understanding how someone could kill their own child. I don't think there's a more heinous crime in the universe.

"Doesn't matter," Anderson said. He finished tying his shoes, but remained in his chair, his body language fraught with tension. "Maybe Konstantin thought he'd be okay with it at first, but when he saw Cyrus taking over his role—and making some decisions he didn't agree with—he realized he couldn't stomach it. He might even think killing Cyrus would make the rest of the Olympians forgive his past mistakes and let him lead them again." He raked his hand through his hair. I don't know if that was a stress reaction, or if he actually thought he was finger-combing it. If the latter, he failed spectacularly.

"You still haven't told me why Cyrus called *you* of all people. And why you're at my doorstep at this hour of the morning."

No, I hadn't. And I didn't want to. My throat tightened up on me, and I couldn't think of what to say. I didn't like the idea of sitting on Anderson's bed, but my shaky knees wouldn't hold me anymore, so I did it anyway.

I told myself I wasn't really *scared* of Anderson. I told myself that I was having a hard time finding my voice because I didn't want to cause him pain, and because I was enough of an emotional coward that I didn't want to be there to *see* his pain. That part was true, at least as far as it went. But the truth was, I *was* scared. He was a freaking *god*! And anyone who has even a smidgen of familiarity with mythology knows that gods don't act like human beings. They routinely kill the people closest to them, and they only sometimes show any remorse for having done it.

Despite my pathetic attempts to put on a brave face, Anderson couldn't help but see my fear. I thought even that might make him angry, but when I sneaked a glance at his face, I saw only gentle compassion. I just didn't know whether to trust it or not.

"You don't have to be afraid of me, Nikki," he said in a tone he might use with a frightened animal. "I can tell you have bad news to impart, and I promise I won't kill the messenger."

They were the right words, delivered in the right tone, and yet I still didn't trust him. "I've seen your temper before," I said, looking at the floor because I couldn't bear to face him. "I saw you torture a couple of people to death. I saw you stand by and watch your wife being killed before your eyes because you were angry at her for betraying you. I saw what you did to all the trees in the clearing." I didn't even mention the times he had threatened to kill me.

He stood up and came toward me, and I had to fight an urge to jump to my feet and run. I was rather proud of myself for staying right there on the edge of the bed until Anderson was an arm's length away. I would have had to look up to meet his eyes, but I felt no temptation to do so.

I practically jumped out of my skin when Anderson reached out and brushed his fingers over my cheek, tucking a stray lock of hair that had escaped my messy braid back behind my ear. The touch startled me enough to make me look up at his face.

"You have seen me get angry," he said, and there was still that look of compassion in his eyes. "You have seen me be ruthless. You *haven't* seen me truly lose my temper. I learned long ago how dangerous my temper can be. I did . . . terrible things in the old days, before I started consorting with humans. I will never let that happen again. That's why I shut down like I did the other night. It's what I had to do to contain myself." He touched me again, a brief caress of my cheek.

"I would never hurt you, or your loved ones, or any of my people, in a fit of anger."

I looked down, unable to think straight when he was looking at me like that. Maybe I was imagining things, but I thought I'd seen a kind of warmth in his gaze that was almost . . . intimate. Was I really seeing something telling in his eyes? Or was I doing exactly what I'd feared I would ever since my conversation with Maggie and letting the power of suggestion make me see something that wasn't there? I didn't know, and I couldn't afford to think about it.

"Tell me whatever it is you have to tell me," Anderson prompted. "I can sense your urgency."

I can't say I was completely convinced. But he wasn't wrong about the urgency, and it was time for me to stop stalling.

"Cyrus killed the Descendant who attacked him, but he didn't do it quickly." My gorge rose as I remembered Cyrus's dispassionate account of using his power as a descendant of a sun god to slowly roast his attacker to death. "While he was suffering and dying, the Descendant raved about how Konstantin would win in the end. And he said Konstantin had used Cyrus to—" My voice choked off for a moment, and I forced myself to look up at Anderson once more. He'd put on his unreadable mask, and I had no idea what he was thinking or feeling.

"You might want to sit down," I said, and despite my lingering fear, I felt an urge to reach out and take his hand to comfort him as I delivered the blow. It said something about what he was feeling behind the mask that Anderson actually took my advice and sat down on the bed beside me.

"What did Konstantin use Cyrus to do?"

I took a deep breath in a futile attempt to steady myself. No amount of willpower could force me to look Anderson in the face. "He used *all* of us," I said. "To frame Emma. He was behind the fires, and behind my abduction. He planted the fake letters on Emma's computer. I thought I'd had a lucky escape thanks to the car accident, but that was all part of the plan, too. He wanted the kidnapper to be caught so he would admit what he was hired to do and say he was hired by a woman. It was all a big setup so that you would kill Emma." Never mind that Anderson hadn't killed her with his own hands. We all knew the decision to let her die had been his in the end. And now, he would have to live with having condemned the woman he'd loved so desperately to die over a betrayal she wasn't even guilty of.

My hand was squeezing the bedpost so hard my knuckles were turning white and my fingers were going numb. My pulse was drumming erratically in my throat, and I had to remind myself to draw the occasional breath as I waited for Anderson's reaction. No matter what he'd promised, I feared an explosion of some kind.

The silence stretched, my heartbeat loud in my ears as I held myself tense and ready—for what, I don't know. I finally couldn't stand it anymore and risked a look in Anderson's direction.

His face had a slightly gray cast to it, and his bloodshot eyes were rimmed with red. His lips were pressed together in a tight line, and I saw no evidence that he was even breathing. But when he met my eyes, there was no sign that he had turned into the automaton of the other night, nor that he was about to explode with temper. There was just pain, and a soul-deep sadness that brought tears to my eyes.

I wanted to say something to break the silence, find some words of sympathy, or comfort. Anything to break the tension, if only for a second. But there were no words.

Anderson blinked rapidly a few times, then let out a slow, hissing breath. "Do you know what the worst thing about this is?" he asked in a hoarse whisper.

I shook my head mutely. Everything about it seemed equally awful to me.

He reached up to rub his eyes, as if he could make the haunted expression in them go away. "The worst part is that this doesn't hurt as much as Konstantin hoped it would. Because you see, Nikki, I've done worse."

TWENTY-THREE

I'd been unsure of a lot of things in recent days. However, there was no uncertainty in my mind now. If Anderson had done worse sometime in the course of his long life, I didn't want to know about it. And while he said Konstantin's trick hadn't hurt as much as Konstantin had hoped, it was obvious that it had hurt plenty. Anderson wasn't exploding in rage, but the pain and sadness that wafted from him made my eyes tear up in sympathy yet again.

Not trusting my voice, I cleared my throat before I spoke again.

"Strangely enough, Cyrus doesn't feel the need to protect Konstantin anymore. He suggested you and I might want to hunt Konstantin down and bury him somewhere that no one will ever find him."

Anderson nodded slowly. "He wants us to do the dirty work for him so he can deny having anything to do with his father's disappearance."

"That was my interpretation. So far he and Mark are the only Olympians who know what Konstantin tried to do, and I think Cyrus plans to keep it that way if he can. I don't know if he's trying not to piss off Konstantin's supporters, or if he just doesn't want to give anyone else ideas.

"Anyway, Cyrus told me Konstantin's been moving around constantly, trying to make it hard for me to get a bead on him. But he was apparently staying at Alexis's old place last night. I'm sure he knows by now that his assassination attempt failed, and he's no doubt on the run, but we have a solid starting point, and the moon is still up."

Anderson raised an eyebrow at me. There was still a haunted expression in his eyes, and his face hadn't fully regained its usual color, but he seemed entirely calm and rational. "You mean to tell me you're willing to hunt him now? His revenge has come to its head, and I doubt you and your family are in any danger from him anymore. He was never really after you in the first place."

My shoulders slumped, and I suddenly felt almost unbearably tired. Until that moment, when Anderson challenged me with it, I hadn't even allowed myself to *think* about what I was doing. The pain and anger that swelled in me when I learned what Konstantin had done were so overwhelming that I'd been acting on pure instinct, letting those swirling emotions guide me. I wanted Konstantin dead, and if I could help make him that way, then I was all for it.

But had anything really changed since I'd refused to hunt Konstantin because my conscience rebelled at the idea of killing for revenge? Sure, Konstantin had hurt more people, but as Anderson had said, his revenge was now complete. At least, it seemed logical to assume it was.

I like to think of myself as a nice person. I've long taken pride in being a bleeding heart, in being a voice of reason when others around me were acting on pure emotion. I'd considered myself above acting out of revenge. And yet even now, when Anderson pointed out the inconsistency of my decision, my conscience couldn't quite rouse itself to try to talk me out of it. Konstantin had hurt too many people, in too many twisted ways. And unlike Emma, or even Justin Kerner, he was not clinically insane. There was no excuse for his actions, not even in my unusually open mind. He was just an evil man, and the world would be a better place without him.

"I still don't believe in revenge killings," I said slowly, thinking over my words carefully. "If there were a way to sentence him to life in prison, I'd be all for it." Even as I said those words, I wasn't sure they were true. Not anymore. In my arrogance, I'd thought there was no situation that could persuade me to believe in the death penalty, ever. Maybe I still didn't. I'd have to wait until my emotions settled down before I would know for sure. But there were exceptions to every rule, and I couldn't deny that in my mind, Konstantin was one of them. "But since we can't imprison him except by burial, which I wouldn't wish even on him, then I guess he has to die. If that makes me a hypocrite, then I guess I'm just going to have to live with it."

Anderson gave me a gentle smile. "I don't think you're being a hypocrite, Nikki. We're being spurred into action by revenge, but that's not all there is to it. Even if he doesn't personally come after us anymore, he will still be an evil person, and countless others will suffer and die at his hands if we don't take him out. There are good, logical reasons to kill him above and beyond our desire to punish him for what he's done."

Everything Anderson said was true. By killing Konstantin, we'd be saving innocent lives, there was no question about it. But I had the sense that I was taking my first step onto a slippery slope, and that there was a long, long fall ahead of me if I wasn't very careful.

"I can wrestle with my conscience later," I said. I glanced at my watch. "We have about an hour and twenty minutes before the moon sets. It'll take us thirty to get to Alexis's place, and that won't leave us a whole lot of time to pick up the trail and figure out where Konstantin has gone." Assuming I could get my power to work on command, which was far from a sure thing.

"Then there's not a moment to waste," Anderson said.

Together, we hurried out into the predawn darkness to hunt the deposed "king" of the Olympians.

I let Anderson drive, on the assumption that once we got close enough to Alexis's mansion for me to start sensing Konstantin, I'd have to do my semiconscious tour-guide impersonation as I'd done with Steph on the night we'd gone hunting together. As soon as we were through the gates, I leaned back in my seat and closed my eyes, trying to let my mind drift in just the right way. The darkness, the early hour, and my exhaustion from a mostly sleepless night threatened to drag me down into sleep. The pressure of the ticking clock, along with the burning need to ensure that Konstantin could never hurt anyone again, kept sleep from winning, but it didn't exactly help me zone out.

The roads were an icy mess, making the drive painfully slow. A couple of times, I felt the car skid, and my eyes opened in alarm. Anderson knew how to drive in the snow and ice, however, and he quickly righted the car.

"Relax, Nikki," he said, reaching over to pat my knee briefly. "I'm not going to crash the car. Trust me."

I gave him a sidelong glance and frowned. The knee-pat had been an almost instinctual, absent gesture, and if he'd realized it was uncommonly familiar, he showed no sign of it. I bit my lip and sank a little lower in my seat. The last thing I needed right now was to distract myself analyzing every nuance of Anderson's behavior when I should be tracking a killer.

"It would be nice if just once I was trying to find someone without being under time pressure," I grumbled. It would be so much easier to relax if it didn't *matter* so goddamn much.

Of course, if it didn't matter so much, then I wouldn't be doing it.

Anderson didn't reply. I let out a long, slow breath and let my eyes slide closed again. I hoped Konstantin hadn't gotten very far away from Alexis's house by the time we got there. We were going to have precious little moonlight left, and if I lost the "signal," we'd be back to square one again by the time the moon next rose. Konstantin was no dummy, and after poking the bear, he was going to be running as fast as he could. With Cyrus mad at him, without the full support of the Olympians, he would have to get out of the D.C. area, and who knew where he would end up? If it were me, I'd get out of the country. And if he left the country, I suspected even *my* hunting skills might not be up to the challenge of finding him.

The urgency made my nerves buzz as if I'd drunk a gallon of coffee. I was tapping the fingers of one hand restlessly against my thigh. I stopped as soon as I noticed the movement, taking another deep breath and urging myself to calm. I searched for that floaty, abstracted feeling I got when I was a passenger on a boring drive.

The car hit a bump, and my eyes popped open again, searching out the dashboard clock before I could stop myself. It was 5:29, and we had less than thirty minutes left before the moon set. My heart sank. Even if Konstantin hadn't found out his assassination attempt failed until Anderson and I had left the mansion—and I was pretty sure he would have known before then—he had a good forty-minute head start. There was no way we were going to catch up with him before the moon set. My powers aren't nonexistent without the moon, but they're spotty at the best of times. I didn't for a moment believe I could find Konstantin during the day. And by nightfall, he'd be long gone, perhaps out of my reach.

The grimness on Anderson's face told me he'd reached the same conclusion, but he wasn't ready to admit it yet.

"Keep trying," he urged me as he turned onto the street that would take us by the front gates of Alexis's home. I would have thought one of the other Olympians would have appropriated it after Alexis's "disappearance," but perhaps Konstantin had wanted to keep it for himself.

I shook my head. "It's too late." I rubbed at my tired eyes, wishing there were some better way for me to control my power. Maybe it would help if I took up meditation. Maybe that would make it easier to relax in tense situations like this one.

"Don't you dare give up on me now, Nikki," Anderson warned in a low growl.

If he thought that was going to make it easier for me to relax into my powers, he was sorely mistaken. But I wasn't in the mood to argue with him, so I closed my eyes. My fingers were tapping away again, trying to vent the nervous energy that still pulsed through my veins. My mind might have decided the search was fruitless, but my body hadn't caught up, still buzzing on the adrenaline of the hunt.

I made only a halfhearted effort to relax myself, knowing there was no way we were going to have time to catch up to Konstantin. Mostly, I was just pretending to try so Anderson wouldn't nag me. My mind was still going a thousand miles an hour, and my token effort to relax hadn't had the slightest effect, when my eyes popped open for a third time, this time with no external prompting whatsoever.

A shiver of dread trailed down my spine as I looked out my window and saw we were passing directly in front of the gates to Alexis's mansion. Once upon a time, I would have considered the fact that my eyes had opened at that very moment to be nothing more than a coincidence. Now, however, I felt sure it meant only one thing.

"Konstantin is still in the house."

Anderson's hands jerked on the steering wheel, and for a moment I feared he was going to take us right into a ditch. He handled the car expertly, smoothly turning into the skid until he regained control and came to an idling stop in the middle of the road.

"He can't be," he protested. "He's arrogant, but not stupid. He had to have arranged for his pet Descendant to contact him when Cyrus was dead, and he *had* to know what it meant when the Descendant didn't do it."

"Maybe he didn't expect Cyrus to sic us on him so quickly," I said doubtfully. Of course, it didn't matter exactly what Konstantin had been expecting. Whether he thought we'd be after him in an hour or a day, he wouldn't be hanging out at his last known location to make it easy for us. "Or maybe Cyrus forced the Descendant to call Konstantin and tell him he succeeded."

"Yes, and he failed to mention that to you when you talked to him. And Konstantin has nothing better to do after assassinating his son than to lounge around in Alexis's house."

Okay, that theory didn't make a whole lot of sense, either. But I really hated the third theory that came into my mind.

There was no parking on the street in this neighborhood, and a snowplow had piled dirty brown snow and ice along the curbs, but that didn't stop Anderson from pulling off the road. The car shimmied and groaned a protest as he forced it over the mounded, icy snow. I clutched the grab bar with one hand and braced against the center console with the other. There was an ominous bang from the undercarriage, and Anderson's side of the car lurched upward while mine lurched downward. I barely kept my head from smacking against the window.

Anderson brought the car to a stop—or maybe the car took the decision out of his hands—and put it in park. We were still at a precarious angle, and I wondered if the tires on his side were even touching anything. Of course, if being hung up on the side of the road was the worst thing that was going to happen, I'd be ecstatic.

"The only reason I can think of for Konstantin to still be here is if this is a trap," I said, giving Anderson a meaningful look. Which would have been more effective—maybe—if he'd bothered to look at me. Instead, he was unbuckling his seat belt with one hand while opening the door with the other.

I grabbed his arm to get his attention. "Let's think about this for a minute before we do something stupid!"

I had no idea what Konstantin was planning. He *knew* Anderson couldn't be killed, not by him, and not by a Descendant. But he must think he had some way to hurt him, some way to prevent Anderson from killing him. There was no other reason I could imagine for him to still be in the house when he had to know we'd be coming after him.

Anderson gave me a steely glare. "Konstantin is here. That's all I need to know."

He turned toward the door again, and again I grabbed his arm. "We also know this has to be a trap. He could have thirty of his closest friends in there with him, just waiting for you to stroll in like a macho idiot."

Anderson snorted. "He'd have to risk letting them find out what I am, and that's something he would never do. He's alone in there. And I suggest you let go of me. I'm in no mood for your interference."

"Well, *I'm* in no mood to get killed because you won't listen to reason."

"Fine. Then stay here." He easily jerked his arm out of my grip and leapt out of the car.

"Dammit!" I fumbled with my own seat belt, uttering a few choice cuss words under my breath. I couldn't just let Anderson walk in there alone. Sure, I was more vulnerable than he was, but I was also a hell of a lot more *rational,* and right now, that seemed like an important factor. "Wait up!" I yelled, pushing my door open and jumping out. Which turned out not to be my brightest move ever. We had come to a stop at the edge of the ditch, the car's undercarriage hung up on a big chunk of ice. The side of the ditch was covered with ice as well, and given my momentum and the severe angle, I ended up doing an inglorious nosedive into the ditch.

I twisted my ankle during the fall, as well as knocking the wind out of myself. Anderson, radiating impatience, reached down and hauled me to my feet before I was ready. I almost went down again.

"Your delay tactics are getting on my nerves," he said, and if he wanted to think my pratfall was a deliberate attempt to slow him down, then I was happy to let him go right ahead thinking it.

"Just give me half a second to catch my breath. That hurt!"

From the looks of him, half a second was all I was going to get, and grudgingly at that.

"So what's your plan, Rambo?" I asked as I gingerly put my weight on my injured ankle. "Go in the front door and hope he's not expecting you?"

He shot me a glare that would have had me taking a hasty step away if my ankle weren't complaining so loudly. Clearly, he wasn't open to suggestion, nor was he prepared to address my objections. I'd never seen him quite like this before, and frankly, it scared me. I didn't want to let him go in there alone, but I didn't want to get killed—or worse, considering this was Konstantin we were going after—charging in like a stampeding bull.

"I don't care if he's expecting me," Anderson said through gritted teeth. "There's nothing he can do to me."

Apparently that was as much discussion as he was willing to entertain. He turned away from me and started marching through the snow toward the house, leaving me to follow or not as I chose.

Wincing in pain at every step, I took off after him.

Our car had come to a stop well past the driveway, and Anderson and I were approaching the house through the woods. I could have reminded him that there were surveillance cameras in these woods and that it might be best to disable one before plowing heedlessly onward, but I didn't think he would listen to me. I just hoped Konstantin hadn't kept up the security detail that was monitoring the cameras the last time I'd trespassed here.

I had already determined beyond reasonable doubt that Anderson wasn't going to listen to me, but I didn't have it in me to just keep quiet as we knowingly walked into a trap without a plan.

"Konstantin obviously thinks there's *something* he can do to you," I said, panting a bit from the effort of walking through the snow, especially at the brisk pace Anderson had set. "Are you 100 percent sure he's wrong?"

"Yes," Anderson snapped.

"What if he's planning to bury you? Or drown you, like he did Emma?"

"He might find me reluctant to hold still for it. Besides, I'm rather hard to restrain." To punctuate his point, Anderson walked straight through the trunk of a tree.

I wished his reminder and demonstration made me feel better. The walking-through-walls thing was a common ability for death-god descendants. Konstantin had to know Anderson, as a death *god*, could do it, and he was waiting in that house for us anyway. To say I had a bad feeling about this was an understatement.

"But you *can* die, at least temporarily," I said. "I've seen it happen." He hadn't stayed dead anywhere near as long as a *Liberi* with similar injuries would have, but still . . .

"Unless his plan is to stand by my side and kill me every ninety seconds or so, it doesn't matter." He came to an abrupt stop and whirled on me. A hint of white glow was leaking out of his eyes, giving me a glimpse of the terrifying, nonhuman creature that lay behind his facade. "Go back to the car. This is my battle, not yours."

Oh, we were back to that again, were we?

"You're being a pigheaded, mindless jackass," I retorted. "Don't you see that Konstantin has been pulling our strings from the very beginning?" I myself was only now beginning to see how thoroughly Konstantin had manipulated us all. "He didn't trick you into killing Emma just to hurt you. He did it because he knew it would make you act exactly like you're acting now." And his attack on Cyrus was never supposed to succeed, was only meant to prompt Cyrus into giving up his location. "This is exactly the endgame he planned. We're here because he wants us to be, and we'd be idiots to fall for it."

Anderson moved so fast that all I saw was a blur. Then there was a hand at my throat and I was being propelled backward until I crashed into a tree trunk. I probably would have lost my footing in the snow and ice, but Anderson kindly held me up. Unfortunately, he was holding me up by the throat, but what's a little choking between friends?

"I told you I would never hurt you in a fit of temper," Anderson growled, the white light in his eyes now bright enough to make me squint. "Don't make a liar out of me."

I swallowed hard. Anderson can be one hell of a scary guy when he wants to be. But I also noticed that the hand around my throat wasn't really digging in, and that my impact with the tree had been much more surprising than painful. He was in better control of himself than he wanted me to think, which was sort of scary in itself. If he was in control of himself and *still* wanted to storm the house, if it wasn't just some hotheaded momentary madness, then there was no chance in hell I was talking him out of it, no matter how sound my reasoning.

Anderson took my silence for capitulation, and he let go of me. When I started following after him yet again, he gave me an exasperated look over his shoulder.

"I'll shut up," I promised him, holding my hands up in surrender. "But I'm coming with you."

I didn't know if I could possibly be any help. Konstantin had to be expecting both of us, after all, and that meant he had a plan to deal with both of us. But I wasn't letting Anderson walk in there alone. I fished my gun out of my coat pocket, rechecking the cylinder to make sure it was loaded and ready to go. Not because I had any doubts, but because I wanted to look tough and ready for action, instead of scared out of my wits.

The show must have been at least marginally convincing. Anderson turned from me once again and started heading toward the house. I followed.

TWENTY-FOUR

We approached the house from the back, staying under the cover of the woods for as long as we could. I tensed as we broke through the trees and onto the back lawn, but no gunshots shattered the darkness, and there was no one lurking nearby to jump us.

My twisted ankle had healed already, but Anderson was

still walking fast enough that it was hard to keep up. I wished I had longer legs, and bit my tongue on a request that he slow down. He'd made it clear he was through waiting for me.

To get to the back door of the house, we had to walk by the pond that had been Emma's personal torture chamber for the better part of a decade. It was completely frozen over, its surface hidden under a layer of snow. Someone not familiar with the house might not even have realized it was there, though if you looked carefully you could see the outline of its banks under the snow.

I'm sure it cost him something, but Anderson resisted looking at the pond as we made our way past it. There was no way he wasn't aware of its presence, wasn't thinking about what Emma had gone through, wasn't thinking about what Konstantin had manipulated him into doing, but he was in a painfully single-minded state, so focused on his revenge his footsteps didn't falter.

There were no lights on in any of the windows that looked out over the back of the house, but that didn't mean there wasn't anyone on the lookout for intruders. I wanted to maybe do the kind of crouching run you often see people doing in action movies, but that only worked if there was cover to hide behind. Anderson and I were two moving dark blotches in a sea of pristine white snow, and if anyone was watching for us, there was no way in hell they could miss us.

The thought made me utter a few more curses under my breath. Anderson could make himself invisible. If he'd been willing to take the time to formulate a plan, perhaps we'd have been able to figure out a way to take advantage of his ability. But no, he'd rather charge in immediately, too impatient for his revenge to waste time on such trivialities as trying to figure out how to get at Konstantin as safely and easily as possible.

We reached the back door without any alarms sounding or traps springing, but that didn't make me feel any better. If Konstantin had set a trap of some sort, it made sense that it would be inside the house.

Anderson tried the door. Surprise, surprise, it was locked, but there was no way that was going to slow down a death god, much less actually stop him.

Anderson walked right through the door, and I had a momentary fear that he was going to leave me outside to find my own way in while he continued on without me. Before the worry took on a life of its own, I heard the locks turning, and Anderson considerately opened the door for me. I had the guilty thought that I'd probably have been better off if he'd stranded me outside, but that didn't stop me from stepping through the doorway.

"What now?" I asked in a bare whisper.

"Take me to him," Anderson responded. The edge of impatience in his voice made me bristle.

"I'm not a bloodhound!" I held up my wrist and pointed to my watch. "The moon set three minutes ago. I have no idea where he is." There was a flash of white light in Anderson's eyes again. "And getting angry at me isn't going to make my powers suddenly come back."

He blinked a couple of times, and the light went away. "The moon may help you, but you aren't powerless without it. You should be able to track Konstantin when he's so close."

He was right, and I knew it. But my pulse was tripping, and my chest was tight with anxiety, and I wasn't in any state to pick up the subtle nuances of my subconscious. My conscious mind was fully in control—telling me I should get the hell out of the house while there was still time—and any subconscious cues I might be getting were drowned out by the yammering.

I made a helpless gesture and shook my head. At this point, I almost hoped Konstantin changed his mind about whatever he was planning and decided to run instead. I was too frazzled to follow him, and it meant I would probably never be able to find him again, but I suspected that might be the lesser of two evils.

Anderson grunted. "Guess we'll just have to search the whole house then."

And what a joy *that* was going to be. The damned house must have been fifteen thousand square feet at a minimum. Searching it was going to take forever. Maybe it would be boring enough that I'd be able to hear my subconscious eventually. Or maybe Konstantin's trap would be in the first room we checked.

Anderson reached out and took my left hand. I wasn't expecting it, and I was jumpy enough that I tried to snatch my hand away. Anderson kept a firm hold, but disappeared from my view. I could still feel him there, still feel the pressure of his fingers against mine, but though I was looking straight at him, all I saw was the wall behind him.

"Be ready to shoot at a moment's notice," his disembodied voice said. "And try not to shoot *me,* even though you can't see me."

"I'll do my best."

There was a noise behind me. I jumped and gasped, whirling in that direction before logic caught up with me and informed me it was just the heater switching on. Luckily, I resisted the urge to pull the trigger.

Anderson made a sound that could have been a snort of disdain or a muffled laugh. Without being able to see his face, I couldn't tell. My hand was sweating in his. I did one more quick scan of the entryway, and that was when I noticed Anderson wasn't completely invisible, as I'd thought. I could sort of see him as a vague shadow, a deep black against the predawn darkness, but only out of my peripheral vision. If I looked straight at him, it was as if he wasn't there.

"I'll go first around every corner," Anderson told me, giving my hand a little tug and leading me through a laundry room that was to the right of the entry.

That sounded almost like the beginnings of a plan. Emphasis on *almost*. Being mostly invisible, Anderson wasn't likely to get shot or otherwise attacked when he walked into a room, so it made sense for him to go first. It would have made *more* sense if we'd had some idea of what we'd do if he rounded a corner and found Konstantin waiting. The way Anderson was acting, I thought it more than likely he'd dispense with any hint of caution and rush into mortal combat. The best I could do in that case was zip in after him and hope I could get a shot at Konstantin before he sprang whatever surprise he had waiting for us.

To say I wasn't happy with our "plan" was an understatement, but I followed Anderson into the belly of the beast anyway.

The house was as huge as I'd expected, and I couldn't help wondering what a single guy needed with all that. My dearly departed condo had been a little over two thousand square feet, and I'd thought *that* was more than enough. The floors, when they weren't covered with Persian rugs, were all marble or hardwood, and my rubber-soled boots made squeaking noises when I walked no matter how carefully I stepped. Anderson and I both ended up taking off our shoes and leaving them in the hallway for the sake of stealth. I left my parka as well.

There was a faint musty smell in the air, and even in the darkness, I could see that some of the furniture was collecting dust. The aura of genteel neglect made me feel like I was picking my way through a haunted house. The unsettling half glimpses I kept getting of Anderson out of the corner of my eye weren't helping any, nor was the feeling of his invisible hand on me. It wasn't just my hand that was sweaty anymore. The heat was turned on too high for my tastes, but it was the nerves that were making me perspire. Whatever was about to happen, I wished it would just happen already.

A thorough search of the first floor failed to reveal Konstantin. I couldn't decide if I was relieved or disappointed. Anderson tugged me toward the staircase leading up to the second floor. I was still taut as a guitar string about to break, but as soon as I'd walked up those first few steps, I felt a strange reluctance to go any farther. Maybe it was just because it was so dark at the head of the stairs that I couldn't see where we were going.

No . . .

"Wait," I whispered, giving Anderson's hand a little tug for emphasis. I tried to sort through what I was feeling, tried to isolate whatever sense made me reluctant to go up the stairs, but the more I tried to focus on it, the vaguer it became, until I wasn't sure it wasn't all my imagination.

"What is it?" Anderson asked when I just stood there.

"It might not mean anything," I hedged. "But for some reason I didn't want to go up the stairs. The feeling is gone now."

I heard a sigh that echoed how I felt. I wished my damn powers would provide blinking neon signs instead of subtle, ephemeral hunches.

"It means something," Anderson said, and I felt him changing direction and starting down the stairs.

When hunting monsters, even those in human form, the last thing I want to do is go exploring dark basements, but it looked like that was what I was going to have to do.

"I don't like this," I muttered.

"Just stay behind me," was Anderson's only reply.

During our search, we'd found two doors that opened on stairs leading down. Whether they led to two separate basements, or were two ways to the same basement, was yet to be determined. I didn't feel any strong preference for one stairway or another, so Anderson and I chose the one closest to us.

There's nothing quite like looking down pitch-black stairs to raise the hairs on the back of your neck, especially when you're stupid enough to be descending them into the darkness. We'd been making our way through the rest of the house with the aid of the predawn light that filtered through the various windows, but we would have no such help in the basement. I hated the idea of lighting a beacon to let anyone in visual range know we were coming, but we wouldn't have much luck finding Konstantin if we couldn't see our hands in front of our faces.

The constant pinging of my nerves was making me punchy,

and I almost laughed as I thought that Anderson couldn't see his hand in front of his face regardless. I swallowed the laugh and tugged my hand out of Anderson's grip. I was holding the gun in my right hand, and there was no way I was putting it away to get my cell phone out of my pocket. Anderson made a small sound of protest.

"Flashlight app," I hissed in explanation. I had my phone set to airplane mode so it wouldn't make any inconvenient sounds that might give us away, but I supposed if I was going to use it as a flashlight, that was a wasted effort.

I worried for a moment that Anderson would try to veto the flashlight, but he had to know fumbling around in the dark wasn't going to do us any good. With another sigh, he became fully visible again.

"Don't suppose there's any point in hiding anymore," he mumbled under his breath. "Stay behind me anyway."

It seemed to me like the person with the flashlight should lead the way, but I didn't think Anderson was going to let me take point. Mutely, I handed him my phone, and he took it without comment. We continued down the stairs.

The light from the phone wasn't exactly powerful, and the darkness of the basement was oppressive as all hell, even once we made it safely out of the stairwell. The stairs opened onto a somewhat puny gym, with a small collection of free weights and an ancient-looking treadmill. However, I smelled chlorine in the air, and sure enough, when we made it through the gym, the next door opened onto an impressive lap pool. The pool was big enough that my light couldn't illuminate the far end of it, but when Anderson and I made a circuit of the deck, we still saw no sign of Konstantin. We peeked behind a couple of closed doors that turned out to be changing rooms, and then we found yet another stairway, this one leading even farther down.

How many freaking floors did this mansion have?

The hairs on the back of my neck prickled yet again. This stairway was far narrower than the previous one, the steps nothing more than bare planks. We weren't going to be finding any fancy exercise equipment down there.

Anderson looked at me, and I shrugged. My instincts weren't talking to me, and I had no idea whether we should continue down these stairs or go back up to the ground floor and try the other stairway we'd seen up there. We hadn't found any evidence of it opening onto this first basement anywhere.

"We might as well check it out while we're here," Anderson whispered, though why he was bothering to whisper when the flashlight was giving us away, I don't know.

He went first down the stairs, and I followed reluctantly. It was so tight and claustrophobic, even with the flashlight, that I had a hard time forcing myself to take each step. The wooden steps seemed rickety, and they creaked, further removing any hope we might have of keeping the element of surprise. Not that I thought we had it in the first place.

I was about halfway down the stairs, and Anderson was about two-thirds of the way down, when suddenly, the pitch-black staircase was flooded with blinding white light, so bright I couldn't possibly keep my eyes open. I heard Anderson's cry of dismay, and heard what I presumed was my cell phone thunking to the floor. I tried to force my eyes open in search of something to shoot, but the light was overpowering after the heavy darkness.

A step creaked behind me, and a gunshot nearly shattered my eardrums. Anderson made a strangled sound, which I could barely hear through the sudden ringing in my ears. I felt the vibration under my feet as he fell. The light hurt, stabbing through my head like ice picks, and there was no way I could open my eyes. I turned, meaning to shoot blindly up the staircase behind me. I didn't know if my supernatural aim could work if I had no idea what my target was, but it was worth a try.

Whoever was behind me moved faster than I did, and something hard and heavy smashed into the side of my face. Pain short-circuited my brain, and I tried to take a step backward to steady myself. Not such a great idea on a staircase. My foot came down on empty air, and I plummeted downward. My reflexes tried to save me, but there was nothing to grab onto, and all I could do was drop the gun. The light dimmed, and I managed to squint my eyes open just a tiny bit.

Enough to see Cyrus, wearing wraparound sunglasses and holding a gun, standing on the stairs and watching me fall.

TWENTY-FIVE

I went down the last of the stairs in a painful and undignified tumble. My ears were still ringing from the gunshot in the enclosed space, and I felt more than I heard the ominous crack a fraction of a second before white-hot pain stabbed through my chest.

There's nothing that hurts quite so much as a broken rib, and if I'd had any air in my lungs I'd have screamed at the pain. The rib jolted again when I landed in a heap at the base of the stairs, my body piled atop Anderson's. The light was no longer blindingly bright, but it was as if I'd stared directly at the sun, the afterimage burned into my retinas. Cyrus was nothing more than a shadowy form descending the stairs toward me.

The pain got the better of me and I blacked out.

I don't think it was for very long. Only enough for Cyrus to reach the bottom of the stairs and crouch over me. He tucked his gun into a holster on his belt, then grabbed mine from where it had landed on the basement floor. He was smart enough to unload it before sticking it in his pocket, though in the state I was in, I wasn't wrestling it away from him anytime soon. My rib screamed with every breath I took, my exposed skin seemed to have gotten a serious sunburn from the bright light, and my face throbbed where Cyrus had hit me. I probably had a bunch of other injuries, too, but my rib and face hurt the worst. My head was a little woozy, and it took me a heartbeat or two to realize I was no longer lying atop Anderson's body.

"I'm sorry about this, Nikki," Cyrus said, flashing me a sad and sympathetic smile. He took off the wraparound glasses and stuck them into his shirt pocket. I guess the light had been so bright that even the descendant of a sun god needed protection from it.

Before I could tell him what to do with his apology—before, in fact, I was conscious and coherent enough to do or say much of anything—he had turned me over onto my stomach. My rib didn't appreciate the movement, and I couldn't suppress a scream of pain, even though the scream itself hurt just as much.

"Sorry," Cyrus said again as he hauled my arms around behind my back and fastened what felt suspiciously like handcuffs around my wrists.

I was in no position to object to his rough treatment, and the breath-stealing pain kept me from retorting. Once my hands were bound, Cyrus sat on my legs, and I felt him pulling up the cuffs of my pants. The clinking sound of metal warned me what he was about to do, but with my hands behind my back and his weight holding me down, there was nothing I could do to stop him from shackling my ankles together.

I blinked away tears of pain and tried to breathe. When Cyrus had turned me over, I'd come to rest with my head facing the base of the stairs, giving me a disturbing view of a large pool of blood. I presumed it was Anderson's, since as far as I knew, I wasn't injured enough to leak that much. It was enough blood that I knew Anderson hadn't moved himself out from under me, and that meant Cyrus wasn't alone.

Steeling myself against yet another blast of pain, I turned my head so that I was facing the main part of the room.

Actually, calling it a "room" was a bit of an exaggeration. It was really just an unfinished, unadorned basement. The floor was ugly gray concrete, and the walls were cheap pegboard, like you might see in some handyman's garage, only there were no tools on any of the pegs.

In the center of the floor was an ominous black hole, about the size of a manhole, though I didn't think there were too many people who had manholes in their basements, and I saw no sign of a cover anywhere. Beside the hole, there was a large collection of what looked like steel girders, only they'd been cut up into little sections, maybe six or eight inches long and piled about three feet high. And beside those girders, looming over Anderson's limp body, was Konstantin.

Having finished securing my legs, Cyrus grabbed me under my arms and pulled me into a seated position, dragging me a couple feet so my back could rest against the wall. I could tell he wasn't actively trying to hurt me, but when you've got a broken rib, *everything* hurts. He winced in what looked like sympathy. Some of my hair was sticking to the tears on my cheeks, and Cyrus reached out to brush it away and tuck it behind my ear. I jerked away from his touch, practically knocking myself out as my head reminded me I'd been pistol-whipped about two minutes ago.

Cyrus pulled his hand away, and I saw that his fingers were wet with blood, rather than tears. "I didn't want the wound to heal around your hair," he said.

How considerate of him.

"Guess everything you told me on the phone this morning was a lie, huh?" I asked. I'd thought after seeing him kill Emma with such cool dispassion that I'd allowed myself to see Cyrus as he truly was, that I'd gotten over thinking he wasn't really such a bad guy. But the stab of betrayal as my head cleared enough for me to figure out what was happening said I hadn't quite gotten there yet.

"'Fraid so," he said, sitting back on his haunches.

"Why?" I shook my head, hardly able to believe how wrong

we'd all been about him, thinking him a lesser evil than Konstantin.

Cyrus glanced over his shoulder briefly, taking in the sight of his father looming over Anderson. When he turned back to me, there was an expression of grim determination in his eyes.

"Because when Anderson's gone, Blake will have no choice but to rejoin the Olympians."

My jaw dropped open. I hadn't even come close to seeing that one coming.

"How I managed to raise a son with a sentimental streak, I'll never know," Konstantin said, and there was no missing the disdain in his voice.

"You don't have to understand," Cyrus said tightly without looking at his father. "You just have to stick to the deal."

My stomach felt like it was doing the cancan, and I wasn't sure whether it was because I was sickened by what Cyrus was doing, or if he'd actually given me a concussion when he'd hit me. Maybe both.

My head wasn't as clear as I would have liked, and my sense of time was definitely out of whack, but I was pretty sure it had been at least a couple of minutes since Anderson had been shot. If I could keep father and son talking long enough for him to come back to life . . .

"I thought you were enjoying your Blake substitute," I said, trying to sneer. I think it came out more like a grimace of pain, but Cyrus was appropriately needled anyway.

"Why settle for a substitute when I can have the real thing? Blake never belonged with you people anyway. He really wants to be one of the good guys, but it just doesn't suit him."

"And you think taking out Anderson and letting your daddy kill the rest of us is going to send Blake running into your arms?" It was a little easier to muster a real sneer this time. I hadn't thought much of Blake when I'd first met him, and I still didn't think a whole lot of him dating my sister. But I *did* think he was basically a good guy, with a good heart. It was hard to imagine what he'd ever seen in Cyrus—at least, it was hard for me to imagine it now, when Cyrus was flaunting his true nature—but I didn't for a moment believe Blake would forgive and forget.

Cyrus shrugged. "If his choices are run into my arms or die, he'll run into my arms." One corner of his mouth tipped up in a fond smile. "He's a survivor." The smile faded quickly, and Cyrus's voice dropped to a whisper. "I'll save as many of your people as I can, Nikki. I'm not doing this because I want anyone to get hurt."

Words couldn't describe how much he disgusted me in that moment. I felt a chill of fear as I thought about what would happen to the rest of Anderson's *Liberi* if Anderson were no longer around to protect them. Leo, Maggie, and Blake might be able to become Olympians, if they could stomach it. They were all descended from Greek gods, which was the primary membership requirement for the Olympians. But Jack, and Logan, and Jamaal . . .

And let's not even talk about what would happen to *me*. I might not be Olympian material despite my ancestry, but I was a rare and useful tool, and I held no illusions that there would be a quick and easy death in my future.

But of course, nothing was going to happen to Anderson. He was a freaking god, and he was going to come back to life any second now. Once he did—

Another gunshot rang out. Cyrus flinched and ducked, his hands going up to his ears. He quickly lowered them again and glared over his shoulder at Konstantin.

"Some warning would be nice next time," he shouted. At least, I was pretty sure he was shouting, because otherwise I wouldn't have been able to hear him over the renewed ringing in my ears. If I were an ordinary mortal, I'd be seriously worried about permanent hearing damage.

Of course, the ringing ears weren't the worst of my problems. Konstantin had just shot Anderson a second time, which meant any healing progress was back to square one. Killing Anderson every few minutes was a surefire way to keep him out of the picture, though obviously Konstantin had something else in mind. The yawning hole in the floor suggested that some kind of burial was forthcoming. Anderson had dismissed potential burial as a threat—maybe he could move through the earth as easily as he could move through walls—but I wasn't exactly eager to put it to the test.

"If you don't like it, hurry up and finish your touching good-bye before I have to do it again," Konstantin replied.

"It's not really a good-bye," Cyrus hastened to reassure me. "You don't have to take my word for it, even. You know you're too valuable to kill."

"Actually, that doesn't make me feel any better," I said between clenched teeth.

"If you can find it in yourself to cooperate, things will go much easier for you."

My rib was still hurting like hell, but I managed to suck in a deep breath of indignation anyway. "You advising me to lie back and think of England?" I growled at him.

He wouldn't meet my eyes. "It's the best advice I can give under the circumstances."

"As if I would ever take advice from *you,*" I replied in disgust, hating myself for letting his charming smile lull me for even a moment. "You're nothing but a liar and a fraud. I should never have believed a single word that came out of your mouth."

"I can't argue that I'm not a liar," Cyrus admitted. "But for what it's worth, I was telling you the truth most of the time. I didn't know my father was behind any of this until last night."

Konstantin interrupted with an exaggerated snort. "Now tell her if it would have made a difference if you had."

"It might!" Cyrus snapped over his shoulder, and his father laughed at him.

"As long as I promised to give you Blake, you'd have done whatever I told you to do."

Cyrus's face flushed with anger. I didn't know why he was getting so pissed off. Did he really think it made a difference whether he'd been lying from the beginning or just since his phone call this morning? "Then why *didn't* you tell me?" Cyrus countered.

"Because I would have had to watch you wring your hands and listen to you whine about it." Konstantin gave Anderson a nudge with his foot, as if to reassure himself that he was still dead. Then he turned to me. "My dear son has pretensions of moral superiority. He doesn't mind making an omelet, as long as he doesn't have to break the eggs himself."

The anger that flared in Cyrus's eyes made me hope he and Konstantin were going to get into a fight. I didn't know exactly how I was going to take advantage of that fight, but I was sure I would find a way to do *something* useful while they weren't looking.

Unfortunately, they weren't stupid enough to give me the opportunity.

Cyrus stood up straight, wiping the remainder of my blood off his hand and onto his pants. "I don't think it's a character flaw that I don't enjoy hurting people."

Cyrus had his back to Konstantin and couldn't see his father rolling his eyes. For once, Konstantin and I were in agreement about something. It might make Cyrus more comfortable if someone else did the dirty work for him, but the fact that he didn't enjoy it and would rather not see it didn't make him a better person. Nor did the fact that he seemed to feel at least a little bad about it.

"You're worse than *he* is," I said to Cyrus. "At least he's not a hypocrite!"

Cyrus hung his head in what looked suspiciously like shame. The look on his face said he actually did feel more than a little bad about what he was doing, and I suspected he was fully aware of the hypocrisy of his own position. The question was, was there some way I could take advantage of his vulnerabilities and turn him against his father? Because I didn't care *what* Anderson had told me about how Konstantin couldn't do anything to him. Konstantin had a plan, and a reason to believe it would work. Anderson might be a god, but that didn't mean he was never wrong, and this would be the world's worst time to prove it.

"Don't do this," I begged. "Blake still cares about you. I can hear it in his voice when he talks about you. You can work things out with him if you want to. But not if you kill all the other people he cares about. You do that, and he'll hate you, and you'll never have what you really want."

My impassioned plea missed its mark.

"He'll hate me at first," Cyrus conceded. "But you know what they say about time healing all wounds. I'm willing to wait." A tiny smile played along his lips. "And I think I'll enjoy the challenge of trying to seduce him and win him back."

Cyrus stepped over my outstretched legs, carefully avoiding the pool of Anderson's blood as he put his foot on the first step. I realized that meant he wasn't going to stick around and watch whatever Konstantin was planning to do to Anderson and me. I also realized that meant whatever unpleasantness was in store for us would likely start as soon as he left the basement.

I did *not* want him to leave the basement.

"Cyrus! Wait!"

I had no arguments left to make, no hope that Cyrus was going to change his mind. In fact, I had only two hopes left: that I could keep delaying things until Konstantin got careless and didn't shoot fast enough to keep Anderson dead; or that Anderson was right and there truly was nothing Konstantin could do to him in the long run. Neither one felt like a spectacularly strong possibility to pin my hopes on, but Cyrus shattered hope number one when he ignored me and started up the stairs.

"I'm sorry, Nikki," he said again, shaking his head.

I let out an incoherent cry of rage and frustration—and not

a little fear—as the stairwell swallowed Cyrus. Moments later, I heard the door at the head of the stairs open and close.

And it was time to find out exactly what Konstantin had planned.

TWENTY-SIX

Konstantin stared at the ceiling. Possibly, he was listening to Cyrus's retreating footsteps, but all I could hear was the rushing of my blood in my ears. My rib still sent daggers of pain through my body with every breath, but I no longer felt blood trickling down the side of my face. All in all, I was in a lot better shape than Anderson was.

To make sure that remained the case, Konstantin shot Anderson yet again.

Anderson's head was a bloody mess. He was never going to recover unless I could find a way to stop Konstantin from shooting him every couple of minutes. My stomach lurched unhappily. I told myself I had a concussion, because a tough chick like me had no business vomiting at the sight of blood. Never mind that I'd once tossed my cookies looking at crime-scene photos.

"Did you tell Cyrus Anderson's big secret?" I asked. Not that I actually cared. I was just looking for an opening, some way to distract Konstantin long enough to let Anderson heal.

For one unguarded moment, I saw shock on Konstantin's face. He hadn't realized I knew that Anderson was a god. He hid his emotions quickly, but I cursed myself for opening my big mouth. Konstantin didn't want anyone to know Anderson was a god, because he didn't want anyone getting the idea that he himself wasn't the most powerful being in the universe. And I might have just signed my own death warrant by admitting what I knew.

The scary thing was, I would probably be way, way better off if Konstantin killed me than if he kept me alive.

"I didn't see any reason to burden him with that knowledge," Konstantin said, giving me a once-over that made my skin crawl. I couldn't have looked that appealing with my face all bloody and my hair scraggling out of its braid. My flannel shirt was blandly shapeless and buttoned to the top for warmth. And yet Konstantin's leer told me he liked the way I looked just fine.

Maybe he just liked how a woman looked in chains.

It was hard not to squirm when Konstantin looked at me like that. I knew he was a rapist, and I hoped like hell that Anderson was going to come back to life sooner rather than later, before Konstantin decided he was in the mood to play.

"So what's your big plan, anyway?" I asked as nonchalantly as I could. "Are you going to stand there and shoot Anderson in the head every couple of minutes for the rest of eternity? Because personally, I think that would get old after a while."

I was trying to get under Konstantin's skin, but his smile said he was finding me more entertaining than annoying. On another man, the smile would have looked genuine and disarming. Konstantin wasn't traditionally handsome, but he knew how to make the most of what he had. His neat black beard disguised what I suspected was a weak chin, and I'd never seen him wearing anything other than designer suits. Today was no exception, though the suit was well on its way toward being ruined. Anderson's blood spotted his pants legs and the bottom of his jacket.

"Actually, I've quite enjoyed it," Konstantin said, his smile morphing into a phony frown. "Though I'd enjoy it more if he were alive to feel it."

I shuddered. Cyrus might not enjoy hurting people, but Konstantin sure did. I wished Anderson had listened to me, though truthfully, I'm not sure what kind of plan we could have made to avoid this. We couldn't have gotten to Konstantin without descending the stairs into the basement, and once we were in the stairway, we were sitting ducks.

Konstantin's smile returned, and there was now an unpleasant gleam in his eyes to go with it. "But no matter. I'm sure I can find other ways to entertain myself once I've removed this thorn from my side."

He tucked the gun into the waist of his pants. I hoped it would go off and blow his balls to smithereens. The damage would heal, but I suspected the pain would distract him for a good long while.

Unfortunately, my hopes were in vain. Konstantin bent down and grabbed Anderson's arm, dragging him closer to the hole in the floor. The man might have looked like a fop in a fancy suit, but he was clearly carrying some muscle underneath, because dragging Anderson's lifeless body didn't even make him break a sweat.

My mouth went dry, and my heart rate jumped to red alert. I was aware of Konstantin watching me, savoring my reaction. I tried my best to keep my face neutral, but I don't think I succeeded. I bit my lip when Anderson's head slid over the edge of the hole, flopping limply into the darkness.

Konstantin kept dragging on Anderson's arm, until Anderson's shoulders crossed the edge and his upper body tilted precariously.

One more tug, and Konstantin let go of Anderson's arm, tossing it into the mouth of the hole. The weight of his arm was enough to tip the scales, and Anderson started slipping into the hole, headfirst. I wanted to howl in rage, but I somehow managed to stifle the sound. Still, a little whimper worked its way out of my mouth as Anderson fell. When he hit the bottom of the hole, there was a metallic clang. I didn't know what it meant.

"Anderson can walk through walls," I said, my voice shaking. "He can get out of there."

If nothing else, he'd be able to brace himself against the

sides of the hole and inch his way up. But I knew there was more to Konstantin's plan than just dumping Anderson in a hole.

Konstantin leaned over the hole and fired three quick shots. It would be nice if that were the last of his bullets, but I didn't think he was careless enough to let that happen.

"It's very hard to keep death-god descendants contained," Konstantin agreed. "I found that out the hard way, as you know. I imagine it's even harder with an actual god." He grabbed one of the sections of girder stacked beside the hole, dropping it down. "I don't know if he has some kind of animal he can conjure to dig him out if I bury him." This time, he used both hands and threw two sections down at once. "But I'm not about to take chances."

"What are you going to do?" I didn't know how tossing pieces of steel down into the hole was going to help keep Anderson trapped, but I had a sick feeling I would soon find out.

"After my mistake with Justin, I've decided a little overkill is in order." He got impatient with throwing the steel down one piece at a time, positioning himself behind a stack of pieces and giving them a mighty shove.

I winced, even knowing that Anderson was currently dead down there and couldn't feel all those heavy pieces of metal raining down upon his vulnerable flesh.

Konstantin looked over the edge of the hole and nodded in satisfaction. "That ought to be enough," he said, more to himself than to me.

He held out both his hands toward the hole. "I reinforced the hole with steel pipe, and put a good-sized layer of girders on the bottom."

A blast of heat sucked all the moisture from my eyes and mouth. I couldn't see very well from where I was sitting, but my skin felt seared and raw from the heat, and the edges of the hole began to glow, first red, then white.

The steel was melting.

I screamed out a protest as the sides of the hole began to melt and run, flowing downward into the hole. I thought of all those pieces of metal Konstantin had tossed down there, melting around Anderson's body, burning the flesh from his bones.

Konstantin smiled and made a big show of dusting off his hands. "Even a god will take some time to recover from the damage all that molten metal will do. And when he does, the steel will have cooled around him. He'll be trapped like a bug in amber."

I was crying again, dammit. I tried to hold on to the hope that Anderson was as indestructible as he'd thought he was. "B-but, he can walk through walls. He can get out of the metal."

Konstantin took one last, satisfied glance at the hole, then sauntered toward me. I wanted to scoot away from him, but there was nowhere I could go. The best I could do was draw my bound legs up toward my chest as he squatted beside me with that smug, sadistic smile.

"Let me explain some basic rules of physics to you," he said. "A human body cannot pass through a solid object. Death-god descendants pass through walls by making themselves incorporeal, but they can't actually move themselves when they're incorporeal. Imagine them like astronauts, floating through the vacuum of space. If you give them a push, then the momentum will keep them going indefinitely. But if you could drop them into the vacuum in complete stillness, then they'd have no momentum to move them, and nothing to push against to give them momentum. A death-god descendant takes a step toward whatever barrier is in his way, giving himself momentum. Only then can he go incorporeal and keep moving.

"Anderson will awaken completely immobilized by his metal casing. He can go incorporeal all he wants, but with no momentum, all he can do is flail around." Konstantin frowned dramatically. "It might have been enough just to immobilize him by burial. After all, Kerner could go incorporeal, but he couldn't get out of his grave until his jackals dug him out. But, as I said, overkill seems like a good idea."

Konstantin sat back on his heels with a happy sigh as I tried to absorb the horror of what he'd just told me. I really wanted to find a flaw in his theory, or at least to believe he was lying. But no, he was way too happy and self-satisfied. He was sure Anderson wasn't getting out of that hole. Ever. And I was beginning to fear he might be right.

TWENTY-SEVEN

I was deathly afraid of whatever Konstantin was going to do next. Even if there was some miraculous way Anderson could escape when encased in solid metal, I was sure it would take a while. Hell, it would probably take a while before he could possibly come back to life. I had no idea how long it would take that molten metal to cool, but I was sure its temperature would be lethal for quite some time.

Meanwhile, I was chained hand and foot and trapped with a man who thought rape and torture were fun. The only other living person who knew where I was was Cyrus, and he'd made it abundantly clear that he had no intention of saving me.

In short, it was looking spectacularly bad for the home team, and I was fighting the very reasonable urge to panic. I tried to wriggle my hands out of the cuffs, willing to take off as many layers of skin as necessary to escape them, but I didn't think I was getting out of them without removing a few pesky bones from my hand.

Konstantin licked his lips, and I couldn't tell if it was an unconscious gesture, or if he was trying to feed my panic. He smiled over his shoulder at the hole in the floor, the contents of which were still emitting a faint red glow.

"I'm sure that will hold him," he said, turning back to me, "but a little more overkill can't hurt."

I tried to flinch away as he reached for me. All I managed to do was tip myself over. Konstantin grabbed me by the waist, then flung me over his shoulder in a fireman's carry. I wished I could struggle more effectively, but it's hard to do much of anything when your hands are cuffed behind your back and your ankles are shackled.

"Patience, Nikki dear," Konstantin said as he started up the narrow stairs. "I'll give you plenty of things to get excited about later, but being carried up the stairs isn't one of them. You might want to save your energy."

Raw terror coursed through my veins with every beat of my heart. There was nothing I could do to get his hands off me. The sense of helplessness and dread was crushing, but I was never, ever going to give up fighting. I struggled and squirmed, not caring that getting free of Konstantin at this moment meant another painful tumble down the stairs, but I'm a small woman, and Konstantin was way too strong for me.

Konstantin paused when we reached the pool deck.

"I wonder how long it would take you to bend to my will if I dropped you in the pool for a while. It certainly helped put our dear, departed Emma in a more accommodating state of mind."

I struggled even harder as Konstantin walked to the edge of the pool. I didn't want to die ever again, and from everything I'd heard, drowning is a very unpleasant way to go. A life that alternated between drowning and being suspended in the airless dark of death wasn't worth living. Maybe I should have been hoping he followed through with the threat, because at least while he was drowning me, he wouldn't be raping me, but I wanted to live. Where there's life, there's hope, right?

Konstantin sighed in mock regret. "Such a shame the pool is too shallow. Of course, there is that lovely pond out back. As you might have noticed, I wouldn't have any trouble melting all that inconvenient ice."

Oh, good, I wasn't going to be drowning in the next five seconds. One could argue that things were looking up.

Konstantin continued on past the pool, carrying me up to the ground floor and then wending his way through the house to the back door. I remembered his previous comments about overkill and wondered what the hell he was up to. If he was planning some additional safeguard to reassure himself that Anderson was trapped, then why was he leaving the house?

I hadn't realized my clothes were damp with sweat until we made it outside and a blast of wind plastered them tightly against my skin. I started shivering almost immediately. Konstantin wasn't wearing a coat, but the cold didn't seem to bother him. Maybe he could generate his own heat using his powers. Or maybe his excitement over whatever torture he had in mind was enough to keep him warm.

I had mostly stopped struggling. I was just too exhausted to keep it up, and while I was determined to fight to the bitter end, I had decided to conserve my energy for that mythical moment where fighting might actually do some good.

Slung over Konstantin's shoulder as I was, I couldn't see where we were going, but then I didn't *need* to see. We were going to the pond, of course. Whether he truly meant to toss me in there or was just trying to push my fear to the max, I didn't know.

I didn't have a properly scaled map of the property in my head, but when Konstantin came to a stop, I knew we weren't anywhere near far enough away from the house to have reached the pond yet. Konstantin let go of me and ducked his shoulder so I would roll helplessly off. I hit the snow with a cry of pain as my broken rib reminded me it hadn't finished healing yet.

"You might want to watch this," Konstantin said, reaching down and dragging me into a sitting position by the collar of my shirt.

I sat panting and shivering in the snow, my eyes squeezed half-shut as I waited out the pain. Konstantin stood slightly in front of me and held out his hands like he had in the basement. Ignoring the biting cold, I let my fingers sift through whatever snow they could reach, hoping to find something I could use as a weapon. There was no way I could throw anything with my hands bound behind me, but I might be able to use my feet.

It was a long shot, no doubt about it. But a long shot was better than no shot, so I kept searching.

Once again, I felt a blast of heat, and something like an invisible fireball shot from Konstantin's hands toward the house. I could track its progress as it evaporated the snow in its path. It expanded as it traveled, growing wider until when it hit the house it was almost wide enough to engulf it.

The moment Konstantin's fireball hit the house, it went up in flames, the walls practically melting away. The fire spread instantly, racing around the walls and over the roof. Windows shattered, and the flames crawled in like living things, all blue and white with heat. I'd been shivering and cold a moment ago, but now I felt like I was sitting in an oven.

In a matter of seconds, the entire house was ablaze, the flames roaring with the fury of a forest fire. Konstantin basked in the glow of the fire for a moment, then frowned.

"Hmm," he said. "Perhaps we're still standing a little too close."

It was almost unbearably hot, and I was more than happy to put some more distance between myself and the fire. I'd have liked it a lot better if Konstantin hadn't moved me by grabbing hold of my braid and dragging me through the melting snow. Despite the pain, I kept trying to sift through the snow with my fingers in search of a weapon. Unfortunately, the snow was covering a lawn, and there aren't a whole lot of useful throwing weapons lying about on your average lawn.

Konstantin had dragged me all of about five feet when there was a deafening, earthshaking *boom*. He let go of my hair and dropped to the ground as the flaming house collapsed, the walls falling in upon themselves. Out of the corner of my eye, I saw

Konstantin covering his head, and I wished I could do the same. There was another blast, even louder than the first, and a huge cloud of smoke and dirt and debris fountained into the air.

I had no way to protect myself as the debris came raining down. The best I could do was curl into the smallest ball possible and hope nothing too big and lethal landed on me. Flaming pieces of house dropped to the ground all around me. A couple of the missiles hit me, including one that nearly lit my pants leg on fire, but I rolled enough for the wet snow to snuff it out.

When the debris rain had lessened enough for me to risk it, I sat up and looked all around me.

The house was completely gone, nothing but a burned-out, debris-filled, smoldering crater where it had once sat. Konstantin had seemed to know the explosion was coming, and I figured that meant he had set up explosives so that the house would fall down directly over the basement where he'd stashed Anderson. Now I saw what he meant by overkill, though to tell you the truth, if being encased in metal didn't keep Anderson contained, I doubted the weight of an entire mansion crumbling on top of him would, either. Still, it made for quite the spectacular show.

I hoped that a stray piece of debris had crushed Konstantin like the bug he was, but he'd actually gotten us pretty close to the edge of the debris field before the charges went off. There were bits and pieces lying on the still-melting snow around us, but most of the heavy stuff had come down closer to the house, and except for his seriously destroyed designer suit, Konstantin was unharmed. His eyes were practically glowing with pleasure as he eyed the destruction.

For the moment, his attention was not focused on me, and I knew I had to take advantage of his distraction in any way I could. The nice, grassy back lawn had been a poor candidate for providing a projectile weapon, but thanks to Konstantin's overkill, there was now a lot of potentially handy debris lying about.

I searched the ground around me. I needed something heavy enough to do some damage, yet small and light enough that I could either lift it with my bound feet, or at least slip my feet under it so I could give it a kick. And it also needed to be close enough that I could get to it before Konstantin noticed I was getting ready to try something.

Moments ago, I'd been glad we were out of the worst of the debris field, but now I wished I had more larger chunks around me. Most of it was too small to do any significant damage. However, I did spot a broken piece of brick not too far away. A normal person wouldn't have been able to do any damage with that piece of brick unless they could really wind up and throw it like a baseball, but I thought it possible that with my aim, I might be able to do it.

Keeping an eye on Konstantin, I wriggled and squirmed my way toward the brick, angling my body so my feet would get there first. Despite the fact that my socks were soaking wet from melted snow and my feet beneath them felt frostbitten in places and burned in others, I was glad I'd taken off my boots while in the house, because I was definitely more agile without them.

I managed to wriggle my toes under the piece of brick, then positioned myself so I could get the best momentum behind my kick/throw. Konstantin was still looking at the crater. The brick felt alarmingly light under my feet, and I knew it was all going to come down to perfect placement. I had to hit Konstantin in just the right spot to disable him, and in my experience, the eye is just about anyone's most vulnerable spot. Lots of soft tissue to damage, some delicate bones that can shatter, and let's face it, there's a certain terror factor to feeling your eye squish.

I needed him facing me, and closer.

"Are you posing for a picture or something?" I jeered, and he finally managed to drag his attention away from the ex-house.

"I was observing a moment of silence for Anderson," he replied with heavy sarcasm, and though he was looking at me, I could tell his attention was still divided. Which was good, because if he realized I had a weapon within my reach (sort of), he might decide to shoot me before coming any closer.

"But if you're impatient to find out what I have planned for you, I'll be happy to hurry things along."

He was smiling his smug smile, jovial, arrogant, secure in his victory. Just the way I wanted him. He took a whopping two steps in my direction before he noticed the positioning of my feet. His eyes widened, and as he stepped backward, he reached for the gun still sticking out of his pants.

I wanted him closer, but it was now or never.

Putting every bit of strength I could muster into it, I scooped up the piece of brick, using the backs of my feet rather like a lacrosse stick, and kicked my bound legs as hard as I could toward Konstantin's face.

I had taken Jamaal's eye out once with a well-aimed toss of a stiletto-heeled shoe, but I wasn't quite as lucky this time. The brick hit Konstantin's eye, and he fell to the ground with a gratifying scream of pain, but though he clutched the socket, there was no sign of blood leaking through his fingers.

I hadn't taken out his eye, but for a few precious moments, he was going to be in too much pain to retaliate. I couldn't let him have time to recover.

I spotted another piece of brick, even smaller than the first, positioned between me and Konstantin. I wriggled toward it and kicked it at Konstantin's head. He was protecting his wounded eye with his hand, but his other eye made a good target.

The second piece of brick didn't hurt him as much. The hand that wasn't clutching his wounded eye pulled his gun from his belt, and I had to duck as he fired a couple of blind shots in my direction. I suspected he'd get me with a lucky shot before I was able to pitch enough debris at him to incapacitate him, so I needed another plan.

I hunched in on myself, making myself as small a target as possible, then tried to contort myself enough to get my cuffed hands down below my butt. I'd tried this maneuver when I'd been duct taped in the trunk of the car and hadn't been able to manage it, but I had a lot more freedom of movement out here in the open. I practically tore both arms out of their sockets to do it, but I managed to get first my butt, then my legs, through the circle of my arms so my hands were in front of me. Still cuffed together, but it was an improvement.

Konstantin fired off another shot, and it splashed up muddy snow way too close to my head for comfort. He tried to fire again, but he was out of ammo.

"Probably shouldn't have wasted so many bullets on Anderson," I taunted, because I couldn't resist.

Konstantin dropped his hand from his eye, and though it was closed and swollen and obviously painful, he was going to be back to full capacity way sooner than I would like.

"I have more," he growled at me, reaching into his pants pocket.

Of course he did.

Bracing myself with my hands, I pushed to my feet. I could move a little by shuffling, but by the time I got anywhere, Konstantin would be reloaded. He might not be able to aim as well as he'd like with one eye swollen shut, but I doubted he'd have any trouble hitting me with a full clip at his disposal. So instead of taking little shuffle-steps, I bunny-hopped.

I probably looked pretty ridiculous, but aesthetics were the last thing on my mind. I hopped toward another piece of debris, then bent to retrieve it and hurl it at Konstantin's hands. I didn't even know what I had thrown. It wasn't big or heavy enough to do damage, but it did cause him to drop his clip in the snow. I thought that was an improvement, until he abandoned the gun and clip and surged to his feet.

Even if I hadn't been bound hand and foot, Konstantin didn't need a gun to hurt me. He was a big, strong guy, and I bet he had plenty of experience wrestling women into submission.

I hopped away from him as fast as I could, my eyes frantically scanning the grass and snow for the perfect weapon.

I saw it about six feet away, a big chunk of concrete that might have come from the foundation. I wasn't going to be able to hop that distance before Konstantin tackled me, so I threw myself forward in a headfirst slide, my hands outstretched.

I might have put a little more oomph into that slide than was strictly necessary. I jammed my fingers against the concrete, breaking a few nails and possibly dislocating my middle finger. I swallowed the pain and wrapped my hands around the concrete, rolling into a sitting position so I could get some momentum on the throw.

At the last moment, Konstantin, who was almost on top of me, seemed to realize he had made a mistake. He tried to skid to a stop, holding his hands out in front of him. I think he was trying to summon another blast of heat, but it was too late.

I put my whole body into the awkward, two-handed, side-arm throw, and the chunk of concrete hit Konstantin right between the eyes.

He staggered and went down to his knees, blood streaming from his nose and from a large cut on his forehead. My throw had been too awkward, and he'd been too close for me to get enough momentum to knock him out. However, it had obviously made him woozy.

He flailed at me as I hopped over toward the chunk of concrete, but I think he was seeing double or triple, because he didn't come close to hitting me. I raised the concrete over my head, and this time I had a nice downward angle for my throw.

The concrete caved in the back of Konstantin's head, and he went down for the count.

TWENTY-EIGHT

I gave myself all of about three minutes to bask in my victory and enjoy the relief that flooded my system. Konstantin wasn't going to get his chance to rape and torture me, and though I was hurting in any number of places, the damage I'd sustained was all superficial enough that it would heal completely within an hour or two. Considering how grim my situation had been when Konstantin had carried me out here, it was quite a gratifying turnaround.

It didn't take long, however, for the logistics of my current situation to sink in.

Konstantin was dead, sure. But I was neither a mortal Descendant nor a death god, so he wasn't going to stay that way. I was still bound hand and foot. My phone was somewhere in the rubble beneath the house. We'd driven here in Anderson's car, and the keys were probably somewhere down there with my phone. Not that I liked my chances of making it to the car before Konstantin came back to life and tracked me down. Hopping wasn't the most efficient means of travel, and my legs were already feeling the burn. It didn't help that my supernatural healing ability sapped so much of my energy. It would probably take me hours, and plenty of rest stops, to get to the damn car, even if I had the keys. And let's not even talk about how I would be able to drive!

I was squeamish enough that I'd have preferred not to look at Konstantin's body. There was a lot of blood, and an obvious concave spot on his skull. However, unless I planned to stand here indefinitely in the freezing cold and conk him on the head every time he started to come back to life, I was going to have to get out of the handcuffs and shackles.

Praying under my breath that he would have the keys on

him, I dropped to my knees beside him and started gingerly exploring his pockets. I kept my eyes narrowly focused on his body, not letting them stray to his ruined head, but my stomach was queasy anyway.

The good news was I didn't hurl. The bad news was, there were no handcuff keys on him. In another case of good news/ bad news, he had a cell phone, but either he'd broken it during our struggle or its charge was dead. I had no way to get out of the handcuffs and shackles, and no way to call for help. It was possible one of the neighbors had heard the blast and called the cops, but I didn't think that would be a good thing. I did *not* want to try to explain the current situation to cops, and if Konstantin came back to life while there were witnesses . . .

I scanned the sky, trying to judge how likely it was that I had to start figuring out a cover story. The blast had been incredibly loud from close range, but in this neighborhood, there were acres of land between houses. I could imagine someone nearby being roused from their bed by the blast. They might even go look out their window in case they could see what had caused it. However, you couldn't see Alexis's ex-house without actually trespassing on the grounds. The fire had burned so fast and fierce that it had burned itself out already, but there was still plenty of smoke rising from the smoldering wreckage. The darkness wouldn't hide the smoke for long, which meant I had until dawn to get myself and Konstantin's body out of here.

I was frankly at a loss for what to do. With a lot of work, I *might* be able to drag Konstantin's body past the tree line, where he was less likely to be found right away. What I really needed was a *Liberi* extraction team to come get me. We would then have to find someplace secure where we could bury Konstantin's body. I still didn't like the idea, no matter how evil Konstantin was, but until we could get Anderson out from under all the rubble and saw through his metal casing, we didn't have anyone who was capable of making Konstantin's death permanent.

I now had something new to add to my list of things I didn't want to think about: how to get Anderson out. We would need a freaking excavation to get down to where he was, and somehow I didn't think it would be so easy to arrange an excavation on land that didn't belong to us.

I'd spent about fifteen minutes dithering, trying to come up with a plan that didn't suck, to no avail. Maybe it was my imagination, but when I forced myself to look, I thought the depression in Konstantin's skull was shallower than it had been.

Hitting a dead man in the head with a hunk of concrete shouldn't bother me so much. It wasn't like he could *feel* it. But it was still remarkably hard to get myself to do it. I'm just not the violent type. However, I couldn't risk him coming back to life.

Closing my eyes and turning my face away, I brought the concrete down on Konstantin's head. The nasty crunching sound it made when it hit his skull made my stomach turn over, and it took everything I had not to throw up. I was just not cut out for this sort of thing.

I put down the hunk of concrete, then lowered my face into my hands, momentarily overwhelmed. It didn't help that the heat from the fire had dissipated. I was shivering, and I couldn't feel my feet. It was bitterly cold out, and ice was forming on the surface of the puddles the melting snow had formed. Frostbite couldn't kill me, but it could make getting myself out of this mess even harder.

I was still hanging my head, my mind cycling through each of the possible things I could do next and hitting the same brick walls, when the sound of a throat clearing behind me made me scream and jump to my feet. The screaming part of that equation worked just fine. Jumping to my feet, not so much. It's amazingly hard to stand up when you can't feel your feet, especially when your ankles are shackled together.

I landed in a heap in the snow.

"I'm sorry," Anderson said. "I didn't think there was any way I could make my presence known without scaring you."

My jaw gaped open, and I turned to look at the smoldering ruins of the house. Then I turned to look at Anderson. My gaze dropped to his feet when I realized he was stark naked. He was standing in a pristine patch of snow about ten feet away from me, past the debris field and past where the heat from the fire had melted the snow. Which made the lack of footprints anywhere around him noticeable even while my mind was trying to encompass the idea that he was alive and free.

"H-how . . ." I gestured at the ruins and shook my head, unable to form a coherent question.

"I'm not sure exactly what happened," he said. He had to be freezing standing there in the snow in the nude, but there was no hint of shivering in his voice. "I take it I was inside when the house came down?"

Of course he wouldn't know what had happened. He'd been dead for most of it. I could have given him a blow-by-blow recap of what he'd missed. But only if my brain had actually been working.

"M-molten metal," I stammered incoherently. "You were encased in molten metal and h-he brought the house down on t-top of you." The fact that I was well on my way to turning into a human Popsicle wasn't making my dialog any wittier or easier to understand.

I saw him nod out of the corner of my eye. He was completely unself-conscious about his nudity, but I couldn't say the same of myself.

"I can see why he'd have thought that might work."

I sucked in a deep breath, hoping it would help steady me. Instead, I merely froze my lungs a little more. "H-he said you wouldn't be able to move."

"He was right about that, at least." There was a hint of smugness in his voice, and I couldn't resist looking at him despite his nudity.

"Then how—?"

"I'm the son of Death, Nikki. There is one way to kill me, and it was not in Konstantin's power to do. But there is no power on earth that can contain me." He walked through the snow toward me—leaving footprints this time—and crouched so he was about at eye level. "You remember the Underworld, don't you?"

I shuddered and nodded. When I'd been hunting Justin Kerner, I'd discovered that some death-god descendants are able to use cemeteries as gateways to the Underworld. I couldn't tell you exactly what the Underworld *is,* even though I've been there, but it's not a place we mere humans can get to without aid. I knew that Anderson was able to use cemeteries that way—after all, he'd come into the Underworld to rescue me—but we weren't in a cemetery right now.

"Neither Alexis nor Konstantin was stupid enough to bury bodies on their own land, so unless we're sitting on top of some ancient burial ground, this isn't any form of cemetery," I said.

"Death-god descendants get to the Underworld by *creating* a gateway. I, on the other hand, *am* a gateway. I can create an entrance to the Underworld wherever I am. I told you Konstantin couldn't trap me by burial or drowning."

"You didn't mention being encased in molten metal."

He smiled. "I'm glad you still have your sense of humor."

I didn't actually find it all that funny. If Anderson had just come right out and *told* me this in the first place, instead of being so cryptic in his impatience . . .

I sighed. It wouldn't have made a bit of difference. He hadn't been able to come back from the dead until after I'd already finished off Konstantin. He wouldn't have been able to help me, and no matter what he'd told me, I wouldn't have believed he could really escape until I actually saw it.

"We have to get out of here," I said, glancing up at the sky. It was still dark, but I thought I was beginning to see the first hints of predawn light.

Anderson stared at Konstantin's inert form. I guess I was getting to know him pretty well, because I knew what he was thinking.

"Unless you can get these shackles off of me," I said, "you're going to have to carry me to the car if we want to get there before next Wednesday. I know you're strong, but can you carry me *and* Konstantin at the same time?"

Anderson was the son of Death, but he was also the son of a Fury. I'd certainly hurt Konstantin when I'd pelted him with bricks and dropped a hunk of concrete on his head, but when Anderson killed someone, they *suffered*. Unless their human shell was already dead, that is.

"A quick death is too good for him," Anderson said through gritted teeth.

"Maybe. But how about you worry about what's good for *us* instead? We really don't want to be here when the police come knocking, and the house is going to be sending up smoke signals like no one's business when the sun rises. We need to go. The sooner the better."

For a moment, I thought Anderson's need for revenge was going to overcome his common sense. He had that angry light in his eyes, and I could feel the malice rolling off of him in waves. Then he shook his head violently and closed his eyes.

When he opened them again, the white light was gone, and he had a look I could only describe as haunted. "I let my need for revenge control me once before. I swore to myself I would never do it again."

He didn't seem to be talking to me so much as to himself. He'd told me before that he'd done "terrible things" in his past, and it seemed like a good guess those "terrible things" had been done in revenge. I was too nosy not to be curious, but now was not the time for questions. And I didn't think Anderson would answer them anyway.

"If it makes you feel any better," I said, "at the last moment before I hit him with the rock, Konstantin realized he'd made a mistake and he was going to get killed by a five-foot-two woman with chains on her wrists and ankles. I suspect that knowledge counts as suffering in his book."

Anderson flashed me a weak smile. Then, his face saying it was killing him to do it, he reached out with a glowing hand to touch Konstantin.

TWENTY-NINE

Not having keys turned out not to be a problem, as Anderson kept a spare set in the glove compartment; however, we had to get underneath and chisel away at the hunk of ice we were hung up on. It didn't actually take all that long, but if another car had come along while we'd been at it, it would have been . . . awkward. It's not every day you see a naked man and a woman chained hand and foot having car trouble by the side of the road. Anderson had helped himself to Konstantin's suit jacket after Konstantin was dead, but it was speckled with blood, which would have been hard to explain if anyone had stopped to try to help us. He'd tried the pants, too, but Konstantin was both taller and broader, and there was no way to keep the pants up.

At least the jacket, bloodstains and all, kept Anderson from looking like he was completely naked when we passed the police cars that blew by us only moments after we'd gotten back onto the road.

As I defrosted in the car on the way back to the mansion, I told Anderson everything he had missed—including that Cyrus had set us up. The fury that darkened his face made me wonder if I should have left that part out. The Olympians had clearly broken the treaty, but even though Konstantin was dead, nothing had really changed from our standpoint. We could *not* afford a war against the Olympians, no matter what Cyrus had done.

Anderson was quiet for a long time, stewing in his rage. I thought about reminding him of all the reasons why we couldn't afford a war, but decided my best course of action was to let him figure that out himself.

Of course, the decision of whether or not we were going to war against the Olympians wasn't entirely up to us. Konstantin had never dared start a war because he knew Anderson could kill him, but Cyrus had no way of knowing our puny little team could actually hurt him and his Olympians, and he was bound to be upset when he found out we'd taken out his dad.

Anderson let out a heavy sigh when we drove through the gates of home sweet home.

"Cyrus is a conniving, selfish, morally bankrupt bastard," he said. "And he's a huge improvement over Konstantin."

"He's going to assume we buried Konstantin somewhere," I replied. "He and his daddy might not have had the most loving relationship, but Cyrus is going to want revenge anyway."

"He might want it, but he won't dare try to get it." Anderson smiled, and there was a touch of cruelty in his expression. "If he kills us—or if he just pisses me off enough—he'll lose all hope that we might someday tell him where Konstantin is buried."

It was the same tactic Konstantin had used with Emma. Anderson had wanted to kill him for a long time, but he hadn't dared kill the one man who might be able to give Emma back to him. The fact that there was absolutely no reason to believe Konstantin would ever do it had never killed the little ray of hope. Maybe Cyrus would fall victim to that same hope. Obviously, I was completely worthless when it came to guessing what Cyrus was going to do.

"What are we going to tell Blake?" I asked as we pulled into the garage. The relief of being home was strong enough to bring tears to my eyes.

Anderson frowned and turned off the car. "The truth, I suppose. I think he's past being disillusioned by Cyrus anymore."

"Yeah, maybe he'll be flattered that Cyrus went through all that trouble just to get him back," I said sarcastically. I didn't think it was possible to find out that your onetime lover had planned to kill or enslave every one of your friends to force you to come back to him, without feeling some serious pain and disillusionment. After all, Blake still seemed to like Cyrus in a guarded sort of way.

"Don't worry, you don't have to tell him. I'll do it myself. He deserves to know."

To that, I had no argument.

I was too exhausted to hop, so I made no objection when Anderson offered to carry me into the house.

EPILOGUE

The email hit my in-box at eight in the morning. I knew we were in trouble the moment I saw the subject line: ANDERSON IS A GOD.

To whom it may concern,

If you're reading this, then I am most likely dead. My murderer is Anderson Kane, and he is a god. His father was Thanatos, the Greek god of death. I never did find out the identity of his mother. He pretends to be one of the *Liberi,* but I have seen him in his true form. He can kill *Liberi* with a touch of his hand, and if the screams are any indication, it's a terrible way to go. Long ago, we negotiated an agreement whereby I would keep this information secret, but my death invalidates that agreement. I don't know why it is so important to him that this information not get out. Maybe he doesn't want to alienate his people with the knowledge of who and what he really is, and my revenge will turn out to be nothing but a petty torment. But I suspect there is more to it than that.

I have arranged for this email to be sent to all of Anderson's people, as well as all the Olympians. But just in case that doesn't inconvenience him enough, I've also arranged for it to be propagated via spambot. Soon, millions upon millions of people will see this email. Most will delete or ignore it or just think I'm a crackpot. But Anderson, if there's someone out there you're trying to hide from, if *that* is the reason you don't want anyone to know your true identity . . . Well, I'm afraid that cat is now out of the bag.

Isn't it funny how sometimes even when you win, you lose?

Konstantin Galanos

DIVINE
DESCENDANT

*To all the readers and fans
who make this wild and wonderful
career as an author so rewarding.
I couldn't do it without you.*

ONE

I stepped up to the door and knocked loudly. "You can't shut us out like this, Anderson," I said. I was standing outside Anderson's study, surrounded by my bewildered, angry, and hurt housemates. I had knocked once politely. When he didn't answer, I decided politeness was overrated. "Let us in, or we're letting *ourselves* in."

My friends recoiled, and there was a chorus of shushing, accompanied by urgent hand gestures. No one spoke to Anderson like that. You didn't have to know the whole truth about who and what he was to tread cautiously around him and what I'd dubbed his Hand of Doom.

"Nikki, what are you doing?"

"Do you have a death wish?"

"Speak for yourself, not for the rest of us!"

Everyone took a step away from me, as if fearing they'd get caught in the explosion if they stood too close. I understood where they were coming from. Anderson could be damn scary even if you didn't know he was a god. Before the posthumous email that Konstantin, the late and unlamented leader of the Olympians, had sent out into the world, I'd been the only one who knew exactly how dangerous Anderson truly was. Now that we *all* knew, the rest of the *Liberi* probably expected me to bow and scrape accordingly. I'm not the bowing and scraping type.

I ignored the protests and warnings, and when Anderson still didn't answer me, I turned the knob and pushed his study door open. I'd expected it to be locked.

Of course, I'd also expected Anderson to be inside, and he wasn't.

In fact, he was nowhere to be found. I tried calling his cell phone, but my call went straight to voice mail. I tried again, listening for the telltale sound of his phone ringing from somewhere in the house, but I couldn't hear anything.

I'd expected Anderson to be seriously upset about his secret getting out, and I certainly expected him to not want to talk to us about it. But it had never occurred to me that he might be too chicken to face us at all.

My housemates and I searched the whole house, just in case he'd turned off his phone and was holed up somewhere unexpected, but he was gone.

With Anderson now AWOL, the most immediate threat my housemates and I faced was Cyrus Galanos, the new leader of the Olympians. He was under the impression that Anderson and I had buried his father, Konstantin, in a secret location he hoped to prize out of us someday. Being buried alive was a hellacious torment for a *Liberi*, who would die, then revive, only to die all over again, but it wasn't irreversible. Cyrus's hope that he might someday rescue Konstantin from that secret grave gave him an incentive not to attack us. However, now that Cyrus knew the truth about Anderson, knew that he was capable of killing *Liberi*, who were for the most part immortal, it was only natural he'd suspect his father might have met with a more permanent fate. I didn't think it would be good for our collective health if Cyrus found out Anderson killed his dad.

Cyrus was not an easy man to put off. He called the house multiple times, and since he had both my cell phone number and Blake's, he called us, too. No one felt inclined to pick up. It wasn't really any of us he wanted to speak to, and since we couldn't produce Anderson for a conversation, silence seemed our wisest option. You see, we all thought the situation was temporary, that Anderson would soon come back from wherever he'd disappeared to and pick up the reins once more. Then it would be up to *him* to figure out what to do about Cyrus and the Olympians.

When Anderson didn't come back the next day, I began to get nervous, and Cyrus got impatient. His phone messages took on a more threatening tone, and I worried he and some of his goons might show up at the front gate. He *probably* wouldn't break it down as long as he thought Anderson was around, but the longer we refused to answer, the more likely he'd get over his fear of getting on the bad side of a death god.

By the third day, I wasn't the only one who was beginning to wonder if Anderson planned to come back at all. And even if he did, I wasn't sure we could afford to wait for him. Cyrus and his Olympians outnumbered us by a huge margin, and if they stormed the house, they and their pet Descendants could slaughter us all and there would be nothing we could do to defend ourselves. Not when they had mortal Descendants—the only people other than Anderson who can kill *Liberi*—on their side and we didn't.

I could happily have gone the rest of my immortal life without seeing Cyrus's face or even hearing his voice again, but it seemed that was not among my options.

"Have you decided what you're going to tell him?" Maggie asked as I pulled into a parking space across the street from the coffee bar where we were to meet Cyrus.

"Hell no," I answered honestly—and perhaps unwisely.

"You're kidding, right?" Logan asked from the backseat. "I thought you said you had a plan."

I shrugged, wondering how exactly I'd come to be our spokesperson in Anderson's absence. "My plan is to find a way not to get us all killed."

"You're not filling me with confidence," he replied, and Maggie snorted in some combination of agreement and amusement.

I wasn't exactly filling *myself* with confidence, either. When I'd spoken to Cyrus on the phone to arrange the meeting, he'd been tense and tightly controlled. I might have felt better about things if he'd shouted and threatened me with death and dismemberment. Once upon a time, I'd allowed myself to forget that Cyrus was one of the bad guys, and the consequences of that oversight continued to ring in my memory. I was through trying to predict what Cyrus would say or do, and that made advance planning challenging, to say the least.

"It all depends on how badly Cyrus wants to believe his daddy's still alive," I said. I didn't wait around for any more questions, darting across the street as soon as there was a break in traffic. I wished Maggie and Logan had allowed me to come alone, as I'd originally planned, but they seemed to think I might need backup. Unfortunately, they were probably right.

Cyrus was expecting to see only me and Anderson come through the door. Somehow, I didn't think he was going to be happy to see me showing up with Maggie and Logan instead. I hadn't specifically lied to him and told him Anderson was coming, but I'd certainly encouraged him to draw that conclusion.

Cyrus had made it to the coffee bar before we did. When I opened the door and looked inside, I realized that he had brought a veritable army with him. There wasn't a single person in the entire place who didn't sport an iridescent—and invisible to non-*Liberi*—glyph on some stretch of exposed skin. Even the lone barista had a glyph in the center of her forehead. The coffee bar was *supposed* to be a neutral site, but right now it looked the exact opposite of neutral. Not a good start to our meeting.

"Shit," I heard Logan mutter under his breath behind me, and Maggie let out a soft gasp of surprise. We were badly outnumbered, and I had no doubt that at least a few of the people in the room were Descendants, and therefore capable of killing us and claiming our immortality for their own. Maybe meeting Cyrus in person had been a bad idea, but it was too late to back out now.

Cyrus was sitting at a table at the rear of the room, facing the door. His legs were stretched out in front of him in a posture that was supposed to look casual and relaxed, but even at a distance I could see the tightness in the muscles of his crossed arms. He sat up straight and looked surprised when he saw me. I half expected him to order his people to attack, but he didn't, instead waving and beckoning us in.

I shared a quick glance with Logan and Maggie. If things went sour in here, the two of them would almost certainly be killed. Cyrus would probably prefer to keep me alive, just as his father had wanted to, because descendants of Artemis are rare and useful. But the life the Olympians envisioned for me made death seem far preferable.

Maybe I should have tried harder to convince Maggie and Logan to stay home. It was one thing to risk myself, quite another to risk my friends. My nerves buzzed with anxiety as I stepped into the lion's den with Logan and Maggie right behind me.

The room was eerily silent as the three of us made our way back toward Cyrus's table. The Olympians watched us with predatory intensity, and the hairs on the back of my neck rose. The espresso machine let out a screech, and I couldn't contain a little start of surprise. The barista laughed out loud at my reaction, and several of the others had a nice chuckle. So much for my plan to pretend I was filled with confidence and not a bit intimidated by the enemy.

Cyrus stood up as I approached the table. There was no sign of his usual deceptively friendly smile, which was just as well. The last time I'd seen him, he'd conked me on the head and trussed me up to hand over to his father. He'd known perfectly well that Konstantin planned to rape and otherwise brutalize me, but he'd delivered me in a neat little package anyway. If he'd tried a friendly smile, I might not have been able to resist putting my fist through his teeth.

"Anderson running late?" he asked with a cock of his head.

"Nope. He's not coming." I met his challenging stare head-on, doing my best to ignore the angry muttering of the Olympians who now had us completely surrounded.

I thought my answer might irritate Cyrus, but he just shook his head. "Why am I not surprised?"

I figured that was a rhetorical question and kept my mouth shut.

"Please, have a seat, Nikki," Cyrus said, resuming his own seat with his back to the wall.

I sat across from him with Logan standing at my right shoulder and Maggie at my left. They weren't much use as bodyguards under these circumstances, but they were doing their best.

Cyrus and I indulged in a brief, silent staring contest. Looking at him, remembering his "advice" that things would go easier for me if I didn't fight Konstantin, I couldn't help feeling sick to my stomach. Turning green around the gills wouldn't do much for my credibility, so I decided to derail the staring contest.

"Aren't you going to offer me a coffee?" I asked him. In the past, he'd ordered espressos for me even though I didn't want them. I glanced over my shoulder at the barista, with her iridescent glyph and her ugly glower. I doubted drinking anything she served me would be a smart move.

The expression on Cyrus's face hardened. "Pardon me if I don't feel particularly gracious today. Right now, you're just lucky to be alive."

"I seem to recall you saying that your daddy *wanted* me alive and that I would be much luckier if I *did* die."

He gaped at me. "You're going to try to guilt-trip me? Who do you think you're talking to?"

"Oh, right. I almost forgot I was talking to a man who only has a conscience when it's convenient." I believed he honestly regretted leaving me to his father's tender mercies—but only to a point. After all, that regret wasn't enough to stop him from doing it in the first place, so it meant nothing. Anger pounded through my veins, some of it directed at myself. I had almost *liked* Cyrus, despite knowing he was the bad guy. I felt hurt and betrayed by what he'd done, then felt pissed off at myself for feeling that way.

He leaned forward and put his elbows on the table so he could glare at me from closer range. "If you're here to talk about my shortcomings, then you are possibly the biggest fool I've ever met."

I tried to be subtle about taking a deep breath, doing my best to stuff all that anger, hurt, and self-loathing into a mental box where it would be out of the way. I had somehow ended up as the spokesperson for all of Anderson's *Liberi*, and that meant I had to keep a level head.

"I apologize for drifting off topic," I said, my voice too tight to make the apology sincere.

"Frankly, I'm not sure what the topic is," he countered. "Your boss killed my father and lied about it. If ever there was a cause for war, that would be it. And, Nikki, I do hold grudges. It may have been your boss who did the killing, but you were there. I don't care how rare and useful descendants of Artemis are. I *will* kill you."

The threat was even more disturbing coming from someone who'd always been so friendly to me before than it would have been from an unrepentant psycho like Konstantin. I won't pretend I didn't feel a chill of apprehension, but I hoped I kept it from showing on my face. When dealing with Olympians, revealing weakness is never a good idea.

"If you weren't worried about what Anderson would do, you'd have killed me already," I pointed out. "He's not a man whose bad side you want to get on. Just ask your dad. Or Emma."

Anderson had made no secret about how much he'd loved Emma, but Cyrus was there when Anderson thought she'd betrayed him and condemned her to die.

Cyrus's eyes filled with anger and his jaw clenched. Instinct told me he was about three seconds from telling his people to kill us all right here. Apparently, I wasn't the only one the thought occurred to, because one of his goons started closing the blinds on the front windows.

"If any of us get hurt, Anderson will hold *you* personally responsible," I warned him. "I don't know how many Olympians he'd kill in retaliation, but I do know you'd be first in line. And *you* know that, too."

The rest of the Olympians in the room started murmuring among themselves, and it occurred to me that maybe coming into what had obviously become enemy territory and issuing threats hadn't been my wisest decision. Then again, coming in with my tail tucked between my legs and begging for forgiveness would have gotten us all killed for sure.

Either way, it was time to change the tone to something marginally more positive.

"Konstantin isn't dead," I said, and my words instantly silenced the buzz in the room.

Cyrus sneered at me. "You expect me to believe that?"

"*I* was there, remember? Anderson didn't want *anyone* to know what he really was." Which was true, to an extent. Anderson had threatened to kill me—and anyone I told—if I didn't keep his secret, and I'd never doubted that he meant it. I suspect I was very lucky he hadn't killed me on the spot when I'd learned his identity. "Do you honestly think he would kill Konstantin with me there to witness it? We buried him, just like we told you before."

Cyrus dismissed that with a wave of his hand. "That's meaningless. Even if it's the truth, it doesn't mean Anderson didn't go back later and do the deed."

"All right, then. Let me put it to you this way: Which is the better revenge? A quick death, or an eternity of dying then coming back to life and then immediately dying again?"

For the first time, Cyrus looked like he might be considering my words. But then he shook them off, saying, "If my father is alive, then prove it. Take me to him."

I let out a bark of laughter. "Yeah, right."

"You think I can't make you?"

I rolled my eyes, though it was hard to maintain my aura of confidence when I was spouting so much bullshit. "I think Anderson is really, really good at keeping secrets. I helped bury your father, but I have no idea where we were. Anderson blindfolded me. For my own good," I finished, with air quotes.

"Funny how everything worked out so conveniently for you."

I don't have to make him believe me, I reminded myself. *I've just got to plant enough reasonable doubt to make him hesitate.* "Convenient or not, it's the truth. You're never going to find Konstantin without Anderson's cooperation, and you're never going to get his cooperation if you kill any of his people."

"It's not like I'm going to get his cooperation anyway."

I shrugged. "Where there's life, there's hope, right?"

The muscles of Cyrus's jaw worked as he ground his teeth, and I knew I had him. He and his father had obviously had their differences, but he still harbored love and loyalty that Konstantin neither deserved nor returned. He *wanted* me to be telling the truth, and that wishful thinking was going to keep his thirst for vengeance in check. For now.

In my peripheral vision, I could see a wide variety of scowls and glares on the Olympians who surrounded us. I doubted any of them felt the faint hope of rescuing Konstantin was worth giving up on their vengeance. Konstantin was respected as a leader, but I sincerely doubt he was ever loved by his people. Cyrus would probably be buffeted repeatedly with that message, and eventually either he would cave to the pressure, or they would stop listening to him. I just hoped I was buying us enough time to find Anderson and come up with a better plan for defense.

"Why did Anderson send the three of you here instead of coming himself?" Cyrus asked. "Maybe you were the ones he thought were expendable?"

I decided to intersperse a little truth with all the lies I'd been telling. "Anderson's been off on a little walkabout ever since that email came in. I figured this meeting of ours couldn't wait until he got back."

I sensed both Maggie and Logan tensing. Letting Cyrus know Anderson wasn't around was a calculated risk. On the one hand, it left us looking exposed and vulnerable. On the other hand, I couldn't think of a plausible explanation for Anderson sending us in his place. He was a freaking *god*. If he didn't want to talk to Cyrus, he'd tell Cyrus to shove it, not avoid him.

"A walkabout, eh?" Cyrus asked, his eyes narrowing. "Coincidentally, I seem to have lost track of two of my Olympians in the last couple of days. Two who were close friends of my father's. You don't suppose Anderson had anything to do with that, do you?"

His face had closed off, and I made an educated guess that meant he was trying to hide what he was feeling. But I could easily imagine what that was: abject fear. For all Cyrus's blustering and his numerous Olympians, if Anderson decided to hunt them all down and kill them one by one, there would be nothing they could do to stop him. Sure, they might retaliate by killing all of us, but that wouldn't bring back the dead.

"I honestly don't think so," I said. If he were going to kill any of the Olympians, he would go for Cyrus first and foremost, though I figured pointing that out would be counterproductive. "There has to be a good reason he kept his identity such a secret, even from *Liberi* who've been with him for decades. I can't imagine what it is, but I have to believe wherever he's gone, it's to deal with the ramifications of that email." I vividly remembered Anderson telling me that if his identity got out, it could cost the lives of everyone on the planet, but that was info I couldn't share with Cyrus.

Cyrus was still trying to keep a neutral expression, but I swore I caught a flash of worry in his eyes. He might be a lying, selfish snake, but he wasn't stupid. If there was someone out there powerful enough to send a god running for cover—or whatever Anderson was doing—then that someone had to be seriously bad news.

Cyrus leaned back in his chair, his brow furrowed. "I'm not sure that makes me feel any better," he said.

"Me either," I admitted. "Your dad may have pulled the pin on something he thought was a grenade but is actually a nuke." Of course, I was being generous in implying Konstantin might have cared what the consequences of his actions would be. He knew he wouldn't be around to face them, so what did it matter to him?

Cyrus nodded and looked grim. "All of that may be perfectly true, but it doesn't change anything. I believe that my father is dead and that you're lying through your pretty teeth in hopes of saving your own ass."

"Konstantin is *not* dead," I insisted. I thought I was being pretty convincing, but I was starting to sweat. It had seemed for a while that Cyrus was considering my story because he hoped it was true. Now I wasn't so sure.

"Prove it!" Cyrus said, pounding the table and making everyone jump. "Give me proof of life, and I won't wipe you all out no matter how much I want to."

It was a frighteningly reasonable request, but obviously one we couldn't grant. There was nothing I could do but stall for time.

"Anderson's the only one who knows where Konstantin is buried," I said. "Until he comes back, there's no way we can give you proof of life."

"Well, then you'd better hope he comes back soon, or use your powers to track down the burial site yourself. If I don't have proof within one week that my father's alive, I'll start picking your people off one by one until you give me what I want or you're all dead, whichever comes first."

"You only have to kill one of us to sign your own death warrant," I replied. "Anderson's the son of a Fury. He's really good at revenge."

"So am I," he answered ominously. "You have one week. Now get out of my sight before I change my mind."

T<small>WO</small>

The meeting with Cyrus had staved off immediate disaster, but we were still in deep trouble. I might be able to stall for time by having Jack, our resident trickster, disguise himself as Konstantin for a proof-of-life photo—his illusion magic was scary good—but I suspected Cyrus would see right through that. We needed Anderson back ASAP. Maybe he could talk (or threaten) Cyrus into leaving us alone.

We tried calling his cell phone, of course. I'm sure all of us left him at least one urgent message, but he didn't respond. I also tried email, though I doubted he would answer an email when he wouldn't answer a phone call or text.

"He'll come back when he's ready," Maggie assured me when I expressed my frustration. "He just needs time is all."

I like to think of myself as a pretty understanding person, but I had my limits, and Anderson had pushed way past them. "Well, we don't have time to wait till he's goddamn ready!" I retorted. "And if he doesn't get his ass back here soon, then I'm going to track him down and haul him in."

Maggie gave me a shocked look, and I couldn't say I blamed her. I probably sounded pretty ridiculous claiming I was going to hunt down a god and force him to do anything. Anderson would come back when and if he felt like it, and we all knew it.

That said, I *was* a descendant of Artemis, and I'd never been good at doing nothing. Maybe there was no way I could persuade Anderson to come back if he didn't feel like it, but I knew I would feel better if I at least had some clue where he was.

I was still hard at work trying to figure out the ins and outs of my powers as a supernatural huntress, but at least with almost three months' experience now under my belt, I was no longer entirely clueless about how they worked. Trial and error had taught me they were stronger at night, when the moon was visible. I had also figured out that they were fueled by intuition, the clues registering only on a subconscious level, which made it tough to summon them on demand. I was getting better at telling the difference between a subconscious clue and a random whim, but I was a long way from being truly confident.

I decided to start my search in Anderson's office, the only room in his wing of the mansion that wasn't strictly off-limits to the rest of us. I had a feeling some of my fellow *Liberi*—most notably Maggie—would take issue with me rifling through Anderson's things in his absence, so I tried to be quiet about it. I wasn't the only one in the house who wanted him to hurry back, but I *was* the only one who would risk doing something that might piss him off to make that happen. (Well, except for Jack, who as a descendant of Loki thought infuriating people was a laugh a minute.) Maybe I have a little trouble with authority. Wouldn't be surprising for someone with my upbringing.

I listened to my subconscious with studied attention as I looked through all of his files and drawers and even his computer. He didn't bother with password protection, knowing that no one in the house would dare snoop, and no outsider who attempted to break in would survive the experience. I looked for any mention of places he might frequent or that might have some sentimental value, but I tried to keep my mind open to anything.

Nothing raised a blip on my subconscious radar.

I could have searched the rest of the Forbidden Zone—which

is what I called Anderson's private wing of the mansion—but if I didn't find anything in his office, I doubted I'd have much luck elsewhere.

My next ploy was to wait until the sun set and the moon rose and then drive around at random, hoping my subconscious would lead me in the right direction. This method usually worked better when someone else was driving, allowing me to space out completely, at which point my elusive power would be triggered and I'd start giving directions without even knowing I was doing it. But for the time being, I wanted to try it solo. Although no one had come right out and challenged me about it, I got a sense they suspected that I'd discovered Anderson's secret before they did. After all, they knew I'd been there the night we "buried" Konstantin. I'd told them the same lie I'd told Cyrus, but they had even less reason to believe me. I didn't want to be trapped in a car for several hours with someone who might start pressing for the truth.

I drove around for a couple of hours, but I didn't stray into any unexpected neighborhoods or feel any compulsion to go one way or another. It was highly possible that my meager powers weren't up to the challenge of tracking a god. It was also possible that Anderson had disappeared to somewhere I couldn't follow. As a death god, he had easy access to the Underworld, which mere mortals like me were unable to enter unless escorted.

Frustrated by my total lack of progress, but glad I had actually made an effort, I returned to the mansion.

Anderson was very fond of his privacy, so you couldn't just drive up to the house without going through a gate first. When I neared the gate, I was surprised to see an unfamiliar car stopped in front of it. It was pretty dark, but I could see the driver's hand reaching out to press the intercom button just in front of the gates. The hand was delicate and feminine, and from the way she punched the button about ten times, I had a feeling this wasn't her first try.

I saw no reason to open the gates for a stranger, so I pulled up behind her instead. From what I could see in the shadows, the car had only one occupant, but looks can be deceiving, especially in the world of *Liberi*.

I was on high alert as I put my car in park. A lone woman might not look all that threatening to most, but I would consider her dangerous until I saw evidence to the contrary. I wished I'd brought my gun for tonight's drive, but I hadn't been sure if I'd end up within the D.C. city limits, where I couldn't legally carry it. There'd been an awful lot of times when I'd ignored that law, but only when I felt I might be in immediate danger, which I hadn't tonight.

I stepped out of my car, leaving it running in case I needed a speedy getaway. The brake lights on the car in front of me dimmed, and I realized the driver had put it in park as well.

The door opened, and the woman climbed gracefully out of the driver's seat. She was tall and curvy, with thick black hair held back in a ponytail. She wore faded jeans and an off-the-shoulder sweatshirt, and yet she somehow managed to convey an aura of class and sophistication. I searched her face and the skin exposed by her sweatshirt, but saw no glyph that would mark her as a *Liberi* or a Descendant.

The stranger was regarding me with equal curiosity, and there was nothing about her facial expression or body language that looked even vaguely threatening. However, I wasn't about to relax.

"Can I help you?" I asked.

"I don't know," she said with a half smile. "Depends who you are."

I raised an eyebrow. She might not be overtly hostile, but apparently she had the privileged attitude I was beginning to think of as the hallmark of all the Olympians.

"I live here," I told her curtly. "*You're* the one who needs to identify herself."

The woman looked pointedly down at my left hand. I

didn't get why until she asked me, "Are you the current Mrs. Kane?"

Oh. She'd been looking for a wedding ring. That seemed to suggest she wasn't an Olympian, because they all knew perfectly well who I was.

"Who's asking?" Maybe I was being stubborn, but I wasn't willing to answer even an innocuous question without knowing who this stranger was.

I saw a flash of annoyance in her eyes, but she quickly quelled it. "I suppose one of us has to concede first, and it might as well be me. My name is Rose, and a long time ago, I was the sister-in-law of the man you know as Anderson Kane."

I had no idea how old Anderson was, except that it was *old*, and I knew he'd had at least one other ex-wife besides the two I'd met, Emma and Erin. But I couldn't help wondering just how many ex-wives and in-laws were still wandering around in the world. I assumed most if not all of them were *Liberi*, because marrying a mortal would kind of suck when you knew they were going to die and you weren't. I looked at Rose more carefully and still saw no sign of a glyph.

"How long ago are we talking?" I asked.

"*Very* long ago," she said, then seemed to be thinking something over. I kept my mouth shut, and eventually she sighed.

"I presume you are aware of the email about Kane that circulated not long ago," she said. I nodded and gestured for her to continue. "Well, the author of that email was correct when he suggested that Kane was hiding from someone. You see, he was supposed to have died a very, very long time ago, and there is someone who's very disappointed to learn that he didn't."

I didn't need any supernatural powers to hear the warning bells clanging away. Hard not to be alarmed when Anderson's words about "every man, woman, and child" kept echoing in my head. No *Liberi* could possibly cause that kind of damage, which meant whoever Anderson was hiding from had to be a god. And having his ex-sister-in-law from "very long ago" parked here in front of the gates gave me a definite sinking feeling.

"That someone wouldn't happen to be an ex-wife, would it?" I asked.

"Yes, it would. And before you ask, yes, that would be my sister, Niobe."

Oh, shit.

I hadn't exactly been an expert in Greek mythology when I'd become a *Liberi*, but just for the sake of self-preservation, I'd done a lot of reading since. Enough that the name Niobe was frighteningly familiar.

"You don't mean *the* Niobe, do you?" I asked hopefully.

"Perhaps we should go inside," Rose suggested. "I have a feeling we have a lot to talk about."

Natural caution aside, I had a feeling she was right. And that I might prefer to be sitting down for this conversation.

When Rose and I entered the house, I went into hostess mode and put on a pot of coffee.

Much of what is recorded in mythology flat-out isn't true. For example, my divine ancestor, Artemis, is known as a virgin goddess, but obviously since she had descendants, that wasn't strictly true. But there's usually at least a kernel of truth buried within the myth, and considering what I knew of Niobe's story, that kernel of truth couldn't be good.

According to mythology, Niobe was guilty of the heinous crime of hubris, overly proud of herself, her status, and her children. She thought herself better than the gods, and they didn't like that. They sent Apollo and Artemis to teach Niobe a lesson—by killing every one of her seven sons and seven daughters before her eyes. The idea that the gods—including my ancestor—thought murdering fourteen innocent people was a fitting punishment for someone they thought was conceited shows just how not-human the gods really were.

When the coffee was ready and Rose and I were sitting at

the table in the breakfast nook, I cupped my hands around my mug and looked her straight in the eye.

"So your sister is the Niobe that the Greek myths talk about."

Rose nodded. "Of course the myths have just about everything wrong about her."

"I figured as much." But I also figured the kernel of truth was going to revolve around the ugliest part of the story, that it was probably *Anderson* who'd killed Niobe's children rather than Apollo and Artemis. That would certainly give her reason to want him dead and be pretty pissed off to find out he was alive.

I didn't want to consider the possibility that Anderson had done something so terrible. However, he'd hinted more than once about his dark past, and I didn't think refusing to hear about it was the mature and responsible choice.

"Niobe is not a mortal woman," Rose said. "She's a goddess, and long, long ago she and Kane . . . I mean Anderson, were married. Together, they had seven sons and seven daughters. But Niobe fell in love with a mortal man, and Anderson caught the two of them together. Niobe begged for her lover's life, and Anderson spared him. Then he went home and killed all of their children, claiming he couldn't be sure they were his."

I'm sure my face went white as a sheet, and my stomach plummeted to my toes. For a moment, I seriously feared I was about to be sick and had to swallow hard to keep everything down. I thought I'd been braced for the worst, but the idea that it was *his own* children that Anderson had killed never entered my mind. And to have done it out of pure spite to punish his wife . . .

I *knew* that when gods did terrible things, they were terrible beyond the imaginings of regular people, but nothing could have prepared me for this. Nothing.

Tears burned my eyes, and I found I had trouble breathing. There was no way Rose didn't notice my distress, but she kept talking anyway.

"As you can imagine, Niobe was heartbroken when she found out what Kane had done, and she was determined to get her revenge. She wanted Kane dead. Gods and goddesses have been killing each other since the beginning of time, but death gods are exceedingly hard to kill. Niobe couldn't just run him through with a sword, so she got together with me and the rest of our sisters, and together we came up with a plan to cause his death."

The floor felt strangely wobbly beneath my chair as it finally dawned on me that Rose was a goddess. My shock and distress were clearly messing with my mental faculties, because if her sister was a goddess, then *of course* Rose was one, too.

"Kane's powers and his very life are all sustained by human death. If we could eliminate death among humans, then he would no longer be able to exist."

Rose was looking at me expectantly, but there was no way I was up to drawing logical conclusions about anything. All I could think about was my friend, a man I looked up to and respected, cold-bloodedly murdering his own children just because his wife cheated on him. I had always been convinced he was one of the good guys, but I knew I could never, ever look at him the same way again. Suddenly his disappearance and his radio silence made a whole lot more sense.

Rose chewed her lip, suddenly looking anxious and uneasy. Her gaze dropped down to her mug of coffee, which had stopped steaming. She hadn't exactly been relaxed before, but she was clearly a lot more tense now, her eyes glazed and a little haunted.

I forced myself to focus, to think about what she had just said. She and her sisters had been determined to kill Anderson—for which I could hardly blame them—but he couldn't be killed as long as human beings kept dying.

"How do you eliminate mortal death?" Rose asked softly, still not looking at me.

My heart gave a hard, almost painful thud as I realized

what Rose was implying. "You eliminate mortals," I answered. For the millionth time, I remembered Anderson's claim that every man, woman, and child would die if word of his existence reached the wrong ears. And now I knew why.

Which meant I was sitting across the table from a goddess who'd thought it was a good idea to kill everyone on the planet in an act of revenge.

"We figured once there weren't any people around to die anymore, Kane would wither away and die himself, and then we'd repopulate the planet and start all over."

Rose reached across the table and lightly touched the back of my hand, causing me to jump and shove my chair back from the table to get away from her. She stayed in her seat and raised both hands to indicate her harmless intent. I knew she hadn't meant anything by that touch, had just been trying to establish a little human contact, but there was no way I was letting someone like her touch me.

"You have no need to be afraid of me," Rose said. "I have lived among mortals for thousands of years now, and it has changed the way I view the world more than you can possibly imagine. You have to understand that we considered mortals little more than animals. We would occasionally adopt one as something of a pet, but we didn't care about them, not really. They were our toys, which we could play with and discard at our convenience. I'm not like that now, but I was back then.

"The problem with our plan was that gods are very possessive, and we destroyed toys that didn't belong to us.

"I don't know how many we killed in total, but it was a lot. The rest of the gods didn't appreciate us killing their pet mortals, but when Niobe explained our grievance, they agreed that Kane was at fault. He was sentenced to death—a sentence only another death god could enforce. Anderson's father, Thanatos himself, carried out the sentence. Perhaps we should have looked askance at Thanatos being willing to kill his own son, but then again that was hardly a rarity among our kind. We all believed Kane was dead, and we stopped killing mortals, but of course none of that could bring back Niobe's children, and her grief was . . . terrible."

Rose's eyes filled with tears and she put her hand to her chest as if her heart literally ached. "You can't imagine the pain she was in, or the pain we sisters felt on her behalf. But the rest of the gods weren't moved by our grief, and those whose mortals we destroyed wanted us punished.

"Eventually, the gods left the Earth in search of new worlds to explore, but they refused to take me or my sisters with them. They renamed us all and made us into fertility goddesses. We were sentenced to remain upon the Earth as caretakers of the humans we'd tried to wipe out. We were each given a territory, and it is our job to ensure the humans within our territories are fertile. Someday, the gods will return to check on us, and if we've done our jobs properly and our territories are appropriately populated, we will be freed from our obligation and allowed to rejoin our brethren."

It didn't seem to me that allowing a bunch of crazies who'd been willing to kill every human on the planet to be our "caretakers" made a whole lot of sense, but then so far I hadn't seen a whole lot of god-logic that did.

"So, Niobe is still around?" I asked. I knew it was a pointless question with an obvious answer, but I felt a need to fill the silence—and maybe shut up some of the yammering that was happening in my brain.

Rose nodded. "I've lost touch with most of my sisters over the centuries, but it's not like there's anywhere for us to go. And we've all kept up with our duties, consecrating our altars each year so that the people in our territories will remain fertile. I suspect most of us have been fully integrated with human society. I know I have, and I don't know how my sisters could not be as well when we have no choice but to live among you.

"When I look back on what my sisters and I did . . ." She shuddered and hugged herself. "That seems like a different person altogether. I can't even remember what it felt like to care so little about human life, to be willing to do such terrible things without even a touch of conscience.

"I think that's one of the reasons why most of us lost touch. We don't want to be reminded of that time. And I know I, for one, have no interest in leaving the Earth, even if our fellow gods do come back for us."

"You said you suspect *most* of you were integrated into human society," I said. "I'm going to take a wild guess and say that Niobe is the exception."

Rose nodded. "She maintains her altar because she knows it's what she has to do if she ever wants the chance to leave the Earth. I haven't spoken to her in at least a couple of centuries, but the last time I did, she was no more remorseful over what we'd done than before. She is still a goddess, through and through. And though she does her duty to further her own goals, she refused ever to use the new name the gods gave her. She will always be Niobe, never Blossom." Rose smiled sadly. "I found we have nothing left in common, and that's why I haven't seen or spoken to her in so long."

I shivered in a sudden chill. "You think she's going to go on another killing spree now that she knows Anderson is alive, don't you?"

To my surprise, Rose shook her head. "I'm not sure the seven of us could have succeeded in our plan the first time, when the Earth's population was vastly smaller. We can cause a lot of damage just because we're goddesses, but how could we possibly kill *everyone*?"

Her words might have sounded like reassurance and made me feel better if there weren't such an obvious *but* coming.

Rose didn't keep me hanging for long.

"But remember, the gods made my sisters and me caretakers of the world's fertility. We have to renew our altars once every year, and if we delay, there will be no children conceived within our territory until we perform the ritual. So you see, we don't have to kill anybody. We can just abandon our altars and let the human race die out all on its own."

I tried to imagine what life on Earth would be like if there were no more babies born, and my mind balked at the enormity of it. Even before the population began to dwindle, the world would become an ugly, ugly place to be. Think zombie apocalypse, only without a clear and present bad guy to rally against, since I doubted anyone would correctly guess that the sudden infertility was caused by a bunch of fertility goddesses going on strike.

"Are you telling me that's what you're going to do?" I asked in a voice little more than a whisper. The answer *had* to be no, because there was no hint of gloating or threat in her, and there was so much worry in her eyes. But I wanted to hear her say it anyway.

"I will maintain my altar as I always have," Rose affirmed. "But unless she has changed drastically—and impossibly— since I last spoke with her, Niobe will not." Rose rubbed her hands together in a very human nervous gesture. "I think my other sisters have become too human to commit such an atrocity voluntarily, but Niobe . . ." Rose shuddered delicately. "She won't be able to cope with the knowledge that Kane is alive. I fear she may try to stop the rest of us from renewing our altars when the time comes.

"That's the reason I'm here," she concluded. "I have one sister who I've been in touch with recently. Her name is Jasmine, and she's responsible for all the islands in the world. She lives in Bermuda, and she's supposed to renew her altar soon. But ever since that email about Anderson went out, I haven't been able to reach her. I've called and called, and I've even gone by her home. There's no sign of her. And I don't think that's a coincidence."

THREE

For the second time in a week, I took it upon myself to call a house meeting. If I wasn't careful, people were going to think I was trying to take over, when in fact it was just dumb luck that I happened to be the one to drive up while Rose was at the gate.

I introduced Rose, and I asked her to tell the rest of the *Liberi* what she had told me. I had the pleasure not only of having to listen to it all again, but of watching the mounting horror on my friends' faces as they found out just what Anderson was capable of.

"It's a lie!" Maggie shouted halfway through, her eyes shining with unshed tears. "Anderson would never . . ." Her voice choked off.

"Perhaps the man you know as Anderson Kane never would have committed such an atrocity," Rose said gently. "But Kane the god and the son of a Fury most definitely did."

Maggie kept shaking her head. I think everyone else was too shell-shocked to react. Either that or they were doing that whole manly stoic thing that gets on so many women's nerves. Including mine.

Rose finished with the kicker about the disappearance of her sister Jasmine—and about the need to renew Jasmine's altar.

"Jasmine and I both love the Earth and its people," she concluded. "I know that if Niobe came to me and asked me to abandon my altar, I would refuse, and I believe Jasmine would do the same." She shivered and crossed her arms over her chest. "I also know that unless Niobe has changed considerably since the last time I saw her, she will not take no for an answer. I'm afraid she may have . . . done something to Jasmine."

I could tell from the looks on my friends' faces that they

were still hung up on Anderson and his terrible past. I won't claim I wasn't pretty upset about it myself, but it seemed to me that feelings of hurt and disillusionment had to take a backseat under the circumstances.

"I don't believe a word of this story!" Maggie said, glaring at Rose. "We have no way of knowing who this woman really is. Just because she claims she's a goddess doesn't mean she is."

Logan, who was usually surprisingly even-tempered for a war-god descendant, was glaring at Rose just as fiercely, his face flushed red and his fists clenched. "Maggie's right. For all we know, you're some Olympian here to stir up trouble."

No, my fellow *Liberi* were not the most trusting sort, and having been on the receiving end of their suspicions when I first joined them, I knew exactly how pigheaded some of them were capable of being. When they don't want to believe something, they work very hard to keep unwanted evidence out.

"Am I the only one who remembers some of the crap Anderson said when he and Emma were fighting?" I asked. "He kept making veiled threats about what had happened to previous ex-wives. And when he found out Konstantin had tricked him into condemning her to death, he told me it didn't hurt as much as Konstantin wanted it to because it wasn't the worst thing he'd ever done."

"Just because he may have done bad things doesn't mean he did *that*," Logan argued.

"But he always was a little funny about how Konstantin treated his own kids," Blake said, and he looked haunted rather than angry. "There was something a bit off in his tone when he talked about the ones Konstantin killed."

I hadn't noticed that myself, but I was just happy that someone was keeping an open mind.

"You're just manufacturing evidence to support the claim you want to believe," Maggie snapped.

"No," Blake fired back. "That's what *you're* doing."

The tension in the air was almost palpable, and it didn't

take a genius to sense the dangerous undercurrents. There were some hot tempers flaring, and we didn't have Anderson around to keep it from escalating. I sneaked a glance at Jamaal, who was the most volatile and dangerous of us all, but he didn't look like he was about to join the fray, which was a good thing for all of us.

"Time out!" I said loudly, making the requisite hand signal. "Is anyone here seriously going to just ignore the threat and hope it's all a big lie? Because if we do that and we're wrong, the consequences would be . . . Well, I don't know of a word big enough to describe it. We're talking the potential end of all humanity here. If we think there's even a sliver of a chance that it might be true, we have to act. Is there anyone here who's convinced they know Anderson so well that they're willing to risk all of humanity on that conviction?"

"Before anyone gives a knee-jerk answer," Jamaal said, "let's all remember that not one of us"—he gave me a pointed look—"knew Anderson was a god until a few days ago." He paused almost imperceptibly, giving me a chance to admit that I'd actually known all along. A chance I had no intention of taking him up on. "The man we think we know doesn't even exist."

"I'm sure he *does* exist," Rose said. "He's lived among humans for thousands of years, just like I have. There may be more to him than you knew, but that doesn't mean Anderson Kane doesn't exist."

Jamaal shrugged. "Whatever. My point is that there's obviously lots about him we don't know. We may not like what we're hearing, but refusing to believe it would be irresponsible."

If you'd asked me a couple of weeks ago if I'd ever imagined Jamaal, with his incandescent temper, being the voice of reason, I'd have laughed you out of the room.

I could tell by the looks on their faces that Logan and Maggie were still resisting the truth, but they kept their mouths shut, and everyone else was trying to make the difficult transition into problem-solving mode. Because let's face it, we had one hell of a big problem to solve.

Deciding to give everyone a hand with the transition, I turned to Rose and asked, "So, you have reason to believe Jasmine may have met with foul play of some sort, and if her altar isn't renewed soon, every woman living on an island in the ocean is going to stop conceiving." Rose nodded her agreement. "What is it exactly you'd like us to do?"

"Well, since you're a descendant of Artemis, I certainly hope you can help me find and rescue Jasmine, if she's still alive. But the first priority is to make sure her altar gets renewed before it loses its power. I imagine it would take a while before people would start to notice the effects, but can you imagine the panic and confusion it would cause if so many women stopped conceiving all at once?"

I winced. I don't know how scientists would try to explain what was happening. Maybe they'd believe it was some kind of disease, though how they would explain its sudden spread through only the world's islands was beyond me. What certainly *would* happen was a mass exodus from the islands, which could only lead to disaster as improvised flotillas of desperate people tried to make it to mainlands that no doubt would be less than welcoming. Especially if enough people believed the islanders were suffering from some previously unknown communicable disease.

"So the altar can be renewed without Jasmine?" Blake asked.

Rose nodded. "It's only necessary that one of the seven of us perform the ceremony. I can stand in for Jasmine."

"If that's the case, then what exactly do you need us for?" he challenged.

Rose seemed unaffected by his tone. "Niobe knows that Jasmine's is the first altar that needs to be renewed. If she's vengeful enough to prevent Jasmine from doing it, then she's vengeful enough to guard against any of the rest of us stepping in."

"If she's dead set against it being renewed, why doesn't she just destroy it?" I asked. That seemed like the easiest solution from Niobe's point of view.

"The altars aren't really physical objects," Rose explained. "They're like the seeds of immortality you *Liberi* carry, existing on a metaphysical level. The heart of the altar is part of the Earth itself. You can destroy its physical vessel, but it will regenerate. Just like the *Liberi* can regenerate and come back to life."

That was the first bit of good news I'd heard in a while. If Niobe could destroy the altars, then we'd already be too late to prevent her from doing it.

"So you want to go to Bermuda and renew Jasmine's altar," I said, and Rose nodded. "And you want us to provide some protection because you're expecting Niobe to have that altar guarded."

"Yes. I'd go by myself, but I know she will not allow me to walk up to the altar and renew it without a fight. She was willing to hurt or maybe even kill Jasmine to stop her from renewing it, and there's no reason to think she wouldn't do the same to me. I was hoping Kane would have the decency to help me, but since he's not here and you are . . ."

"So basically what you want is bodyguards?" Blake asked.

"Yes, that, of course. But I also need a man to perform the ritual with me. Ordinarily, I would use a mortal, but I can't in good conscience lead a mortal man into what may become a battle of immortals."

Cue another round of shell-shocked looks. I don't suppose any of us had yet put any thought into what kind of ritual would be needed to renew a fertility goddess's altar, but in retrospect it was pretty obvious.

"You want one of us to have sex with you on the altar," Blake said with a cold look that sat awkwardly on his pretty-boy face.

Rose blinked in evident surprise. "Is there any man here who *wouldn't* want that?" she asked, and I didn't think the innocence on her face was feigned. She was stunningly beautiful and alluringly voluptuous, and under other circumstances and with no existing attachments, I'm sure any of our men would have leapt at the chance.

I couldn't help surveying all their faces to see how they were taking this oddly uncomfortable proposition. Leo, our resident hermit and computer nerd, was blushing to the roots of his hair. He was uncomfortable even with eye contact, and the idea of him having public sex with a goddess was unthinkable. Jamaal was looking at the floor, his arms crossed over his chest in what I felt sure was a defensive posture. He had intimacy issues worse than Leo's, and it was almost nice to see that I wasn't the only one he balked at having sex with.

Blake was involved with my sister, Steph, and though he was a descendant of Eros with a promiscuous past, his face was a picture of stubborn refusal. If he felt any temptation whatsoever, he was keeping it well buried.

Logan might have seemed like an obvious choice: an unattached manly man who was both very nice to look at and driven by a sense of duty. I was surprised to find he was pointedly refusing eye contact and trying to disappear into his chair.

That left Jack, who was always eager to prove he didn't take *anything* seriously. After letting a moment of uncomfortable silence pass, he rose to his feet with exaggerated ceremony and did his best preening peacock imitation.

"I will selflessly volunteer my services," he said in a booming voice, just in case he didn't already have our full attention. "I will joyfully fall on my *sword* in the service of mankind." He put his hand over his heart and raised his chin high. "It will be a *hard*ship above all others—"

"Oh, shut up and sit down," Jamaal growled, never Jack's biggest fan. "I'm sure you can think of a dozen more penis puns, but they're not exactly original. Or funny."

"What if I said I'm *up* to the task? Would that be funny enough for you, or would you still have a *bone* to pick?"

There was a collective groan and more than one "shut up, Jack." All of which only served to encourage him.

"Hey, I want Miss Rose to know she's getting the best *bang* for her buck," he said, stepping forward and making a sweeping bow in Rose's direction. Interestingly, while the rest of us were groaning and rolling our eyes, Rose's lips were twitching with a barely suppressed smile.

"And prove you're cock of the walk?" she asked, letting the smile bloom.

Jack was almost always smiling or laughing, his eyes twinkling with humor, but the way his face lit up now was like nothing I'd ever seen before. For someone who made such a point of trying to annoy people, he seemed to really like having Rose share his humor.

"A woman after my own heart!" he declared, forgetting to work in another pun. "Excuse me while I swoon."

Jack put his hand to his forehead and threw his head backward, then crumpled to the floor in a boneless heap. Rose rewarded him with a warm laugh. It looked like Jack was officially part of this expedition, which could turn out to be quite a headache for anyone else who went along.

"So, how many bodyguards do you suppose you'll need?" I asked, hoping comedy hour was over. "What kind of ambush are we talking about? I mean no offense, but I can't picture a fertility goddess as some kind of assassin-ninja."

Rose smiled again. "No. Niobe herself isn't much of a threat—there's nothing she can do that I can't do equally well. She couldn't have harmed Jasmine without help, and I presume she will bring whatever help she used before. They will likely be mortal men who are so enthralled by her that they'll obey her every command."

Blake looked at her skeptically as Jack, no longer the center of attention, rose without fanfare and returned to his seat. "So you're telling me a bunch of mortal men can kill or kidnap a goddess?"

"No," Rose said with a shake of her head. "But though we are stronger than mortal women, we are still vulnerable to superior numbers. If Niobe brings three or four men with her, they can likely restrain me long enough for her to kill me. She may well anticipate that I won't come undefended, so I suspect she will have more than three or four men with her."

"What about *Liberi*?" I asked, remembering suddenly that Cyrus had said a couple of his Olympians had gone missing.

Rose looked thoughtful. "It would likely be difficult for her to enthrall *Liberi* men, at least not with any great security. *Liberi* have enough of the divine in them not to be so susceptible to a goddess's charms."

Then again, Cyrus had said the ones who went missing were Konstantin's cronies, most of whom wouldn't give a rat's ass about the fate of the human race. If Niobe offered them something tempting in return, she wouldn't need to use supernatural powers to convince them to help her.

"We have to plan for the worst," I said, looking around the room and assessing who would be most useful to have in a fight. "I should go. If I can somehow figure out how to take a gun with me, I can take out a lot of men in a short amount of time." Assuming I could get over my squeamishness about shooting people. I'd forced myself to kill before, but it would never be easy for me—at least I hoped not. "I'd say bringing a war-god descendant is a no-brainer," I continued, indicating Logan. "And Jamaal and Sita might be scary enough to make mortal men run for their lives instead of sticking around." As a descendant of the death goddess, Kali, Jamaal was scary enough all on his own. He'd recently learned how to channel his death magic into a phantom tiger named Sita, who was one hell of a mean kitty. She also hated my guts, so letting her loose when I was around might not be the brightest idea.

"Well," Jack said, "since *I'm* going, you don't have to worry about getting weapons through security. I can make 'em look like ladies' underwear until we actually need them."

I raised an eyebrow. "And your illusions will fool the high-tech scanners at the airport?"

"Yep." He grinned. "And even if they don't, what TSA agent is going to hold up a pair of panties and try to convince people they're actually a gun?"

I gave him the dirty look he'd no doubt been hoping for. "Will it fool the scanner, or will they just not be able to find the gun the scanner's revealed? You can't have it both ways." He gave me what was supposed to be a mysterious grin, but looked more like a smirk.

I was pretty sure he'd meant it when he'd first replied that the scanner would be fooled, and he'd only tacked on that last bit about the panties because he was being his usual annoying self. But though it was hard to say I really *trusted* Jack, I did believe in the power of his illusion magic. One way or another, he would get us through security with every weapon we could possibly need tucked in our luggage.

I wasn't exactly thrilled to be planning a hasty trip to Bermuda when the problem of Cyrus and his one-week deadline was still hanging over our heads. I would have liked to take some more time to try to hunt down Anderson, but with my subconscious not divulging any clues, I wasn't sure I would do much good. Besides, I still harbored the hope that Anderson would soon get his head out of his ass and come back before the deadline. What would happen when he did was anyone's guess, but at least it would be *his* problem to solve, not mine.

According to Rose, Jasmine's altar was due to be renewed in three days' time, which added a certain frantic note to the preparations.

"If we're a couple of days late," Rose said, "the effects won't be too bad. But the longer it goes untended, the longer it will take to get it activated again, so sooner is better than later."

It would have been nice to have at least a week to plan our little excursion, but with Anderson MIA, Cyrus ready to go on the warpath, and the altar's juice failing, time was a luxury we didn't have. I wanted to be in Bermuda before the altar expired, and back from Bermuda with at least a couple of days to spare before Cyrus's deadline.

I arrived in Bermuda with Jamaal, Jack, Logan, and Rose one day before Jasmine's altar needed to be renewed. With a little help from Rose, Leo had rented a set of luxury cottages for us about a mile down the road from Jasmine's house, a gorgeous Bermuda-sand-pink stucco house on a cliff with a breathtaking view of the ocean.

From the beach below the cottages, we could just make out the house in the distance. We didn't know what kind of resistance to expect. Rose informed us that the altar could only be accessed from the basement, which concealed a secret chamber.

As soon as we arrived, we went down to the beach, and Logan used some military-grade binoculars to look over Jasmine's house from a safe distance.

"It's hard to see much," he said when he lowered the binoculars. "Too many trees in the way. The place looks empty, but there could be an army hiding in the bushes and I wouldn't be able to tell."

I bit my lip. Going in there blind was out of the question. We knew Niobe would have help guarding the altar, and we suspected some of that help might consist of the missing Olympians, but that wasn't enough information to go on.

"I can do some recon before we go in," Jack volunteered.

He promptly disappeared, and an ugly orange tomcat appeared in his place. He looked up at me and let out a plaintive, high-pitched meow. Then he trotted over to Jamaal and started winding himself around and between Jamaal's legs while purring like an outboard motor. He was lucky not to get booted in the face for his troubles.

"Not a bad idea," Logan said. "No one's going to pay any attention to a stray cat wandering around. Can you look around inside the house, or just outside?"

Jack turned back into himself while still practically standing on top of Jamaal, who shoved him away. Jack gave him a mock wounded stare, but thankfully let it go at that. He was being relatively well behaved, at least by his standards.

"Not as a cat," he said. "I'm not *really* turning into a cat. I can't slip through small openings or anything. I'm sure I can get in, but not without spoiling the 'I'm just a harmless cat' illusion."

"Stay outside, then," I said. "Recon does us no good if you get caught."

It didn't occur to me until after the words were out that I'd spoken as if I were somehow in charge. I would have apologized for the presumption, except no one else seemed to notice.

"Should I go now?" Jack asked. "Or should I wait until we're ready to go for the altar?"

Everyone looked to me for an answer, which made me squirm inside. "Both. We'll come up with a plan based on what you see tonight, then we'll double-check to make sure nothing's changed before we go in tomorrow."

Jack nodded. "You got it, boss."

I'd have objected to the term, but Jack had put on his cat disguise and streaked off into the bushes before I had a chance to say anything.

FOUR

Jack's recon gave us *nothing*. There were no guards lurking in the lush foliage that surrounded the house. Nor did he see any signs of life inside the house itself, despite having peeked through every window he could reach in his cat disguise.

"I could have gotten to the second-floor windows," he said, "but it might have looked pretty unnatural—and likely suspicious—if someone saw a cat climbing a drainpipe."

I had to agree that caution was the best choice. Niobe probably had at least two Olympians with her, and they might very well guess an illusion was at work if they saw a cat behaving in an un-catlike manner around the house.

"What about video surveillance?"

Jack shook his head. "Not that I could see."

"So whatever Niobe's got in store for us," I said, "it's probably inside the house."

Just because Jack hadn't seen any video surveillance didn't mean there was none. I knew just how small spy cameras could be. But at least we wouldn't have to worry about an ambush the moment we set foot on the property, assuming nothing changed between now and then.

"If you want, I can spend more time casing the place tomorrow," Jack said. "Maybe if I make myself comfortable in a tree for a few hours during the day, I'll see something interesting."

It was worth a shot, but I wasn't feeling terribly hopeful.

"If we don't learn anything new tomorrow," Jamaal said, "then we'll have to go in anyway. We don't have time to watch the place for days. We've got too many other problems to deal with."

I didn't like feeling rushed, but Jamaal was right. This couldn't wait.

"Once we get there," he continued, "Sita can check out the inside of the house. She won't be able to tell us what she sees, but if anyone's waiting in ambush, she'll definitely flush them out."

It sounded like a pretty good plan—if we could trust Sita. It would suck—especially for me—if we counted on her helping us and she decided she'd rather maul me instead.

We all agreed it was best to go to bed early and get a good night's sleep, but I was too uncomfortable with the Sita situation to be that practical. Instead, I made my way over to Jamaal's cottage and knocked on his door. When he opened it and saw me standing there, he looked wary. I restrained my urge to roll my eyes.

"Come down to the beach with me," I said, pointing to the narrow stone stairway that led from our cottages to the beach below.

Jamaal's eyes narrowed with suspicion. "Why?"

This time, I *did* roll my eyes. "Because we're in Bermuda, and it's a beautiful, clear night, and we have our own private beach."

He looked at me like I was nuts. "Do I look like the kind of guy who likes romantic walks on the beach?"

"You don't look like a guy who likes going to art museums, either. Looks can be deceiving."

There was no way Jamaal believed I wanted nothing more than to snuggle on the beach . . . though that certainly would have been nice under other circumstances. But despite his long list of hang-ups, he truly was beginning to emerge from the rock-hard shell he'd hidden behind for so long.

"Fine," he grumped, as if this were all some great inconvenience. "We'll go for a moonlit walk on the beach."

I tried not to look too smug as he stepped outside and closed the cottage door behind him.

"Don't you want a sweatshirt or jacket or something?" I asked. He was wearing his usual jeans and plain short-sleeved T-shirt, but though it was nowhere near as cold here as it was at home, the air still had a definite nip.

"I'm fine," he said, tucking his hands into his pockets while shrugging. "Don't try to mother me."

I held my hands up in a gesture of surrender. I'd seen Jamaal walk around outside in the snow with just a T-shirt on. He was made of much sterner stuff than I.

I led the way down to the beach. My nerves were pretty jittery, because I knew how terribly wrong this conversation was capable of going, but even so I couldn't help drinking in the beauty of my surroundings. The moon was bright enough to light our way without completely drowning out the blanket of stars. The stairway to the beach was surrounded on both sides by bushes, some of which were flowering and fragrant even in January.

When we emerged from the bushes and my feet hit the sand, I let out a little sigh of contentment. The water was calm, gently lapping at the beach, and though the moon provided enough light to see by, you couldn't see very far, which made our cove feel even more secluded.

Despite the chill in the air, I found I couldn't help slipping off my sneakers and rolling up my pants so I could feel the sand between my toes. I was surprised when I saw Jamaal following suit, and almost collapsed in shock when he reached out and took my hand. He grinned at me. *Grinned.* Jamaal doesn't grin. Ever.

I sniffed for the scent of clove cigarettes or pot, both of which he smoked when his temper was on a knife's edge. Not that I'd ever seen a hint that either one of them mellowed him out *this* much. And all I smelled was salt air and the faintest hint of some flower I didn't recognize.

Still holding my hand, Jamaal shrugged. "Okay, I'll admit it: I do actually kind of like moonlit walks on the beach. The atmosphere is very . . . soothing."

Was this really Jamaal beside me, or was it Jack in disguise pulling a prank? I wouldn't have put it past the trickster, but I knew in my heart that Jamaal was the real deal. I just didn't know what to make of his calm.

Hand in hand, we walked till we found the firm damp sand just beyond the reach of the waves. Even in my fleecy pullover, I shivered at the chill as a gentle ocean breeze blew through my hair, but I wouldn't have missed this moment for the world. Tomorrow could turn out to be total hell, and this peaceful night might be the calm before the storm, but that made me appreciate it even more.

I marveled that Jamaal was not only willing to hold my hand but had actually initiated the contact. Before, I always had to make the first move, and he would resist like his life depended on it, afraid showing any sign of connection to me would enrage Sita. I often wondered if Sita's dislike of me was fueled by Jamaal's own fear of intimacy. Did the tiger really have a mind of her own, or was her mind a reflection of Jamaal's?

In the end, it was a moot point. Whether Sita's jealousy was fueled by Jamaal's subconscious or her own independent mind, it could potentially turn disastrous tomorrow.

I squeezed Jamaal's hand. "So, what's changed?" I asked him, risking a brief glance at his face before looking away so he wouldn't feel cornered. The moonlight softened the sharp angles on his cheekbones and made him look less forbidding. "Why are you willing to hold my hand, when usually you act like there's a restraining order keeping you at least fifty feet away?"

Jamaal made a soft growling sound under his breath. "I don't!" he protested.

"Uh-huh. When was the last time you voluntarily touched me?"

He came to an abrupt stop and, not surprisingly, let go of my hand. "That would be the time Sita came without being called and nearly bit your head off. There's a reason I keep my distance."

"I know that," I responded. Using Sita to vent his death magic had definitely helped Jamaal calm his temper, but I still thought the price was too steep if she wouldn't let him get close to anyone. I'd voiced that thought before and been shot down, so I kept it to myself this time. "So why did you take my hand tonight?"

He folded his arms across his chest and glared down at me. "Are you complaining?"

Jamaal is a pro at conversational diversionary tactics. Unfortunately for him, I was used to it, and refused to be diverted. "You know I'm not. And now I'm wondering why you're trying so hard to avoid answering the question."

He shook his head. He usually wore colorful beads at the ends of his shoulder-length braids, but tonight he'd gone with black ones, and only the sound of them clicking together reminded me they were there.

"Why do you always have to ask so many questions?" he asked. "Can't you just take something at face value for once?"

I reached my hand out toward him as if to shake. "Hello, my name is Nikki, and I'm a private investigator. Nice to meet you."

He glared at my hand until I dropped it back to my side. He's one of the more strong-willed people I've ever known, but he'd met his match in me.

Jamaal let out a frustrated huff. "All right, all right. I just . . . I have a bad feeling about tomorrow. I don't like walking into what we know is a trap without having any idea what's lying in wait." He put his hands on my shoulders, looking down into my eyes. "Sita already hates you. I don't think us holding hands will make it any worse than it already is, and I just . . . wanted something nice in case tomorrow really sucks."

I reached up and touched the side of his face, eyes locked with his. I wanted to go up on tiptoe and kiss him, but the difficult conversation had to come first. He might not want to kiss me afterward, but that was a risk I had to take.

Still cupping his cheek, I took a deep breath and then waded in. "We need to talk about Sita," I said.

I guess he heard something ominous in my tone, because his hands dropped from my shoulders and he took a small step backward, enough so my hand could no longer reach his cheek.

"What is there to talk about?"

"I need to know that if we go in there tomorrow, she's going to attack the bad guys instead of attacking *me*."

Jamaal put on an offended look, but it was clear from the expression in his eyes that he was worried, too. "She's not stupid. She'll know who the real threat is."

"But will she *care*?" Jamaal started to respond, but I cut

him off. "I think she and I need to make peace with each other, and I think we need to do it now."

His eyes went comically wide. "Please tell me you're not suggesting what I think you're suggesting."

"I'm suggesting that you summon Sita now so she and I can have a little heart-to-heart before we potentially go into battle tomorrow."

He took another step backward like he was prepared to bolt. "You're *crazy*! That's the dumbest idea I've ever heard from you, and that's saying a lot."

I reminded myself that he was feeling cornered and that I shouldn't take anything he said personally. "Yeah, letting her out tomorrow in the heat of battle when all our lives depend on it and we don't know if she can be trusted is a much smarter idea," I countered. "If you can't keep her under control tonight, when you can put your full concentration on her, then she and I can't both go tomorrow."

Figuring out which one of us shouldn't go would be a challenge—Sita would be able to wade in without risk, but unlike me she wouldn't be able to take out multiple targets in quick succession—but I was really hoping it wouldn't come to that. Sita had proven before that she had way beyond an animal's intelligence and seemed to understand what people were saying to her. I just had to hope that intelligence ran deep enough for her to see the logic in making peace with me.

Of course, first I had to convince Jamaal, who looked like he was near panic.

"We have to try," I told him in a soothing a voice. "She can't do me any permanent harm if it turns out you can't control her, and I promise I won't hold it against you if that happens."

I rested my case on those words, knowing that I needed to give Jamaal a little time and space to think it over. I would be the one in physical danger if Jamaal lost control of Sita, but it would do some serious damage to his psyche if I got hurt. He had always been ashamed of his inability to control his temper and his death magic, each of which fueled the other in a sometimes-unbearable feedback loop. Losing control of Sita would mean he hadn't improved as much as he wanted to think, and that would hurt like hell. But sometimes we have to swallow unpalatable truths, and this was one of those times.

Stuffing his hands into his pockets, Jamaal walked away from the water and plopped down onto the dry sand. "This is *such* a bad idea," I heard him mutter under his breath, and I realized I'd won the argument. Hooray for me.

Now that I'd gotten my way, adrenaline began to rush through my veins and my breathing shallowed. All well and good to build a logical argument for why we needed to do this, but that didn't mean the prospect didn't scare the bejesus out of me. I'd seen Sita in action before, and if she didn't feel inclined to listen to my rational argument, this could get very ugly very fast.

I moved a little farther away from Jamaal, closer to the water's edge. I didn't know if the water would discourage a *real* tiger, much less a phantom one with human or near-human intelligence, but if she came after me, I figured I'd dive in and find out. The edge of a wave lapped against my bare heel, and it was all I could do not to jump and yelp at the sudden cold. Diving in would not be fun, and I hoped like hell it wouldn't be necessary.

Sitting cross-legged on the sand, Jamaal closed his eyes. It used to take considerable time and effort for him to summon Sita, but the process was getting faster. Five hundred pounds of surly tiger appeared on the sand beside him before I felt even remotely prepared to face her.

Sita greeted me in the usual way, with a tooth-baring snarl that made my bones rattle. Her eyes fixed on me with unnerving intensity, and she lowered herself into a crouch as she began stalking toward me. Jamaal opened his eyes and reached out to her, touching her flank.

"Let her be, Jamaal," I said. Inside, I was practically gibbering with fear, very aware that I was prey in the presence of an apex predator, but I think I sounded relatively calm. "She and I have to work things out between ourselves."

I don't know whether Jamaal did as I asked and let her be, or if Sita just chose to ignore him, but she kept stalking closer, ready to pounce at a moment's notice. My pulse pounded in my throat, and it took a hell of a lot of willpower to stop myself from backing away.

I held my ground and met Sita's eyes, hoping she wouldn't take that as some kind of challenge. "I'm not your enemy, Sita," I told the tiger. "You and I both love Jamaal." Internally I winced at hearing myself use the L word. I hadn't intended to, but now was not the time to act embarrassed and equivocate. "I want what's best for him, and I hope that's what you want, too."

Sita snarled again and kept coming toward me. This time, I couldn't stop myself from taking a step back, even though it put me within reach of the chilly waves. A little cold water was the least of my problems.

"You're *hurting* him," I said. Sita didn't appreciate that, and her snarl turned into a mini roar. "I know you don't mean to," I hastened to continue, "but you are anyway. Humans need contact with other humans, and Jamaal has been isolated for so long. You've helped him so much with managing the death magic! Because of you, he can finally have real friends without worrying that he's going to lose control and hurt them." I hoped phantom tigers liked flattery as much as most humans do.

"But the problem is you won't let him. He's not afraid his own temper is going to be dangerous anymore, but he has to worry about what *you'll* do, and that's just as bad."

Sita was still moving toward me, but I was mildly encouraged by the fact that she hadn't attacked me yet. She could cross an enormous distance with a single bound, so I was already well within her kill zone. Either she was listening to me, or she was playing with me. I took another couple of steps backward just to give myself a little more space. I now had water up to my ankles and I had to fight for balance as the sand shifted beneath my feet, but at least Sita didn't speed up her approach.

"You *know* him," I told her. "Better than anyone else. Think about how he would feel if you hurt someone he cared about. Do you really want to put him through that?"

Sita paused and narrowed her eyes at me. Her tail twitched, and she showed me her teeth again.

"We both want what's best for him," I said, and this time I was determined not to back away any farther. "There's going to be a fight tomorrow, and he's going to need both of us there to keep him safe." Jamaal probably would have bristled at the suggestion that he needed our protection, but my slow retreat toward the water had put enough space between us that he probably couldn't hear me over the waves. Either that, or he was giving me one of those looks that kill, but I wasn't about to take my eyes off Sita to check.

Sita started forward again, and I dug my toes into the sand to keep from retreating.

"Please, Sita," I said. "Let's work together. Jamaal deserves so much better than what he's gotten from life."

I was being consciously manipulative, and yet my own words made my throat tighten and my eyes burn. Jamaal had suffered so, so much over his life, and though he wouldn't appreciate anything that resembled pity, I hoped he could at least tolerate some empathy. Aside from practical matters, I *wanted* this for Jamaal, wanted him to have Sita and still be able to have relationships with other people, to be loved.

Sita was close now, and a wave lapped at her front paws. She looked down at them with a soft snarl, lifting and shaking first one, then the other. I fought a sudden urge to giggle. She started toward me again, and another wave wet her paws. Once again, she flicked the water off before taking another step. And another. Step, flick. Step, flick. Step, flick. I had to suck my cheeks in to keep from laughing. It's hard to look dainty and menacing at the same time, even for a quarter-ton tiger.

I swallowed past laughter and fear and took my life into my own hands. "How about if I come to you, since you don't like the water?"

Sita froze in midflick. I'm not much of an expert in reading feline facial expressions, but I interpreted the way she looked at me then as total shock. There was no question that she understood what I'd just said.

Gathering my courage, I took a cautious step closer to Sita. Her lips twitched with a warning snarl, but I ignored it and took a second step. She finally put both her paws down, now ignoring the water that lapped at them. Behind her, I could faintly see the man-shaped shadow that was Jamaal, and I could almost imagine him holding his breath.

I was ashamed to feel the quivering in my knees as I continued to approach, one careful step at a time. Sita wasn't leaping to attack me, but the narrowed eyes, bared teeth, and twitching tail didn't look all that welcoming. Maybe I was just shivering because I'd been walking in the cold ocean water and not because I was quivering in fear. Yeah, that was it.

"Can we make peace?" I asked her softly as I took a final step, one that put me solidly within reach of her dishpan-sized paws. She looked up at me and made eye contact.

Her sudden snarl caught me by surprise, and I made an embarrassing bleating sound as she lunged. She moved so fast that I had no warning, couldn't even take a step backward.

The top of her head made solid contact with the center of my stomach, knocking the wind out of me while not actually hurting me. However, the blow was easily hard enough to push me off my feet, and I landed on my butt in the water. Sita did the lift-flick thing with each of her front paws, sending sprays of water right into my face, then turned around and sauntered back onto the beach, where Jamaal awaited her.

FIVE

I sat stunned and chilled in the shallow water. Sita looked back at me over her shoulder once, then disappeared, leaving Jamaal and me alone.

Jamaal was on his feet, and he probably would have come and given me a hand up if his first step in my direction didn't make him sway dizzily. He had a much easier time summoning Sita these days, but it still took a lot out of him and he needed some recovery time afterward.

Teeth chattering, I climbed to my feet. I'd fallen in ankle-deep water, which was more than deep enough to soak my jeans through and through. I'd caught myself with my hands, which meant my fleece sleeves were wet practically to the elbow, and the water Sita had flicked in my face dripped off my chin and the end of my nose.

I tried in vain to wring the water out of my sleeves one by one as I made my way back onto the dry beach, but even if I could get them to stop dripping, I'd still be soaked. I was also now a sand-magnet and could feel the abrasive rubbing where it had gotten under the waistband of my jeans.

When I was finally close enough to Jamaal to see his face in the moonlight, I found that he was smiling broadly. Which I supposed was better than laughing out loud, but not by much.

I shoved a damp tendril of hair out of my face and willed myself to stop shivering. "Why don't you go take a seat in the ocean and see how much *you* like it," I grumbled at him.

His smile remained firmly in place. Jamaal with a smile on his face can take a woman's breath away, and parts of me started heating up despite the soaked and sandy clothes.

"I still haven't figured out if you're brave or stupid," Jamaal said with a shake of his head.

"I didn't realize the two were mutually exclusive."

He enveloped me in a hug, and I let out an incoherent sound of protest as I tried unsuccessfully to hold him off.

"I'm all wet!" I reminded him, as if he could possibly have forgotten.

"Ask me if I care," he mumbled into my hair, holding on and sharing his delicious body heat.

I took him at his word and wrapped my arms around his waist, pressing the side of my head against his chest. The steady thump of his heart was as delicious as his warmth, and my shivering eased.

"So I'm going to guess the message was Sita will tolerate me for the greater good," I said. I couldn't decide whether shoving me into the water was supposed to be a playful gesture or just a reminder that she still held me in contempt. But I was willing to settle for anything that didn't involve ripping my head off.

Jamaal pressed a kiss to the top of my head. "That's my takeaway, too. And though I hate to admit it, I guess this means you were right."

I grinned against his chest and squeezed more tightly with my arms. I was pleasantly surprised Jamaal deigned to admit it, and I knew both of us would feel a whole lot safer tomorrow now that Sita and I had forged some kind of truce.

I would have loved to preserve that moment for another hour or so, would have loved to just stand there on the moonlit beach and enjoy the feeling of Jamaal's arms around me. Unfortunately, while my shivering had calmed somewhat, it hadn't stopped. The otherwise lovely ocean breeze was making my jeans and my sleeves into air conditioners, and my lips were probably turning blue. I considered taking the jeans and fleece off—I knew Jamaal wouldn't complain—but I doubted I'd be much warmer without them. And though my truce with Sita might make it possible for Jamaal and me to explore our attraction further, it probably wouldn't be smart to go too fast. Especially not when we were in for a fight tomorrow.

Reluctantly, I pulled away. For the first time I could re-member, things felt almost peaceful between Jamaal and me. The silence as we made our way back to the cottages above was distinctly companionable.

Jack kept watch on Jasmine's house for all of the next day and saw no sign of anyone moving, inside or out. That didn't make me—or anyone else—feel any better. There was no way Niobe had left the altar undefended, and we'd all have felt a lot better about things if we had some clue what to expect. Personally, I worried that there was some kind of booby trap set up inside the house. Sita would go in and explore before any of us tried it, but would she recognize, say, a bomb if she saw one?

Because we feared we might need to make a speedy get-away, we drove our rental car over to Jasmine's place for our attempt at reaching the altar. Not the stealthiest approach, even though Logan killed the lights before we turned into the drive-way and rolled toward the house.

Logan stopped the car in the middle of the driveway instead of pulling off to the side to park. We gathered our weapons and piled out of the car, our eyes straining in the darkness as we tried to spot any hidden threats Jack might have overlooked.

The house was surrounded by lush tropical vegetation, with beautifully manicured bushes and flower beds all around. There was a narrow strip of lawn on each side of the driveway, but that lawn ended abruptly with a wall of junglelike green-ery: trees, vines, and untamed bushes that looked eager to spill over and reclaim their territory.

Jamaal summoned Sita, and I tensed in case our truce had been a figment of my imagination. She gave me a glare and curled her lip to show me her teeth, but thankfully that was the full extent of her aggression. Hell, for her that was practically a friendly greeting.

The night was alive with sounds, from the steady chorus of frogs and insects to the crash of the waves far below to the rustling of the leaves in the breeze. The moon and the stars were obscured by clouds, and we had to take a few minutes for our eyes to adjust to the darkness before starting forward.

Sita took the lead, and we made sure Rose stayed behind us. She was much harder to kill than the rest of us, but she was also a noncombatant. Logan had tried to arm her, offering to teach her how to shoot, but she had staunchly refused. Probably just as well. Who wanted an amateur with a gun running around in their midst?

Logan, Jack, and Jamaal each carried an intimidating automatic—Logan had told me what kind, but the array of numbers and letters had promptly slipped my mind. Instead of my usual revolver, I was carrying a Glock semiauto.

We crept up the driveway toward the house. When we were at the base of the front porch, Jamaal crouched beside Sita and whispered instructions. She then padded silently up the steps and walked right through the door into the house, her body insubstantial whenever she wanted it to be. We all held our breath, waiting for the sound of screams, as a light rain began pattering down.

Even knowing that there had to be trouble awaiting us inside the house, I still had the nagging feeling that this had been too easy so far. I kept scanning the darkness around us, looking for some clue as to where our enemies were hidden, because surely they had to be hidden somewhere. Never mind that Jack had thoroughly checked the area and seen no one.

The rain intensified, making the visibility even worse. I shivered and wished my jacket were waterproof as the wind kicked up. We should have gone ahead and stormed the altar last night, when the sky had been clear and bright.

I heard the soft *thunk* of a car door closing somewhere in the distance. I glanced over my shoulder, but the only car in sight was our rental, and all four of its doors were hanging open as we'd left them, ready for our quick escape. The sound must have come from a neighbor's place.

There were still no screams from inside Jasmine's house, which meant that Sita still hadn't located anyone lying in wait. My gaze kept darting around anxiously, and that's when I saw it, carefully concealed within the branches of a tall bush.

A spy camera. So small and hidden I probably wouldn't have noticed it if I didn't have personal experience with the things.

What if the enemy wasn't waiting for us inside the house? What if they were just hanging out nearby somewhere, where no one could see them? What if they were watching the feed from that spy camera, waiting for a threat to present itself?

And then I remembered the sound of the car door closing, and I knew we were in deep shit.

"Everyone get down!" I suddenly shouted, taking a couple of running steps toward Rose and grabbing her hand. I dragged her to the ground, but not before a *boom* nearly deafened me.

There was a sickening, smashing-melons sound, and Rose's hand went entirely limp in mine as we both hit the ground. I turned to ask if she was okay, my brain not quite ready to register the shower of hot liquid that splashed all over me.

Rose's head was gone, as was a large portion of her upper chest and shoulder, scattered in little bits and pieces of blood and flesh and bone, forming a garish red splash over Jasmine's pretty green lawn. It was too dark to really see the colors, but my imagination had no trouble filling in the gaps.

I'd seen more blood and gore in the last few months than I'd ever seen in my life, and I wasn't as squeamish as I used to be. But nothing could have prepared me for *this* level of horror, and my entire body just froze up on me. I couldn't speak. I couldn't move. Hell, I could hardly even *breathe*, and I certainly couldn't *think*.

Everyone around me dove for cover, but I just sat there and dripped, staring at what was left of Rose's body, unable to process anything. I was vaguely aware of Jamaal yelling at me. I knew I had to move, that I was a sitting duck, but I couldn't seem to force my limbs to do anything.

I had forgotten about Sita, who must have heard the shot and come running. She barreled into my back with the force of a freight train, knocking me flat on my face. The lawn made a disturbing *squooshing* sound under me that I hoped was just because of the rain soaking the grass. A streak of blinding light came shooting from somewhere near the head of the driveway, electricity crackling the air around it. The lightning passed right through where I'd been sitting a moment ago. It hit the pavement with a crack so loud it left my ears ringing, and was quickly followed by a burst of automatic-weapons fire.

And then, because the situation wasn't bad enough already, everything went dark.

I don't mean natural dark, like the night. I mean inky, solid, absolute dark, the kind where you literally can't see your hand in front of your face. I knew this particular brand of darkness, having experienced it before. Emma, Anderson's most recent ex, had been a descendant of Nyx, the Greek goddess of night, and she'd had the power to create impenetrable blackness.

With the wreckage of Rose's body now hidden from my view, I was able to get my brain back online. It was still raining pretty hard, but no way had that bolt of lightning come from the sky. That meant the enemy included at least two *Liberi*, one descendant of Nyx and one of Zeus. Based on the sheer volume of gunfire, I estimated they had at least two or three others with them, whether *Liberi* or mortal I had no idea.

The good news was that in the unnatural darkness, the bad guys couldn't possibly see what they were shooting at. The bad news was that none of *us* could see, either. I had dropped my gun when Sita knocked me flat, but I found it again with a little groping. The artificial darkness was so dense I couldn't even see the muzzle flashes as the enemy kept shooting at us in short, intense bursts.

I aimed toward the sound of one of those bursts, and my finger tightened on the trigger. My supernatural skills allowed me to target accurately based on sound, but at the last moment,

I changed my mind and slipped my finger off the trigger. I might well hit whoever was shooting, but I had no idea where Jack or Jamaal or Logan were, and I didn't know if my power would prevent me from accidentally shooting one of them if they were in the way.

I started crawling forward on my belly, looking for an end to the swath of darkness the Nyx descendant had created. Emma's had always been pretty small, so maybe I could crawl clear of it and get a visual on the shooters.

I hadn't gotten very far when I followed the logic of my own thoughts and realized something was off. If the patch of darkness was that small, then surely two or three guys raking it with automatic-weapons fire ought to have hit *someone* by now. Maybe they had—my friends weren't shooting back or making any noise to help the enemy find targets—but I'd had no sense of bullets whizzing past or making impact with the ground near me.

Either they were the worst shots in history, or they weren't really trying to shoot us. So why would they form this pool of blackness around us and then not shoot into it?

Rose!

In the heat and the horror of the moment, I'd allowed myself to forget that Rose was a *goddess*. That bullet might have made a wreckage of her body, but unless it was fired by Niobe herself, Rose would not be dead for long. Which meant that our enemies had to get their hands on that body to exact a more permanent solution to their problem.

My conviction that they weren't shooting into the darkness wasn't so strong that I was willing to stand up straight, but I rose into a crouch and tried to orient myself. My sense of direction had always been good, and it was pretty close to flawless now that I was *Liberi*. I took a couple steps toward where I knew Rose's body was lying, meaning to stand over it and guard it with my life.

Unfortunately, my understanding of the enemy's tactics

had come too late. The darkness suddenly lifted, and I heard the gunning of an engine followed by the screech of tires.

Rose's body was gone.

Logan and Jack were both crouched near the bushes, unhurt. Jamaal was lying facedown on the lawn. Sita was parked on top of him, shielding him with her body and holding him down with one massive paw on his back as he tried to get out from under her. The sight might have been comical in another context.

I entertained the brief notion of diving into our car and taking off in pursuit, but one look at our sorry rental showed that was not an option. The car was riddled with bullets, glass shot out of every window and all the tires thoroughly flattened.

We weren't going anywhere.

SIX

It wasn't long before we heard the sound of emergency vehicles making their way toward us. Thanks to our shot-up car in the middle of the driveway, there was no way to cover up our presence at the crime scene.

"Can't you hide it with one of your illusions?" I asked Jack, but he shook his head.

"I can cover it with an illusion, but it'll still be there, and someone's bound to run into it. That would get weird, don't you think?"

I didn't like it, but he was right. And a bunch of foreigners carrying illegal firearms and standing in the middle of a violent crime scene was going to be bad, bad news. I didn't want to get an up-close-and-personal view of the Bermuda jail system.

"I can't hide the car," Jack said, "but I *can* hide the weapons." He looked me over from head to toe. "And *you*."

I shuddered, trying not to think about what I might look like, what might have soaked into and stained my clothing. I looked at the area where Rose's body had lain and saw that our enemies had gathered up any significant chunks that the bullet had left. I wondered if it would have been possible for Rose's life force to return to one of those chunks instead of her captured body. Maybe that was why there was so little left behind. The rain was doing a decent job of washing away the blood on the grass, or at least diluting it so much that you couldn't really see it in the dark, but I didn't think it was having a similar effect on me.

"We don't have much time," Jack said. "Hand over the guns and let's find some secluded place where they're not likely to trip over them—or us—while they process the scene."

"What about Logan and Jamaal?"

But they were both handing their weapons to Jack and me and making shooing gestures. I hoped Jamaal's temper was up to the challenge of dealing with the police, and that he wouldn't collapse from exhaustion after having summoned Sita.

"We'll deal with it," Logan assured me, and since the sirens were getting uncomfortably close, there wasn't time for an argument.

Jack and I crouched at the far edge of the property, well away from where all the shooting had happened, the weapons piled at our feet while he created some illusion I couldn't see.

Pretty soon, a veritable army of police and emergency vehicles swarmed the place. Logan and Jamaal were immediately taken into custody, and crime scene techs started scouring the place, taking pictures and otherwise collecting evidence. The rain continued to fall, sometimes with more intensity, sometimes with less. Jack and I watched the process carefully, but we saw no evidence that the police noticed any of the blood or other . . . stuff left over from where Rose had been shot.

"If they had some reason to look," Jack whispered to me, "like a body, or a witness saying someone was shot, they'd probably find something. Tonight, they just want to get out of the rain."

I figured he was right on that score and wondered how they were explaining the bizarre scene to themselves. There were hundreds if not thousands of rounds fired, and yet apparently no one was hurt. Jamaal and Logan would no doubt claim they were in the wrong place at the wrong time, which wouldn't do much to help the cops figure out what had happened.

The police towed our defunct rental and cordoned off the entire area with crime scene tape, leaving a few hapless souls to keep watch. My guess was that they decided to save the more thorough examination of the crime scene for daylight.

The cops left guarding the scene were at the head of the driveway facing out, which gave Jack and me the chance to creep back to the area where Rose had been shot and look for anything that might clue the cops in that someone had been hurt here and cause them to look closer. It was a good thing we did, because I found the bullet that killed Rose, buried in the trunk of a small tree by the porch. It was the size of four or five bullets put together, and if the crime scene techs had found it, it definitely would have stood out—and given them an idea where to focus their investigation.

As it was, I pried the bullet out of the tree and hoped no one would be interested in the hole that was left. Jack and I then made our way back to our cottages on foot with the weapons shielded from sight by another of his illusions.

Although it was clear to everyone involved that the police weren't happy about it, they eventually had to let Logan and Jamaal go. There was no evidence that either of them had committed a crime, and ostensibly they were just a couple of American tourists who'd accidentally gotten in the middle of something that had nothing to do with them.

The police instructed Jamaal and Logan not to leave the

country, but they had no grounds to insist. I hated to leave the altar dying, but without Rose there was nothing left we could do. Besides, we still had pressing problems waiting for us at home, seeing as Anderson hadn't miraculously appeared while we'd been gone.

By the time Jamaal and Logan finally got back to the cottages, Jack and I had packed everything up so we could go straight to the airport and catch the next flight home.

"Tell me you didn't let Jack near my stuff," Jamaal said as he eyed the suitcases suspiciously.

"Of course not," I assured him. I could only imagine what kinds of "hilarious" pranks the trickster would have played if I'd let him pack anyone's belongings but his own. "I packed your bag myself."

But things were bad. That altar was losing its juice, and we no longer had a helpful fertility goddess ready to lend us a hand. And even if we did, Niobe and her accomplices would still be keeping a careful eye on the altar to make the second attempt as disastrous as the first.

The best-case scenario would be for Anderson to emerge from wherever he was hiding and somehow fix the enormous mess he had created, but there was still no sign of him. Barring that, we had to find another one of Niobe's sisters, convince her that renewing Jasmine's altar was the right thing to do, and then actually *get* to the altar to perform the ceremony. We knew Niobe had at least two *Liberi* on her team as well as two or three others, one of whom was apparently a sniper. When I showed the bullet I'd dug out of the tree to Logan, he said it was a .50-caliber round fired from a sniper rifle, probably from a significant distance. The shooting, the lightning bolt, and the darkness had all been used to blind and distract us while they hauled Rose's body away so Niobe could kill her more permanently.

We went over all these details when we got back to the house, still reeling from our dismal failure.

"How could we possibly have gotten around the trap they set?" I asked, shaking my head.

"If we'd known what was coming," Logan said, "we could maybe have kept better track of Rose and made sure she was always surrounded."

Jamaal dismissed the idea quickly. "We'd still have been totally blind, fighting someone we couldn't see. And even if we hadn't been, there were at least two gunmen and then whoever was in the distance with the sniper rifle. Nikki might have been able to take out the guys with the automatic weapons if it weren't for the dark, but she couldn't have done anything about the sniper. Not with a handgun."

We'd been doomed since the moment we turned into that driveway, and there was no reason to think we wouldn't be just as doomed if we tried a second time.

"The fact is," Logan said, "there just aren't enough of us to fight our way through to that altar. Not when they're all set up and ready for us. We're going to need more people."

"Well, we're all we have," I countered. The moment the words left my mouth, I understood what he'd been getting at, and my jaw dropped. The moment Rose had shown up at the house, I'd pushed Cyrus and his ultimatum to the back burner of my mind, trying to focus on one problem at a time. I was still aware of his deadline, the clock ticking away, but I kept telling myself I'd deal with it later—all while clinging to the hope that Anderson would show up so I didn't have to deal with it at all. Asking Cyrus to help with our current crisis would never have entered my mind.

"No way!" I said, glaring at Logan.

"As soon as you come up with a reasonable way to get us to that altar without any help, you can reject my suggestion out of hand," Logan said. "So, what's your suggestion?"

He had me there, and he knew it. There were probably ways individual members of our merry band could get safely into that house, thanks to our various powers, but the problem was we had to get someone *else* in, and not just for a couple of minutes. The ceremony would take time, so even if we miraculously snuck another goddess in there, she and Jack would be sitting ducks for however long it took. Assuming we could find another of Niobe's sisters and convince her to cooperate.

"In case you need a reminder," I said, "Cyrus and the Olympians are the enemy. He's planning to start killing us off one by one if we can't prove his daddy's alive, which we can't do."

"Keep in mind his highest priority," Blake said. "Cyrus wants what's best for Cyrus, at all times." Blake should know, considering the twisted friends-with-benefits relationship he and Cyrus had once had going—and that Cyrus would stop at nothing to resume. The whole reason Cyrus had turned me over to his father was that Konstantin had promised to "give" him Blake as a reward.

"All the more reason why he'd laugh us out of the room if we asked for help."

"Not if you take the long view," Blake argued. "He and the rest of the Olympians don't give a shit about anyone but themselves, but that doesn't mean they'd enjoy a world completely devoid of human beings. They need mortals to do all kinds of stuff for them, like provide food and housing and entertainment. In a world without mortals, the Olympians would have to provide for themselves, and I guarantee you that isn't something they're interested in doing."

I chewed my lip as I considered Blake's argument. I had never thought about it that way before, but he was right. Olympians might consider mortals on par with cattle, but that didn't mean they didn't want the cattle around for their convenience. And there were a hell of a lot more Olympians than there were of us. With greater numbers and a larger variety of powers at our disposal, we might actually stand a chance. Hell, Cyrus was a descendant of Helios, the sun god, and I had seen him create something like a sunburst before. Maybe his light could counter the Nyx descendant's dark.

I wasn't happy about having to negotiate with Cyrus, especially not from a position of weakness. But if nothing else, getting him to lend us some of his people might buy me a little time before I had to deal with our inability to prove his father was alive.

SEVEN

I'm not sure how I ended up being Anderson's stand-in while he was gone, but I was the one who called Cyrus and asked for a meeting, and none of Anderson's *Liberi* seemed to object to the way I was taking charge. I did a little fancy verbal footwork on the phone and allowed Cyrus to believe that we were meeting so I could personally give him the proof of life he'd been demanding. I figured he'd be more willing to show up if he didn't know he'd be facing a request for help.

We met in the same coffee shop where we'd met before, under very similar circumstances. I had Logan and Maggie with me, and every person in the shop was an Olympian. I suspected Cyrus had bought the place or he probably wouldn't have been able to take it over so completely. They had more than enough firepower to mop the floor with us, and I reminded myself of the need to be at least marginally diplomatic despite my loathing for Cyrus.

As with last time, there were no preliminary pleasantries or offers of coffee. Cyrus merely gestured me into the seat across from him, his stare uncommonly cold and unfriendly.

"Three more of my Olympians have gone missing since we last spoke," he growled. "I don't think proof of my father's life is going to be enough anymore."

Ah. So I wasn't the only one who'd shown up under false pretenses. I realized there was a good chance Cyrus was planning to kill me and my friends right on the spot in retaliation for what he was assuming was Anderson's killing spree. I also realized that we now most likely had at least five *Liberi* working with Niobe, and I wasn't happy to learn the odds were stacked even more heavily in her favor.

"I'm afraid I've figured out what's happening to them," I said calmly, "and it's not good for any of us. The first two who went missing were a descendant of Zeus and a descendant of Nyx, right?"

Cyrus's puzzled look told me this was not at all how he'd expected me to take the news. He'd expected fear and excuses, maybe even desperation. It took him a moment to process my words, then he cocked his head. "And how exactly would you know that?"

"Because I was recently in a fight that involved someone who could throw lightning bolts and someone who could create dark just like Emma used to. I made the logical assumption."

I gave him as basic and brief an explanation of the situation as I could manage. "I'm sorry if I led you to believe on the phone that I had proof of life to give you," I concluded. "I decided the current crisis has to take precedence. I hope you agree."

Cyrus snorted. "First you have to convince me that this isn't all a load of bullshit you're feeding me to stall for time."

"Some of it is pretty easy to verify," I said. "I'm sure you have people who can confirm that we were in Bermuda and that Logan and Jamaal were questioned by the police about a bizarre shooting incident where about a zillion rounds were fired and no one was hurt."

Cyrus gave one of his flunkies a commanding look, and the flunky took out his smartphone. His thumbs started flying, and in about sixty seconds, he held his phone out to Cyrus. Cyrus read whatever the flunky had found, and his anger and skepticism transitioned into something more like curiosity and calculation. It was very like Cyrus to hear that the human race was in danger of extinction and try to figure out how he could use the situation to his advantage.

"I think Niobe is recruiting your people," I said while Cyrus tried to process all the information I'd given him. "I don't know what she's promising them to make them think wiping out all of humanity is a good idea, but it's gotta be something. I don't think even your dad would want that, and he's pretty much my mental poster boy for Team Evil."

Cyrus scowled at me, but at least he had the good sense not to argue. That he loved and was loyal to his father didn't mean he was blind or stupid. Still, it probably wasn't smart of me to keep poking at him.

"I'm here because I'm hoping your people and mine can put our differences aside long enough to deal with this crisis. It doesn't mean we have to like or trust each other, and when we've finished saving the world we can go back to business as usual."

"What exactly are you asking us to do?"

"I'm asking you to lend us some of your Olympians to help us get through to the altar in Bermuda. They should be people whose powers can counter those who've gone missing, because I think it's safest to assume they're all with Niobe."

"Aren't you getting a little ahead of yourself?"

"Yes, yes, I know. I have to find another of Niobe's sisters first and convince her to do the right thing. But that'll be a lot easier to do if I can offer her a substantial number of *Liberi* to guard her."

Cyrus thought long and hard before he spoke again, and I had to fight not to hold my breath. If Niobe now had five Olympians at her beck and call, then there was no way I and the rest of Anderson's *Liberi* were getting to that altar without help. If Cyrus turned me down, I had no plan B.

"There's another problem, of course," Cyrus said, then raised his eyebrow at me as if challenging me to guess what he was talking about.

Not that it was a hard guess. "What is this, a pop quiz? I think we need to worry about the altar that's out of juice right now and figure out what to do about the larger problem of Niobe and all those other altars later."

"Somehow I doubt that's a problem any of us is capable of fixing," he said, voicing the nasty truth that I myself was trying not to think about too much. "As long as Niobe wants Anderson dead and this is the only way to kill him, we'll be fighting a losing battle."

"I know," I admitted. I hoped it was a good sign that he had said *we*. "Finding Anderson and getting him to take care of this mess is on my to-do list. Right after finding another of Niobe's sisters."

"I would argue that finding Anderson and fixing the problem at its source is of higher priority."

"And I would argue that taking care of the immediate problem has to come first. Especially when we know how to solve the immediate problem and we have no clue how to fix the big one." Not to mention that I'd already come up empty in my attempts to find him.

Cyrus started to say something, but I cut him off. "*I'm* the one who'll be doing the finding. Unless you've suddenly acquired an Olympian who can do what I do."

"Touché," he said, holding his hands up in surrender. "If you find a goddess who's willing to renew that altar, I'll lend you a team that'll help you get to it."

I looked at him askance. Was it my imagination, or had that been too easy? He wasn't the kind of guy who did anything out of the goodness of his heart, and though I believed stopping Niobe was in his best interests, I was surprised he hadn't made any demands.

Not surprised enough to look the gift horse in the mouth, however. When I got back to the house, I took Blake aside and asked him if I should be worried about Cyrus's seemingly easy cooperation. He gave a snort of laughter.

"Five of his Olympians have deserted, and so far he's had no luck finding them. You're offering to draw them all out for him. He's not in it to save the world—he's in it for the easy revenge."

Blake's humor quickly melted away. "He's going to try to take them all alive so he can bring them back here and torture them before letting his favorite mortal pets harvest their immortality."

I shuddered. Suddenly, it all made perfect sense. I was not going to feel good about aiding and abetting the gruesome murders of five *Liberi*, but we had limited options. Whether I liked it or not, we needed Cyrus's help. I'd just have to deal with the moral consequences later.

Why is it that every time I have to use my power to find someone, there's a Countdown of Doom happening in my head?

If I had plenty of time and wasn't overwhelmed with stress, I was pretty confident I'd eventually be able to find another of Niobe's sisters. But knowing that even now, women who lived on islands had stopped conceiving—and realizing we had no idea which altar would be the next to come up for renewal and when—made a stress-free search impossible.

Searching for the sister in charge of North America seemed like my most logical choice, as she was the one we'd be able to get to the quickest. But North America was kind of big, and I didn't know what to search for. Usually I have at least a name and a starting point, but in this instance, I had nothing.

I don't know how much time I wasted fighting my own panicked fear of failure, but it was hours. I paced my suite and tried to think, to force myself to come up with an off-the-cuff idea that would turn out to be one of those significant hunches that were my trademark. I'd had enough experience with frantic searches already to know that forcing it didn't work, but there's nothing like trying relax to make you as tense and strung-out as possible.

Finally, I sat down in front of my computer in desperation and Googled *fertility goddess North America*.

I listlessly scrolled through the search results. Not surprisingly, they were all links to sites about Native American fertility deities. Completely useless for my purposes. I chewed my lip and considered throwing my laptop out the window to work off some of the stress. Then I began deleting my search terms one character at a time, hitting the delete button with more force than necessary.

For no particular reason I was aware of, I stopped deleting when just the word *fertility* was left. With a shrug, I hit enter. Not surprisingly, I ended up with a list of fertility centers and fertility treatments along with a few stray fertility goddess entries. Just as useless. And yet I had stopped deleting my search terms and hit enter with no particular thought behind it. Was it possible there was some subconscious hint to be gleaned?

I stared at my screen, mentally commanding it to cough up some answers. I was looking for a fertility goddess, and my subconscious had prompted me not to erase that word from my search criteria. If I assumed my subconscious actually knew what it was doing, then I had to think that a search with the term *fertility* in it would lead me somewhere useful.

"What do I know about this goddess?" I asked myself aloud. That was, after all, how I would perform any search: start with what I knew. It was just that, usually, I actually *knew* something.

The sum total of my information about Niobe's sister was that she was a fertility goddess who lived somewhere in North America. I added *North America* back into my search and hit enter, not expecting to find anything useful.

The first hit on the search terms *fertility North America* was a map of fertility rates in North America. And a crazy thought hit me: what if having a fertility altar nearby made women more fertile?

I racked my brain trying to remember which African

country Rose had said her altar was in. I hadn't paid much attention at the time, because everything else she'd had to say was so earth-shattering. I did a quick search for the fertility rates in African countries, and found that it was highest in Niger, which I was pretty sure wasn't the country Rose had mentioned. But just seeing the map of Africa jogged my memory, and I remembered she'd talked about having a home in Johannesburg.

There was no way Johannesburg had the highest birthrate in Africa. And come to think of it, there was no way Bermuda had the highest birthrate of any island. Which logically meant that searching for the place with the highest birthrate in North America should be a dead end.

And yet my power had never once steered me wrong, and I was getting better at telling the difference between an ordinary hunch and one fueled by my divine ancestor. This hunch was one of the latter, I was sure of it. So I dug deeper into my North American search results. I still wasn't really sure what I was looking for, except that anything I could find that might narrow down my search could only be for the better.

Figuring that the effect of the altar might be pretty localized, I ignored the question of which *country* had the highest birthrate and focused instead on cities. I made notes along the way, trying to make sense of conflicting data and different methods of reporting, and in the end, I couldn't tell you which city actually had the highest birthrate. But I *did* notice that I'd written down one of the candidate cities, Memphis, more than once on my list of notes. Maybe it was just because by the time I got to the end I was so brain-dead I'd forgotten I'd already put Memphis on my list. Or maybe Memphis had some significance?

As was the case pretty much every time I did one of these searches, my results felt flimsy, my reasoning ridiculous. If I tried to explain it to someone, they'd probably laugh at me. But until I found some way to use my power with conscious intention, there was nothing I could do but listen to my subconscious hunches, no matter how silly they seemed.

Apparently, another road trip was in my near future.

EIGHT

I had no further clue how to narrow my search. I can't say I had a ton of confidence in my own methodology, but since we literally had nothing else to go on, I started organizing a trip to Memphis. I would have been happy to go alone—I was still getting used to this whole working-as-a-team thing—but I knew I needed at least one other person with me to do the driving. With no empirical evidence to follow, I was just going to have to listen to my gut, and that wasn't something I could do reliably while driving a car.

I didn't know what to expect from Niobe's sister even if we found her, so I wasn't sure who should come with me to Memphis. I finally decided on Jamaal, partly for obvious reasons, but partly because I knew he'd be able to sit in a car with me for hours as we drove around aimlessly without feeling the need to make conversation. If my subconscious homing beacon was going to lead me to the goddess, the last thing I needed was a bored *Liberi* interrupting my concentration.

Time was of the essence, so I decided we should fly into Memphis instead of making the thirteen-hour drive. Leo worked his computer magic and got us a flight within four hours of me coming up with the idea.

Jamaal and I climbed into our rental car at the Memphis airport just after dark. The weather was perfect and the moon was shining bright, so the conditions for the search were ideal.

"Where do you want me to go?" Jamaal asked as we made our way toward the airport exit.

"Just drive toward the city," I instructed him. "Hopefully, I'll start giving you directions before we get there, but if not, just keep driving around. If we're in the right place, and if I can find my Zen, I'll eventually catch the scent."

He did me the favor of not showing any hint of the skepticism I was sure he was feeling. Hell, I was feeling plenty of it myself. Maybe someday—a few years, or maybe even decades down the road—I'd develop some confidence in my powers, but I wasn't close yet. It was with great effort that I closed my eyes and focused on my breathing, trying to block out the million-and-one negative thoughts that assailed me.

Jamaal drove in silence for I don't know how many miles. The soothing hum of the tires against the pavement, the quiet, and the darkness would ordinarily have lulled me right to sleep, but tonight I was way too keyed up. Instead of sitting there peacefully and letting my mind drift, I kept searching my mind for a clue, examining each random thought with way too intense a focus.

This is the way you always *start,* I reminded myself. Just because I began tense as piano wire didn't mean I would stay that way. But tonight, the doubts were stronger than I was.

Before when I'd tried this kind of search, I'd always known my quarry was within reach. Maybe my powers were being difficult, but I knew if I could just get them to cooperate, I would succeed.

Tonight, logic kept insisting that there was no way on earth Memphis was the right place to search. North America is so huge, and I never would have found either Jasmine's or Rose's altars using the ridiculous method I'd used to pick Memphis. If the goddess we sought wasn't in Memphis, then this was all a spectacular waste of time. Time that we didn't have to spare. Time that perhaps I should be using to search for Anderson, although so far my attempts to find him hadn't produced anything.

I was locked in a vicious cycle of desperation and frustration when Jamaal started singing softly.

He has a voice that simultaneously gives me goose bumps and makes me feel like I'm cuddling up in a warm blanket. On more than one occasion, he'd used that gorgeous voice of his to help me sneak past a wall of trauma and find my way into sleep. Ordinarily, I'd let myself latch on to that voice and drink it in, but tonight I opened my eyes and turned my head toward him.

"Not that I don't love listening to you sing," I said, "but if you keep doing that, I'm going to fall asleep, and that won't do us much good."

He risked a quick glance at me before returning his eyes to the highway. Traffic wasn't heavy—especially not compared to D.C.—but it wasn't nonexistent, either. "You didn't seem to be having a whole lot of luck," he commented. "And don't think I didn't notice how fidgety you've been. You're not even close to getting into the zone."

I squirmed in my seat. "You try relaxing when the fate of all humanity is resting on your shoulders."

The weight of that thought nearly took my breath away. It sounded like a total exaggeration. Certainly way too much to be sitting on *my* shoulders. Even if I found another goddess and we successfully renewed the altar in Bermuda, the larger problem of Niobe would still exist, and that was beyond my ability to handle. But I *felt* like it was all riding on me, and maybe that wasn't completely unreasonable. After all, no one *else* seemed to be doing anything to try to improve the situation.

"I'm trying to help you relax," Jamaal said, with a patience I never would have expected from him only a short time ago. "We're no worse off if you fall asleep than if you sit there stewing and getting frustrated. And maybe if you start falling asleep, it'll lower your guard enough to let your power shine through."

I took a deep breath and let it out slowly. He was right, and I felt foolish for arguing. Right now, my mind was practically cannibalizing itself as I tried to force myself to relax. Finding something external and soothing to focus on might be just what I needed.

"Okay," I agreed. "It can't hurt to try. But wake me up if I start drooling or snoring or something."

He smiled without looking at me. "All right, then. Any requests?"

I had no idea what kind of music Jamaal liked. The only thing I'd ever heard him sing was the lullaby I'd just interrupted. It was a song from his childhood, before everything went wrong, and since he didn't even know what language it was in, he assured me he was butchering the pronunciation. But it was beautiful, and I loved it.

"How about you finish the lullaby and go on to whatever moves you after?" I suggested.

"Agreed. Now close your eyes."

I came back to myself as Jamaal was pulling up to the curb in front of a stately Victorian house. I blinked to clear away my confusion. I had no idea how we'd gotten here or how long we'd been driving, nor did I feel the grogginess or heaviness behind the eyes I'd expect if I'd fallen asleep.

The house was large without being huge, and it looked old without being decrepit. We were in a neighborhood that screamed suburbs, with the houses sitting on what I'd estimate to be an acre of land and everything neat and well kept.

"Where are we?" I asked, glancing over at Jamaal, who shrugged.

"Don't know. I was just following your directions."

I suppressed a shudder. There was something strangely unnerving about me giving driving directions without ever having been conscious of it.

"You think this is the place?" I asked pointlessly. It wasn't like Jamaal had any more clue than I did.

He leaned over toward my side of the car a bit to get a better look at the house. His proximity made me want to reach out and touch him, but I resisted the temptation. Now was definitely not the time.

"Whoever lives here seems to have a green thumb," he commented as he sat up straight once more. "Those are some pretty spectacular gardens."

I'd been too preoccupied to even notice, but now that Jamaal mentioned it, they were pretty amazing. There were two beds of flourishing pansies, one on each side of the driveway along the sidewalk, and the entire front of the house was lined with flowering shrubs of some sort.

"That seems kind of fertility-goddess-like," I said. It could also be the sign of an ordinary expert gardener, but I'd take any hopeful sign I could find. I used my phone to make a Wi-Fi hot spot, then dug out my laptop and performed a search on property records. Property ownership is public record, so I didn't even have to tap into any of the databases I was still subscribed to thanks to my PI days.

"The owner of the house is named Violet Hawthorne," I announced after a few minutes of searching. Jamaal and I shared a significant look. Rose had told us that she and her sisters had all been given flower names. "That seems unlikely to be a coincidence."

He put the car in park, then turned it off. "Agreed. Let's go see if she's home."

He reached for the door, but I stopped him with a hand on his arm. Jamaal may be drop-dead gorgeous, but he's one hell of an intimidating guy, big and muscular with a face better suited for scowling than smiling. If Violet was who we thought she was, then she'd be in no danger from any mortal or *Liberi*. But she would know from the crescent moon glyph on his forehead that he was a descendant of Kali, and that might make her . . . less than welcoming.

"Why don't you wait here for now," I suggested. "We don't want to spook her, and I'm about as harmless looking as you can get. You, however, couldn't look harmless if you had flowers in your hair and were carrying an armload of kittens. And that face you're making proves my point."

I wasn't sure if that harsh, guttural sound he made was supposed to indicate amusement or annoyance.

"I'm not going to wait in the car like I'm your chauffeur," he growled.

"You don't have to wait in the car with the nice heater going if you don't want to," I said. "I'm just asking you to stay out of sight until I've convinced Violet I'm not one of the bad guys."

There were definite disadvantages to choosing Jamaal as my driver. He'd done an admirable job of helping me relax and not interrupting my concentration, but his temper would always be an issue. It probably would be wiser to insist he wait in the car, because if Violet balked at all about what we were asking her to do, he might explode and make matters worse. However, I knew better than to suggest such a thing when he was looking at me like that.

I was tensed and ready for Jamaal to pick a fight, and was pleasantly surprised when he took a couple of deep breaths and stepped away from the edge. "All right. I'll stay out of sight."

It was after eleven at night, but the house was still brightly lit, so I didn't think we'd be waking anyone. Jamaal and I walked up to the door, and I had him stand to the side while I rang the doorbell. He had his arms crossed over his chest and looked all tense and broody. It looked like he needed a cigarette, or maybe some alone time with Sita to vent his death magic.

I didn't hear any approaching footsteps, but the porch light turned on, and moments later the peephole darkened. There was an obvious and deliberate pause before the door swung open to reveal a beautiful olive-skinned woman with dark, pixie-cut hair and eyes that instantly reminded me of Rose. Any remaining doubt that I had found one of Niobe's sisters disappeared.

"Let me save us both some time and aggravation," Violet said. "The answer is no."

Warned by her tone, I had my foot wedged in the door before she managed to slam it in my face. Beside me, I could feel Jamaal bristling, and I prayed he'd stay out of sight. There was enough tension in the air already without him looming over her.

"How do you know the answer is no if you don't even know the question yet?" I asked. I gave her my best innocuous smile and held out my hand as if inviting her to shake, though I knew full well she wouldn't. "I'm—"

"Nikki Glass," she finished for me, startling me into silence. "Yes, I know who you are, and I know what you want. And my answer is still no."

She tried again to close the door, but I didn't think she was putting her whole strength into it or she probably would have crushed my foot. I put my shoulder against the door for extra leverage, just in case.

"If you know who I am, then you might as well accept that there's no short version of this conversation," I told her. "I'm not leaving, so you'll get rid of me faster if you just let me in and get it over with."

I didn't like the fact that Violet knew who I was. I imagined she'd gotten her information from Niobe, who must have researched Anderson's people. Which meant Niobe knew who was important to Anderson. I was probably lucky she was too busy trying to end all humanity to stop by and slaughter us all.

"Fine," Violet said with a disgusted snort, pushing away from the door and turning her back to us. "Come on in," she called over her shoulder.

I stepped inside, with Jamaal close behind me. Either Violet didn't hear the heavy tread that could not possibly come from my feet, or she just didn't care that I wasn't alone. She kept walking, and we followed. I thought maybe she was going to try to leave through a back door and run away. However, she led us into a first-floor turret room that was some combination of library and den. A wood fire crackled in the fireplace, and a tattered paperback lay open and facedown on the seat of a cozy chair in the corner. The matching ottoman looked like it had been casually shoved aside, and I made the educated guess that Violet had been sitting by the fire and reading when we came knocking.

Violet stood in front of the fire with her back to us, staring into the flames. Jamaal and I shared a look and simultaneously shrugged, not sure what to make of her behavior.

"How did you know who I was?" I asked, despite having deduced the answer.

"Kane mentioned you," she said to the fire. "Told me you might come knocking."

"You mean Anderson?" I asked with a gasp. "You've seen him? Do you know where he is?"

Violet turned to face me. She glanced briefly at Jamaal, her eyes darting to his glyph. I would have introduced him, but she started speaking before I could. "I mean Kane. Yes, I've seen him, and no, I don't know where he is now. I expect he's visited as many of us as he can find to try to plead his case. I don't suppose you'd be here if you didn't know he's a murderer of innocents."

A tiny pinprick of white appeared in the center of her pupils then quickly disappeared. It was something I'd noticed happening with Anderson a couple of times when he was angry, a bit of his true self leaking through his human disguise. A lot of time had passed since Anderson had slaughtered his children, but it looked like Violet still held quite the grudge. Not that I could blame her.

"I know the story," I told her, trying not to think about it too much. "I can totally understand why you and your sisters might want him dead. But—"

There was that spark in the middle of her pupils again, and it lasted a little longer this time before disappearing. "Don't try to tell me how he's changed, how he would never do such a terrible thing again. I'll tell you the same thing I told him: it doesn't matter. He killed my nieces and nephews, destroyed my sister's heart, out of pure malice, and he deserves to pay for that crime!"

Rose had seemed more saddened than angry at what Anderson had done so long ago. Such was obviously not the case with Violet.

I held up my hands in a gesture of surrender. "I'm not arguing with you. I'm not here because I'm trying to save Anderson's life."

To tell the truth, I couldn't entirely sort out *what* I felt about Anderson right now. If Niobe and her sisters had some means of killing him without the entire human race dying out, would I step in and try to protect him? The man I'd thought was my friend was nothing but a fraud, and I wasn't sure I could forgive the atrocity in his past no matter how much he may or may not have changed.

"I just don't think it's right that billions of innocents should suffer and die because of what he did," I said.

"No one will suffer and die because my sisters and I neglect our altars. They just won't have children."

"Cut the crap," Jamaal said before I could respond. "You're not a lawyer arguing about the letter of the law, and you know perfectly well what will happen if children stop being born. Who do you think will be blamed for it? Because you know people will want to find someone to blame. You can bet there'll be people pointing fingers at every minority group in the world. Religious fanatics will say God is punishing us and we have to eliminate people who don't share their beliefs. People who already hate the West will decide it's all some American plot gone wrong and start blowing more shit up. These are just the possibilities I can come up with off the top of my head. There will be plenty of suffering and plenty of death."

Violet folded her arms in what I thought was a defensive

posture despite her still-belligerent expression. "There's always been plenty of suffering and death."

I could almost feel Jamaal's temper poking its head up and looking around, so I put a calming hand on his arm. I doubted the situation would be much improved by a shouting match. He tensed under my touch, and I feared it had had the opposite of the desired effect, but at least he didn't rise to Violet's bait.

"It's my understanding that you and your sisters are going to be trapped on Earth forever if you don't take good care of it," I said. Violet's eyes narrowed in a barely perceptible wince. "Forever is a long time, and the world is going to be pretty boring if there are no people in it, don't you think?"

Violet let out a huge sigh, and some of the fight went out of her. Her arms dropped back to her sides, and her shoulders slumped. "It's not like I *want* it to happen," she admitted. "But I've always been a pragmatist. I only fight the battles I can win. This isn't one of them. My sister is nothing if not determined."

At least she'd admitted she didn't want to destroy the world. That was progress, wasn't it?

"We'll find a way," I promised her. "But to solve the larger problem, we're going to need time, and that means getting Jasmine's altar renewed before it's too late."

Violet shook her head. "I'm not going anywhere near that altar. Niobe would see it as yet another in a long list of betrayals, and she is not the forgiving sort. I love my sister, but I also know what she's capable of, what she became after Kane murdered her children."

"We'll protect you," Jamaal said.

"Like you protected Rose?" she fired back.

I suspect Jamaal and I wore similar expressions of surprise. It hadn't occurred to me that she had any way of knowing we had already tried to renew the altar once before and failed.

"How do you know about that?" I asked.

Violet turned away from us and faced the fire. "Because Niobe wanted to make sure all of us knew what would happen to us if we didn't cooperate. She sent pictures." Even with her back turned, I could see Violet's shiver of fear. "I don't want to cause the extinction of mortals, but better that than risk crossing Niobe."

"Wow, that's some attitude," Jamaal said with equal parts shock and disgust. "You're really so selfish that you'd rather let billions of people die than risk your own life?"

I had to admit, Jamaal was right. It was almost impossible for me to imagine how someone could live with themselves if they were that cowardly.

She's a goddess, Nikki, I reminded myself. Goddesses don't think like human beings, and Violet was living proof. She might have lived among humans for thousands of years, but she wasn't one of us.

"You can shame me all you want," she said, turning to face us once more. Tears shimmered in her eyes, but none fell. "But renewing that single altar will do no good, and it's just not worth the risk. Even if you could get me through, what happens when the next altar wanes? And the one after that? How many times do you think you can fight your way past a goddess?"

Violet blinked away the tears. "I will happily renew the altars that have been left empty, but only if I can do so safely. You'll have to either talk Niobe into forgoing her revenge, or find another way of stopping her. Without hurting her!" she hastened to add. "If you harm Niobe in any way, I swear to you neither I nor any of my other sisters will ever set foot near an altar again."

Jamaal gave Violet a glower that would melt an iceberg or freeze a flame. "So you'll happily just sit back in your chair reading a book while panic spreads throughout the islands and people start dying because of it."

She lowered her head, unable to meet either of our gazes. "Happily? No. But I *will* be staying home."

Jamaal, visibly shaking with barely suppressed fury, took a

menacing step in Violet's direction. I don't think he was planning violence—as angry as he was, he wasn't out of control—but Violet took no chances. White light leaked from her eyes, and suddenly a blinding white brightness stabbed my eyes, causing me to cover them with my forearm.

The brightness quickly eased off, and when I risked opening my eyes, the Violet we had been talking to was gone. In her place was a towering, vaguely humanoid pillar of white light. Jamaal let out a string of curses and hastily backed away. I would have done the same if I hadn't seen Anderson in this same form once before.

"*Get out of my house,*" the pillar said in a voice that reverberated through my bones.

I had no idea what Violet could do in her current form, but I suspected she was capable of some serious smiting. I didn't want to give up, but it was plain to see there would be no reasoning with her. Not right now at least.

"I'm going to leave my card in case you change your mind," I told her, fishing through my purse. I was pretty sure I still had some business cards in there from my PI days.

"*I won't change my mind.*"

"Just in case," I repeated as my fingers found a beat-up, dog-eared card at the bottom of my purse. I straightened it out as best I could, then dropped it on an end table.

"*Out!*" she said, pointing one glowing arm at the door.

This time, Jamaal and I obeyed.

NINE

Jamaal and I had no choice but to retreat to the hotel Leo had booked for us. We hadn't bothered with a real dinner, having settled for sandwiches grabbed at the airport, but we weren't much in the mood to sleep, so we ordered room service just after midnight.

We were in a two-bedroom suite, and while we waited for our food to arrive, Jamaal retired to his room for a shower. I felt mildly grungy myself after all that travel, but I decided I'd rather do something more productive than freshen up.

Violet was right, and getting the altar in Bermuda renewed was only a Band-Aid on the much larger problem. I was mildly heartened to learn that Anderson had been out and about since his secret was revealed, and glad to know he was at least *trying* to do something to save the world. However, I was still royally pissed at him for going Lone Ranger on us. Would it have killed him to at least send one of us a text or an email letting us know he was on the job?

Maybe Anderson thought this conflict between gods was something too big for his *Liberi* to handle, but it didn't seem to me that whatever solo solution he'd come up with was having a whole lot of success. We needed to work together to keep Niobe from destroying humanity, and that meant Anderson had to grow a pair and face us, whether he wanted to or not.

I opened my laptop and let my fingers hover over the keys, waiting for inspiration to hit. Playing around on Google had helped lead me to Violet, so maybe it could help lead me to Anderson as well. I started performing searches almost at random, typing in any word that popped into my head, hoping one of them would lead to search results that piqued my interest.

I was still trying when Jamaal emerged from the shower, and I'd probably have kept at it if our food hadn't arrived at the same time.

"So, no luck, huh?" Jamaal asked as soon as he closed the door after the delivery guy.

I was tempted to toss the metal dome that covered my plate to the floor in frustration. When my weird searches actually worked, I never felt confident in them, never felt secure in my own reasoning. Tonight, however, I was quite sure none of the random thoughts that had come to me was a supernatural hunch.

"Absolutely nothing," I said, sitting cross-legged on the sofa with my plate on my lap. I'd ordered a burger because I thought the decadent overindulgence might help soothe my frustration, but my stomach was so tied up in knots I wasn't sure I could eat it. I nibbled on a lukewarm fry and tried to give myself permission to just relax and focus on my food for a few minutes.

"Maybe he's too far away for my powers to sense him," I mused. "He's apparently trying to visit all of Niobe's sisters, and they're scattered all over the world. He could be *anywhere*."

I'd been talking more to myself than to Jamaal, but when I played my words back in my head, I realized I knew exactly why I hadn't been able to get even the slightest hint of a lead on Anderson's location.

"He's traveling all over the world," I groaned. "And unlike us, he isn't going by plane."

Jamaal frowned at me and put down his own burger, which he'd already partially demolished. "What do you mean?"

"He's in the Underworld." No wonder I couldn't find him. He was spending most of his time in a place I couldn't possibly reach.

I don't know exactly where the Underworld is, or even *what* it is, but I know that Anderson could create portals into and out of it, and that those portals would allow him to travel around our world with amazing speed.

It was Jamaal's turn to groan as he got it. "He knew you'd be looking for him, so he's hiding out in the one place he's sure you can't find him."

There are some death-god descendants who can open portals into the Underworld, but Jamaal wasn't one of them. At least, not that I knew of.

I cocked my head at him. "Do you suppose there's any chance *you* can open a portal to the Underworld? You are descended from a death goddess, after all."

"I think that if I could, I would have figured it out by now," he replied.

"Just like you figured out how to summon Sita all on your own?"

He scowled at me, but he knew I had a point. When I'd first asked him if he thought he could summon some kind of spirit animal, he'd categorically dismissed the suggestion. And I'd kept on him about it, because I knew of another death-god descendant who seemed to be able to vent some of the death magic through a spirit animal. Eventually, Jamaal had caved and tried, and that was how he found Sita.

"I suppose I can try," he admitted. "I'm not sure what I'd have to do, but then I didn't have much idea when I started looking for Sita, either. The only thing I know for sure is that we'd have to be in a cemetery."

Anderson could create portals wherever he was—he'd once told me that he himself actually *was* a portal—but apparently *Liberi* needed to draw power from the dead to do it.

"I'm sure we'd have no trouble finding a cemetery in this area," I said.

Jamaal gave a little start. "You want to try it *tonight*?"

I rubbed my eyes. I hadn't been the least bit tired until that moment, but now the idea of slipping into bed seemed very appealing.

"Jasmine's altar is already barren. I think that's a crisis worth pulling an all-nighter for, don't you?"

Jamaal suppressed a yawn. Amazing how tired you get when you realize you're not going to be getting to sleep anytime soon. "When you put it that way . . ."

Jamaal and I found a small cemetery not far from our hotel. It was situated behind a picturesque Baptist church, and the area was so quiet and abandoned at one in the morning that I felt like we might be the only two people left alive. It was a disturbing mental image for a pair of immortals who were facing the possibility of mankind's extinction. If we didn't find a way to fix this unholy mess, we would not only have to watch the human race die out, we would also still be walking the Earth when it was all over. I had no clue what the total number of *Liberi* in the world was, but I knew it wasn't very large, and even if we started breeding like bunnies—a difficult prospect when *Liberi* descended from different gods can't have children together—we'd never come close to re-creating what we'd lost.

Based on the wear and tear of the headstones, the cemetery we'd chosen had been around for at least a century or two. It would probably have been lovely in the daytime, situated on a gentle hill and surrounded by ancient trees that would provide welcome shade. At night, however, it was a different story. The only illumination came from the ambient light of downtown Memphis, miles away, and from the tiny porch light over the church's front entrance. In fact, it was so dark I had to use a flashlight app on my phone so we wouldn't trip over any of the weathered headstones.

I could tell almost from the first moment we set foot in the cemetery that Jamaal was feeling the presence of the dead. The dead called to his death magic, bringing it closer to the surface—and loosening his hold on his temper. His shoulders were tense, and his fingers were constantly in motion with subtle fidgets. I'd hoped his practice with Sita would make him better able to deal with the atmosphere of the cemetery, but that seemed not to be the case.

"Are you going to be all right?" I asked.

He slanted a look at me. "I'm surrounded by the dead in the middle of the night hoping to pull a previously unknown power out of my ass. What could possibly go wrong?"

I smiled at him, feeling absurdly proud of that little flash of humor. Sure, it was dark, sarcastic humor, but when I'd first met him, Jamaal would have needed a dictionary to figure out what the word *humor* meant, so this was a big improvement.

"Don't forget that the fate of the world is resting on your

shoulders," I told him cheerfully. "I know that always helps *me* relax and concentrate."

He snorted, but didn't otherwise respond. We made our way to the approximate center of the cemetery, and then Jamaal waved me away.

"I have no idea what I'm doing or what might happen," he warned. "Best if you keep your distance and turn that flashlight off."

I swallowed hard at the thought of being in the cemetery without the security blanket of my feeble light, but I saw the sense in Jamaal's request. The last thing he needed was anything resembling a distraction.

I picked my way over to an inviting patch of grass and sat down, then reluctantly turned off the light on my phone. The air felt immediately colder, the darkness heavier. I zipped my jacket a little higher and stuffed my hands into my pockets. I had a feeling I was going to be freezing by the time this little adventure was over.

Whatever efforts Jamaal was making to open a portal, they were silent. All I could hear was the rustle of branches from the occasional breeze and the distant hum of traffic from the highway about half a mile away.

At first, I couldn't see Jamaal at all, even though I was no more than fifteen or twenty yards from him. His dark jeans and coffee-brown leather jacket were invisible against the night. My eyes adjusted after the first few minutes, and though I couldn't see very well, I could at least make out vague shapes here and there.

Jamaal was on his feet, visible as nothing more than a blot of greater darkness in the night. He didn't appear to be doing anything other than standing there, but I knew he was trying to tap into his power, just as I'd seen him do when he'd been learning to summon Sita.

It was hard to measure the passage of time. The darkness and stillness made every minute feel like an hour, and the cold that was now seeping into my butt from the ground wasn't helping matters. I considered checking the time on my phone, but didn't want to risk the glow distracting Jamaal. It was dark enough that my phone would probably look bright as a beacon.

Too chilled to remain still, I pushed up to my feet and tried to move around a little to keep warm without making any distracting noises. Jamaal was still standing motionless, although every once in a while I thought I saw him sway a bit. Not a good sign. When he'd been trying to summon Sita in the beginning, the effort had practically made him pass out a few times. I chewed on my chapped lip and forced myself to stay put. This was an effort Jamaal had to undertake on his own.

The swaying became more pronounced, and despite my best intentions, I found myself inching slowly closer. Maybe it was time to interrupt him. If he were going to open a portal, he would have done so by now, right?

I kept my jaws clamped shut. The risk of Jamaal exhausting himself to the point of collapse was worth taking if the reward was getting into the Underworld and finding Anderson. I still didn't know how it had happened, but somehow I seemed to have taken charge of his *Liberi* in his absence, and I wanted nothing more than to shove all that responsibility back on his shoulders where it belonged. It had taken a god to make this mess, and I was convinced it would take one to fix it.

I had covered maybe half the distance between myself and Jamaal when I suddenly noticed a patch of unnatural blackness forming at his feet. Hope leapt within me, and I covered my mouth to make sure I didn't make any sound. The only other time I'd seen a portal to the Underworld, it had manifested very much like this one. Jamaal was on the right track.

Except apparently he wasn't.

The pool of blackness resolved itself into the shape of a tiger.

Sita leapt out of the way as Jamaal pitched forward and landed on the frozen ground in a heap. I cried out in dismay and took a couple of running steps toward him before Sita inserted herself between us and snarled at me, warning me off. I skidded to a stop and held up my hands.

"I just want to make sure he's okay," I told the tiger, not entirely sure our truce was still in effect.

Sita snorted at me, then dismissed me from her attention, turning to Jamaal and nuzzling his shoulder. He was out cold and didn't move an inch.

I sidled closer, keeping a wary eye on Sita while making sure I made enough noise that she knew I was coming. I didn't think startling her would be good for my health. She gave me the evil eye and a halfhearted snarl, then used her head to try to turn Jamaal over onto his back.

"I think that'll be easier to do with hands," I told her when her effort failed. "But he's pretty heavy, so I could still use your help."

Her narrowed eyes screamed distrust, but Sita allowed me to come close and crouch on the ground next to Jamaal's prone body. I slipped my hands under his shoulder and upper chest, pushing with my legs to move his dead weight. As soon as I got him partway raised, Sita shoved the top of her head under him, and together we got him turned over onto his back.

He was breathing steadily, and when I touched my fingers to his throat, his pulse was speedy, but strong. I tried to arrange him as comfortably as possible, not sure how long he would be out. Sitting this close, I could see the sheen of sweat on his face and knew that even once he woke, he'd be weak and shaky.

I looked at Sita, who was watching my every move like a hawk while she lay down beside him across from me.

"You know he was trying to open a portal to the Underworld, right?" I asked. She just blinked at me. "I thought he was succeeding, but then you appeared. Was the darkness I saw a portal forming, or was it you all along?"

No, I wasn't expecting her to answer me. I was talking more to myself than to her, but then I reminded myself that she seemed perfectly capable of understanding me.

"Do you know if he can create a portal?" I asked her. "Nod or shake your head."

Sita growled at me, showing off her impressive teeth.

"Please," I added hastily. Apparently, she didn't like being given commands, especially not by me.

She gave me the evil-eye stare for another long moment, then lowered her chin in what I decided to interpret as a nod.

"Can he do it?"

Another pause, then she moved her head subtly from side to side. I decided she understood the gestures of nodding and shaking her head but wasn't exactly used to communicating that way.

"Can *you* do it?" I asked in a sudden burst of inspiration.

Sita sighed loudly and made another awkward side-to-side head motion.

"Just to make sure I understand: are you saying there's no way you or Jamaal can get us into the Underworld?"

Her chin-dip confirmed my understanding. If I wanted to get to the Underworld to search for Anderson, I was going to have to find another way.

Ten

Jamaal had really worn himself out. When he finally regained consciousness, he was so weak he couldn't stand on his own and I had to help him to the car. I knew he was in bad shape when he accepted help from anyone, but especially me. He was a little better when we arrived at the hotel, and though his face was ashen, he made it to the elevators unassisted. However, that effort took the last of his strength, and he had to lean on me the rest of the way to our suite.

He uttered a mild protest when I led him straight through

the sitting room and into his bedroom, but I ignored him. Maybe his pride would have felt better if I'd plopped him down on the sofa until he was ready to walk unaided again, but I've been known to have little patience with overblown male pride.

Jamaal groaned in relief when we made it to his bed, and he flopped bonelessly on top of the covers, still wearing his leather jacket and his black lace-up boots. As he lay on the bed and panted, I started unlacing one of those clunky boots.

"Stop that," he protested, making a halfhearted effort to pull away.

I ignored him and kept working on the laces. Even in his weakened state, he was more than strong enough to pull away if he really wanted. I worked the boot off and dropped it to the floor beside the bed, then started on the other one.

"You don't have to mother me," he said.

I rolled my eyes at him. "Why don't you give the alpha-male crap a rest and let me take care of you," I said, pulling on his laces without pause. "Is it that big a deal to let me take your boots off?"

He grumbled something under his breath. Probably just as well I couldn't make out the words. It had been a long, long time since Jamaal had experienced true care from a fellow human being, and he was obviously uncomfortable with it. Which was just tough. Being cared for was something he was going to have to get used to.

The second boot joined its mate on the floor.

"Let's get you out of that jacket," I suggested.

I hadn't turned on the bedside lamp, but there was enough light leaking in through the open bedroom door to reveal the mulish look on his face.

"Just let me rest, would you?"

"You'll rest easier if you aren't wearing a heavy leather jacket indoors. Tell me you're not roasting already." I'm cold-natured, but the thermostat was set comfortably high, and I quickly shed my own coat to set a good example.

"You're a real pain in my ass," Jamaal said as he laboriously sat up and tried to get out of his jacket without help.

I crossed my arms over my chest and gave him my best look of long-suffering patience as he struggled to find the energy to get his shoulders out of the jacket. His face was sweaty again, whether from the effort or just because he was wearing a winter jacket indoors I didn't know.

Jamaal is capable of amazing displays of stubbornness, but the jacket quickly got the best of him, and he let his arms fall back limply to his sides. He couldn't quite bring himself to ask for help, but he gave me an imploring look that got the message across.

While I helped him wriggle out of the jacket, I couldn't help but notice that his clothes beneath—a loose-fitting T-shirt over a long-sleeved thermal knit—were soaked with sweat.

"Let's get you a dry shirt while we're at it," I suggested.

Jamaal tensed, and I knew he was fighting his inner demons. His back and chest were covered with scars from his days as a slave long ago, and he was enormously self-conscious about it. That I'd seen them before didn't seem to make letting me see them again any easier for him, but he eventually let out a long, shaky breath and nodded.

That simple show of trust warmed me on the inside. I was careful not to touch any of the scars as I helped him peel the double layer of shirts off together.

"I'm going to hang these in the bathroom or they'll never dry," I told him. "Then I'll bring you another shirt." The scars bothered Jamaal enough that he always wore at least an undershirt to bed.

"Thanks," he said almost reluctantly as he lay back down and closed his eyes.

When I came back from hanging his shirts in the bathroom, I thought he might have fallen asleep. I went for his suitcase anyway, and he said, "Don't bother. Too tired."

My heart warmed for a second time as I realized how far

he had come in such a short time. I doubted he was exactly *comfortable* lying there without his shirt on with me in the room, but that he was even *willing* to do it was a tremendous improvement.

I should have left him to rest then, but instead I went to sit on the bed beside him. I wasn't surprised to find him looking tense and wary. There was easily enough light for me to see the ridges and valleys that had been carved into his flesh, and though I didn't want to look at them, I didn't want to *not* look at them, either. I took his hand and squeezed it while a lump of mingled sympathy and fury rose in my throat. I wanted to go back in time and kill whoever had done this to him. I'm a self-proclaimed bleeding heart, and my mind simply wasn't able to encompass how one human being could do something like that to another.

"It was a long time ago, Nikki," Jamaal said gently as if he could read my thoughts. "I've outlived every one of those fuckers, and I've even pissed on some of their graves. In the end, I won."

I squeezed his hand again and forced a smile. That was an unusually positive way of thinking about it, especially for Jamaal, but the emotional scars ran so much deeper than the physical ones. He was letting me see the scars on his body, but he had yet to let me touch them, which spoke of much more baggage he still had to dump if he was ever going to find real happiness.

Jamaal swallowed hard, and his breathing quickened. Before I could figure out what to make of it, he jerked my hand up to his chest and practically slammed it down on his sternum. The scar tissue was an obscene texture under my palm and fingers, marks of unspeakable brutality. Jamaal held my hand in place. His eyes were closed, his skin was clammy, and his heart pounded like a drum beneath my palm.

I wanted to tell him that he didn't have to do this, that it was okay if he didn't want me touching him, that I was willing to wait until he was truly comfortable instead of forcing the issue. But I kept my mouth shut and swallowed the words. If Jamaal was going to break free of the memories that haunted him, he would do so at his own pace, and only he knew what that pace was.

He held my hand in place for a long time, his body rigid with tension as he fought his inner demons. He'd told me he once had an owner who'd been turned on by the scars. That was all he'd said about it, but it was clear she'd acted on her desires against his will. To tell you the truth, I didn't *want* to know exactly what she had done to him. I didn't want to share him with his past, didn't want its shadow constantly clinging to us, didn't want it weighing him down and interfering with his happiness.

Eventually, the pounding of his heart slowed and some of the tension eased from his muscles. He opened his eyes and met my gaze. I was terrified that I would say or do the wrong thing, and I hoped it didn't show in my eyes. His hand slid away from mine, and he let his arm come to rest at his side.

It was humbling, to say the least, to have Jamaal trust me enough to give up control. It was up to me to figure out how to handle that without screwing anything up.

Eyes locked with his, I brushed my fingertips over the scars I could reach without moving my hand. Jamaal tensed again, but he made no attempt to stop me or pull away. Nor did Sita make a sudden and unexpected appearance, which was the surest way to spoil a mood, as we'd found out before.

Once again, Jamaal's tension eased, his body accepting my touch. How long had it been since a woman had touched him like this? He'd been *Liberi* for more than a century. I liked to think that there had been other women before me to ease his loneliness and isolation, but I wondered if he'd ever been able to let down his guard.

Watching carefully for any signs of distress, I allowed my hand to roam, slowly stroking the length of his sternum. There were so many ridges and valleys that if I hadn't known what I was touching, I'd never have been able to figure it out. Jamaal broke eye contact so he could watch the progress of my hand.

"It doesn't disgust you?" he asked in a hoarse voice that hardly sounded like his. "Touching them like this?"

I rejected the facile denial that first leapt to my mind and allowed myself to think a moment before answering. "It disgusts me to think someone did this to you," I said. "But I'm not touching the scars—I'm touching *you*."

Jamaal shuddered and closed his eyes, but not before I glimpsed the shimmer of tears. Abruptly, he turned over onto his side, facing away from me. I knew it wasn't a rejection, that he was simply trying to hide his emotions. He liked to pretend anger was the only emotion he was capable of.

I knew better.

Instead of letting him retreat, I carefully brushed his beaded braids out of the way and lay down behind him, my arm around his chest, my face nestled against the back of his neck. I could almost feel him fighting his urge to pull away, to reject the intimacy I offered, but instead he held still. I closed my eyes and inhaled the scent of him, reveled in the warmth of his body.

When I'd first met Jamaal, he had been broken, a man with nothing to live for but his endless rage. The death magic was eating him alive from the inside out, and he had for all intents and purposes given up. Only an idiot would have fallen for him under those circumstances, but from the very beginning, I had seen in him a reflection of myself. He was what I would have become if the Glasses hadn't been willing to accept an angry, rebellious eleven-year-old hellion into their home, hadn't loved me and tamed me and given me a sense of self-worth after my birth mother abandoned me.

He wasn't exactly all about unicorns and rainbows now, but he was in a vastly different place than he had been a few months ago. He had hope, even if he was sometimes reluctant to admit it, and I no longer felt like I needed to *justify* my feelings for him. I wasn't ready to officially stamp the L word on those feelings—never mind my Freudian slip when I'd made peace with Sita—but the combination of warmth and yearning that flooded me as I spooned Jamaal—and he *let* me—came pretty damn close.

When Jamaal's breathing slowed and evened out into the rhythm of sleep, I knew that tonight's had been his biggest breakthrough so far.

Apparently, I fell asleep. The next time I opened my eyes, it was to see the bedside clock flashing 4:35. I blinked, momentarily disoriented and not sure what woke me up. That was when I heard the gentle clatter of Jamaal's braids and noticed him crouching by his suitcase. He'd changed out of his jeans and put on a pair of plaid pajama bottoms and was now staring indecisively at an undershirt. I smiled when he shoved it back into the suitcase.

When he stood up, he took a quick glance over at me, then cursed under his breath.

"Sorry," he said. "Didn't mean to wake you."

I yawned and sat up. "No problem," I said. "If I slept in these jeans any longer, I'd have permanent seam marks by morning." I tugged at the waistband and winced when I felt the angry divot the button had dug in my abdomen while I slept. And let's not even talk about what the hardware in my bra had done to me.

I swung my legs over the side of the bed and hesitated. Jamaal was obviously fine now, so there was no reason not to go back to my own room and my own bed. Except that I didn't want to. Jamaal had had an obvious breakthrough, but I didn't want to jeopardize that by being too pushy. I wished there were more light so I'd have a better chance of reading his face and body language.

Sometimes there's no better way to get an answer to your questions than to abandon subtlety and ask.

"Do you want me to stay?" I blurted out.

Jamaal froze, his body nothing but a silhouette against the light that shone through the open bedroom door. "Only if you want to." There was an edge of uncertainty in his voice, like he was worried he might be imposing on me in some way.

I laughed softly. "Good to know you're not planning to tie me to the bed to keep me here against my will."

He made a grunting sound that may have been an indication of amusement. "You know what I mean. If you'd be more comfortable in your own bed . . ." He let his voice trail off.

I stood up. "I'm going to assume that because you haven't thrown me out on my ass, it means you'd like me to stay, even if you won't come out and say it. Feel free to correct me if I'm wrong."

I didn't wait for an answer, instead pulling back the rumpled covers. I wasn't sure enough of Jamaal's state of mind to get naked, but I quickly shed my jeans and socks. A few awkward contortions allowed me to get my bra off while still mostly covered by my sweatshirt. I still couldn't see Jamaal's expression thanks to the backlighting, but he wasn't telling me to stop. I'd have loved to dump the sweatshirt, too, but took a cue from the fact that he was wearing jammies and slipped into bed without further stripping.

Jamaal closed the bedroom door, and in the darkness I heard rather than saw him pad around to the other side of the bed. He pulled back the covers, the sound not quite covering the nervous deep breath he took. And then the bed shifted under his weight as he got in. I was pleasantly surprised when instead of keeping shyly to his side of the king-sized bed, he slid over to me, slipped an arm around my waist, and pulled me up against him, my back to his chest.

Let me tell you: when you're five two and your guy is six three, it's a lot cozier to be the spoonee than the spooner. The feeling of him wrapped around me like that was almost good enough to make me forget that our mission here in Memphis had been a total failure. My head was tucked under the curve of his chin, my body tight against his. It felt great, but I wished we had more skin against skin.

Don't get greedy, Nikki, I told myself. This was already more progress than I could have hoped for, and I should be fully satisfied with it. I wondered how long it had been since Jamaal had cuddled up to a woman in bed. Hell, with his past, I wondered if he'd *ever* done it before.

He pulled me a little more tightly against him, and I had the feeling he was enjoying the contact as much as I was. His hand began idly stroking the skin of my arm, where the sleeve of my sweatshirt had been pushed up. As erogenous zones go, it wasn't much, but my whole body prickled with awareness anyway. I'd been feeling sleepy not that long ago, but just that tiniest caress made sleep the last thing on my mind.

I wriggled my hips so I could fit more perfectly in the curve of his body, and the sudden hardening against my butt told me Jamaal enjoyed that small motion. He was still in his jammies, and I was still in my underwear, but the material was thin enough that I could feel the steady rise in temperature as his blood rushed downward.

I held my breath, wondering if this was some kind of spell that would quickly dissipate, but Jamaal was still pressed against me, and with his chest against my back I could feel the renewed pounding of his heart. The erection I felt against my butt told me that this time, his tension rose from a completely different source.

Jamaal's hand wandered, finding its way to my breast. I obligingly moved my arm out of the way so he could have free access. Which it turns out isn't all that great when you're wearing a sweatshirt. I could feel his hand all right, but the touch was unsatisfying. To us both, apparently. He quickly lowered his hand so he could snake it up under the sweatshirt, and I let out a quiet groan when his hand closed over my breast.

His fingers caressed my nipple, which was already pebbled,

and his sensuous lips brushed the place where my neck and shoulder joined. I arched my neck to give him better access, then groaned again when he gently pressed his teeth against my skin in an inflammatory nip.

I wanted to turn around, look him in the eye, but he held me still, and I didn't have the will to protest. With him, I'd take whatever he could give me, whenever he could give it. His hips had begun a subtle bump and grind, which I encouraged as best I could. His hand continued working my breast, teasing mercilessly while I struggled to find my breath. Never had I wanted out of a piece of clothing as much as I wanted out of that sweatshirt. His lips felt divine on the skin of my shoulder and throat, but I wanted them elsewhere, wanted them all over my body.

"Please," I whispered. "I've got to get this damn sweatshirt off."

His breath was warm on my skin as he chuckled at my urgency. "What's the rush? If we're going to do this, shouldn't we do it right?"

Do this? Do *what*? Did that mean he intended to follow through on the promise of these kisses and caresses? Was he going to get out of those jammies and stop being afraid? Or was he going to put the brakes on the moment things became too intense for him?

I was overthinking things, but then what else was new for me?

I let out the breath I was holding and tried to let go of all expectations. Jamaal's touch was worth encouraging, and that meant I shouldn't let any complaints pass my lips.

His small sound of approval made me smile. Then he pinched my nipple between his thumb and index finger, the slight tweak of almost-pain instantly soothed by a caress. I hummed my approval and arched my back, trying to obtain a firmer touch.

"You're really impatient, aren't you?" Jamaal whispered in my ear. He nipped my earlobe, and I practically saw stars.

If I was getting this turned on by the foreplay, I wasn't sure how I was going to survive the main event. Assuming we managed to *get* to the main event. Every time things seemed to be rolling between us in the past, something had intervened, and though I hoped it wouldn't happen again this time, I couldn't be sure.

"Have you ever seen any sign that I'm full of patience?" I quipped.

"Compared to me?"

Okay, that was a fair point. "I want you," I said simply. "I want to make sure you know that."

"I want you, too," he replied, proving his point with a thrust of his hips. "And I'm tired of denying myself what I want."

But was he really? We had come so close that time when Sita had appeared on the bed beside us. As hot and bothered as Jamaal sounded now, I couldn't help wondering if his inhibitions were going to come rushing back—and if I was going to react badly if they did.

"Can we please get me out of this sweatshirt?" I asked. "It's not a question of patience, it's a question of comfort. It's lumpy to lie on."

Which was true, as far as it went, but I don't think either one of us believed that was why I was so desperate to take it off. I hoped Jamaal wasn't keeping it on me because he was still worried about contact with his scars.

"All right, fine," he said as if conceding a major victory. "Sit up and I'll get it off you."

I did as I was told, lifting my arms above my head so that Jamaal could pull the sweatshirt off. He tossed it aside, then cupped both my breasts and pulled my back up against him once more. I could feel the ridges of scar tissue, and I knew from the tension in his body that he knew it, but he didn't move away, and after a few seconds, the tension eased out.

His hands roved up and down my body while his lips caressed my jaw. I turned my head so his lips could meet mine, and he obliged, his tongue darting in for a taste as his hands molded my breasts and his breath grew shorter and shorter.

As much as Jamaal had lobbied for patience, it was he who finally decided it was time to get serious and maneuvered me onto my back.

Our eyes had adjusted to the dark, and Jamaal spent a long moment sitting over me, drinking me in with his eyes. I could feel his gaze almost like a caress, sweeping over my body. I took similar advantage, admiring his shape and muscle tone while trying not to think about the scars and about how he'd gotten them. Even with them, he was beautiful to look at, and the tent that had formed in his pajama bottoms was tantalizing.

After he'd looked his fill, Jamaal lay down on top of me, kissing me into a frenzy, then kissing his way down my throat as one hand teased my nipples again.

His braids brushed over my skin with every movement, and though I was prone to being ticklish, I had no urge to laugh this time. I was caught up in the pleasure, and before I knew I was going to do it, I'd put my arms around him, my hands each landing on a mass of scar tissue on his back.

We both tensed, waiting to see if he would freak out, but when he didn't pull away immediately, I knew I had won.

Jamaal paused only for a second or two before he resumed kissing me, and when his lips found my nipple, I reflexively dug my nails in and made an incoherent sound of pleasure.

I'm usually a big fan of foreplay and a slow buildup, but tonight I felt like my body was on fire and only Jamaal could quench it. I reached down and found the drawstring on his pajamas and ruthlessly tugged it open. My hand snaked in and found the hot, hard length of him, and we both groaned in unison.

"I can't wait," I told him.

Jamaal raised his head from my breast, and for a fleeting moment I thought I saw a hint of panic in his eyes. But the expression quickly passed, his eyes narrowing in pleasure as I stroked him.

He would have to climb off me to get my panties off, but apparently he didn't have the patience for the effort. He hooked his fingers into them and with a swift and easy pull tore the flimsy material out of his way. I'd have protested the loss of an expensive pair of undies, but I had other things on my mind. I spread my legs, pressing the inside of my knees to his hips.

"It's been a while for me," he gasped as he lowered himself into position. "Don't know how long I can last."

"Don't care," I muttered, rising up so I could kiss the words from his mouth. I figured if the first time went too fast, we could always try, try again, but my mind was too fuzzy to form the words to tell him so.

I could tell that Jamaal was still trying to restrain himself, still trying to slow down, but he was having a gratifyingly hard time of it. He pressed gently against my entrance for a moment, his whole body quivering with need. I arched my body up to him and squeezed him tightly between my thighs as I thrust my tongue into his mouth.

His control shattered, and Jamaal entered me in a shockingly hard thrust that might have been painful if I weren't so out of my mind with desire. I was glad we were in a suite and didn't have to worry that someone next door would hear the banging as he started to thrust, hard and desperate. I probably made some obscene sounds of pleasure, but I don't remember. All I remember was that it was glorious, and that as Jamaal warned, it didn't last nearly long enough. Within minutes, his thrusts reached a crescendo and he let out a long, low moan of pleasure.

I shared in his ecstasy, drinking in the look on his face even though I was still a long way off from reaching my own climax. It was enough for me to know that he'd finally broken through his barriers, that he was no longer bound and determined to keep me at arm's length. An orgasm was a fleeting thing, but this change in our relationship was not. Arousal still screaming for release, I wrapped my arms and legs around him and held on tightly as he sucked in air and the sweat cooled on his skin.

He raised his head and met my eyes, brushing away a strand of hair that had gotten stuck at the corner of my mouth. There was no wariness on his face, no fear in his eyes, and I couldn't remember ever seeing him like this before, so open and relaxed.

"Sorry I was so quick," he said with a rueful smile. "Take it as a compliment."

I returned the smile and tried not to squirm with my own unfulfilled need. It was a battle I lost, and though the movement was slight, the flare in Jamaal's eyes said he felt it.

"The good news," he said in a hot whisper, "is that I'm more than hungry enough for seconds." Sure enough, I felt him hardening again, still inside me. "And this time I'm going to be old-fashioned and say, 'ladies first.'"

I shivered pleasurably at the promise in his voice. He kissed me then, his lips deliciously soft and warm, his tongue teasing and urging me on, stoking the fire that hadn't been banked yet. I dug my fingers into his coarse braids, holding him to me. Good Lord, but could that man kiss when he put his mind to it.

To my intense disappointment, he ended the kiss, raising his head to look deeply into my eyes once more. He was still hardening within me, his eyes dark with desire, but there was something else shadowing his expression, something not so pleasant. I reached up and stroked my fingers down the side of his face.

"What's wrong?" I asked, pushing my own frustrated needs aside. That we'd already had a major breakthrough was clear, but it was unrealistic to expect the shadow of his past to completely disappear at the drop of a hat.

"I'd like to exorcise one more demon, if I can," he said.

"How can I help?" My body still cried out for release, wanting the pleasure he'd been promising me for so long, but I wanted to heal his psyche and chase that shadow from his eyes.

"The woman . . . The one who liked my scars . . ."

"The bitch owner who abused you, you mean."

Jamaal winced but didn't argue with my terminology.

"She . . ." He cleared his throat and broke eye contact. "She liked being on top, so she could see the scars real clearly while she . . . When I couldn't get it up for her, she gave me more scars. And when that didn't get her what she wanted, she started hurting *other* people to motivate me."

He closed his eyes and swallowed hard again. I willed myself not to cry for him, for his past or for his pain. He huffed out a deep breath and opened his eyes with what seemed like a great effort.

"For more than a century, I've lived with that memory, with the image of her on top of me, forcing me to participate to keep her from hurting some innocent bystander. Could you help me replace it with a different image?"

A hint of panic fluttered in my chest. Tonight had been a breakthrough on about a thousand levels, but we could ruin it all by trying to take it further. It was on the tip of my tongue to gently decline, to tell him we should take things one step at a time. I swallowed the words at the last moment, realizing that wasn't my call to make. Only Jamaal could know when he was ready to face this particular demon, and he said he was ready now. The worst thing I could do was imply that I didn't trust his judgment.

I lifted my head enough to kiss him gently on the lips. "I'll see what I can do," I murmured, trying to make my tone sound more playful than terrified. I hoped like hell I was making the right decision not to protest.

Jamaal held me close and turned us over so that I was on top. Anxiety and bad memories had combined to leach the arousal out of him, and I feared we were already at a disadvantage.

He lay stiff and tense below me as I rose to my knees. I didn't want to know what evil images were flashing across his mind.

The demons may have been nibbling at him, but Jamaal was nothing if not determined. He reached up and cupped my breasts. I leaned into him, giving him full access. Even with all the uncertainty, his touch was incendiary, and I made a small, needy sound as arousal came rushing back into my system. My nipples hardened under his touch, and if the stirring between my legs was any indication, Jamaal liked that.

"You are so fucking beautiful," Jamaal said in a hoarse whisper as his eyes raked up and down my body.

I couldn't help smiling at the compliment. I raised my arms over my head and stretched languorously, pulling all my muscles taut. Jamaal's hips lifted slightly, letting me feel the erection that was well on its way back to full mast. I'd never thought of myself as particularly pretty or sexy, but his quick reaction made me feel like a cross between a cover model and a porn star.

I wrapped my hand around his erection to steady it, keeping a careful watch on his face in case I accidentally triggered something unpleasant, but his eyes were wide open, staring at me with undisguised desire, and I knew that he was firmly here with me in the present.

Carefully, I lowered myself onto him, and we both groaned with the pleasure of it. Jamaal closed his eyes and threw his head back with abandon, but almost instantly came back to himself and fixed his gaze on me once more. I gathered it was easier not to drift into the past if he could keep his eyes on me and constantly remind himself who he was with.

I began moving my hips in a slow, easy rhythm, teasing us both with the pace. Jamaal's hands slid down my body, and one of them found its way between my legs and brushed over my sensitized nub. I gasped and couldn't help moving faster.

"No fair," I panted. I wanted to make this last, but it would be damn hard to do with him touching me like that.

"You don't like this?" Jamaal asked with exaggerated innocence.

If he could play with me like this, he wasn't desperate enough. I forced myself to slow down just a little and reached up to massage my breasts. I was not at all surprised when that made him gasp out a soft curse and his hips bucked beneath me.

"No fair," he moaned, but not like he really meant it.

Thinking that surely we were now completely clear of the shadow of his past, I ground myself against him and thrust faster. Never mind the slow, languid buildup. I'd had about as much teasing as I could take.

"Touch my scars," Jamaal panted out, and that threw some water on my fire.

"What?"

"She liked . . . touching my scars while she fucked me."

He was still hard as a rock beneath me, but I could almost feel his past trying to rush back in and claim him. He meant for me to replace his memories of his bitch owner with images of me, but I had to draw the line somewhere.

"I'm not her," I told him. "I'm doing this *my* way."

Maybe he would have tried harder to get me to follow his script, but I leaned back to get a better angle, and that apparently pressed his buttons in just the right way. He forgot all about giving me stage directions, his hips lifting to meet me as he toyed with my nub with one hand and used his other to clamp on to my butt with a death grip.

Desire and pleasure crowded out every other thought and emotion. Our bodies moved in tandem as we thrust, the bed creaking beneath us in a way that would have made me self-conscious if there were room for that in my mind. Jamaal was breathing so hard, the cords of his muscles so tight, that I was sure he was going to come any moment.

But he was a man of his word. He'd told me I would be going first, and he waited until I was already tipping over the edge myself before he cried out in climax.

ELEVEN

Jamaal and I were a little stiff and awkward with each other in the morning, trying to adjust to the new dynamics of our relationship. There would be no more fighting our attraction, no more trying to act like there was nothing more than friendship between us. It was new, it was different, and I was glad our flight back home didn't leave until the afternoon so that we had a little time to get used to it.

I checked my phone obsessively to see if Violet had had a change of heart, but there were no messages. Jamaal and I stopped by her house again, but she didn't answer the door.

"I can go in anyway," Jamaal suggested, referring to his ability to pass through doors when he wanted to.

"And do what?"

Jamaal shrugged helplessly. Breaking into her house would not endear us to Violet, and pissing off a goddess wasn't going to help our cause. Maybe she just needed a little more time to think things through.

Going back home with no progress to report sucked, but what else could Jamaal and I do? We told our housemates what had happened—including our attempt to enter the Underworld—and though we were met with disappointment, no one seemed especially surprised by Violet's attitude.

"Why would we expect a goddess to be *less* selfish than the Olympians?" Logan said with a shake of his head. "So, what's our next move?"

I fought to quell a surge of panic as everyone looked to me. As if I was somehow more likely to come up with a plan to save the world than any of them.

"I don't know what to do," I was forced to admit. "I think

Violet was right about one thing: renewing the altar in Bermuda doesn't address the primary problem."

"That doesn't mean it's not worth doing," Blake said. "I don't know if it's even in our power to stop Niobe, but we *can* get that altar taken care of."

"Not as long as Violet is more interested in protecting herself than protecting mankind," I countered. "I'll spend some time this afternoon trying to get a hint where we can find another sister, but I don't know whether we're likely to get a better response from one of the others. Not if Niobe is sending them gruesome photos of what she did to Rose and Jasmine."

"And meanwhile the clock is ticking," Blake said. "How long do you think it'll take before people start noticing a sudden lack of pregnancies and the panic begins?"

It was hard to know, especially when the effect wouldn't be geographically isolated, at least not in any way that made sense to ordinary people. "Any answer I give would be only a guess."

"Considering the time that's already passed, I'd say we don't have more than a week or two before the first signs start showing up," Blake answered for me. "The number of new pregnancies will start declining, and it'll seem like a fluke at first. But when it *keeps* declining . . . My guess is that within four to six weeks, the panic will start building and the conspiracy theorists will start coming out of the woodwork. That's when it's going to start getting ugly."

I rubbed my eyes, tired both from lack of sleep and from stress. "I don't know what else I can do but start another search and hope I find a sister who's willing to cooperate. I haven't had any luck finding Anderson yet, and as long as he's hanging out in the Underworld, I don't expect that to change."

Blake made as if to say something, then changed his mind and clamped his jaws shut. He looked away from me and shook his head.

"What?" I asked him. "What were you about to say?"

Blake squirmed. "You're not going to like it," he warned, still not meeting my eyes.

I'd always thought Blake's moral compass was just a bit bent, and he rarely showed discomfort like this unless he was talking about his relationship with my sister, Steph. I knew that meant he was right, that I wouldn't like whatever he'd chosen not to say. But I also knew that at a time like this I had to hear it whether I liked it or not.

"Tell me," I said.

"Don't!" Maggie interrupted suddenly, snarling at Blake.

Her sudden vehemence surprised us all—except for Blake, who met her narrow-eyed gaze with one of his own. Tension crackled in the room, and I took a quick glance around at my fellow *Liberi*. Everyone looked as baffled as I was, except for Leo, whose face had gone white and who was staring intently at the floor as if trying not to be noticed. Not that the latter was rare for him with his distinct lack of people skills.

In a burst of insight, I realized that the tension was emanating solely from the members of our band who were ex-Olympians, and that clued me in to Blake's intention without him having to say a word. If I were an Olympian—someone completely self-centered who found moral codes inconvenient and irrelevant—what would I suggest under the circumstances?

"You think we should kidnap Violet and *force* her to renew the altar," I said.

I'd thought there'd been tension in the room before, but it was suddenly ten times worse.

"I told you you wouldn't like it," Blake said. "And I don't think the situation is that desperate yet. But in a couple of weeks, if we haven't found another solution . . ."

"That is *not* an option," Maggie spat, and if she squeezed the arms of her chair any harder, she would probably break it. Her head whipped around in my direction and she aimed her fiery stare at me. "Tell me *you* don't consider this an option."

My stomach flopped like a grounded fish, and images of my

sister lying battered and naked in Blake's arms after she'd been raped by Alexis hammered at me. What Blake was suggesting lacked the malice and cruelty of what had happened to Steph, but I doubted that or the presence of a good cause would make Violet—or the rest of us—feel better. It was an unthinkable solution, but the alternative was pretty damned unthinkable, too.

"Keep in mind that Violet is a goddess, not a human being," Blake said. "She doesn't think like us, and she doesn't have the same psychology. Remember, she thought it was worth killing every human on Earth to punish Anderson. It wouldn't necessarily be traumatic for her like it would be for a human woman."

"I can't believe you're suggesting this!" Maggie spat at him.

"I don't *like* it!" he shouted back. "I'm saying if the choice is do something awful to one person or let something even worse happen to millions of people, maybe it's better to do something awful."

There was a tremor in Blake's voice, and I realized with some relief that it was costing him a lot to voice this particular option. If he'd suggested it with cool pragmatism, I'd have been tempted to kill him on the spot. He'd made rape threats before, both to men and women, using his powers to force an unnatural lust on people. I called it weaponized sex. He'd told me once that he would have followed through with the threat as long as it was against an Olympian who had done as much or worse, but I wondered if that had just been bluster. We hadn't exactly been on good terms at the time, and he had been trying to intimidate me.

If you looked at the situation with cold logic, Blake's argument made all kinds of sense. The good of the many and all that. But everything within me recoiled at the thought. Any answer I came up with in my own head seemed wrong. Never mind my doubt that it was even *possible* if Violet turned into a pillar of white light. Blake had never seen a god or goddess without the human disguise, didn't fully understand how non-human they truly were.

"I think we all need to take a step back from the edge," Jamaal said. His voice was remarkably cool and even compared to the angry vibe in the room. "Violet didn't object to the idea of renewing the altar. She's just scared to take the risk of going there. If we can get her there safely, I have the feeling she'd be willing to renew it. After all, she wants the population to be healthy so the gods will let her rejoin them someday."

I sucked in a shaky breath, stepping back from the edge just as Jamaal suggested. He was right, and though Violet had once been vengeful enough to try with her sisters to kill off all mankind, she now had a personal interest in keeping the status quo.

"We'd still have to get her to the altar against her will," I said, looking at Jamaal. "You saw her when she stopped pretending to be human. How do you suggest we kidnap *that*?"

"And what do we do if you're wrong?" Maggie asked. Anger still sparked in her eyes, and her chin still jutted out stubbornly.

"We don't have to answer that now," Jamaal said, still calm. People were starting to look at him funny, unused to him being anything resembling a peacemaker. "Like Nikki said, part one of the plan still has a gaping hole in it. No need to worry about the rest if we can't patch that hole."

"Well, I want to know what part two would be!"

"Why?" Jamaal countered. "There's no right answer here, no answer that will satisfy anyone. So let's concentrate on making sure we never have to answer it."

"Who are you, and what have you done with Jamaal?" Blake muttered just loudly enough for everyone to hear.

The question made more than one of us smile, if only faintly, and a little more tension eased out of the room. Maggie seemed to be the only one still struggling, the rest of us content to run away from the moral dilemma as fast as we could.

"I think Jamaal went and got himself laid," Jack said. He'd been unusually silent throughout our meeting, and I'd thought maybe even *his* sense of humor had been affected by the dire subject matter. Too bad it hadn't.

I shot Jack a glare that would have done grumpy-Jamaal proud. You know, just in case someone in the room thought Jack was just kidding or dead wrong. Always cool under fire, that's me.

Jack grinned unrepentantly. And then Sita appeared in the middle of our circle of chairs, looking straight at Jack and snarling. More than one chair was hastily pushed back—Sita is one hell of an intimidating creature—but of course Jack stayed right where he was. I took a quick peek at Jamaal's face, making sure his expression wasn't genuinely murderous, and was relieved to see no sign of an imminent explosion.

Sita snarled again, the sound deep and rumbling, triggering every avoid-being-lunch instinct in my body even though for once it wasn't directed at me. She took a menacing step in Jack's direction, and though he was trying not to show it, I could tell that even he was feeling the fight-or-flight instinct.

One thing I'll say for Sita's appearance: she instantly put the kibosh on any speculation about whether Jamaal and I had done the deed. Which I suspect is exactly what Jamaal intended when he summoned her. Jack had a unique skill for getting on his nerves, but the new calmer, more rational Jamaal wouldn't kill him for it. Probably.

"I think Sita objects to your tone," Jamaal said. "Maybe that's a sign that it's time for you to shut the fuck up." There was a surprising lack of heat behind the words, and I was pretty proud of his restraint.

Jack opened his mouth for a response, and Sita's roar made the paintings on the wall rattle. His eyes widened in mock fear that probably wasn't as mock as he wanted us to believe, and he made a zipping-his-lips gesture. My guess was that Jamaal wasn't convinced, because Sita lay down on the floor about a yard from Jack's feet, her eyes narrowed and fixed on his face while the tip of her tail twitched.

I cleared my throat, drawing attention back to myself, though it was hard to ignore the irritated tiger in the room.

"I don't think kidnapping Violet is a viable option, no matter what," I said. "She's too powerful for us to handle. The only person who could drag her to that altar against her will is Anderson. Which means we *have* to find him."

"How?" Jamaal asked. "I think you're right and he's in the Underworld, and we've already established you can't follow him there."

I let out a whoosh of breath, because I really didn't like my own idea. "I can't get there without the help of a death-god descendant who can open a gate. You might not be able to do that, but maybe Cyrus knows someone who can."

Anderson had made it sound like the ability was fairly rare, but there were a lot of Olympians out there, so maybe I'd get lucky.

"Seriously?" Blake said. "You're going to ask Cyrus to help you save the world after everything he's done? He might help you get to the altar because it helps him capture and punish his defectors, but he doesn't get anything out of lending you one of his people."

"You have a better idea? Because we're scraping the bottom of the barrel as it is."

"Just because I don't have a better suggestion doesn't mean asking Cyrus for help is a good idea."

"A bad idea is better than *no* idea," I said, and Blake had no argument for that. "I'll try to find another of Niobe's sisters first, see if one of them is willing to cooperate. If not, then I have no choice but to talk to Cyrus one more time."

I put in several hours in front of the computer, trying to force my subconscious to cough up another lead, but I had no success. It's hard to overstate how much I wanted to find a solution that didn't involve me traveling to the Underworld in search of Anderson, but I was also painfully aware that finding a fertility goddess willing to renew Jasmine's abandoned altar would barely scratch the surface of the trouble mankind was in. I don't think doubts of that level are conducive to making my power flow, so my lack of success may very well have been my own fault.

I kept searching, even after I'd already called Cyrus to set up a meeting for the next day. I could always cancel if a better idea popped up.

Instead of eating a proper dinner, I munched on the junk food stash I kept in my mostly empty filing cabinet. A word to the wise: sleep deprivation, end-of-the-world stress, and a dinner of Ding Dongs and potato chips do not go well together. My head was aching from staring at the screen for so long, my stomach rumbled unhappily, and I was too tired to yawn.

About the last thing I needed to face under the circumstances was more drama, but apparently the universe had it in for me, because as I was wallowing in frustration, there came a knock on my door. Instinct told me that knock did not portend good news, and I was halfway tempted not to answer.

Then again, it wasn't as if I were being productive.

"Come in," I said wearily.

My exhaustion evaporated when the door opened and I saw my sister standing there with tear-reddened eyes. I shoved my chair back and jumped to my feet.

"Steph!" I cried in alarm. "Oh, my God, what's wrong?"

I went to hug her and she practically collapsed in my arms, sobbing for all she was worth. I stuck out my foot to kick the door shut without letting go of Steph, terrified that we'd just had a death in the family. Our parents—well, *Steph's* parents, my adoptive parents—had recently moved to California to take care of our ailing grandmother. I'd been trying with limited success to fully embrace the Glasses as my own parents, but I'd never come close to forming that kind of bond with extended family. Maybe it was selfish and mean-spirited of me, but I couldn't help hoping the bad news related to extended family rather than the Glasses themselves. I wasn't sure I could bear a loss on top of everything else I was dealing with.

Unfortunately, Steph was crying too hard to form words, and I knew from long experience that I'd have to wait until the worst of the storm passed before I'd be able to get an explanation. All I could do in the meantime was hold her and murmur nonsense about how it was all going to be all right. I wished Steph would hurry up and get it together so she could tell me what was wrong. I'd never been much of a crier myself, and it always took effort on my part to tolerate and understand people who were more open with their emotions.

When Steph's sobs slowed to heavy sniffles, she pushed away from me and scrubbed at her eyes. I grabbed the box of tissues from my desk, and wordlessly she snatched a handful and blew her nose.

"What is it?" I asked. "Did something happen to Mom or Dad?" I still wasn't comfortable calling them "Mom and Dad"—I'd always called them "Mr. and Mrs. Glass"—but I was trying to change that long habit.

Steph's swollen red eyes widened. "No!" she exclaimed hurriedly. "It's nothing like that." Her lower lip quivered dangerously, and she swallowed hard. "Blake and I broke up."

The tears started flowing freely once more, and she grabbed more tissues while I tried to deal with my own welter of confused emotions. I had made no secret of the fact that I disapproved of Blake and Steph's relationship from the beginning. Things might go great between them now, but what would happen in twenty years, when Steph was middle-aged and—physically at least—Blake remained unchanged? Blake might not be as young as he looked, but would he still want Steph when she was a little old lady?

If Blake were just some mortal boyfriend I didn't like, I wouldn't be so torn up about the potential future of their relationship, but thanks to Eros, Blake's divine ancestor, no woman who slept with him more than once would ever be satisfied with another lover. Which meant that if Steph fell in love with him and then later changed her mind, she would end up alone for the rest of her life. He wasn't someone she could try on for size, and that made him dangerous to her emotional well-being.

The two of them had been together for a couple of months now, and I knew they had somehow resisted the temptation to have sex—possibly because Steph wasn't ready yet. But as her psyche healed and her relationship with Blake deepened, things were bound to change. In my opinion, ending it now while Steph still had choices was a terrific idea, but that didn't mean I liked seeing my sister heartbroken. Her misery sparked an almost physical pain deep in my chest.

"I'm so sorry, Steph," I said. "Do you want to tell me what happened?"

I'd been through enough breakups myself to know that sometimes you wanted to talk and sometimes you just wanted silent support, and I was fully prepared to provide whatever Steph preferred.

Taking the whole box of tissues with her, Steph flopped down on my sitting room sofa and kicked her shoes off with an almost angry motion. I took that as an indication that she wanted to talk, so I joined her on the sofa and told myself in no uncertain terms that I would not let any indication that I thought the breakup was a good thing leave my lips. Steph knew I wanted the best for her, but she'd never appreciated my sisterly advice on the topic of Blake.

Steph started shredding the wad of tissues in her hand, and I quietly reached for the trash can beside my desk and plopped it down on the floor between us. The gesture prompted a ghost of a smile, and Steph tossed her first few shreds in while continuing to work on the rest.

"Blake told me what he suggested," she said, her voice hoarse from all that crying. "At your meeting this afternoon," she clarified when she saw my puzzled look.

My jaw dropped, and I was momentarily at a loss for words. Steph had been forcefully dragged into the world of the *Liberi*, so it was no surprise that she knew all about the current situation. But I couldn't *imagine* a reason why Blake would tell a rape victim—the woman he supposedly loved, no less—that he had suggested kidnapping and raping a goddess.

"What the fuck was he thinking?" I asked out loud.

Typical of my softhearted sister, Steph immediately rose to Blake's defense. "He was all quiet and broody this evening, and I kept bugging him to tell me what was wrong." She gave the tissues in her hand a vicious tear, sending a flurry of shredded tissue bits into the air. "Eventually, he gave me what I asked for." She frowned at the tissue-snow that now covered the seat of the couch and the floor at her feet. "Sorry," she said sheepishly, and began picking up the pieces and tossing them into the trash can.

"You don't have to do that," I told her, but she ignored me. Maybe it made her feel better to focus on a task.

I'd been on the receiving end of any number of Steph's inquisitions in the past, so I knew just how persistent and annoyingly persuasive she can be. But even knowing that, I couldn't imagine how Blake could be so stupid. Okay, yeah, he was a guy, and sometimes guys can be awfully dense about women's feelings, but still . . .

"I know you think he shouldn't have told me," Steph said. "But I think I deserved to know just what kind of a man I was involved with."

I found myself in the unfamiliar position of defending Blake. "To be fair, we are talking about the potential end of all human life, so the situation is as extreme as it's possible to get."

Steph slammed her handful of tissue pieces into the trash can, then pulled another from the box so forcefully she tore it in half. "So *you* think it's a good idea, too?"

"No! It's a terrible idea, and it's not going to happen."

Which was an easy thing to say, but it was a little tricky to find the moral high ground on the issue. If that was the only way to keep the human race going, was it really morally superior to *not* do it?

My deepest, most fervent wish was that I not have to answer that particular question, because I was guaranteed to hate myself no matter which answer I chose.

My quick and emphatic denial seemed to satisfy Steph, so apparently I was doing a good job of hiding my own doubts. Her lips started quivering again. "I can't believe the man I thought I loved would do that. Not after what happened to me."

I gathered Steph into my arms so she could sob some more, realizing her distress had less to do with Blake than it did with her own terrible experience. She never talked about it, and though logic told me that not nearly enough time had passed for her to take more than a couple of baby steps toward healing, she'd done a good job of pretending to be her normal, cheerful self. I like to think that if my own life hadn't been in constant danger and turmoil, I'd have had the wits to realize she still needed help and done a better job of supporting her.

Anderson had forbidden me to tell her that he had killed Alexis, the man who raped her, but in spite of his dire threats, I hadn't been able to resist telling Steph that Alexis was dead, though I shared no details. Now that Anderson was AWOL, I figured the gag order no longer applied, and I could give her all the details she deserved.

"Let me tell you how Alexis died," I murmured as I rocked her back and forth like a child.

I doubted hearing how long and how loud Alexis had screamed when Anderson killed him would do anything to heal the wounds the bastard had left on my sister's soul, but at least she would know he'd paid for what he'd done. None of which would make things better between her and Blake, who I was tempted to go shoot in the nuts.

Why the hell had he told Steph any of this? What good could he possibly have thought it would do?

Right now, the only thing I could do was hold her and show her every scrap of the love I felt for her. But I was already making plans to show Blake just how big a mistake he'd made by breaking my sister's heart.

TWELVE

I was getting mighty sick of the damn coffee bar Cyrus always insisted upon as our meeting place. It was far from the "neutral site" he'd once claimed it to be. However, there was no way I was inviting Cyrus to the house, nor was I willing to set foot in his, and we couldn't have this conversation in public.

I'd decided to make a show of good faith by bringing only Maggie with me, leaving Logan back at the mansion, but Cyrus hadn't done me the similar courtesy. The coffee bar was packed to the gills with glyph-marked, scowling Olympians, and I wondered if I'd made a tactical error. Maggie was strong enough to crush bricks with her pinkies, but I didn't know if that made her any good in a fight.

"Was it really necessary to bring a platoon with you?" I asked Cyrus as I pulled up a chair and sat at his table without waiting for an invitation.

He gave me an unrepentant grin. "You can never be too careful."

I shook my head. I had absolutely zero desire to play games, and I was going to have to work hard to hold on to my patience. There was no point in letting Cyrus get under my skin so easily, but somehow I couldn't stop myself from snapping at him.

"Look, I've had a really lousy week trying to save the world, so is there any chance we can skip the posturing and other bullshit and just talk like grown-ups?"

His eyebrows arched comically high. "My, someone got up

on the wrong side of the bed this morning. Should I offer you an espresso, or will that only make things worse?"

"I guess expecting you to care about saving the world was asking too much."

Cyrus's perma-smile lost a little of its wattage. "If I didn't care, one of your people would already be dead by now and we wouldn't be having this meeting. I care my way, you care yours. It'll work out better for both of us if we just accept our differences, don't you think?"

Cyrus was a total prick, but unfortunately, he was also right. I closed my eyes and took a quick, deep breath, doing my best to push aside my somewhat frayed state of mind. I was here once again to ask the enemy for help, so coming in with virtual guns blazing was a bad idea. It was time for me to dial it down a notch.

"You're right," I said. "Sorry I was so pissy, but I'm just too stressed out to be a model of self-control at all times."

He cocked his head, now looking more curious than amused. "Why are you so convinced it's *your* job to save the world, as you put it? Shouldn't that be up to Anderson, seeing as he got the world into this mess himself?"

"I would love nothing more than to make this all be Anderson's problem," I said fervently. "Actually, that's what I'm here to talk to you about. I've been doing everything I can to locate Anderson, and it's just not working."

"And you think *I* can help?" Cyrus asked.

"Sort of. I think maybe Anderson's hanging out in the Underworld because he knows it's somewhere I can't find him. Not without help, at least."

The metaphorical light bulb went on over Cyrus's head. "Ah. Please, do go on."

I didn't like the calculating gleam that lit his eyes, but it wasn't like I could back down now. I swallowed my foreboding and met his gaze. "I don't know all of your people, but I'm hoping that you have a descendant of Hades you can lend me, one who can create a gateway to the Underworld."

Cyrus nodded sagely. "You want one of my Olympians to come into the Underworld with you and help you search for Anderson, is that what you're telling me?"

What part of that wasn't clear? I wondered, but thankfully I was able to keep the thought to myself. "Yes."

"And what do I get in return?"

I blinked at him for a moment. I'd had enough dealings with Cyrus to know he was self-interest incarnate, but I'd halfway convinced myself that the stakes were high enough that he couldn't possibly be selfish enough to ask what was in it for him. Even though Blake had warned me he would be.

"You do realize we're talking about saving the world here, right?"

He shrugged. "I'd say that's up for debate. Sounds to me more like we're talking about finding Anderson, which isn't the same thing."

"But I want to find him because I think he's the only one who can fix this mess!"

"And you think he's just sitting in the Underworld with his thumb up his ass sulking about his big secret getting out?"

I opened and shut my mouth, but no words came out.

"I'm not sure I can say I really know a guy who I only recently found out was actually a god in disguise," Cyrus continued, "but I'm pretty sure Anderson is doing more than just sulking. He's not the kind of person to sit on the sidelines and eat popcorn while the world goes to hell."

Like you are, I thought, but again refrained from saying out loud.

"Maybe if you and Anderson put your heads together, you'll have a better chance of solving the problem, but that doesn't mean finding him is the same thing as saving the world. So if you're going to lead one of my Olympians into danger, into the unknown country of the Underworld, then you're going to have to give me something in return."

I sputtered. "I'm not planning to lead anyone into danger! I just need someone to open a gate!"

"And go in with you, because if you don't find Anderson you're going to need someone to get you back out. I don't know much about the Underworld, and when I've heard it described to me, it doesn't sound like a very nice place to be. It's the kind of place a death god would go to hide out, and there's no way you can convince me a trip there would be safe."

I swallowed a few choice responses. The only bad things that had happened to me during my one trip to the Underworld had all been caused by the death-god descendant I'd been chasing, but even so the place had given me a major case of the creeps. The very air I'd breathed had been thick with the scent of you-don't-belong-here, and I had no idea who or what aside from Anderson might be lurking there.

"You owe me," I said. "You lured me into a trap, hit me over the head, and handed me over to your father when you knew exactly what he was going to do to me." When I flashed back to the image of Cyrus walking away, leaving me tied up and helpless at his father's mercy, I broke out in a cold sweat.

Cyrus chuckled. "Nice try. But if you want to borrow one of my Olympians, then you're going to have to pay for the privilege. I hold all the cards right now, and I'm perfectly happy to walk out of here without an agreement. Can you say the same?"

I wanted to kill the bastard, but unfortunately that wasn't an option. I knew he was telling the truth. He could walk out of that coffee bar without helping me and not feel even a twinge of remorse over it.

It was a game of chicken, and we both knew I would swerve first.

"I'll never get used to the idea that people can be as selfishly mercenary as you're being right now," I said.

"Sticks and stones, yadda yadda yadda. I'll never get used to the idea that some people are so worried about everyone else that they never even *try* to get what they want. I think that's kind of sad."

What can you do with someone who thinks being selfish is a *good* thing?

Nothing. There was no point in appealing to Cyrus's better nature. He didn't have one. Which meant I had to accept the bitter reality that if I wanted his help, I had to bribe him.

"What is it you want?" I asked, the words forced out through gritted teeth.

Cyrus gave me a triumphant smile. "What I've always wanted, of course." He looked at me expectantly.

Cyrus was not on speaking terms with subtlety, so it was no secret what he wanted. No, *who* he wanted. "You want me to give you Blake," I said. I was pissed as hell at Blake for breaking Steph's heart, and I fully intended to find some time to let him know just what I thought of him, but that didn't mean I was prepared to hand him over like a slab of meat.

"Of course."

"No. Think of something else."

He sighed dramatically. "We've been through this already, Nikki. The person who's willing to walk away has all the power, and in this scenario, I'm that person."

"I can't just *give* you a human being!"

"Sure you can. If it makes you feel better, you can even ask for his consent before you give him to me. I think under the circumstances, he'll come willingly, since he's playing the hero these days."

He was probably right about that, but no, it didn't make me feel any better. It was clear that Blake had a lot of conflicting emotions about Cyrus. I'd never asked how long the two of them had been "friends with benefits," but I had the impression it had been a long time, and that there was plenty of regret and heartache on both sides when it ended. I saw no sign that

Blake had any interest in resuming their relationship, but I also saw no sign of the knee-jerk rage that often accompanied a bad breakup.

If I asked Blake to do this, he would do it. Especially now that he and Steph had broken up and he wouldn't have to worry that he was betraying her. But how could I ask him to do it?

Cyrus leaned forward in his chair, putting his arm on the table and lowering his head in an obvious attempt to regain eye contact. I hadn't even realized I was staring fixedly at the table-top until he put himself into my field of vision.

"It's a fair trade, Nikki," he said. "It's not like I'm going to hurt him."

No, I didn't think Cyrus had any intention of physically hurting Blake. But the amount of psychological damage he could do . . .

I shuddered. "You might not hurt him, but you can destroy him."

Cyrus was under the impression that if he had Blake all to himself, he'd be able to win him back over time. But it was clear to me that he couldn't do that without breaking him, and I just couldn't allow that to happen. Somehow, I had fallen into Anderson's shoes, and one of my duties had to be to protect the rest of his *Liberi*. And Cyrus was right: finding Anderson felt very important to me, but it wasn't necessarily the key to saving the world, no matter what hopes I might have.

"I might be able to destroy the mask he's been wearing ever since he left the Olympians," Cyrus said, "but that's not the same as destroying *him*. And before you voice your outrage, let me also point out that it would take considerable time. I'll be letting you borrow one of my Olympians, so how about if I just borrow Blake as well? I do insist on getting the better end of the deal, so I would like to keep him for three times as long as you keep my Olympian. So if you can track down Anderson in, say, eight hours, I'd get to keep Blake for twenty-four hours. How much damage do you really imagine I can do in that amount of time?"

Putting a time limit on the deal made it feel slightly less morally bankrupt. But I had no idea how long it would take to find Anderson, nor did I know what kind of trouble we might run into in the Underworld. If something were to happen to the Olympian I "borrowed," I might never be able to get Blake back from Cyrus's clutches.

"Ask him," Cyrus urged. "It doesn't have to be your decision."

Yes, it did. Unlike Cyrus, Blake definitely had a conscience and a sense of responsibility. If I brought this proposal to him, he'd agree to it, so I was basically making the decision as soon as I decided whether or not to ask him.

Cyrus reached into his back pocket and pulled out a cell phone, laying it on the table in front of him. "I'll even make it easier than that," he said. "*I'll* ask him. Whether you want me to or not. The fact is that it's not really your decision to make; it's his."

If I didn't know better, I would swear there was a hint of compassion in Cyrus's voice, that he was genuinely trying to take the burden of the decision off my shoulders. Blake had told me once that Cyrus was capable of being a nice guy when he wanted to and when it didn't inconvenience him. I wouldn't go that far, but I will admit he didn't go out of his way to be nasty, like many of the Olympians did.

"I'll ask him," I said, my voice raspy as I tried not to cry. Maybe Cyrus was right and I could shrug off any responsibility for what I was asking Blake to do—if I were a different person. But, dammit, it was my bright idea to ask Cyrus for help, and if Blake was going to have to pay for it, then I was going to have to live with the guilt. I owed it to Blake and to myself to be brutally honest about it.

How I was going to deal with Steph when I was forced to admit to her what I'd set in motion, I had no idea.

I wasn't exactly eager to talk to Blake, for more reasons than one, but putting off the conversation wouldn't make it any easier, so as soon as I got back to the mansion, I marched myself to Blake's suite. I didn't give myself time to think about it, just knocked on his door and held my breath. I'm ashamed to say part of me was hoping he wouldn't be there. Just because my rational mind knew delaying the conversation wouldn't help anything didn't make me eager to get on with it.

He answered the door within seconds.

Usually, Blake is what I'd describe as a pretty boy, well dressed and impeccably groomed, with his hair messy in that special, product-laden way that said the look was intentional.

Today, he hadn't bothered to wash and primp. He wore a simple T-shirt with wash-faded sweats, his cheeks were pebbled with stubble, and his hair was sticking up in ways that had nothing to do with style. His eyes were slightly bloodshot, and he smelled of stale booze instead of expensive aftershave.

In other words, he looked terrible. As much as I hated him for breaking Steph's heart, it was clear to see he had broken his own right along with it, and I surprised myself by feeling sorry for him.

"If you've come to give me hell about Steph, please skip it," he said. "I feel shitty enough already." His words weren't slurred, but the scent of alcohol on his breath told me he was still in the process of drowning his sorrows. I wished I could just leave him to it.

"That's not why I'm here," I answered.

Blake pushed away from the door, leaving it open in a silent invitation. He didn't stagger as he made his way to his sitting room sofa, so I presumed that though he wasn't technically sober, he wasn't out-of-his-mind drunk, either. That was good, because I'd hate to have this difficult conversation with him only to have to repeat it later because he couldn't remember.

There was a half-empty bottle of vodka sitting on his coffee table, and I glimpsed an empty one stuffed into a trash can discreetly hidden beneath an end table. Other than that, his sitting room was neat and tidy.

I was about to take a seat when a flash of red caught my eye and I came to a sudden halt. On the opposite side of the sofa from the trash can was a lined wicker basket, and in that was a ball of red yarn with a pair of knitting needles stuck into it. My heart gave an unpleasant squeeze when I saw the lacy red scarf that lay beside the yarn.

I knew that he'd been knitting that scarf for Steph, meaning to give it to her on Valentine's Day. He'd told me once that he'd taken up the hobby as a rebellion against his father, who had told him that boys don't knit.

The scarf was obviously finished, and it was beautiful. I didn't want to know how many hours he had put into knitting it, and I certainly didn't want to think about the depth of feeling those hours implied.

"Are you all right?" I asked him in the kind of gentle voice I'd use with a trauma victim.

Blake gave me a withering look. "Do I *look* like I'm all right?"

I winced and shook my head. "I don't get it. Why on earth would you think it was a good idea to tell Steph about our meeting? I mean, I'm all for honesty and everything, but . . ."

Blake saw me looking at the scarf and gave a little snarl. "You wanted to break us up, didn't you? Well, your wish came true, so stop complaining."

Call me oversensitive, but I sensed a bit of hostility being aimed my way. Not that I'd ever been particularly subtle in my disapproval, but I'd done my best to keep my opinion to myself, and I certainly never *tried* to break them up.

"I won't pretend I thought you were good for Steph in the long run," I said, "but I do know you were taking good care of her after . . . what happened." In some ways, I wondered if the sexual limitations Blake's divine ancestor imposed were part of his appeal to Steph. At least she didn't have to worry about finding a way to be comfortable with sex again anytime soon. And Blake had always been gentle with her psyche in ways that other men might not have been. So the long-term outlook hadn't seemed too good, but in the short term he might well have been just what the doctor ordered. If he hadn't gone and screwed it up by opening his big mouth.

"But you were happy when Steph told you it was over, weren't you?" Blake prodded. "Admit it."

I remembered Steph's heartbroken sobs, and it was hard to describe my own emotions as "happy."

"No, I wasn't happy that you broke my sister's heart!" I snapped. "She was comfortable with you, she trusted you. Hell, I'm pretty sure she *loved* you. And then you had to go and tell her how low you'd be willing to sink, when you had to know how she would feel about it . . ."

My words petered out as I thought about exactly what I was saying. Blake *had* to have known how badly Steph would take his suggestion. I've known plenty of insensitive, clueless men in my time, but Blake wasn't one of them, especially not where Steph was concerned.

"You *did* know how she would take it," I said. "And you said it anyway."

I couldn't interpret the look on his face, except that it was hard and closed off. "I'm not a moron," he said.

"But then why did you do it?" And then I answered my own question. It was clear to anyone with eyes that Blake was miserable, which meant he wasn't tired of Steph or anxious to break up with her. He'd obviously hurt himself almost as much as he'd hurt Steph, and he'd done it with his eyes wide open.

"You purposely caused her to break up with you," I said. "You knew how strongly she'd react to what you'd said, and you said it anyway."

Blake rose to his feet and started to pace restlessly, unable to hold still. "Of course I knew how she'd react. I realized that you've been right all along." The expression on his face was pure agony. "I love her. More than anyone else who's ever been in my life. And if I love her that much, I can't risk ruining the rest of her life by tying her to me. Nothing good could come of it, so I decided to end it. But in a way that felt like it was her idea."

It made a twisted kind of sense, and I almost had to admire the genius of it. Steph was badly hurt now, but she'd probably be even more heartbroken if Blake had initiated the breakup. Making it seem like her idea would eventually help dull her pain, at least in theory. To be perfectly honest, I never would have guessed Blake had it in him. And it made it even harder for me to ask him what I knew I needed to ask him.

"You said you didn't come here to give me hell about Steph," Blake said. "So what *did* you come here for?"

From one unpleasant topic to another in quick succession. I told him about my meeting with Cyrus, watching his face closely the whole time, trying unsuccessfully to read him. He could be a tough man to read when he wanted to be. I was certain he had strong emotions about the subject, but you'd never have guessed it from his studiously neutral expression.

"What do you think?" I asked when a long and uncomfortable silence had settled on us. "Should we take him up on the offer?"

"How can we not?"

"Well, there's no guarantee that I can find Anderson in the Underworld. I have no idea whether my power will even work there. It's not like there's any moonlight to fuel it. And even if I do find him, I'm not sure how much good it will do. If he could fix things himself, I suspect he would have done it by now."

Blake offered a nonchalant shrug that I didn't believe for a moment. "If it's something he can do alone. Maybe he needs help and he's too much of a lone wolf to ask for it. I mean, it doesn't sound like Niobe is open to sitting down and having a chat with him to work things out. Hell, I doubt he can even get near her if he doesn't have some manpower to help him get through her followers."

"So you're really willing to do it? Willing to let Cyrus take you?"

Another of those too-casual shrugs. "He won't hurt me. I've done a lot of distasteful things in my life. This will just be one more."

He was being so stoic and closed off about it, but I knew that wasn't how he really felt. He had to be tied up in knots. I didn't think he'd ever been in love with Cyrus—though I suspected the reverse wasn't true—but there had certainly been genuine friendship between them, and there was still a spark there, visible to anyone. The emotional damage of being forced into Cyrus's arms might never heal.

"It feels wrong to me," I said. "Cyrus is right, and it's your decision to make rather than mine, but . . . no one should have to do what he's asking you to do."

The corner of Blake's mouth tipped up in a smile. "He's asking me to have sex with him," he said. "There are a lot worse things that could happen to me in the hands of the Olympians."

Physically, sure. But being strong-armed into having sex with your ex did not sound like the healthiest thing in the world.

"I'll be all right, Nikki," he said with a sigh. "I can't have the woman I love, but at least I can do something useful. A little meaningless sex is a small price to pay for the chance to find Anderson and fix this mess."

There was no way in hell he was going to convince me that going with Cyrus would be nothing but "a little meaningless sex" to him. I knew it would be painful and damaging, and I also knew that even though Blake and Steph had broken up, they would both be hurt by it.

Jeez, how was I going to tell Steph about this? She was going to hate me.

"Don't tell Steph until after it's too late," Blake said, reading my mind. "She's . . . not going to take it well."

"No shit, really?" I could hardly bear the thought of seeing Steph's face when she learned about this. Maybe if we found Anderson really quickly and Blake wasn't missing for too long, I wouldn't have to tell her at all. But I knew how hard it was to keep secrets, and too many people would know about this one to realistically hope Steph would never know. The only thing worse than hearing it from me would be hearing it from someone else.

"We both love her," Blake said quietly. "If we tell her about it while there's still a choice, one or both of us might not be able to go through with it. We can't let ourselves back out just because we can't stand to hurt her. It's too important."

I wondered if it was possible Steph would ever forgive either one of us for this. But if she didn't, Blake and I were both going to have to suck it up and deal.

THIRTEEN

My second journey to the Underworld began at Rock Creek Cemetery. It was a cruel irony that we ended up having to hand Blake over to Cyrus on Valentine's Day of all days.

My plan had been to go to the Underworld alone rather than risk any of my housemates, but I should have known Jamaal would veto that idea.

"No way you're traipsing around the fucking Underworld with some Olympian shitbird as a guide and no backup," was how he put it.

I didn't want to put Jamaal—or anyone else, for that matter—in danger, but I had to admit he made a hell of a nice security blanket. And I doubt I could have convinced him to stay home anyway.

We met Cyrus and several of his goons at the cemetery. One of them turned out to be the Olympian we were borrowing.

Oscar was a descendant of Hades, and he looked like the kind of guy who might find employment as a mob enforcer. Big. Intimidating. Buzz-cut hair. Deep-set glower.

Despite his imposing build and weaselly eyes, there was still an aura of power to him, and I knew that suit he was wearing hadn't come off some department store rack. So he might be a mob-enforcer look-alike, but he was an especially well-dressed and -groomed one.

"Seriously?" I asked him when Cyrus made the introduction. "You're going to the Underworld wearing a suit?"

I was wearing a pair of old jeans and a sweatshirt over a sleeveless top. The last time I'd been to the Underworld, it had been uncomfortably hot, so I figured layers were the key.

"What do you care what I wear?" Oscar countered. He looked me up and down with a little sneer, letting me know he was not impressed by my own wardrobe choices. "If I mess up this suit, I'll buy another."

No, it would never occur to an Olympian to take good care of his belongings. Everything—and every*one*—was disposable to them.

"Play nice, children," Cyrus said with an indulgent chuckle as he gave Oscar a pat on the shoulder. Oscar tensed almost imperceptibly, and the muscles in his jaw worked.

I looked the Olympian straight in the eye, which he didn't seem to like much. "I'm not taking you with me if you're not a volunteer," I said, because the vibe I was getting from him suggested he wasn't. Not that I was in any position to turn up my nose at any aid Cyrus chose to offer, but I didn't much like going into the Underworld in the first place, and I liked the idea of going there with a hostile, resentful Olympian in tow even less.

"Of course he's a volunteer!" Cyrus said before Oscar could

answer. "We Olympians are not known for doing things we don't want to do."

True enough as far as it went, but they did have a hierarchy, and I doubted Cyrus had any qualms about pushing his people around. Especially not when manufacturing a volunteer would win him some alone time with Blake.

"And yet you felt compelled to answer when I wasn't talking to you," I said, narrowing my eyes at Cyrus. "If he's a volunteer, why didn't you just let him say so?"

"I'm a volunteer," Oscar snapped. "Now can we just stop yapping and get this over with?"

Oscar wasn't winning any acting awards in the near future. There was no hiding the anger that lurked behind his eyes, and I suspected some of his belligerence was born of fear. Or maybe I was just projecting my own feelings.

"Let it go, Nikki," Jamaal advised quietly. "We have to do this."

Maybe I was stalling just a bit. Diving into a portal to the Underworld in the heat of battle had been a lightning-quick decision on my part, and therefore much easier than walking in now with my eyes wide open.

"All right," I agreed reluctantly. "Let's go."

We all took a quick glance around to make sure there wouldn't be any witnesses to the impossible thing that was about to happen. Luckily, there aren't that many people who like walking around cemeteries at night. Even if there had been, they'd have had to be practically breathing down our necks to see the pocket of inky-black darkness that formed and blotted out the sea of headstones as Oscar opened a portal.

I had to fight a sudden urge to take a step or ten back. Even Cyrus seemed affected by the dread that emanated from that portal, his perpetual mask of good-natured humor slipping away. *Abandon hope all ye who enter here,* I thought, then shook my head violently to clear that thought from my mind.

The Underworld wasn't Hell, I told myself, but not very convincingly. I was hard-pressed to say exactly what the Underworld was, so it was difficult to be any more convinced of what it *wasn't*.

Cyrus shuddered dramatically. "Have a nice trip, kids," he said. He was trying to regain his usual aura of nonchalance, but he wasn't fooling anyone.

I took a step toward the portal, still fighting my natural reluctance, but Cyrus held out a hand to stop me.

"First things first," he said, then held out his hand to Blake, who hadn't uttered a peep since we set foot in the cemetery.

Blake rolled his eyes and didn't take Cyrus's hand. "I'm here. There's no reason I have to hold your fucking hand." He crossed his arms over his chest.

Cyrus cocked his head. "So you mean to be difficult about this?"

"You expected something different?" Blake replied, his jaw jutting out stubbornly.

There was a wealth of undertones I didn't fully understand, and once again I worried about Blake's safety. We all knew Cyrus wanted him for something other than the pleasure of his company, and if Blake resisted . . .

Cyrus sneaked a glance at my face and chuckled. "Tell Nikki it's all right for her to go. I think you've triggered her mother hen instincts."

Blake waved me toward the portal. "It's fine, Nikki. And while I won't take Cyrus's hand, you three might want to hold hands. Wouldn't want Oscar to make the portal go away at an inconvenient moment."

That won him a particularly withering glare from Oscar, which he totally ignored. Not trusting Oscar as far as I could throw him, I decided to take Blake's advice and grabbed his hand. The glare shifted to me, but I wasn't inclined to pay it any more attention than Blake had.

Jamaal took my other hand and led the way into the forbidding darkness of the portal. I followed, wishing like hell I could fight off the waves of dread that kept washing over me.

The Underworld had not magically transformed into a verdant paradise since I last saw it. The portal tossed the three of us out into a gray stone tunnel, the impact jarring enough to send us all to the floor. I lost my grip on Oscar's hand, but nothing short of the Jaws of Life would pry Jamaal's fingers loose.

It took a minute to get my breath back, but when I did, I sat up and had a quick look around. There was nothing to see. There was a dim ambient light in the tunnel, with no discernible source, but it was barely enough to reveal our immediate surroundings. Both sides of the tunnel disappeared into total darkness a few yards from where we all sat, and if the tunnel had a ceiling, that, too, was invisible.

The air was stale and unmoving, just hot enough to be uncomfortable.

"So this is the Underworld," Jamaal said, giving my hand a squeeze. "Charming. I can see why Anderson would like to hang out here."

I managed a weak smile. "There's more to it than this." Not that I had any idea how *much* more. On my previous trip, I'd seen a tunnel just like this one—maybe even the very same one, for all I knew—and a massive abandoned city. If Anderson was spending his days here, I was sure it would be in a city somewhere. Which would have been more useful knowledge if I had any clue how many cities there were and how to get to them. However, there was no point in being negative about it.

Freeing my hand from Jamaal's, I rose to my feet and dusted off the seat of my pants. Oscar and Jamaal followed suit.

"Which way?" Oscar asked, looking at me expectantly.

I had no clue. Both sides of the tunnel looked exactly the same, and I felt no strong inclination to turn one way or the other. Not a promising start to our expedition.

I wasn't even close to trusting Oscar, so I quickly decided I didn't want him to know I was clueless. He'd made little effort to disguise how unhappy he was that Cyrus had ordered him to come with us, and I imagined it would take little provocation to cause him to run home. Cyrus might not even be mad at him if he left Jamaal and me behind.

"This way," I said, trying to sound decisive as I took a step to my right. Jamaal slanted me a strange look, and I realized he saw right through my attempt at subterfuge. But that was only because he knew me so well. He'd been on enough hunts with me to know I was *never* certain, so just the fact that I acted certain meant I had no idea where I was going. Luckily, Oscar didn't know that.

The tunnel was so monotonously the same that it felt something like being on a treadmill—we walked and walked and walked, and it looked like we hadn't moved an inch. I kept mentally prodding and poking at my subconscious, hoping to get a feel for whether we were going the right way or not, and I got nothing. As far as I could tell, we were walking aimlessly, with no more guidance than we'd have if I weren't descended from Artemis.

When the tunnel branched off with one way going straight and one to the left, I decided to keep going straight with no particular instinct guiding me. That sinking feeling inside me kept saying this was a pointless endeavor. If my power wasn't guiding my footsteps, then I was just wandering through an immense world and hoping I would accidentally bump into Anderson along the way.

There was a part of me that thought I should give up right then and there. Though we had seen nothing even remotely threatening, there was a pervasive feeling of *wrongness* to this place. A sense that we as living beings didn't belong here. I could tell Jamaal felt it, too, because he was all nervous and fidgety as we walked. Kind of like he was when he spent too much time in a cemetery.

"Are you doing okay?" I asked him quietly. The dead, flat

air seemed to swallow the sound of my voice. I should have considered how Jamaal's death magic would respond to a place like the Underworld before I agreed to bring him with me. Then again, I didn't think there was any way I could have persuaded him to stay behind.

Jamaal stuffed his hands into his pants pockets and shrugged. "I'm uncomfortable," he admitted, "but I'm not anywhere near losing control."

Oscar just loved hearing that—especially the unspoken "yet"—and he scowled at us. "I'm not staying down here with a death-goddess descendant who's out of control!" Sweat beaded on his forehead and upper lip. I didn't know if that was from the heat or just from his nerves. He was as jittery as Jamaal, although he'd been like that from the very beginning.

"He's not out of control," I said. "And you're a death-god descendant yourself, so stop being such a weenie. This place ought to be right up your alley."

Oscar clenched a fist, and I think he was considering throwing a punch. A quick glance at Jamaal made him change his mind, so he tried to kill me with his laser glare instead.

"This is not right up my fucking alley!" he shouted. His voice should have echoed in this tight space with stone walls and floor, but it didn't. "This is not up anyone's alley! Can't you *feel* it? We don't belong here."

Yes, I could feel it. I would have thought a death-god descendant would feel less out of place, but apparently that wasn't the case. "Maybe we don't, but you've been here before and lived to tell the tale, and so have I, so there's no reason to panic. Let's just keep moving."

I didn't wait for him to agree, just kept moving forward into the darkness ahead as if unaffected by the dread that permeated the Underworld. Oscar followed, but if footsteps could sound sullen, his did.

"You'd better know where you're going, bitch!"

The friendly rejoinder was quickly followed by a startled

bleat and the sound of flesh slamming into stone. I whirled around and saw that Jamaal had grabbed Oscar around the neck and pinned him to the tunnel wall.

"You watch your fucking mouth or I'm going to teach you some manners!" Jamaal barked, his nose about an inch from Oscar's.

Oscar was built like a bruiser, but there is nothing as intimidating as Jamaal in a rage. His build was much more aesthetically pleasing, but no less muscular, and he was almost a full head taller than Oscar. He also had a glare that had been honed to a fine edge over years of abuse and decades of bitterness.

Oscar held up his hands in a gesture of surrender, his eyes wide with fright. Personally, I'd have been inclined to let it go, because I didn't think we needed any more ill will. But I knew from experience that with Jamaal's temper, it was sometimes best to just stand back and let it run its course.

"Do you understand what I'm saying to you?" Jamaal growled, giving Oscar a little shake for emphasis.

"Yeah, yeah, I get it," Oscar said. He was trying to snarl back just as fiercely, but it's hard to sound fierce when you're quaking in your boots.

Jamaal abruptly let go and started down the tunnel. The look Oscar gave his retreating back was not promising, his fear transforming into fury. He didn't act on that fury, but I knew I'd have to keep a careful eye on him. Add one more problem to my ever-growing list.

Fourteen

In the outside world, I was so used to using my phone to check the time that I never wore a watch. I felt sort of silly pulling my phone out while wandering through the Underworld—I'd totally freak out if I got a signal here—but the resolute monotony of the light and the blank features of the tunnel had my sense of time so screwed up that I just had to see what time it was.

I wasn't entirely shocked that my phone didn't work at all. The laws of physics as I knew them didn't seem to apply in the Underworld—or else there would be no light whatsoever—so why should I expect my phone to function? Oscar saw me checking and snorted.

"Nothing with a battery works in the Underworld," he said. Amazing how he could look so freaked out by the place and still manage such a convincing tone of condescension.

"Thanks for the heads-up," I muttered back.

The unpleasant reality was that though I couldn't say exactly how long we'd been at it, my aching legs and confused sense of time were sure it had been several hours already. And we had seen nothing but the endless gray tunnel. Occasionally, we came across branches that veered off, but whether driven by intuition or just the fear of getting lost, I kept going straight. I had no sense as to whether we were getting any closer to Anderson or whether my power was working at all.

I thought I was hiding my uncertainty well, and maybe I was, in the beginning. However, as the hours—however many of them there were—passed by one by one, my ability to hide my increasing frustration and decreasing hope weakened.

"You have no idea where you're going, do you?" Oscar challenged when I once again chose to ignore a branching tunnel.

"My power works strangely," I informed him. "I've learned to trust it, and you're just going to have to do the same."

"And maybe *you* need to learn to quit while you're ahead," he said. "This isn't working, and it's time for us to get the hell out."

Jamaal pierced him with one of those patented glares of his. "Are we going to have to have another come-to-Jesus moment?" he growled.

Oscar ignored him and kept talking as if there'd been no interruption. "Every minute we're here brings him another step closer to the edge," he said, jerking his thumb at Jamaal. "This place is bad enough for someone who doesn't have death magic, but he's going to lose it eventually."

It was true that Jamaal was getting steadily more agitated. He'd even broken out the clove cigarettes and smoked a couple of them to try to steady his nerves. Not that smoking had ever had as much of a positive effect as he might hope.

"I'm not losing it anytime soon," Jamaal snapped in return. "Not unless you keep poking at me and pissing me off, that is."

I made a calming gesture at both men. There was too much at stake for me to back out now, no matter how fragile my hopes had become.

"We're going to keep going," I said. I turned to Jamaal. "Do you think it would help if you brought Sita out?"

As fierce as she was, the tiger had helped Jamaal so much in the effort to control his temper . . . but he shook his head.

"It's not really *me* who's being affected by this place," he said. "It's the death magic. And Sita *is* the death magic. I'm not sure letting her out is safe."

I wasn't about to argue with him. His temper problems often had to do with fighting to keep the death magic contained, which was why summoning Sita, letting the magic out, had had such a positive effect. But as bad as Jamaal could be when he lost control of his temper, it would be that much worse to be faced with a furious phantom tiger.

"Standing here arguing about it isn't doing anyone any good," I said. "Let's keep moving."

Oscar made no attempt to hide his disagreement, but I didn't much care what he wanted. Maybe I was on a fool's mission, destined to fail, but at least I felt like I was *doing* something. There was no way I could abide sitting around at home and giving up while the existence of the human race was in danger.

Not long after that, the tunnel finally opened out into a vast cavern within which sat an entire city. I had been hoping to find one, as it seemed the most logical place for Anderson to hang out. Even so, the sight of it raised the hairs on the back of my neck and jolted adrenaline through my system.

The tunnels and the very air we breathed had filled us all with a sense of not belonging, but that was nothing compared to the dread this city inspired.

The city was laid out in a grid pattern, with roughly paved streets and a multitude of stone and marble buildings, some of which looked like simple residences, and some of palatial proportions that suggested they might be temples. The unpleasant gray light of the Underworld was enough to reveal the first few blocks of the city, but the rest of it faded into the distant darkness. There was no sign of life, no sign of movement. No bugs, no scurrying creatures, no green things.

I stood side by side with Jamaal at the opening of the tunnel. I couldn't have told you which of us initiated the action, but we ended up holding each other's hands. Both of us had sweaty palms, and Jamaal was holding tight enough that I could feel the thud of his pulse through his fingers. Descendant of a death goddess he might be, but this place felt as wrong to him as it did to me.

"You didn't do this place justice," he whispered, staring out at the city and shaking his head.

I didn't want to let the city cow me, so I answered in full voice instead of giving in to the urge to whisper. "I don't think this is the same place I was in last time. That city was smaller."

Jamaal gave me a pointed look, telling me without words that that wasn't what he'd meant. I knew he was referring to the way the place made you feel rather than to the appearance, but I was afraid acknowledging the dread would make it worse, make it more real. If I were the only one feeling it, then I could at least pretend it was a figment of my imagination.

"Bet Oscar is just loving this," I muttered under my breath. I looked over my shoulder to see how our reluctant Olympian guide was responding to the city.

It was a good thing I did. If I'd waited even a few seconds longer, he'd have been gone.

"Hey!" I yelled at his retreating back. He was heading toward a patch of blackness that I very much feared was a portal.

Jamaal whirled at the sound of my voice, and before he had time to take stock of what he saw, Sita appeared out of thin air, positioning herself between Oscar and the portal and giving a roar that, unlike the sound of our voices, echoed through the tunnel.

Oscar came to an abrupt halt, windmilling his arms to fight his forward momentum and keep himself from slamming into Sita. She roared again, and the portal disappeared. I supposed it was hard to concentrate on keeping a portal open when you were faced with five hundred pounds of angry tiger.

Oscar held his hands up and to the sides and started slowly backing away. For every step he took back, Sita took one forward, stalking him and snarling.

"I think maybe you should put her away," I said to Jamaal. "I seriously doubt Oscar will try that again."

"Um, I didn't actually summon her," Jamaal said.

Okay, that was bad. Sita was dangerous enough when Jamaal had her under his control, but if she was acting on her own, this might get very ugly, very fast.

"You should try to put her away anyway," I urged. Oscar was backpedaling rapidly, and it wouldn't be long until he was in full-scale retreat and triggered Sita's instinct to give chase.

"You think?" Jamaal gave me a brief, irritated eye roll, then turned his attention back to Sita. "Sita! Come here!"

She didn't even look at him, much less obey him. She gave another bone-shaking roar, and that was when Oscar completely lost his nerve. With a yell, he turned around and started running full speed in the only direction that led away from Sita—toward the city.

Jamaal called to Sita again, but again she ignored him, her eyes fixed on her fleeing prey, her body crouched and ready to spring. I entertained a brief hope that things might turn out okay when Oscar blew past Jamaal and me and Sita hadn't given chase yet. Then I realized she was just playing with him, letting him get a head start so she could have a more entertaining chase.

"Sita, no!" Jamaal shouted as she took off in pursuit. "Stop it!"

Jamaal planted himself firmly in Sita's path, holding his arms up as if to stop her from jumping over him. Not that it would have worked—I've seen Sita jump before, and with her supernatural nature, I'm sure she could have cleared that hurdle just fine. But in her current state of mind—or mindlessness—she apparently didn't feel like hurdling. So instead she just ran Jamaal over, knocking him to the cavern floor and continuing down the main street of the city.

I ran to Jamaal's side, shocked by what Sita had just done. She'd knocked the wind out of him, but otherwise he seemed unhurt as I helped him sit up. He blinked and shook his head as if to clear the cobwebs.

Oscar screamed, a high, shrill sound of abject terror. Jamaal used my shoulder for support and jumped dizzily to his feet, calling Sita's name. I looked on in horror, covering my mouth with my hand to keep myself from screaming. Oscar made it about ten yards past the tunnel opening before Sita caught up to him and knocked him off his feet with one easy swat of her paw.

A swat that tore through the backs of his legs like tissue paper and sent a shower of blood splashing against the nearest building, a many-columned structure that had to be a temple.

Sita swatted Oscar again, this time across his back. More of his blood spattered the front of the building and the columns.

Still shouting Sita's name, Jamaal ran full tilt down the street toward them. I wasn't sure running toward Sita at a time like this was a good idea, but I'm not much of a fan of playing the helpless bystander, so I followed him.

Sita continued playing with Oscar like a cat torturing a

mouse, raking her claws over him and biting without doing enough damage to kill him. I don't know if it was shock or blood loss that silenced him, but he wasn't screaming anymore, though his pathetic attempts to crawl away proved he was still conscious.

Sita acknowledged Jamaal's presence for the first time when he was a few yards away, still frantically shouting at her to stop. She was looking straight at him when she closed her mouth around Oscar's neck. There was a sickening crunching sound, and Oscar's struggles abruptly ceased.

"No!" Jamaal yelled, still running toward her, though he had to know as well as I that it was too late to save Oscar.

Her jaws still locked in Oscar's neck, Sita leapt impossibly high, landing on the roof of the temple at least twenty feet above her. Oscar's blood-soaked, torn body slammed against the bas-relief that decorated the temple's upper reaches. Sita gave the body a tug until enough of the weight was supported by the roof so it didn't fall, although one leg still dangled over the edge, dripping down blood like rain.

I caught up with Jamaal, and we both looked up at Sita and our now-defunct ticket out of the Underworld.

"He can heal from that, right?" I asked Jamaal in a small voice. I'd died twice since becoming *Liberi*, and both times I had come back. It was not a fun process, but it was better than the alternative.

"Maybe," Jamaal said doubtfully, and I looked at him in alarm. He shrugged. "We're in the Underworld, in a City of the Dead, and Sita is death magic incarnate. I'm not so sure I know what the rules are right now."

Perched on the roof with her kill at her feet, Sita began calmly licking the blood off her fur. I hoped that meant she was done killing, because I was suddenly feeling awfully small and vulnerable.

"Sita, honey, will you come back to me now?" Jamaal coaxed, beckoning to her with his hand.

It took all my willpower to keep still when Sita cocked her head at him, then leapt easily to the ground. Her paws left bloody prints as she walked up to Jamaal and gave him an affectionate head-butt. Jamaal reached down and touched the top of her head, and she disappeared. Apparently, Oscar's death had satisfied the death magic, at least for now.

I looked up at Oscar's body. "You should have had her bring him down with her. I don't know how we're going to get him down from there when he recovers." I refused to think of it as *if* he recovered.

"Shall I summon her back and have her fetch him?" Jamaal asked caustically.

If I weren't all weak-kneed and queasy, I might have managed a clever comeback. As it was, I had to settle for silence.

FIFTEEN

There wasn't any point in going anywhere until Oscar recovered, so Jamaal and I sat on the steps of a modest white marble building across from the temple to wait. I still didn't know how we were going to get him down, but perhaps the matter would sort itself out. In his precarious position, he might well fall to the ground when he woke up—which would probably kill him again, but at least we wouldn't have to fetch him.

I leaned against Jamaal's side, and he put his arm around me. Despite the hot, stifling air, I shivered, wishing I could be anywhere but here. My eyes kept being drawn to the massive quantities of Oscar's blood that had splashed all over the temple's front stairs and supporting columns, and that was even now leaking from his dead body and leaving streaks on the bas-relief.

I tried to focus on the temple instead of the blood, but that was no less disturbing a proposition. If you didn't look at it too closely, it would look like your typical Greek- or Roman-style temple, with maybe a hint of Egyptian thrown in, because the columns were etched from floor to ceiling with intricate battle scenes. But when you took a second look, you couldn't help noticing that all the etchings and carvings and bas-relief featured skeletons rather than living people. Even the animals—horses mostly, though I also spotted what might have been a lion or a large dog—were rendered as skeletons.

My eyes roamed all over the temple, looking for some hint of life, some reminder of the outside world, and my eyes finally picked out one figure that had flesh on it. Partially obscured by a splash of Oscar's blood, the carving appeared to be of a ferocious dog. Its head was at an odd angle relative to its body, and something sprouted out of its neck only to be hidden by the blood. After staring at it another minute, I realized that thing sprouting out of its neck was another neck. This was Cerberus, two of its heads blotted out by blood.

Jamaal withdrew his arm from around my shoulders and jumped to his feet, shaking out his arms.

"I'm too restless to sit still," he said, and I noticed that his fingers were twitching ever so slightly.

I stood, too, though my feet hurt and I wouldn't have minded sitting down for a week or two. "Maybe we should wait back in the tunnel. This can't be a good place for you to hang out."

Jamaal moved his head from side to side, and the clacking of the beads at the ends of his braids couldn't drown out the snap, crackle, pop of his neck. "No, it's not. But if Oscar wakes up and we're not here, you know he's going to create a portal immediately and disappear."

I wasn't sure he'd have the strength to do that so soon after coming back to life—dying and healing take a lot out of you, and even lifting your head can feel like a challenge at first—but it wasn't a chance I was willing to take. Even though my own sense of restlessness and discomfort seemed to be getting worse by the minute.

"Why did Sita have to drag him up to the roof?" I grumbled. If Oscar's body were somewhere we could reach, we could carry him away into the tunnel and maybe escape the city's aura of malice. I kept looking around, expecting to find hostile eyes boring into me from the darkness.

"That was probably my fault," Jamaal said. "She saw me coming toward her kill and wanted to make sure I didn't take it away from her."

I shuddered, realizing we were probably lucky she didn't eat the body. Maybe Oscar would have come back from that, too—I had come back after my body was burned—but it would have taken *days* rather than hours.

I gazed up at Oscar and hoped to view signs that he was beginning to heal. Sita had torn the entire back of his leg open, but between the shreds of fabric, the copious blood, and the insufficient light, I couldn't get a good look at the wound to see how it was doing.

Jamaal was pacing now, his hands twitchy and never still. The air felt more stifling than ever, and for no discernible reason, I felt the distinctive sensation of adrenaline leaking into my blood. My breath came shorter, and I found myself continually checking over my shoulder, afraid something was sneaking up on me. Jamaal was doing the same.

The City of the Dead had had a distinctly unwelcoming vibe from the moment we set foot in it, but it was exponentially stronger all of a sudden.

"You feel this, too, don't you?" Jamaal asked, his eyes wide as he tried to look all ways at once.

There was no pretending this was a figment of my imagination. *Something* was happening, even if I couldn't tell what. I nodded and moved closer to Jamaal. "Yeah, I feel it."

I kept looking around for the threat my body insisted was near and found that my gaze kept returning to the temple. It took me a second to see what had caught my eye, but when I did, I grabbed hold of Jamaal's arm.

"The blood!" I said in a choked squeak. The sense of dread reached a crescendo, and I couldn't force out a more coherent statement. Not that Jamaal could possibly miss what I was seeing.

Oscar's blood had been splashed willy-nilly all over the front of the temple, marking the stairs, the floor, the columns, the walls—even the roof. The blood had operated according to the laws of physics, with trails and droplets streaming downward toward the ground. But physics had apparently taken a coffee break, because instead of those drips and streams pointing toward the ground, many of them were now headed sideways or even directly upward. I swallowed hard. The blood had formed a large, rough circle and was trickling inward toward the center. Toward the figure of Cerberus that I'd noticed on the temple wall. The figure looked larger than it had when I'd first spotted it, and as more blood touched its outline, it grew larger still.

"It was Cerberus's job to guard Hades," I said. My voice shook, and the air felt so thick and heavy I couldn't get the words out in one breath. I loosened my grip on Jamaal's arm and groped for his hand instead. His fingers closed tightly over mine, and he edged backward.

"Don't think we should"—gasp for breath—"be here when all that blood is absorbed."

The blood circle continued to contract, continued to move closer to the carved Cerberus. And Cerberus continued to grow, its features becoming disturbingly lifelike as it did.

Jamaal gave my hand a tug and started backing down the road away from the temple, toward the tunnel through which we had entered.

"But Oscar . . ." I protested. And yet even with that protest, I found myself not resisting Jamaal's pull, every instinct within me crying out for me to get moving, to get out.

Jamaal and I both kept backing up at a brisk pace. We could have moved a lot faster if we'd just turned around and run. I assume that Jamaal didn't do it for the same reason I didn't—I couldn't stand the idea of having that temple at my back, of not knowing what was happening behind me.

We were about halfway back to the tunnel opening when a massive slate-gray figure leapt out of the wall and landed in the street with a loud thump.

About eight feet tall at the shoulder—and weighing who knew how much—Cerberus was literally as big as a house. Well, maybe only a mobile home, but that was more than big enough. Three snarling wolf heads fixed their yellow-eyed gazes on Jamaal and me, and the growl that massive body produced was enough to shake the buildings.

We continued to back away, but by silent mutual agreement we moved more slowly now. If Cerberus had anything in common with Sita, the worst thing we could do was trigger its predatory instincts by running away.

"Maybe it'll be satisfied just to chase us out of the city," Jamaal said.

I swallowed the knot of fear in my throat and nodded, hoping that was the case. I had no viable weapons on me, and even if I had, I doubted any would affect a creature like Cerberus. Jamaal had Sita, but even if we could trust her, Cerberus was big enough to make her look like a fluffy house cat.

The middle head lifted up and howled like the loudest siren you can possibly imagine, and the other two quickly followed suit. Worse, that howl was echoed by other voices throughout the city.

"We are fucked," Jamaal said.

Cerberus stopped howling and fixed its attention on us once more, stalking forward. I glanced at the tunnel over my shoulder, trying to calculate the odds of us reaching it before Cerberus got to us. We might have a shot at it, though it wouldn't be much help if the creature planned to pursue us past the city's limits.

"I think it's time to run now," I said, and we turned in unison and charged for the tunnel.

Cerberus let out a ferocious roar that made Sita's sound dainty by comparison. The creature was so massive the pavement beneath our feet vibrated under its thumping footsteps as it gave chase. The tunnel that had seemed so close a moment ago now looked about a mile away.

"Go go go!" I yelled at Jamaal, and tried to give him a little shove to hurry him up. With his long legs, he could easily outrun me, but he had slowed his pace to match mine and refused to go ahead. I lowered my head and poured on every bit of speed I could conjure. I didn't have to look behind me to know that Cerberus was gaining fast.

Cerberus was so close I felt its breath against the back of my neck when Jamaal and I barreled over what we hoped would be the finish line, the opening of the tunnel. Naturally, we kept on running as fast as we could. And naturally, because pretty much nothing had gone right since we'd entered the Underworld, Cerberus pursued.

There was no doubt in my mind we were about to die. And there was a lot of doubt as to whether it was the kind of death we could come back from. I wished Jamaal would run ahead, wished he would let my own death buy him some time, but even if I'd had the breath to speak, I knew he wouldn't do it. We would face our hideous fate together.

All of a sudden, a blinding white light speared through my eyes, and I thought my head would explode from the piercing pain of it. Jamaal cried out, and behind us Cerberus let out a pained yelp.

I closed my eyes tight against the burn of the light and held my arm up to try to block it out. I kept moving in the direction I hoped was forward, but despite the terror behind me, I couldn't force myself to run full speed when I was blind.

I crashed into something solid, and yet slightly yielding, and something that felt like an oversized arm wrapped around my shoulders to hold me still. Beside me, I heard Jamaal curse and his heavy footfalls ceased.

I tried opening my eyes just a tiny crack. The light was still painfully bright, and all I could see was a white blot, as if I'd just looked straight at the sun with my naked eyes. I quickly shut them and tried to wriggle out of the arm—or whatever it was—around my shoulders. Weirdly, it seemed smaller than it had when it had first landed on me, but it was just as strong, holding me tightly in place.

Once again, I cracked my eyes open. The light was less blinding, and I was suddenly aware that I was pressed up against the source of it. Three sets of yellow eyes glowed in the brightness, but even Cerberus seemed unable to look directly at the source, its heads bobbing side to side as it backed away.

All three sets of eyes vanished, and I heard the sound of clawed feet against stone as Cerberus finally retreated.

The glowing arm released me, its dimensions continuing to shrink until it was human size, the light receding so I could make out the vaguely humanoid figure from which it was emanating. And with Cerberus no longer literally breathing down my neck, my brain finally made sense out of what I was seeing.

"Anderson!" I gasped.

The light was fading, the shape at its center becoming more distinct until I could finally make out the form of a familiar man. Naked, of course, because Anderson's godly form and clothing were incompatible. Jamaal stood on Anderson's other side, gaping at him as the glow subsided.

Anderson crossed his arms and looked stern, which was a neat trick when he didn't have a scrap of clothing on him. Although he spared a quick glance at Jamaal, most of his attention focused on me. "The Underworld has felt agitated all day, and I figured that meant some moron of an Olympian was wandering around," he said. "Good thing for you I decided to check out the disturbance. How the hell did you get here?"

He looked and sounded like the same man I had known

for these last several months, and he certainly had the scolding tone down. But after learning his history, I didn't know if I could ever look at him the same way again.

"We had help," I told him. "Cyrus let me borrow one of his Olympians so I could look for you."

Anderson glowered at me. "Did it occur to you that I was here because I didn't want to be found?"

"Did it occur to *you* that it's not all about you and what you want?" Jamaal snapped in reply. He had to be incredibly pissed off to use that tone with Anderson, who had always commanded his respect.

I shot Jamaal a look of warning. Anderson was no longer trying to pass as an ordinary *Liberi*, and maybe if he was no longer trying to fly under the radar, he wouldn't be as tolerant of our human foibles. Now that we knew what Anderson was capable of—no matter how long ago that was or how much he had changed—it seemed wise to treat him with a certain degree of caution.

Jamaal showed no sign of having noticed my warning, but thankfully Anderson didn't get his back up. Instead of getting all alpha and bossy, he swallowed the rebuke with relative grace.

"You have no idea what I'm dealing with," Anderson said. "I don't have time to—"

I cut him off, forgoing caution. "If you're referring to Niobe, then I'm afraid that cat's already long out of the bag."

Anderson was rarely speechless, but he'd obviously been spending too much time in the Underworld and had no clue what had been going on above in his absence. His first expression was shock, followed quickly by dismay. Maybe there was some shame in there, too.

"We didn't come here for shits and giggles," Jamaal said, and though Anderson had just saved our lives, Jamaal looked like he was contemplating murder. "We came here because we thought it would be better if we worked together to solve the problem. Sorry if we're interrupting your sulking."

"I'm not sulking!" Anderson snapped. "I'm trying to find Niobe!"

Jamaal was considerably larger and more imposing than Anderson's human form, and he used that to his advantage as he loomed into Anderson's personal space. "Oh? And why would you want to go looking for a fertility goddess in the Underworld? Doesn't seem like a very fertile kind of place. But I suppose you have magical tracking abilities you never told us about and that's why you think you should go hunting for her all by yourself." The sarcasm in his voice was thick enough to eat with a spoon. "Hell, you lied about everything else, so why am I surprised?"

It was hard to tell whether the flush that crept into Anderson's cheeks was from anger or shame. There was a little of both in his body language as he glared at Jamaal and hunched his shoulders.

"Back off, Jamaal," Anderson said. The centers of his pupils went white. Maybe that was an intentional threat, or maybe it was a sign his defensive anger was getting the best of him. Either way, I thought backing off sounded like a great idea.

I put a hand on Jamaal's arm. "Let's—"

Jamaal jerked away from my touch, unwilling to let go of his righteous outrage.

"No, I will *not* back off!" He took his life in his hands by reaching forward and poking Anderson in the chest. "You were too much of a chickenshit to face us and tell us the truth, so you tucked your tail and ran and left us to try to fix everything ourselves."

The white in Anderson's eyes grew, and his right hand started to glow in a way that would make any sensible *Liberi* backpedal. Even those who didn't know he could kill with that Hand of Doom, as I affectionately called it, knew you were in for a world of hurt if he put that hand on you. I'd seen him use it on Jamaal once before, and I never wanted to see anything like that again.

"Back. The. Fuck. Off," Anderson grated with careful enunciation.

If Jamaal were in one of his death-magic-fueled rages, he wouldn't have even *noticed* the threat, much less given in to it. But though he was angry enough to spit nails right now, it was a rational anger. I saw his glance drop to Anderson's glowing hand, saw that he was fully aware of the threat.

He threw a punch anyway.

Sixteen

Jamaal's fist connected with Anderson's jaw, sending him to the floor.

I covered my mouth with both hands and struggled against the new flood of adrenaline in my blood. Even *Cerberus* had been cowed by Anderson, and now Jamaal had to go and *hit* him? And not in a fit of mindless rage, either. I racked my brain trying to think of a way to defuse the tension before Jamaal met with a painful and untimely end, but no bright ideas leapt to mind.

Sprawled inelegantly on the floor, Anderson shook his head as if seeing stars, then put his hand to his jaw and worked it back and forth a couple of times. If he were human, I'd say he was checking to make sure nothing was broken, though I doubt a god had much to worry about on that score.

Jamaal looked down at the man he'd showed such deference to for decades, completely unrepentant. "I, and all the rest of your *Liberi*, have every right to be pissed at you right now." Though the words were blatantly aggressive, his voice was mild. "Maybe you should just man up and take it instead of getting your bully on."

Anderson snorted and sat up. I was pleasantly surprised to

see that neither his hand nor his eyes were glowing. "This from the man who just decked me."

"Oh, like you weren't threatening to do worse to me."

Anderson winced and looked sheepish. "I wasn't *threatening* you, I was just . . ." His voice trailed off, which was just as well, because we all knew that was exactly what he'd been doing, even if he hadn't put the threat in words. He looked small and vulnerable, sitting there in the nude while Jamaal towered over him. But I knew it was all an illusion.

Jamaal offered him a hand up, then pulled off his T-shirt, revealing his ubiquitous wifebeater, and held the shirt out to Anderson.

"I don't like fighting with a dude whose dangly bits are showing," he said.

Anderson laughed and put the T-shirt on. Thanks to their size difference, it was long enough to just barely hide the "dangly bits," as Jamaal called them. He looked sort of ridiculous swimming in that too-large tee, but I agreed with Jamaal that it was better than nudity.

"So we're planning to fight some more?" Anderson asked with an inquiring raise of his eyebrows.

To my surprise, Jamaal looked at me. I figured that meant he was done expressing his personal outrage and it was time to move on. I had plenty of personal outrage of my own, but I put that aside and kept the acid out of my voice. Mostly.

"I guess it kinda depends what you're going to do next," I said. "If you're planning to run off again and leave us to try to clean up the mess without you, then I suspect we're going to have a problem."

Anderson's eyes flashed, and he opened his mouth as if about to issue a heated reply. Then he thought better of it and tried again. "I was never leaving you to clean up the mess without me," he said evenly. "This is beyond your ability to handle, and I'm doing everything I can to take care of it."

"No, you're not," I countered. "If you're looking for Niobe

and you haven't asked for my help, then you're definitely not doing everything you can. Unless you really *do* have some secret hunting talent I don't know about."

"I don't," Anderson said with exaggerated patience. "But your power isn't mature enough to handle this kind of global search yet. Traveling through the Underworld lets me get from place to place quickly and efficiently, and you would not be able to withstand spending the kind of time here that I have. This is no place for the living."

I couldn't help my curiosity, despite being annoyed at his lame excuse. "But *you're* living."

"True, but I'm not human and I'm the son of Death. The rules are different for me. So you see, this really is a hunt I have to do on my own."

Jamaal spoke before I had a chance to calmly point out that Anderson's explanation was total bullshit.

"What are you planning to do with her if you *do* find her?"

Anderson thought a moment before answering. "I'll try reasoning with her, of course, but I have no reason to think that's going to work. If she's still willing to destroy the human race—along with her own and her sisters' chances of ever rejoining the rest of the gods—to get her revenge, then I don't see her being talked down from that particular ledge."

"So you plan to kill her," Jamaal said, more stating a fact than asking a question.

"I doubt she'll leave me any alternative."

"And killing her would help the situation how?" I asked. "It would make for one more abandoned altar and possibly some very pissed off sister goddesses. Killing Niobe doesn't help get those altars taken care of."

Anderson shrugged. "If push comes to shove, the altars can all be maintained by one goddess. They may hate me even more than they do now—if that's possible—but once they see that I am both willing and able to kill them, they'll have no choice but to take care of both their own altars and the abandoned ones."

I wasn't convinced by Anderson's logic. Violet had come right out and said she and her sisters would refuse to renew their altars if Niobe was killed. Taking out more of them to try to bully the rest into doing their duty seemed like it could backfire on an epic scale. The sisters might not be willing to risk their lives for the greater good, but they just might do it for the sake of revenge.

"No matter what you plan to do with her, you have to find Niobe first," I said.

"Exactly," Anderson replied. "And the time we're spending on our nice little chat now is—"

"Not a waste, so don't even go there," I finished for him. "You don't have to *search for* Niobe. All you have to do is get one of her sisters to an abandoned altar, and you can be sure she'll show up to stop it from being renewed."

Anderson opened and closed his mouth a few times, but no words came out.

He's not an idiot, I swear. He's just single-minded—and apparently very good at lying to himself. Chasing Niobe pointlessly through the Underworld gave him the excuse he needed to avoid having to face the people he'd disappointed. Gave him a way to hide from us while still convincing himself he was putting up a fight, trying to solve the crisis his past actions had triggered.

"The problem isn't finding Niobe," I said. "The problem is *getting* to her." Anderson's power was awesome and frightening, but it wouldn't be very useful in a battle. It took too much time, and he could only use it on one person at a time. I was certain Niobe was continuing to recruit additional support and that the next time we faced her, our odds would be even worse.

"You're doing no one any good in the Underworld," Jamaal said. "It's time you come back to the mansion and face the music. And then we can all work together and see if we can come up with a way to get to her."

Anderson eventually agreed that it made sense to stop pointlessly chasing after Niobe through the Underworld. When he finally conceded that, he no longer had any excuse not to come back with us. I honestly didn't know how that would go, whether the rest of his *Liberi* would be able to accept him. Hell, I wasn't sure if *I* could, and he hadn't been lying to me anywhere near as long as he'd been lying to them.

Anderson was ready to open a portal right then and there, and I wanted out of the Underworld so bad I was sorely tempted to let him.

"We have to go back to the city and get Oscar," I said, not at all looking forward to the prospect. I was sure we'd be safe with Anderson by our side, but I doubted his presence would make the city *feel* any better to my already hyperactive nervous system.

"Oscar?" Anderson said. "That would be the Olympian guide you were telling me about?"

"Yeah. He tried to ditch us, and Sita didn't like it." I chose not to mention that she'd been out of control and killed Oscar intentionally and against Jamaal's will. "We had to leave him behind when Cerberus showed up."

"Then I'd say he got what he deserved for trying to leave you here with no way out," Anderson said. "He can find his own way home when he recovers."

"Ordinarily, I'd agree with you," I lied. We both knew I was too much of a bleeding heart to leave a member of our party behind, even when the guy was a son of a bitch. It didn't escape my notice that Anderson had said "when he recovers," to make it sound like a certainty that he would. But Anderson had chased Cerberus away, not killed it, and I didn't like Oscar's chances of getting out while it was on duty.

I told Anderson about the deal I'd made with Cyrus, and I

thought we were in for another godly temper tantrum based on the look on Anderson's face. Jamaal leapt to my defense before Anderson could let me know what he thought about my decision making.

"Before you start throwing stones, remember that the only reason we even had to consider making a deal with Cyrus was because you chose not to stick around."

Anderson cocked his head and regarded Jamaal with obvious curiosity. "When Nikki first found out what I was, she tiptoed around me like I was some unstable explosive that might go off if she looked at me funny. Why don't you try the same thing?"

"I used to let you boss me around because I respected you. That changed the moment you disappeared on us. Now let's go get Oscar and get out of here."

I knew Jamaal's words had to hurt, and maybe in the past Anderson would have lashed out to reassert his authority. But he no longer had solid ground to stand on, and he knew it. He kept his mouth shut and started down the tunnel toward the city.

Jamaal and I looked at each other, and I saw my own reluctance to go back to the city mirrored in his eyes. However, after all the trouble we'd taken to find him, there was no way we were letting Anderson out of our sight. Jamaal took my hand, and we gave each other squeezes of encouragement before falling into step behind Anderson.

Our hands stayed locked together when the City of the Dead opened up in front of us, and I couldn't help looking around in search of Cerberus. There was no sign of it, which didn't do much to calm my unease. The city really, really wanted us gone, and every step was an effort.

When we reached the temple, there was no sign of Oscar. His blood had been completely absorbed by the building, and his body was gone.

"Could he have woken up already and gotten out?" I mused out loud. I didn't think he'd had enough time to manage that.

Anderson shook his head. He looked at me, and I saw him

notice for the first time that Jamaal and I were holding hands. Maggie was convinced Anderson was secretly in love with me, though he'd never made any overtures. I imagined if she was right, seeing me and Jamaal openly acting like a couple must have been another blow. If it was, he hid it well.

"He's still here," Anderson said. "You just can't see him."

"Huh?" Jamaal and I said in unison. It might have been funny if we'd been anywhere but where we were.

"It's the City of the Dead because it's full of dead people," Anderson explained. "Their spirits, anyway. The living can't see them, but that uneasy feeling you get when you enter the city is them trying to push you out."

"But *you* can see them," I said.

He nodded. "And although I don't know your Olympian friend, I'm pretty sure that must be him, because he seems to hate your guts in a very personal way."

"Okay, so his spirit is here, but where's his body?"

"It's gone and it's not coming back," Anderson answered. "His spirit wouldn't be here otherwise. Cerberus must have gotten to him, and that's a death from which he cannot recover. The Underworld isn't safe for the living, even *Liberi*."

Unlike Jamaal, I kept my string of curses contained, but inside I was screaming my lungs out. What had I done? And how the hell was I going to tell Steph that I'd basically gambled with Blake and lost?

SEVENTEEN

As a god of death, Anderson has a control over the Underworld unlike even the most skilled *Liberi*, and the portal he created as soon as we stepped out of the city opened onto the mansion's front lawn.

It had been just after sundown when Jamaal and Oscar and I entered the Underworld, and I expected to emerge from the portal into the dark of night, knowing despite my confused sense of time that many hours must have passed. Instead, we stepped out of the portal in a gray light not much brighter than that within the Underworld. Being an early riser, I knew that it had to be the first light of dawn. I'd been dead tired to start with, but realizing we'd spent what was effectively the entire night in the Underworld without a wink of sleep ratcheted my exhaustion level up to max.

I yearned for a hot shower, a hot cup of coffee, and a long nap, not necessarily in that order. I expected I'd be lucky if I could get one of the three, and I wasn't wrong.

A subtle change overtook Anderson the moment we stepped through the front door, and he immediately started to take charge.

"Why don't you make some coffee, Nikki?" he suggested in a tone that made it more of an order than a suggestion. "I'm going to go put some clothes on and wake the others. I don't want Blake in Cyrus's hands a minute longer than necessary, so we might as well get any other drama out of the way as soon as possible."

Maybe he was hoping everyone would be too bleary eyed to tell him what they thought of him if he rousted them out of bed. But I doubted it was anything his people would *say* that Anderson would have trouble dealing with. Most of them were too used to deferring to him to be as openly angry as Jamaal had been. Their anger and their sense of betrayal would come through in the way they looked at him—or maybe even in the way they *wouldn't* look at him.

I wished I could just take time for some well-earned rest. However, the altar in Bermuda had been dead for five days now, and catching up on my sleep was not a high priority.

I did as I was asked and brewed a pot of coffee, extra strong. Jamaal wasn't much of a coffee drinker—caffeine was a really,

really bad idea for him—but he stayed with me anyway, and having him there was a balm even though he didn't speak. I was still struggling with my guilt over having let Cyrus take Blake. Anderson seemed to be taking it for granted that we were going to get Blake back despite Oscar's unfortunate demise, but I wasn't so sanguine. Maybe it was just as well that I not have any time alone with my thoughts. They might well have eaten me alive if I gave them a chance.

One by one, the rest of Anderson's *Liberi* trickled into the kitchen. The expressions on their faces ranged from anger, to sadness, to calculated blankness. I really hoped Anderson was groveling and apologizing as he explained himself, though that wasn't exactly his style. Even if he *was* doing it, it didn't look like it was helping much.

Maggie, her eyes rimmed with red like she'd been crying, was the last of the *Liberi* to arrive. She went straight for the coffee without speaking or making eye contact with anyone. She probably could have used a hug, but that didn't come that naturally to me, so I settled for passing her the sugar and giving her an encouraging smile.

Anderson made his appearance about ten minutes later. No one was talking, and I had my back turned while pouring myself another cup of coffee, and yet I knew the moment he appeared in the kitchen entryway. It was like something changed in the air itself, and I felt almost like I could reach out and touch the tension in the room. Slowly, I turned around.

Anderson looked much like he always had, dressed in a wrinkled shirt and nondescript khakis. And yet he was somehow different. Maybe it was the almost tentative expression on his face, or maybe it was just the way everyone was looking at him. He just seemed *lesser* somehow, and I found myself missing his aura of quiet authority.

A fraught silence filled the room as Anderson looked us over one by one. I don't think anyone other than Jamaal and me made eye contact with him. If my own feelings about him weren't so mixed, I almost might have felt sorry for him.

"Look," he finally said, "I know you're all angry, and you have every right to be. Maybe it would be good for us to do some kind of big group therapy thing where we all share our feelings and clear the air. But we don't have time for that right now. When Blake is safely home, and we've worked out a plan to deal with Niobe, we can have it out."

"Who says you get to decide when we can have it out?" Maggie challenged, startling me. She was the most deferential of us all, and she was the absolute last person I'd expect to use that tone with Anderson. I actually felt kind of proud of her.

"If you think telling me I'm a shit is the best use of our time at the moment, then by all means let me have it."

But for once, Maggie refused to be put in her place. "Okay. I think you're a shit."

Anderson blinked, and the two of them spent a few seconds indulging in a staring contest. The room was so quiet I could practically hear everyone's heartbeat. It might have been gratifying to see Anderson continue to squirm, at a total loss for the first time since I'd met him, but he was right, and we had better things to do.

"Everyone who thinks Anderson is a shit, please raise your hand," I said, raising my own hand high above my head. Jack and Jamaal both quickly followed suit. Logan gave me a brief, incredulous look, but his hand went up as he nudged Leo into action with his elbow.

"Great," I said with false cheer. "Now that we've established that, what's next on the agenda?"

"This isn't funny," Maggie snapped.

"Do you see me laughing?" I countered. "Look, if it makes you feel any better, Jamaal already decked him when we were in the Underworld, so we made our opinion pretty clear." That won Jamaal a few wide-eyed looks. "Can we please just concentrate on getting Blake back and leave the public flogging for later?"

I don't think anyone was exactly eager to let go of their grievance, but for Blake's sake, they did it. When it became clear that we were ready to move on, Anderson fell back into his easy habit of taking charge.

"As soon as it's a decent hour," he said to me, "call Cyrus and request a meeting. And don't tell him that Oscar didn't make it back."

I blinked at him. "You're going to try to bluff him? He already thinks you've lied to him about Konstantin, so—"

"No bluff. I just want to make sure he brings Blake with him, and if he knows Oscar is dead, he might not."

There was no reason I should feel bad about lying to Cyrus, and it wasn't like I hadn't done it before. But the combination of stress and lack of sleep made me decidedly cranky. "Why don't *you* call him and set up this meeting? I think it's well established that you're a better liar than I am."

Anderson gave me a reproachful look but didn't deny my accusation. "I think it's best if he doesn't know you found me. We want him to feel really secure and in control. He mustn't feel it necessary to hold Blake back and use him as a hostage." He cast a look around the assembled *Liberi*, most of whom still refused to make eye contact. "I know I've failed you in many, many ways. But I won't fail you in this. I *will* get Blake back."

It was a sign of how much had changed that not a single person in the room looked like they believed him.

Thanks to Cyrus's favorite meeting place, I was in danger of associating the wonderful aroma of freshly ground coffee with the stress I felt when I walked through the coffee bar door. It was impossible to enter that lion's den filled with Olympians and not have my pulse start racing, even though I knew that for once, I would not occupy center stage.

The knots in my stomach pulled so tight I couldn't breathe

when I paused in the doorway to assess the situation—a habit I retained despite having Anderson right behind me—and saw Cyrus sitting at his usual table.

It wasn't Cyrus who made my stomach knot, though. It was Blake, who stood close by his shoulder. And was wearing a dog collar. Worse, there was a leash attached to it, and Cyrus held the other end.

I wished I had Jamaal's power and could summon an angry tiger to rip Cyrus limb from limb. It was probably a good thing I hadn't brought a gun to the meeting, or I probably wouldn't have been able to resist shooting the bastard.

My fury and outrage must have shown on my face, because Cyrus's posse went on high alert, watching me with the clear intention of pouncing on me if I made a hostile move. Frigid air breezed in from the open door, but I was struggling too hard against my rage to step inside and let the door close.

Blake made a big show of rolling his eyes and crossing his arms over his chest, leaning his hip against Cyrus's chair to show how relaxed he was.

"Don't be so easy, Nikki," he said with an ironic grin. He plucked at the leash. "You know he just put this on me to get a reaction out of you."

Yes, I did know that. If Cyrus had meant the leash to wound Blake, he'd obviously failed. I'd seen evidence before that Blake had as much testosterone-fueled ego as any other man, but unlike many, he was able to turn it off when it behooved him.

The spectacle Cyrus had created derailed me so much that I almost forgot about Anderson. I'm short enough that Blake and Cyrus could see him behind me, but thanks to my dramatic reaction, they hadn't bothered to look. I could see the moment that changed; both their jaws dropped open in surprise.

Anderson gently nudged me aside and stepped into the coffee bar. His rumpled clothes and messy hair were a disguise within a disguise, making him seem unremarkable and non-threatening. But of course now that everyone knew who and what he really was, the glamour lost its power to fool.

The assembled *Liberi* and mortal Descendants gave out a collective gasp, and weapons were whipped out of pockets and holsters and waistbands. Cyrus pushed back his chair and jumped to his feet, dropping Blake's leash. Blake calmly reached up and removed the collar, letting it and the leash drop to the floor. Cyrus was far too fixated on Anderson to care.

The mind-blowing array of guns that were pointed our way would have daunted just about anybody—except Anderson, who had stepped in front of me. Shielding me with his own body, I realized.

"You all know what I am," he announced in a booming voice that barely sounded like him. "Your guns can't hurt me, so you might as well put them away."

That wasn't technically true. I'd seen Anderson die from a gunshot wound to the head before. But that death hadn't lasted long, and if he burst out of his mortal disguise, I wasn't sure what bullets could do to him.

Every weapon in the room remained pointed in our direction. Cyrus tried to regain his composure and look confident, but there was too much fear in his eyes to make that work.

"I see Nikki was not completely honest with me when we spoke on the phone," he said.

"Very observant," Anderson answered. "Tell your people to put their guns away."

"Why would I want to do that?" Cyrus asked with an inquiring tilt of his head. "They might not be able to kill *you*, but they can kill *Nikki*. I'd be sad if that happened, but I think you'd be sadder."

"You'd be too dead to be sad," Anderson said. He stepped out of the way so that suddenly I was completely out in the open, a sitting duck. "If that's a risk you're willing to take, then have your people fire away."

And I thought *I'd* gambled with someone's safety when I'd

bargained with Cyrus. Some of the people aiming guns at me were mortal Descendants, though I couldn't tell which ones. Any one of those Descendants would be *thrilled* to shoot me dead and steal my immortality.

"Don't be stupid, Cyrus," Blake said. "He *will* kill you. I know you can see that in his eyes as well as I can."

Cyrus was faced with the same dilemma his father had faced before him, the one that had kept Konstantin quiet about Anderson's identity for so long. It's a tough thing for someone who's trying to be the alpha dog to admit in front of the people he leads that someone else is stronger and more powerful than he is. I wondered if Anderson could have handled this in a more subtle and tactful manner, but it was too late to change strategy now.

I could almost see the thoughts swirling around Cyrus's mind, and I imagined he was looking for some way, *any* way, to save face. But there wasn't one.

"Put the guns away," he growled. Most of his people obeyed promptly, if with obvious reluctance, but there were a couple who hesitated a moment. A fierce glare from Cyrus put them in their place, and soon all weapons were out of sight, if not out of mind.

Anderson nodded his approval. Maybe he'd had no doubt that Cyrus would give in rather than shoot me, but *I'd* had plenty of doubt. I'm sure it was much easier to feel confident when you weren't the one in danger of dying.

Without waiting for an invitation, Anderson took a seat at Cyrus's table and gestured for the other man to sit. It was an imperious, arrogant move that was not lost on the gathered Olympians. More than one dark look was thrown my way, and hands twitched with the desire to pull those guns right back out.

Once again, Anderson had left Cyrus with no way to save face. With a sour look, Cyrus yanked back his chair and sat. Usually, he managed to keep an easygoing, almost friendly facade even when tensions were running high, but today he couldn't do it. His jaw was so tight I could see its outlines under his skin, and the look in his eyes said he would strike Anderson dead right then and there if only he could.

"I think it best we keep this conversation private," Anderson said, making a sweeping motion at the small army Cyrus had parked in the coffee bar. "It'll be easier for both of us to speak freely without an audience, and it's not like they serve a useful purpose."

Cyrus considered Anderson's suggestion for a long while. I doubt he liked the thought of ordering his people to leave at Anderson's request, but he'd already had ample evidence that having an audience wasn't in his best interests.

Eventually, practicality won out over pride, and Cyrus dismissed his goon squad. There was some grumbling as they filed out into the cold, and I doubted they would go far, but I for one was happy not to have to worry about being shot in the back.

"I'm going to be completely honest with you," Anderson said when we had the place to ourselves.

Even in his fury, Cyrus managed a short laugh. "Well now, that's a change, isn't it?"

Anderson made a dismissive gesture. "We don't have time for games or posturing. I know Nikki told you what's at stake, and I know you care or you wouldn't have been as cooperative as you have.

"I killed Konstantin," Anderson said. Blake and I both gasped to hear him admit it so baldly, and Cyrus's face went white. "I had good cause, and I'm sure everyone—including you—knows that."

Cyrus did his best to hide the pain and grief Anderson's words caused, but his best wasn't good enough. How a sadistic bastard like Konstantin with a penchant for killing off his own kids had won Cyrus's love and loyalty was a mystery I would never understand.

"He was my father," Cyrus said in a hoarse croak.

Anderson's voice gentled, but only a little. "Feel free to hate me as much as you want. You'll probably live longer with him out of the picture, but I don't expect you to thank me or even forgive me."

Cyrus's hands clenched into fists, and I could hear his quick, shallow breaths as he tried to control what he was feeling. I wouldn't have been surprised if he'd leapt across the table and gone for Anderson's throat, despite knowing what Anderson could do to him.

Apparently, Blake had the same thought, because he put a hand on Cyrus's shoulder. Cyrus jumped at the touch, and his head whipped around so he could glare at Blake.

"Don't get yourself killed over this," Blake said, and I saw his fingers tighten as he squeezed Cyrus's shoulder. "You already knew in your heart that he was dead. Nothing has changed."

For a tense moment, I thought Cyrus was going to bite Blake's head off. Instead, he let out a gust of breath and sanity returned to his eyes. "That's the second time you've held me back in the last ten minutes. One might almost get the impression you cared about me."

Blake hastily jerked his hand away and scowled. "Don't get carried away."

But I was pretty sure Cyrus was right and Blake *did* care. Kind of amazing considering Cyrus had had him on a leash not so long ago.

"While we're being honest," Anderson said, "I must also tell you that your Olympian—Oscar, wasn't it?—didn't make it back from the Underworld."

Cyrus blinked. I think it was the first time he even noticed Oscar wasn't with us. Which probably said something about how important Oscar was to him: not at all.

"He got himself killed while trying to skip out on Nikki and Jamaal," Anderson continued. "I'm sure you'll agree that attempting to strand two of my people in the Underworld is sufficient cause for us to demand a refund." He looked point-edly at Blake. I struggled with the feeling that we were once again treating Blake like no more than a slab of meat, but no one else in the room—including Blake—seemed to share my concern.

"I have only your word for it that Oscar tried to strand them," Cyrus said, but the argument sounded halfhearted to me.

"I just admitted to murdering your father. Why would I bother to lie about Oscar?"

"Because you'd do anything to get Blake back," Cyrus snapped.

"Yes, I would," Anderson admitted. "And since you know what *anything* entails, you might as well acknowledge that you have no choice in the matter. If your Olympian had stuck to the agreement, then I'd feel honor-bound to do the same. But he didn't."

I don't think anyone, much less Cyrus, was convinced Anderson would have given up on Blake if Oscar had died without trying to abandon us, but it at least *sounded* plausible. Even so, Cyrus looked near to hyperventilating. Anderson shook his head and leaned forward conspiratorially.

"Come on, Cyrus. We both know you wouldn't have sent him if he was someone you valued. Is he really worth risking your life over?"

Cyrus kicked a chair in frustration but didn't say anything.

"He's lost a lot of people already," Blake said to Anderson, looking at Cyrus with concern in his eyes. "Konstantin's cronies are leaving in droves—probably to join Niobe. If he lets you bully him into letting me go, his Olympians are going to see it as a sign of weakness, and more of them will likely defect."

Cyrus pinched the bridge of his nose. "Thanks for sharing things told to you in confidence."

Blake snorted. "Like hell it was in confidence. You knew I'd share any intel I got." He turned his attention to Anderson. "The last thing we need is to feed Niobe's little army. I'll stay with Cyrus until we've dealt with her one way or another." He glanced at Cyrus. "No one has to know it's voluntary. But you're not putting that fucking leash on me again."

The fight—and the energy—had drained out of Cyrus, and he sat there with shoulders slumped and a lost look on his face. I'd have felt sorry for him if I didn't remember him clubbing me over the head, tying me up, and leaving me to his father's tender mercies.

"If you're willing to keep up the appearances," Anderson said to Blake, "then I have to agree that's probably for the best." He looked at Cyrus. "The best way to regain control of your Olympians is to stop Niobe before she lures any more of them away."

A hint of life returned to Cyrus's eyes. "Oscar was a slimy little weasel, and I won't shed any tears for him, but I wouldn't have loaned him out if I didn't agree she needed to be stopped."

"Yes, she does," Anderson said. "And I won't be able to get through her army of ex-Olympians without your help."

Cyrus laughed, the sound verging on hysterical. "You show up here, treat me like I'm your bitch in front of my people, admit to murdering my father, and you want my *help*?"

Anderson smiled wryly. "I have to admit, it sounds rather presumptuous when you put it that way." The smile faded quickly. "The fact is when you get right down to it, this is what's best for *both* of us. You need Niobe to stop siphoning off your people, and I can make that happen. If you can help me get to her."

I could see that Cyrus still wanted to argue. I could also see that he no longer had the will or energy to do it.

"Fine," he said with a resigned shake of his head. "I'll assemble a team whose abilities are a good counter to the people I've lost. It may take me a couple of days. I'd hate to make the wrong decisions and have people turn on me at inopportune moments."

"Understood," Anderson said. "I'm going to need some

time myself to set things up." He pushed back his chair and stood. Cyrus remained seated and stared at the tabletop. He might be agreeing to help, but he wasn't even close to happy about it.

"If I offered a handshake," Anderson said, "would you accept it?"

Cyrus found the will to summon a fierce glare. "No way in hell."

"All right, then. I won't offer." He looked at Blake. "You're sure you're willing to stay?"

Blake nodded, then shot a glance at me. "If there's any way you can avoid telling Steph about this . . ."

But we both knew there wasn't.

EIGHTEEN

If I'd had my way, we'd have been on a plane bound for Bermuda that very day, but Anderson and Cyrus were in agreement that this expedition of ours required thought and careful planning. I can't rightfully say I disagreed, but I begrudged every moment that went by.

Leo had set up some complicated algorithm searching for evidence that might indicate people on the islands were starting to notice the lack of new pregnancies. It had been only about two weeks since the altar went dormant, but already signs were starting to show. All Leo found were a few offhand comments here and there from OB-GYN clinics and midwife services noting that business was a little slow lately, but those offhand comments would soon turn into something more like complaints, which would then morph into worries. If we didn't stop Niobe soon, the panic was going to start, and my mind balked at considering how bad it would get.

Cyrus sent us an inventory of the missing Olympian *Liberi* and Descendants, and it painted an ugly picture. Most of the *Liberi* had been Konstantin's closest associates. That meant they were the oldest and most experienced—and that they had the least amount of conscience. I couldn't believe they were willing to wipe out the entire human race in return for whatever reward Niobe was offering them. Then again, these were people who thought it was okay to murder Descendant children on the off chance that those children might grow up to be a threat to them someday. Cyrus had never been and would never become a good guy, but he was about a thousand times less cruel than his father, which meant that he'd been putting the reins on the worst of the Olympian excesses. Something Konstantin's associates had to resent.

All in all, it seemed that thirteen of Cyrus's *Liberi* had defected, along with six mortal Descendants, who would be their most lethal weapons. If it came down to a battle, those Descendants would be especially eager to make a kill and steal another *Liberi*'s immortality. There would be at least nineteen people standing between us and that altar, and if we were really trying to fight our way through them and then hold them off long enough for the renewal ritual, I would not have liked our chances.

Not that our plan to draw Niobe out was what you'd call easy. We were confident she would be nearby so that she could swoop in for the kill as soon as her followers got hold of Violet, but nearby wasn't good enough. We had to get her out in the open so that Anderson could attempt to negotiate with her, and that probably wouldn't happen unless we fought our way through enough of her people to make ourselves into a real threat.

To increase the chances that Niobe would put in an appearance, we gave her advance warning we were coming by renting the same cottages we had stayed in during our previous attempt. Anderson's *Liberi* and a handful of Cyrus's people would travel to Bermuda by conventional means, but Anderson would bring the rest over through the Underworld to hide our numbers.

Unfortunately, Cyrus would not be providing as many warm bodies as we might have hoped.

"I can only bring people I feel one hundred percent certain won't turn on us," he told Anderson in one of our strategy meetings. "Even some of the most loyal of my people have friends who have defected, and I don't trust them not to try to warn those friends."

"And these are the people you want to spend your immortal life with," Blake muttered in a voice Cyrus was obviously meant to hear.

Cyrus cast him a quick, dark look, but didn't otherwise respond. "I have six people I'm absolutely sure will keep their mouths shut."

"That's it?" I asked incredulously. "Six people? When we're facing nineteen? Are you—"

"Six *Liberi*." He was definitely testy. I suspect he was finding it unsettling to take such a close look at the people he led and find how little loyalty existed. "It's the mortal Descendants who'll be the most use to us anyway, and it's much easier to incentivize them."

Of course it was. They were all waiting for their chance to become *Liberi*—a chance that some of them would never get and that some would wait a long time for—and if they were offered the opportunity to kill some of the Olympians they had once served, they'd jump at it.

"I'll bring a dozen of my most loyal candidates, but I'm not going to tell them in advance. The more people who know what we're planning, the more chances it will leak to Niobe."

"So you're just going to show up on their doorsteps on the day of the attack and say, 'Hey, I'm going on this exciting little adventure today, wanna come, too?'"

"Something like that," Cyrus replied, failing to bristle this

DIVINE DESCENDANT   1003

time. "I'll make them an offer they can't refuse, but I don't imagine any of them would be inclined to refuse anyway. Their job will be to take down any Olympian they can, but I'm particularly worried about one of my father's closest friends. His name is Jonathan, and he's descended from Hephaestus. He can create and control fire, and none of my people has a good counter to that power."

Anderson furrowed his brow. "You have several descendants of Poseidon, don't you? We'll be right by the water, so can't they—"

"I *had* several descendants of Poseidon. They're all on the wrong side now."

"So we've got a guy who's going to try to set us all on fire and who we can't do anything about, and we've got several descendants of Poseidon when we're going to be conveniently close to the ocean," I summarized. "What could possibly go wrong?"

"That's why we have to concentrate on taking them out first," Cyrus said patiently.

"What about the Nyx descendant?" Jamaal asked. "No one can do much of anything in the kind of dark that guy can create. Assuming it is a guy, since none of us saw who did it."

"I'm a descendant of Helios," Cyrus reminded him. "I'm the perfect counter. It also means I'm going to be kept very busy fighting the darkness and won't be much use otherwise."

"Don't forget," Anderson said, "I'm going to be there, too."

"No offense," I said, "but you're not that great in a battle."

"How would you know?"

He had me there. But still . . . "Do you have powers I don't know about? Because your Hand of Doom takes a while to work."

Anderson shrugged. "Maybe so, but I can certainly keep someone occupied and keep them from using their own powers. After all, they know what I can do, and they won't want any part of me."

"So you're basically going to run around chasing people?"

The glance he tossed my way was distinctly annoyed. "Look, we can make elaborate plans, but until we fully know what we're up against, our plans are mostly useless. Niobe's had plenty of time to prepare, and she knows the house and the surroundings better than we do."

"Anderson's right," Cyrus agreed. "I'm going to bring the people who can best counter the ones Niobe has won over, but beyond that we're going to be reduced to winging it. Thanks to Anderson bringing people in through the Underworld, we may manage some measure of surprise, and that's the best we can hope for."

I was not what you'd call excited about this so-called plan. There didn't seem to be much more to it than "show up and hope for the best," which was pretty much what Jamaal and Jack and I had done the last time, and look how that had turned out.

"I can do some surveillance before we go in," Jack said. "They'd notice any human who tried to get a good look at the place, and they probably figured out the cat thing from last time. I'll have to go as something even smaller and less conspicuous. Like a mouse, maybe."

"It's not like they don't know about you and about what you can do," Cyrus reminded him.

"Knowing about me and stopping me are two very different things," Jack said. "What are they going to do? Kill every living creature that tries to set foot on the property?"

"I wouldn't put it past them," Anderson muttered.

"As long as Jack doesn't call undue attention to himself in whatever form he adopts," Cyrus said, "his plan ought to work. Like he said, they can't kill every living creature they see, so even knowing that he might try to sneak a look, it'll be just about impossible for them to stop him. It's worth the risk if we can get some idea what we're up against and what kind of booby traps they might have in store for us."

"Easy to say when you're not the one taking the risk," Anderson said, and I feared things were about to get testy.

"I'm the one who brought it up," Jack said. "I'm willing to take the risk."

It says something about how dire the situation was that Jack actually stepped in to stop people from bickering. Usually, he enjoys egging it on, as if it's a vital requirement of the trickster's code of conduct.

So we had something that vaguely—and I do mean vaguely—resembled a plan. Unfortunately, there was one vital component of the plan that we hadn't fully worked out: Violet.

To make our appearance at Jasmine's house into a legitimate threat, one that Niobe had to counter personally, we had to have one of her sisters with us. Based on our last conversation with her, I didn't think Violet was going to volunteer her services, especially when our plan was so ill-formed.

"I don't plan to give her a choice," Anderson said when I voiced my concern. "Once everything is ready, I'll go get her. I don't want her to have a chance to warn Niobe."

"I'll come with you," I said.

I wasn't surprised when Anderson shook his head. "That won't be necessary."

"I know. But I'm going anyway."

Violet hadn't exactly warmed to me, nor I to her, but she sure as hell liked me better than she liked Anderson. "No offense, but Violet hates your guts, and she might be more willing to listen if *I'm* the one doing the talking."

"There's only one thing she's likely to listen to," Anderson said, holding up his right hand. The Hand of Doom.

"You promised you would try to reason with Niobe before doing anything . . . drastic. Is it too much to ask for you to give Violet the same courtesy? She has every right to hate you after what you did, and there's no reason to be more of an asshole than you have to be."

I was pleasantly surprised when Anderson looked sheepish.

"You're right. I'm sorry. It was a lot easier to live with myself back in the days when I could almost convince myself it never happened. Though I suppose you of all people know about using anger as a coping mechanism."

I'd have been stung by the words, except I knew I didn't use my anger as Anderson was doing, didn't lash out at people who didn't deserve it. Not since I was that angry little girl getting shuffled from foster home to foster home anyway.

"So you'll try to find a better way to cope when we talk to Violet? Is that what you're saying?"

"When *I* talk to Violet. Or don't you trust my word?"

I wasn't sure I did, but it would be undiplomatic to say so. "If you're going to be calm and rational, then there's no reason for me *not* to be there, is there? And maybe I'll be able to keep the two of you from falling into old patterns. I know you've been to see her at least once already, and it didn't go well."

Anderson scowled. "I'm going to travel through the Underworld to get there. Haven't you had enough of the place already?"

I suppressed a shudder. Yes, I'd had more than enough of the Underworld. It wasn't like I expected to do a whole lot of good, but I hoped Anderson would be more inclined to control his guilt-fueled temper if I was around. There was too much riding on this not to do everything possible to create the right environment for success.

"I'm sure just this once our trip through the Underworld will be uneventful," I said.

Anderson groaned and rubbed his eyes as if tired. "You are relentless."

"Thank you."

"Fine. You can come with me. But I'm not going to tell Violet the whole truth. If she knows I'm using her as bait to draw Niobe out, we'll have to watch our backs the entire time."

"So what are you going to tell her instead?"

"That we're making a second attempt to renew Jasmine's

altar. Maybe she'll be more cooperative if she knows I'll be there to protect her."

And maybe Niobe would have a sudden and inexplicable change of heart and decide we should all hug it out. Hey, it could happen.

NINETEEN

I was no fonder of the Underworld this time than I had been any other time I'd traveled through it, but I had to admit it was damn convenient. Instead of taking hours to get from D.C. to Memphis, it took a little less than five minutes. And I didn't have to go through a TSA virtual strip search to get there.

Anderson's portal let us out practically on Violet's doorstep. I found myself unable to resist asking the really stupid question, "What if she won't answer the door?" The lights were on, so I was pretty sure she was home.

Anderson gave me a dry look. "Do you really think a closed door would stop me?"

No, of course not. He probably could have made the portal open up directly in her living room if he wanted to. Knocking on her door like an ordinary visitor was kind of a courteous gesture. Not that I thought Violet would see it that way.

Anderson's first knock was polite. His second was firm. His third threatened to break down the door and convinced Violet she had a limited number of choices.

She threw the door open, but didn't invite us in. Her fierce glare communicated without words how glad she was to see us—or at least Anderson. I got the feeling in present company I was basically beneath her notice.

"I have nothing more to say to you," she growled at Anderson. "I have no intention of getting between you and Niobe."

Unwisely, she went for the door-slam. Anderson stopped the door with his hand, and she tried slamming it again. I was reminded once again that these were not just ordinary people when the door hit his hand so hard his fist went straight through. And he didn't even flinch.

Violet made a frustrated huffing noise. She frowned at the door as Anderson calmly pulled his hand back through, scattering a handful of splinters.

"You're paying for that," she said irrelevantly, then turned away and stomped into the house. This was not unlike the greeting Jamaal and I had received, although that had come with less door splintering.

Apparently Violet was feeling even more unwelcoming this time than she had before, because instead of leading the way into her comfortable living room, she stopped in the foyer, crossing her arms over her chest as she turned to face us once more. Her mouth was set in a sullen moue, and when she looked at Anderson, she didn't quite meet his eyes. She spared me nothing but a brief, reproachful glance, as if it were somehow all my fault Anderson was standing here in her living room. I tried an encouraging half smile in response, but shockingly, that didn't win her over. I closed the door behind me, which would have done more good if the fist-sized hole weren't letting in a wintry breeze.

"What can you possibly say that you haven't said already?" Violet asked. Everything about her, from her face to her body language, was closed off, screaming that she was not prepared to listen.

Anderson can be extremely persuasive when he wants to. Believe me, he's persuaded me to do any number of things I very much didn't want to do. But apparently when he'd promised to be reasonable and diplomatic about this, he'd been lying through his divine teeth.

"How about this?" he asked with menace oozing from

every pore. "You're coming with me to Bermuda and you're going to renew Jasmine's altar."

Violet's spine stiffened, and the look on her face became positively forbidding. I wondered if it would be safer for me not to be standing so close to Anderson. The air felt charged with intensity and danger, and being anywhere near a battle between gods was not good for anyone's health. Reminding Anderson that he'd promised not to be an asshole would be even worse.

"What makes you think—"

Anderson cut her off, taking a step closer to her. His eyes were starting to glow white, which was a bad sign. His hand was starting to glow, too, and that was an even worse sign. He'd never had any intention of trying to convince her to come voluntarily. No wonder he hadn't wanted me here to witness it.

"I'm through trying to be reasonable and diplomatic about this," Anderson said. "There's too much at stake. You have two choices: you come with me and do your fucking duty, or I kill you right here and now." He held up that glowing hand of his.

Violet's eyes went wide and frightened, and she took a hasty step backward to stay out of Anderson's reach. Her face had gone pale, and she put her own hand in front of her in a defensive gesture that had no hope of doing her any good.

"You wouldn't dare," she said not very convincingly.

"Why the hell not? I'm sure once I've demonstrated my willingness to kill, I can persuade one of your sisters it's in her best interests to take care of that altar."

"They would never help you if you killed me."

Anderson grinned, and it was not a nice expression. "Want to bet your life on that?"

Neither one of them seemed to care—or even notice—that I was standing there. Which was probably a good thing. I doubted I was having much luck hiding the turmoil that was chewing away at my insides.

I liked and respected Anderson. At least, I liked and respected the man I'd once thought he was. But this man who stood before me and coldly threatened to commit murder to get his way was a stranger to me.

Yes, it was of vital importance that we get Violet to that altar and lure Niobe out. I did not need to be reminded that the fate of all mankind rested on it. But this was now the second time I'd seen Anderson pull the "do what I want or I'll kill you" tactic, and it triggered all sorts of unpleasant thoughts in my mind.

For all that he was supposedly one of the good guys, Anderson had a terrifying amount of power. He was truly immortal, and as the son of Death, he could kill *anyone*—mortal, *Liberi*, or goddess—who stood in his way. Once upon a time, he'd had to keep his identity a secret, and that had forced him to keep his power—and his ability to abuse it—under wraps. But such was not the case anymore. I was disturbed and disappointed to see the change in him. Or maybe it wasn't a change. Maybe this was finally the true Anderson Kane I was seeing, and the one I'd thought I'd known was nothing but an illusion.

Violet swallowed hard and put her hand to her throat. "Niobe will kill me if I set foot near that altar. Just like she killed Jasmine and Rose."

"We'll protect you," Anderson said. I noticed he didn't bother to say anything about who "we" were. If he were really trying to offer her any comfort, he would have elaborated, given her more of a reason to believe she'd be safe. He was still in full bludgeon mode.

"But caring for that altar will only delay the inevitable!" There was desperation in her voice, and I almost felt sorry for her despite the selfishness she had displayed.

"It sounds like you're still under the illusion that you have a choice."

Violet's eyes shimmered with tears. She hugged herself and shivered. I'd had a pretty harsh and judgmental opinion of her before, but I now had a greater degree of sympathy. She was a goddess, but not a particularly powerful one, and we were going to drag her into the middle of a battle. The battle might not kill her, but she could certainly get hurt, and if we came out on the losing end, Niobe would not forgive her. She was in a difficult spot, no two ways about it. No wonder she was scared. If I allowed myself to think about what we were planning to do, I'd probably run screaming from the room. And I wasn't being forced to do it by the man who'd killed my fourteen nieces and nephews in a jealous rage.

I took a step toward Violet, putting myself between her and Anderson. She jumped, and I realized she had literally forgotten I was there.

"Anderson's being a bully and an all-around asshole," I said, causing her to gape at me in shock. Maybe giving Anderson my back while insulting him wasn't my wisest decision ever. I had visions of that hand of his landing on me, but I stood firm anyway. "But he's also right, and we have to do this. I'm a lot easier to kill than you are, and I'm scared out of my mind, but I'm going anyway. I know you don't want to live in a world without humans any more than I do, and I know you don't want to go through the decades-long nightmare that would lead to human extinction. You certainly wouldn't be able to live peacefully in this beautiful home, or—"

"You don't have to persuade me," Violet interrupted harshly. "Like Anderson said, I don't have a choice if I don't want to die."

I wanted to slap Anderson silly for having led with a threat instead of a negotiation. "Maybe not, but you'll have a better chance of living through it if you quit feeling like some helpless victim who's being dragged into a fight that doesn't concern her.

"We won't be going in with only a handful of people this time, and we wouldn't be going in at all if we didn't think we had a chance of succeeding. And we will protect you. Getting to that altar would be pointless if you're not around to perform the ritual."

I was genuinely trying to comfort her, but I suffered a twinge of guilt anyway, because while I wasn't lying, I wasn't being entirely honest, either. If we succeeded in drawing Niobe out, there was a good chance Anderson was going to kill her. Oh, he'd promised to try reasoning with her first, but he'd just shown me how reliable his promises of good behavior were.

It would be an exaggeration to say Violet relaxed in the face of my reassurance, but at least she backed away from the edge of abject terror. I would be a lot happier if we didn't have a screaming damsel in distress with us for this little adventure.

"Niobe has gained more supporters since last you faced her," Violet said.

"I know. But so have we." In a manner of speaking, at least. I was still having a little trouble wrapping my brain around the concept of Cyrus and his Olympians as "supporters," but I supposed for the time being that was what they were.

Violet seemed to have latched on to me and was now completely ignoring Anderson. Under the circumstances, I couldn't blame her. "I still don't think taking care of that one altar is worth the risk."

And if that were really what we planned, I'd probably agree with her. I hoped she didn't start putting things together and realize renewing the altar wasn't our objective after all. If she decided to call Anderson's bluff, and he decided to show her it *wasn't* a bluff, she could end up dead and we'd have to start all over with *another* sister.

"We desperately need to buy time," I said. "If that's the best we can do for now, then that's what we have to do, even if it's risky."

I mentally crossed my fingers. Surely some part of her had to know we were gunning for Niobe. But maybe she just didn't want to know and that was why she swallowed my reasoning despite the gaping holes in it.

She heaved a dramatic sigh. "I suppose you have a point," she said grudgingly. "I still think this is a fool's errand, but it looks like I'm coming along whether I want to or not."

There was no question in my mind that without Anderson's threat hanging over her head, she would have refused. I guessed that meant Anderson had been right all along, but I still felt like a bully and wished we could have found a more benevolent way to win her cooperation.

On the day before we planned to storm Jasmine's altar, our "advance forces" flew to Bermuda, giving Niobe ample time to realize the attempt was coming. Unless she was a total idiot—which Anderson assured us all she wasn't—she'd find it suspicious in the extreme if we didn't have significantly more people with us than we had for our last attempt, which ended so badly, so all of Anderson's *Liberi*, including Leo, who would not join us for the fight, made the trip with us. We traveled by private jet, but anyone on the lookout for us would know we'd arrived. Anderson, Cyrus, and Cyrus's trusted Olympians would arrive the next day via the Underworld—and hopefully take Niobe by surprise.

As soon as we were all checked in to our cottages, it was time to do some recon. Jack turned himself into a mouse and made his way over to Jasmine's house to scout. He was gone for hours, which wasn't completely unexpected if he was being thorough, but we were all on tenterhooks waiting for him. He'd been very convincing in his argument for why it wouldn't really be that dangerous, but I kept thinking about all the worst-case scenarios. Jack was annoying as hell and not exactly what I'd call a nice guy, but that didn't mean I wanted anything to happen to him.

When he finally arrived back at the cottages, we let out a collective sigh of relief. Until he turned back into his human form and told us what he'd found.

"I don't know exactly what's going on over there," he said,

"but I wasn't able to get a good close look at the house. Every time I got near a door or window, some plant would suddenly have a ridiculous growth spurt and block my way. I thought maybe I could push past, but when I tried, a vine pulled a boa constrictor on me. I barely got away with my life."

Ordinarily, I would have thought that was one of his exaggerations, but not this time. He looked genuinely freaked out, and that was not something I'd expect from him. He'd never met a situation, no matter how grim, that he didn't treat as a joking matter. I was not happy we'd found the exception to that rule.

"It's Niobe's doing," Violet said. "We all have a way with plants, but Niobe's the one who really excels. I guess it's because she likes plants more than she likes people."

"Can you try with something even smaller?" Jamaal asked. "A cockroach maybe?"

"Is that a suggestion, or are you editorializing?" Jack inquired, his sense of humor never quelled for long.

"Both," Jamaal deadpanned.

I swallowed a laugh. Not that long ago, Jamaal would have bristled at Jack's use of humor at inappropriate times, and now he was giving it back. Whatever else might be going wrong with the world, Jamaal was getting better, finding some modicum of peace and control. I kind of wanted to hug him for it, though now clearly was not the time.

"Remember, it's an illusion," Jack said. "Just because I *looked* small as a mouse didn't mean I *was* small as a mouse. Making myself look even smaller wouldn't help."

Of course, Jack's "recon" was an illusion all on its own. We had no intention of fighting our way into that house. All we had to do was trigger a battle on a large enough scale that Niobe felt inclined to join in. It was good news that the plant life was giving us reason to believe Niobe was nearby, maybe even inside the house itself. Though if she could use plants as weapons, Bermuda was not the optimal place to fight her.

Violet gave me a penetrating look, and I wondered if we were all taking Jack's failure a little too easily. Maybe we were tipping our hand, giving her reason to think the altar wasn't our objective after all.

"Well, maybe there's no way to sneak in and get an early look at the lay of the land," I said, "but if all goes well, it shouldn't matter much. They won't be counting on Anderson opening a portal to the Underworld in the middle of their living room."

Violet let it go, but I didn't like the way she was looking at me. Maybe I'd laid it on a little too thick. If she figured out Anderson was planning to kill her sister, things could get ugly fast. We were going to have to keep a careful eye on her lest she stab us in the back. It's always great to go into battle with a bunch of people who might turn on you at any moment. If the stakes were any less overwhelming, I might have been running for the hills myself.

TWENTY

Those of us who were already in Bermuda had the dubious pleasure of getting to Jasmine's house first. The idea was that we would head over, get the party started, and maybe find out where all the bad guys were and what kind of weaponry we would be facing. There were enough of us to make it look like a halfway legitimate attempt to get into the house, and hopefully it would never occur to them that there were more of us than they saw.

In theory, once we'd gotten the enemy's attention, we would text Anderson, who would be ready and waiting to lead Cyrus and his band of Olympians into the Underworld and emerge out of nowhere to save the day. It seemed like a pretty good plan to me, especially when Anderson could open that portal inside the house. The last time we'd tried to get to the altar, the house had been empty, but the fact that the plants had interfered with Jack's attempts at recon suggested that was not the case this time. Hell, if we were lucky, Niobe would be hunkered down in that house, sitting out the battle feeling safe, and Anderson would come out of the Underworld right in front of her.

I wasn't sure I entirely bought into that theory, but since I lacked better ideas, and since every day we waited increased the danger that the fertility crisis in the islands would be noticed, I went along with it.

We started preparing at sunset, after a tense meal that I couldn't help thinking of as the Last Supper. Everyone except for Violet loaded up with weapons provided by Logan, and he decked us all out in body armor as well. It wouldn't protect us if we got hit by the kind of sniper fire that had taken Rose out, but it should at least help us survive lesser wounds. The stuff was heavy and hot and awkward, and there was a little grumbling, but everyone saw the sense in it.

Logan offered to give Violet a gun and teach her how to shoot it, but like Rose before her, she refused. Although she had half accepted the necessity of her presence, she made no pretense that she was a willing participant, and she was so terrified I worried she might freeze up under fire. We had promised to protect her, but I had a feeling I was the only one who really meant it. Not that the others would hang her out to dry or anything, but let's just say that keeping her safe wasn't a high priority. As usual, my bleeding heart was showing, and I planned to stick to her like glue.

We went on foot this time, because it was stealthier, and because it allowed us to periodically send Jack ahead in mouse form to see if we were about to stumble on an early ambush. Most of Niobe's forces would be focused on protecting the house itself, but we assumed she had people keeping an eye on the surroundings, too.

Because the road was too obvious a route—and because it was so narrow we were likely to be run over as we crept along its nonexistent shoulders—we fought our way through the dense foliage that grew up wherever it wasn't aggressively cut back. If we'd had to hack our way through with machetes, I'm not sure we'd ever have gotten to the house, but Violet finally found a way to make herself useful, using her powers to coax the plants out of our way.

Seeing branches pulling themselves to the side and vines slithering like snakes to make room for us creeped me out, but if that was the worst thing I was going to see tonight, I'd have one hell of a party tomorrow. The body armor made me feel like some kind of cyborg, and a klutzy one at that. Even with foliage clearing out of my path, I still managed to trip and nearly face-planted more than once. I wasn't the only one struggling, and we were probably about as sneaky as a herd of elephants.

This isn't a stealth mission, I reminded myself for the twenty-fifth time. We were a scouting party of sorts, but we were also the bait in the trap, and what good is bait if no one knows it's there?

Even so, I winced every time someone tripped, or their weapon clanked, or they couldn't hold back a mumbled curse. It was probably a lovely, temperate night, but thanks to the body armor and nerves, I was soaked with sweat, my hair and clothes sticking to me. I hadn't had a good night's sleep in forever, and I was scared enough to practically pee myself. And if *I* was that scared, I couldn't imagine how Violet felt. It was her choice to go in there unarmed, but then I don't think having a weapon in hand would have made her feel much better.

How does someone who was born immortal cope with the fear of imminent death?

Not very well, if the chattering of Violet's teeth was any indication. I reached out to give her a silent pat of encouragement, and she practically jumped out of her skin. At least she didn't scream.

When we judged we were about fifty feet away from breaking through the foliage and getting our first look at the house, we sent Jack ahead to take yet another look at our path and make sure we weren't about to stumble onto any surprises. He returned with grim news.

"There are men with automatic weapons stationed on the roof," he told us. "They've got at least one guy facing each direction, and several of the windows are cracked open. I couldn't see in, but I don't think they're open for the sake of the refreshing ocean breezes. They're definitely waiting for us."

If that was our greatest threat, we might not have been too worried. The Olympians were not trained soldiers, and as long as we didn't present them with clear shots, they were liable to miss way more often than they hit when it was dark and we had such thick cover. But as soon as that first shot went off, all hell would break loose, and that meant the magical attacks would begin.

Jack looked at me. "I bet with your aim you could pick some of them off even when they supposedly have the more advantageous position."

"Probably," I agreed. My supernatural aim was so good I didn't think the dark would do much to hinder it. "But unless they're all clustered together like morons, I'll be lucky to get more than one or two of them before the rest get under cover and lightning bolts and other fun stuff starts raining down on us."

"Well, we *are* here to get things started," Logan said. "We *want* them to engage with us so that Anderson and Cyrus and the rest can come at them from behind."

Yeah, that was the plan, and the plan had always involved a certain amount of sitting duckness. It would be nice if we could even the odds just a little bit before we started drawing fire, though. Something that would distract the gunmen—who were likely mortal Descendants and therefore didn't have magical powers they could bring to bear—so that I'd have a chance to take at least some of them out before they knew what hit them.

"We need Blake," I said, realizing that he would be perfect for the job. As a descendant of Eros, Blake could create a lust so overpowering that no one, not even the most powerful *Liberi*, could resist it. The guys on the roof might even drop their weapons in their haste to get to each other and have some action.

Too bad Blake was with Cyrus and the rest, waiting for our signal to step into the Underworld.

"Sounds more like a job for Sita to me," Jamaal commented. "She can make one hell of a big distraction, and she can take a couple of those guys out with one swipe of her paw."

Instantly, a vision of Sita playing with Oscar like a house cat with a mouse entered my mind, and I tried to think of a tactful way to tell Jamaal that I didn't exactly trust her after that. But one rarely gets a chance to come up with something tactful when Jack is around.

"Are you sure letting Hell Kitty loose in the middle of all this is a good idea?" he asked. "No offense, but if she's gotten a taste for killing people . . ."

"She hasn't 'gotten a taste' for it," Jamaal said in a fierce whisper. "The Underworld had a bad influence on her, but we're not in the Underworld now. You don't seriously think I'm going to go into a fight without her, do you?"

His voice had risen to something above a whisper, and I put my hand on his arm and squeezed a silent warning. I had some of the same worries as Jack, but I wasn't about to ask Jamaal to go into a battle without Sita, and if Sita was coming out, she might as well get in there early and start causing some chaos. You'd have to be in a freaking coma not to be terrified when she came after you, and there was that extra bonus of being invulnerable to bullets.

"And what if something happens to Jamaal?" Jack persisted. "Or if things go on too long and he passes out from exhaustion?"

"Fine," Jamaal snapped. "*You* go in and create a diversion."

That stopped the argument. Hopefully before it got loud enough to be overheard. The two of them weren't doing much for the stealth factor.

We started moving forward again, more slowly now as we tried to be quiet. The night was alive with sounds, with insects and frogs and the crash of the waves down below, but I still felt like every footstep made too much noise, and I half expected the gunfire and lightning to start before we were ready.

Despite my worries, we made it to the edge of Jasmine's property without being attacked. It was oppressively dark within the shade of the jungle, but the moon was nearing full and it was a clear night. There were no lights on, either inside or outside the house, and the guys on the roof were wearing black or dark gray to blend into the background, but that full moon meant I could see them if I looked hard enough. I counted five, although there was no way of knowing who else might be lurking behind the ominously open windows. I thought I saw a flash of movement from inside, but that might have been my imagination.

"I have a bad feeling about this," Jack muttered. I wondered if he thought anyone here had a *good* feeling about it, because I sure didn't.

If I were an ordinary human—you know, like I was just a few months ago when I was so blissfully ignorant about the existence of the *Liberi* and all things magical—I would never in a million years have thought to try to shoot guys dressed in dark clothing, lying flat against a roof in the dark of night. I probably would have looked a lot more badass if I'd had some macho military rifle, but when your aim is literally flawless, you can be deadly with a peashooter. Not that the Glock Logan had bullied me into using was a peashooter.

I found the best available vantage point, then took aim through a thick veil of leaves at the gunman who was the most exposed. A human sharpshooter would have had trouble making that shot with a handgun, but I was confident I could do it.

If I could get myself to pull the trigger, that is. I am not a big fan of shooting people. Even when I know they're bad people who probably deserve it.

Everyone else hunkered down in the darkness behind me. Logan insisted we not stand too close together and make ourselves into easy group targets, but I'm sure I'm not the only one who didn't like the way the others seemed to melt away into the darkness as soon as they moved a few feet away. There was the disquieting feeling that they were all abandoning me. Except for Violet, who refused to budge from my side.

"They're going to be panicked for a few seconds," I warned her, "but after that, they're going to start firing back, and it won't just be with guns."

Thanks to the flash suppressor Logan had installed on my gun, they wouldn't be able to target me that way, but someone throwing lightning bolts didn't have to make a direct hit to put me—and anyone around me—in a world of hurt.

"You should go with Logan." As a war-god descendant, he was better able to protect Violet than anyone else. And unlike me, he wouldn't immediately be drawing fire.

Violet shook her head. "You're the only one who actually cares if I live or die. I'm sticking with you."

I winced internally, because that was pretty much true. I still thought she'd be safer with Logan, but there wasn't time to argue.

Sita shimmered into existence on the lawn a couple of feet away from the thicket of vegetation that kept us all hidden. One of the rooftop gunmen saw her and let out a cry of mingled alarm and warning. I should have started firing right then and there, but I was still fighting to overcome my resistance to shooting a fellow human being.

Everyone on the roof started scrambling in search of the source of the alarm, and the guy who'd spotted Sita fired on her. No bullet could hurt Sita, and she and I were hardly what I'd call friends, but maybe just because I saw her as part of Jamaal, I felt a surge of protective rage that suddenly made pulling the trigger not so hard.

The guy I'd taken aim at had risen to his knees, the better to swivel around and face the threat. He also gave me a target I could have hit even without my supernatural abilities. My bullet went through his head, and he went instantly limp, his body sliding off the roof and landing on the grass below with a thump.

Everyone else who'd been scrambling suddenly remembered why they'd been keeping such a low profile in the first place and dropped back down. I didn't have a good shot at anyone, the angles of the roof keeping the most vulnerable body parts protected, but then Sita did one of those impossible leaps of hers and vaulted all the way from the ground to the middle of the roof, inches from one of the gunmen. He let out a scream of abject terror and tried to bring his gun around to bear on her—not that it would have done him any good—but Sita let out an earthshaking roar and lunged for his throat.

I was glad it was dark so I couldn't see the fountain of blood that must have erupted as his cry was abruptly cut off.

The rest of the guys on the roof started firing those automatic weapons of theirs, but they were panicked, unaimed bursts. They must have had some idea where my shot had come from, but either Sita was too distracting for them to bother with trivial things like aim, or they were imagining phantom movements in the dark, because despite the spray of bullets, nothing even came close to my position.

I took out a gunman as Sita chased another right off the edge of the roof. The enemy wasn't exactly showing grace under fire, and I was reminded again that as frightening as the Olympians and their followers could be, they weren't as a general rule combat trained. They were used to living the good life, not *fighting for* their lives.

I suppose I was getting a little complacent already, watching our enemies fall so easily, but of course those guys had been exposed on the roof because they were considered expendable.

The next burst of automatic-weapons fire came from the windows, from people who didn't have to worry—yet—about having Sita rip their throats out. And though it was clear they still couldn't pinpoint where my shots were coming from, they had a general idea. Bullets ripped through the foliage around me, and I lowered myself to a crouch, making as small a target as possible.

Sita continued to wreak havoc on the roof, and no one there was even trying to shoot at me, too busy trying to stay alive. I took a moment to look around, hoping to spot Jamaal even though I knew better. I could barely see Violet, who was right there with me. How I hoped to see Jamaal, who had presumably moved to a safe distance, I don't know.

Gunfire from the open windows continued to strafe my approximate position. Broken branches and torn leaves rained down on me, and I wondered if the tree I was using for cover could survive the repeated assaults. My fellow *Liberi* were now shooting back from their scattered positions, making it harder for the gunmen to concentrate on a single target. I hoped everyone was keeping safe and covered—especially Jamaal, who would start to weaken over time from the effort of controlling Sita.

Sita dispatched the last of the rooftop gunmen and began looking around for her next target. We had certainly achieved our goal of getting the party started, but we hadn't drawn out their big guns yet. Being shot at with machine guns wasn't what you'd call a pleasant experience, but the guns weren't our biggest concern, and what we were really trying to do was draw out and engage the *Liberi* defectors, who were the true threat. As long as they settled for using guns, we knew they were keeping their most powerful people in reserve. It was Logan's job to signal Anderson via text to head into the Underworld. I wondered if Logan had sent the signal yet. It would take a few minutes for Anderson and the rest to make it here, and those were going to be a long few minutes.

I dared to peek out around the cover of my spindly tree and scrutinized the windows, trying to see who was inside, but all I saw were muzzle flashes that left spots in my vision when I looked away. We had to eliminate the gunmen before things started to get real, and even with my aim, that was going to be tough to do when they had such good cover.

Sita jumped down from the roof, drawing a hail of fire that passed right through her. The windows weren't open wide enough to let a tiger through, but Sita never let such trivial things as closed doors or windows stop her. She made another impressive leap, this time aiming for one of the second-story windows. The gunfire intensified, which seemed kind of pointless to me considering how many rounds they'd already wasted on her with no effect, but I suppose they didn't have anything useful to do.

Sita sailed through the window as if it didn't exist, and I heard the screams from inside even over the continued gunfire. Apparently, having Sita actually inside the house convinced the bad guys that they needed a more potent weapon.

The darkness came out of nowhere, so dense I might as well have been suddenly struck blind. The gunfire sputtered out, since no one could see anything. Through the ringing of my ears, I could still hear screams coming from the house. I didn't know if it was as dark inside as it was outside, but Sita didn't need to see to be deadly.

The only person who could see in this total dark was the Nyx descendant himself, and he was probably taking advantage of it somehow. Niobe would want Violet dead for her betrayal, and I had visions of the Nyx descendant walking right up to her and shooting her in the head without me ever knowing he was there. I reached out to put a hand on Violet to make sure I didn't lose her in the dark, then closed my eyes so they would stop straining to see.

Without speaking, I backed up and tugged on Violet's arm. She got the hint, and I heard the plants around us rustling as they made room for us to retreat farther into the cover of the jungle. When we were about ten feet back from the edge, I urged Violet into a crouch once more and made sure to position myself between her and the house.

Even with supernatural night vision, the Nyx descendant would have to be almost on top of us to see Violet now. He would also have to venture into the jungle, which he couldn't do without making a fair bit of noise, as we had learned earlier during our short trek. I hunkered down next to Violet and, with my eyes still closed, strained to hear the sound of leaves rustling in something other than the breeze.

Although the gunfire had stopped, the night was still far from silent. There wasn't as much insect noise as there had been before the shooting began, but there was some, and I heard the distant crash of the waves from below. And of course, the screaming and the occasional roar from inside the house. But those sounds were all distant, and I was listening for something much closer, for the sound of a man forcing his way through the trees and bushes, confident he was safe in the darkness he had created. When I'd had to play cat and mouse with Emma and her manufactured darkness once, I'd learned that I could do a pretty good job of finding a target by sound alone.

I'm convinced my plan would have worked out nicely and I'd have been able to take the Nyx descendant out of the picture at least for the space of time it would take him to heal a severe gunshot wound. But even in the sweaty heat produced by too much adrenaline and heavy body armor, I went completely cold when I heard a single gunshot and a distant roar from Sita, one that sounded pained instead of furious.

I'd been assuming the Nyx descendant was coming after Violet, but though killing Violet would have foiled our presumed attempt to get the altar taken care of, it would not have eliminated the biggest threat that was facing Niobe's impromptu army right now: Sita. As far as we knew, she was completely invulnerable. Which meant the only way to stop her was . . .

"Jamaal!" I croaked, not meaning to say it out loud.

I wanted to run to him, to protect him, but I had no idea where he was. If I could have calmed the panic that throbbed in my veins, I might have been able to use my power to find him even in this dark, but I was in no state to be still and focus on vague subconscious clues.

Another gunshot rang out. Sita let out an unearthly scream and fell suddenly silent.

I lost all semblance of logic and reason, my brain completely short-circuiting.

"*Jamaal!*" I screamed, leaping to my feet regardless of my blindness.

I would have taken off into the darkness at a dead run, frantic to get to Jamaal even if there was nothing I could do for him, only Violet anticipated me and grabbed my arm, yanking me back down onto my ass. I hit with a teeth-clacking thump just as a concentrated burst of gunfire cut through the space I'd been occupying. I'm not the only one who can target based on sound.

Violet's quick action probably saved my life, but I wasn't in a grateful state of mind. Hell, I don't know if my mind was even *present*, much less functioning. Despite my close call with death, I struggled against her grip, desperate to get to my feet once more.

Violet might not be the most powerful goddess ever to walk the Earth, but she had more than enough strength to restrain a puny human like me, and my struggles were to no avail. She wrestled me to the ground and clapped a hand over my mouth so I wouldn't shout again. Then she put her mouth right up against my ear.

"He's *Liberi*, Nikki. He'll recover."

The words didn't get through to me at first, so she repeated them, and finally my brain came back online.

As long as it wasn't a mortal Descendant who pulled the trigger, Jamaal would recover from even the worst gunshot

wound. I was almost certain it was the Nyx descendant—
a *Liberi*—who'd done the deed, unless he'd been dragging a
mortal Descendant around with him, which seemed unlikely.
So Jamaal might be dead at the moment, but it wasn't a permanent thing. At least it wouldn't be as long as we didn't lose this
battle.

With Sita no longer wreaking havoc inside the house, Niobe's crew finally went on the offensive. The darkness was so
complete I couldn't *see* the barrage of lightning bolts thrown in
our general direction, but I could feel the electric charge in the
air, and I could sure as hell *hear* them as they crashed into the
trees and bushes and shook the ground. I smelled a combination of smoke and ozone in the air, and after what Cyrus had
told us about the former Olympian who could control fire, I
was not a bit happy about the smoke part of that equation.

If the dark was so total it could make lightning bolts invisible, then we wouldn't even be able to see any fires that might
pop up. I hoped that Logan had given Anderson the signal, and
that our reinforcements were even now pouring into the house.

A wall of light, blinding after the total dark, appeared out
of nowhere, pushing the dark away before it. The dark pushed
back, the line separating the two shimmering back and forth as
each fought for supremacy, night against day. That could only
mean that Cyrus was here, and for the first time, I felt almost
hopeful. We had lost Jamaal and Sita—*temporarily*, I reminded
myself—but Niobe's losses had been greater, and her people
were now outnumbered.

Either Cyrus won the battle against the Nyx descendant,
or Niobe's people decided the dark was no longer to their advantage, because the heavy black darkness disappeared all at
once, leaving me squinting and covering my eyes against the
sun brightness Cyrus had created. I wondered briefly what the
hell the neighbors were making of all this.

I forced my eyes open and tried to find something to shoot
at, but because we'd moved back so far into the trees earlier, I

couldn't see anything but leaves and vines in the artificial daylight.

Cyrus's light abruptly winked out, moments before a very visible bolt of lightning streaked through the air. I guess bringing the sunlight was very much like bringing a flashlight, giving the enemy a clear and easy target in the night. I hoped the fact that Cyrus's light had gone out before the lightning hit meant he'd gotten out of the way in time.

Violet and I crept forward through the trees once again, taking up a position right at the edge where we could see the house but still have cover. On the far left edge of the jungle, right next to the cliff, a dead tree was on fire, filling the air with smoke. Ordinarily, I didn't think this lush jungle landscape was in much danger of catching fire, but the situation was far from ordinary. If that fire started to spread, it would flush us all out of the cover of the trees.

From my position, there wasn't a whole lot to see except for the dead bodies Sita had left in her wake. I fought off an almost dizzying sense of dread, wishing I could find Jamaal and stay by his side for the duration. I didn't know how many mortal Descendants were left alive in that house, but all it would take was one to steal Jamaal's immortal life.

Focus, Nikki, I commanded myself. The stakes in this battle were too crushingly high for me to allow myself to be distracted by my own fears or even by the fate of a single man. No matter how much he mattered to me.

Lightning streaked from two of the open windows into the jungle. Zeus, having been a horny bastard, seemed to have more descendants than any three other gods put together. I noticed for the first time that the house's front door was swinging in the breeze. Left open by Cyrus, no doubt, when he left the house to push back the darkness. But if our reinforcements were in the house, then why were there still people throwing lightning bolts at us from inside?

I noted with alarm that the fire was spreading and a couple

of living trees were now engulfed in flames. I silently pointed it out to Violet, who chewed her lip in worry. If we wanted to stay within sight of the house, we had about fifty yards' worth of cover before we'd reach the driveway and be forced out into the open.

The idea had been for us to drive Niobe out from cover, not the other way around, but so far she obviously felt safe enough in her fortress—and confident enough in her allies—that she felt no need to come out and confront her sister personally. We were going to have to turn up the heat, so to speak.

In a night that had been dead calm, there was suddenly a gust of wind so strong it almost knocked me over. The trees all creaked and groaned with it, and vines whipped through the air. I glanced at the sky and still saw the clear, bright moon hanging above, with only wispy, slow-moving clouds obscuring it. And yet the wind brought an unmistakable hint of moisture, mistlike drops of water that blended with my sweat.

I licked my lips and tasted salt. At first, I assumed it was the sweat, but then as the water in the air grew thicker, carried by the swirling wind, I realized that the water itself was salty.

Seawater.

I remembered that Niobe had a couple of Poseidon's descendants in her court, and I didn't much like the implications.

While the salt water continued to swirl in the wind, it didn't seem to be bothering the fire one bit. When the wind gusted the right way, I could feel the first edges of heat and knew we had to start moving. Thanks to the light from the fire, we weren't as invisible as we'd once been. The bad guys would have a harder time picking us out of the foliage if we just held still, but the fire was quickly taking that option away.

We had to move out of sight of the windows before I felt safe enough to start creeping closer to the driveway, and I had no idea how we were going to get across that driveway without being shot or electrocuted by lightning. However, that was a problem I'd worry about when the time came. I wished I knew what was going on inside the house. I could hear yelling and occasional bursts of gunfire, but Anderson and his reinforcements obviously hadn't taken out the most dangerous *Liberi* yet. The salt water in the air had now gathered itself into a waterspout that was starting to tear into the vegetation at the far side of the driveway, where I presumed some of our people were still taking cover.

I thought Violet and I had drifted far enough backward into the greenery that we would be practically invisible to anyone from the house, but apparently I was mistaken. A bolt of lightning came to ground much too close for comfort, the force of its impact sending both of us sprawling. My ears rang and my head felt a little woozy, but it hadn't been a direct hit and all my body parts seemed to be attached.

The lightning had cut an impressive swath through the foliage, and the fire was now close enough to reveal our location to hostile eyes. I grabbed Violet to help her up, and we both plunged into the cover of the surrounding jungle just as a second lightning bolt blasted by.

"Keep moving!" I gasped at Violet, but she wasn't inclined to stay still any more than I was.

We'd never have been able to go more than a few feet into the densest vegetation if Violet weren't able to coax the plant life out of our way. Impressive that she could manage it while under this kind of stress.

I kept waiting for a third lightning bolt to hit nearby, but it didn't. A serious sense of urgency made me want to keep moving as far and as fast as possible, but since the immediate threat seemed to have been removed, I slowed down and tried to get my bearings. To get back to the fight, we had to angle back to the right.

"Hold up," I said, coming to a stop so abruptly Violet practically plowed into me from behind. "There's no reason to keep running away. We just have to head back and find a better position." I expected Violet to argue, since she wanted no part of the battle to begin with. Instead, she looked in the direction I was pointing, a crease of intense concentration forming between her brows, followed by a look of alarm.

"The plants aren't responding to me," she said.

I had the instant suspicion that she was lying, trying to trick me into fleeing—which is basically what she'd wanted to do all along. The plants in the direction we'd been running were still moving, clearing a path for us. Violet followed the line of my gaze and barked something out in a language I didn't recognize. I suspected it was a curse of some sort.

"*I'm* not doing that," she said.

That was so not what I wanted to hear. If Violet wasn't doing it, then there was only one other obvious suspect. What if we'd been wrong, and Niobe had never been *in* the house?

I'd lost track of how many shots I'd fired, but I decided now might be a good time to change the mag even if it wasn't empty yet. Not that I had any reason to think a bullet could hurt Niobe, but it was the only weapon I had. Maybe I understood why the hapless gunmen had continued to fire on Sita once she had made it quite clear bullets weren't doing any good.

"Can you make a path in some other direction?" I asked. I wanted to get back to the others, but not as much as I wanted to not be following a path Niobe had created for us.

Violet concentrated a moment, then shook her head. "It's not working. Niobe was always better at this than the rest of us."

"My kingdom for a machete," I muttered.

"What?"

"Nothing. I guess we're going to have to force our way through." I reached out to shove a tree branch out of the way, and a vine clinging to that tree suddenly whipped out and wrapped itself around my wrist. I yanked free easily enough, but clearly forcing our way through the foliage would be no easy task.

"We have to try," Violet said as if reading my thoughts.

Even in the darkness, I could see how pale and frightened she was. "You are not capable of defending us against Niobe."

I knew that. Hello, puny human here. Not going to come out ahead in a fight against a goddess. Getting cut off from the herd and being forced to face Niobe with just the two of us had not been part of the plan.

I cupped my hands around my mouth and bellowed out Anderson's name, but I had no reason to believe anyone could hear me. The gunfire had started up again with renewed vigor, and I worried I was going to have permanent hearing loss from the constant supersonic cracks the lightning bolts made.

My reward for yelling was another lightning bolt tossed in our general direction. We were deep enough into the trees that its force dissipated before it got to us, but it left me disinclined to shout again.

Violet cursed, and I realized I could see her better than I had a few minutes ago. I looked over my shoulder and saw that the fire was advancing on us at an alarming pace. It aimed at us like a missile, trees catching fire one by one in a straight line of the sort never seen in nature.

We were being pushed ahead, and we had no choice but to let it happen.

Twenty-One

We tried several more times to veer off the path Niobe was creating for us, but she wasn't about to let it happen. The plants resisted Violet's every attempt to control them, and the fire continued its inexorable pursuit. The sounds of battle grew more distant, though the lightning was still earsplittingly loud. I wondered how all of my friends were doing, and most important of all, I wondered if Jamaal was going to be okay. I *had* to assume it was a *Liberi* who shot him and not a mortal Descendant. And I tried not to think about him dead or just barely alive, lying helplessly in the path of the fire.

Jamaal had already died three times during his immortal life—once from being shot to death, once from being hanged, and once from being beheaded—the last two at Anderson's orders when Jamaal's death magic had led to a tragic loss of control. It wasn't fair that he had to go through it yet again, and I would happily shoot Niobe for chasing me away from his side when he needed my help.

Not that shooting Niobe would do a hell of a lot of good, and that, of course, was where the difficulty lay. In theory, her sister goddess should be equally powerful and able to put up a fight—defending *me* instead of vice versa—but Violet did not strike me as a pillar of strength, and her inability to forge us a new path through the plant life did not bode well.

Somehow, I had to find a way to get reinforcements to our side. Specifically, Anderson, the only one among us who had the strength to defeat Niobe in a fight as well as the power to kill her. I'd objected before to the idea of killing her, worried that her surviving sisters might decide they had to avenge her, but right now I was thinking it might be the lesser of two evils. A selfish way of thinking, perhaps, but I was not eager to die, and whatever I might think of Violet, I felt at least partially responsible for her. I'd promised to protect her—a textbook definition of hubris, now that I thought about it—and keeping my promises was important to me.

I had no clue where Anderson was or what he was currently doing. He might still be inside the house, futilely searching for Niobe. Yelling again was unlikely to get me anything but another lightning bolt, and it wasn't like I had a flare gun I could shoot into the air for help.

I almost came to another abrupt halt when the obvious answer practically slapped me in the face. Running headlong down the barely cleared path while being pursued by a line of fire with a will of its own made getting my phone out of my back pocket an awkward proposition. The bulky body armor Logan had insisted we all wear made it impossible.

"Hold on a sec!" I said to Violet, halting her with a hand on her shoulder.

"Are you crazy?" she asked, pointing at the fire and then trying to yank me back into a run.

"Wait!" I yelled as I tore at the Velcro on the body armor, trying to get enough mobility to get to my back pocket. I resolutely refused to follow Violet's pointing finger, because if I could see how close the fire was getting, I was afraid I'd panic and start running again. I'd been dead the last time my body was burned, and going through that while alive was not on my bucket list.

I was rushing too much to get the body armor off completely, but I at least managed to loosen it enough so that I could get into my back pocket. As soon as I had the phone in hand, I looked over my shoulder and saw the fire was practically nipping at our heels. Waves of heat rolled off it, preparing the way.

Violet yanked on my arm again, and this time I had to agree that running was a great idea, no matter what unknown terror we were running toward.

Adrenaline and exertion had left me with shaky hands, and even having Anderson on speed dial, it was hard for me to find the coordination to turn the phone on and make the call while running for my life. I prayed Anderson wasn't in the middle of hand-to-hand combat. And that he could hear his phone ring over the gunshots, lightning bolts, crackling fire, and howling wind.

I held the phone to my face, panting so hard I was wondering if I'd have enough air in my lungs to speak if I managed to get through to him. The fire was getting closer, gaining on us no matter how fast we ran. The air felt more like scorching desert than tropical jungle, and the fire spat occasional sparks and cinders like fireworks.

I heard Anderson's phone ring once, twice, then a third time. Just before the fourth ring, his voice came on the line, snapping an abrupt, "What?"

He had to know I wouldn't make a phone call in the middle of an apocalyptic battle if it weren't damned important, but he sounded irritated as hell anyway. I'd tell him that he was being a jerk when I had a moment to spare.

My first attempt at forming words failed, my throat too parched from the heat and the run to function properly. I cleared my throat and swallowed hard, hoping to find some moisture, and I think my second attempt to speak would have succeeded, only I didn't get the chance.

Something darted out of the foliage beside me and wrapped itself around my ankle, yanking hard. I pitched forward and instinctively put my hands out to try to stop my fall.

The phone flew out of my sweaty palm and landed face-down on the ground just out of reach. I could hear the faint hum of Anderson's voice, but the speaker was facing away from me and I couldn't make out any words. I tried to throw myself toward the phone, but the vine that had wrapped around my ankle held firm.

"Violet!" I shouted as I tried in vain to get to my feet. "Help!"

She had so far shown no sign that she had the ability to countermand her sister's power, but at least she could lend me some extra body weight to try to rip the vine out of the ground. The fire was so close now the heat was almost unbearable. I sat up and clawed at the vine that held me captive, terror coursing through me as my likelihood of burning to death increased.

I didn't really expect Violet to help. She was not the type to risk her own skin for someone else. Especially not someone like me, an annoying human who had variously insulted her, bullied her, and guilt-tripped her. But maybe she was made of sterner stuff than I gave her credit for. Instead of leaving me to save her own ass, she whirled around and stumbled back *toward* the fire.

Violet fell to her hands and knees beside me and grabbed the offending vine with both hands. She gave a violent yank, and the thing all but disintegrated in her hands. I'd forgotten that she was a hell of a lot stronger than I was.

She didn't wait for me to climb to my feet, instead flinging my arm over her shoulder and half dragging me. I thought she was just doing that in a frantic effort to get away from the fire, but when I tried to get my feet under me and support my own weight, my ankle buckled and I would have gone back down without her help. I had too much adrenaline in my system to feel much in the way of pain, but clearly that vine had done some damage—or I'd hurt myself in my effort to pull free.

Violet kept my arm slung over her shoulders, keeping me upright while we both lurched into an awkward, limping run. A whimper of fear rose from my throat, because there was no way we were going to outrun the fire at this pace. I'd have told Violet to leave me and save herself, only it turned out I wasn't as noble as all that.

The wind changed, bringing with it a choking cloud of smoke that made both of us cough. I had no idea how far we'd run or even what direction we'd run in. It seemed that we shouldn't have been able to go this far without running into one of the neighboring houses or falling off the cliff, but for all I knew Niobe had us running in circles. We were incapable of running in any direction she didn't want us to go. If she'd wanted us to burn to death, all she'd have had to do was stop making that clear path ahead of us. I wished I thought her failure to do so was a good sign.

Just when I thought it was all over, that the fire was upon us and we couldn't possibly survive, the single line of flames split into two, each line swerving around us and suddenly outpacing us. Ahead, the trees and bushes and vines all pulled away, shrinking back into the surrounding jungle and forming a wide, barren clearing bordered by fire.

At the far side of the clearing stood a woman. About six feet tall with glorious auburn hair warmly lit by the fire, she wore a long white gown belted at the waist and draped over one shoulder, looking very much like a figure that should be gracing the Parthenon, or at least the Ancient Greece exhibit at the National Museum. Her eyes glowed white, and in her hands she clasped an enormous bronze sword I probably wouldn't even be able to lift.

Violet and I came to a halt as the fire continued to outpace us, creating perfectly carved arcs on both sides of us and curving inward to form a solid wall behind Niobe.

We were trapped in a seething circle of fire with a seriously pissed-off, sword-wielding goddess. It was time for the endgame, and from where I was standing, it didn't look good for the home team.

TWENTY-TWO

Niobe took a few graceful, gliding steps closer. It looked like her feet weren't even touching the ground, though I assumed that was just an illusion. Thanks to the wall of fire, the artificially created clearing was about the temperature of your average pizza oven. Niobe would have looked a little more human if she had the grace to sweat in the heat, but it might as well have been a temperate spring day for all the discomfort she showed.

Violet was a different story. Her hair was disheveled and her clothing torn from our long run, and her makeup was melting in the perspiration that dripped down her face. I desperately wanted to get out of the goddamn body armor—it certainly wouldn't do me any good at a time like this—but getting all the Velcro loose would require taking my eyes off Niobe, and that didn't strike me as the best idea in the world.

"I am very disappointed in you, Sister," Niobe said, and

no one would ever mistake that resonant voice for something human. She might be wearing a human mask over her godly form, but she wasn't exactly making an effort to pass.

Beside me, Violet stood up straighter and lifted her chin. I knew how scared she had to be, how scared she'd been earlier, but she did an admirable job of hiding it.

"*I'm* the one who's disappointed," Violet responded. "You know I would be happy to dance with you on Kane's grave, but the cost is too high."

Niobe gave a snort of disdain. "You have been living among the animals too long if you think the cost is too high."

"That's not what I mean, and you know it."

It took me a second to grasp her implication, and when I did, I winced. *Goddesses do not think like humans,* I reminded myself for the bazillionth time. Of course in their worldview the inconvenience of being forever trapped on the Earth was of greater consequence than the extinction of all human life.

Neither goddess seemed to be paying attention to me at the moment, so I drew my gun, knowing a bullet would be about as effective against Niobe as a spitball.

"Don't even think about it," Violet muttered, barely moving her lips. "She's angry enough already."

I doubted it was possible to make Niobe any angrier than she already was, but since I had no reason to think shooting her would improve the situation, I kept the gun down by my side. I was reluctant to let Niobe out of my sight, but I kept stealing glances all around me in search of a way out.

The wall of fire that surrounded us was solid and thick, and from what I could see, there was no hope of getting through it without being burned to a crisp. It didn't seem like I had much choice but to rely on Violet to get us out of this. Relying on others has never been my favorite thing, and I racked my brain for some way I could take action and save the day. Unfortunately, it was pretty hard to come up with anything when the enemy was a freaking goddess.

"Have you forgotten what Kane did?" Niobe asked. "Fourteen precious, innocent children he took from me! A true and loyal sister would be willing to sacrifice her own desires to avenge them."

Interesting how her definition of loyalty didn't seem to include any responsibilities on her part. Like, say, not murdering sisters who didn't see things her way. Maybe Niobe's problem wasn't so much that she was angry but that she was batshit crazy. I've never met anyone with taste in women as epically bad as Anderson's. If he had a thing for crazy women, couldn't he have at least stuck to ones who weren't homicidal?

"I would love nothing better than to see Kane dead," Violet said. "I loved my nieces and nephews, and I love *you*. But I want to have a future. And I want *you* to have a future, and Iris and Lily and Poppy. We all deserve better than to be forced to live on a barren world for all eternity."

Niobe waved the objection off as if it were completely beneath her notice. "We will have each other, and that is enough. And more than anything, my children deserve the justice they have so long been denied. It saddens me to find you can't see that."

She didn't sound sad, and she certainly didn't look it. The glow in her eyes intensified, and though there was no missing her fury, I was sure I saw more than a hint of glee as well. Niobe had so far been unable to hurt Anderson, but she was clearly taking pleasure out of finding other targets for her rage. That did not encourage me to hope for a peaceful resolution to the current conflict.

I'd been watching the sisters talk, my head turning back and forth as though I were at a tennis match while I kept hoping I could magically come up with a way out of our situation. I hadn't noticed the gap opening up in the wall of fire behind me. Not until something wrapped around my already sore ankle and squeezed tight.

I whirled around so fast I fell down, and my eyes widened

at what I saw. A section of the fire wall, about four or five feet wide, had opened up, and through that section poured a seething mass of greenery, vines and branches and roots heading for Violet and me like a green tidal wave. The vine that had grabbed my ankle was in the vanguard, and two more of the tendrils leading the charge latched on to me as I struggled.

Beside me, Violet gave a cry of dismay as she, too, was suddenly lashed with vines. Being much stronger than I am, she was able to pull free of the first couple of tendrils, but before she could retreat, several more grabbed on, pulling her down.

Violet screamed as the boiling wave of greenery grew thicker, more and more tendrils finding a hold until there were enough of them that she couldn't generate sufficient momentum to rip free.

I was being grabbed, too, but Niobe obviously didn't consider me much of a threat—and rightly so—because I was receiving nowhere near as much attention as Violet.

I found a use for my gun, taking several quick shots to sever the vines that held me, but all I succeeded in doing was letting Niobe know that she needed to direct more of the flood of foliage my way. For every vine I severed, three more whipped out to grab me. Eventually, one vine wrapped around my hand and one around the gun, tearing it out of my grip.

Violet, however, was faring even worse. Her body was completely invisible now beneath a blanket of green. All I could see of her was her horrified face as she writhed and squirmed to no avail.

Things were looking mighty bad. And then they got worse.

Standing just behind the gap in the fire wall was the shadowy figure of a man. He was no one I knew, but in the light of the crackling fire, I caught a glimpse of an iridescent glyph on his cheek. At first glance, I couldn't tell what the glyph was, so he conveniently turned his face to the light so I could better see the stylized hammer and anvil that marked him as a descendant of Hephaestus.

The *Liberi* smiled at me triumphantly in a display of the typical Olympian sadism, though I supposed technically he wasn't an Olympian anymore now that he'd joined forces with Niobe. He made a sweeping gesture with his hands, and the fire began creeping up the tangle of vines—making its leisurely way toward where Violet and I were held captive.

We were about to be roasted alive, and I saw no way we could possibly get out of it.

"Sister, please!" Violet shouted, but if there was more to that sentence, she didn't get it out. She made a choking sound that suggested one of the vines had wrapped around her throat.

As far as I knew, the fire couldn't permanently kill either one of us, seeing as it was wielded by a *Liberi*, but it would be an excruciating death, and I sincerely doubted our situation would have much improved when we came back. I'm not ashamed to admit that I cried as I watched the fire's inexorable approach and struggled in vain to free myself from the tangle of vines.

My vision blurred with tears that evaporated in the heat moments after they left my eyes. I couldn't tear my gaze away from the fire that continued to crawl closer, burning down the vines that held us like a spark traveling down a fuse. Violet was screaming in terror, and the flames that surrounded us roared. My heartbeat drummed in my ears, and at first all those sounds drowned out another scream.

I blinked in an effort to clear my vision and coughed from a cloud of smoke that wafted my way. The combination of ultra-hot dry air and smoke made my eyes burn so fiercely I could barely keep them open, but my survival instinct had refused to give up on me, so I was still in search of a way out. I had to know who else was screaming and why.

I tore my eyes from the trail of fire and squinted against the pain until I could see the gap in the wall, where the *Liberi* who controlled the fire stood. Or rather, where he *had* stood. Now he was on his knees, his back arched, his hands clawing uselessly at the air in front of him while he howled in agony. Behind him stood Anderson, whose glowing hand was clapped to the back of his neck.

Death by Anderson Kane's hand was not quick, and it most certainly was not painless. I suspected that the *Liberi* suffered more than I would have if the fire had engulfed me, but I could find no pity in my heart for him.

Anderson wasn't looking at the man he was killing, nor was he looking at me or Violet. Instead, his eyes were fixed on a point above my head. I took a quick glance behind me and confirmed that yes, it was Niobe whose gaze he had caught.

The screams finally died down, and the *Liberi*'s body disintegrated into nothingness, leaving only a pile of empty clothes. Violet and I were still trapped in the vines, but the fire stopped its relentless march toward us. The flames around us started burning a little lower—and, unfortunately, creating more smoke. My guess was that without the *Liberi*'s help, the fire was disinclined to use wet living foliage as fuel.

Paying not the slightest attention to Violet or me, Anderson strode through the widening gap in the fire wall, his hand still glowing with the power of death.

"It's time for this to end, Niobe," he said.

She spat out a few un-goddesslike curses, then said, "It will end when you are dead, and not before."

"You have that backward," he replied calmly, holding up that glowing hand. "Your choices are to give up your vendetta, or die. I don't much care which you choose."

This was becoming a disturbingly familiar tactic on Anderson's part. He seemed to have forgotten that he had said he'd try to reason with her first. Not that I had any reason to believe negotiation would work, but I would have felt better if he'd made a good-faith effort just in case.

Niobe laughed. "You always were a blind fool. My sisters might not all be in perfect agreement with me at present"—she waved her hand toward Violet, who was exhibit A—"but the one sure way you can unite them against you is to kill me. Murdering me after slaughtering my children will hardly endear you to them."

"I don't need to endear myself to them," he scoffed. "I just need them to renew their altars. I'd rather they do it willingly out of the kindness of their hearts and their respect for human life, but you don't actually think I would hesitate to force them if necessary, do you? Having known me as long as you have? Don't forget I am the son of Vengeance, my dear, and my mother taught me well."

I shuddered. I'd been having a hard time reconciling my image of Anderson with the atrocity I knew he'd committed in his past, and I'd been telling myself he had changed so much he bore little resemblance to the spiteful, angry god he'd once been. But here he was threatening to rape Niobe's sisters, and there was not an ounce of regret or reluctance in his voice.

To my shock, Anderson's threat made Niobe smile. "I know exactly what you're capable of. But you were not present when my sisters and I were assigned our penance. You were supposed to be *dead*." She spat that last word with such venom I half expected Anderson to reel as if slapped.

"Our altars cannot be renewed by force," she said triumphantly. "We must tend them *willingly*, or the rite will fail. Whether you kill me or not, our altars will fail one by one, and you will die the slow and agonizing death you deserve."

Anderson's fists were clenched by his sides, and anger poured off him in almost palpable waves. "I only need one sister alive to renew all those altars," he growled. "Perhaps as I kill them one by one, those who survive will eventually come to see the error of their ways."

I was still thrashing and squirming, trying to free myself from the vines. The struggle had seemed pointless at first, but the more attention Niobe focused on Anderson, the weaker the vines' grips became. I now had some bona fide wiggle room, and I could almost stretch my arm enough to touch my fingers to the butt of my gun. I was still uncertain what possible use a gun could have in this conflict between gods, but if nothing else it would be nice to have hold of my security blanket. It certainly didn't look like the "negotiation" was going very well.

Niobe shook her head and clucked her tongue. "You are still under the misguided impression that you have some power in this situation. I regret to inform you that you have none."

The vines that had been holding Violet melted away. I'd been too engrossed in the confrontation between Anderson and Niobe to pay much attention to Violet, but one look at her face told me Niobe wasn't as delusional as she sounded. Violet's eyes were practically throwing sparks, and though it was Niobe who had just tried to burn her to death, it was Anderson she stared daggers at. She struggled free of the last of the vines and rose to her feet.

She was filthy, her clothing torn, her makeup smeared, and yet she had no trouble exuding power, confidence, and fury.

"You *lied* to me," she spat at Anderson. "This was your plan all along, to kill Niobe and then threaten me and the rest of my sisters with rape and death."

She spit at Anderson's feet and strode over to stand by her sister's side to present a united front. For the first time, I thought I saw a hint of uncertainty in Anderson's eyes. I had told him that killing Niobe and otherwise making threats wasn't the wisest way to resolve the problem, and he hadn't listened to me. I wished I could derive even a modicum of satisfaction from having been right.

"I think you're lying," Anderson said to Niobe. He was trying to sound firm and convinced, but I could hear the shadow of doubt in his voice. "I think you're just saying all that to save your own life and Violet is playing along to save herself."

Niobe walked steadily forward, coming to stand within arm's reach of Anderson before dropping to her knees.

"Go ahead and kill me," she said softly, looking up at him

from her position on the ground. "You stole from me my one and only reason to live. Do you honestly believe threatening me with death frightens me? Put your hand on me. I will die happy knowing that my suffering will finally be over and yours just begun."

Niobe was no longer putting any effort into controlling the vines, and I was finally able to fight my way free of them. I grabbed my gun and climbed stiffly to my feet. No one even bothered to look at me, and there was no missing that I was completely insignificant to these gods. Even to Anderson.

Niobe was a madwoman, and though I'm no psychologist, I had little doubt she would qualify as psychotic. But as she knelt there at Anderson's feet declaring how little her own life meant to her, I couldn't help but pity her for the soul-deep pain she'd been suffering for untold centuries. There was no way my mind could encompass the depth of the grief she carried with her, nor the guilt that must go hand in hand with it, whether she expressed it or not. She had cheated on her husband knowing he was the son of a Fury. It was he who had committed the atrocity, but she was not completely without responsibility in the death of her children, and I couldn't imagine the torture of that knowledge.

I believed her. Believed that she would happily die, happily sacrifice all her sisters' lives, if it would end her pain. I also believed she was telling the truth about the altars, that they couldn't be renewed by force. She wanted Anderson's death more than anything, and if she weren't 100 percent certain her own death would eventually lead to his, then she wouldn't be so willing to die.

I did a mental double take at my own line of thought. My impression of the discussion so far had been that she wanted Anderson's death more than anything else, and if that was truly the case, then the human race was already well on the road to extinction. So the way to save humanity was to find something Niobe wanted more than Anderson's death.

"If you could have absolutely anything in the world," I asked Niobe, making everyone jump because I think they had literally forgotten I was present, "what would you ask for?"

Glowing, inhuman eyes turned to me and I had an instant and almost overwhelming desire to shut up and run away. The wrath of a goddess is never an easy thing to face, and she didn't have to tell me how unwanted my input was. I hoped Anderson would help me if she decided to take drastic action because I'd had the gall to speak to her.

"Anything at all," I prompted. The vines popped back to life, grabbing at me.

"I don't recall giving you permission to speak," she said with a sneer as the vines threaded their way up my legs, squeezing painfully tight.

"What can it hurt to answer a simple question?" I asked, keeping my voice as calm as possible and trying not to let her see that she was causing me pain. I didn't even bother to struggle against the vines. "Just tell me what you want more than anything in the world."

Her eyes glowed more brightly, twin lasers that should have sliced through my flesh. Anderson was looking at me, too, his face a picture of shut-the-hell-up.

"If you can honestly say that there's nothing you could possibly want more than Anderson's death," I persisted, "then I promise I won't say another word. Can you say that?"

"I want my children back!" she snarled at me. "But since I can't have that, I'll settle for revenge. I may not be the child of a Fury, but I have learned my craft from the best."

I could see the moment Anderson caught on to what I was implying, because his jaw suddenly dropped open and his eyes widened. I nodded at him ever so slightly, urging him to pick up the ball I'd just tossed. He shook his head at me, but it was in amazement, not denial. It seemed there *was* something Niobe wanted more than Anderson's death after all.

Anderson turned to Niobe, and there was still a hint of

wonder in his eyes. "I can't give you back the children I took from you," he said. "But I can give you *new* children."

For the first time, Niobe was struck speechless. No ordinary woman—at least no ordinary woman who had any business being a mother—would think of her children as objects that could be replaced. But hadn't I thought to myself a million times that gods and goddesses do not think like ordinary people? After all, no ordinary human being, not even the most psychotic, would think it a good idea to kill every living man, woman, and child to get revenge on an ex.

Anderson saw the first chink in Niobe's armor, and he pressed on. "I would happily give you a child for each one you lost."

"That you murdered, you mean," she spat, but there was considerably less heat in her voice, and the white glow in her eyes dimmed as she rolled the possibilities around in her mind.

"That I murdered," Anderson agreed quietly. "I can never make up for the sins of my past, and though I know you won't believe me, the only person who hates me more than you is me. If I could die without taking several billion innocents with me, I would give myself to you without hesitation and let you do whatever you wanted to me. But I can't do that. I've caused the death of innocents before, and I will never allow that to happen again."

Her eyes shimmered with what might have been a hint of tears, and while it didn't exactly make her look human, it made her look less *in*human. The rage that had been wafting from her since I'd first caught sight of her had all but disappeared. Anderson reached out and put his hand lightly on her shoulder—and she *let* him.

"Let me give you something better to live for than revenge," he begged. "It's never as satisfying as you hope and often leaves you feeling worse than when you began. Take it from someone who knows all too well."

The glow was completely gone from Niobe's eyes, replaced

by a glimmer of something that looked suspiciously like hope. "You must promise me at least seven sons and seven daughters."

Anderson nodded his agreement. "Of course."

"I will share you with no other woman until you have fulfilled your obligation."

"Done."

But Niobe shook her head. "No. That is too easy. Just because I am willing to consider a compromise doesn't mean I don't want to see you suffer. I will share you with no other *person* until you have fulfilled your obligation."

Anderson eyed her suspiciously. "Just what exactly is your definition of *sharing*?"

"You will see no one. You will speak to no one. You will, in fact, be my prisoner."

This was a pill Anderson did not swallow as easily, and it was clear he was about to balk.

"If you wish me and my sisters to maintain our altars and to care for those of Rose and Jasmine as well, then you have no choice but to accept my terms."

Anderson cut a quick glance over to me before returning his attention to Niobe. "Agreed. But I would ask you to give me seven days to get my affairs in order before I withdraw from the world."

Despite everything I had learned about Anderson, I still felt a distinct pang at the thought of him withdrawing from the world for the years it would take him to father all those children.

Niobe thought about it a moment, and then nodded. "I'll accept that condition, but no others. I will make the rules, and you will obey."

Anderson let out a deep, shuddering breath. "Then it sounds like we have an agreement."

TWENTY-THREE

The battle between Cyrus's handpicked Olympians and the ones who had deserted to join Niobe raged on while Niobe and Anderson came to their arrangement, and by the time it was all over the good guys—if you can even use that term when referring to Olympians—had won the day.

I left Violet, Niobe, and Anderson to work out any additional details in the agreement and made my way back down the smoldering trail of ash toward Jasmine's house. The crushing vines had left a circle of swollen, aching bruises around my ankle, but being *Liberi* has its advantages, and those bruises ached a little less with each step I took. The way back felt considerably shorter—probably because I wasn't running for my life.

I no longer heard any gunfire, nor did I hear thunder from thrown lightning bolts, but I approached the area with caution anyway. I could tell we had won because I caught sight of Logan and Maggie sitting side by side on the grass in plain sight. They had both removed their body armor and put away their weapons, so I stepped out of the jungle and onto the grass to get a better look at what this night's combat had wrought.

The house and its environs looked every bit like the battlefield it had recently been. There were char marks and bullet holes on every wall, and I couldn't see a single unbroken window. Two trees had fallen. From the black scars around their bases, I guessed they'd been taken down by lightning bolts. The lawn and driveway were spotted with puddles and scattered with leaves and broken branches, as if a hurricane had just blown through.

And then there were the bodies.

It looked like Cyrus's men were in the process of laying all those bodies out in an orderly row, having moved the ones that Sita had killed so that they were all lying side by side. As I watched, a couple of Cyrus's men emerged from the house, carrying bodies over their shoulders and then slinging them roughly to the ground beside the rest. I was glad not to recognize any of my friends among the dead, but I very much wanted to see them with my own eyes. Especially Jamaal, who was at least wounded even if he wasn't dead.

I spotted Cyrus strolling down the driveway from the street, and I rushed over to meet him. His clothes were drenched and his hair looked like it had been put through a blender, but except for the haunted look in his eyes and the exhausted droop of his shoulders, he seemed unhurt.

"Have you seen Jamaal?" I asked as I caught up to him. Then I realized I was being almost as selfish as an Olympian, because Cyrus had no way of knowing that we'd convinced Niobe to give up her vendetta. He'd put himself and his closest friends at risk to help save the world, and he deserved to know that his efforts had not been in vain.

I hurried through a quick explanation that probably didn't make a whole lot of sense, but at least it made me feel marginally less insensitive. Of course I ended by repeating my question about Jamaal, so I'm not sure I earned all that many brownie points.

"He'll be all right," Cyrus said, and it was all I could do not to burst into tears. "He took one shot to the shoulder and one to the chest, but by the time we found him the wound was already starting to heal. Maggie laid him on a couch inside so he'll be more comfortable when he comes to."

I wanted to run directly to Jamaal's side, but I would be useless there. Even not having firsthand knowledge of how severe his wound was, I knew he wouldn't be regaining consciousness anytime soon.

Two more men emerged from the house carrying bodies. My stomach considered raising an objection to the sight of so much blood and guts, and I wasn't completely happy to discover that my recent life had desensitized me enough to make the reaction manageable.

"Did we lose anyone?" I asked. "For good, I mean."

"No, *we* didn't lose anyone," Cyrus said with a bit of a bite. "*I*, on the other hand, lost two good men to a couple of Descendants I wouldn't have trusted to tie my shoe even *before* they betrayed me."

"I don't suppose their newfound immortality did them a whole lot of good."

Cyrus's smile was unusually fierce for him. "No, it did not. My own Descendants held their own in the battle, and I was happy to be able to reward each of the survivors as he or she deserved."

By which he meant he'd allowed those survivors to kill the wounded traitors and steal their immortality. I looked at the collection of bodies that was still growing larger. "How many Descendants did you end up bringing with you?" There seemed to be an awful lot of dead people.

"Not quite enough to take care of *every* traitor. We'll have to take a couple of them back to D.C. and harvest them later."

I tried not to shudder. If I had to die, I'd much rather it be in the heat of battle with as little warning as possible. I didn't think the last days and hours of the traitors' lives were going to be much fun.

I'd held still and gathered information for as long as I could bear. It wasn't that I didn't care about the fates of others, but I couldn't pretend any of them were half as important to me as Jamaal was. And what I needed most right now was to see him and reassure myself he would be all right.

On my way back to the now thoroughly beat-up house, I forced myself to stop one more time and give Maggie a hug and tell her I was glad she was safe. She had a lot of blood on her, but it turned out none of it was hers. She'd gotten sick and tired of seeing the men trying to carry the wounded around and had insisted they let her do the heavy lifting.

She led me inside, and I saw why our invasion force had been occupied for so long. There were barricades everywhere—now all destroyed, of course. There wasn't a single room our men inside could have entered without a fight. Maybe Niobe had been expecting Anderson all along. That would explain both the barricades and her decision not to be inside the house for the battle.

Jamaal was lying on a torn couch in a debris-strewn living room. I told myself I wouldn't cry, but when I saw him lying dead on that sofa, I practically collapsed with sobs. Maggie stayed with me, hugging me and murmuring soothing sounds I couldn't decipher.

"He's healing nicely," she told me when the worst of the crying jag was over. "He'll be as good as new in no time."

I knew it was true, but logic was a poor weapon to combat the visceral punch of seeing him like that.

Jamaal is a large man, and finding room for myself on the couch beside him was a challenge. However, I wriggled, squirmed, and pushed until I got enough of my butt onto the couch to sit.

Maggie had pried him out of the body armor and had obviously cleaned up the worst of the blood. There were dark, crusty stains on the torn-up remains of his undershirt, but the skin around the open wounds was pristine, and his face had been washed clear of blood and sweat and grime. I touched his cheek gently and shuddered to find it cold. Then I forced myself to look at the bullet wound that had killed him, the one straight through the center of his chest. The edges were visibly puckered, and it looked like it was at least a few days old. It was undeniable visible evidence that he was healing, that he was still *Liberi*, that he would soon be coming back to me.

I took one of his hands and clasped it between mine, even though he couldn't feel the touch. Then I bent and touched my lips to his, wishing I could kiss him awake like a prince in a fairy tale.

I didn't consciously notice any sound, so I'm not entirely sure how I knew I was no longer alone. I sat up and turned my head without letting go of Jamaal's hand. The wound had healed enough by now that the spark of life could come back at any moment, even if consciousness was still an hour or more away. Maybe he couldn't feel my touch while he was unconscious, but damned if I was going to let go.

I wasn't surprised to see Anderson standing there in the shambles of what had probably once been a cozy living room. He looked different to me somehow, older and more worn. Or maybe that was all just in my head. I knew things about Anderson now that I could never un-know, and though he had manned up and offered a considerable sacrifice for the good of everyone, I couldn't forget how he had bludgeoned Cyrus and Violet and Niobe with his threats. Considering his frightening level of power, it wasn't entirely surprising to find out he had the heart of a bully, but it wasn't a comfortable thing to know, either. I couldn't entirely say I was unhappy that he would be going away for a while, even if I knew I would miss him once he was gone.

"You have put me to shame more than once in recent memory," he said quietly, giving me a sad little half smile.

I didn't know what to say to that, so I said nothing.

Anderson looked down to where my hands were wrapped around Jamaal's. He nodded and put his hands in his pockets, looking unsure of himself. It was an expression that sat oddly on his face. I'd never entirely bought into Maggie's theory that he had the hots for me, but I was long past the point of dismissing the notion out of hand. Maybe that was longing in his expression, or maybe it wasn't. Either way, it didn't matter.

"You're good for him," Anderson said with what sounded like approval.

"We're good for each other," I corrected, squeezing Jamaal's hand between my own. Maybe it was my imagination, but I thought perhaps his skin felt just a touch warmer.

Anderson cocked his head as if thinking, then nodded. "I never would have expected it, but I suppose you're right."

A long, uncomfortable silence descended, and I didn't know how to break it. The house creaked with footsteps and echoed with voices as Cyrus and his surviving men continued the cleanup. After the place had been turned into a supernatural war zone, I would have expected to have emergency vehicles coming out of our ears, but there was not a siren to be heard. I had no idea how Cyrus managed that, but I was too exhausted and wrung out to care.

Anderson took another couple of steps into the room. I wished he would just go away and let me sit with Jamaal in peace. As important as Anderson had become in my life over the last few months, I found now that I had nothing to say to him. Unfortunately, the same could not be said of him.

"Do you have any concept of how many lives you saved today, Nikki Glass?"

I understood where he was coming from, but honestly, I hadn't *done* much of anything.

"Don't sell yourself short," he scolded, although I still hadn't said anything. "You came up with a mutually acceptable solution when it seemed no such thing existed. There's far more to you than meets the eye."

"Thanks. I think." I hoped he wasn't expecting a big hug-it-out session, because he wasn't getting one. I certainly didn't hate him, but I couldn't say I much liked him anymore, either.

"I want to . . . hire you to manage my affairs while I'm gone."

That threw me for a loop and seemed to come out of nowhere. "Huh?"

"I'll need a trustee. Someone who has the legal right to make decisions about the house and property in my absence."

I frowned. "Isn't that more up Leo's alley?"

"I'll ask him to manage my finances, but the house I want to leave in your care. I'll put my things into storage and you can take over my wing."

I sat there and blinked up at him, very aware of the undercurrents beneath his words. Sometimes a house isn't just a house.

"Don't you think you should put that on someone who's lived in that house for more than, like, five minutes? You have several to choose from."

He shrugged. "My house, my rules." It was a common refrain, one we'd all heard more than once. He fixed me with a penetrating look. "And while you're the caretaker, *your* house, *your* rules."

Yup. Definitely more than a house we were talking about. "I don't think—"

"Please do this for me. There is no one I would trust more."

I huffed out a sigh. "You're making an awful lot out of what was just a last-second burst of inspiration."

He had the nerve to laugh at me. "I'm making a lot out of you coming up with the idea that saved the lives of billions of people? Really?"

Okay, when you said it that way it did sound like a pretty big deal. But it didn't make me into an automatic candidate for queen of the universe, or whatever it was Anderson thought.

"Who did everyone look to when I was in the Underworld?" Anderson asked, trying a different tactic. One that made me squirm because it was hard to deny his implications. "You're the right one for the job, Nikki. You know I'm right."

Never in a million years would I have seen this . . . complication . . . coming. I didn't want to be the new Anderson. How does one step into the shoes of a god?

I had no freakin' clue. But it seemed I didn't know how to say no, either. I'm not sure my halfhearted chin-dip was much of a yes, but it seemed to satisfy Anderson.

"Thank you," he said with quiet dignity. Then he left me alone with Jamaal, who had just started to breathe again.

Jamaal was alive but unconscious when I asked Maggie to help me get him out of that house and back to the comfort of the cottages. There was still plenty of cleanup happening at the scene of the battle, but I didn't offer to lend a hand. Maggie, with her Herculean strength, had no trouble carrying Jamaal's unconscious body all the way back to the cottage she and I were sharing.

Maggie is a good friend. She knew without asking that I'd want Jamaal laid out in my bedroom rather than his. She also spontaneously volunteered to go back to Jasmine's house to see if she could be of use. We both knew it was an excuse for her to let Jamaal and me have some privacy when he came to. I'm not generally a hugger, but I hugged her before she left.

After removing the remains of his undershirt and tossing the bloody mess in the trash, I lay down beside Jamaal, who seemed to be resting comfortably enough. I put my hand on his chest and felt the steady beating of his heart, the gentle rise and fall of his breath. I was so grateful he was alive I couldn't hold back tears, and I clung to him tightly.

I realized I'd been tap-dancing around my feelings for too long, calling them a crush or lust or just a flat-out bad idea. But the terror that had seized me today when I knew he'd been killed was like nothing I'd ever experienced before in my life. I did not have "a thing" for him. I was in love with him, pure and simple.

Jamaal's body jerked, and he drew in a gasping breath. He was awake.

I knew exactly what he was going through, knew he was struggling against the memory of the breathless paralysis of death, the absolute nothingness of it. I clung to him even tighter, reminding him that I was here, that he didn't have to face the terror alone.

This was not the first time Jamaal had died. I don't know if that made it any easier for him or if he was just being stoic, but the tension eased out of him, and his quickened pulse slowed. With a groan of effort, he turned onto his side to face me, throwing an arm around me and snuggling me against his chest. He sighed contentedly, as if all was right with his world.

Dying takes a lot out of you, and I knew he would be asleep

again in moments. He was probably at least halfway there already.

"I love you," I whispered softly against his chest, not expecting him to hear.

These were not words I spoke lightly. Hell, the only ones who'd ever heard them before were Steph and our parents, and even then only rarely. For all my long list of failed relationships, I had never once given my heart to someone like I had with Jamaal. I figured it would take a while before I gathered up the courage to say them loud enough for him to hear.

Which was why I nearly passed out when I heard his whispered, "Love you, too."

I raised my head to look into his face, my eyes wide and my pulse thudding in my throat. But he must have fallen asleep the instant the words left his mouth.

Twenty-four

I officially moved into Anderson's wing of the mansion seven days after the battle in Bermuda, when he left to begin his time as Niobe's prisoner . . . and stud. I was more than a little overwhelmed by the massive undertaking I had committed myself to, but I was determined to take things one day at a time.

Before Anderson left, we had a meeting with Cyrus. No more posturing or intimidation—this time we met at the mansion, just the three of us, and discussed how we could manage to build a peace between us that wasn't based on threats.

It wasn't as hard as I'd expected. Cyrus was probably never going to get over his fury with Anderson for killing his father, but he reluctantly agreed he'd had good cause. It helped that all of Konstantin's closest allies—the ones who would have put the most pressure on Cyrus to get revenge—had died either in the battle or in the days following it, their immortality given to Descendants with more moderate views.

The Olympians would never be the good guys. Cyrus had no intention of using his own or his people's powers to make the world a better place. We would continue to have significant philosophical differences, and no doubt there would be times when we would clash. But during that meeting, we agreed that we'd stay out of each other's way as much as possible and hopefully solve any conflicts by negotiation instead of violence.

"If you're ever tempted to go back to the old ways," Anderson warned Cyrus, "just remember that I won't be Niobe's prisoner forever. I will be back someday . . . and I'll hold you personally responsible for any harm you or your Olympians do to my people."

Cyrus then flashed me a wry smile. "I won't miss having him trot out that old chestnut every five minutes."

I almost smiled back but managed to catch myself. I wouldn't miss having Anderson continually bullying his way into getting what he wanted, either, but that didn't necessarily mean having that threat hanging over the Olympians was a bad thing. Maybe it would help keep them honest.

I wasn't sure I trusted the agreement, and Anderson concurred that tempering any optimism with caution was a wise plan, but it was a hopeful beginning. Cyrus made a big deal out of handing Blake over as some kind of grand gesture to symbolize the start of our new peace, but I suspect even his own people knew that it wasn't a true concession. What he wanted from Blake couldn't be taken by force, and I think Blake's brief stint as his prisoner had proven that to him.

Steph wasn't speaking to me. I hoped that was only temporary, that she would eventually come to realize I'd done the best I could in an exceedingly difficult situation. I know Blake tried to contact her as soon as Cyrus let him go, but she made it clear I had company in the doghouse.

I expected that to be the last I saw of Cyrus for quite some time, which was a happy prospect. However, as I was in the process of moving into Anderson's office, Cyrus called from the mansion's front gate and requested a moment of my time.

"Really?" I asked over the intercom. "You're going to start testing me when Anderson's been gone all of half an hour?"

"Nope, no testing," he promised. "I come bearing gifts."

"Yeah, right."

"I mean it. It won't take long, and it'll be more than worth your while."

Be wary of Olympians bearing gifts, I told myself, but I had to admit I was curious. He sounded sincere, although tone of voice doesn't necessarily carry that well over an intercom. Still, it wouldn't bode well for our new policy of peaceful coexistence if I told him to shove it.

I buzzed him in and hoped he wouldn't make me regret it.

I brought him up to Anderson's study. No, *my* study now, though I supposed it would take a while for me to start thinking of it that way. I felt like a little kid playing dress-up when I helped myself to Anderson's chair. I hoped the awkwardness and unfamiliarity didn't show on my face.

"So . . . what was it you were saying about bearing gifts?" I inquired. He wasn't carrying any packages, which I took to mean that the word *gifts* had been metaphorical.

He surprised me by pulling an envelope from the inner pocket of his sport coat. He looked at it with strange intensity and didn't immediately hand it over. Something about his demeanor caused my pulse to kick up.

Cyrus looked away from the envelope and met my eyes. "I know you're aware of my father's policy toward Descendants."

"You mean the one where you search out Descendants and their families and slaughter them all—except for the children you feel are young enough to be brainwashed into drinking the Olympian Kool-Aid?"

"That was my father's doing," Cyrus reminded me, "and I put an end to it the moment I took charge."

"You put an end to killing the *children*," I corrected, knowing it was true, but wondering just what constituted a child in the current Olympian view.

"I did that first," Cyrus agreed. "But I decided to put a stop to the practice altogether. Most of the Descendants we hunted were no threat to us, and killing them so they couldn't kill us first was a precaution that bordered on paranoia. But never mind that for now. My point is that my father's policy was to eliminate any and all adult Descendants he could locate and all but the youngest Descendant children."

My pulse went from slightly elevated to racing in no time flat. "So what's your point?"

"Even without a descendant of Artemis on our payroll, we were damn good at finding Descendants and eliminating them. But as good as we were, sometimes our quarry got away."

"As evidenced by your father giving me a list of names and trying to strong-arm me into finding them." My heart was pounding hard enough that I could practically hear its drumbeat, and my voice came out tight and breathless.

"Exactly." Cyrus cleared his throat. "One of the ones who got away was a descendant of Artemis."

I squeezed the arms of my chair.

"She eluded us and went on the run with her young daughter and infant son." He put the envelope on the desk and pushed it toward me. "She must be a remarkably resourceful and clever woman. We never did find her. Or her children."

My eyes blurred with tears as I stared at the envelope before me. My mother had abandoned me in a church far from where I grew up when I was only four years old. I hadn't known my own last name, and I was so far from home that no one could possibly recognize me, so the authorities had never been able to determine who my mother was or where I had come from.

All my life I'd hated her for that abandonment, for the repeated childhood traumas I endured as I was passed from foster home to foster home, becoming more of a problem child each time. I'd been on my way to becoming a juvenile delinquent at best, a career criminal at worst, when the Glasses found me, took me in, and tamed me. But all the years of kindness and love since then hadn't even begun to erase the bitterness and hurt that resided deep within me.

Until I had become *Liberi*, I hadn't once considered the possibility that my mother had abandoned me for any reason other than that she didn't want me. It was a terrible and painful conviction to grow up with, but it seemed the obvious conclusion from the facts I had available.

Once I'd learned about Konstantin and his purges of Descendant families, I entertained occasional fantasies that my mother had left me in that church to escape the Olympians' clutches, but I had never really *believed* it. Back when she'd been speaking to me, Steph kept badgering me to use my newfound powers to find my birth mother, and I had repeatedly rejected the idea. I was terrified I'd find her and discover that my initial assumption was right, that she hadn't wanted me and that noble sacrifice had had nothing to do with it. Bad enough to *think* that was what happened. I couldn't bear to *know* it.

"What's in the envelope?" I asked with a hoarse croak.

"It's your family tree. What we know of it, anyway. It's also got your mother's name and her last known address."

In other words, everything a person with my abilities would need in order to locate both my birth mother and my little brother.

With shaking hands, I picked up the envelope. Cyrus hadn't bothered to seal it, which was probably a good thing or I might have torn it apart trying to get it open. Neither my body nor my brain was working at full capacity at the moment. I had to scrub at my eyes before they could focus enough to read.

There was indeed an intricate family tree drawn out, but I had little interest in anything but its very last branch. I saw my name and my brother's—*William*—at the very bottom and traced up one generation to find the name *Jessica*.

My mother.

I noted there was a question mark where my father's name should have been. I had no memory of him, so whoever he was, my mother had clearly split with him—if they had ever truly been together in the first place.

My mother had had two sisters and a brother, all younger and childless. And all of whom had apparently died in the same year. The year my mother had abandoned me.

"Oh, my God. The Olympians killed my aunts and uncle," I whispered.

"Yes," Cyrus whispered back. "I'm very sorry. I had nothing to do with it, but I know I am complicit anyway."

Another shock—I traced the tree up a little farther and found my mother's surname: *Mallory*. I recognized the name Jessica Mallory, and it wasn't because I finally remembered it from my childhood.

Jessica Mallory. That name and William's had been two of the names on the list of Descendants that Konstantin had given me to hunt down for him. My mother, and my little brother, Billy. If I had given in to Konstantin's demands, he would have killed them both. And oh, how he would have reveled in the cruelty of what he'd had me do.

"My father and all his followers are dead now," Cyrus said. "If you want to find your mother and your brother, you don't have to worry that they'll come to harm."

He pushed his chair back, but I didn't have the strength or will to do the same. I was shaking, my thoughts whizzing around in my head like a fly trapped in a jar.

"I'm going to assume you need a little time to yourself," Cyrus said. "I know I would in your position. I'll see myself out." And because this was Cyrus and he couldn't resist being a smartass: "Don't worry about the silver and china. I have plenty of my own."

If I were being my normal, ornery self, that quip would

have made it necessary for me to personally escort him to the door, but this time I wasn't up to it, and I just let him go.

My hands still shaking, I put down the family tree and smoothed it against the desk with both hands.

Should I look for my family?

So far, I hadn't exactly been superconfident of my abilities, but I knew deep down that I could do it. And Lord, how I wanted to. I imagined a tearful reunion full of hugs and laughter. As hard as it had been for me to grow up without my mother, how much worse must it have been for her? By abandoning me—and, I presumed, Billy as well—she had made sure that even if the Olympians caught her, they would never be able to find her children. What a heartbreaking—and courageous—decision that must have been.

Just thinking about it made me start weeping in earnest. All these years, she'd had no way of knowing what happened to us, whether we found good homes, whether we were loved, whether we were happy. She deserved to know that all the pain she'd been through had been worth it, that we had survived and flourished—assuming my brother had done as well as I, but at least he'd been a baby when she'd left him. It was much easier to find a good home for a baby boy than for a four-year-old girl who was just old enough to know what she'd lost.

And yet . . .

Cyrus had told me the Olympians would not seek out and murder Descendants anymore, and I believed he'd been sincere. But just because he said it was safe didn't mean it was the truth. He'd made some drastic changes to the makeup of the Olympians when he'd killed off his father's cronies, but I was sure there were still plenty of bad apples left in his orchard. And his command of his Olympians wasn't as absolute as his father's had been or he'd never have had so many deserters. It would kill me if by finding my mother and my brother, I ended up leading the Olympians straight to their doorsteps. For all

I knew, my mother had more children now, who were every bit as vulnerable as Billy and I had been. Hell, Billy would be a little young for it still, but it wasn't impossible that he had children of his own.

I felt like I would be playing Russian roulette with the lives of my family if I went looking for them as I so desperately wanted to.

I took a deep, shuddering breath and wiped away my tears. It had been more than twenty years since I'd been left in that church. Just because I now had the ability to find her didn't mean I had to make a decision about it *today*.

I slid the family tree back into its envelope and tucked it deep into the desk drawer. I had plenty of time to think about it before I acted. And maybe, over time, I'd get a better feeling for how much change the Olympians were capable of. Maybe Cyrus would surprise me and have no trouble maintaining control. And maybe he would continue getting rid of the bad seeds, replacing them with those who at least knew what a moral compass was, even if the ones they possessed were rusty and disused.

I had a whole life ahead of me, and it was destined to be a long one. Maybe it would never be safe to search for my biological family. If that was the case, then I'd learn to live with it. But for the first time ever, I was filled with a genuine sense of optimism. And I had a support system, people who would be there to help me figure out what I really wanted to do.

With that in mind, I decided installing myself in my new office could wait. What I needed now was to pour my heart out to someone who would understand exactly what I was going through. Lucky for me, I had someone who fit that bill perfectly, waiting patiently for me to be done fussing so that we could christen my new bedroom.

There would never be a better time than now.